A DARK ROMANCE

THE THALIA SERIES

THE COMPLETE COLLECTION

USA TODAY BESTSELLING AUTHOR
JENNIFER BENE

Text copyright © 2018 Jennifer Bene

All Rights Reserved.

No part of this book may be reproduced in any form or by any electronic or mechanical means including information storage and retrieval systems, without permission in writing from the author. The only exception is by a reviewer, who may quote short excerpts in a review.

This book is a work of fiction. Names, characters, places, and incidents either are products of the author's imagination or are used fictitiously. Any resemblance to actual persons, living or dead, events, or locales is entirely coincidental.

ISBN (e-book): 978-1-946722-27-0

ISBN (paperback): 978-1-946722-26-3

Cover design by Laura Hidalgo, https://www.spellbindingdesign.com/

The Thalia Series

Security Binds Her
Striking a Balance
Salvaged by Love
Tying the Knot

Short Stories included in The Thalia Series Complete Collection:

Christmas at Purgatory
The Branding
A Kalen and James Flashback
James at The Auction

"Look at how a single candle can both defy and define the darkness."
— Anne Frank

The Thalia Series holds a special place in my heart, and it always will, because it was the first time that people outside of my friends responded to the stories in my head. They loved the darkness as much as I did, and it fed me in ways I cannot fully describe. It fed my heart, my soul, my creative spirit, my muse, my mind, and my courage. I had always been afraid to write the words in my head, all of the dark and twisty, but something about Thalia touched people, burrowed deep, and held on — just like she had with me. I am infinitely grateful for every person that commented on Literotica with the original version of this story, for every person that has found Thalia since and loved it. Whether they bought it in secret, shared it with a friend in a devious whisper, wrote a review, or took the time to email or message me about it.

Each and every one of you have made me the author I am today, and I love you for that.

I look forward to many more years writing about the darkness and the light, lovelies, and I hope you will be right there with me.

A DARK ROMANCE

SECURITY BINDS HER

BOOK ONE OF THE THALIA SERIES

USA TODAY BESTSELLING AUTHOR
JENNIFER BENE

Text copyright © 2015 Jennifer Bene

All Rights Reserved.

No part of this book may be reproduced in any form or by any electronic or mechanical means including information storage and retrieval systems, without permission in writing from the author. The only exception is by a reviewer, who may quote short excerpts in a review.

This book is a work of fiction. Names, characters, places, and incidents either are products of the author's imagination or are used fictitiously. Any resemblance to actual persons, living or dead, events, or locales is entirely coincidental.

ISBN (e-book): 978-1-946722-15-7

ISBN (paperback): 978-1-946722-23-2

Cover design by Laura Hidalgo, https://www.spellbindingdesign.com/

"Light is meaningful only in relation to darkness, and truth presupposes error. It is these mingled opposites which people our life, which make it pungent, intoxicating. We only exist in terms of this conflict, in the zone where black and white clash."
- Louis Aragon

This is a dark book. It is the first of a series that tackles the darkness and the light, suffering and recovery. I've always had the darkness in my head, but I've found it has always helped me to see the light more clearly. It defines it. With that in mind, I am so grateful to everyone who supported Thalia's story when it first appeared on Lit. Who accepted the darkness and fell in love with the twists and turns along with me. This story brought me the possibility of a future as an author, an amazing group of authors, and introduced me to the loveliest group of readers on the internet!

It is an absolute truth that without all of you, Thalia's story would have never been told.

The darkness, or the light.

Prologue
THALIA

Thalia stretched as she woke and buried her face into the pillow trying to grab just a few more minutes of sleep before the day started.

Wait.

She sat bolt upright. This was not her bed. It didn't smell like her bed, it was more subtle, more masculine. She was in the center of a king-size four poster, and fear slammed into her chest despite the pleasant surroundings. It was a nice room, like a fancy hotel. Nicer than any place she'd ever stayed before.

But she didn't want to be here at all.

Thalia quickly rolled off the bed and lunged for the curtains on the wall, but they were an illusion. There was no window.

The room would have been pitch black except for a small night-light plugged into the wall that revealed two doors. Thalia ran over and yanked open the first one, her body arguing against the movement as she was achingly reminded of the night before.

Thalia bit down on the urge to cry. She didn't want to remember asking, begging him to let her come, or the humiliation of touching herself in front of him.

Her eyes focused, staring into a beautiful bathroom that was as big as her bedroom at home. A large garden tub, a shower with six heads, a long vanity, and a small, enclosed toilet. How could a place so beautiful belong to someone so evil? After using the toilet, she stepped back into the main part of the room and caught herself in the mirror.

Her light brown hair was limp and hanging past her shoulders without much of the curl she had added to it the morning before. Her hazel eyes were bloodshot and empty, and they told the same story her body did. Pain. Shame. Purple bruises ringed her wrists darkly as if they were bracelets, faint lines could be seen on the pale skin of her breasts and ass from the crop and his belt. She covered her mouth as she started to cry again.

How could any of this be real?

Thalia shut the light off to end the sight. She couldn't bear to look at the evidence of the night before. Memories slammed into her. Handcuffed in the stairwell, his hands on her, him re—cuffing her to the car and punishing her. The torment in the trunk, touching herself for him. The spanking.

And coming for him.

She didn't need the mirror to know she had flushed bright red. He had made her come, and she had, like an idiot, asked for it.

She hated herself. She was ashamed. The loud sob surprised her when it burst out of her mouth, but she wiped the tears on her cheeks as she approached the only other door.

Reaching for the handle she mumbled, pleading with the world, the powers that be, or any god that felt like listening, "Please open…"

Of course, it didn't.

Despite the obvious futility Thalia still grabbed the handle with both hands and tried again and again to get it to turn. Turning back to the room the panic ramped up in her chest. She was trapped. There was no way out. The air seemed thin, it was hard to get a full breath into her lungs, and she could hear it whistling in her chest.

Flipping back to the door she slammed her fists on it, "HELP! Someone please help me! I'm trapped! Let me out! Let me OUT! Someone open the door!" She kicked it repeatedly, realizing somewhere in her mind that he had taken off her heels. He had to be out there. Somewhere in the house. "Open the fucking door you sick asshole!"

Screaming loudly, she let out the frustration and rage and fear and guilt in a long wail that strained her voice. Tears were flooding down her cheeks, all the panic and shame combining until she felt like she was coming apart at the seams.

A loud bang on the door surprised her, and she yelped. With her hands still resting on its surface, she'd felt the vibration in the wood from the force of the strike.

Thalia was shaking as she waited for something else to happen, but she heard the low murmur of a voice outside. Stepping forward cautiously she pressed her ear to the door, but it was hard to hear.

"— at least a few weeks —"

"— I'm not ready to share yet."

"— they're already live, and —"

He seemed to move farther away for a moment and it was difficult to discern any specific words. Her pulse was pounding so hard in her ears she was shaking. This was what fear felt like. A horror movie couldn't match this. This is what it was like when it was real.

The strong snap of a lock being disengaged warned her to step back a second before the door opened. Thalia became painfully aware of her nakedness as his blue-gray eyes danced across her skin. His dark hair was perfect, and he wore a gray shirt and black pants that hung low on his hips. They reminded her of the military. Numerous pockets, black hardware. He seemed amused, the edge of his mouth lifting before he spoke.

"Good morning, Thalia." His voice was warm with humor. A morning person. How fucked up.

"Let me go," Thalia demanded, aiming for strength. She wouldn't cower from him, she wasn't just going to placate him like she had the night before. She was going to be brave.

His eyebrow arched neatly as he stepped into the room, his size and his presence made her want to step back, but she didn't. He stopped just in front of her, almost close enough for his shirt to brush against her chest. "No. And did you already forget the lessons I gave you last night little whore?"

"I am not a whore!" Thalia screamed and slapped him. The crack of her palm connecting with his cheek seemed to echo in the room.

She immediately regretted it.

Chapter One
THALIA

The Night Before

It was after six, and Thalia was working late. Again. The plain gray of her cubicle walls were about as depressing as the stack of documents yet to be entered, but what had she expected when she took a data entry job? College dropouts didn't get high paying jobs in nice offices. They got temp work. Short-term assignments that meant you were lucky to spend six months in the same office. Which meant being left behind when all the permanent employees grabbed lunch, or gossiped in the breakroom, or did *anything* as a group.

She was good at it though. She always received high praise at the end of a contract, and several times they had kept her résumé in case there was an opening. No one had actually *called* yet, but they kept her résumé. She typed at almost a hundred words per minute, and she would always knock out the work quickly. Well, she could if her current boss wasn't always 'dropping by' at the end of his day to lean over her cube and talk to her. If he didn't do that, maybe she'd actually leave on time. Even wearing a button down with no cleavage, a knee-length skirt, and minimal makeup — he still bothered her every single day.

He'd targeted her the day she'd started a few months before, and even moved her desk to be right near his office. He'd asked her out to lunch twice, and both times she'd refused as politely as possible. She may not have friends in this office, but she definitely didn't need enemies because the boss was paying her special attention. His retaliation seemed to be little last minute *emergencies* like the ones he'd laid on her desk today.

As if data entry was ever that urgent.

"Asshole," she hissed under her breath as she flipped over the next file folder he'd left her with when he'd stepped into her cube, squeezed her shoulders, and left to go home. Of course, if she didn't get the information entered in their system then she'd be in his office in the morning, getting eye-fucked while he asked her questions like, *'what kept you from accomplishing your tasks, Thalia?'* or *'maybe a less stressful position would help you?.'*

Corporate asshole speak for *'I can cancel your contract in a second if you even think about complaining.'*

Thalia groaned as she started typing again, it wasn't worth it to go home now and deal with him. For the hundredth time that month she thought about how she needed to just sit down that weekend and start applying for jobs. Real jobs. Permanent jobs. Her Netflix marathon of *Breaking Bad* could wait one weekend.

It was two hours later when she finally stood up from her desk, smoothed out the dark gray skirt and slipped her heels back on. The windows outside were pitch black and she knew it would be well after nine by the time she got home. Only enough time to water her plants, take a quick bath and collapse into bed.

No gym tonight.

She muttered about her boss as she shut down her computer and grabbed her purse to leave. Out in the hall she pressed the elevator button, but it didn't even light up. Pressing it again she groaned when nothing happened. It looked like she'd get a work out anyway. Four flights of stairs in heels.

"What a day..." Thalia muttered and pushed open the door to the concrete stairwell, her heels ringing out loudly on the metal steps, echoing off the walls as she started down. She stopped when she thought she heard another door open. The building should have been empty this late at night, so she waited, but she didn't hear footsteps and shook her head. Paranoid and tired, great combination.

Opening her purse, she dug through it as she rounded the last turn to exit to the parking garage. As soon as her heels hit the concrete floor someone grabbed her from behind and shoved her forward into the wall. Her head cracked against the concrete and for a moment she was too stunned to do more than try and keep her balance. Then the hand tightened in her hair, gripping it at the base of her skull and pressing her forward against the wall.

She screamed, listening to her voice echo up the stairwell as she tried to push back, but the man pressed himself against her, pinning her to the wall with his broad body. His erection jutted into her backside, and it made her stomach flutter with fear, a whimper rising out of her as she realized she wasn't able to move back at all.

A soft chuckling came from him, his breath moving against her ear. "You can go ahead and scream. No one else is here. All the good boys and girls have gone home already."

"Please, please just let me go…" she begged, still trying to shift against him, to twist enough to get to the door so she could run. He pressed his hips harder against her, and she stilled.

"I don't think so." He wrenched her head back and kicked her feet farther apart until her skirt started to slide up her thighs.

"I haven't even seen your face, you can just let me go. I won't call the police." Thalia winced as he forced her against the wall, wrenching one of her arms up behind her back until she yelped in pain.

"I know you're not going to call anyone." He shoved her purse to the floor and lifted her other arm above her head, the ratcheting sound of a handcuff clamping around her wrist was accompanied by the painful pinch as it was tightened too far.

She renewed her fighting, kicking back at him until he yanked her arm up higher on her back and she cried out. He seemed to be unbothered by her struggle, where she was already breathing hard in panic. *This couldn't be happening.*

This. Could. Not. Be. Happening.

The arm he had behind her back was suddenly pulled up to join her other and she looked up to see his hands loop the cuffs over a pipe above her, and then he secured the other cuff around her left wrist. That was when she started crying. Murmuring pleas as his hands slid down her curves. "Stop! Please don't—"

He clenched a fist in her hair, bending her head back until she saw him. It was the night security guard. She knew from the few times he'd walked her to her car after working late that he was ex-military, unmarried, and liked movies. He'd always been so nice to her. He'd always been friendly. Even now he was smiling at her like everything was normal, but then he kissed her hard. Struggling, she bit his lip and he pulled back, a red swipe of blood across his lower lip. She could taste the copper in her mouth as a sick feeling filled her stomach.

He laughed as he wiped his mouth on his arm. "You're going to regret that. Trust me, you're going to do whatever I tell you to."

Thalia was on her toes already as she tried to relieve the pain in her wrists, but she jumped when his hand came up her skirt and swiped at her panties. Shuddering when she realized they were damp, unsure when that had even happened. She tried to bring her knees back together, and he chuckled in her ear — his feet were in between hers, holding her legs open. "Why are you doing this? Why?!" she half-screamed it at him.

"Because, I chose you." The guard's voice hummed against her shoulder, and her anger surged forward again. Lifting her heel she tried to bring it down on his foot, but all she could make contact with was a boot, and he was totally unfazed.

His hand instantly tightened in her hair. "Be still. If you try to kick me again I'm going to take the heels, and I'm not sure you could reach the floor without them. So, unless you want to hang by your wrists, behave." His words made her shiver, and she felt a whine rise up in her chest. He nudged her heels a little wider and the strain on her wrists grew worse. The guard started to rub her clit through the thin fabric and her hips bucked involuntarily. Groaning, she gritted her teeth, doing her best to use her fear to push back the inklings of sensation he was pulling from her.

"That's right. I knew you were a slut." His mouth trailed down her neck under her hair. His other hand squeezing her breast through the shirt as his fingers continued to torment her. She shook her head. She wasn't enjoying this. She wasn't. It was just some terrible betrayal of her body causing the heat to blossom in her lower belly as his fingers slid underneath her panties. When he pressed on her clit, moving his fingers in a tormenting circle, she moaned and promptly bit her tongue to cut it off.

"No." The word came out as more of a whine. He ignored her and jerked hard on her shirt until several of the buttons snapped, revealing the light tan lace of her bra. The guard flipped the cups in so they held her breasts up for his touch, and she screamed again, begging him to stop, but he only answered by thrusting a finger inside her. Her hips tilted forward, trying to ease the angle and she shook her head, tears streaking her cheeks as she tried to keep her body under control, but he was playing her body against her. Like he knew it.

Knew better than she did.

"You can keep screaming, but it's only going to make me fuck you harder." He growled the words in her ear as he thrust a second finger inside her, pinching one nipple in his fingers until her back arched. She was getting wet, and she could feel herself crying as that realization settled over her. She didn't want this, she couldn't want this.

His thumb pressed against her clit and she tried to stifle a moan, but her hips bucked against his hand, shifting so his fingers thrust deeper inside her. Fighting against the urge to push forward toward the pleasant sensation, but she was subconsciously doing it anyway, her breaths growing short as pleasure tried to short-circuit the fear inside her. Then he suddenly pulled his hand away.

"Whoa now, Thalia, you need to learn some control. Now, clean up your mess." Holding his fingers in front of her mouth, she shook her head, keeping her mouth tightly closed. He might be able to make her body respond, but he couldn't make her participate. She felt his hips move back from hers, and he bunched her skirt around her waist. Then she heard his belt coming off.

"No, no, no!" she screamed, thinking he was about to fuck her, but instead the belt cracked against her ass, making her jump and drop back down, bruising her wrists in the cuffs. She was crying again as the belt came down on her other cheek. She tried to twist away from it, but he pressed her to the wall with a hand between her shoulder blades.

"You don't refuse me. Understand?" The belt cracked across her sensitive skin one more time and she found herself nodding as she pressed harder against the wall trying to get away. This time when he placed his fingers in front of her mouth she opened and sucked them, tasting herself. Without noticing, she had tried to bring her thighs together but he kicked the inside of a heel. "No, keep them spread."

When he took his fingers from her mouth, she gasped a breath and realized with a hushed sob that she was still crying. Cold metal scraped up the inside of her thigh and she whimpered, jumping as she heard the sound of fabric tearing and then the cool air of the stairwell hit her pussy as he grabbed the remnants of her underwear. The black lace was in a ball as he reached around her. "Open," he demanded.

She did without argument and he pressed them into her mouth, and once again she could taste herself, this time on the fabric. Thalia was ashamed of herself, her mind tearing her apart. She'd always thought she'd be the one to fight, to run, to *win*. To be the one who defeated her attacker with yet undiscovered martial arts skills like some female Jason Bourne. But here she was, wet and arching into his touches? Obediently opening her mouth? What was wrong with her? His hips pressed against her again and his hand tightened in her hair. Then she heard his zipper and she whimpered.

"You are such a good slut, already soaking wet and I've barely touched you. If I'd known you'd be this willing I wouldn't have planned so much." He positioned himself behind her, reaching between her legs to rub her clit until she was grinding against his hand. Just as she caught herself and stopped, he thrust deep inside her in one movement. She cried out because it hurt. It had been months since she'd even had a date, it had been a year since she'd had sex. Her body remembered the feeling of fullness though, and the tingling rush from his circling touch on her clit confused it.

'*Stop, please stop…*' Thalia begged, pleaded, trying to be clear through the muffling effect of fabric in her mouth. She needed him to stop, because it was starting to feel good. That was the worst part. It couldn't feel good, that was wrong. He pulled back and thrust in again and she pulled on her arms trying to distract herself with the pain in her wrists, but it somehow only made it all worse. The pain and pleasure combining and ratcheting up the intensity until she was moaning through clenched teeth with each thrust.

His fingers found her clit again and she came without warning. The orgasm was surprising, blinding, her muscles tensing and her legs shivering to the point that she wobbled in her heels. He grabbed her hips and held her still against him. Thalia tried to muffle the moan through the panties gagging her as she felt her pussy clenching him in waves, and he laughed in her ear before he started thrusting again. "Such a little cockwhore," he growled, "I'll have to punish you later for coming without permission."

Hand tightening in her hair, he held her still and started to fuck her hard. The rocking of her body faded to the background as her mind took over the torture. She was appalled at herself for coming. She whined, sniffling and shaking her head against his grip. Shame washed over, threatening to drown her. She hated herself. Hated him. Hated the universe for letting something like this happen. Tears streaked her cheeks even as she felt a second orgasm rising up, the tightening in her lower belly making her lift onto her tiptoes. He yanked her head back and kissed her hard, biting her lower lip in return.

"Do not come again or I'll make you suffer." He spoke through his teeth against her ear and she arched her back as he thrust over and over, trying to ignore her body's urges to fall over the edge again. Then, mercifully, she felt him pause inside her, holding himself deep as he came. She squirmed in his grip. He hadn't had a condom on, she'd felt that. She screamed, cursing at him through her underwear as he pulled out of her and stepped back.

"Go ahead and be angry. We both know you liked it, and I prefer a bit of fight. All the more fun to break you." He yanked her skirt back down over her welted ass and pressed her forward against the wall. "Ready for your punishment, Thalia?"

He stood silently behind her, as if he were actually waiting for her to answer. She hung by the cuffs, her arms limp from her wrists to her shoulders as she ignored the ache of the metal digging in and the tingling in her fingertips. Thalia kept her chin tucked against her chest as she heard him putting himself away, the belt returning to his pants.

"I asked if you're ready for your punishment." The guard grabbed her face and pulled her panties out of her mouth.

"Please don't hurt me anymore. Just let me go." She weakly twisted in the handcuffs, whispering, "I just want to go home."

He gripped her face a little harder and leaned in close. "You clearly don't understand the situation." The guard dropped his hand from her face and painfully twisted a nipple until she cried out. "You will learn though." Reaching up he unlocked one of the cuffs and her arms were so exhausted they just dropped, but she still lunged for the door out of a desperate instinct.

It was stupid. *So fucking stupid.*

He caught her around the waist as she tried to move past him and threw her to the floor with barely a grunt. In an instant he'd flipped her onto her stomach so he could pull her arms behind her and recuff her as she screamed in futile frustration.

"Let me go you fucking psychopath!" Fighting wildly on the floor, he did nothing. Letting her fight for a few minutes, screaming and cursing at him until she started to wear out. Her breasts rubbed against the concrete floor as she fought him, her nipples growing hard and chafing. She hated that he wasn't even putting forth much effort to keep her down, it was a statement without words. The guard finally sighed in exasperation and spanked her hard. Covering her mouth with his hand, he bowed her back, his knee pressing in at her waist until she whimpered from the strain. Pain radiating up her spine until it stretched like agonizing claws across her ribs.

"Alright, that's enough. You already have a punishment owed for coming without permission, and another for fucking biting me." He bit down on her shoulder, hard enough that she screamed against his hand as cold fear settled in her stomach like she'd swallowed ice cubes. "So don't push me, or I'll take your pretty little ass next, without a warm up, and you'll still get punished."

That made her still, and she tried to nod against the death grip he had on her face. When he let go of her he stood up and then hauled her to her feet by one arm, the strain in her shoulder and wrists making her cry out.

Scooping up her purse, he shoved her through the door to the garage. It was unbelievably empty, and her silver Camry was parked against the back wall as usual. The guard fished out her keys as she made prolonged eye contact with every camera in the garage. He laughed when he finally noticed. "I disabled the cameras. As far as anyone is concerned there was a technical glitch tonight. Someone will undoubtedly fix it tomorrow."

"Why are you doing this to me?" Thalia choked on the urge to cry again. Fear of the punishment he'd promised and a slow realization that no one was even going to try and help her made her sick. No one was even going to know he had taken her. He could do whatever he wanted and no one would find out. No one was going to know.

"Why? Because you need this. I'll show you. You'll understand." His fingers dug into her arm as he reached her car. "You just need someone to make you understand what you are."

He moved his hand to the back of her neck and bent her over the trunk, immediately thrusting two fingers inside her. She cried out, and he teased her, quickly bringing her back to the edge where he'd stopped her second orgasm. A moan slipped out of her mouth until she closed her lips against it, but her hips wiggled seeking just a little more, to get his touch just a little deeper.

Just as she was about to come he pulled his fingers back and spanked her pussy hard, making her body jolt against the car. Thalia started crying again. Something was wrong with her. No one was supposed to moan when they were being attacked. They definitely weren't supposed to encourage them.

"You want me to fuck you again? Answer honestly." He leaned down and whispered right against her ear. The low growl in his voice did funny things to her, making her stomach flutter and heat pool between her legs again.

"No!" she shouted at him, and he huffed.

"Liar." He chuckled under his breath. "You're not this wet for no reason. Open." He pressed his fingers against her lips and she whimpered as she opened them to suck the mixture of them both off his fingers. When he pulled away again he yanked her back by her hair. Thalia cried out and then he pushed against the back of one of her legs so she dropped to her knees hard on the concrete. Pain starburst across them and she gasped.

"Please, just stop," Thalia begged as he reached behind her and undid one of the cuffs. A spark of hope bloomed inside her and she looked up at him, his gray-blue eyes staring back at her with amusement.

He wasn't releasing her.

Her hope went out like a snuffed candle. Stretching her handcuffed hand under the car he hooked the other half of the handcuff to something and locked her to it. From the back of his pants he pulled another set of handcuffs and stretched her free arm to the other side of the car, pressing her back against the bumper as he locked her there. She panicked and jerked against the handcuffs as he moved back in front of her, her arms stretched to either side.

"Let me go! Let me go, just let me—"

"No, Thalia, I'm not letting you go. Shut up, and don't be stupid." He sounded exasperated. "You're going to be punished before we leave, don't make it worse."

Her world went sideways. He had said *'we.'* He was planning to take her with him. Tears ran down her cheeks as she looked up at him. His uniform was easier to see as he stepped back, dark fabric clinging to a lean, muscular body. When he'd walked her to her car in the weeks before, she had noticed it, had noticed how big his hands were when he pushed the door open for her. The smile he would give her as he had let her get in her car on those other days. She'd thought he was cute, even hot, and she cursed herself for it now. How had she not seen this in him? How had she been that stupid? That blind? Because of his fake kindness, a joke about some stupid movie, a nice smile?

She felt like such a fool.

And he wasn't smiling now, his eyes had a predatory gleam to them, and it made her quiver with fear. He turned and walked out of her view, and after a couple of minutes she became very aware that she was unable to move, and that he had left her breasts popping out of the top of her bra. The cool air of the garage was moving over the moisture between her legs, and it made her even more aware of how wet she was after the stairwell. Thalia pulled her thighs together to shield herself just as she heard his heavy footsteps echoing out through the garage.

He dropped a duffel bag next to the car, unzipped it, and out came a riding crop.

"No!" Thalia panicked and jerked hard on the cuffs, bruising her wrists badly as she bent forward as far as she could to try and shield herself, the strain of the cuffs limiting her movement.

The riding crop came down hard on her shoulders and she screamed and sat up to protect her back against the trunk.

"Keep your back against the car. If you pull away I'll add a lash to your punishment." Then he flicked the crop against her right nipple and she screamed, but he didn't pause before he hit the left nipple just as hard. They hurt so much already she couldn't imagine him continuing, but he did. The crop came down on her nipples, the sides of her breasts, and then he brought the crop to the sensitive part underneath the breast. She was sobbing when he suddenly paused, and she tried to catch her breath as the burning ache spread across her chest.

"Thalia. Tell me why you're being punished." His voice was calm and cold.

"What?!" she screamed at him, and he immediately brought the crop down between her legs, striking her pussy hard. She sobbed again, clenching her thighs together. She hadn't realized her thighs had spread during the torment.

He gripped her by the hair and brought the crop down hard across both breasts. "You will spread your legs and you will answer me. Now."

She cried out again and slid her knees apart, the pain spreading across her chest as bright red lines lit up on her pale skin.

He brought the crop down between her thighs, landing with a blinding strike of pain on her clit, and her body shook with the strain of not closing her legs or lifting her back from the car. She was sobbing as she tried to answer him. "I — you said I, umm…" She couldn't say the words out loud. She'd orgasmed, she'd come without his permission.

"You came," he filled in.

"Yes, umm, wi—without your p—permission. An—and I bit you." She was shaking, but she felt her pussy flood as she thought of how hard she'd come against the wall. She was soaked between her thighs, and knew it was impossible for him not to notice. There was something wrong with her body.

"Say it all together, slut." He said it plainly, but her stomach turned at speaking the words. She must have taken too long because the crop slapped against her wet pussy again, making her cry out in pain.

"I came without your permission! I bit you!" She yelled it through her tears and he cupped her chin, lifting her head so she looked at him. He was smiling at her, and the boy-next-door charm of it eased some of the tension in her stomach. He wasn't angry anymore?

"Good girl." He threw the crop back onto the duffel bag and then swept her hair back from her face where her tears had stuck some of the strands to her cheeks.

"Please." She whimpered. His gentle touches were almost worse than the riding crop.

Running his thumb over her bottom lip she tried to turn away from him, but he grabbed her face and turned her back. "At least you're pretty when you cry." He let go of her face and smiled at her. "Time to go."

She dropped her head, too sore and exhausted to fight him. This time when he undid the cuffs she didn't try to run, and when he pulled her to her feet and she wobbled he just lifted her into his arms as if she weighed nothing at all. Her body pressed against his hard chest and she felt empty, and vacant, like someone had pushed her out of herself.

He popped the trunk and laid her inside. Panic started to rise but he covered her mouth with his hand. "Don't fight me. I don't want to punish you again. At least not *yet*." Running his thumb over her swollen lips, he released her mouth, and she just stared into his eyes as he reached behind her. He took the handcuffs on her wrists and latched them to her ankles which had her bowed backward in the trunk and mostly unable to move.

"One more thing." He stepped away and then came back with something small and silver in his hand, which started to buzz.

"No, no, no!" She squirmed and tried to shift away but there was no space in the trunk and she could barely move her arms and legs with them handcuffed together.

Reaching between her thighs he pulled her knees apart and she felt the cool metal slip easily between her wet lips, burying itself deep inside her. He draped a cord over her hip, which led to a tiny battery pack that strapped to her thigh. "This isn't strong enough to make you come, but it should keep you right on the edge for me. And girls on the edge are so much better behaved."

He leaned down and pressed a kiss to her lips and stood back up smiling. Then he dropped her purse into the trunk behind her.

"See you soon," he said, and then the guard slammed the trunk.

Chapter Two
THALIA

Thalia was tightly bound. The handcuffs linking wrist to ankle made her feel like she was about to be sacrificed.

Maybe she was.

She could hear the guard moving around the car. A door opening, something landing on the backseat, and the door shutting.

Buzzzzz.

The vibrator in her pussy was keeping her so wet, she clenched her thighs together trying to get just a little more pressure, but it didn't work. It was small, and he had been much larger. She already felt sore from the stairwell — *dammit*, thinking of the stairwell was a bad idea. The memory of his weight against her as she came made the torment of the vibrator even worse. She tried to reach for the fear and panic she had felt, but it was like she was numb to it, like she had passed through the other side of fear and her mind was now only focused on the physical. And the physical was centered between her thighs.

Another door opening, closing, and then the engine started. He was whistling. The bastard was whistling, minutes after he'd attacked her and beat her. She tried to kick the walls of the trunk but only hurt herself, yanking the handcuffs hard into tender flesh. She gritted her teeth against the pounding ache in her wrists that she had just amplified with her attempt at a tantrum.

Suddenly the radio kicked on, some top 40 station blaring Katy Perry as he turned up the volume to an obnoxious level. Then Thalia felt them moving, the sway of the car with each turn started to make her nauseous. And then there was the constant humming between her legs, the heat building at the core of her, but never enough to push her over the edge.

She could feel her heartbeat between her thighs, every sense focused in trying to get just a little more sensation from the little silver vibe. Thalia realized she was moaning, a high-pitched noise that reminded her of begging. Her thighs were sawing together, her back bowing and contracting as much as possible — all so she could come.

She knew if she came without his permission he would hurt her again, but even thinking of the crop made her groan. The way the burning ache had spread across her breasts. If she could just tilt a little she could rub her nipples against the floor of the trunk, any kind of touch would be better than this.

She gave a little frustrated scream as she realized there was no room to turn enough to rub against anything, and then screamed again when she realized how ridiculous it was to even want to try. It was an impossible tension to escape, her body was wound up with sensation, still taut with the after effects of her orgasms.

As the car kept moving, and the buzzing continued deep inside her she started to take rapid breaths, panic sliding in under the haze of arousal.

Where was he taking her? What was he going to do to her? Would he fuck her again?

Did she care right now?

Another quiet scream which dissolved into sobbing. If she could just come she could think clearly, but everything in her body was focused at the pounding of her clit, begging for attention.

Time seemed to move torturously slowly. She felt like they drove forever until her body was a network of humming nerves, begging her brain for release. By the time the car rocked to a stop, and she heard the engine turn off, the absence of the loud music left her in an eerie quiet where her fast, shallow breaths filled her ears. Crying silently in the dark, barely a shudder to each inhale and exhale. The muffled sound of a garage door shutting came just as his door opened and closed.

She felt raw. Every nerve ending painfully sensitive, but not enough. It wasn't enough!

All she wanted was to come, just so she could think straight. She wanted the little vibe out of her, but she also wanted it pressed to her clit — just for a moment — so she could finally fall over the edge.

Heavy footsteps came to the back of the car and the trunk popped open. He was smiling down at her in the dim light. The reason why slammed into her and she groaned in despair. She hadn't screamed for help and he was happy about it.

But what if someone on the streets at night had heard her? What if she could have been rescued?

She was so stupid.

"Well, Thalia, how did you enjoy the car ride?" His hands were on his hips as those blue-gray eyes slid over her, stopping on her wet thighs before returning to her eyes.

"Go fuck yourself." She spat it out, because facing him again made it all real once more. This was really happening. Cold steel filled his gaze and he gripped her arm hard to pull her toward him. When he did the cuff dug sharply into her wrist and ankle and she cried out.

"I'd much rather fuck *you* again." His voice was cold too, and she wanted to stay away from him. This version of him was terrifying. Reaching behind her he quickly uncuffed her ankles from her wrists and pulled her out of the trunk, letting the cuffs dangle at her sides. She shook with fear and the steadily beating arousal between her thighs. Her legs were so wobbly that he kept a hand on her to keep her upright.

The gush of wetness that came from her when she was standing was embarrassing, she felt it on her upper thighs and he didn't miss it. Slamming the trunk he turned back to her and swept his right hand up her thigh, collecting some of the juices before palming her pussy. He tugged out the little vibe and ripped off the battery pack before pocketing both. Then his hand returned to pressing gently against her. She almost mourned the vibe's absence because she was still shaking with her urge to come.

"You're very wet, slut, aren't you?" His fingers dug into her arm, demanding an answer.

"Yes," she muttered weakly, staring at the car and not his hands or his belt or his hips.

"Yes, *sir*," he corrected, and his palm rubbed against her clit just enough to make her moan.

"Yes, sir," she repeated, her entire being focused between her thighs once again. Just as quickly as the pressure from his hand had been applied, he took it away again, leaving her gasping. She dissolved into tears again as he pushed her through the large garage.

Now that she could look to the side she saw four other vehicles, all very nice. Three cars of various styles, and a big SUV. She couldn't have named them, but they all looked luxury.

When he pushed her through the door she stepped into an incredibly beautiful house. It distracted her momentarily from the throbbing heat between her legs.

Gray floors and light wood in a huge floor plan. Everything was obviously custom made, the shelves, the entertainment center. Through a doorway to the right she saw the hint of a massive kitchen.

"Kneel." He let go of her arm and pointed at the floor in front of her. As she dropped to her knees she tried to tell herself it was because her legs were wobbling, not because she was obeying him. She was not giving in.

He nodded at her and stepped into the kitchen, returning a second later with a pair of scissors. Thalia jumped and tried to stand, but he grabbed her hair firmly and held her still.

"I will not have you in clothes in my house unless I have requested it." He relaxed his grip on her hair and his fingertips rubbed her scalp where it still tingled. "You don't need them anymore."

"Please don't," Thalia begged. The clothes weren't covering her much, but they were her last barrier.

"I'll ignore that you didn't address me as 'sir' that time. I know you're learning." He crouched in front of her, and her eyes couldn't escape the steel in his. "Answer me this, have your clothes stopped me from doing anything I want with you?"

She shook her head slowly and felt a sob rising in her throat, she fought it, but it still came out as a small cry.

"Then why do you care if you have them?" His question seemed sincere, his face wasn't angry, and she felt a fraction calmer staring into his eyes when he wasn't furious with her.

She opened her mouth to answer but couldn't bring herself to agree with him. She still wanted her clothes, even if they hadn't helped her at all.

His sigh made her jump. "Stay still, I do not want to cut you." The scissors started at the bottom of her skirt and moved to the top where he held the fabric away from her skin. As soon as the last snip was made he pulled it away, leaving her naked from the waist down. His hands tugged at the button down and the last of the buttons broke easily, and then he simply tugged it off. Cutting the sleeves to allow the cuffs to come through. Her bra was half pressing her breasts out of it, one of the cups still inverted to hold her breast up and out.

He was right, her clothes had done nothing for her.

A snip at the center of her bra, and at each strap and it came away in pieces. She was nude, kneeling before him as he stood up.

When he returned to the kitchen with her ruined clothes she looked around at what she could see. Information could help her. The house looked expensive, much nicer than her little apartment, and she was confused as to how he owned it.

Security, even for a big company like the one she was at, couldn't pay enough for this place.

"Stand up." His voice was made for commands, strong and direct, but Thalia had no idea why she was listening. When she wobbled to her feet she realized he had left the heels on. "Follow me." He turned and walked into the other room with the entertainment center.

She stayed still for a minute as he moved ahead of her. It took her mind a minute to process that at the moment she had no idea where she was, the few windows she could see were pitch black without even the hint of streetlights. The urge to run back into the garage was there, but by the time the door rose enough for her to get out, he'd have caught her. She silently cursed herself, but worried if she waited much longer he'd hurt her again, so she walked after him, keeping her steps painfully slow.

As she entered the living room she looked around, trying to see if there was anything that would help her. No pictures. No papers. There were empty couches and chairs and a huge, dark rug in the center of them all. No coffee table, just open space. He pointed at it, and she moved there.

When he stepped behind her she whimpered, his hands sliding down her sides as his hips brushed against hers. He was getting hard again. Already.

"Are you still wet for me?" His left hand reached between her legs and she shook with the urge to fight him, knowing it would be pointless. When his fingers delved between her lips her hips lifted she sighed, his touch instantly bringing back the driving arousal of the trunk, the urge for just a little more so she could come.

Suddenly the vibe was in his right hand, and when she heard the buzzing she jerked back against him. He held her there as he pressed the vibe to her clit and she screamed something unintelligible. Just as she reached the edge, teetering toward oblivion, he pulled the vibe away and she started crying again like she had been in the trunk. Desperate to come, she whimpered and actually laid her hand over his, trying to wordlessly beg him to touch her again.

"Tell me what you want."

"Please," she begged, breathlessly, and shifted her hips against him. He seemed unbothered, despite the erection pressing into her.

"Words, Thalia."

She made a frustrated little sound which was so childish and petulant it surprised her. "Please touch me."

"Sir," he corrected.

"Please touch me, sir."

He chuckled and stepped back from her, tucking the vibe away. "No."

She gawked at him as he walked around her and dropped into an oversized chair directly in front of her.

"Touch yourself for me. On your knees." He sat back and waited.

The pounding heat between her legs made it hard to think, hard to feel embarrassed as she lowered herself to her knees. She still felt herself blush, her skin always quick to turn pink and then crimson when she was in an uncomfortable situation. He stared at her as she laid her hand on her thigh, not wanting to do something so intimate in front of him. When she hesitated he leaned forward, cracking his knuckles. The threat was apparent — either obey or be punished. She closed her eyes and her fingers slid between her folds and pressed against her clit. Her hips bucked and her head dropped back as she finally felt herself moving toward the sweet escape of release. The aching tension from the trunk had been simmering under her skin for too long.

She clenched her eyes tight, trying to ignore the penetrating stare of his eyes on her. Her breaths came harder, her pulse ringing in her ears as she slid her hand farther down, thrusting two fingers inside herself and rubbing the heel of her hand against her clit. Then she brought the wetness back to her clit and focused on what she always did for herself. It didn't take long until she felt herself shake and moan, the release coiling up her spine and then snapping like a cable wound too tight, bursting into sparks. Sending her gasping into the afterglow with rapid breaths and a humming sensation in her skin. The fog in her head cleared, the haze of arousal evaporating to leave only reality behind, and she whimpered — unsure as to how she had actually managed to come while kneeling on a carpet in front of a monster.

When she opened her eyes she saw him smiling. Coldly. Maliciously. He stood slowly and walked toward her, snapping her head back painfully with a harsh grip in her hair.

"What did you forget, Thalia?"

She grabbed onto his wrist, trying to ease the strain, but he slapped her hands away. "I did what you asked!" she screamed, crying again. How could he be angry at her already?

"What. Did. You. Forget." His voice was angry now, right at her ear and it made her shake with fear.

Oh no.

She had come without permission. Again. He had only told her to touch herself, not to come. The fear of the riding crop made her start sobbing, but a tug at her hair reminded her to respond. "I came without your permission."

"I thought I'd given you a lesson you wouldn't forget, maybe you need another one?" He tilted her head to the side, reaching down to pinch her nipple harshly until she squirmed and cried out. "Something to also remind you to address me as 'sir' perhaps?"

"I'm sorry, sir. I'm so sorry, please don't punish me again. Sir." Thalia was babbling, she knew she was, even as he dragged her forward on the floor by her hair. Stepping around her, he dropped into the chair and suddenly she was over his knee. Her head hanging toward the floor, the blood pounding in her temples. He trapped her legs under one of his own and linked the cuffs from her wrists to a bracket that had been installed on the chair.

It struck her that this was not random. He wouldn't have a chair like this unless— SMACK.

The first strike of his hand across her ass made her scream and buck, but she couldn't move. SMACK.

Thalia shook her head, burying her face into the leather of the chair. She hadn't been spanked since she was a child and it had never hurt this much. SMACK.

His hand was leaving stinging welts wherever it landed, the heat would spread and the next time the strike overlaid on a place he had already spanked it hurt worse. Not as bad as the belt, but he just kept going. SMACK.

"Sir, please, please! I'm sorry! I'm so sorry! Sir, please, stop!" She was begging, but her thighs were also soaked, she knew if it was soaking into his lap that he would know. He would know she was wet, and Thalia had a terrible feeling that it wasn't just from her masturbation in front of him. SMACK.

This time his hand rubbed the place he had struck and it was soothing. Thalia suddenly realized she wasn't fighting anymore, a humming buzz was moving through her body. She wasn't scared anymore, she'd passed beyond that, she just *was*. She had let go, resigned herself to this humiliation, to the heat and pain in her ass. SMACK.

He was rubbing again, and impossibly she felt an orgasm growing in her lower belly. The tingling heat building and building with each— SMACK.

She moaned, biting her lower lip hard, clenching her fists in the cuffs as she twisted in his lap, but he only held her down more firmly. SMACK.

More rubbing. SMACK.

Oh no. Not again.

"Sir, please, stop! I can't hold it." She could hear how strangely sexual her voice sounded, lower and breathy. Almost... *needy?*

"Are you saying you want to come, Thalia?" His voice had an edge of laughter to it. He was *enjoying* this as his warm hand moved in circles across her sore skin.

She clenched her teeth, her hair brushing the floor as she felt her face heat up. If she said yes she was consenting to this.

She couldn't.

His hand dipped between her thighs, soaking wet, and he brushed his fingers across her clit. So lightly, too light, but she moaned loudly.

"Thalia?" There was a warning in his voice.

"Yes! Yes, sir, please! I—" she took a shuddering breath, filled with shame but craving the oblivion he could give her. "Sir, I want to come. Please, may I come?"

His fingers began lightly touching her again, and she moaned. "I may not always say yes, Thalia, but you may always ask me. And when you ask it properly…" He thrust two fingers inside her and his thumb brushed harshly against her clit. The sentence trailed away, and as his hand moved against her he breathed a single word in her ear, "Come."

She came hard, her body arching on his lap. It was so much more intense than the one she had given herself, and his fingers didn't stop until he had wrung every small convulsion from her. Leaving her gasping and shivering on his lap.

She heard his soft chuckle above her and his hand gently moved over her hair, like he was petting an animal. "When you ask properly, if I am willing to provide it, I will ensure you are satisfied."

"Yes, sir." Her body was giving up, she felt the dark edge of unconsciousness creeping toward her. It had all been too much. Too much stress, too much fear, too much forced pleasure, too much insanity. Her mind was finally checking out.

She felt him petting her, and heard him say softly, "Good girl," just before the darkness overwhelmed her.

Chapter Three
THALIA

Now

She had slapped him.

After everything he had done to her, after all of the threats, the punishments — she had slapped him. She had slapped the man who had kidnapped her and locked her in a fucking room. She was an epic idiot.

His eyes when they came back to hers were ice cold and rage came off him in waves. All urges to be strong and brave fled her and she only focused on self-preservation.

Thalia tried to turn and run away from him but he was too fast, his hand catching in her hair and wrenching her back hard. When she looked at him again she saw the pink outline of her hand across his cheek. His lips pulled back from his teeth as he hissed, "You are so right, Thalia."

Her confusion must have been evident on her face, even amidst the fear that was making her shake and cry, because he kept talking.

"You are not a whore. I wouldn't pay any bitch who was as disobedient and ungrateful as you." His hand tightened in her hair and he turned her toward the door. "I was gentle with you last night. You may not believe it, but you're about to learn just how true that is."

The security guard turned and dragged her out of the room and down a hallway by her hair. She stumbled occasionally as she begged him, murmuring pleas as she tried to stay upright, but he never stopped dragging her.

"Please, sir, don't," she whimpered.

"Suddenly remember your manners, slut?" He slammed her into the wall next to a door and held her there by her throat. As he opened the door, he spoke through his teeth. "I gave you a beautiful room. I allowed you to sleep unbound. I have done *everything* to make this transition easier for you."

Thalia sputtered, trying to beg him against the choking sensation in her throat.

He wasn't interested.

The guard tightened his grip on her throat and threw her into the room. She gasped as she fell in front of him. The room was rather large and the floor seemed to be lined with dark foam tiles that were not as sharp on her limbs as the normal flooring. A huge bed filled the center and along the walls were... things. Cabinets and contraptions, a giant wooden X covered in straps. Too much to take in and all of it terrifying.

"I'm so sorry, sir, I'm sorry. Please don't hurt me, please." Thalia begged but he slammed the door and turned back to her, delivering a slap so hard that her ears were ringing when she looked back to him in shock.

"Just returning the favor. *That* was not your punishment." He stepped past her to a post that went from floor to ceiling, and he started to attach a pair of leather cuffs linked by a metal chain.

"You don't have to do this. You can let me go. I'm sorry I slapped you!" She moved back across the floor away from him until her back pressed against the dark wall. She could feel the ache in her chest from the sobs she was trying to stifle.

"Come here, Thalia." He pointed at the floor next to him. After a moment he looked back at her and his anger ratcheted up. "Now."

When she still didn't move he took three long steps to her and grabbed her by the hair again, she immediately started crying as he dragged her toward the post. "You are only making this worse for yourself." Wrapping one arm around her waist he lifted her off the floor and pressed her forward against the post.

His weight against her back brought flashbacks from the night before and she fought him. He crushed her harder against it until she couldn't breathe, her hands quickly dragged above her again to be clamped inside the leather cuffs.

At least they were softer than the handcuffs.

Once she was restrained he stepped back and more flashbacks hit her as she heard his belt unwind. She was begging him when the first strike landed on her ass. She jumped forward into the post and started sobbing louder.

The next strike landed just below her ass at the top of her thighs, the next criss-crossed that one. "Tell me, Thalia, how many times did you come last night?"

She was shaking her head and crying quietly when the belt landed across her back, forcing her to think, to count. "Th— three times, s—sir." Her face flushed with shame again.

He struck her again and she yelled, but his voice continued oddly calm. "Then it seems to me you enjoyed last night quite a bit. You didn't seem to fight me on your knees in my living room."

She moaned in embarrassment, and he cracked the belt across her ass again. Her skin was aching and burning all at once. Each line burned like fire for a moment and then ached fiercely.

"You will always respond to me when I speak to you. You may say 'yes sir' or 'no sir.'" Another strike of the belt across her back that made her arch as much as possible as she screamed.

"Yes, sir!" Thalia almost yelled it.

"Good. So are you saying you didn't enjoy when you came for me?" His voice was controlled rage, and she hated him for it. Another strike on her thighs. "I seem to remember you asking, *begging*, to come."

She sobbed as another strike laid fire across her sensitive flesh. "Yes, sir."

"Two of those times you came without my permission," he growled, and the next strike seemed to overlap a previous one, making her hiccup as she continued crying.

"Yes, sir. I am sorry, sir. Please stop!"

"Not done yet, Thalia. Tell me, how many times did you make me come last night?" Another strike that stole her focus and she whimpered. Forcing herself back to those memories, to his hands on her, and she felt herself getting wet. She clenched her hands, digging her nails into her palms to try and distract herself.

CRACK. Another strike across her ass.

"Once, sir!" Thalia shouted, trying to control her sobbing. But everything hurt, her entire backside from the top of her back to the backs of her thighs was on fire and aching. The remnants from the belt yesterday had not faded completely, and this was only enflaming them further.

"So you came more than I did last night. Slept in a luxurious room that I carried you to after you collapsed in my lap. Received minimal punishment despite numerous defiant acts — and still you strike me and speak to me with disrespect?" He was suddenly right next to her, growling in her ear. "That will not be tolerated. You are mine, Thalia. Mine. I am not letting you go, and I will break you and enjoy myself while I do it. The sooner you give in the happier you will be."

"No!" she screamed. The idea that he wanted to keep her made panic clench her lungs in a vice, her chest aching with it.

"No?" His voice was vicious and a hard snap of the belt across her ass made her jump, but she shook her head anyway.

"No! I don't want to be here, I'm not some *thing* that you can own!" Thalia kept her eyes clenched tight, and she jerked on the cuffs even though her bruised wrists protested.

"That's where you're wrong, Thalia." His voice was right against her ear, "I'll break you down. It may take time, but I will."

She drew in a breath, calming her cries for a moment as the stinging faded to heat in her skin, before asking softly, "And if I don't break?"

"You will." He said it with the finality of a door slamming.

Then he bent her head back by her hair and delivered a rapid series of blows down her backside, making her whimper until her voice failed her. She started to feel light headed, her skin humming all over as he pushed her further than she thought she could stand. Then just as quickly as he had started, he dropped the belt. His breathing was harsh in her ears as he reached up and unhooked the chain linking her leather cuffs to the pillar. Thalia slid to her knees because her legs wouldn't support her, and he ran his hand over her hair. Petting once again.

"Do you understand why you were punished, Thalia?" His voice held an edge to it, but his hand was so soothing on her hair, and she was finding it hard to focus with her body thrumming to the beat of her pulse.

"I slapped you. I was disrespectful. I didn't say sir." She cited the things he had listed. Her own voice sounded empty, and although she could still feel tears on her cheeks she wasn't actively crying any more.

"Good girl." His hand lifted from her hair. "Now bend forward, on all fours."

Thalia whimpered and his hand returned to tighten in her hair, pushing her forward until she was in position.

"You will learn it is much better for you when you don't fight me." When she was in position he spanked her ass hard and she cried out from the pain of her welts. His hand rubbed slowly, and she could feel the texture of her skin from the belt. "Although it is delightful to get to punish you so."

He knelt behind her and she wanted to move away from him, wanted to turn and beg him not to touch her, but she already hurt so badly she couldn't risk more pain. She just hung her head down and tried not to stare at the dark leather cuffs and the chain that linked them.

"Spread your legs wider," he commanded. She did and he groaned quietly when he saw how wet she was. "Even with a punishment you're so responsive."

His fingers swept up her cleft and she hated the little moan that escaped her. After so much pain his touch felt amplified. When his fingers moved over her clit she bit her lip and tried to stop the buck of her hips. His low chuckle made her flush with embarrassment, and then he gripped her waist. There was a shift behind her that she tried to ignore and then his cock was pressing into her again.

He made a deep sound as he slid inside, and she whimpered. Still so sore, still hating herself for reacting. When his fingers found her clit, she bucked back against him just as he thrust forward. A clap of skin and he was quickly buried to the hilt inside her. His size stretching her and filling her. More circling pressure to her clit as his thrusts increased in pace, and despite the pain in her backside, and the agony of his clothes against her raw skin, she moaned.

She fucking moaned underneath him. *Again*. She was broken, disgusting, wrong.

Biting down on her lip she tried to stop, but as his thrusts picked up she couldn't deny the intensity of the friction inside her and against her clit. The stinging pain from the welts added another layer to the sensations. Her body rebounded between pain and pleasure so fast she couldn't stop the moans anymore.

He chuckled above her. "You can deny this all you want, but tell me, Thalia, have you ever come this hard before?" He thrust deep inside her, over and over and over, and then he hissed in her ear as he applied pressure to her clit again. "Come for me, Thalia."

And she did.

Her body vibrated with the strength of it and she was dimly aware of him stilling inside her as the world whited out, his fingers tight on her hips as she came. For one blissful moment there was nothing. No guard, no kidnapping, no torture room — but good things never lasted for people like her. Whimpering beneath him as their heavy breaths intermingled in the silence of the room, dragging her back to reality, she bit down on the inside of her cheek to stop the surge of tears.

Sliding out of her, still hard, he pulled her back against him. She didn't fight as her sore skin went flush to his, and as his hand started to smooth over her hair she heard him sigh. "I allowed you to come again, Thalia. What should you say?"

"Thank you, sir." The words came from somewhere inside her. She wasn't this person, she didn't want this. But her heart still leapt when he said…

"Good girl." He let go before he stood behind her and moved to the door. The realization hit her that he hadn't come. Why? Why fuck her and not finish? He snapped out a command, "Face me. Kneel with your knees apart and your hands on your thighs."

She turned around to comply, feeling the wetness slippery between her thighs, but when she tried to sit back on her ankles she yelped in pain. Clenching her teeth, she shook slightly.

"Normally I would have you sit back so I could see you more easily, but I know you're in pain. We will take care of that later *if* you behave." He put his hands on his hips and she was again surprised by how handsome he was. He couldn't possibly need to kidnap women to get laid.

Then again, how many women wouldn't run screaming from a room like this?

He was staring at her expectantly and she almost jumped as she hurried to respond. "Yes, sir," she whispered, hoping she'd said it fast enough, and it seemed to work even though he sighed.

"You will sit like this in any room you enter unless I have told you otherwise. You already know to address me as sir, but you may also call me Master."

Her mouth dropped open at the word and fear coiled in her belly. "Master?" She said in shock.

"Yes?" He responded to it like it was his name. *Bastard.*

"I can't do that." She felt sick all over again. He wasn't going to let her go. He thought he was her *master*. Thalia's eyes locked on the leather cuffs on her wrists and she realized she was crying again.

"Say sir, Thalia."

"Sir," she responded automatically, her mind somewhere else trying to look at the situation objectively. How had she gotten here? What had she done? "Why me, sir?" The last question was out loud.

"I knew what you were after the first time I saw you. You only confirmed it the first time I took you to your car. You don't realize it yet, but you need this as much as I want it." His eyes were steady on her. He believed every word he was speaking.

"No, sir." Thalia shook her head slowly and he sighed again. She hoped her response wouldn't make him hurt her again.

"I'll ignore that for now. I know this is still new, and I'll look forward to hearing you call me Master when you're begging me for my cock." He leaned back against the door and crossed one ankle over the other, just watching her for a moment. She gritted her teeth and he continued. "You will crawl after me, and you'll keep the cuffs on. Now."

Turning on his heel he opened the door and started walking down the hall. Fear shot through her as he disappeared around the doorframe. For a moment she couldn't move, but as the heavy footfalls started to fade she rushed forward.

Her backside screamed, but when she got into the hall she saw a hint of movement to her left and her knees ached against the hard floor. She crawled, the chain between the cuffs shortening her ability to reach forward, and she felt a blush flood up her chest. She turned a bend in the hall and found him standing near a door. He smiled at her when she sat up in front of him.

"You know the position, Thalia." His voice held humor again. It grated her, but it was so much better than the rage of before. She spread her knees and ignored the pain as she sat back on her heels.

His smile reflected in his eyes. "Good girl." The guard pushed open the door he stood by and she saw a different bedroom. Darker tones, drapes over real windows where sunlight peeked around the edges. A massive bed, an armoire — and then he was moving forward and her observations were cut short. Thalia crawled after him and wished she could disappear into the floor when he stepped into the bathroom. It was all glass, and dark wood, with smooth stone gray walls instead of tile. He opened the glass door to a massive shower, which could easily fit two or more people, and turned on the water.

"We really need to clean you up, Thalia. That was my plan for your morning. A shower, breakfast, a conversation about your new situation." His hand tested the water and he beckoned her forward.

For a moment, she thought about how much better that version of her morning would have been. His shirt came off and she stared up at his body. He was strong, but not overly muscled. His body was lean and fit. He smiled at her appraisal of him and she dropped her eyes to the floor, where his pants pooled. Leaning down he unclasped the leather cuffs from her wrists and left them on his clothes.

"Get in the shower, stand, and face the wall."

Thalia felt like she should cry, but she obeyed. Stepping into the streams of water that came from all sides. The water was simultaneously soothing and painful against her raw skin, but she stayed still. The traitorous fluttering in her lower belly betrayed her body's anticipation of what would come next.

Why was she reacting this way?

The door shut behind him with a clap and she jumped. One of his hands grabbed the back of her neck and held her still as the other began to soap her skin with a smooth bar. It smelled so clean, not perfumed or flowery like her body wash. This almost smelled like herbs, more natural than anything she could buy at Target. His hand massaged the back of her neck and she relaxed the muscles in her shoulders she hadn't noticed were tense.

"Relax, Thalia. Breathe. I've already punished you, and unless you break one of my rules again you have nothing to fear." His hands worked magic on her skin, somehow making the burning in her back not so bad. He let go of her neck and his hand rubbed her shoulder.

Her mind protested; he *had* punished her for breaking rules, rules he hadn't even told her yet. How was she supposed to obey him when she didn't know the rules? She wanted to ask. She wanted to argue, to scream at him. She wanted to shove him away from her.

She didn't do anything.

"Put your hands on the wall, above your head," he ordered, and she did. A little grateful for the ability to brace herself as his ministrations moved down her legs. The movement of his hands over her welted ass and thighs made her whimper, but he didn't let up. Suddenly his hands were between her thighs, rubbing her with soap, his fingers delving inside her, which made her thighs quake. He made an appreciative sound behind her.

"You respond so quickly to my touch." His other hand slid around to her front and rubbed her clit. She hated that it felt good. She hated that her body accepted it as pleasure, firing the synapses and flooding her with endorphins. How was he so much better than any of her exes? He knew exactly where to rub her, she didn't have to guide him. Didn't have to squirm to try and get his touch back on point. Her hips bucked against his hand and she tried not to moan. She hated even more that he knew what he was doing to her.

She really was a slut. No one else would act like this in her situation. The shame made her start crying again. There was something intrinsically wrong with her.

He took his hands away and she almost opened her mouth to speak, to ask him why he made her enjoy it, but she shut her mouth hard. He set the soap down and leaned her head back under one of the shower streams, his fingers pushed through her hair and then there was a strong, clean smell of shampoo. His fingers rubbed against her scalp and sent a pleasant chill rushing down her back. The soap flooded over her front and one of his hands cupped her breast, pinching her nipple until she gasped and her hands started to come off the wall. He twisted her nipple hard.

"Hands. Wall. Now," he growled in her ear and she pressed her palms back to the stone wall of the shower. Heat flooded between her legs, and she lifted her breasts into his hands unconsciously. He let go without another word and returned to rinsing her hair. When he was done he stepped back and she smelled another wave of the clean soap, followed by splashing water as he washed himself off.

"Are you going to be obedient, Thalia?" His voice was closer to her than she had thought and her muscles jumped. She could feel his presence against her back but he didn't touch her. She wanted him to.

No. She didn't.

"Yes, sir." She dropped her head down as a voice inside almost laughed at her. She wanted to be touched, but she wasn't going to beg him no matter what he said. No matter how wet she was, no matter how much her nipples ached for attention.

"Get on your knees. If you please me, I'll rub down your ass and thighs with a cream that will help you a bit." He spoke clearly and she turned and slid to her knees, his cock already at eye level. She caught herself biting her lower lip, her tongue darting out over the place where her teeth had been. "If you disappoint me, I'll leave you to heal on your own. If you bite me, I'll do things to you that you can't even imagine."

"Yes, sir." Fear and a faint trace of excitement brimmed inside her, she was starting to recognize that this was just what he did to her. Maybe *this* was what he meant about her, what he kept saying she was.

She wanted to come, she wanted away from him, but she knew she had to please him first.

"May I use my hands, sir?" Her voice wavered and he smiled down at her and nodded.

"Yes, you may." His voice jerked as she wrapped her hand around the base of his shaft, her fingers barely touching as she tongued the head of his cock. She tasted precum as she moved her hand up and down his length, sliding him into her mouth and beginning to swirl her tongue.

His hips twitched slightly and she liked the power she had over the guard in that moment. She brought her other hand up to cup his balls, tracing her nails gently over the sensitive skin as she sucked him deeper into her mouth. He let out a quick groan and she picked up the pace, drawing his cock in until he bumped against her throat. She squeezed his balls gently and swallowed to let him into her throat. He moaned and his hand landed on her head, but he didn't hurt her. Thalia held her breath and moved his cock in her throat until her eyes watered and then she pulled back.

Then his fist clenched in her hair and pulled her forward again, pressing against her throat insistently.

She had to please him.

She gagged slightly, swallowing again to let him in and he thrust against her, bruising her throat as he started to move. As he worked toward his climax she tried to beg him to let her breathe, but the vibrations seemed to only encourage him. Just as her vision started to edge in he pulled back enough to let her gasp and then he thrust back. She whimpered and laid her hands on his thighs in a silent plea and he finally came in her throat. His groans above her promised air soon and she swallowed fast, his taste filling her mouth before she could finally gasp.

He pulled out of her mouth, his hand still clenched in her wet hair. "That was pretty good, slut. You'll get better with practice."

In the most fucked up way his comment hurt her feelings, a blush burning her cheeks, and it was worse when he chuckled. "Don't act offended, I'll give you plenty of opportunity to practice, and based on what I know about you it's not like you've had much lately."

"What do you know about me?" she asked before thinking, still on her knees in front of him, then she remembered to add, "Sir?"

He smirked at her and flipped the water off before he opened the door, drying off quickly. Then he shook out a fresh towel and held out his arms. "Come here."

She rose to her feet and stepped into the towel and he patted her dry. Thalia noticed how careful he was not to rub her welts too much. He wrapped her hair in the towel and squeezed to wring it out, then he hung the towel up and walked into the bedroom. "Follow me, Thalia." He called from the bedroom.

Her legs shook with fear but she remembered to drop to her knees and crawl after him. He was standing by the bed, having pulled on some cloth pants already. But at least he smiled at her.

"Good girl. Now get on the bed, on your stomach, and I'll answer your question while I rub down your welts."

She stood and crawled onto the bed, and he never took his eyes off her as she lay down. Then he walked around the bed and secured her spread eagled with soft leather cuffs. She couldn't help but whimper, and she wanted to bring her limbs back in, to try and refuse him, but her skin burned and ached and she wanted him to help her. To be nice, just for a little while.

In a moment she was bound, and he had climbed onto the bed to sit next to her. "I'm sure you've noticed I don't need the security job, but it let me get close to you."

Thalia almost spoke but the first stroke of cold cream across her skin almost had her purring like a cat. It felt incredible on her welted skin. His strong hands massaged it in and loosened the tense muscles underneath.

"I knew you were submissive when I first saw you. It was on the street near the office building. I think you were coming back from lunch, and you stood out to me." His voice was a drone as his hands moved over her skin, such a sharp contrast to the pain he'd caused. But his words ate at her.

He had watched her?

Taking a breath, he started speaking again. "After I got the job at the building you only confirmed it for me. Little signals in the way you responded to male attention, even more that you turned them all down for dates." More cold cream spread across her ass, and he gripped the firm skin making her groan into the bed. What could she have possibly done to make him think she wanted *this*? She barely talked to anyone at the office, and the few who had asked her out to lunch or dinner in the past months had never done it publicly. "Are you still listening, Thalia?"

"Yes, sir." She tried to lift her head but couldn't turn to see him very well.

"Let me see… it's probably safe to say you've never been happy in a normal relationship. You don't know why you're not as sexually satisfied as the other women who talk around you." He was describing her too well. She buried her face in the bed as she remembered coming so hard just moments after he'd beaten her with the belt. Was she really this fucked up?

"Not that women are likely that fond of you. It's hard for you to have strong friendships with women that aren't similar to you, because you might distract the men in their lives with the potential of what they could do to you." His fingers delved inside her and she moaned loudly before silencing herself. "That is, if they had the balls to take it."

"Sir…" she whined. She wanted him to stop talking, to stop stating all of it like it was a fact. How could he know any of this? How did he know she'd always struggled to have friends at all? A few good friends, yes, but they had faded after high school, and working full time during her short stint in college had left her alone most of the time.

"Don't interrupt." He spanked her lightly, and she wiggled as the tingle broke through the cold cream. "I researched you specifically as well. Mother died when you were young, father is a waste and doesn't even talk to you. No close friends. You don't even have a goldfish."

His strong hands worked the cold cream into her back and she was stunned that her life could be reduced to so little. That she had so little. That realization hurt worse than the marks on her skin. Instead of stopping, his next words cut like a knife. "No one is going to look for you, Thalia. It's like you prepared yourself for me. And, even better, your doctor's records showed you were clean and on the birth control shot."

At that Thalia jerked in her bonds. "You got my medical records?!" This time when he spanked her it was much harder and it made her whimper and pull at the restraints.

"Thalia, don't presume that because I'm showing you mercy at the moment that I won't drag you back into the other room if you're disobedient."

"I'm sorry, sir. Please don't take me back in there." Thalia's voice was muffled as she buried her face into the bedding, fear turning her stomach.

"Then behave, Thalia. Stop fighting me. And of course I had your records checked, you think I'd fuck just anyone?" More cold cream smoothed down her thighs, but the comfort had disappeared.

"You planned—" she choked on the words, crying again.

He got off the bed. "Of course I planned, Thalia. I am not stupid, and I'm *hoping* you're not stupid." His hand was between her thighs again and she cried out when her hips lifted to meet his touch. "I couldn't have planned for how responsive you'd be though, it's quite a pleasant surprise."

Something cold slid inside her pussy and she bucked — it then vibrated suddenly, growing more and more intense, and then cut off again. Her heart rate increased, and then the thing kicked back on, bringing her closer and closer to the edge. She heard herself moan and then it stopped, leaving her frustrated.

He laughed next to her. "Don't feel the need to be quiet, Thalia. Everyone watching would prefer if you made noise, but that vibe shouldn't let you come. If you manage to though, I'll punish you."

Watching?!

She jerked hard on her bindings but she couldn't move, she craned her neck and saw him pointing to the ceiling above her. "Cameras. Always on. I have a lot of friends who like to watch."

Thalia screamed into the bed and he laughed. When she cursed at him he swatted her ass. Then the vibe came to life inside her again and she squirmed on the bed, finding herself gasping when it stopped. A set of straps wrapped around the tops of her thighs, securing the vibrator inside her, making it inescapable.

"Be a good girl and I'll be back to feed you lunch. Misbehave and you can squirm there all day until you beg me to fuck you." His voice was final, no arguments allowed. She whined into the bed, and he spanked her again. "What do you say, Thalia?"

"Yes, sir." The words were hollow, her body trembling as she heard him walk away from her. Then the door clicked shut, and although the room was empty, now she knew she wasn't alone.

People were watching her.

Chapter Four
THALIA

Thalia was trying to count in her head the time between the vibrator cutting off and turning back on. The spacing was never the same, but she was trying to fight the urge to scream and the counting helped in the silence. Her muscles were shaking from the stress of being tied down on her stomach for what felt like several hours, and she was hoping this would be the time she would finally slip over the edge.

Five-one thousand, six-one thousand, seven-one thousand, ei—

"Oh no..." Thalia moaned as the vibrator inside her turned on again, her wetness was pooling underneath her, but as she felt herself building toward that glorious edge, her body tensing and her breath coming in pants and moans — it stopped.

She screamed in frustration, bucking against the restraints and ignoring the sting of the welts on her back.

Thalia had no idea how much time had passed since her punishment that morning, after she'd slapped him, but being kept on the edge for so long had her emotions raw, and her body shivering with need. For a while she had stayed silent and as still as possible despite the vibe's persistent humming inside the core of her.

Eventually she had stopped caring about cameras and people watching, and had focused on trying to come, just to get the relief and ease the tension in her muscles. At this point she'd even take whatever punishment he had planned if she could just be done with the endless cycle of getting to the edge and being dropped back.

She tried to make herself count again, but her brain argued against it. She was thinking about how he had reduced her life to so little when he had spoken to her. How sad to be that girl that disappeared without anyone caring. Would she even be reported missing? Or would her father be grateful to not have to make small talk with her every month or so? Would the temp agency she worked for keep calling her, or just erase her in their database?

There was a girl at the gym that usually talked to her on the Tuesday and Thursday yoga classes. She looked for her and laid her mat out by Thalia each time. Would she wonder where she was?

Of course not.

Thalia couldn't even remember the girl's name. She gritted her teeth as she tried not to sob, the strain of holding it in making her chest ache.

The vibe came back on and she screamed again, "Please, please, let me come! Please, sir!" It wasn't the first time she had begged in the time, and she had thought it was what he wanted, but then he hadn't come back. It had to be lunchtime by now, somewhere under the tingling of her ever-impending orgasm, the strain of her muscles, and the ache of the welts on her back — she was hungry.

Doing what it had done a few times before, the vibe shifted the rhythm and intensity to torture her in a new way. The tension coiled in her lower belly and teased her with the edge, making her gasp and moan and buck her hips against the soft, useless bedding. "Master, please, let me come!"

The vibe turned off again and she gasped, weakly pulling on the restraints as the beats of her heart waited out the time before the next torturous hum. Instead, she heard the door open somewhere behind her amidst the heavy sound of her breaths. She tensed as she heard his footsteps approach her slowly, lazily.

"You've put on quite a show this morning, Thalia." His voice held power in it, he knew exactly what she wanted and as she squirmed on the bed he talked to her like he was discussing the weather.

She really wanted to tell him to go to hell, but that would be incredibly stupid considering she was tied to a bed and had been begging him to touch her for hours. Instead of calling him a series of creative names, she whispered, "Yes, sir."

His touch on her thigh caused a tremor to run through her entire body, she was wound tight as a guitar string and he was plucking her. "You called me Master, Thalia."

"Yes, sir." She gritted her teeth, realizing that was what he'd been waiting for. He had even *told* her it was what he wanted after her punishment. His words came back to her through the haze of her arousal, '*I'll look forward to hearing you call me Master when you're begging me for my cock.*'

"So you want to come?" His touches were too light, barely brushing across her skin and she was so close she didn't even try to stop herself as she lifted her hips toward him.

"Yes, sir," she moaned, gasping as his fingers glanced over her thighs.

"Saying *sir* didn't bring me back in this room, Thalia." His hand left her skin and she released a scream of frustration, her hips lifting and then dropping back to the bed as the muscles of her stomach argued with the strain.

"Yes, Master. I want to come — please!" She was begging. She was calling him Master. She was pathetic.

And who knew how many people were watching her do it.

When his hand slid between her thighs again and flicked something on the vibrator she would have jumped off the bed had it not been for the cuffs at her wrists and ankles. She moaned loudly and it dissolved into curses as he slid the vibe in and out of her.

His clothes dropped to the floor and he ran his hands down her body. His touch making her moan even louder, and then she felt him behind her.

"What do you want, Thalia?" His fingers grazed her clit slightly, but it was clear he knew how close she was because he gave her no pressure.

"Please fuck me." She said it quietly, and his soft laugh made her clench her eyes closed against it. If she'd had her hands free she would have covered her ears.

"Are you going to finish that request appropriately?" His voice warned.

"Please fuck me, Master." She whimpered as his hand turned the vibrator to a low setting that kept her wet but didn't push her any closer to the edge. His fingers gathered her wetness and one pushed against her ass. She jerked in the bindings as much as possible.

"Don't fight me, Thalia. You asked for this." One of his hands was gathering her hair in a fist to hold her down, as his finger pressed insistently, her body arguing and tightening as he pushed harder and finally delved inside her. Whimpering, she bit down on her lip as he invaded her. No one had ever touched her there, and she squirmed to get away as he eased his finger in and out. Over and over.

"Relax," he whispered against her ear, and it was a command, not a request. With a flick he increased the vibe in her pussy and for a moment it refocused her attention and she moaned. He took the opportunity to thrust a second finger inside her and it dragged her back from the edge again as she cried out against the bedding. The aching stretch becoming the focus of her whole world for a moment.

He kept going, methodically, whispering at her to relax. It burned, but as he slid in and out of her ass, the insistent pulse of the vibe inside her, the pressure of his fist in her hair, and his deep voice in her ear started to change the dull pain into something else. Her pussy throbbing with each pulse of his fingers.

"Please," she whimpered, and she wasn't sure if she was asking him to stop or to keep going until she finally moved past the edge he'd held her over all morning. Her legs quivered and then he pulled his fingers from her, his weight shifting on the bed until she could feel the dip made by his knees taking position.

His hand tightened in her hair and he leaned close to her ear, speaking quietly, and for a flash she wondered if it was to keep his voice from the cameras. "Relax for me, Thalia. It will hurt so much less. Take a deep breath for me now and push back."

She took a breath and then she felt him pressing against her; too big, too big! Clenching her fists in the cuffs she tightened despite his warnings, trying to shake her head even as he held her down. He leaned down to her ear and hissed again, "Relax."

Closing her eyes, she consciously focused on relaxing each muscle group — starting with her hands, then her shoulders, her back, and then he pressed inside her. The pain was sudden and she screamed a little and tightened again, but he just groaned and pressed forward further. He was so much bigger than his fingers and it hurt, the pain making her still; she wanted it to be over. The hand not in her hair held him up on the bed, and his muscles seemed as tense as hers.

"Thalia..." His voice had an edge to it, like he wanted to say more but couldn't. He was moving slowly, and she knew that was for her sake, she knew he could make it hurt worse. She imagined it could hurt so much more. That was what made her relax again and he slid deeper, muttering curses behind her shoulder, his own breath shuddering.

"Sir, just do it." Thalia clenched her teeth to prepare herself as he made a sound and thrust forward until he was buried completely inside her. She had made some sound between a moan and a scream and she could feel her body stretching to accommodate him. She was full and the burning continued as his girth strained her. Again he waited, his own body arching against hers as he held himself still until she adjusted. He pulled back agonizingly slowly and Thalia whimpered beneath him, then he eased forward again. The smooth movements allowed the vibrator's pulses to make an impact on her again. As if he knew her clit ached for attention he let go of her hair and reached under her to rub the focal point of her body.

"Oh God!" she screamed and he may not have been prepared for how hard she bucked back against him. His arm gave out under him and he bit into her shoulder to stifle himself. His weight on hers drove him deeper and pressed his touch harder against her clit. There may have still been pain but her brain mercifully focused on the wave of pleasure that had been cresting in her body all morning.

"You are incredible, Thalia." His voice was growling as he pushed himself back up. He swung his hips back and forward again, driving himself inside her. Fingers circling her clit, making her moan louder and louder. "You can come. Go on. Come."

His touch, the vibe, his thrusts, and even the ache from the welts built and built until she came apart. The orgasm blinded her and she had no idea what she yelled out as her body tightened, gripping him in waves as she finally fell into that glorious abyss. Bright sparks crackling behind her eyelids, neurons misfiring in a chaotic blur, every nerve ending finally firing with the most intense orgasm she could remember that left her body humming and blissfully relaxed. He moved behind her again, a deep thrust, and then he came as she heard him clip off a curse and his cock jerked. The warmth of his release filling her was a strange sensation that was quickly lost in the buzzing in her skin.

Breathing brushing against her hair, she felt him stretch past her and her hands were released. Blood tingled in her fingertips and Thalia knew she must have pulled too hard on them as she'd come. He leaned up, sliding out of her slowly, and then he removed the vibrator, finally clicking the soaked silver object off. Two more quick movements and her ankles were unlatched.

His weight shifted to the edge of the bed and she curled on her side, ignoring the sting of the welts and her ass as she instinctively pulled her legs toward her chest.

When his hand returned to her skin she jumped, every nerve ending still raw. Too much sensation in the last day, too much for her brain to process.

He didn't seem to care as he curled against her body and she tilted her head to see a black circle in his hand with a single button, it beeped softly when he pressed it. "You are so beautiful." He nuzzled against her neck and she shuddered. "And you respond better than I could have ever hoped."

"Yes, sir." She muttered bitterly.

"Thalia, you can't deny how you respond. This is what you were meant for." His voice was right against her ear, his breath brushing over her neck like a lover's, but she recoiled from the truth in his words.

"I hate you," she said and winced as her willful nature overwhelmed her logical, self-preserving side. She added, "Sir", as if it would negate what she'd already said.

His body jerked back, and she curled tighter into a ball as she prepared for him to hurt her again, waiting for the sound of him unwinding his belt from his pants on the floor. Instead, she heard the soft beep of the remote he'd pressed before and felt his weight leaving the bed. The jingle of him gathering his clothes had her shaking.

"I'm not going to punish you, Thalia. You did," his throat cleared, "very well."

A wave of relief flowed through her. "Thank you, sir — Master."

"Good girl." His voice seemed strained and she heard him move to the door and open it. Her head lifted out of curiosity and caught a full view of his toned backside. He sat a covered tray inside the door and then glanced back at her.

"Eat and shower if you want. I'll come back later." He spoke gently and she laid her head back down, listening to him shut the door. The lock clicked into place, but it was a relief. At least she'd know when he returned.

Thalia shifted off the bed, uncomfortably aware of how sore she was as she went to grab the tray of food, moving it back to the bed to eat the grilled chicken and cauliflower and fruit before she fell asleep in a semi-circle around it. Exhausted and empty, even with her stomach full.

Hours later she awoke and moved the tray back to the door and tried the handle, but of course it wouldn't budge — he'd just locked her in a different room. But she wasn't cuffed to the bed and she had free range of the bathroom. Running herself a hot bath, she filled it with some soap that smelled of herbs again and she soaked, letting her mind drift as her muscles relaxed. The heat soothed the aches in her body. When it started to cool she got out and showered quickly to rinse. Thalia left the lights off so she wouldn't have to see the marks on her body and just listened to the quiet of the house. If he wasn't sleeping in this dark, masculine toned room, where was he sleeping?

She thought of banging on the door, of asking him to come back so she wasn't alone, but she didn't. Even as she dried herself, carefully moving the cloth over her sore skin, she was aware of the cameras. It didn't matter, they'd seen everything. She lay down without clothing and took stock of the pains in her body as she peeled the sheets back and curled up beneath them.

No show tonight for anyone who was watching. She was too tired. He had exhausted her, which was probably his plan. But she slept free of dreams, or memories, in the dark abyss of unconsciousness.

Her version of morning came harshly. There was no light coming from the curtains when she woke up again, but the loud click of the lock being turned was better than any alarm clock she'd ever owned.

Her body stilled on instinct, some primal part of her brain urging her into physical and mental quiet as the sound of his steps filled the room. The door clicking and locking back into place. For a moment she couldn't place him in the massive space around her and then she heard him beside the bed, breathing evenly. She could picture his broad chest rising and falling and she wondered if he was dressed or not. If he would touch her again.

Part of her wanted it, wanted to be brought over the edge again and again no matter how he took her there, the other more logical side only spoke of the fear she should feel — still trapped, still undressed, still at his mercy.

Chapter Five
HIM

Thalia was beautiful even sleeping. Her still form under the sheets was athletic and he could remember the feel of her body against his in numerous positions. Her long, light brown hair was cast over her shoulders and slightly across her face. Damp at its thickest points because she had showered. She had been terrified when he'd left her, but he'd had to. He had wanted to curl against her and sleep but she had pushed him away in the only way she could.

I hate you.

Her words rebounded in his head and he could think of no way to argue her. He had taken her against her will, shown her the side of herself she had yet to recognize, but he had done it by force. The primal side of himself howled at the success of his time with her, the way her body had yielded to his, the way she had come against his hands and his cock.

She was so damned responsive.

Of any woman he had taken and trained she was his greatest success, in twenty-four hours she had submitted, she had begged for him, called him Master. Even his brother was impressed and had called to tell him so.

It's why he'd used the remote to stop the cameras. He'd wanted a few minutes of not being observed to tell her how beautiful she was, how incredible he thought she was — but she had shunned him with three words.

Yes, she had added the address of 'sir,' but even that he had taught her through punishment, it had been for her own survival to add it. And he had accepted it, and turned the cameras back on, and left.

His brother had assured him that most of their girls, especially the feisty ones, fought back in any way they were able. Submitting with their bodies, but not their will — never the core of who they were.

But he wanted Thalia. Wholly, completely.

Mine.

Something inside him roared as he stared down at her. He wanted to pin her down and take her again and again until she submitted to him fully. Until she didn't challenge his dominance of her, not with a look or a word or a movement.

Since he had first seen her walking in front of the office building, that was all he'd been able to think about. She'd put on her business smile, nodding at someone on the sidewalk, in those four inch heels, and the core of him had wanted her. It had only been fed as he'd overheard complaints from her boss and male coworkers as they'd talked about her refusals of lunch and dinner dates. His brother's computer skills had turned up no love interests, no real family, no real friends to speak of. It had marked her, he'd wanted her.

And here she was.

But she still wasn't fully his. He'd taken her in every way but one, and her will had still appeared. She had begged for him, not just once, but over and over. Other women had broken to his will, caving to the pressures of his commands, crawling on their knees to him, unable to even think of saying the things she'd said.

Even on her knees Thalia wasn't broken. She had crawled after him and faced him with the same serious, hazel eyes as the night before when he'd cuffed her to her car.

At the memory of the stairwell his cock jumped to attention. He remembered her lithe body held aloft by the handcuffs, the skirt slipping up her milky thighs to reveal her ass, her moans as he'd thrust against her — even the fact that she'd fought to escape him afterwards. It had fed the animal inside him.

The chase.

She was always running from him even when there was nowhere to go, and he was able to overpower her again and again. Something deep inside him purred in satisfaction as his hand moved up the outline of her thigh under the sheet.

Mine.

Her breath jumped and he saw her ribs rise and fall more quickly. He didn't speak as he pulled the sheets off her, but she didn't either. Her pale skin was revealed in the dim light of the room, a small nightlight on the wall revealing the curve of her hips, the long slope of her thigh. He kept the cotton pants he had tugged on when he'd left his room, but he still shifted onto the bed and she stopped breathing. He didn't have anything with him — no cuffs, no belt, no gag. He didn't want those things.

He wanted Thalia.

She didn't fight him as he touched her hip, his fingers wrapping around the curve of her to make her lie flat on the bed. Her knees fell open so as not to challenge him, and he was both appreciative and frustrated by that fact.

Part of him wanted her to resist, and part of him wanted her to welcome him.

With her laid out he moved further onto the bed, his hands moving up her thighs to hold them open beneath him. Then he touched her pussy, still warm and wet to his touch. His fingers slid over her clit and her hips lifted slightly although she made no noise.

For a moment he thought he should click the cameras off, but his brother and their customers would be angry if he did, and he didn't want to explain it away.

He couldn't resist the urge to taste Thalia though, the only thing he hadn't had the chance to do.

Lowering his mouth, he glided his tongue against her cleft, opening her up slightly. She let out the quietest of sounds as his tongue grazed her and he fought down the fire in his belly, the aching of his balls that demanded he take her.

He swept his tongue up the lips of her pussy, using his shoulders against her thighs to keep them open even though she wasn't fighting him at the moment. When his mouth found her clit her hips bucked against him and he grabbed them to hold her still under his assault. The soft moan that followed fueled the fire inside him.

He wanted more.

He delved his tongue deeper, slipping inside her as he lapped. Her pussy was as sweet and wet as he imagined it would be against his tongue. Her moans rose and her hands clenched into the sheets and it felt like victory as he continued. She moaned again when he brushed against her clit, sucking it into his mouth, pressing his tongue against it over and over until she lifted her hips from the bed to press herself more urgently against him.

He could hear her breaths increasing, his own heart pounding in his ears as he felt her getting closer to the edge. He lapped again, sucking and licking against the core of her, her juices starting to flow and overtake his senses with her taste. Soft and warm. The tang of her filling his mouth as she really started to get wet. He was so hard it hurt, but he pinned his erection between his stomach and the mattress, shifting his hips a little to give himself the slightest of attentions. She cried out when he thrust a finger inside her.

The way she responded to him made him want to roar. And the way her heat flooded his mouth as his tongue moved against her pussy, those hips lifting — it was incredible.

Then her hand found his hair. He almost sat up but her fist clenched and held him there, her hips lifting against his mouth, and he couldn't resist the urge to cup her ass and lift her pussy to meet his tongue. He sucked on her clit drawing loud moans as he thrust his fingers deeper. She was rising, almost at the edge. He could tell by the way her thighs clenched, her stomach tightening as she rolled her hips against his mouth.

He'd never had a woman direct him the way Thalia was with her hand clenched in his hair, but he wasn't stopping her. It made him feel strange, different.

"Come, Thalia…" he mumbled against her. The tone of her moans changed as she grew closer and he lapped harder, the thrusts of his fingers curled to touch that bundle of nerves and then she came apart in his hands and under his mouth. Her thighs tightened against his shoulders, the space near her knees tightening around his head to hold him in place as her juices flooded his mouth and hands. She soaked the bedding below and he was in awe of her.

His own cock jerked against his stomach, demanding attention, wanting him to bury himself in the hot, wet place that his tongue was bathing. Instead he pushed himself up above her to see Thalia's hazel eyes out of focus as she stared at the ceiling.

This was how he wanted to leave her. Not in fear of what he had planned next, but with an understanding of the pleasure he could bring her.

It took more willpower than he thought he had to drag the sheet and cover back over her long legs and the sweet apex of her thighs. Adjusting himself inside his pants he moved back to the door, pushing the code into the lock and opening it before grabbing the empty food tray and stepping into the hallway. He set it down outside and waited for the door to relock before gripping his cock through his pants. It took a moment to convince himself not to go back inside, not to push her thighs apart and bury himself inside her until he could feel her coming against him. He gripped harder and stroked himself, then stopped.

Not here.

It was a stiff walk back to his room where there were no cameras. He could smell her all over him. He could taste her with every breath, and he knew he had to shower or he'd never sleep. The shower kicked on and he rinsed his face, fighting the urge to just bite the soap to forget what she tasted like against his tongue, to forget the way she felt against his mouth.

His hand moved down his stomach and gripped his cock, dragging down his length as he fisted and thrust into his grip. Again and again, but what he was picturing was the shape of her hips as her muscles lifted them, the way her mouth parted when she moaned, the pained expression as she orgasmed and how she panted and whimpered as she came hard against his mouth. Despite his efforts, memories of her body quaking beneath him that morning in the punishment room came back. The way she had cried out when he'd struck her with the belt. The clean pink lines on her pale skin that each strike left behind. The way her mouth had stretched around his girth when she'd swallowed him in the shower. Those soft words in her perfect voice.

He came hard. Bracing against the shower wall as strands of his come came out with no warm place to seek but the empty shower. He groaned and leaned his head against his other arm on the shower wall.

The girls weren't supposed to get to him like this. He could have one any time he wanted, the one he was training shouldn't be in any type of control over him.

But Thalia was.

And even as he washed himself clean, his mind was thinking of her body, the sounds she made against him, her voice as she begged him, and the taste of her on his tongue.

And he just wanted more.

Chapter Six
THALIA

Music started quietly at first and quickly increased until the classical was blaring so loudly that Thalia was sitting up in the bed with her ears covered.

"I'm awake! Shut it off!" she tried to yell over the music, but her voice just seemed to be swallowed by it. Her eyes scanned the walls and she saw little speakers embedded in the corners of the room.

Surround sound as torture. Lovely.

The door across from her opened and the guard looked a little surprised by the music, then he smiled and she was shocked again by how handsome he was.

It was just the abusive, psychotic personality that kept him from being charming.

He balanced a covered plate on one hand and pulled his phone from his pocket with the other. Slowly the music fell to a tolerable level, and then he turned back to the door and locked it.

"Good morning," his voice rumbled, and she remembered his mouth between her thighs, and how she'd clenched her fist in his hair to keep him there. A blush flushed up her chest, heating her cheeks and she gritted her teeth.

"Morning, sir," she mumbled and hoped it was obscured by the music still playing.

"Well, now, you're much more polite this morning," he said as he walked toward the bed. He wore a thin white cotton shirt that didn't veil his hard body, and black pants that reminded her of pants some martial artist might wear. As he reached the bed he flipped the cover off the plate in his hand with a dramatic flair. "And look, I brought breakfast as promised."

Thalia scooted away from the end of the bed until her back touched the headboard, the sore skin making her flinch. He sighed and set the plate down on the bed. It looked delicious — fresh sliced fruit, some kind of omelet with cheese and thin strips of meat she couldn't identify. Not bacon.

"Prosciutto." He pointed at where she had been staring. "You need to eat."

"I'm not hungry." *Lie.* Her stomach practically roared, she'd burned through the food he'd given her in the late afternoon yesterday and wanted more, but she wouldn't beg.

"Come here, Thalia." He sat on the edge of the bed and patted the spot just behind the plate.

Edging forward slightly she stopped just short of where he wanted her to sit. He sighed and took a plastic fork out and speared a slice of strawberry, holding it out toward her. Thalia reached forward with her hand and he pulled it back, shaking his head a little.

"Tsk tsk. With your beautiful mouth, please." He extended the hand with the fork again and Thalia crawled a little farther forward and bit down. He had drizzled the fruit in honey and she made a soft moan at how good it tasted. Her eyes had closed and she opened them again to find a smile curving the edge of his mouth, those blue-gray eyes looking playful as she trailed her teeth against the fork and sat back. "Do you like it?"

"Yes, sir." She swallowed the slice of strawberry and her tongue licked along her bottom lip to grab the errant honey that had stuck there.

"I said I'd tell you the rules here. You know some already. First rule to discuss today is that you should really call me Master. Sir is for others. The faster you get used to saying it, the better." He speared a blackberry and held it out to her.

Leaning forward she almost got the blackberry into her mouth before he pulled it back. It hovered just in front of her face, and she ran a hand through her hair, pushing it back from her face. Her irritation at him not letting her feed herself was growing. The plate was only about six inches from her hand and she lunged to grab another strawberry but he caught her wrist and twisted it sharply in the hand not holding the fork. Thalia cried out and whimpered as she felt the fine bones grind in the strength of his grip.

"What do you say when I speak to you, Thalia?" It took him no effort at all to restrain her, and she knew he'd just keep tormenting her until she said it.

"Yes, Master. I'm sorry, Master." Thalia said it through her teeth, but he let go of her wrist and held out the blackberry again. She took it into her mouth, and it was just as delicious.

"Good girl." He stabbed another piece of fruit and held it out, smiling as she took it. "I'm only trying to prepare you for what's to come."

Swallowing the fruit he'd offered, she spoke, "What do you mean, Master?"

Thalia could tell he was consciously being patient with her as he took a breath. "Second rule is that you really shouldn't speak unless it's 'yes master' or 'no master.' If you want to ask a question like that, first ask — 'May I ask a question, Master?' then only if you're given permission you may ask it." He held out a bite of the omelet this time and it was also heavenly as she bit into it. He had to be the one cooking, she hadn't heard or seen anyone else, and she was kind of impressed.

"May I ask—" Thalia started but he cut her off.

"It's fine, I'll answer you. I'm teaching you how to behave so that when you meet others like me, they will want you." He held out another bite of omelet, but Thalia didn't move to take it.

"Others? You're bringing others here?" She was starting to panic at the idea of other people being here, touching her like he did.

He was planning on sharing her with his friends. The ones who watched her on the cameras.

Her mind was racing when he leaned forward and grabbed her by her hair, tugging just hard enough to get her attention. It silenced her mind as she waited for him to yell, or hurt her, or something.

"Thalia, you're not behaving. I'm trying to have a nice conversation over breakfast with you since you did so well last night. If you won't behave then I can't be nice." His voice stayed calm even as he gave her hair a sharp tug. Then he relaxed his hand and ran his fingers over her scalp where it tingled and he leaned back.

"I'm sorry, Master. May I ask a question, Master?" She felt fear stirring in her stomach, but she knew the best way to get answers was to follow his rules.

"Go ahead, Thalia." He seemed irritated, but not so much that he'd hurt her.

"Why don't you just let me go, sir, I mean, Master? I'm not good at being obedient, and no one will want me, I'm sure they won't. You could just let me go home, and I won't say anything." She pointed at the ceiling, tears threatening to spill over as she fought the panic in her. "I mean you've got me on video doing — *things* — and I don't want those videos out. That guarantees my silence! Just let me go, Master, and I promise I won't tell anyone. Ever!"

"Even if I were to let you go, which I won't," his voice was solid as he slammed the door on her request, "it's not like you have anywhere to go."

What did he mean by that? She opened her mouth to speak and he held up his hand to stop her.

"Thalia, listen to me, you have nowhere to go. You resigned from your job two nights ago via email." His eyes were watching her steadily.

"I didn't!" She stared at him in shock but he pinched her thigh hard and she yelped. His irritation showed on his face as the red mark bloomed on her pale skin.

"Don't interrupt. You did resign as far as anyone knows. The email came from your work email address, you told your boss you were moving back home. You've also given your apartment a thirty-day notice and have already paid the last month. The apartment will be empty by the end of this weekend, and your car is already on its way to Mexico." Every time he calmly crossed off one of the tether lines to her life, it felt like a hammer ringing a bell in her ears. Each time shutting down more of the hope that had been keeping her together. She didn't even realize she was crying at first until she felt the drops on her arm.

"Someone will look for me," Thalia said and sniffled, trying to hold in the urge to cry even harder.

"Who? Your coworkers never talked to you outside of work, you have a few people you might call friends but you rarely saw them because you worked all the time. And you haven't talked to your father in two months." He tilted his head like he was concerned. It was obviously an act. How long must he have followed her to know all this?

"Someone—"

"You're mine, Thalia. The sooner you accept that, the easier all of this will be." His voice was falsely comforting, but nothing about what he said was okay. Underneath the panic and the desperate urge to scream, she was so very *angry*. It bubbled up inside her, burning underneath her skin, stretching it until she thought she might explode if she didn't do something.

"I do NOT belong to you!" Thalia shouted as she kicked the plate to the floor. The sound of the plate breaking made her pulse race even faster, her rage making her shake.

"Yes, you do, Thalia." He was talking through his teeth as he tried to maintain his calm. "You haven't accepted it yet, but you were always meant to be a slave. I know you're not ready to hear that yet, but you need this. No other relationship would ever fulfill you like submitting will." His fist was clenched next to him, the only outward sign of his anger toward her.

Thalia's breaths came in shallow gasps as his words sunk in and she fought against them. That wasn't true. It wasn't. Unbidden, her mind reminded her of how frustrated she had been by the boyfriends she'd had. How they were so syrupy sweet, wanting to cuddle with her on the couch and in bed. It had actually turned her off, and she'd thought something was wrong with her, because they hadn't acted like she wanted a guy to act. She wanted — she slammed the brakes on that train of thought. She did *not* want this man in front of her, she did not want him at all and she wasn't going to fall into some twisted version of reality that had her as his slave and him as her Master. *No way.*

"No. I won't. I won't be your slave, I won't be anyone's, I WON'T!" She'd started off talking calmly, but it quickly rose until she was shouting at him. He reached into his pocket and pressed the button again. She'd heard the soft beep of it.

"I already told you I don't like it when you tell me no." He was almost growling at her, his eyes blazing, and she knew she should be afraid, that she should stop, but she couldn't shut her mouth.

"What does that button do?! Does it turn off the cameras? What don't you want them to see? Don't want them to see that I'm never going to be a *good girl?*" She was yelling as she threw his words back at him. He brought his hand back and slapped her hard. The pain shocked her as it spread across her cheek, and she grabbed her face and whimpered as he started shouting at her.

"I'm trying to help you, Thalia! I'm trying to teach you what they expect so you can perform well and someone will want to buy you who will actually take care of you!" He was yelling at her now that the cameras were off, his calm façade slipping away. "You think I'm bad? I'm NOTHING compared to some of the men out there, Thalia. And if you keep acting like a defiant little brat, the nice Masters won't even want to look at you, you'll only get the harsh ones interested. The ones who want to punish you, just to see if they can break you."

"YOU said you want to break me!" she shouted, and his shoulders rose and fell as he made himself breathe deeply.

"I am so much more gentle than some of them. You have no *fucking* idea, Thalia."

"I don't care!" she screamed through her tears, still trying to shield her face in case he hit her again.

"You better care, Thalia, I'm the only one who can teach you what you're supposed to do, and right now I *am* your Master no matter what you choose to think." He was trying to maintain his calm again, but she didn't care. Her self-preservation had disappeared somewhere between him telling her she no longer had a job and him reminding her no one would even report her missing for months, if even then. It's not like her dad and her were ever close. The fear and anger at her situation rose up and she looked him straight in the eye, sitting back up and dropping her hands to her sides in fists.

"I *hate* you, I will NEVER be yours!" she roared, and he was on her in an instant. His hand ripped into her hair, yanking her backward to hold her to the bed. His knees were between hers quicker than she could try to close them, and he pressed her there with the lower half of his body until she lay squirming beneath him, unable to do more than push at his shoulders and then try desperately to unwind his fist from her hair.

"Don't say that to me, Thalia," he growled down at her, his mouth barely inches from hers. "I could do so much to you, things you can't imagine." His hips were pressing against hers, and she could feel how hard he was, and she hated herself for getting wet in response.

"I DO hate you. Why wouldn't I hate you?!" Even pinned under him, knowing it wasn't going to do anything but make things worse, she kept yelling at him. She hit his shoulders with all her force, pushing as hard as she could, but he didn't even shift above her. She hated feeling so weak, and hated even more the little part of her that was aroused. Her body was a traitor.

He let go of her hair and grabbed her arms, pinning her wrists to the bed above her with one hand. His free hand grabbed her chin and he made her look at him. "I'll let you decide your punishment for this outburst. Tell me the rules you can remember. Based on what you can tell me I'll decide what you've earned." His voice was controlled rage, and her body was shaking underneath him despite all her bravado in shouting at him. The adrenaline was just making the panic worse. "Now, Thalia."

"Please—"

He gripped her chin harder, shutting her mouth as he angled her head up. "Rules. Name all of the ones you can remember since you arrived."

She tried her best to nod against his grip and he relaxed his hold enough that she could speak. "No clothes."

"Are you going to make me hurt you? You know how to address me." He growled out the words at her.

"No clothes, Master." She blinked away the tears, feeling them slide down her temples into her hair.

"Continue."

"I must call you Master. I must always respond with 'yes, Master' or 'no, Master.' I must ask for permission before I ask a question, Master." She hiccupped as she tried to talk through the urge to cry. "I must never come without permission, and I must crawl when you tell me to follow you, Master. I must kneel in a room if you do not tell me otherwise, Master."

He smiled down at her, but it was cold, and he continued to hold her chin as he placed a chaste kiss on her lips. "You are smarter than you pretend to be, Thalia. Now that you've admitted you know the rules, I will not accept any further mistakes. Do you understand?"

"Yes, Master." Now that the anger had left her she felt cold with fear. She couldn't decide if it was brave or completely stupid for her to fight him the way she did. His hips pressed against her again as he pushed himself off her and slid off the bed. Thalia sat up slowly, staring at the floor because she didn't want to meet his gaze.

"Clean up the mess. I'm going to make a phone call." He walked to the door without looking back at her and she heard it unlock, shut firmly, and lock again.

Chapter Seven
THALIA

※

She was still shaking when she slid from the bed and started gathering the remnants of the plate into a pile, gathering the food onto one of the larger pieces of plate. She quickly ate the food that still seemed clean, trying to fill her stomach before he came back. It took longer than she thought as she tried to clean up the smooth wood. She carried the mess gently into the bathroom and put it in the trash, and she was washing her hands when the door opened again, and his voice thundered out. "Follow me. Now."

He stood by the door as she came out of the bathroom and waited until she slid to her knees to crawl. "Yes, Master."

Nodding, he left the door open and began walking down the hall. It was the same path she'd taken before, but in reverse. He stopped at the room he'd punished her in and she was terrified of what he had planned. She stopped and knelt the way he had taught her, looking up at him. Wanting to beg him, but knowing it wouldn't help.

"Rule three for today, you don't look at me unless I ask you to or make you look at me. Understand?" His voice was so angry still, and she tried to be quiet as she dropped her eyes to the floor and started crying again.

"Yes, Master," she said shakily. The door opened and he moved inside, she crawled until she was just inside the door and then she knelt again. Knees spread, hands on her thighs, back straight, head down.

He slammed the door next to her and she jumped, expecting him to hit her. He didn't. He just walked away from her and she heard something being dragged, but she didn't dare look up. It felt like forever as she heard the clank of metal, the sound of a cabinet being opened and closed, a drawer. Finally he commanded, "Come here."

Thalia whimpered but crawled forward until she saw his shoes and then she sat back into position.

"Good girl, now stand up." As she did she noticed the heavy metal frame next to her. There was a bar just above her head leading to two large triangular sides in front and behind her that seemed to balance and hold the thing steady. Leather cuffs hung from the top rung, and toward the floor was a lengthy of shiny rope. "Straddle the rope, Thalia."

"Yes, Master." She did and he quickly grabbed her wrists and locked them in the cuffs, her hands bound above her head but not fully extended. He leaned down next to her and slid something on the frame in front and behind her as he brought the rope up between her legs. A knot had been tied in it, and he moved it to just below her pussy. Then he reached behind him and revealed another silver vibrator, she immediately jerked on the cuffs and started shaking her head.

"Master, please—" She had planned on begging for mercy but he slapped her. It stung sharply for a moment and then she was left with the shock of it.

"Already forgetting the rules? I told you I wouldn't accept any more of your slips." He moved close to her body, the fabric of his shirt brushing against one nipple and it hardened. His hand slid between her legs and her hips bucked as he pressed against her clit, she was already wet and he laughed softly. Shame made her blush and bite her lip.

"Such a good little slut." He slid the vibe inside her easily and secured it with a set of straps around both thighs again. Then he flicked it on and she squirmed as her body reacted instantly. A soft moan escaped her lips and she heard a beep just before he grabbed her hair and kissed her. It was rough, his tongue sweeping into her mouth to meet hers and then pulling back again so he could bite her lip before turning his head and kissing her hard again. She found herself moaning and pulling at the cuffs. She wanted her hands in his hair again, so she could lean into the kiss. The kiss was nice, so much better than when he was angry. His palm cupped her breast and pinched her nipple, she gasped but he tilted his head again and kissed her harder. Then his hand moved to the other breast and repeated it, she was squeezing her thighs together as the sensations ran together.

Then she screamed.

A violent pain came from her nipple and she looked down to see a clamp on it, leaving it dark red, a thin chain came from it and he ran this over the bar above her head. "On your toes, Thalia." When she paused he reached behind her and spanked her, waking up the bruises that were still fresh. She rose up on her toes and he pulled the chain and then latched the other clamp on. She screamed again, and as she tried to lower her heels to the floor she realized the chain was too short. If she lowered herself much at all the clamps pulled on her nipples painfully. Her tears had started again and then his hand returned to her clit, and with her pussy filled with the vibrator she was assaulted by the pleasure. It twisted in her head with the pain from her breasts and she moaned.

"It could be like this all the time, Thalia. If you'll just obey me." His fingers worked magic over her clit, moving her closer to the edge, her breath coming in fast pants. "Then you'll find you can be happy here. So. Very. Happy." He punctuated his last words by pressing the vibe harder inside her each time.

"Yes, Master." She gasped as she neared the edge, and he stopped his fingers. Then he removed his hand completely and her hips tried to follow. She bounced in the restraints out of frustration and was only rewarded with pain as the clamps dug in.

She heard another beep.

He'd turned the cameras off again? To hide what he'd said? Or the kiss?

"Yes, Master," she said, as he placed the rope up against the lips of her pussy. Then he slid the rope between them, adjusting it until the knot rubbed against her clit. The sensation was odd. It was nowhere near as satisfying as his touch, but every slight shift of her hips made the knot rub against the bundle of nerves. He adjusted something on each side of her and the rope seemed a little more taut between her thighs.

"You have my permission to come as many times as you can manage." His hand ran down her backside, squeezing her ass as he walked past her. "I'll be back when I think you've had enough."

"Yes, Master. Thank you, Master." She was so confused, how was this a punishment? The clamps weren't comfortable, but as long as she stayed on her toes they didn't hurt much.

"Good girl." His voice was closer to the door, and then she heard it open and shut behind her. Then music came on, some kind of low thrumming beat with wordless vocals mixed in. It was beautiful in an eerie way.

Shifting her hips Thalia grazed the knot again and the pressure on her clit sent a shudder of pleasure through her. He had wound her up and left her wanting, but this time he'd told her she could come.

Probably so she'd put on a show for his friends.

She yanked on the cuffs above her, but only made the bruises on her wrists tender by doing it. She contemplated just staying very still and waiting for him to return, but then there was no difference to the other tortures he'd put her through. She knew she'd end up grinding against the little knot between her legs eventually.

As if her body knew what she was thinking her hips twitched forward and her clit rubbed against the bundle of rope. She gritted her teeth to stifle the little moan that rose up inside her. The vibe grew stronger and she found herself trying to press harder against the knot, but as she pushed down toward the rope her breasts were pulled upward by the clamps. She winced and lifted herself back up on her toes and away from the firm pressure against her clit. She whimpered as the intensity of the vibe changed and her pulse was suddenly pounding between her thighs, her pussy gushing and her hips twisting as she tried to get more pressure.

"Please..." she whispered to the empty space around her. Her back arched and she bit her lip to press herself against the knot, rocking forward even as the pinching in her breasts got worse. Instead of the pain pulling her back from the edge she imagined his hands on her nipples, pinching them as he thrust inside her. And as the tension rose in her belly she didn't even care that it was his voice she heard in her head.

Then she came, hard, her legs buckling momentarily which caused the clamps to pull tight on the chain. Her moan became a scream and she pulled herself up by her arms until she could stabilize on her toes again.

"Dammit!" she shouted, exhausted already as she fought to still her shaking legs. This was the punishment. She'd drive herself to orgasm but her body would fail her in that moment, yanking her back from the pleasure with a too sharp pain, only to start the cycle over.

The vibrator had backed off for a moment after she'd come, her breaths coming harshly, and then it revved up again, her body still too close to the edge, her pussy hot and even wetter. It was hard to think clearly with the overlapping sensations, the tightness in her nipples and their sharp ache from the clamps, the insistent vibration inside her that teased her to the edge, the way the vibe pressed deeper when she sank down onto the rope — and that center of her brushing against the knot again and again. The rope was slick with her juices, and it made it even easier to rub against, the rough pattern of the knot drawing her back to the edge again.

The second time she came she tried to prepare, tightening her arms as her legs tried to give out in the wave of pleasure that overwhelmed her. She half-screamed and half-moaned as her body fought the urge to stay standing.

She had been an idiot to think this wasn't a part of his plan, that anything he did would result in only pleasure for her.

Except for last night.

Her mind gave her that memory suddenly. In the middle of the night, when he'd crawled onto the bed between her thighs. He hadn't spoken other than to command her to come, but his mouth and his fingers had sent her flying. The fear of what he might do had kept her so tense that the orgasm had rocked her hard.

Then he had just left her there, panting breathlessly as her heart pounded in her ears. She had been awake for at least an hour after, waiting for him to come back, to finish what he'd started. But he never had.

Thalia lost track of how long she stood there, alternating between feet to try and save the strength in her legs. Despite her best efforts to stop the orgasms she came again and again from the combined efforts of the vibe, the clamps on her nipples, and the incessant rubbing of the soaked rope between her legs. The orgasms had crossed the boundary of pleasure and pain, each rub a too intense brush against her clit.

Her body shook with the stress of it, her mind hazy with a swirling mix of pain and pleasure. Purples and reds and blues whirling behind her eyes. As the morning passed she was using her arms more than anything, but no amount of yoga or Pilates prepared you for trying to hold yourself up for this amount of time. As the vibe changed its attack again she screamed between her teeth, arching her back as she desperately tried to relieve the ache in her arms and legs. The pleasure had faded completely; her clit was so sensitive it just hurt now and her body hummed with the after effects. Her thighs were slick from her juices, her throat dry from breathing through her mouth. She'd called out to him once or twice as she'd come, yelling *Master*, but he hadn't returned. Her whimpers filled her own ears, and she briefly wondered if the people on the cameras could hear her over the music. Then her body started to shake, taunting her with the abyss again.

This time she begged.

"Master! Please, Master, please stop..." Her heels were threatening to drop to the floor again as her legs fought to keep her stable, she was at war with her own body. Her chin dropped to her chest and she took in another shuddering breath and screamed louder, "MASTER, PLEASE! I'M SORRY, I'M YOURS, JUST PLEASE STOP!"

Her arms shook and then she slipped and the clamps tugged her nipples sharply, dragging out a harsh gasp as she weakly tried to pull herself back up. The vibe lowered its intensity and she realized her body was quaking with her efforts to stay upright. It was going to hurt when she collapsed.

A minute later the door opened and shut quickly and then she felt his arms around her, lifting her up enough that her legs didn't have to bear her weight. "Shh, Thalia, shh... you did so well." He pressed a kiss to her temple as the rope fell away from her. A moment later the vibe shut off and he undid the straps on her thighs to remove it. She was crying quietly, but his strong grip around her waist held her still against his bare chest.

His lips pressed against her ear as he whispered, "Take a breath, this will hurt."

She gasped just before he removed one of the clamps. Pain seared her as blood flooded back into her nipple, and before she could react the second was released as well. Screaming, she sagged against him as he held her tighter, kissing her hair as his palm rubbed gently over her aching nipples.

"It's over, just breathe."

"Master…" she whimpered and he removed the cuffs so her arms could finally collapse. Leaning down he scooped her up until she rested in his arms, much like she had the first night. Her head leaning on his chest as he walked to the bed in the room. It had nothing more than a fitted sheet, no other bedding to be in the way as he crawled on top of it and laid her down in the middle.

"You are so beautiful," he mumbled against her skin. His mouth trailed kisses down her ribs, over her hips where he nipped at her hipbone, and then he was pushing her thighs apart. Her legs quivered as she tried to shut them but he pushed them apart with little effort. "Don't, Thalia."

She was so raw and too sensitive. When his mouth landed directly on her clit she screamed and bucked her hips, but his fingers dug into them and held her down to the bed. His tongue lapped at her, but it didn't even feel good this time. She put her arm over her eyes and could feel the warmth of tears against her skin.

"Please, no, Master…" She was whispering, terrified of making him angry so soon after he'd stopped the punishment.

His mouth stopped and she felt him above her, his hand pulled her arm away from her face and he kissed her. She tasted herself on him, and the kiss was so soft at first. Bracing himself above her with one arm, he used the other to cup her face and hold her lips to his. She kissed back and it was almost soothing in the chaos of her body, with her hands free she pushed them into his hair like she'd wanted to before and he groaned against her mouth, taking control of the kiss as he opened her mouth and swept his tongue against hers. This was good, and simple. Why couldn't he be like this? Why did he have to be so angry? Why did he have to hurt her?

"Thalia…" His lips moved against hers as he said her name with an ache in his voice.

"Yes, Master?" she replied on a whisper, his forehead pressed against hers for a moment and she became aware her hands were cupping the back of his head, holding him to her. She let go and he pushed up from her.

"You said that you're mine." His voice was rough, and he was looking down her body so she couldn't see his expression.

"Yes, Master," she whispered.

"Was that the truth?" He still didn't look at her, and she shifted underneath his gaze, the heat of his body barely an inch from hers.

She bit her lip, as she thought about why she'd screamed it. It had been out of desperation, fear of her body giving out. But... if what he'd said that morning was true, then she had nothing. He had access to her entire life, and even if she could get out — and he'd said he would never let her leave — she would have nowhere to go.

Sometime during her punishment that reality had settled around her, and she'd realized that fighting him was only going to lead to more suffering. More anger, more pain.

When he wanted to, he could be so kind to her, and the things he could make her body do were surprising. Even now he had carried her gently to the bed, he had kissed her with tenderness. If she would just give in, it didn't have to be so traumatic. Whatever she was now, whatever side he had drawn out of her had changed her fundamentally. She wasn't the same person she had been, she barely knew the person she was now, but she knew he was in control. In the last few days he had made that incredibly clear to her. Her breath hitched as her answer solidified in her mind and realigned her thoughts.

"Yes, Master, I am yours." Thalia said it quietly, but he moaned and kissed her hard. His hand slid between her thighs and she tried to make a noise as she was too sore for it to be enjoyable, but it was muffled against his mouth. She grabbed his shoulders, but she couldn't budge him as he slid his fingers inside her. She was more than wet, coming over and over had left her slick and her thighs damp. He groaned against her mouth and she felt his knees spread her thighs apart and then he removed his fingers from her as he pushed his pants down his hips. He paused to look at her, and then he kissed her again as he held her hip in place and thrust inside her. That's when he broke the kiss, and she winced as he rubbed against her raw clit with each deep thrust, his size stretching her again and making her ache even deeper.

"Mine," he whispered against her hair as he thrust hard. He gathered her hands from his shoulders and held them down beside her. She arched up against him, trying to ease the pressure on her most sensitive parts but he pressed her harder to the bed with his next thrust, and eased her thighs wider apart as he widened his own stance to push deeper inside her. Impossibly, her body seemed to be tightening toward another orgasm.

"Yes, Master." She verified his claim and in that instant he slammed into her harder. When she felt him come, the sticky heat of his seed filling her, she came too. It wasn't as strong as her others, her body was too weak, but he sighed against her ear as he took rapid breaths.

"Mine." He kissed her as he slid from her, pulling her tight to his front as his arm wrapped around her waist. This time she said nothing for a moment, his face was in her hair, she could feel his breath on her neck, and she knew this was what he wanted.

"Yes, Master," she mumbled as she finally slid toward sleep, her exhausted body mercifully dropping her into the emptiness of dreams.

Chapter Eight
HIM

He still had Thalia tightly pressed against him when he woke up. For a moment he was surprised she'd stayed in his arms. Some part of him had imagined her pulling away in the night to sleep on the other side of the bed, or on the floor. Which would have pissed him off, but here she was, her warm body pressed against his bare chest.

She had submitted to him. Finally admitted it was what she was meant for, and his primal side felt victorious. His erection pushed against the soft flesh of her ass through his pants, and he wanted her again.

Nudging his face into her hair he kissed along her neck, occasionally nipping her skin. "Thalia..." His voice rumbled in his chest, still rough from sleep.

Her head lay buried in the crook of her arm, her light brown hair across her face and she squirmed against him as a soft "*Hmmm?*" came out of her in response. Part of him wanted to spank her for not responding properly, but she was beautiful as she was waking up and he was enjoying watching her. Her eyebrows scrunched together as her body shifted against him again and he fought the urge to groan at the friction.

Pushing the waist of his pants down he reached between them to grip himself; cock hard and aching to be inside her again. He wanted to hear her say it again though. *Had* to hear her say it again.

Nipping her neck, he grabbed a fistful of hair and tugged her back against him, just sharply enough to wake her up. Hazel eyes opened wide and she started to roll her hips away from him, but he growled softly in her ear and tugged her back against him by her hip. The bare skin of her ass rubbed against his cock and he bit down on the sound he made. He needed her to say it. "Thalia?"

"Yes, Master?" Her own voice was more sultry from sleep, and he smiled against her hair as she remembered how to respond properly.

"Who do you belong to?" Fingers sliding over her hip to glide between her legs, his erection kicked as he found her warm and wet already. She was incredible. No one responded this well.

Her throat worked to swallow before she answered, "You, Master." That pink tongue flicked out over her soft lips and he rewarded her by pressing his fingers over her clit, moving in tiny circles that quickly had her hips shifting against him with each movement. She was tormenting him and she didn't even know it. Her whimpers were the delicious balance of the pleasure he was giving her, and what he imagined was a lingering sensitivity from the punishment the day before.

"Say it again," he demanded, low against her ear as he pushed his leg between her thighs to open her up, continuing the friction against her clit that now had her making tiny panting sounds of pleasure. She was driving him crazy, and he didn't want to wait, but he just wanted to hear it once more.

"I'm yours, Master." The words were almost a moan and he was undone.

Yanking her hips back further, he bit down on her shoulder as he thrust inside her hard. She was wet and welcoming and her hips bucked back against him as he bottomed out. Thalia moaned loudly and he pulled her back by her hair so she was tight against his chest as he started to move. Her eyes were clenched tight, her lips parted as she panted for breath, making little noises as he rubbed her clit and then thrust again.

This was the side of Thalia he was amazed by, she responded perfectly and his body craved her. Her pussy tightened around him as she arched her back and started to beg for more. He groaned in her ear, loving to hear her little pleas, and bit down on her shoulder again. She only moaned louder as his teeth pressed into her skin, his hand clenched tighter in her hair, and he thrust again and again. Her pussy hot and slick around him.

"Say it again," he breathed hard, and she moaned loudly as he picked up speed inside her. The friction making his balls ache.

"I'm yours! Master! Please!" She was much louder now, her words coming between smaller moans as he felt her muscles tighten, her pussy contracting around each thrust as he felt the edge of his own release rising to meet them. She whimpered, saying words between short breaths, "May I? May I come, Master?"

"Yes," he growled against her skin and his balls tightened as she came and her pussy gripped him tight. Her body pulled him over the edge with her. Groaning loudly against her neck, while she screamed something that might have been a thank you.

Thalia's breaths were coming fast as she came down from her orgasm, little murmurs escaping her mouth. Body quivering against his, and he looked down and saw the shape of his teeth in her skin, the two imprints almost overlapping. They would fade quickly but with her pressed to him he liked that they marked her as his.

"You are incredible, Thalia." He hid his face in her hair so she wouldn't see the smile he knew spread across his face.

"Thank you, Master," she breathed as her warm body turned to liquid against his in the glow after she'd come.

He opened his mouth to say something else when he felt the irritating little vibration of his phone. Sliding out of her slowly he released her hair and leaned back, shoving his pants completely off and onto the floor. If his brother was calling, he could fucking wait and enjoy the show.

Once on his back he watched as Thalia pushed herself up to look at him. She shouldn't be looking at him, but the way she looked he didn't care to make her stop. Her hazel eyes were wide, her pupils still dilated from the orgasm and her cheeks flushed from their efforts. Her hair was tangled from having his hand in it. The overall effect made her look like something straight out of his imagination.

He wanted to kiss her. He already wanted to fuck her again until she was shivering, his cock refusing to go soft. He wanted her taste to fill his mouth again. He wanted to take her ass again with her wrists bound behind her back.

He wanted her. Period.

Staring at her lips he knew what he wanted at the moment, the rest could wait.

"Clean up your mess, Thalia." Fighting the smile that curved the edge of his lips, he watched as her eyes moved down his abs and settled at his hips. She pulled her bottom lip into her mouth and he almost grabbed her hair to tug her warm mouth down, but she beat him to it.

"Yes, Master," she said softly, pushing her hands through those light brown tangles as she twisted her hair over one shoulder; then her hand was on him. Her touch was gentle and his hips lifted slightly off the bed as she stroked him base to tip. He let out a curse when her mouth slid over the head of his cock, her tongue swirling against the underside of him as she started sucking. He was viciously sensitive, but it was an incredible torture. Her fist still moved up and down and her other hand came up to cup his balls as he slid farther into her mouth. He bit down on a moan as her lips stretched around him and slid over his cock.

"Good girl." He could hear the faint buzz from the floor of his phone going off again, but he just pushed his hand into her hair as she moved her mouth over him. Couldn't his brother see he was fucking busy?

She paused when his hand tangled in her hair, and he knew why. She was waiting for him to grab hold of it and guide her, make her move the way he wanted. In that moment he was proud of her for already taking to her training so well. She was submitting beautifully.

He moaned as her tongue flicked against him, and even after coming inside her he was hard and aching again inside her warm mouth. He dragged his nails over her scalp to encourage her to continue for now, and she did. Easing him farther into her mouth again she made him groan, her nails grazing softly across the skin of his balls. She started to pick up speed and he was tempted to take control and push into her throat when a racket burst out in the room. Thalia gasped and thankfully removed her mouth without hitting him with her teeth.

It took a second for him to realize it was a phone ringing; the incredibly loud sound of a phone ringing was being pumped through the speakers of the house. His brother.

Asshole.

Thalia had sat up and she looked at him in confusion as she winced slightly from the volume. He really should correct her, make her avert her gaze, but he was distracted. Her mouth and chin were wet with saliva and he was even more pissed at having to leave her like that unfinished.

"Stay here, I need to get that."

She nodded and he slid off the bed and yanked his pants on, ripping the cell phone out of the pocket as he stomped toward the door. *What the hell could be so damned important?* Behind him he heard a breathy, "Yes, Master," that made his balls ache.

Unlocking the door he stepped out and slammed it. Listening to it automatically relock as he pressed the button on his remote so no one would eavesdrop on their conversation — but the beep from the little device didn't sound. His cell phone buzzed again in his hand and he answered it.

"What is your problem?" he hissed into the phone as he walked down the hall in case she got curious and came to the door.

"My problem?" His brother's smooth voice came out of the phone and he gritted his teeth. "Have you completely forgotten what you're supposed to be doing?"

"She's performing perfectly," he snapped. At least she *had* been when he'd interrupted them with the sound of a phone.

"I can see exactly how she's performing, and so can every one of our customers and potential buyers. And as lovely as she is to watch, you have her shouting out that she's yours over and over. Have you lost your damn mind?" His brother's voice was about as angry as he'd ever heard it. The man didn't shout, he was cold to the core, but it was obvious. As the younger brother he was the one who had inherited the temper and his brother always called him out on it.

"I'm making her accept the idea of ownership, just like we always do." It sounded like a lie even to his own ears. His primal side had shouted a claim to her, and he had wanted to hear her accept it.

Over and over and over.

"I don't care what you *think* you're doing, but you're going to piss off our customers, so stop. Now." His brother was using the commanding tone that had women cowering. But he wasn't some submissive kneeling at his brother's feet.

"I think we've established over the years that I know what the hell I'm doing." He clenched his teeth, irritated that his brother would dare challenge him after every submissive he'd trained and sold successfully.

"Don't forget who brought you into this world, who taught you how to train them, who got you the houses, the cars, the money. You'd still be in a desert somewhere in fatigues without me, that was the only other job you've ever kept more than a month in your entire life." His brother sounded bored as he outlined exactly why he was in charge. In a fistfight he'd take his older brother easily, but when it came to politicking and business — his brother knew it all and did it *very* well. In just six years he'd developed a reputation for the quality of submissives he could deliver. Making their training available for those who paid to view the cameras only brought the money in faster and attracted lists of potential buyers.

All of which were his brother's ideas.

His singular talent had been discovered in how quickly he could break them down, taking his brother's three months down to a few weeks. Now if they were on track, they could deliver almost one girl a month.

"Are you listening to me?" His brother's voice snapped across the phone.

"Yes."

"That's it. I'm coming out there." The frustration in the man was clear to him, but he almost growled at the idea of his brother coming to take over part of her training. Things normally happened like that, but — *shit*. The realization hit him suddenly.

He didn't want anyone else touching Thalia.

The thought slammed into him, and was only made worse when he heard himself say, "No."

"Excuse me?" His brother's voice revealed his shock, even though it stayed calm. He knew the little changes in his tone well.

"Things are fine, I don't need you here." He tried to speak evenly but his voice wavered as his own internal confusion warred. What was he planning to do with her if he didn't want anyone to touch her?

"She is just another slut, you idiot, and you need to remember that. In fact," he heard his brother typing, "I'll be there in two days to remind you, and I'm going to move up the sale. You clearly can't handle this one for some reason." His brother blew out an irritated breath and he heard him typing again.

"I have it handled," he spat out through his teeth.

"You better have it handled, because if she can't behave when I get there you know how I'll deal with it."

He remembered how his brother got the girls he trained under control. Suspension, water, electricity. Breaking them down through terror, torture, and very little pleasure. "She's behaving," he said.

"Good. Make sure it continues." He thought he was going to hang up on him, but then his brother laughed quietly, "Oh, one more thing. I don't know what you've been doing with her when the cameras have been having their little issues, but I went ahead and disabled your controls in the house so our paying customers don't miss anything. I'll see you soon."

The call ended and he gripped the phone in his hand. He wanted to throw it, but he knew his brother was watching to see his reaction. If he couldn't get this situation back under control his brother would just 'surprise' him by showing up sooner.

He thought of Thalia sitting on the bed in that room, waiting for him to come back and he felt angry. She was supposed to be his for at least another week. Who knew what his brother would do when he showed up? He never played nice with the girls. And as well as she was doing, she was still far from his brother's standards.

Chapter Nine
THALIA

Thalia stayed in the center of the bed, still confused as to what had happened. The actual house had rung like a phone.

Loudly.

He had seemed so irritated as he'd stormed out and time was moving slowly without him there. Her pulse thrummed between her thighs, her clit aching from the punishment the day before and his attentions when he'd woken her up. Just thinking about how he'd held her by her hair and taken her made her shiver.

He had made her say it again though, made her tell him she was his.

'Well, aren't you?' her mind asked the question, and she recoiled. She still wanted to fight this, but when she tried to think of options… there were none. He locked the door to every room, and even then she had no clothes and no idea where she was. And she had nowhere to go. He'd made that clear.

The door unlocked and swung open and then he slammed it shut, hard. She jumped, and fear washed over her like a bucket of cold water. The pulsing between her thighs stuttered and she knew that the man at the door was not the one who had whispered in her ear that morning or had his mouth between her thighs.

What had she done to make him angry? What was the phone call about? And what would make him upset with her when she'd obeyed him since he woke her up?

"Come here." His voice was harsh, and he pointed at the floor in front of him. The fear was making her shake as she slid off the bed and onto her knees. As she started crawling toward him tears gathered in her eyes. She'd been good! She hadn't fought him at all, she'd done everything right, followed every rule. She stopped where he pointed and kneeled while stifling a whimper.

"What did I do, Master?" she asked, her voice on the edge of tears, and then he slapped her hard. Her head cracked to the side and before she could recover he grabbed her around the throat, and panic clenched her chest.

"I told you I wouldn't accept any more mistakes, Thalia. What are you supposed to say if I give you an order? And is *that* how you're supposed to ask me a question?" He leaned forward and hissed the words at her. She was clenching her fists and fighting the urge to claw at his hand on her neck, but she shook her head as much as she could in his grip.

He let go and she collapsed, gasping. She couldn't understand why he had turned on her, he had been so good to her that morning, and she had behaved. She knew he had moments where he was better, and this time she'd done nothing to earn his rage. *Nothing!* Her voice shook, "Master?"

"Shut up. You need to listen to me very carefully. Our time table just got a lot shorter, and you can't make mistakes anymore." She was staring at the floor, confused about what time table he was referring to, and then he grabbed her hair and wrenched her head back so she looked at him. "I can't be lenient with you. If you're not perfect the consequences will be much worse than anything so far."

"May I ask a question, Master?" she asked bitterly. She had behaved, she had done nothing wrong, and he still hurt her.

"No." His jaw was clenched tightly as she looked up at him, his fist tight in his hair. The expression on his face was so confusing, his eyes weren't cold, they almost looked concerned. Underneath her fear she was growing angry, he had told her if she behaved it would be better. But here he was, hurting her again for *nothing*.

"Master, I just want to know what time table you mean?" Thalia asked it as steadily as she could, but while his eyes had seemed concerned, his face was full of rage, and his voice was harsh with his anger when he grabbed her throat and shoved her back to the floor.

"You do not have permission to speak, slut." Lifting her by her throat, he slammed her head back down. "If you keep defying me, you're going to make me hurt you. Do you understand?"

Thalia arched her back, trying to relieve the pressure on her throat. She couldn't breathe. She still didn't understand what she'd done but she knew she couldn't fight him — so she nodded.

He gripped her throat harder for a moment and then yanked her back to her knees by her hair. "You're here to learn to serve, Thalia, and you will be sorry if you fail me."

She whimpered, the cold fear of what he would do to her settling in her stomach. "Yes, Master." Her voice cracked as the ache in her throat affected it.

He was once again terrifying, the small kindness he'd shown her before was gone. She couldn't imagine what she'd done to earn this.

The rules. She just had to follow the rules. Perfectly.

He let go of her hair and she dropped her eyes to the floor. She heard him growl in frustration, or anger, and then he spoke again, "Follow me, Thalia."

He yanked the door open hard enough for it to bang into the wall behind it, and she winced. He was moving and she crawled after him, expecting him to go left back to the dark toned room she had been in, but he went right. He walked with heavy steps as he took her back to the room that resembled a hotel. The one she had woken up to her first morning.

How did that seem so long ago? It was just a couple of days.

Unlocking the door, he shoved it open and gestured inside. Now that the lights were on she could see that it was falsely sunny with a pale yellow wall color. There was no window though, she remembered that, and she had no idea what time it was. Thalia hiccuped as she kneeled in front of him, the fear and the uncertainty of what she'd done to set him off making her feel off balance, unsure. She had to fix this. She couldn't handle this version of him. Not when he was the only person she ever got to see.

She moved forward slightly until her knees were almost touching his bare feet. Keeping her eyes low she shook with fear as she lifted her hands to the waist of his pants. He grabbed her wrist and twisted it sharply and she yelped.

"What are you doing, Thalia?" His voice was rough, but she didn't dare look up. She wanted to yell at him, scream at how unfair he was being when she was trying, but she didn't want him to hit her again. If she finished what they'd started that morning, maybe she could be on his good side again. Her mind raced with how she could answer him within the rules, her pulse pounding in her ears. Her voice wavered when she finally spoke.

"May I, Master?" She was afraid she spoke too softly for him to hear her but he let go of her wrist and he stepped back against the doorframe. She heard a quiet thump and thought he must have dropped his head back against the wood.

"Yes." He was quiet, but she heard the edge to his voice. He wanted her, and if she could please him, maybe she could calm his anger. It was too terrible to be in this house with that anger. She inched forward on her knees and reached for his waistband again, slowly, worried he might hurt her again if he changed his mind.

A quick tug and his cock sprang free, growing before her eyes as he got hard before she'd even touched him. She almost forgot to respond to him, but she muttered a "Thank you, Master" before she gripped him.

Running her hand toward the tip she licked the head. He hissed between his teeth and she saw his fists clench at his sides. She didn't wait for him to second-guess his decision. She drew his cock into her mouth and ran her tongue along him as she pulled him deeper. Gripping his shaft more firmly she moved back, bringing her lips to his tip and stroking him with her hand before she took a breath through her nose and pushed forward. When he hit her throat she swallowed and took him deeper, he moaned above her and she heard him hit the door with his hand. She fought the urge to flinch at the sound.

Thalia lifted her hand and ran her nails up his thigh tugging his pants lower. Sliding her mouth back and forth again, swallowing him deep, she cupped him and he groaned.

"Dammit," he whispered and his hand was in her hair again. His hips bucked against her throat and she ignored the urge to gasp for air as he held her there. Her other hand clenched in the fabric of his pants, but then he mercifully pulled her back enough so she could gasp a breath and then he thrust deep into her throat again. She didn't even care that her body fought to breathe. Her eyes tearing as she moved her tongue against him, he was moaning above her. He thrust again and again, her body gaining small gasps of air when he pulled back far enough, her mouth filling with saliva as she swallowed against him. His fingers were tight in her hair, but the faint pain actually made her squirm, that errant pulse coming to life between her thighs.

He pulled her off, sliding from her mouth, and then he yanked her to her feet by her arm. "Move." His voice was harsh and she closed her eyes so she wouldn't look at him as he pushed her forward into the room. His fist remained tight on her skin and she stumbled but he steadied her. In a few more steps her legs ran into the bed. Bending her forward he growled, "Get up on the bed. Spread your knees wide, arms above your head."

With no warning he thrust all the way inside her and she moaned, squirming under him. He didn't ease into it with her like he had that morning; he fucked her hard and pulled her head up by her hair to bow her back. She bit her lip as the hard pounding stirred up heat between her legs. He groaned behind her and she knew if he continued with the deep, hard thrusts she was going to come.

"Master, may I come?" The request came out breathy and begging, her voice sliding into a moan as she tightened her thighs against the rising orgasm.

"No, Thalia. Wait." He ground out the words and she whimpered, trying to ignore the friction, the waves of sensation as he thrust deep inside her. She was panting and moaning, squirming against his grip as she tried to focus on anything else. His hand landed on her hip and he dug his fingers in hard enough to bruise, but it only made her cry out louder.

Her hand clenched in the bedspread as she moaned again, and she brought her arm to her mouth and bit down, holding off the urge to come for a moment more.

He slammed into her hard and growled out, "Now, Thalia!" She let go and came screaming, trying to muffle her voice against her arm as her hips bucked back against his. She felt him fill her and her head swam, angled back sharply by his grip in her hair. His moans behind her were low, and his grip in her hair slowly relaxed so she could lay forward on the bed again, breathing harshly.

"Good girl," he said and she felt relief. She had not come without permission, he likely wouldn't hurt her if he said she'd done well.

"Thank you, Master." She mumbled and he moved back, his hand sliding from her hip over her ass before he squeezed the round of it. Then he stepped back completely but she was afraid to move, to make a mistake again, to find out what he'd meant by consequences.

"You should shower and rest, Thalia. I'll come back." His voice sounded off, but she didn't even have the chance to respond before she heard the door close and lock.

Her legs shook as she tried to stand and she leaned back on the bed, looking around at the room she'd first woken up in. Well-furnished with bright, feminine colors. She remembered the ample bathroom and decided she'd just soak in a bath until she was clean and the throbbing between her legs dulled.

Thalia still wanted to know what she'd done. How could she avoid his anger again if she didn't know? She just had to obey him enough that he wouldn't hurt her. At least until whatever time table he had mentioned revealed what was next for her. As far as being obedient, he'd told her to shower, and so she would.

The rest she'd have to wait to figure out.

Chapter Ten
THALIA

Thalia had never realized just how much she depended on clocks. She'd had the alarm clock in her room, the one on the microwave, the little one in the living room on the DVR. And her phone.

She missed her phone.

She missed her apartment.

For a brief moment a panicked sob clenched her chest so tightly she didn't think she could breathe. Wrapped snuggly in the large towel from the bathroom, curled up under the sheets, she was covered in more cloth than she'd been allowed in days, and all she could think about was everything she didn't have.

And wouldn't ever have again, according to the guard.

She had no idea how long he'd been gone. *No clocks.* Her stomach was growling because he only seemed to feed her when he wasn't angry with her, and she had no idea if he was still mad now or what he was planning to do next.

The sob escaped from her chest and she bit down on the soft pillow under her head. She hated herself. She did. Why wasn't she fighting him with everything she had?

'Because he'll beat you,' her mind reminded her. But he hurt her anyway. He hurt her even when she was trying so hard to follow his rules and behave. What if he was the only person she ever saw again? What if she could never figure out what the hell he wanted, and he just punished her at random? What if this was going to be her entire life? What if whomever he was bringing to this nightmare house was worse?

Another sob slipped out and she realized her tears were soaking the pillow she had buried her face in. The lock clicked and she jumped. He didn't slam the door open this time, which told her maybe his anger had cooled. He turned and gently shut the door and locked it.

Thalia had her face hidden in the pillow, but from the corner of her eye she could see he was standing by the door. Waiting.

For what?

"Thalia..." His voice had an edge of warning to it and her stomach filled with anxious butterflies, her pulse firing in time with their beating wings. "I know you're not asleep. Get on your knees."

She didn't try and fake it. Sitting up, she kept her eyes down to the bed and pushed into a kneel, keeping the towel clutched tightly across her body. "Yes, Mast—"

His stern voice interrupted her, "What did I say about covering yourself in my house?" She flinched as her hands let the towel down slowly until it pooled at her waist, and she sniffled trying to stifle the tears that had been flowing freely before he came in.

"I'm sorry, Master." She spoke quietly, not trusting herself to speak any louder.

"Get on the floor." He had the cold edge of command that she'd first heard in his voice, and it made her muscles quake as she slid off the bed leaving the towel behind. Forming into the proper kneel, she paused and then he snapped his fingers. "Come here."

"Yes, Master." Her head was spinning trying to remember everything she should and shouldn't do. He grabbed her hair when she arrived at his feet, tilting her head up so she had to stare into those blue-gray eyes. Completely detached, that's what he looked like.

He pressed his lips against the shell of her ear and hissed, "I will teach you more today, but do not forget the other rules or I will punish you severely."

She nodded against the grip in her hair, biting her lower lip to try and stop the crying. "Yes, Master," she said on a quiet, shaking breath. He didn't even give her a second look when he let go of her hair, unlocked and opened the door. Then he started walking.

Her knees ached as she followed him across the wood back into the huge open living room where she saw that it was daytime. An entire wall of the room was made of floor to ceiling windows and beautiful sunlight flooded into the space. Outside were woods, and she couldn't see another house. "Eyes down!" he snapped, and she winced and dropped her eyes back to the floor to continue after him as he walked into the kitchen.

When she arrived he slapped her, just hard enough to shock her, but not enough for lasting damage. He was frighteningly good at walking that line when he wanted to. She realized she hadn't responded to his command about the windows.

"I'm sorry, Master. I will keep my eyes down, Master." She leaned her head a little lower as he pushed out a frustrated breath.

"Do you know how to cook?" He paused in front of her. "Stand up and look around the kitchen."

She stood slowly and looked over the pale wood counters, the glass paned cabinets that displayed beautiful glassware and plates and bowls and a variety of colorful kitchen tools. "Yes, Master. Some things."

"What can you make us for breakfast?" His voice had an edge to it that had not been there before — as if he were already angry with her. The anger had appeared after the phone call, and now she wanted to know more than ever what had been said and who had called. But it wasn't like she could ask, so she tried to focus on his question. *Breakfast.*

"Eggs?" she said nervously, then continued, stumbling over her words, keeping her eyes away from him and training them on the fridge as if it could offer her support. "French toast, omelets, bacon, sausage, and I can make pancakes if you have a mix, Master." Her body quivered with tension, he was unpredictable now. What was a good answer, and what would make him punish her?

"French toast. I believe the ingredients are here. Make it. There's fresh fruit in the fridge as well. Do not eat until I return. When I return you will kneel and await my permission to continue." He spoke quickly, and she nodded.

"Yes, Master," she said. Then — he left. He left the room. Left her alone in the wide-open space of the kitchen, which flowed into a dining room and then the massive living room with all its windows. She had no cuffs, no confining walls, no locked room without windows. In her fear she waited a moment for him to return, but he didn't.

Moving mechanically to the fridge she took out eggs and milk. She found the pantry and was surprised at how deep it went. Grabbing bread, spices, vanilla, and piling it all by the stove to start making breakfast.

Thalia's mouth was watering as the first piece was cooking, but since she just had to wait she started to look around the kitchen again. There were big windows in here too — and a door.

A door!

She ran to it. A sliding door to a deck, and she pulled on it hard; it didn't budge. Her heart was racing as she fiddled with the small twist lock at the handle and then she tried again. The door rocked slightly under her assault but still didn't budge. She ran her hands around the frame looking for a secondary lock, or a pressure lock like she had at her apartment.

Nothing.

Nothing?!

Then why wouldn't it open?! Tears were streaming down her face again, she was so close to freedom and she wasn't going to miss her chance. Hurrying back to the cabinets she quietly opened the one that held a large, red, KitchenAid mixer. It was heavy in her arms, and as weak as she was from lack of food, the fatigue of holding herself up the day before, and her overall exhaustion, she was worried she wouldn't be strong enough to do what she planned.

Lining herself up at the door, she took a deep breath and tested the weight of the mixer in her arms. It was oddly shaped, but definitely the heaviest thing in the kitchen she could wield. Thalia stared at the glass and breathed a quiet prayer to any god who felt like listening, then she twisted back and threw it as hard as she could.

The crash of the glass breaking almost gave her a heart attack. She crouched down, covering her ears as the mixer slid over the deck amidst hundreds of shards of glass. The glass in the doorframe crashed to the floor, tinkling over the wooden floors. The frame was jagged and Thalia turned quickly to grab the metal spatula she was using for the French toast and started knocking out huge chunks of the glass to make it safe to crawl through. A shard sliced her foot but she yelped and didn't care.

"THALIA!" She heard his voice boom through the house and lunged for the door, slicing both of her feet on glass before she felt his strong arms grab her around the waist and throw her backward away from the door. She hit the floor hard, already sobbing in fear, as she flipped to her stomach and scrambled up, ignoring the pain in her feet as she tried to get away from him. It took him no time to grab her by her hair and pull her out of the kitchen and throw her down again. She hit the floor with a sharp pain in her shoulder and tried to get up again, but he was already there. He kicked her hard in the stomach and she curled on her side, sobbing as she coughed and tried to drag air back into her lungs.

"YOU STUPID SLUT! Did you really think I'd leave that door unlocked? Or that I wouldn't be watching you?!" He was shouting above her, and she knew she had no chance to outrun him, or fight him, but she had been so close. *So close.*

"I HAD TO TRY!" she screamed and he yanked her head back by her hair until she cried out from the pain of it. Flipping her to her stomach he grabbed her arm in his other hand and twisted it up behind her back. She fought him like she had the first night, bucking and twisting until he slammed his knee into her back and pulled her arm higher. He moved it further and she thought her shoulder would tear under the strain.

"You are so stupid!" he screamed down at her, and she couldn't control the sobbing. "It was a test, Thalia! You stupid little bitch, it was a TEST! And you failed me, you failed me miserably!"

She tried to twist under him, but he used his knee to press her harder into the floor until it was difficult to breathe. "I WANT TO GO HOME!" Her voice broke as she screamed, and he growled in anger above her.

"YOU DON'T HAVE A HOME! It's gone, Thalia! Everything is gone! Give it up and accept this life or you're going to end up in a hell of your own making!"

She screamed in frustration, tears threatening to choke her. "THIS IS HELL!"

He leaned down and wrapped his arm around her throat, dragging her back with him as he sat down and her legs moved underneath her. She was pressed back firmly against his chest, his knees on either side of her, holding her in place. He applied pressure to her throat until she could barely breathe, and the blood in her head pounded behind her eyes and in her ears. She dug her nails into his arm, trying her best to draw blood, but he didn't relent. He hissed in her ear quietly, seeming unfazed by the pain of her nails. "You have no *idea* how kind I have been to you. The things people have requested I do to you would terrify you. The things people want to see me do to you."

Thalia squirmed, whining against his arm across her throat, trying to block out the things he was telling her. He kept going.

"I am trying to train you so you'll have the best chance at a good life, a life you may actually grow to enjoy. But if you keep this up," he viciously twisted her nipple until she screamed weakly through his hold on her throat, "I'll let my partner sell you to whatever whorehouse in whatever country will buy you. You disrespectful, disobedient, DEFIANT little cockslut!" His voice dropped as he hissed against her ear, "And they will use you until you break completely, and then they'll kill you! Is that what you want?"

His words sunk in, burrowing into her as fears she'd never had words for came to life inside her. Not just one man, but tens, hundreds, doing things to her. Being forgotten in some country across the world where women being treated that way was normal. And how did those countries feel about American women? She kicked her feet in front of her, leaving streaks of blood on the gray floor. Adrenaline must have been suppressing the pain, because as it faded she felt her feet burning, her ribs aching where he'd kicked her, a multitude of bruises littered across her body. She was sobbing but couldn't make much noise behind the pressure of his arm against her neck.

"Is that what you want, Thalia?!" he shouted at her, and her vision started fading at the edges. Her fingers and lips tingling. She finally shook her head and he let go of her, shoving her forward from him as she curled into a gasping ball.

"Fuck!" he shouted and with her first breaths she could smell smoke. He stood up quickly and she heard him walk back to the stove, turn it off and drop the pan into the sink. He came back to her and pulled her to her feet by her hair. She buckled the moment she put pressure on her feet and screamed in pain as he dropped her back to the floor. Her knees whined at the impact and she looked up to see his fist buried in his own hair. When she locked eyes with him she cried out in fear and looked down immediately. He had never been this angry. Not even after the call.

What had she done? Stupid, stupid—

This slap was much harder, her ears rang and she could taste the copper of blood in her mouth. "Keep your eyes down, slut. If you move from this spot I will whip you bloody, and then sell you as is. Do you understand?"

She whimpered and nodded, mumbling "Yes, Master" before she heard his footsteps retreat. It had been a stupid attempt, she would have been running through the woods with her feet sliced up with glass, completely naked under the sun, with no food, no water, and no idea where a road or help could possibly be.

She should have just made breakfast. Her stomach growled in agreement, and she cursed herself.

A moment later his angry steps were returning and she cowered, curling in on herself. "I'm sorry, I'm sorry, I'm sorry…" she whimpered over and over.

He didn't respond, he just yanked her arm behind her back and latched a cuff to her forearm. Pulling her other arm he stacked them on top of each other and latched the other cuff to her other forearm. The cuffs pulled her shoulders back, lifting her chest, and making it much harder to move since her arms were higher. "I don't want to hear it, slut. I warned you there would be consequences if you failed me—"

"Please don't whip me, Master, please—"

He pulled her head up and slapped her hard on the other cheek, she whimpered and let her head fall forward as he released her hair. "Do not speak again unless I ask you to."

Chapter Eleven
THALIA

Leaning down he put his shoulder into her stomach and his arm behind her ass and stood easily, as if she didn't weigh anything. She ended up hoisted over his shoulder, dripping blood off the bottoms of her feet across the house. Something inside her was deeply happy about tracking blood through his pristine house, as if the blood revealed the truth of the place — even though she knew he'd likely clean it up.

He opened the door to a small room, and he dropped her hard into a chair without a back. But he immediately fixed that by sliding a thin plank between her arms and her back, pulling them even tighter as he locked the rear of the chair into place. Then came a leather strap around her waist, her neck, her ankles. Each thigh was bound separately and she could see the bottom of the chair was missing a v-shape between her thighs. She whimpered quietly as it quickly became apparent that she couldn't move.

"Since you can't seem to use your mouth properly today." He held up a small rubber ball gag, and he grabbed her face hard. "Open." She did and he pressed it between her teeth, securing it behind her head.

Then he mercilessly attached clamps to each nipple, a small scream muffled behind her gag each time. His fingers rubbed her clit and she shook her head from side to side, the muscles of her thighs shaking in their effort to close. He thrust two fingers inside her and her hips tried to buck ineffectively in all the bindings. He returned to her clit, pinching and rubbing it until his other hand spread her lips and the pinch of a clamp on her clit had tears in her eyes as she screamed loudly.

"Hush. You're already making so much noise and the punishment hasn't even started." He gathered wires from somewhere to her left that she couldn't really see and began attaching them to the clamps. Dread filled her and Thalia shook her head, pleading through the gag. He ignored her. "My partner has serious doubts about you, and this is one of his favorite rooms in the house. Since you failed me so miserably this morning, I've decided perhaps my methods are too gentle for you." A humming started somewhere behind her and she jerked against the bindings as cold fear filled her. *Too gentle? Was he kidding?* He stood next to her, one arm extended behind her as he stared down at her. She openly stared, trying to plead for mercy with her eyes for whatever he had planned.

He didn't flinch.

"I warned you," he hissed, and pain shot through her entire body, focused on the three points of the clamps. Her muscles strained for a moment against the straps and then it stopped and she collapsed back, crying against the gag. "That was an electric shock, Thalia. You're going to keep receiving them until you've learned your lesson. Once you have you *might* earn pleasure."

On the wall in front of her he unrolled a long poster, tacking down the bottom so she could see it clearly in the harsh light of the room. In large font were the rules in a long list that covered the height of the wall. Thalia started to read them in her head:

"You are not your own, you are property."

"You will address me as Master. Everyone else as Sir or Ma'am."

The pain tore into her again and she screamed against the gag, twisting her head to the side to see him looking at his phone. Thalia glanced back at the list as the pain faded.

"You will kneel in all rooms, and again whenever your Master enters."

"You will crawl when told to follow."

"You will ask permission to speak, to ask a question, to orgasm."

The guard was in front of her when the pain went off this time, her nipples pulsing with the ache, and her clit had a heartbeat of its own tied nothing to pleasure. She could feel the tears running hot down her face. He was detached when he looked at her again. Cold and furious. She couldn't handle it, and her eyes flicked back to the wall.

"You will wear no clothing unless provided by your Master."

"You will thank your Master for all punishments."

"You will keep your eyes down at all times unless directed."

Blinding pain, her muscles strained against the straps and a keening cry tore out of her behind the gag. She felt hoarse already. His hands were on his hips when she looked up for a moment, but she quickly dropped her eyes.

The guard hadn't triggered it.

Thalia's eyes snapped up to the ceiling, tracking along the edges until she found the small cameras in two corners. She screamed again, knocking her head into the chair back as she realized who had to be doing this. The guard grabbed her face, and she knew his contact with her skin was momentarily saving her from another shock.

"You did this. *You* made this choice." He stepped back and she tried to twist, to beg him to let her go, to take control away from his partner. But sometime during the next surge of pain that burned through her body, he left the room. He had left her alone with the one who had control.

A small screen turned on next to the rules and it showed her the camera feed. The cameras didn't show the wall she stared at, because they were aimed at her. She was completely exposed in the chair. The dark leather straps a sharp contrast against her pale skin, her cheeks flushed from the escape attempt, the fight, his slaps, and her pain. She closed her eyes and pain surged through her instantly, making her scream until her voice broke behind the gag.

She was breathing harshly through her nose when it stopped and she looked up to see text appear on a black strip at the bottom of the screen: 'Looking away will result in punishment.'

Thalia widened her eyes and looked up at the cameras, futilely pulling against the restraints again. The text changed: 'Your Master has been gentle with you.'

She rolled her eyes and a sharp shock went through her that was what she imagined a stun gun must feel like. She suddenly had sympathy for those criminals on Cops who had been brought down by the electric current.

'Do not be disrespectful. It will only result in pain.'

Thalia breathed harshly, staring at the screen, trying to zone out from her own image. Her breasts rising and falling. Her mouth stretched around the gag, her thighs spread. She tried desperately not to think of the people watching her.

She wanted to know where the guard was. She wanted him to come back.

Which proved she was insane.

'You must behave, or we have no use for you. Nod if you understand.'

Thalia pressed her teeth into the gag, making her jaw ache. Another man wanting her to submit. This one from halfway across the world as far as she knew. A sharp warning shock went through her and she arched up as much as the bindings allowed. When it stopped she nodded slowly.

'Good girl.'

The clamp at her clit began to hum low with an electric current, creating a thrumming at the core of her she was helpless to ignore. It felt good despite the aching of her body. She whined against the gag, her hips lifting slightly, until she saw herself writhing on the camera and she stilled. The hum stopped and the text changed again.

'Your Master is right that you are beautiful. But disobedience will not be tolerated.'

Thalia glared at the screen, huffing out a breath as her tears dried up in her anger.

'Nod if you understand.'

She held her head still. All they wanted was her body. They thought she was pretty to look at, they were happy to use her body, but wanted to crush everything inside her. It didn't matter if the guard may have been right about some things, that some of the things he'd done with her had felt incredible. Had filled a need she was unaware of. Maybe she did crave some of this, but not at the risk of losing herself completely. And this asshole, sitting behind a computer somewhere, he didn't know her at all. He'd watched her on cameras making decisions about who she was. She didn't have to bend to him. Even if—

Pain. All-encompassing pain. Her brain shorted out with it, her vision went white, she felt a sharp pain in her throat and then there was nothing.

Sometime later Thalia became aware of shouting. It seemed to come from far away. She couldn't really feel her body; it was like she wasn't fully connected to it, but floating half in and half outside of it.

"Thalia?!"

The guard. His voice came into focus a little and it sounded panicked, concerned. About her. He cursed and she heard his voice moving away again.

She wanted to open her eyes, but her body didn't react. What had happened? She remembered the pain, the text on the screen, the chair.

"Fuck you! It's done. No! No more, I'll handle it!" His voice came from the hallway. He was angry with whomever he was talking to. Suddenly his voice was close again, filled with an odd mix of concern and leftover anger. "Thalia. Can you hear me? — Shit! Come on, wake up."

Something popped near her and the sudden scent of ammonia and a strong lavender perfume hit her and knocked her back into her body. Her head slammed back against the chair, and she winced. The guard was crouched in front of her, holding a small white thing in his hand. *Smelling salts*. Relief washed over his face for a second, and then it disappeared as he schooled his face into a blank expression.

He dropped the packet on the ground and started untying the straps from her. He wasn't talking anymore. Thalia stared at him, her body shaking. She had never felt pain like that, never been in so much pain she'd fainted. When her legs and her body were unstrapped, she heard two clicks and the chair back slid up and he set it aside, allowing her arms to relax a little. Her shoulders ached from the strain they'd been under and she noticed all of her muscles felt like she'd run for hours. She realized the clamps must have been removed while she was unconscious, but the pain from those points seemed to blend into the overall pain of her body.

A constant, never-ending stream of strumming nerves.

He didn't even try to make her stand, he just scooped her up over his shoulder and walked out of the horrible small room with that evil chair. She felt a twisted sense of relief at being back under his control. He had tried to warn her about the others, but she hadn't believed him. There *were* worse things, and she was sure there was more than the chair.

He had stopped it, but she didn't know what he would do with her now. She wanted to tell him thank you, to beg him not to hurt her anymore, to apologize for trying to run — but he'd left the gag in. He was clearly not interested in letting her speak. He brought her into the dark toned room again, and she whimpered against the gag as the door shut and locked. The guard stepped into the bathroom and the bright lights hurt her eyes as he laid her down on the tile next to the tub. With her arms bound she ended up uncomfortably arched off the floor, but he didn't care.

The silence was driving her crazy. She tried to say she was sorry but it came out as nothing more than a garble and her throat burned at the effort of making the small sounds.

"Stop. I don't want to hear you talk." His voice was cold again, all the concern from when she was unconscious gone. He walked back to her with a handful of first aid supplies. Sitting on the edge of the tub he grabbed one of her feet off the floor and, using a pair of tweezers, he pulled out a sliver of glass that made her scream. The screaming hurt worse than her foot. There was something wrong with her throat. His handsome features were pulled together in concentration as he slowly went over her foot, pulling out glass. Then he did the same with the other foot. Lifting her again he laid her down in the tub and began to run warm water, letting the tub fill a few inches.

She'd been an idiot to try and walk over broken glass naked and barefoot. She was lucky that when he'd yanked her back he'd thrown her clear of the glass and she was cut nowhere else.

He gently rinsed the blood off her feet, and then grabbed a razor. She started to close her legs, but he pinched her thigh and she winced. He didn't even speak to her as he lathered between her legs and began shaving her most private place smooth again with confident sweeps. She looked up at the ceiling and started counting to ten thousand, anything to not be present in this humiliating moment. "You will keep yourself shaved. Understand?"

She just nodded.

The guard continued and shaved her legs with a surprising confidence, moving the razor in quick swipes. He rinsed her off and then let the water out. Drying her off in the tub, he tucked the damp towel under her and checked the soles of her feet once more, tilting them both. When he was satisfied he used an antiseptic that made her wince and writhe, and he pinched her calf to still her but he still didn't look at her face. After wrapping one foot in a bandage, he repeated the process with the other.

When her feet were bandaged he picked her up under the arms, like one might a child, and set her on her feet. It hurt, but not impossibly. She had a new scale for pain after the chair. He still scooped her up and brought her into the bedroom. Dropping her on her stomach on the bed, he spoke coldly, "Don't move."

She swallowed behind the gag, the excess saliva pooling and threatening to choke her if she didn't. She was perfectly still, aware that it was only him keeping his partner at bay.

At least *he* had never hurt her like that.

He came back naked, and hard. His cock glistening in his hand as he stroked himself. He stayed silent and grabbed her hair pulling her higher on the bed, forcing her to move only on her knees with her arms bound behind her back. When she was where he wanted her, he moved onto the bed behind her, but he didn't speak. No comforting words, no commands to follow. *Silence*. His hands moved over her waist, pulling her toward him so that her face was pressed into the bed, her hips high in the air.

His cock pressed against her ass and she shook her head against the bedding, whimpering behind the gag as she tried to pull away. He hadn't done anything this time to make it easier for her, no vibrator to distract her, no touches to her clit. His fingers dug into her hips and he spanked her hard enough that she could feel his handprint. When he pulled her back again, he immediately thrust the head of his cock inside her ass and the pain made her clench her fists and press her face into the bedding as she let out a broken scream. He had obviously used lube, or she knew it would be worse, but the pain was constant and burning as he pushed himself further. Her voice was raw as she cried again behind the gag. He groaned behind her and pressed his hips forward slowly until she felt him flush against her.

She shook her head again and begged through the gag, trying to make her body relax consciously so it hurt less.

"Shut up, Thalia. I want you to understand"—he withdrew and moaned quietly as he thrust forward hard— "that I give you pleasure by choice, but I don't have to." He thrust hard again and she nodded against the bedspread. Compared to the last time, this was so much worse. She wanted him to touch her clit, to give her something else to focus on, something to turn this into pleasure. "I can use you any time I want, and it is not necessary that you enjoy it."

He thrust inside her again, and she whimpered, driving her shoulder down into the bedding as her body shook. Too much pain already today. Too much.

His hand was suddenly in her hair and he yanked her back, without her arms the strain on her back was impossible, it held him deeper inside her, stretching her around his cock and making her cry out against the gag. The guard let her go without warning and leaned over her, biting into the skin over her ribs as his fingers tangled in her hair. The pressure of the gag faded and he reached into her mouth and pulled it out, at the same time he thrust again. Her voice cracked when she made a sound.

"You don't get pleasure unless you earn it, do you understand, slave?"

The term made her cry harder but she nodded against the bedding. "Yes, Master," she said, but her voice had a breathy quality and was a little lower than usual. Her throat was incredibly sore from the screaming in the small room.

He pressed in again and she clenched her teeth, her jaw so sore from the gag. Mercifully, he reached under her and slowly began to circle her clit as he stayed still inside her. She'd been in so much pain that although on some level she knew it felt good, she couldn't really react to it. She waited for it to overwhelm the pain, but even after several focused minutes it never seemed to. He continued rubbing her for a minute more and then removed his hand. He muttered something and slid out of her slowly. Whimpering, Thalia tried her best to stay still on the bed as he moved away.

When he returned a moment later he had pants on and he unbound her arms. Her shoulders argued with her as she rotated them forward to brace herself on the bed before he gently pushed her to the side so she would roll onto her back. His silence was unbearable, his suppressed rage a constant fear, but she didn't even have the energy to fight him, he could do what he wanted.

As if he'd heard her, his fingers slid inside her and her hips twitched, but the liquid heat his touch normally drew out of her didn't come. When his thumb started circling her clit, the bundle of nerves made her hips kick once but she just took even breaths and trained her eyes on the headboard as he continued. After a moment he made a frustrated sound and spanked her pussy hard, she gasped and clenched her teeth against the pain in her throat.

"What is wrong, slave?" His words threatened violence and she wanted to scream at him to just kill her if he was really going to sell her to some whorehouse. She couldn't handle this. She couldn't handle not knowing what he'd do next, she couldn't handle anything like the chair again. Fear kept her quiet though and she only whimpered. He grabbed her chin to make her look at him. "Why aren't you responding to my touch?"

"I'm sorry, Master." She could barely get her voice behind the words.

"Tell me why you're not responding." His fingers were tight on her jaw and she could swear there would be bruises, but she wanted to scream at him that she didn't know. She'd never understood why she HAD responded to his violence. *Wasn't this reaction more normal?* "Slave!" he shouted into her face and she winced.

"Pain, Master?" she offered the obvious solution and he let go of her. Her body quivered as she waited for him to hurt her, training her eyes up at the headboard.

The guard cleared his throat. "Then rest for now, slave. But know that if you ever try to run again I will ensure you end up in a nightmare."

"Yes, Master." She didn't try to close her legs or move at all, she kept her eyes on the headboard as she heard him leave the room. She had been emptied, all the fear and adrenaline had hollowed her out, and she didn't know what it would take to bring her back.

She didn't know if she could come back from this.

Chapter Twelve
HIM

"You broke her!" he shouted into the phone, but his brother only laughed.

"The slut needed a real lesson. She tried to run. *She broke your door.*"

"You could have killed her, she fucking passed out!" His grip on the phone was dangerous, and so he made himself pace through his bedroom again.

"I've never killed a slave." His brother's voice held a warning edge to it, but he ignored it.

"No, but you broke Beth so badly you had to keep her. Does she still not even respond when you speak to her?" He gritted his teeth against the memory of the little blonde his brother had tortured so badly that something in her just shattered. After that she didn't respond no matter what his brother had done, it was like she wasn't even there anymore.

"I don't know. I sold her to a brothel in Thailand. At a loss to our investment, but better than me having to deal with her."

"You sold her like that?" He was shocked, the last time they'd discussed Beth his brother had said he was trying to bring her back around.

"What did you want me to do? She was useless. There all she has to do is lay on her back, and she can do that." His brother's icy tone made him flinch. The man really had no soul to speak of.

"You're not doing that to Thalia." His stomach clenched at the way she'd been completely unresponsive to his touches. That had been the most amazing thing about her. If his brother had broken her…

"If she's too weak to handle one real punishment, then she'll break anyway." His brother spoke so casually, like he hadn't invested money and time into acquiring her.

"You went too far and you know it."

"You're defending this slut to me?" His brother's voice was threatening.

"I'm defending our investment. She was doing just fine before you interfered this morning." He let out a frustrated laugh before his brother could interrupt. "If you hadn't made me shut her down this morning she would have passed the kitchen test." He wasn't just saying it, he knew it was true. She'd been submitting to him in the early hours, before the phone call, and before he'd been suddenly harsh with her.

"Maybe she would have if I hadn't interrupted, but that's being generous. I knew she wouldn't pass the test the way she was acting, it's why I made the bet."

He knew it was true, his brother had wanted to play with Thalia his own way and had wagered exactly that on whether or not she'd pass the kitchen test.

His brother sighed. "I want her out of the house, she's messing with your head. And, despite all of her obvious faults, we actually have people interested. We need to capitalize on it before she completely breaks if that's where this is heading. I know a few of these buyers won't be interested anymore if that happens." His brother was typing again in the background. "It seems we can have a good group of buyers two days from now. I'll be there soon."

"You have to give me time to fix her! I have to get her to depend on me again or the auction will be a disaster." *Two days wasn't enough.* He needed more time with her. The anxiety made his stomach twist, and he was grateful he still hadn't eaten after the fiasco in the kitchen.

"You don't have any more time. If you'd handled her like you handled the others we wouldn't be in this situation." His brother was snide, but it wasn't like he'd been that different. Sure, he hadn't been able to resist fucking her in the stairwell. He probably should have just taken her, but when he'd felt her against him he couldn't stop himself.

"What about your precious reputation? We've never turned a girl around this fast. She's going to bear our mark. If she can't perform it reflects on both of us." He had found himself back at the computer monitors that showed the various cameras in the house, including the one that was live. Thalia was still curled in a ball on the bed — she hadn't moved.

"Well, I suggest you work on getting her up to our standards. Do whatever you have to." His brother wasn't even paying attention to the conversation anymore as he flippantly gave his own commands.

"Let me talk to her off camera, explain things to her."

"No."

He slammed his fist down on his desk in frustration. "Dammit, would you just trust me? I've never failed you and I don't plan to."

"And what exactly are you going to *explain* to her?" His brother put more emphasis on 'explain' than necessary.

"The options available to her when we sell her. The reality of it. I don't need the potential buyers listening to me talking about them, they get sensitive." That was true, and the discussion would help, but if he was honest with himself he also wanted to make her feel better. He wanted her responsive again, he wanted to fix the damage he and his brother had done. He pulled up the non-live version of the camera in her room and zoomed in on her. She was asleep again, her brows pulled together like she was having a nightmare. Probably about him.

After all, he was the monster in her bed instead of under it.

"Fine. I've activated your remote again. Abuse it and I take it back. I'll speak to our potential buyers about the party and explain that the cameras may have gaps." He muttered something and then his voice came back to the phone. "Make sure she doesn't embarrass me. She's quite lovely when she's writhing. I'd hate to waste her overseas."

"I'll make sure she's ready." The call cut off without his brother saying anything else.

He cleaned up the blood around the house first, nauseous at how much there seemed to be. He never liked to see a girl bleed. Welts, bruises — absolutely, but blood just reminded him of a battlefield. When the blood was gone he swept the glass up, put the mixer back in the cabinet, and sealed the door with tarp and tape. It had been incredibly ballsy of her to break the window like that. In all his years even the ones who had tried the door had never gone that far. Just another way Thalia was unique. He made calls for what he'd need done before the party while he was cooking. When he was done he grabbed a Vicodin and powdered it, dumping it into her glass of orange juice. If pain was causing the issues with her responses, he could take care of that.

It was mid-afternoon by the time he came back to the room with a tray. She didn't even wake up when he unlocked the door. Her breathing was even, her ribs rising and falling in a slow rhythm and he was instantly angry at himself as he saw the bruise forming on them from when he'd lost his temper and kicked her. The more he thought about the kitchen test, the more his rage at her trying to run started to come back — but he calmed himself. He'd caught her. The predator in him knew she was still trapped. Still his.

For now.

He pushed away the thought of selling her for a little while longer. He needed to see if he could even get Thalia back first. Setting the tray on a table against the wall he lifted the whole thing and moved it as quietly as he could to the edge of the bed. No temper tantrums with the food again. He pressed the button in his pocket and was satisfied when he heard the beep.

Without the weight of his brother and the customers watching him he let himself feel how much he wanted her. How much he wanted her to respond to him. Moving to the side of the bed she was closest to he gently pushed her hair back from her face. That woke her and she jumped, her body tightening and then slowly relaxing.

She had her eyes down. Good.

He lifted her chin up and gently kissed her mouth, Thalia was stiff but he hadn't expected her to be otherwise. He moved his mouth along her jaw line, his face burying in her hair as he moved down her neck. The tension eased out of her slowly and when he returned his lips to her mouth she was a little more relaxed.

"I want to talk to you," he said the words against her mouth, and her hazel eyes found his. She looked so empty, and he wanted the fight back in them.

"Yes, Master," she breathed in a slightly more sultry voice than she'd had before she'd screamed her throat raw under his brother's ministrations.

He sat at the end of the bed and gave her room to sit up and still have some breathing room, even though he wanted her in his lap. "This morning was," he sighed, "not handled well by either of us."

Panic filled her eyes and she reminded him so much of an animal about to flee that he suddenly wanted to hunt her. Chase her down through the house and pin her — *No.* He stopped that train of thought. The goal was to bring her *back* from being terrified, not turn her into a frightened, useless, little rabbit.

"I'm sorry, Master," she whispered, her eyes on the bedding by her knees.

"Look at me," he commanded and she did. "I should not have put you in the chair, I should have handled your defiance differently."

Meaning he should never have taken his brother's bet.

Her mouth opened, and then closed. Her eyebrows pulled together and tears filled her eyes as she frantically tried to find a way to respond. Her panic actually bothered him, so he raised a hand.

"It's okay, you don't have to respond right now. I've turned the cameras off so we can speak freely." Her eyes widened a little, and she nodded slightly as he handed her the orange juice. "Drink that, all of it. You need the sugar." *And the Vicodin.*

He took a breath. "You deserved to be punished for trying to run, you understand that, right?"

She was drinking the orange juice but stopped to respond. "Yes, Master. Th-thank you for my punishment, Master." She shook slightly as she said it and he wanted to curse his brother and his damn poster of rules, and his fucking fetish with electricity.

"Good girl," he replied, but only because he couldn't counter his brother's rules. Having her thank him for a punishment that could have killed her made him sick. When he'd heard her screaming like that he'd had to turn off the audio, and then he'd seen her go limp and his heart had jumped into his throat.

Bastard. He'd probably done it on purpose.

"Thank you, Master." Her muscles were shaking and he knew it was exhaustion. He'd put her through too much. She didn't have enough fuel for her body and she was already lean. He was lucky she wasn't in shock. He was glad when he saw her drinking more of the orange juice.

"I brought food as well. Someone suggested French toast this morning, and I went with it." She flinched, not even a hint of a smile at his poor attempt at a joke. "Will you let me feed you?" *And not kick the plate onto the floor while screaming*, he added silently.

Her stomach growled and he tried to hide his smile. She finally muttered, "Yes, Master."

Cutting off a corner of the French toast, he held it out to her on the fork. He wanted to move closer to her as weak as she was, but he knew he couldn't change their dynamic that much. She winced as she eased forward slowly until her pink lips closed over the bite and she sat back to chew. More orange juice to wash it down. He cut another piece for her. "I want you to know that as long as you address me properly, you may ask me any question without the risk of punishment right now."

She swallowed and nodded. "Yes, Master."

He continued to feed her as he spoke. "My partner will be here soon." She flinched back from him, but he continued. "I will do my best to limit his interactions with you to avoid another incident like this morning. But you must behave."

She nodded and spoke after another bite. "I will, Master. Are you really going to sell me to someone, Master?"

His heart raced at the question but he made himself answer steadily, "It is what you are here for."

"Do you... want to sell me, Master?" She was either incredibly observant, or he was as obvious as his brother had said. Or maybe she just wanted to stay with him? An odd flare of hope lit inside him, but he snuffed it out.

"What I want doesn't matter. You're here to be sold."

She bit her lip and nodded, tears sliding down her cheeks. She finished the orange juice, and he took the glass from her to set it aside.

"Can you tell me, wi-will they hurt me like that, Master?" She closed her mouth against a sob, and he was strangely relieved to at least see her willingness to talk coming back, and she was reacting emotionally. She wasn't like Beth.

'Yet,' his mind taunted him.

"I don't know." He watched as the fear washed over her, but he'd decided not to lie to her in this free moment they had. He couldn't guarantee who would win the auction, after all.

"I'm sorry I tried to run, Master." Her shoulders were shaking as she tried to suppress her crying. He had never really felt compassion when others cried, but he found that he wanted her to stop, no matter how beautiful she looked.

"I shouldn't have given you the test after the issues this morning. I tried to make a point to my partner that you were obedient, and it backfired." He pushed a hand through his hair as she took another bite he offered her. "It's why I punished you so severely."

"I didn't mean to fail you, Master. I won't do it again, just please don't put me back in the chair?" Her eyes were down once more, and he silently cursed his brother again.

"No more chair."

She nodded, biting her lower lip. "Thank you, Master, I just— thank you." She tugged at the bedding under her knees. "May I ask what happens next, Master?"

He sighed. "The auction will happen in two days according to my partner. You have to be ready by then. Do you understand?"

There was a pause, and it grated his nerves that she wasn't responding to a direct question, but he made himself wait. She finally spoke softly, "How, Master?" Thalia was staring at the bed, speaking so quietly with her breathy voice that he almost misunderstood her. He debated on what to tell her, he wanted to tell her nothing. He didn't want anyone to want her, but he knew if she didn't behave by the time his brother arrived the chair would be the least of her concerns.

"Be obedient. If you're not obedient you're going to deter the interest of any Master who may treat you well." He tried to bite his tongue, but the next part came out of his mouth. "You shouldn't try to seduce any of them either. If they want you, they will want you. If no one buys you at this auction, we will hold another."

And I can keep you in the meantime.

He wanted to slap himself. His brother would never let him keep her. With her here he wouldn't train another girl. That meant no money.

No money meant no house, no cars, no life.

No girl was worth that.

Not even Thalia.

"Yes, Master." She nodded, looking at the now empty plate, and biting her lip. He wanted to bite her lip for her.

He realized he'd fed her the entire plate of food as they'd talked, and she looked a little steadier. That may also have been the Vicodin kicking in though to dull the pain. Her mouth was perfect, and she looked better now that she'd stopped crying, even though he liked the way her nose and cheeks turned pink, and how her eyes were more vibrant, the way she took little gasps of breath while she cried.

His cock was a stiff bar in his pants, and he knew it was twisted that thinking about her crying had got him there. But after their fight in the kitchen he'd wanted to fuck her to make her submit again. He also hadn't finished earlier when she'd stopped responding, and he'd purposefully avoided coming when he'd showered. Which wouldn't have happened without the damn chair, but his brother's request if she failed the kitchen test had left him with no choice.

He should never have bet against his brother, he always lost.

His heart slammed in his chest as he looked over her, he wanted her so much he was salivating.

"Lay back." The command was rough. She didn't argue, but she shook slightly as she lay back and he pushed her thighs apart.

"Yes, Master." Her breathy voice made his cock jump. He wanted her but he knew he had to get her back first. When he stroked her thighs, he felt her muscles shake. She wanted to close her legs on him but wouldn't dare now that she knew what else was waiting for her. The chair had done something good at least. If he'd completely broken her though, it was all for nothing.

He ran his tongue up her slit, his hands pushing her thighs farther apart. Her hips shifted slightly, and he focused his attention on her clit. The little bundle of nerves making her muscles quiver regardless of what she wanted. He slid his tongue inside her, tasting her again and groaning against her flesh. His thumb pressed gently against her clit, moving in rolling circles that made her hips shift in time.

It may have been the rest, the food, the conversation, or more likely the Vicodin, but she finally started to respond.

After a few minutes a soft moan came out of her and he returned it, tasting as she grew wet against his mouth. He looked up the plane of her body, her stomach tightening and relaxing as she moved her hips against his mouth. Her breasts rising and falling with her breaths. Her head was tilted back so he could see her throat working while he pulled quiet sounds of pleasure out of her. He didn't regret telling her the reality of her future, he hoped it would keep her in line or he'd never be able to keep his brother's hands off her. He wanted to be the one to touch her.

A wordless, breathy moan came out of her, dissolving into a whine as she clenched her hands in the fabric to either side of her. He moved his mouth back to her clit and reveled in the way her hips bucked against him. To think he'd risked *this* to satisfy his brother. He'd much rather satisfy Thalia. He thrust a finger inside her slick pussy and her moan changed, her back arching off the bed and easing back down with a tilt of her hips. He slid a second finger inside her heat and she started murmuring the little pleas that made his balls ache.

"Please..." she moaned softly, and he knew she was likely not aware she'd said anything. Her fists tightened in the bedding and he wanted her hands in his hair again, but he didn't want to break the moment. She gasped, and her hips tilted back from his mouth.

"May I?" Another gasp as he pressed his mouth to her clit again. "May I? Master?" she whimpered, and he curved his fingers upward and gave her what she wanted as he spoke against her flesh.

"Come," he commanded, and she did. Her walls tightened around his fingers, and he felt her pulsing. Running his tongue along her, tasting her juices as her sticky wetness coated his face and fingers. He groaned and fought the urge to mount her. He'd just pulled her back, he could have her again tomorrow.

Maybe *only* tomorrow.

A heavy feeling settled in his stomach with the idea that in two days she could be gone — she could be under another man. The rage that idea summoned inside him was dangerous and he forced it back.

Pushing up, he held himself above her. A flush had crept up her chest and into her cheeks with the orgasm, lips swollen from how often she'd bit them. He kissed her, hard, nipping them himself, but she moaned quietly against his mouth. He knew she could taste herself on him, and he settled his hips between her thighs. Her body instantly stilled under his, but he just wanted to feel her. To know she was his for a little while longer. Biting her bottom lip made her gasp, opening her mouth so he could thrust his tongue inside her.

Moaning into the kiss, he pressed his cock against her through his pants, but he broke the kiss and leaned his head against the pillow by her head, his face in her silken hair. If he didn't get up he was going to take her, and not gently.

"Thank you, Master," she whispered against his shoulder, and it almost undid him. He tightened his fingers in the sheets on either side of her and kissed her again before pushing himself back. Looking down at her body was its own form of torture.

"Good girl." He cleared his throat and sat up between her knees, but this view was even worse. He wanted to touch her, to fuck her until she only wanted him.

He was out of control. His brother was right.

He made himself get off the bed, ignoring the erection that was beginning to border on painful. "Promise me that you'll behave."

"I promise, Master." She had pushed herself up on her elbows, and he groaned to himself. Why wasn't he fucking her right now?

"No more issues. None."

"No, Master." She shook her head a little.

"We'll try cooking again later, rest for now. You have a busy day tomorrow." He said it smoothly, and she opened her mouth to ask a question and then stopped. He couldn't handle being as close as he was to her anymore, so he was grateful that she didn't push.

"Yes, Master." Her hazel eyes were locked on his and he tried to remember her like this. Submissive, and satisfied.

Who knew how much longer he'd get to look at her?

Chapter Thirteen
THALIA

Thalia woke up flushed under the covers and threw them off. Her skin was damp, she could feel a blush in her cheeks, and as her dream came back to her she felt the sticky residual wetness high on her thighs. She let out a little frustrated scream and pressed the heels of her hands to her eyes.

She'd been dreaming of *him*. His hand between her thighs, his lips on hers, her hands in his hair as she moaned against his mouth.

What the fuck was wrong with her?

Under her hands she could feel the tears starting and she let out another little scream as she kicked her legs to untangle them from the sheets. He was insane, and horrible. He'd hurt her over and over. He'd let his partner hurt her in that nightmare of a chair. He'd threatened to sell her to a whorehouse in God knows where, and he was *actually* planning on selling her to someone just like him. Maybe worse than him.

And she was fucking dreaming about him?

'Because he's the only person to ever make you come so hard and so often,' a little voice inside reminded her.

Thalia gripped her hair as she fought the urge to snap. She didn't want to think of the truth in that little voice. She couldn't fight him. She definitely couldn't outrun him even if she got outside. She was trapped. She was *his* — at least for now.

What was the phrase? Better the devil you know, than the devil you don't? The idea of his partner, or someone like him, getting her was even worse than the guard's twisted possessiveness and penchant for punishment. At least he seemed to want her to feel pleasure, to come for him. He'd been upset the day before when she'd stopped responding, and he'd been gentle with her after that.

It felt wrong for her to even think it, but he really had treated her well the night before. After he'd gone down on her, and her body had shuddered with a release she had not been sure she was capable of anymore, she had prepared for him to fuck her... but he'd left her alone.

A couple of hours later he had returned and taken her back to the kitchen. She had been frustrated by how well he'd cleaned up. No blood on the floor, no glass. The gaping hole in the sliding door neatly covered by tape and tarp. It was the only sign anything had happened except for the cuts and bruises on her body. He'd reviewed the rules with her, that even if she were cooking or cleaning if her Master returned to a room she must kneel until he gave permission to continue. He had her cook dinner, and tested the process several times. Leaving and returning. Leaving and returning. Then she had knelt by him on a pillow at the dining room table and he had fed her by hand.

She'd felt like a dog, but she had been so hungry she had still told him thank you. She'd fucking *thanked* him. Why did she keep thanking him?!

She could hear a whine in her chest as her thoughts tore her apart. "Dammit, Thalia, what is wrong with you..." she whispered to herself, as she wiped her eyes and sniffled.

The loud click of the door unlocking made her heart race. She didn't want to make him angry again so she wiped her face on the sheets and knelt on the bed, head down. When the door opened she fought the urge to look at him. He was silent for a moment as she heard him set down a tray. Her stomach growled at the opportunity for food, despite the fact that she'd eaten more yesterday than any other day he'd kept her.

"You put on quite a show this morning. What were you dreaming about?" The laughter in his voice made her flinch. As wet as she was she could only imagine what she'd done, or possibly said, in her sleep. For all the cameras to see.

"I don't remember, Master." Her voice shook with the lie, but like hell she'd admit it was him. She wouldn't be so stupid as to yell at him again, and she wouldn't try to run — that would be suicidal — but she wouldn't provide something voluntarily.

"Is that the truth, Thalia?" His voice was closer and it held a dangerous edge. Her heart rate increased and fear crept up her back.

"Yes, Master," she lied, but her voice was still shaking.

He was by the bed, and his hand brushed over her neck gently, his fingers moving into the hair at the back of her head. She waited for him to grab it, to yank her head back, but he didn't. He moved his fingers against her scalp, sending a chill down her spine.

"Thalia... I think we both know who you called out for." The laughter in his voice was too much. Heat flushed her chest and her cheeks but she kept her eyes down. She bit down on her lip and he made a low noise in his throat and leaned in, kissing her hard. His thumb pulled her lip free, and she knew she shouldn't look at him but she couldn't resist. He kissed her again and then pulled her lip between his teeth, biting just hard enough to make her groan. Then he let go of her completely, leaving her breathing hard and her heart racing.

"Come have breakfast, Thalia." His voice was smooth, and calm. *Damn him.*

"Yes, Master." Her pulse was pounding in her temples as she watched him walk to a small table against the wall. It had one chair and he fell into it casually, leaning back as he waited for her to obey. He pushed a hand through his dark hair and leveled his stare at her to watch her. It was almost cruel that he was so attractive. For some reason aesthetic appeal made people seem nicer, but he wasn't nice.

She repeated it in her head for good measure: *He isn't good, he isn't nice.*

Thalia dropped her eyes and slid from the bed to crawl to him. He ran his hand through her hair when she knelt next to him, and then he offered her a slice of melon.

Part of her wanted to take it from him and feed herself, but then he probably wouldn't feed her, and he'd hurt her, and — it just wasn't worth the effort. She took the melon with her mouth and chewed slowly, savoring it.

When she swallowed, her stomach growled in response, demanding more.

He laughed, and she clenched her teeth wanting to cover her ears against the sound. He didn't seem to feel guilty at all about the day before, despite his 'secret' talk with her where he admitted he should have handled it differently. As if having his partner electrocute her for fun was the same as choosing a different paint color. "Hungry, Thalia?"

"Yes, Master." At least that she could answer honestly, and he continued to feed her by hand. Placing small bites in her mouth as he started talking.

"We're going to have guests today." Her stomach dropped and he noticed how tense she became, her heart rate climbing again. Panic bloomed in her chest and she opened her mouth to speak but he put another bite in her mouth to cut her off. "My partner will likely not be here until tomorrow. Relax." His hand brushed through her hair gently.

"Yes, Master," she responded automatically, her mind yanking her back to the pain in the chair. She didn't want to meet his partner. *Ever.*

"You're going to be on your best behavior, and not embarrass me in front of my friend and his girls. Right?" His voice was smooth and confident, but she had no faith in the humanity of anyone he called a 'friend.'

"I will behave, Master." She opened her mouth again as he slid a bite of strawberry inside.

"Good girl. They're only here to help you be prepared for the auction." He popped another bite in her mouth but a finger followed. She didn't bite down as he slid his finger in and out. His blue-gray eyes were locked on to her mouth, and she lowered her gaze quickly so she didn't have to watch him.

"Don't worry, Thalia. It's just a test run today. The auction isn't for another day or two." His voice had lowered, and the edge was back in it. She nodded and his other hand slipped down to her breast and pinched her nipple. She made a noise but kept her lips wrapped around his finger, until he pulled it away and released her. Her mind was racing with all of the questions she wanted to ask. Who was coming? What would they do with her? What would his partner do when he arrived?

She cleared her throat. "May I ask a question, Master?" Her voice was still shaking, because her body had flooded with adrenaline in her panic.

"No. There's nothing more you need to know about today," he answered bluntly, and when she opened her mouth to speak he grabbed her chin firmly. "Finish your breakfast, Thalia." He held out more of the food and she gave in as he continued feeding her until she finally shook her head. Since she'd barely eaten in the last few days she couldn't eat as much as he'd brought. He used a fork to finish the omelet and fruit on the plate.

She sat in silence next to him, his hand moving through her hair, and then gripping it loosely to hold her next to him. "You're such a good girl, Thalia, when you *try*. Promise me you'll behave today, so I don't have to punish you?"

Thalia chewed on her lip and swallowed, terrified of a repeat of the day before. She knew her body was tinted with bruises all over, her feet still wrapped in bandages. She didn't have the strength for a repeat. "I promise, Master."

His mouth was on hers before she finished speaking, his tongue darting in and she murmured against him. The way he kissed could almost distract her from the day ahead, the possibilities of what his friend might do to her, and the terror of his partner's arrival. He stood up and pulled her up with him, his fist in her hair making sure he never lost contact with her mouth. His other hand pressed her against him, and she could feel how hard he was. He broke the kiss with a run of smaller kisses across her jaw and down her neck that had her body humming. She was already wet again, and she silently cursed herself for responding to him like she did.

His grip on her neck pushed her toward the bathroom and she moved with him. When he got to the shower he flipped the water on and pulled his shirt off revealing the lean muscles of his chest and stomach again. Her eyes drifted to his waist as she felt her heart rate increasing again. When he pushed his pants down his cock sprang forward, and he smiled at her when he saw her eyes on him. Thalia turned her head away and he laughed as a blush raced up her chest again.

"Yeah, we both know who you were dreaming about." He knelt in front of her and removed the bandages from her feet; his touch was ridiculously gentle. His thumbs brushing against her ankles as he balanced her and it made her body thrum.

"As you say, Master," she muttered and his eyes blazed when they looked up at her. His touch wasn't gentle when he pushed her into the shower, and he immediately pressed her chest against the wall with his body. The water was warm as it poured over her from various showerheads, soothing some of the aches she felt, yet it didn't change the situation. She pressed her palms against the wall, tensing, but stopped herself before she tried to push back and fight. He probably wanted her to fight, and she wouldn't give him the satisfaction.

"You don't remember calling out for me?" His hand moved between her thighs and she moaned when he rubbed her clit. "You called me Master, Thalia." As his fingers circled that bundle of nerves her hips bucked, but she gritted her teeth against the urge to confirm it. His mouth trailed down her neck and across her shoulder, and he bit down as he thrust two fingers inside her. Her body jerked with the contrast of pleasure and pain, and she pushed back from the wall. It was what he'd wanted, his fist tightening in her hair as he pressed her hard into the wall. His cock rubbed against her hip as he slid his fingers from her and returned to rub her clit.

"You woke me up calling for me." His voice rumbled low against her ear, and she whimpered, not wanting to admit to it, and hating herself for calling out for him. Her stomach tightened as she felt herself moving closer to the edge, but before she could even ask for permission to come he stopped touching her. The frustrated scream that came out of her was involuntary.

"Admit you dreamed about me, and I'll fuck you." He bit her ear lobe and she groaned, pressing her hips back into him. She wanted to refuse him, but he chose that moment to tease her clit again, and she moaned. "Admit it," he growled against her ear, tightening his fist in her hair. She could hear the anger seeping into his voice and she whimpered.

"I did, Master," she whispered against the wall, and he pulled her head back so she was looking at him.

He was smiling.

"Did what, Thalia?" His fingers rubbed against her clit again, and the heat coiled in her belly. She wanted the release. She'd dreamt of the release he could give her, and she hated herself for it — she hated herself for wanting it now.

"I dreamed of you, Master," she muttered and he pressed her against the wall again, fist tight in her hair, positioning himself behind her. Her body tensed as she waited for him to take her.

"I know you did." He thrust inside her and she moaned, her hips pressing back against him to get him deeper. She was obviously a slut, damaged, completely messed up… no one else would act this way. "Did you dream of this?" His cock filled her, making her moan louder as he pulled almost all the way back and then thrust in again with a vicious snap of his hips. "You wanted this, Thalia, didn't you? Say it."

She was crying against the stone tiles as her orgasm coiled around the base of her spine, threatening to release inside her at any moment. "May I come, Master?" she ground out the plea in a shaking voice, and he thrust deep and held himself there.

"You can come if you say it." His lips were against her ear, and she tried to twist her head away from him but his grip in her hair was too tight. "Say it," he repeated and she wanted to scream.

"Yes, Master," she whispered.

"Yes what, Thalia? You know I want you to use your words. Don't act stupid, it's unattractive." He ground his hips against her, teasing her closer and closer to the edge again until she let out a small gasp.

She'd begged him before, but for some reason this felt different and she was fighting it. Her mind chose that moment to remind her of the pain in the chair, of the alternative to the guard, and her resolve collapsed. "Yes. I want this, Master. Please, may I come, Master?"

He moaned his satisfaction at her response. "Yes, Thalia, you may." His hips began to move again and his fingers found her clit, and quickly her body was shifting against him in time to his thrusts. He groaned and whispered against her shoulder, "You're incredible."

Then she fell apart as she came, her legs almost buckled but he'd been ready and he held her against him by her waist as her pussy clenched around him and he thrust again and again until he fell over the edge after her. Hot pulses of his seed filling her as he held her up and pressed her harder into the wall. She realized she was still crying and he held her back against him, using her hair to crane her head back.

"There's no point in crying, Thalia. I told you that I wouldn't have chosen you if I didn't see a submissive slut inside you. You just need to accept it, stop fighting it." He held her until she nodded, and she hated the part of her that agreed with him.

From the first night she'd responded to him, she'd been questioning *why*. In so many ways it was nice to know what to do, and not have to make decisions in bed, to have a man control her in the ways she'd apparently always wanted but never had the words for. But he hurt her too, and he let others hurt her. She gritted her teeth and tried to pull herself together.

Whether or not he was right about her, crying wasn't helping. She needed to stop crying. "Yes, Master." His hands slid over her and soon she smelled soap, and she tried to relax into his firm touch as he massaged her sore muscles.

"Good girl."

Chapter Fourteen
THALIA

After their shower he gently rebandaged her feet and the dichotomy between when he'd hurt her the day before, and how gentle he could be as he cared for her, was incredibly confusing to her mind. She wanted to just blindly hate him, and he made that so difficult when he helped her, or acted concerned for her, or when he made her come so hard she saw stars. Eventually he left her in the room while he went to change, but he wasn't gone long. When he returned she made sure she was already on her knees, made sure she followed him through the house on her hands and knees, made sure she kept her eyes down. With her behaving there wasn't much for him to talk about, and he only spoke to her to guide her. She'd knelt by him for about an hour in his living room while he'd read, and he'd done nothing more than occasionally run his hands through her hair as it air dried.

He had her cleaning the kitchen from the breakfast he had made when the bell chime of a doorbell echoed through the house. He stepped into the kitchen and she dropped to her knees and she could hear the satisfaction in his voice. "Good girl, my friend has arrived. Come to the door with me to greet him and his girls."

"Yes, Master." She followed him and her mind was busy wondering what girls he was bringing. Was he referring to the man's children? Hopefully not. She imagined a wife and the shame that overwhelmed her at another woman seeing her kneeling, naked, at the feet of the guard made her want to throw up. But the girls he referenced could be slaves like her.

Like her?!

Her heart pounded in her chest as she stopped where he pointed and she fought the urge to scream. When had she accepted that title? When had it become something she identified herself by?

Before she could analyze her moment of insanity any closer, the guard was opening the door and a man walked in smiling wide. "Thomas!" The guard laughed as the man approached him.

He was overly cheery, his voice loud in the living room. "Ah, my friend! I'm so glad to be invited to your home again so soon! Where is the latest acquisition?" They clapped each other on the back and then two beautiful young women stepped in behind him, each carrying a black box.

They were wearing thin dresses that didn't exactly hide their forms at all. Not that it mattered because as soon as the guard shut the front door they set the boxes down and they both slid the straps off and the dresses dropped to the floor almost in unison. The two girls folded the colorful dresses and stacked them against the wall by the boxes before kneeling like the guard had taught her to. This left them only wearing wide matching cuffs on their wrists, and a thin leather collar around each of their necks. Their eyes stayed down, and it made Thalia uncomfortably aware that she should be doing the same. They were slaves, definitely slaves, and much better at it than she was.

She dropped her eyes just as the man, Thomas, bellowed again, "There she is!" His booted feet were suddenly in front of her and he tilted her chin up with a soft touch. "She's gorgeous. It's terrible that she hasn't been very obedient. Bruised to hell, but at least her face is still pretty."

Her eyes stung with unshed tears, but she bit her tongue to hold them back. Her Master appeared at Thomas' side and he shrugged a little. "All that will heal, no scars other than her feet, and what's most important is how well she responds."

His friend grinned down at her, a finger stroking her cheek. "And I have enjoyed watching how well she responds. Any chance you'll let me test her myself?"

Thalia tried to keep the panic off her face as her stomach twisted. The guard laid a hand on Thomas' arm and he dropped his hand from her chin. "You can come by for the auction and bid if you're that enamored. You know our deal."

His friend laughed loudly. "I know, I know, I just get to watch my girls get her ready and do my thing. I always have to ask though, who knows, you may take pity on me one day!"

The guard chuckled, but she knew his reactions well enough to know it was forced. He subtly stepped between her and Thomas, but the other man didn't react, he just walked back to his girls. Thalia dropped her eyes again, but not before she'd seen the other girls clearly. One was very small framed, of Asian descent, with long, straight black hair to the middle of her back. The other was her opposite, tall and pale and white-blonde. They were both fit, but she saw neither of them had any marks. No bruises, no bandages.

"Anna and Kaia. Why don't you take Thalia and start working with her? We will come by to check on your progress in a bit." Thomas' voice was warm when he spoke to them.

"Yes, Master," they said in unison.

The blonde turned and grabbed the box behind her, and then spoke in the softest voice. "May I walk to carry the box, Master?" She kept her eyes down but he cupped her chin and she looked up at him with something like — love?

No way.

"Of course, Anna. You and Kaia may both walk to escort Thalia." He took her hand to help her stand and kissed her. Thalia felt incredibly uncomfortable as the kiss continued, it was passionate and Anna was definitely moaning.

Kaia squirmed on the floor next to them and let out a whine. "Master?"

Thomas laughed softly as he broke the kiss and pulled Anna back by her hair. The blonde dropped her eyes as he helped Kaia to her feet and leaned down to kiss her as well. Kaia wiggled, her thighs pressing together as Thomas wrapped his hand in her hair. Her little murmurs were obviously from pleasure, not fear. Thalia felt herself grow wet, her pulse pounding between her thighs as she stared. The guard was grinning when he turned to look at her. When he arched an eyebrow, she dropped her gaze to the floor, using her hair as a shield to hide the flush in her chest.

"Girls. We're here to help Thalia and her Master." Peeking through her hair she could see them both staring at Thomas with a look of infatuation, of devotion.

Both girls sighed. "Yes, Master."

He laughed again and turned back to the guard. "My friend, let's catch up while the girls get started with her." Thomas grabbed the other box and they walked past her. Her Master ran his hands through her hair as he passed by, but he let go quickly.

This left Thalia facing off with the two girls, at least six or seven inches different in height, but absolutely beautiful. Thalia stayed on her knees as they approached, both of them moving their eyes over her. Anna made a tsk'ing sound and adjusted the box to her hip. "You've been fighting him hard, haven't you?"

"He's not a bad Master, you know. He's just trying to train you. You should listen to him," Kaia spoke up, one hand gently tugging at her mouth as she stared at Thalia. Neither of them had an accent, and both seemed incredibly comfortable being naked. Thalia was almost frozen in fear, because she didn't know how to respond to the girls. Would they get her in trouble?

Anna sighed and grabbed Thalia's arm, tugging her to her feet. "Come on, we need to figure out what we can do with you."

Kaia gasped and knelt down next to her. "What happened to your feet?!"

Thalia suddenly felt self-conscious about her injuries. Both of them seemed so satisfied with their situation, and she didn't want to explain her failed attempt at escape or discuss what had happened after.

Anna sounded haughty when she spoke again, "Fine. Don't talk, but you have to come with us."

Kaia looked concerned, but kept her mouth shut as she stood and led them through the house to the yellow walled room. "It always looks exactly the same," she mumbled to herself as they maneuvered her into the bathroom. Anna set the box on the counter, unsnapping the lid to open it up and she started taking out makeup and brushes and creams and things that Thalia had never even seen before.

Kaia's words finally sunk in through her shock and Thalia's voice broke when she finally spoke, "You were here? You were with him?" She stared into Kaia's dark brown eyes and the girl brushed Thalia's hair back with a wistful little smile.

She started pulling a brush through her tangles before she answered. "Yes, almost two years ago now. I've been with my Master, and Anna, since then." That strange little smile stayed on her face. "He's very strict, but if you obey him he's extremely giving." Thalia looked at her in the mirror and saw that she was blushing prettily.

"She's obviously not obeying him. Look at her, Kaia. Master was right, she's a mess. How are we supposed to make her presentable?" Anna spoke with unveiled disgust as she lifted Thalia's arm and showed Kaia the purple and green bruises circling her wrists from the handcuffs on the first night. "Who is going to want to buy her when her body tells anyone who looks at her that she's disobedient? Even if she fakes it for the auction, it's obvious."

Thalia opened her mouth to argue, but Kaia spoke up from behind her. "I had my share of bruises under his training as well, Anna. Not all of us came to this life voluntarily."

"He took you too?" Thalia twisted around to stare at Kaia. She was a few inches taller than the small woman, and a few inches shorter than Anna — but standing between the two of them, one dark and kind, one light and uncaring, it was clear they still had way more in common with each other than she had with them.

"Yes. He did." Kaia pulled at her lips again. "But he was right. This is what I was meant for, and I'm very happy now."

Thalia realized she was crying when Anna handed her a towel, and Kaia frowned at her. "Stop crying. I need to put makeup on you." Anna was so stern, and she held Thalia's face still as she began brushing concealer and powder across her. Kaia continued working on Thalia's hair, working some kind of product into it that somehow captured the natural wave without weighing it down, or making her look like a crazy, unkempt club kid. It actually looked nice, but Thalia still couldn't get over the fact that Kaia had been here, in this house, this room, with the guard.

Maybe Thomas would buy her and she could be happy like them.

"You should be grateful for your Master, not disobedient. He produces very high-quality slaves." Anna was moving quickly on the makeup, using an array of hues on her lids to exaggerate the colors in her hazel eyes.

"You're so sweet, Anna." Kaia blushed and smiled at Anna in the mirror.

"I didn't want this. I didn't ask for it," Thalia mumbled softly. It was so difficult to articulate her panic and her fear when the first people she'd seen since he'd taken her were so accepting of her new situation. And they expected *her* to accept it as well. Hell, Anna apparently expected her to be grateful.

"You wouldn't be here if he didn't believe you were meant for it, Thalia. Our Master has always said your Master has an eye for natural submissives." Kaia smiled as she washed her hands in the sink. "He was right with me, he has been right with every girl we have helped prep for the auctions, and I am sure he is right with you."

"You should accept it, or your new Master may not be so gentle with you." Anna's voice dripped venom as she squeezed Thalia's cheeks and then brushed color across her lips.

"Gentle?!" Thalia almost screamed at Anna. She wanted to tell her about the chair, scream at her that he had kidnapped her, raped her — but she heard Thomas' boisterous voice in the hall and her Master entered the bathroom a moment later.

Chapter Fifteen
THALIA

Anna and Kaia dropped smoothly to their knees the moment her Master entered the room. Thalia took a moment longer but she knelt between the two girls as Thomas arrived, still laughing. An aura of cigar smoke filled the air around them, pungent and a little nauseating in the mix of all the lotions and makeups in Anna's kit.

"Oh, lovely girl, you *are* making my friend's life very difficult, aren't you?" Thomas spoke directly to her, and she knew she was supposed to respond, but she didn't know what would be appropriate. A flutter of panic rose up, reminding her of her Master's demand for obedience. She went with the least offensive thing she could think of.

"I'm sorry, sir." Her voice was quiet, but luckily Thomas just laughed again.

"He's had it way too easy lately. You're challenging him, keeping him on his toes." A friendly punch to her Master's arm, and then Thomas continued. "Whoever buys you is going to need patience, or a stern hand, or both! But they will be lucky, because as my girls have drawn attention to... you *are* beautiful."

"Thank you, sir." Thalia kept her eyes down.

"Girls, please continue." Thomas said it warmly and they both stood, but Thalia stayed on her knees.

"Good girl, Thalia. You may stand and continue as well." The guard sounded pleased with her, and she was grateful she'd passed this test. Now she understood why he had made her practice as she had cooked dinner the night before.

When she stood, Anna began putting the final touches on her makeup. She had closed her eyes so Anna could work on her eyelids again when Thalia felt Kaia pinch her nipple. She yelped and looked at Kaia who laid a hand on her shoulder, squeezing in a silent urge for Thalia to relax. There was rouge on Kaia's fingers and she rubbed it around Thalia's nipples, occasionally pinching her.

"Will we be piercing her? She'd look lovely with some." Thomas' voice was low with lust, but the guard's voice cut in quickly.

"She's not mine to make that choice about. It'll be up to whoever wins the auction." His voice sounded deadly serious and sent a chill down her back. Her new Master might pierce her? "You know what I need you to do, Thomas."

"Of course."

Thalia wanted to ask what they meant but Kaia's fingers suddenly slipped between Thalia's legs and as she started to move away, the rouged fingers began to slowly but methodically apply the color to her inner labia. Anna dug her nails into her arm as she began brushing a lavender scented powder all over her skin. It left a faint shimmer everywhere, which would have been nicer if her skin didn't sporadically blossom into blues and purples and sickly greens from her random bruises. They were right, she looked like she'd been beaten repeatedly, because she *had*. Which only meant one thing in this world of theirs — defiance.

Maybe her behavior had cursed her. Maybe she was already doomed.

Anna and Kaia stepped back and knelt, and the guard was suddenly right next to her, the smell of smoke engulfing her. "You look beautiful, Thalia. Thank you, Anna, Kaia, you've done beautiful work." He coiled one of her waves around a finger and then released it. "Girls, will you take her to the bedroom for the last items." He turned back to Thomas as Anna and Kaia took her arms gently. Thalia wanted to ask what was going to happen, but fear had her tongue-tied and she didn't want to embarrass the guard and suffer the consequences.

"Yes, sir," Anna and Kaia replied in unison and led her from the bathroom. Kaia pushed her to get on the bed, but fear twisted her stomach.

Acting like she was adjusting Thalia's hair, Kaia leaned in and whispered quickly, "It only hurts a little, and if you fight he'll hurt you again. Behave, Thalia, *please.*"

What only hurts a little?!

Kaia's attempt at kindness had only increased her fear. Her heart was pounding in her ears and she suddenly felt dizzy as Anna pushed her flat on her back on the bed. Thomas approached and Thalia tried to sit up, until she saw the guard behind him.

"Stay still, Thalia." His tone held an edge of anger, and she whimpered in fear as she forced herself to lay back, her muscles shaking regardless.

Thomas' hands on her thigh and hip made her jump, but she bit her lip and stayed still. His loud laugh only made her flinch. "She's pretty when she's terrified."

"She looks even better when she cries." The guard's voice dropped, rumbling in a way that urged her body to respond.

A swipe of a cold cloth on the inside of her hip made her look down, watching as Thomas dragged a razor over the skin there and then he coated it with a clear substance. A small piece of paper was laid on and then peeled off revealing a small design on her skin.

A tattoo?!

Thalia tried to sit up again and Kaia grabbed her shoulder and pulled her back down, shaking her head. Tilting Thalia's head toward her, Kaia pointed at a small design on her hip. It matched the one that had just been laid on her own skin. An elegant bold script 'W' with a crown on top, and what at first looked like a slash underlining the small design was actually, on close inspection of Kaia's hip, a riding crop. It was a concise little logo, and it was about to be permanently etched into her skin.

The first bite of the tattoo needle felt like she was being pinched over and over. As Thomas' smooth movements against her skin continued, she started crying. His other hand brushed soothingly over her opposite hip, but it wasn't helping. Even if she got away, the guard had marked her. She was his. Anna made a tsk'ing sound again and began to brush the tears from under Thalia's eyes. It didn't take long at all before Thomas was sitting up.

The guard approached her and Anna and Kaia backed away. Thomas started packing his bag, and suddenly the guard was kissing her. She could taste the ash of the cigar he had apparently smoked. His hand was in her hair, lifting her up to his mouth. She heard herself moan softly against his mouth, and realized she was not so different from Anna and Kaia when Thomas had kissed them. She was weak. "You bear my mark now. You represent me." His thumb traced along her bottom lip. "Don't disappoint me," he threatened before he kissed her again, biting her lower lip hard enough to sting.

Thomas clapped his hands and his voice boomed as the guard smiled down at her and straightened. "I can see why you're still so invested in her despite her disobedience. She's... fascinating."

"Just one more thing and she's perfect." The guard walked over to a table against the wall and brought over a small, black, lacquered box. He pointed at the floor next to him. "Kneel."

"Yes, Master," she whispered, sliding from the bed, awkwardly aware of the sore place on the inside of her hip where the fresh tattoo shined. When she knelt in front of him she heard him open the box.

"Give me your wrists, Thalia."

She raised them and he wrapped dark cuffs around each of them, tightening them until they fit her wrists, the straps weaving back into the cuffs so they resembled broad, leather bracelets. He touched her chin and made her look up at him. The same leather collar that Anna and Kaia wore was placed around her neck.

She was wearing a collar.

Looking down at herself, the cuffs and the tattoo made her painfully aware of what she was. There was no question. It all screamed *slave*. She bit the inside of her cheek to fight the urge to cry.

"She looks great. Do you want Anna and Kaia to come back before the party to duplicate it? Your—" Thomas paused and chuckled. "Your partner emailed earlier that it will be tomorrow night."

She'd be sold tomorrow night? Her heart effectively stopped, and she suddenly couldn't breathe. Muscles trembling no matter how hard she clenched her fists, driving her nails into her palms. *No, no, no.*

Her Master seemed to ignore her distress. "Yes, if you can spare them Thomas."

"As long as I can stay to observe the party, I'll be happy." Thomas laughed again. "Speaking of happy, before we leave did you want some time with Kaia?"

Thalia's head snapped up, but no one was looking at her anymore. The guard's eyes were on Kaia, and she was breathing rapidly as if the idea of being with him excited her.

She couldn't decide if she felt confused or relieved or shocked when she heard the guard say, "No, Thomas, it's alright. You all should head home."

And they did.

Thalia stayed behind in the sunny toned room, but he locked the door on her. He came back to discuss how he expected her to behave perfectly the next day, but she was numb. Nodding and replying appropriately as he outlined his requirements. Then he kissed her again, but he pulled back a second later and sighed, lifting his shirt to his nose to smell it.

"I'll be back in a bit to bring you dinner, but I need to clean up. Thomas always convinces me to smoke a cigar with him." He had that smile again, the one where he looked so normal, so *nice*. It was such a lie.

"Thank you, Master," she whispered, and he traced his fingers over one of the cuffs before he left the room.

When the door locked she was alone again, and emotionally exhausted. She'd avoided punishment so far that day, but at such a high cost. Letting Anna and

Kaia paint her like a doll, letting Thomas tattoo her permanently with the guard's mark. Listening to the other slaves admonish her behavior like *she* was the one in the wrong.

Thalia laid down, twisting in the sheets of the bed as her thoughts tore her apart. She was supposed to fight. She wasn't supposed to give in to him — even though she did. Repeatedly. She'd even begged him to touch her on numerous occasions.

She was shameful. Disgusting.

The lock on her door clicked and she quickly sat up in bed and kneeled, but she didn't try and hide her tears. If she tried to wipe them away she'd probably just smear the makeup and upset him. The door shut sharply and her eyes lifted to peek through her hair.

Immediately her body froze, her stomach tightening in fear.

Not her guard. Not her Master.

Terror choked her for a moment, and then she knew she had to move. She slid backward, and the moment she shifted he started walking forward.

"Master?" She raised her voice a little and the man in front of her shook his head.

"He's busy. I wanted some alone time with you, Thalia." The man's voice was cold, and the way he said 'alone time' triggered another surge of fear inside her. Every instinct she had urged her to run, and she slid farther back on the bed. It hit her suddenly that this had to be his partner. The same partner that had hurt her in the chair. The one her Master had said he would do his best to protect her from.

And she was alone in a room with him.

Fear so potent that she thought she might be sick took hold of her. As if he could sense her terror, he moved around the bed and she tried to counter him by launching herself across the bed, trying to get to the door. He lunged for her and caught her ankle, yanking her hard back toward him across the sheets.

Desperate she took in a breath and screamed, "Master! MAST—"

His hand slammed down over her mouth, the other fisting in her hair to jerk her off the bed. "Shut up, slut. Shut. Up."

She begged for him not to hurt her. Begged and pleaded as fear made her dizzy, but her words were muffled against him palm. He calmly slammed her into the wall by the bed, hard enough to knock the air out of her, sighing as if the effort irritated him. His body pressed against her, a little taller than the guard but with a firm, lean frame, and she ended up staring at his chest as he pinned her with his body.

"I guess you've figured out who I am? That I'm your Master's partner in this little enterprise?" he asked calmly. She whimpered behind his hand and nodded slowly. The look he gave her as he tilted his head promised pain, violence, and she struggled against him. Shoving desperately against his ribs to no avail. He sighed and released her mouth for a moment to gather her wrists, but she didn't waste the chance.

"MASTER! PLEASE!" Thalia screamed as loudly as she could manage and the man brought his knee into her side hard enough that air coughed out of her and her ribs ached. She couldn't draw another breath at first. He crushed her wrists against the wall with one of his hands and returned the other to her mouth. He gripped her face painfully, but he still looked calm which only increased her panic.

"Think, Thalia. I know you're remembering our time in the chair, but tell me, who strapped you in? Who connected the clamps and the wires? Those weren't my hands on you." He had blue eyes, like chips of ice, and he leaned down until she looked at him. His hair was dark brown and a little long, and he seemed a little older than the guard, but definitely colder, more terrifying. His eyes reminded her of a remorseless predator, there was nothing more than the desire to hurt her. He didn't even look aroused. *Sadistic fuck.* She tried not to cry, knowing that would likely make him happy.

"Now, think. Why would my partner help you now, when he gave you to me yesterday?" His thigh pushed between hers and rubbed against her core, but she was too afraid to react. Her body was quaking with the fear of what he'd do to her.

Where was the guard? She'd behaved all day. He was supposed to keep his partner from her. He'd told her he would. He'd admitted the chair was wrong of him! He would never let his partner hurt her, he wouldn't, *so where was he?*

The man against her made a sound and released her wrists to slide his hand between her thighs and she screamed into his palm, letting the pain of straining her voice push her. His fingers brushed over her clit, but she just shook her head, begging him to stop. For once she didn't get wet, and she was grateful. Her fear of what the guard's partner would do to her overwhelmed any kind of physical response. The only issue was that it seemed to be making him angry underneath that cold exterior. He thrust two fingers inside her and she lifted onto her toes trying to avoid his touch, wincing as her pussy wasn't wet enough for his harsh touch.

"Do you want me to tell your Master you didn't behave, girl?" His voice was cold, but her body still refused to respond to him. She whimpered behind his hand, her body shivering with fear.

Where was the guard? Where was her Master?

Thalia started crying again and the small smile that lifted the edge of his mouth turned her stomach cold with fear. "What's wrong, Thalia? Does it hurt?"

She screamed again, shoving hard at his shoulders, but he didn't even move. Thalia's mind wouldn't release the memory of the chair. The blinding pain, the inescapable torment, and fear coiled around her lungs and squeezed. Even if he didn't take her back to the chair, what was he going to do to her?

Chapter Sixteen
HIM

The water was probably too hot, his skin was turning red under the onslaught, but he needed it. He needed to feel clean before he went to Thalia again, then he could explain the auction, and why it had to happen. He was scrubbing his hair and skin a second time to try and rid himself of the lingering smell of cigar smoke. Thomas was a good friend, but he always tempted him with cigars, and the bottle of scotch he'd left with him would be a nice way to distract himself before the auction. After he didn't smell like an ashtray and after he'd had Thalia in his bed again. He had to have her again before the auction. Just in case—

"Master! Please!" Thalia's panicked voice bled through the sound of the shower and he flipped the water off. For a moment he thought she might just be frustrated with him for leaving her in the room after the tattoo — but then he didn't hear anything else. No muttering, no little temper tantrum, no crying.

He pushed the shower door open and stepped into his bedroom to check the cameras.

No signal?

Every feed was black with the same small white text in the center: No Signal.

His heart stuttered in his chest. His brother was here. He had to be. His brother was here and he was with Thalia.

She'd screamed for him.

Fuck!

He was dripping water all over the floor, but he managed to grab a pair of pants and yank them on as he unlocked and threw the door open and ran down the hall to her room. His head was racing with every fucked-up thing he'd ever seen his brother do, and Thalia's scream replayed in his head.

He'd promised her that he would keep his brother away from her. If he'd hurt her—

Punching the code into the door, he slammed it open. Rage made it difficult to process what he saw. His brother had Thalia against the wall on the far side of the bed. His hand was clamped over her mouth, and his other hand was between her legs. She was crying and had both of her hands against his brother's shoulders trying to push him off.

She'd pushed at him like that before. *Just like that.* His stomach turned for a moment, but then his anger overwhelmed those thoughts.

"What the FUCK are you doing with my slave?" His voice cracked across the room, dripping with rage. As if a switch had been flipped the tension in his brother's shoulders melted away and he took his hands from her and stepped back. She slumped slightly against the wall as his hands left her, like Thalia wanted to make herself smaller. His brother's eyes stayed on her though. She looked weak and afraid, which might as well have been a neon sign to attract his brother's attentions.

"Thalia, come to me. Now." He couldn't calm his voice down, and she looked terrified as she responded. While she moved toward him he was concerned his brother might grab her, might challenge him about her immediately. But he didn't. She stumbled before finally sliding into a kneel at his feet. Her breathing was ragged next to him, and he wanted to comfort her — but any attention he paid to her would only attract his brother further.

"Good evening." His brother had turned to meet his eyes, that cold voice moving like oil across the room. "I was surprised you didn't meet me at the door. Were you busy?"

Motherfucker. He'd known exactly where he was. He gritted his teeth against the things he wanted to yell at him, because he needed to get Thalia out of the room and away from him.

"Thalia, kneel in the hallway outside this door. Do not move."

She was slow to respond, and he was so angry he almost slapped her, but he forced himself to remember she was terrified. His eyes stayed locked on his brother across the room as she finally obeyed. As soon as he heard her settle outside the door, he kicked it shut.

"What the fuck do you think you were doing?" He knew he was shouting too loudly. He knew Thalia could probably hear him, but it was either yell or hit his brother repeatedly until he needed corrective surgery… or a body bag.

"I told you I'd arrive soon." The bastard had a small smile tugging at the edge of his mouth.

"Don't pull that. You turned the cameras off so I wouldn't hear her!" He walked toward him but stopped on the near side of the bed. He wasn't completely sure he wouldn't hit him yet, and no amount of violence could fix what was wrong with the man.

"I wanted a little privacy with her too." His brother slowly licked his fingers and smiled coldly. "She tastes like fear, have you noticed?"

"I think you bring that out in her." He spoke through gritted teeth, because the urge to break his brother's hand was almost strong enough to make him move toward him.

"She wasn't very responsive, and while it was endearing that she called for you — that won't make us much money." His brother wiped his hand on his pants.

"Then you should cancel the fucking party and give me enough time to repair the damage YOU caused," he shouted again, but his brother didn't even blink.

"Now, now… which of us made the bet that put her in that chair? Which of us carried her to it, strapped her down, hooked her up, and handed over control?" His brother's silken voice was handling this fight like a business meeting, but he wanted to handle it a lot more physically. That just wasn't an option. His brother could do so much damage.

"Go to hell," he growled and turned away from him to stomp to the bathroom. The fucker wasn't going to make this all his fault. Every time his brother told him to do something, there was an unspoken 'or else.' There were always consequences.

"You know I don't believe in that ridiculousness." His brother's voice carried in from the bedroom as he grabbed a towel and rubbed his hair with it. Of course not, believing in hell guaranteed them *both* a spot.

His body was wet and he did his best to dry off, and calm down, before he approached his brother again. The asshole always out-maneuvered him when they talked.

"I'm not changing the party. I have nine — NINE — confirmed for tomorrow. That's two more than your last girl, and she was here three weeks. Apparently you're not the only one infatuated by Thalia." His brother had settled into a formal chair near the curtains that gave the illusion of a window to the room.

He made himself lean casually against the doorway to the bathroom, schooling his voice into a level response. "I'm not infatuated with her."

His brother's frigid laugh set his teeth on edge. "You can lie to yourself all you like, but I know you and you want to keep that girl. You're picturing sunsets and beach vacations with her kneeling at your feet."

"I just want more time to train her properly!" He came off more defensive than he'd meant to, but he didn't want to admit how much he wanted no one to buy her so she would stay with him longer. He wanted to wake up with her tucked against him again. He wanted to hear her call out for him in the night again… maybe even say his name.

"Then bring her back in here and let me have her," his brother offered smoothly, and he felt the trap his brother had so carefully set snap shut around him. It was hard to breathe through the haze of anger that filled him.

He was fucked no matter what he said. If he told his brother no, he proved his point that he was infatuated with her, which only proved the necessity of selling her sooner rather than later. If he said yes, he'd have to turn Thalia over to his brother for the night, or maybe longer if he cancelled the auction. He'd have broken his promise to Thalia. And who knows what fucked up things his brother would do to Thalia just to test him, to see if he'd come to her rescue again.

Damn him!

He turned back into the bathroom and a roar tore out of him as he slammed his fist into the tile. His hand exploded in pain. "Shit!" He groaned loudly and shook out his fist, noting that he'd successfully split the knuckle on his ring finger and a swipe of blood was left on the wall.

His brother's voice was closer. "You're pathetic. Letting this slut get you so confused. She's lucky there is so much interest in her or I'd break her just to teach you a lesson on getting attached."

He turned and lunged for him, grabbing him by the shirt and shoving him backward. His brother barely reacted, as if he knew he wouldn't hurt him. Rage burned in his chest and he shouted into his brother's face, "I'm not con—"

"You are confused." His brother interrupted him calmly and grabbed onto his wrists, gripping firmly. "The sooner she's gone, the better it will be. You'll forget about her in no time. Have you picked another girl off your list yet?"

His stomach twisted. He hadn't even looked at the list of potentials since the first night he'd brought Thalia to the house. From the moment he'd seen her she'd gone to the top of the list, he had been impatient to hunt her. He'd left the previous girl locked up, alone, far longer than he should have as he had learned Thalia's movements. Not like he'd ever admit that. He shoved his brother back and they let go of each other.

"You haven't even looked at another girl, have you?" His brother sighed as he shook his head. "This is why I moved up the sale. I know you, apparently better than you know yourself. This bitch is in your head."

"Shut up. I just — I want a little more time with her. Alone." He said the last word quietly, and shoved his fist into his hair, turning away from his brother's stare.

"No amount of time will be enough, and you know it." His brother paused for a long moment and then clapped his hands together, taking a step toward him. "I don't know why I'm even entertaining your shit, but fine. I'll leave for tonight, but I'll be back in the morning to make sure she's ready for the auction. And if you can't handle selling her, I'll do it for you. And if she doesn't sell, I'm taking over."

"I've got it handled," he growled.

"Are you sure?" His brother's voice lifted a fraction, his doubt obvious.

It made his blood boil again.

"Get the fuck out. I've got it. She'll be ready tomorrow." As his brother moved toward the door he remembered Thalia was in the hall. "Wait." Stepping in front of him, he blocked his brother's exit. "I'll move Thalia and then you can leave after."

His brother lifted his hands and shrugged.

Turning away from the bastard he yanked open the door, and Thalia's soft gasp was like a punch to the stomach. "Follow me, Thalia."

He stalked through the house, leaving his brother behind. As he walked he couldn't help but hear her soft murmurs as she followed on her knees. When he got to his door, he unlocked it with the code and pushed it open. She crawled inside and knelt, but he didn't follow her.

"Thalia…" He started to speak and he heard her whimper.

"Master?" Her voice was shaking. Part of him wanted to drag her to the bed and take her, to clean away his brother's touch with his. But he'd hurt her right now, he knew he would.

"Stay in here. He can't come in this room if he tries to come back." He started to shut the door, but then he realized what was inside. His notes, his computer, the camera feed, *everything* he kept with him when he moved from house to house. He knew he sounded harsh when he spoke, but he couldn't keep the anger out of his voice. "Don't fucking touch anything. Get on the bed. I'll be back later."

Her perfect mouth opened slightly and then shut. "Yes, Master."

He slammed the door, hearing the lock engage automatically. Then he walked to the front of the house and waited until he couldn't even see taillights on the drive out front.

"Motherfucker..." he mumbled to himself as he replayed everything his brother had said. He'd responded badly, not even remotely calm, but he'd been so worried about her.

Worried? Fuck.

What was worse about the whole fucked up situation was that he was right. The asshole was right. Thalia was in his head, and she wasn't the only one having dreams. If his brother wasn't here, he'd shut the lights off, lock the house down, and pretend no one was home when the customers arrived. Then he'd tie her up and fuck her until he worked her out of his system. He always got bored with them eventually, but something inside him laughed at the idea. He knew it wouldn't be that way with Thalia. She was under his skin.

He saw the bottle of scotch that Thomas had left on the table and he went for it, grabbing a glass from the kitchen before he settled into the oversized chair in the living room.

He had to sell her tomorrow.

He poured an inch of the honey colored liquid and drank.

Maybe he could convince his brother to let him keep her? No chance.

More scotch.

He'd just have to deter interest in her. He nodded to himself as he drank again. He wouldn't say any of his normal sales pitches, no highlight reel of her training, no demonstration.

Then no one would make an offer and she'd stay with him, and he'd just refuse to let his brother have her. He'd keep her locked in his room.

He didn't want anyone else to touch her.

Ever.

Chapter Seventeen
THALIA

Thalia was curled in a ball on the bed. *His* bed. She knew it was his because it smelled like him, a mix of his soap and the way his skin smelled when he was warm and sweating and pressed against her. She trembled slightly, burying her face into his pillow, and for the moment all of it was oddly comforting. He was the lesser of two evils, and she'd choose him over his partner any day.

So, she stayed where he'd told her to. Curled up under the covers, still waiting. She knew it had been over two hours because he had an alarm clock that currently read 10:14 in glowing blue numbers. It wasn't very late, and she didn't hear shouting any more, but she didn't know where the guard was, or his partner.

Even *thinking* of his partner made her throat tighten in panic.

He was more terrifying face to face. She had known it was him the moment she saw him, like some kind of base level survival instinct. Tears streaked her cheeks in silence as the buzz of fear hollowed her out. What if the person who bought her was like his partner? Her body hadn't responded to him, and the ideas that came to her on what he would have done without the guard's interruption made her whimper. He had wanted to hurt her. She should have screamed for the guard right away, she should have screamed as loud as she could as soon as that monster walked in the room.

Remembering the guard's arrival calmed her a little. He had been so angry, but not at her. He'd yelled at his partner about her, about touching her. The rest had been hard to understand through the thick door, but she had been able to hear how angry the guard was, and the odd, cold voice of his partner.

It sent a chill down her back to remember it.

Shaking her head to try and stop crying she looked around the room again. *His* room. It had books on a short bookshelf, an impressive computer station with large screens that were segmented into smaller windows. Probably the cameras, although everything was black. She had imagined his room messy, but it was actually clean and organized. His bedding was a mix of pale blue and light gray. It reminded her of fog. The flooring was the same throughout the house, but his bed was a simple wooden frame. The desk was a dark gray wood, and there was a cell phone. She noticed it as the screen lit up for a moment and then faded.

Her heart pounded. It was at least ten feet away, but he could have left the house. She could call for help and the police knew how to triangulate cell phone calls, right? Or they could track his number and find her.

'Or he could catch you with it and beat you and turn you over to his partner for punishment.' Her head was so helpful.

Her hands were shaking when she slid off the bed. She couldn't believe she was going for the phone, trying to decide if she was being brave or suicidal or both. *Probably both.* He had to wonder where it was, she had always checked her phone throughout the day. Her heart beat so loudly in her ears she was sure it could be heard outside of her.

Just as her hand touched the desk, she heard the click of the door lock. Thalia jumped back from the phone but found herself stranded between the desk and the bed where she was supposed to be. Frozen like a deer in headlights as the door opened.

He was nothing but a silhouette with the light from the hall behind him, but she could feel his eyes on her. "Thalia."

"I'm sorry, Master. I—"

"It's not your fault…" His words slurred together as he shuffled toward her. *Was he…?* The smell of alcohol hit her when he was still a few steps away.

He was drunk.

His large hands landed on her shoulders and then he pulled her against him and — hugged her. She stayed still, unsure of what to do as her heart battered against the inside of her chest. "Master?"

"It's my fault. I picked you. I shouldn't have picked you." His voice was even more muffled with his face buried in her hair, his nose burrowing against her neck.

"It's okay," she said soothingly, and then his arms tightened around her almost painfully.

"It's not okay."

Thalia let out a squeak of pain as he compressed her ribs, but she continued trying to soothe him so he would stay calm. "You're right, it's not okay."

Was he admitting what he'd done was wrong?

"You're not addressing me properly." The phrase would have been more threatening if it wasn't so heavily slurred.

"I'm sorry, Master," she murmured and then he pulled her head back hard, his fist tightening painfully in her hair.

"He wants you." Those blue-gray eyes were staring down at her, and terror seized her. She saw a flicker of pain move across his face and then he kissed her hard. Lips bruising under his assault, his tongue swept into her mouth and she tasted the sour sweetness of liquor. He pushed her back until she was pressed against the wall, groaning as he wrapped his hand around her throat, but he didn't squeeze. He just held her there as his mouth trailed down. "I won't let him have you." The words slid out against her skin, and she felt a flood of relief along with the anxiety his touch always fueled.

"Thank you, Master," she said quietly, and then gasped as his mouth found her nipple. He bit her and she yelped as the sharp spike of pain suffused her breast, but his hand tightened across her throat and pressed her a little harder against the wall. Heat bloomed low in her belly, her pussy growing wet as if it recognized his touch.

His tongue flicked against her nipple, soothing the ache, and his breath chilled her skin as he spoke. "I don't want anyone to…" Trailing his tongue across her skin, he latched onto her other nipple. Her back arched slightly as his tugs against her hardening bud were torturously close to painful. "But he'll hurt you if I try to…" his voice trailed off, still heavily slurred.

The guard lifted his head again, straightening to his full height as he looked down at her. His eyes showed her how drunk he was, a little glassy and shiny in the dim light. And while his words weren't making much sense, they were terrifying her.

"I just wanted you so much," he mumbled and pressed his forehead against hers and she realized she was breathing hard, the panic still urging her to get away before he figured out what she had tried to do. Groaning, he lifted his head again, tightening his grip on her throat until her pulse pounded behind her eyes. "I had to have you."

"Yes, Master," she whispered, voice shaking.

He shifted his hand from her throat to her hair, and he pulled until her neck was bared to him. "You're wet for me, aren't you?" His mouth moved along her neck and then he took a long breath against her skin. "I can smell it."

"Yes, Master." She felt her pussy flood and pressed her thighs together as a flush spread up her chest into her cheeks.

"Spread your legs, Thalia." His voice was slurred, but there was no mistaking it as a command. She obeyed, and he clumsily moved to his knees in front of her. Confusion controlled her for a flash, but then his mouth was on her. His tongue slipping between her folds as her hips bucked, a moan escaping her lips. He grabbed on to her thigh and lifted her leg so he could delve deeper. Dropping her head back against the wall, her shoulders pressing hard into it as his mouth closed over her clit, she moaned again, hand clenching in his hair for balance.

"Master!" she cried out and he thrust two fingers inside her. His touch was so different from his partner's. She knew the guard at least wanted her to feel pleasure. She was more than a little afraid of what he had planned, but that had become a normal undercurrent of his presence. His partner would only hurt her, but this felt good even through the fear. She tightened her fingers in his hair and felt his satisfied growl against her clit.

He wasn't gentle. His thrusts inside her were hard enough to make her feel bruised, and after a moment he thrust a third finger inside her and she rose up on her toes and cried out. He bit down on her clit and pulled her pussy back to his mouth. The orgasm surged inside her and she tried to close her thighs, fighting against his grip on her leg. His fingers thrust again sharply and he breathed against her clit. "Come for me."

And she did. Her body released and her head snapped back against the wall as waves of pleasure made her shake against him. His tongue dragged it out, lapping at her as he held her up because the leg supporting her was quivering. Just as the orgasm was winding down, he curved his fingers inside her and bit down on her clit and she fell over the edge again. Gasping, crying out, moaning like the traitor she was as she rolled her hips against his mouth. She knew her fingers were painfully tight in his hair, but she needed the center as she fell apart above him. He was merciless, licking her until she was murmuring little pleas for him to stop. Her body too sensitive for more, her legs shaking.

Finally, he tilted his head away from her grip and she released his hair quickly, suddenly afraid that he was angry with her for it. But he stood up and she could see the way his eyes darkened with lust. His mouth was wet with her, and he kissed her flooding her mouth with the taste of herself, and the alcohol, and him. That dark, masculine taste of his skin. With his mouth on hers he slid his hands under her thighs and lifted her against the wall, pinning her there at his waist. He pulled back from her lips to stare at her.

"Master — thank you." Her breathing was still ragged from the intensity of the orgasms he'd given her, and she knew her pussy was slick and hot pressed against his hard abs.

"Don't thank me." His voice was rough as he dropped her slightly and impaled her on his cock. With her weight in his arms he bottomed out instantly, a sharp ache inside as he went painfully deep. She moaned and he lifted her and thrust hard again. Keeping her against the wall with his shoulders he fucked her hard. Mercilessly. He stretched her in this position and she ached in the best of ways as he filled her over and over. Eventually she was caught by the waves of pleasure that began to pulse inside her every time he bottomed out. She was moaning in time with him, listening to his breath coming faster and faster as his muscles bunched under her hands.

Another orgasm crested inside her and she bit down on her lip to try and hold it back, but he could feel her, and his voice growled in her ear, "Come, Thalia." He thrust again, driving her hard against the wall and the wave hit her. Arching against him, screaming with the release, but he was bigger and stronger and he pinned her against the wall as his cock pulsed inside her. The heat of his seed filling her. Her body was exhausted and shivering between him and the wall. Trapped, vulnerable, and completely his.

"Master..." she whispered, and he wrapped an arm around her back and started walking with her back to the bed. He dropped her there, still inside her and just looked down at her. Even through the haze of her arousal she could tell he wasn't himself, and it wasn't just the drink. He was staring at her in a different way. He slid out of her and laid his head on her stomach. Reaching up he grabbed her hand and pushed it into his hair as his warm cheek heated her skin further and his breath blew out over her hip.

"I'm sorry," he mumbled.

Her breath caught as he spoke, and she moved her fingers through his hair automatically. A soothing gesture, but there was nothing else she could do. Nothing else she *would* do. She couldn't forgive him, especially not as his fingers began to trace the tattoo he'd had Thomas do that afternoon. But if he really felt sorry, then maybe he'd keep her safe. Keep her from his partner.

His fingers dug into the outside of her hip in a warning and she winced.

"Yes, Master." The words were coated in her urge to cry, but he ignored it, or didn't care. He slid up her body and kissed her again, gently but deeply as his weight pressed her into the bed and his hands wound carefully in her hair, holding her to him.

Her thighs were slick with the remnants of their orgasms, but he moved his hips between them anyway and then he stilled; his body flush to hers. He took a few deep breaths, grinding his hips against hers, and then he kissed her again and slid off her to her side. She was staring at the ceiling trying to calm her heart rate when he twisted to lay on the bed properly.

"Come here." His voice was slurring even more, and it was low and satisfied. She shifted up the bed and he grabbed her by her hair to bring her down next to him.

It hurt but she bit her lip against the complaint. The state he was in, she wasn't sure how much it would take for him to want to punish her. His arm snaked around her waist and pulled her tight to the front of his body. His grip was almost suffocating and they were both still so hot, but she didn't fight him.

"Master?" She didn't know what he wanted, but she knew she didn't want to risk him giving her to his partner, despite his drunken promises.

His hand pushed between her thighs and rubbed her swollen clit, her hips bucked against his hand even though she really didn't want any more attention. He groaned into her ear, "Don't move. I want you in my arms all night…" His voice was heavy with sleep, and she was taken aback by how strangely sweet the command had been.

"Yes, Master," she whispered and tried to get comfortable with one of his hands buried between her legs and the other loosely tangled in her hair. She listened to his breaths as they lengthened and slowed, eventually settling into the slow rhythm of sleep. She wasn't sure how much longer it took her to fall asleep, or how many times his fingers moved against her clit and woke her up in her sleep. But she did sleep, eventually, pressed tightly against him.

Chapter Eighteen
THALIA

The loud knocking on the door jerked her awake a half-second before the guard's fist tightened painfully in her hair. She yelped and he groaned, burying his face against her shoulder. It was almost cute, if she ignored the stinging of her scalp, or the way his hand cupped her between her legs. She knew he had to be hungover and he was hiding from the light and the sound by pressing himself against her skin.

"Open the door. Now." His partner. She couldn't possibly forget him. The cold voice was unmistakable and as he gave the command through the door it made her heart stutter.

The guard lifted his head and leaned back from her body, removing his hands from her. She watched as he stretched back, and he grabbed something from the table by his bed and hurled it across the room. It broke as it crashed into the door with force. His alarm clock.

She jumped at the loud sound of it breaking and he flopped back to the bed next to her, muttering a stream of quiet curses.

"Where's the girl?" His partner's voice came through the door again, unbothered by the crash.

"In here, dammit!" The guard yelled at the door and immediately seemed to regret it, covering his eyes with his arms. She winced when he yelled but he got out of bed and walked to the bathroom without looking back at her. The door slammed shut, leaving her alone in his room with his partner at the door. She was shaking again, and she hated herself for being so weak. The screens on his desk were on again and she could see the whole house in tiny frames.

Getting out of bed she crept over to them and jumped as another round of banging sounded from the door. "Thomas is here with his girls."

Just as the partner said, she could see them sitting in the living room in one of the little screens. Thomas was on one of the couches with Anna and Kaia kneeling on either side of his feet. He was looking at something in his hands, likely a phone. Her fingers itched to grab the phone on the desk, but there was no way she'd get away with using it.

She heard the toilet flush and water running. Then the bathroom door opened and she dropped to her knees, keeping her head down. The guard didn't speak to her, he just tapped a code into the door and opened it with a jerk. "Then bring the girls so they can get her ready."

"I can take her to them." His partner's voice could have frozen water. "You don't seem to be in the best condition this morning."

"No. Bring them here," he demanded gruffly, and then slammed the door in the man's face.

She heard him move toward her and she flinched. He pushed the hair out of her face gently and then lifted her chin to look at him. "Thalia, you have to be perfect today. Do you understand?"

"Yes, Master," she whispered, and she noticed he looked pale, eyes bloodshot and red. Definitely a hangover.

"I—" he paused, swallowing. "I will not be able to keep him from you if you misbehave."

She nodded, fighting down the urge to cry again. Today was the day. Someone was on their way to buy her. The right words came out of her mouth again, but her voice shook as she said, "Yes, Master."

"Good girl." He let go of her face, his thumb tracing her jaw softly before he stepped back.

A soft knock came at the door and he went to it. When he opened it this time, both Anna and Kaia were kneeling at the door, and the guard was still naked. Kaia blushed prettily and spoke. "Sir, we're here to help with Thalia if you still have a need for us."

"Come inside, girls." He stepped back from the door and they crawled forward, dropping back into kneels. He shut it quietly behind them. "I need you to keep Thalia in her room until the party. No questions. If anyone other than myself or your Master comes in, you should call for us. Do you understand?"

"Yes, sir," they answered in unison, and the fear that had appeared when she'd heard his partner's voice again grew stronger. He actually seemed concerned for her and what his partner would do.

"Good girls. You may take Thalia, and you may walk to the room. Go now." He opened the door again and stood aside as Anna and Kaia approached and gently helped her to her feet. She twisted to look at him as they left but he had turned away, moving back toward his desk. Then Kaia shut the door and guided her down the hall.

The moment they were inside the sunny room, Kaia grabbed her arm hard, pulling her out of Anna's grasp. "Why were you in there with him? Why did he have you in there?"

"What?" Thalia was confused. Kaia almost seemed angry with her.

"That is HIS room!" Kaia dug her nails in more sharply and Thalia winced trying to pull her arm back. "Why would he have you in there?!" Her voice ratcheted up a notch, a tone of anger definitely present.

"He wanted me in there! Kaia, you're hurting me!" Thalia grabbed on to Kaia's wrist and pulled at her hand.

"Kaia, he took her in there. Let it go, you have a new Master." Anna's voice was the gentlest she'd ever heard it, and Thalia slowly realized that Kaia was upset because she'd been inside the guard's bedroom.

"Did he not take you in there, Kaia?" Thalia asked gently, not understanding why Kaia was upset when she had someone like Thomas taking care of her.

Kaia let go of her and turned away, wiping her eyes. "No one is allowed in there but Mas— but him."

"I didn't ask to go in there," Thalia said defensively and tried to explain, but Kaia turned back and glared at her.

"Then WHY did he?" Kaia shouted, clearly upset.

"His partner came for me, he was keeping me safe." Before she was even done talking Thalia knew it had been the wrong thing to say. Anna grabbed Kaia as she lunged for her and Thalia stumbled backward until she hit the wall.

"WHAT?!" Kaia screamed and Anna covered her mouth to silence her, holding her back against her chest. Kaia started sobbing and slumped to the floor and Anna followed her down, mumbling soothing words in her ear.

"You should go shower. Now. Make sure you're completely shaved." Anna's voice was serious, and she pointedly looked at the door to the bathroom as she cradled the now sobbing Kaia. Thalia took the suggestion and quickly left them alone.

She stayed in the relaxing heat of the water long after she was done. Her mind was racing. Kaia clearly cared about the guard and was angry that he'd taken Thalia into his room.

She'd been even more upset when she'd found out why.

There was only one reason for that… the guard hadn't kept his partner from Kaia — and he'd definitely never taken her into his actual bedroom. The bathroom door opened and Anna stood in the doorway with her arms crossed.

"Breakfast is here, if you'd like to actually get out of the shower." Anna rolled her eyes and walked back into the bedroom. She left Thalia to flip off the water and dry herself as much as she could, trying to get the towel under her cuffs and the collar. A set of fresh bandages had been left for her feet and she wrapped them quickly the way her Master always did.

She was rubbing the towel through her hair when she stepped into the bedroom. Both girls were sitting on the floor around a tray of food, and Anna was using her kit to touch up Kaia's makeup.

"Come eat," Kaia said weakly and pointed at the blank side of the triangle they were forming around the tray.

"I'm so sorry, Kaia," Thalia mumbled as she sat down by them. She didn't know what else to say. Her own response to the guard was complicated. A mix of fear and hatred and lust for the pleasure he gave her. No matter what though, if Kaia had been with his partner, Thalia knew it couldn't have been good.

"It's not your fault, but you're lucky. You should just know that you're very lucky." She sniffled and looked away. Anna leaned over and brushed Kaia's thigh before gesturing at the food.

They ate and then talked about the rules for the party that the guard asked them to review. She learned that Anna and Kaia wouldn't be there because it would confuse the guests. Thalia had then double and triple checked that this did, in fact, mean that she would be alone in a house full of men who wanted to buy her. They had both shrugged and nodded, reminding her that Kaia had been through it as well.

When she asked them what would happen at the party they refused to answer. Kaia said it wouldn't help to know, and that made Thalia's stomach drop.

As the day passed Thomas came by to check on the tattoo, and immediately noticed Kaia's distress. He wrapped her in an embrace that seemed genuinely affectionate and kissed her gently. She even heard them have a quick conversation about whether Kaia wanted to leave earlier than planned, but she declined. The care he showed was real, and Anna had apparently chosen him of her own free will. Kaia had mentioned it the day before, and Thomas also always seemed to be fair. He made sure he kissed Anna before he left, murmuring in her ear, and even winked at Thalia with a reassuring smile when he left three covered dishes for lunch.

Thomas seemed to be an example of how this life could be. Not like walking on eggshells, not living in fear moment to moment. She was irrationally jealous of the girls.

Soon after lunch Anna and Kaia went into the whirlwind of getting her ready. They made her lay on the floor and reshaved her, which left her blushing and sent Anna into a huff about not knowing where to apply blush if she couldn't see natural skin tone. Thalia was in a daze though. The guard was going to sell her and she didn't know how she felt about that.

He also hadn't come to see her at all.

After his drunken half-confessions she'd imagined him never leaving her side today. She'd thought he would guide her through what would happen at the auction, prepare her mentally and maybe bed her one last time before he sold her. Part of her had looked forward to it, even though it was hard for her to admit. One last chance with someone who might be at least a little gentle, who might care about her pleasure.

Anna snapped her kit shut and it brought Thalia back to reality. "You're an idiot, but you really are beautiful." Her delicate hands tucked a wavy strand of Thalia's hair behind her ear.

"The party will start soon," Kaia said and gave a half smile.

"What? It's only the afternoon!" Thalia turned to them and they smiled.

"Many of the guests have planes to catch or have to return home. And whoever buys you will want to spend time with you tonight." Kaia shrugged like it was obvious. And it was, it made much more sense to have it earlier, but Thalia had imagined it as some secret meeting in the middle of the night, where everyone would drive away unseen. Dark and clandestine.

But this wasn't a movie.

She didn't need a frightening setting to make her realize her situation was serious. It could be sunny in his beautiful living room, and she'd still be terrified. Worried she'd end up with someone closer to his partner than someone like Thomas.

"We have to leave, Thalia." Anna could see the panic on her face and she shook her head. "It's going to be okay, just wait for your Master, alright?" Anna squeezed her shoulder with something almost like kindness.

Kaia just hugged her, and the feeling of the other woman's naked body against hers was different. She'd never hugged a naked woman. It almost made her laugh after everything she'd been through in the last week to be taken aback by a hug. It was also the second one she'd received since he had taken her. "Make sure you don't embarrass him, Thalia. It'll only hurt you in the long run."

"I won't. Thank you both for trying to help me," Thalia murmured and nodded as Kaia released her. They smiled and left a little awkwardly. The door clicked shut and she was momentarily jealous that apparently the guard trusted them with the code to lock and unlock the doors.

Then again, she had shattered a sliding door trying to escape. She hadn't exactly tried to earn his trust.

Chapter Nineteen
THALIA

Without the girls there with her, time dragged. She found herself staring into the mirror. The bruises were distracting, but Anna was right, she did look beautiful. Her lips looked pouty and alluring, her eyes popped with colors she'd never realized were in the hazel mix. Her nipples were rosy thanks to the rouge and remained hard in the chill of the air. And the magic Kaia had worked on her hair was incredible. Her light brown tresses fell in soft waves over her shoulders to the middle of her back. She had never viewed herself as sexy, not really. But she couldn't deny it now. Especially with the cuffs and the collar, which made her more of a sexual object than just being naked ever would have.

She looked good. Which was the whole purpose after all. Hard to sell a girl who looked like a complete mess. With that bitter thought Thalia yanked her eyes from the mirror.

She had walked around the room looking for anything of interest but it was empty. No books, no magazines, not even a deck of cards. Nothing to do but think about the party, and what it would be like, and who would buy her. Her stomach flipped and roiled in her anxiety.

The door finally opened with a click and Thalia dropped to her knees, glancing up for a moment to ensure it was the guard and not his partner. He looked much better than he had that morning. A lot better. He was in a button-down shirt and slacks, but he'd rolled the sleeves up and still looked like himself. Just a sleeker, less hungover version.

"Everyone's here. It's time for your presentation." His voice was short and harsh. Not even one comforting word.

"Master?" Her voice wobbled as the fear of walking, or rather crawling, into the party loomed in front of her.

"What, Thalia?" he snapped at her and she cowered a little. He sighed and seemed to avoid looking at her as he glanced back at the door. "I've never misled you. I brought you here so you could be trained and sold. It's happening faster than normal, but you should take it as a compliment."

She didn't know what to think. He changed so fast he made her dizzy. One minute protective, the next abusive. Worried about her, then reminding her she was nothing but a commodity. Gentle then violent. Soft then harsh. What about last night? What about the half-spoken apologies? The way he'd touched her last night hadn't been educational, that hadn't been to train her! He had wanted her and had wanted to give her pleasure. Now he was acting like he didn't care? Fine. If that's who he wanted to be right now, then *fine*. She gritted her teeth and nodded, refusing to cry and smear her makeup.

"Yes, Master," she growled through her teeth, but he didn't seem to notice. He simply turned and held the door open.

"Follow me," he commanded, and she did.

Crawling after him as the sound of people talking and low music came from the living room. They arrived too quickly to the little gathering. Her heart pounding in her ears as she heard the conversations slow. Her cheeks heated as she could feel eyes landing on her. She both wanted to look up and see who was watching her, and at the same time wanted to hide behind the guard and keep her eyes down until they mercifully ended the party.

He stopped near the wall and she knelt beside him. His hand brushed through her hair once and then his touch abandoned her. She was shivering with anxiety and fear and he had to know it, he had to.

He just didn't care.

Thalia lifted her eyes carefully to peek through her hair at the people gathered in the room. Several of them had picked their conversations back up, but their eyes continued to evaluate her. A heat flushed over her as she realized someone was focused solely on her. A good looking blond man, maybe in his thirties, was staring at her across the room. He was leaning back in the chair, his long legs planted firmly on the floor as he watched her. She knew her eyes should be on the floor but his gaze was insistent. She could feel it like a feather touch over her breasts, her thighs, between her legs.

The man raised a hand and beckoned her over, and she almost obeyed without thinking. She glanced up at the guard, unsure of what to do in the situation. His jaw was clenched tight, his arms crossed and she could see how tight his shoulders were. He didn't even look at her, or reprimand her for lifting her eyes, he just spoke steadily. "Go to him, Thalia. He's asking for you."

She was shocked. He was sending her to another man? He hadn't even let Thomas touch her. Somewhere her brain remembered to mumble, "Yes, Master."

Her eyes dropped and she felt nauseous as she crawled to the man. She felt everyone in the room staring at her, and her stomach fluttered with fear as she finally knelt at the man's feet. He was sitting in the black chair the guard had spanked her in the first night that she was in the house, and the memory made her instantly wet. Her blush intensified with the realization.

"Hello, Thalia." He had an English accent, and it caressed her name. "I must say you are even more beautiful in person." His voice was clear and hinted that he was well-educated. It was a voice for boardrooms and corporate takeovers. Cool, calm, and collected.

"Thank you, sir." She kept her eyes down, staring at the shine on his black shoes.

"He will not let me talk to you long, so I'm going to get right to the point. I've enjoyed watching you on—" he halted suddenly, and she heard him lean forward toward her. "Wait, you don't know your Master's name, do you." It didn't even sound like a question, he was simply verifying.

"No, sir."

"Interesting." She could imagine him smiling. His voice was inches away from her and it sent a pleasant thrill down her spine. "Well, my name is James. I think you should know my name but remember not to use it."

"Yes, sir," she answered softly, a little surprised the man had given his name so freely. Her mind repeated it the way he'd said it in his accent. *James.*

"I've enjoyed watching you on his cameras. I have questions though... has he given you any drugs while you've been here?" He asked the question smoothly, but Thalia's head bounced up in surprise and she met his eyes. Green like sea glass, and they lit up when she locked eyes with him. He slowly arched an eyebrow at her and she felt panic flutter in her belly as she dropped her eyes back to the floor, tensing in preparation for his anger.

Stupid! Stupid! Her heart raced.

"No, sir, no drugs that I am aware of, and I'm sorry I looked at you, sir." She swallowed, digging her nails into her palms to try and stay calm. He might hurt her despite the apology, but she hadn't expected him to ask that. It had been nice though, because she couldn't deny that, after the up-close look, he was gorgeous. Like someone in a Ralph Lauren ad who should be standing on a sailboat with the wind in his face.

What the hell was she thinking?

His hand was suddenly in her hair, and she flinched, but his fingers just moved along her scalp, bunching her hair beneath his palm and then releasing it as he flattened his hand again. He didn't wrench her head back, or yell at her. This was… nice? Almost soothing as her heart rate slowed considerably.

"So, you're trained to keep your eyes down, that's fine. But you don't need to be worried. I obviously surprised you with the question. I'm not upset with you." She was surprised he didn't immediately punish her, and that he'd blamed himself for her mistake. His fingers were making her scalp tingle, and his voice was hypnotizing. Even more so since she couldn't see his expression, and she found that she wanted to. She wanted to look at his eyes again, figure out the exact color of his hair, his eyes, and maybe stare at his mouth as he spoke. She'd never known anyone with an English accent before.

His voice was quiet, meant only for her. "I only asked the question because you've been incredibly responsive to this lifestyle, Thalia, and I didn't know if that was natural or chemically induced to attract the attention of those at this little party for your debut." His trimmed nails grazed her scalp and made her shiver. "And everyone here is looking at you, Thalia. I think you've made quite the impression."

"Thank you, sir." Her heart was tripping over itself and she couldn't exactly pinpoint why. His touches were so gentle, but they still had an edge to them, as if they could switch to something more aggressive in an instant. She had no foolish ideas about him, though. She knew he wouldn't be here if his interests weren't aligned with her Master's… but he'd already told her his name. *That* was different.

"I understand you didn't plan to end up here, but I need you to be honest with me. Do you enjoy it?" His fingers continued to move in her hair for a moment while she sat there in silence, slightly in shock at the blunt question. Her mind raced as she tried to answer. It was hard to separate the fear of everything her Master had put her through from the undeniable moments of pleasure. Her body had reacted in ways she would have never expected to the things he did, and when she thought of all the unfulfilling relationships she'd had before — they were like ghostly images and the week she had spent in this house was in full color. Just looking at the chair the man was sitting in was making her squirm, her mind still stuck on the memory of the guard in it. It made her think of being spanked again. Even in front of everyone.

And if she was honest with herself, *that* idea turned her on.

Her situation had been a nightmare, but the side of her it had awoken was real. His hand lifted from her hair and it pulled her back to the moment.

"I don't know, sir." She felt like she needed to be honest with him, that it was incredibly important, but she could barely think. She knew there was something that kept her anticipating the guard's touch, even though he hurt her. "Maybe, sir?"

He tilted her chin up until she was looking at him again, and she was stunned by the intensity of his stare. Those sea green eyes traced over her features and then moved down the rest of her body. Just like before it felt like he was actually touching her wherever his eyes landed. His lips looked soft, and they tilted at the edge for a moment like he might smile, but he stopped. "Your Master has always had a talent for finding women with a natural inclination toward submission. I've never found myself particularly interested in one of his girls until you though."

His lips were even better when they were moving and she didn't know if she was so mesmerized because it had been so long since she'd seen another person this close, or if he really was this fascinating. His words sank in slowly. "May I ask a question, sir?"

"Yes." This time a small smile made it across his face and she felt a warm flush in her stomach that she'd apparently made him smile.

"I don't know what to do, I just need to know — can you tell me why you are interested in me, sir?" Her breath hitched when she finished speaking, because she was suddenly terrified. She didn't know this man, but she didn't know the guard either. She didn't know anything and she was still so afraid of what the guard would do to her if she did something wrong. And what if this man wanted to hurt her like the guard's partner?

"Thalia..." He blew out a breath and smiled a little as his hand moved from her chin to his thigh. "You are feisty. After all, I saw the incident with your Master's patio door. And as far as obedience? I would say that you are lacking." His words were calm and clear, and she dropped her head as fear overtook her. What would happen if no one bought her? Would he really sell her to a whorehouse in some foreign country so she'd disappear?

His partner absolutely would.

She felt sick.

James lifted her chin again so she looked at him. "But I don't like women who are completely broken down. There's no passion left, no spirit, and that's no fun at all."

His thumb traced across her bottom lip and her breath caught at his words. He didn't want her broken? Did that mean he wanted her like she was? She suddenly wanted to taste his skin with his thumb against her lip, but just as her tongue brushed over her bottom lip his thumb moved.

"That's why you caught my attention, Thalia, and I have abandoned quite a bit of my work in the last week in order to watch you." He let go of her chin and sat back and she swayed forward as if her body wanted to follow his touch, but then she caught herself and looked at the floor again.

He shifted in his seat for a moment, and then he leaned forward again, his fingers trailing over the collar around her neck. "If I wanted to touch you, what would you say?"

"It would be up to my Master, sir," Thalia answered confidently, finally back on stable ground where she knew the responses to give.

"He's trained you well. If he gave permission, would you be okay with it?" It sounded like an earnest question. He was actually asking her if she wanted him to touch her. And she realized she did. She wanted to know what someone else's hands would feel like in this world, how someone else might treat her. She'd wanted it from the moment she saw Thomas with Anna and Kaia.

She was whispering as she replied, her body taut as a bowstring. "Ye— yes, sir."

"That's... very good, Thalia. Look at me." The last command snapped out in his smooth voice, and she obeyed instantly. He sighed and sat back from her a little.

"Yes, sir?" she murmured. His eyes hovered at her lips and he leaned forward again, his fingers gently tangling in her hair. His touch subtly kept her from looking away from him, and for a moment she thought he might kiss her and her pulse thrummed through her body.

"I want you to know that your Master and I have had conflicts in the past about how he acquires his girls." A tick in the muscle of his jaw drew her attention, and then he continued. His accent shaping the words, his voice so quiet she found herself leaning toward him to hear him better, he continued. "I haven't watched his cameras in a while due to that conflict. But I saw you slap him, and I was impressed by you, as foolish as that move was. After that... let's just say I was hooked." A wicked smile crossed his lips and she felt her mouth go dry.

"Yes, sir?" she prompted him to continue and he brought his eyes back up from her body, gaze tracing her mouth before he locked eyes with her again.

"I know you don't know me, but I'll ask you to not panic. I'm going to speak to your Master." His voice was smooth confidence, but his words still opened up a pit in her stomach.

"Yes, sir," she said shakily and his fingers ran up the back of her neck into her hair, leaving a trail of shivers down her back as he stood up next to her and then walked away toward the guard.

Chapter Twenty
THALIA

Thalia kept her head down, but she lifted her eyes to watch him through the curtain of her hair.

James was an inch or so taller than the guard and as he stepped up to him they shook hands. The guard's partner stepped up next to them and both seemed to listen intently to James. Suddenly her Master's face flashed rage. She knew what it looked like when he was close to losing his temper and his partner grabbed the guard's shoulder. She could hear the guard's voice being raised, but she couldn't make out what he was saying.

James was completely calm though, not reacting at all. Even though she could only see his profile, his blond hair lit up by the lights, it was obvious that he wasn't bothered by her Master's anger. The guard and his partner suddenly turned away from him to move into the kitchen.

She was momentarily terrified that James had told them the things she'd said, or that she'd looked at him without permission. Her stomach twisted as he walked back to her, sitting down in the chair by her and immediately returning his hand to her hair. This time his touch was much firmer, his fingers tracing along the back of her head and occasionally gripping her hair, but never hard enough to hurt. It was like a tease, the sensation just enough to rouse her interest, to tingle, but never enough to really change the level of their interaction. "Thalia, do you know the man who was with your Master?"

"His partner." She tilted her head slightly into his touch and his grip tightened in her hair, making her hips shift involuntarily.

He laughed softly. "You are so responsive, and your Master is revealing too much of himself. Normally that man that was standing next to him is here to help train the girls, but your Master didn't let him touch you." His fingers tugged lightly at her hair until she looked up at him, her breath coming in little shallow pants as heat gathered in her lower belly. "Why do you think that is?"

"Master told me this party had to happen, but that he would keep me safe from his partner. He... he said he shouldn't have let his partner hurt me in the chair." The words were out of her mouth before she realized what she'd done. Panic seized her chest and her eyes watered as tears threatened. Biting her lip hard she looked into his eyes and found a calm strength. With his free hand he cupped her face and pulled her lip from between her teeth with his thumb.

"Don't worry, pet. I won't tell him you told me, and I thank you for your honesty. Would you like to know what I asked for that has him so upset?" He relaxed his grip in her hair and his fingers traced her scalp again as the tingling sensation of him pulling her hair faded.

"Yes, sir." She dropped her eyes back to the floor.

He must have leaned forward because his mouth was against her ear. "I told him I wanted to taste you." His words made a pulse appear between her legs. She was wet and his words only built the fire burning down low in her stomach. He laughed softly in her ear and she felt the strongest urge to turn and kiss him. "And your Master didn't want to share you. So, I offered to buy you right then. He and his associate are discussing it."

He'd offered to buy her? Her head turned and she found herself barely an inch from his lips — he pulled back first. "Sir?" she asked for clarification the only way she could think of.

"I know all of this started badly for you, that you were forced into this. I've never been happy about that aspect of their enterprise." One of his fingers swept down her cheek, and he spoke quietly so the others in the room couldn't hear. "I want you to know that with me you could have something consensual, but I will be honest that my appetites are very similar to his. What would change is your right to stop it. You could stop me with a word."

His voice was serious, and his eyes were hungry. A visual of him between her thighs suddenly flooded her mind and she wanted to squeeze her thighs together to hide how wet she'd become.

"My request has him quite upset, so I need you to be brave, no matter what happens." His eyes looked past her for a moment and then returned. "Do you want to stay with him, Thalia? Answer me." His voice carried the command with such power that her body arched slightly just hearing it and his eyes trailed over her.

"THALIA! Come here!" Her Master's voice rang out like a whip crack across the room, and she jumped. His partner was standing behind him with a face now filled with irritation. The man next to her, *James,* immediately lifted his hands from her and sat back in the chair, not even looking at her anymore but staring across the room at her Master.

Fear filled her like cold water as she crawled toward the guard. When she reached him, he grabbed her by her hair and almost lifted her off her knees with the force of his pull. She yelped loudly and started to lift her hands to grab at his but stopped herself. The guard raised his voice so the room could hear him. "It seems my newest girl, Thalia, has already attracted an offer my friends. Would any others like to bid?"

The guard's blue-gray eyes were filled with steel as he challenged anyone else to speak, then he stared right over her head and she knew he was locking eyes with James. Her body arched and she whimpered, trying to ease the pressure from her hair without breaking her kneel.

"What was the offer?" A man with a dark complexion asked as he leaned against one of the walls drinking a glass of wine. His voice was rich and exotic, with a hint of a French accent. She could see him staring hard at her as she twisted.

"The current offer is — substantial. My brother is very interested in accepting it, but as the party has just started we don't want to end the festivities so soon." Her Master's voice had the cold edge of rage in it, and although the words were pretty she knew he didn't mean them. She wanted more than anything to hide from him or plead with him to not be upset with her.

Wait… had he said brother?

Her eyes shifted to his partner standing behind him, and it clicked. Slightly older than her Master but the same hair color, the same shoulders, not as muscular as her Master but more refined, more contained. Both had blue eyes.

He had a brother, and James had said he normally helped the guard train the girls, but the guard hadn't let him. He had argued with his own brother over her.

"We haven't even seen her in action up close, how do we know your little camera feeds have not been edited?" A male voice behind her with a different accent spoke up. The words made her whimper.

"Excellent point." Her Master shoved her to the floor hard, and she caught herself on her hands with a gasp. She waited a moment before slowly pushing herself up into a kneel again. He had told her to go to James. She hadn't done anything wrong. Why was he so angry?

His brother stepped up and she heard him whisper in her Master's ear. "You are not in the right frame of mind to conduct this. Let me."

Her Master turned and glared at his brother but the man didn't back down. His blue-gray eyes flicked down to her and she immediately dropped her gaze as terror dragged its claws through her.

Not his brother. Not again.

"Fine. You wanted the party, you have it. You want to showcase her, you can. As always, you're in charge." Her Master's voice hissed the words between his teeth before he brushed past him and walked toward the kitchen. The brother stepped toward her and she felt herself tense in fear.

She was crying, she could feel the tears. She knew it was a bad idea but she cried out for him, desperate to avoid his brother, "Master! Please!"

The guard paused for a moment but then he disappeared through the doorway to the kitchen. He left her with him. She felt sick as the pit of fear opened wider in her stomach.

His brother leaned forward and wound his fist into her hair. The grip was firm, and completely controlled, pulling just hard enough to hurt as he tilted her head up to look at him. He leaned down and whispered close to her face, "I've watched you. If you misbehave and embarrass me in front of our guests, I will sell you somewhere where my brother's actions will seem like a glorious vacation. Do you understand?" He was cold. There was no anger in his voice, he almost sounded bored, and she had no doubt he could and would do exactly what he threatened.

"Yes, sir." She quivered under his touch and then he let go of her, clapping his hands loudly as he addressed the small group.

"Friends, you know that my brother and I provide consistently well-trained submissives. Thalia, as you've observed, is especially responsive." He moved to the center of the room on the black carpet and snapped his fingers. "Come here, Thalia."

She crawled forward until she knelt next to him, her breath hitching as she fought to suppress the urge to cry again.

"Down." His voice was short, an obvious command, but the guard had never used it so she was unsure what to do. She decided to bow, her head touching the floor with her arms stretched in front of her. She quivered as thoughts of what he'd do if she were wrong filled her head. He sighed and his hands grabbed her hips and lifted them until her ass was in the air, her pussy exposed as her knees were still spread. Then he thrust two fingers sharply inside her and she winced as flashbacks of the night before hit her.

"Gentlemen, she's already wet and we haven't even played with her yet," he announced, and the chuckles she heard from the room were much closer now. Her face heated instantly. She wanted to lift her head and find James, but she knew she wasn't allowed. His fingers slid forward and back slowly but she shook her head against the floor. She didn't want him to touch her at all, she wanted to disappear into the carpet under her.

Thalia whimpered as the guard's brother worked his fingers inside her, and she was a little happy when her body didn't react to him. He circled her clit with his thumb and her hips jerked automatically, but she was quickly losing any arousal James had created with his firm touches and his powerful words.

"The girl is not being very responsive today, is she now?" One of the voices above her.

"Maybe you scared her too bad. That's been an issue for you before, hasn't it?" Another voice, a hint of mockery evident in it.

The brother's fingers left her and he grabbed the back of her neck and squeezed, pressing her into the floor. Panic brimmed inside her, threatening to burst out in sobs. She was embarrassing him, he was going to hurt her, refuse James, and sell her off to some nightmare. It wasn't her fault she couldn't respond to him!

"She's given us a little trouble, as you all know, but we have turned her around rather quickly. She just needs a little incentive to behave." His fingers dug into her skin and she yelped.

"If you wouldn't mind, I'd be happy to do the demonstration. It is what I asked your brother for, after all, and I am the high bid." James' voice was close by, smooth and calm. "As long as no one else objects, of course?"

"Let the Brit show her off, he got the ball rolling on this party anyway." Another voice, that one was clearly American. Thalia had closed her eyes so she wouldn't have to see them gathering around her.

She was shaking, and she knew it was from adrenaline and fear and the proximity of the guard's brother and his whispered threats. A quiet sob slipped from her lips as his hand released her, and she heard him take a slow breath.

Chapter Twenty-One
THALIA

"Of course, you should have the opportunity." That cold voice couldn't fully disguise his anger that she'd failed to respond to him again. The same frustration from the night before appearing.

James' voice was above her, warm and soothing. "Thank you. Thalia has been quite responsive to her Master, you are right." His fingertips traced her spine and sent chills down her back. "I think she's just feeling a little shy with everyone here."

His hand trailed back up her back and wound into her hair. "Up," he commanded her gently, and tugged slightly on her hair as she moved back into a kneel and then stood. He had to be six feet tall as short as she felt next to him. He guided her back to the chair he'd been in, and he smoothly pulled her across his lap as he sat down. His hand brushed through her hair and trailed over her back making her shiver. "Spread your knees."

She did, and as he pulled her toward him on his lap so she was more secure, she felt his erection press against her side. His palm moved over the round swell of her ass and she squirmed, but his fist tightened in her hair to hold her there. "Stay still, Thalia."

"Yes, sir," she answered and hid her face in the curtain of her hair.

His hand slid between her thighs and cupped her, teasing her for a moment with a small amount of pressure. She started to wiggle her hips to get a little more, but he brought his hand back and spanked her ass. She jumped as the sting turned into heat, and he rubbed in a circle. "Stay still."

Nodding, she murmured against her arm, "Yes, sir". His hand returned between her legs and she could feel herself growing wet as he teased her with gentle touches, never enough to do more than entice her. A small whine came out of her throat after only a couple of minutes of the gentle, rhythmic pressing of his hand against her.

"What do you want, Thalia?" His voice had changed a little, deepened by his arousal. She could blatantly feel just how aroused he was by the erection pressing against her stomach.

"More, sir," she said and tilted her hips a little. He spanked her and she jumped, but it only increased the heat between her thighs.

"Of course, if you stay still." One of his fingers slid between her folds and she moaned softly, fighting the urge to lift her hips, to wiggle to get him to touch her more. He brushed her clit and she moaned louder.

"Sir?" Her breaths were starting to come in pants, her fists clenching as she tried hard to stay still.

Another finger as he circled her clit, applying more pressure as pleasure started pulsing between her thighs. "Do you like this, Thalia?"

"Yes, sir." It came out on a moan and she could hear voices talking around her, but she focused on James' voice and his touch. The world dissolved until she was centered at her core, her orgasm slowly starting to build. He moved his hand, and his fingers slid inside her pussy, her slick heat shaping around his touch. She moaned, biting down on her lip so she wouldn't push her hips back against him. He moved torturously slow, and even when his thumb began to press on her clit it was too light. She moaned and twitched her hips forward against his hand trying to get just a little more. He pulled his hand away completely and spanked her.

"Her skin colors beautifully."

"Perfect handprint."

The voices of the men around her made her blush again, and she felt her face heat as she hid it against the chair. James' hand returned to her and immediately gave more pressure to her clit as his fingers slid deep inside her. She moaned louder as he started to stroke his fingers inside her, focusing pressure on her clit in tight little circles that had her heart racing. She felt herself moving toward the edge, and his fingers tightened in her hair. The tingling, and the reminder of his power over her body only pushed her closer to her climax. His words were in her head. He promised things like this, only consensual. He would give her a way to stop him, and she believed he *would* stop. Even for this moment he had asked if she would be okay if he touched her. And if he touched her like this? She would always say yes.

Her orgasm was winding tight at the base of her spine, she just needed a little push. Her hips bucked against his lap when he increased the friction on her clit. But again, his hand came back and spanked her. Her wetness coating his hand and making the pop of it even louder.

"I'm sorry, sir," she whined, hoping his hand would return to her.

"You are lovely, Thalia." His fingers thrust a little harder inside her, but she was slick and the sensation made her moan even before he began circling her clit again.

"Thank you, sir." His hand was firmly in her hair, the strain of it just enough to tingle. She leaned her head forward further so the pull was a little sharper. She heard him laugh softly above her as he increased the strain on her hair and she moaned. Each thrust of his fingers, the delicious friction against her clit, and the ache of his control in her hair were too much. She gritted her teeth when she felt herself almost fall over the edge as his fingers pressed down on that bundle of nerves inside her.

"Sir, may I come? Sir?" The words were breathy and filled with need, but he didn't reply right away. He held her at the edge by gentling his touches for a moment. Her pants and moans were moving her body, she knew she was squirming against his hand but he kept going this time.

"Come for me, Thalia." His fingers brushed deep inside her curling down against those nerves and she came hard across his lap. She bit her lip to try and be quiet as her body arched with the strength of it, but she still made enough noise to have masculine groans echoing around her. His touch drew out the last quaking of her body until she was limp in his lap. Soft moans slipped from her as she wound down from the bliss of the orgasm. His fingers scraped across her scalp softly, leaving a tingling buzz behind, and her mind was a warm puddle for one glorious moment before reality started to seep back in.

"Thank you, sir," she said weakly and she heard his laugh.

"My pleasure. You taste so sweet." James' voice summoned a pulse between her thighs, and she bit back a moan at the idea of him licking his fingers. "You should kneel again, pet."

His strong arms helped her move to the floor and she knelt on shaky legs, her thighs coated in her wetness. Everyone seemed to start talking at once in a hodgepodge of accents. The brother's voice was clear, discussing offers and bids which she tried hard to tune out. All of her fear was coming back as the high of her orgasm fizzled.

"We have a new high bid. Will you counter it?" The brother's voice broke through the haze, and she hoped he was speaking to James.

"I need an answer to a question I asked her before I bid again. Thalia, do you want to stay with your Master?" His voice was warm and soothing, but it didn't matter. Her face flushed instantly because he'd asked it out loud. In front of everyone. The guard could have heard the question. Fear took hold of her lungs and squeezed until there wasn't enough air for her to even cry. She just felt the tears spring up, marking hot trails across her cheeks before they fell to her thighs. Lifting her head, she looked around and found the guard standing against the wall. His arms were crossed, his face unreadable. Her eyes dropped back to the floor and more tears fell.

"Thalia…" James leaned down in front of her, touching her chin to make her eyes lift to him. "I'm only asking for your honesty. Do you want to come with me?"

It was a life raft.

A week at sea in violent waters and James had handed her a life raft. If fear kept her from taking it, she knew she'd drown. She'd barely made it a week with the guard with her sanity intact. Barely kept her head above water. She pulled a shuddering breath through her tears and forced herself to speak. "Yes, sir."

"NO!" the guard shouted from the wall.

"I'm taking her. I'll outbid anyone, understood?" James stood instantly and her eyes followed him up. This was how he must be at work — decisive, intense. The other men backed off immediately.

"She's not for sale!" the guard shouted above her head and she cowered, dropping her eyes to the floor.

"She, in fact, is, and I accept the bid." His brother's voice was cold, but the guard seemed to ignore him. He grabbed her arm sharply and she yelped as he started to pull her up. This had been what she was afraid of when she spoke.

She'd betrayed him. He was going to hurt her.

"Don't touch my property, Marcus." James grabbed the guard's wrist in a tight grip. A few intakes of breath from the guests accompanied Thalia's gasp at James' use of the guard's name. It may have been the guard's own shock at hearing his name that caused him to release her. James gently helped her to her feet, and her legs felt like jelly as he pushed her slightly behind him. Now that she was standing up she could see the pain and fury in the guard's, *no*, Marcus' face.

"Thalia, please, just stay with me. Things will be different, I promise, just choose to stay." He was begging her. She'd never even remotely heard that tone in his voice, but she didn't want to stay. She didn't want to stay where she would never feel safe again, where the rules shifted with his moods, where the threat of his brother was hanging over her if she made a mistake.

She was taking the life raft.

His brother was speaking to him in a low voice and began to push him backward by his shoulders. Marcus suddenly pulled his arm back and punched his brother hard enough to send him to the floor. "Fuck you, Anthony!"

Her heart was in her throat and she found herself clutching the back of James' shirt. He took a step back with her still behind him, and she noticed the other guests had begun to move toward the door, not wanting to be a part of the aftermath. His brother, Anthony, stood back up quickly and turned his eyes to them. His mouth was bloody at the edge, but she was glad someone had hit him. He deserved a lot worse. "Take Thalia and leave, Dr. Hawkins."

"No! Thalia, do not leave." Marcus made it a command and took two steps toward her and she flinched, stepping farther behind James. He stopped like she'd slapped him.

"I told you your methods weren't perfect." James spoke the words calmly, but they struck Marcus. Thalia watched as his face paled, the red flush of his anger bleeding out.

James turned to her and she realized she had been holding her breath. When she breathed in again, it came as a gasp. He leaned down a little to look in her eyes and gave her a reassuring smile as he slid the cuffs off her wrists and they dropped to the floor. The collar he left on, and then he spoke again. "Let's go to the car and talk."

She nodded, wanting away from the brothers. Anthony raised his voice, still speaking with the cold reason she'd identified him with, despite the bloody mouth. "The auction is over. We look forward to continuing a business relationship with each of you. Drive carefully." It was a dismissal. He was still standing extremely close to Marcus as if prepared to stop him if he went for her again.

The other guests let them leave first, and James leaned down and lifted her into his arms to walk over the rock covered driveway. "I am sorry that did not go more smoothly. I knew he was attached to you…" He laughed softly against her hair. "I just didn't know how much."

Thalia couldn't even think straight as he set her down next to an SUV. He opened the passenger door and he helped her climb inside, then he went around to the driver's side. Her mind was whirring and her eyes were trained on the door of the house. The right half of the building seemed to be covered in glass, while the left was solid wood with very few windows. It was modern construction, slightly lifted off the ground with stilts to where the ground sloped up to meet it at the back. The sun was setting and orange light peeked over the tree line as the sky faded into a kaleidoscope of colors.

"Thalia?" Her head turned sharply and she was worried he'd said her name once before.

"Yes, sir? Um, I mean, Master?" Her voice shook and he reached over and cupped her chin.

"Calm down, pet. It will take a bit for us to get to know each other, and while I wouldn't call myself gentle..." His hand slipped into her hair to pull her toward him. "I am understanding."

Then he kissed her. It wasn't sweet, it was full of heat. His other hand tilted her chin back so he could kiss her deeper, his fist tightening in her hair to make her moan against his mouth. It was so many promises in one moment. He wouldn't punish her needlessly, he wanted her to know who he was, and he wanted to learn about her too. And the kiss promised more than what he'd done with her at the auction. When he pulled back from her she swallowed. His green eyes were a shade darker and focused on her mouth.

"All I ask from you is six months. Give me six months as my submissive and then you can decide if this lifestyle is for you." His mouth moved, and the words came out in that incredible accent, but her mind had some kind of car accident trying to process it.

"You? What? I can... what?" she babbled not so eloquently at him.

"Six months. Commit to me for that long, and then you can choose. Go free, figure out what vanilla life you want to live. I'll even help you rebuild it. Or you can choose to stay with me. My original offer doesn't change, this *will* be consensual." His thumb brushed over her lips. "You can always stop me with a word."

"What word?" she asked breathlessly.

"Your choice, pet." He smiled at her wickedly and heat roiled in her belly again at all the promises his mouth made.

"Chair," she answered confidently. He leaned into the back seat and handed her a small plastic bag. Inside were clothes and shoes.

He laughed a little. "Why chair?"

"I'd like to focus on good memories of that word, instead of bad ones."

He tilted his head, his eyes moving over her. "You're very brave, pet." He kissed her again as she was pulling a shirt from the bag, and as he continued her hands slid into his hair. His blond hair was a little longer than the guard's, he smelled like a different soap and the tang of a men's cologne. And she wasn't afraid of him. She was excited at what he might show her, especially as his hand slid between her thighs again and made her arch against the seat, moaning into his mouth. He made a frustrated sound in his throat and leaned back from her, leaving her panting in the passenger seat.

"You should put the clothes on so I don't make a poor decision, and then we can leave." He adjusted a sizable bulge in his pants as he twisted back to the steering wheel.

"Yes, Master." The clothes fit rather well, and she slid them on in the passenger seat while James watched attentively. She blushed as she buckled her seatbelt, and then she saw Marcus standing in the doorway of the house. Her heartbeat stuttered as he stared at the car. Others had filtered out, cars turning down the driveway while they had sat in the SUV.

"I understand why he's so angry. You're incredible, Thalia." James brushed her cheek as he started the car. Marcus never moved as he backed the SUV out and turned it to head down the narrow driveway.

"He told me that too, Master." Her eyes greedily devoured the forest and the fading sunlight, and the inky color of the night sky as it appeared. James sighed, and tucked her hair behind her ear.

"He may have said it to you, Thalia, but I plan to show you."

And she believed him.

THE END

End Notes

First, thank you so much for reading the beginning of Thalia's story! I still remember the chaos that this ending threw people into in the early readings of Thalia's story on Literotica. I promise you, there's a long road ahead for Thalia, and like all the best things in life the road to the end isn't always easy.

In 'Striking a Balance' (Book 2 of The Thalia Series), we follow Thalia as she leaves the auction, learns more about James, and struggles not to lose herself completely in her efforts to understand the side that Marcus forced her to recognize. We've seen the darkness, now it's time to start working toward the light.

Jennifer Bene

A DARK ROMANCE

STRIKING A BALANCE

BOOK TWO OF THE THALIA SERIES

USA TODAY BESTSELLING AUTHOR
JENNIFER BENE

Text copyright © 2015 Jennifer Bene

All Rights Reserved.

No part of this book may be reproduced in any form or by any electronic or mechanical means including information storage and retrieval systems, without permission in writing from the author. The only exception is by a reviewer, who may quote short excerpts in a review.

This book is a work of fiction. Names, characters, places, and incidents either are products of the author's imagination or are used fictitiously. Any resemblance to actual persons, living or dead, events, or locales is entirely coincidental.

ISBN (e-book): 978-1-946722-14-0

ISBN (paperback): 978-1-946722-24-9

Cover design by Laura Hidalgo, https://www.spellbindingdesign.com/

"The best way out is always through."
- Robert Frost

Thank you, the reader, for continuing with Thalia's story and moving to the second book in this series. In this book we start to leave the darkness behind, but if it were easy to leave darkness behind it wouldn't be something we respect.

I really hope you enjoy meeting James and all the other characters in this book. As always, I want to thank all my friends that helped make this book possible, because I know they put up with my insanity with a smile (usually) and that is something I don't always deserve.

Last, I want to thank all the lit readers who encouraged me, and all of those who listened to me talk their ears off for hours about this story and still urged me to keep writing.

All of you make me feel incredibly lucky.

Chapter One
THALIA

The Night of the Auction

The ride away from Marcus' house and the chaotic auction was surreal. For the first part of it Thalia had been glued to the window watching the vibrant colors of the outside world dim as night took over, and then she'd sat slumped against the door staring up at the night sky. James, her new Master, had graciously given her the quiet she didn't even realize she needed. Her mind wouldn't shut up despite the alluring calm of the road noise and the dark, tree lined highway that they were on for about half the drive.

It suddenly hit her as she saw a sign signaling their approach to the city that the auction was over. The threat that Marcus had held over her was gone. The threat of Marcus himself, and his twisted brother, Anthony, was gone. A hysterical little laugh bubbled up in her chest and burst out without warning. She covered her mouth quickly, but James had jumped in his seat at the sudden noise before composing his face back into his calm demeanor as he looked over at her.

"Care to share the joke with me, pet?" His voice was warm silk, and she almost giggled again as his English accent shaped the words. She remembered his hand between her thighs, his mouth against hers and she tried to ignore the flush in her cheeks.

"I—" She started to respond and realized she didn't know how to explain herself. Her mind was swirling with all the panic and anxiety she'd built up about the auction, all the terrible things she'd imagined — and then there was James sitting next to her and calmly waiting for her answer. And thirty minutes ago he'd had her moaning under his touch. He was ridiculously handsome. The kind of handsome you saw in social circles that cared about 'good breeding' and trust funds and yacht clubs and, well, pretty much everything Thalia had never been close to associated with. His blond hair was artfully tousled so that it constantly seemed like he had just run his hand through it. But, actually, it had been her hands in it last when he'd kissed her and slid his hand between her legs and made her want to beg him to keep going. He had green eyes that looked like sea glass the first time she'd seen them, and like green bottle glass when he was aroused. A shiver went through her, and she noticed she was still incredibly wet from when he'd made her come at the party. On top of his accent, his looks, his social status, and the skill he'd shown her with his hands and his mouth... *he had asked her permission.* He had given her a choice to go with him. He had even asked if she'd be okay with him touching her before he'd even approached Marcus!

The hysterical laugh was threatening to burst out again.

In a million years she would have never imagined leaving Marcus' house with someone like James — there had been days she wasn't sure she'd be leaving alive at all. She psychotically felt safe with James. She knew that was insane. She didn't know James, fuck, she didn't know anything about Marcus except for his violence. She had only known both of their names for, what, an hour?

The laugh came out. She slapped both her hands over her mouth and leaned forward in the seat as her head swam and her ribs ached with the effort to quiet it. They were in the city now and the bright lights of buildings flashed by as James maneuvered the luxury SUV smoothly through the traffic. He glanced back over at her and arched an eyebrow, but he didn't pressure her to speak.

She was glad, because she couldn't answer him at the moment. Nothing was funny. She didn't know why she was laughing. Of all things right now, she shouldn't be laughing. Her breathing grew shallow as her situation came into focus. She was in a car with someone who was basically a stranger, a stranger who had purchased her from a really horrifying situation, but why would he have been there if he wasn't the same? He turned into the parking lot of a very large, nice hotel and she finally felt the tears seeping through the shirt she was wearing. She was crying.

"Thalia..." His voice was soft as he pulled into a spot far from the entrance.

His gentle voice didn't help. She folded forward, hugging her knees as sobs started coming out. Somewhere in her mind she had thought the auction was the end of it, but it wasn't. She belonged to James now, and he would do whatever he wanted with her. Whether that was more of what he'd done at the party, and in the SUV, or if he was more like Anthony — she'd just have to find out. A sob choked out of her as fear washed over her again.

"Thalia." His voice was suddenly stern. It wasn't like the soft one he'd used with her since the auction. But it effectively short-circuited the cycle of fear and panic that was escalating inside her and she sat up in response, gasping a breath. His voice came again, "Look at me."

She tilted her head so she could look at him through the curtain of her hair. He sighed and reached for her, but she flinched and he stopped his hand.

"Thalia. Tuck your hair behind your ears so I can see your face." He took his hand back as he said it and allowed her to sweep her hair out of her face and quickly swipe her hands under her eyes, a black blur of mascara and eyeliner marking her hands. "Thank you." He said, still in that calm, direct voice.

Thalia opened her mouth to speak, but every time she started a sentence she would remember the need to address him as Master, which only tumbled her back into her panic. Her chest hurt as she tried to breathe, and the air in the SUV seemed stifling. She grabbed at her throat, and she heard James curse and unbuckle his seatbelt. His strong grip was at the back of her neck as he pulled her seatbelt slack and pressed her head forward between her knees.

"Shh, Thalia. Take a deep breath, you're hyperventilating. Shh." He still sounded stern, but it was actually helping. The high-pitched whine she was hearing was her own breaths rapidly whistling in and out of her lungs. His calm, controlled voice was so different from her panic that she found herself trying to cling to it in the fog of her head. A few minutes like that and her head wasn't swimming any more, her pulse had dropped a little and her chest didn't hurt quite so much. Her breathing quieted slowly and she licked her lips before she spoke.

"Thank you, Master." She murmured and he released his grip on her neck and she sat up.

He rubbed a hand across his face before he gripped the steering wheel. "Thalia, I am not going to hurt you. Well, I will not hurt you anytime soon, and certainly not ever in any way you don't want. I want you to heal. When you are healed and want to try submitting to me we'll talk before anything happens. I promise you that."

She bit her bottom lip and nodded, wiping her cheeks again and sweeping her hair back from her face. "Yes, Master. Thank you, Master."

"God, Thalia." He brushed his thumb across her lower lip and she forced herself not to pull back. He had not hurt her yet or shown any inclination to. "We're going to go upstairs and talk, and I want to check and make sure you're okay. Can you handle that, can you handle walking in there with me?"

"Yes, Master." She nodded and took a deep, shuddering breath to try and calm down the rest of the way.

"There's my brave girl." His thumb swiped across her cheek before he turned the car off.

It was a blur as he came around the car and helped her out. He walked toward the building and she followed him but being around so many people after being deprived of interaction made the panic start coming back. After the longest elevator ride ever, where she hid against the wall while James effectively blocked anyone's view of her, he finally tugged her elbow and they exited. The moment she was inside his room she dropped to her knees, the adrenaline making it a sharper movement than she meant it to be.

James shut the door behind her and she felt her muscles tense in response. He moved in front of her and she saw a physical change in him too, the same she'd seen when he had taken charge at the party, and bought her, and stood up to Marcus. He seemed larger standing over her, and she wanted to apologize for breaking down in the car. She was grateful he took her away from Marcus, and he did seem much nicer. She wanted to explain she was just afraid.

"Thalia, tell me your safe word." The command surprised her.

"Umm… it's ch—chair, Master," she stumbled through her response.

"Good. If at any point you need me to stop what I'm doing, say it. I will stop immediately, and we will talk about why you needed to stop. After we may continue, or we may not. Do you understand?" He was so calm and direct, it was comforting on a variety of levels. What he said, and how honest and confident he sounded when he said it.

"Yes, Master." She nodded along with him, keeping her eyes low. Her mind repeated 'chair' over and over.

"Good. Stand up and undress." He spoke clearly and then moved away from her to what she assumed was the bedroom behind a set of French doors. Thalia stood back up and slipped off the clothes he'd given her, folding them and setting them by the wall on top of her shoes. She'd spent the last week without clothes and the pinch and press of the fabric had felt strange, and so it was almost comforting to be naked again. Which was insane, and some part of her brain knew that. She moved back into a kneel, a little more gracefully, as he stepped back into the living area.

He stopped in front of her, towering over her, still fully dressed. She kept her eyes down, but just his presence sent a thrill through her, heat gathering in her lower belly as she anticipated what he would do. Then he spoke in that low, direct voice, "Good, pet. Come with me."

She'd expected him to turn and start walking so she would follow, but he didn't. She saw his hand at the edge of her vision and she looked up at it, careful not to raise her eyes too high. He wanted her to stand? He was helping her up? Her mouth opened to ask the question, but she stopped herself, "May I ask a question, Master?"

"Is it about the crawling?" He asked it smoothly and she nodded. A sigh escaped his lips, "You don't have to crawl in my presence, pet. While the view is delightful, and I may ask for it sometimes for that reason, it's not necessary."

"Umm... th—thank you, Master." At least that was one more mark in the good column, one less resemblance to Marcus or Anthony. Her hand was shaking when she took his, but his grip was firm and strong as he tugged her to her feet and led her to the bedroom where the sheets were pulled back so there was a large white expanse of clean flat sheet.

"Lay down. On your stomach." She did and she waited to feel his hand between her legs, her eyes clenched tight, even as her pussy grew wet with the memory of his touch at the party and in the car. Instead after she heard movement to her left she felt his warm hands on her shoulders, slippery with some kind of oil. She jumped at first before his strong hands started moving confidently. His thumbs dug into the tight knots of her shoulders and she realized how tense she was, how every inch of her body had been coiled tight in anxiety and fear for a week.

A massage. He was giving her a massage. This was... confusing, and at the same time incredible. He was good at this.

A soft moan escaped her lips as he started to move his hands masterfully over her shoulders, sliding up the sides of her neck under the collar. For long minutes he silently worked the muscles in her shoulders before his hands slipped down her left arm. Her pulse slowed down, and she felt like she could finally breathe after the insane tension of the day.

At her bicep James paused, leaned down, and kissed her skin, his lips barely brushing her. It was a comforting, soothing kiss that surprised her in how gentle it was. He did it again at her wrist. On her right arm he kissed both sides of her wrist. When his hands returned to her back, his thumbs gliding along her spine he muttered a curse under his breath.

She tensed, and he brushed his fingers softly down her back, shushing her. "May I ask what's wrong, Master?"

He didn't answer her immediately, his lips brushing across her back over and over and over in soft kisses that followed where his hands worked her sore muscles. "Nothing is wrong, pet. You are such a brave girl, Thalia, so strong."

Chapter Two
THALIA

It wasn't until she heard him call her brave that she realized the twinges of pain she was feeling weren't just sore muscles, but bruises and healing welts. His mouth was tracing each of them.

"Master?" Breathing the single word was all she managed.

"I wanted to get you away from him earlier, pet, but Anthony refused my calls at first." His fingers continued their gentle pressure across her body, easing each of her muscle groups, kissing each mark on her body. His mouth moved against her skin when he spoke again and his fingers tightened on her hip, "He didn't even try to take care of these, or of you." He sounded so angry when he said it that her hands clenched into fists and her toes curled involuntarily as she waited for his anger to turn into action. The tone made the panic return, the fear, but he quickly brushed soothing hands down her sides.

"Fuck, Thalia, I'm sorry. I'm not upset with you at all, pet, I'm upset with Marcus. It was his responsibility to care for each and every mark he gave you." A soft touch traced what must have been a line across her thigh, and then his lips kissed it. "I told myself I'd learn each welt and each bruise he'd left on you, but I hadn't imagined you'd have so many in a week."

"I—" she started but he stopped her. Her mind raced back to the last time she'd looked at herself in the mirror before the auction. The collection of marks on her body had changed gradually over the week and had blurred into nothing more than background noise to her reflection. But Anna, and Kaia, and Thomas, and now James had commented on it.

She must look worse than she imagined.

"It's okay, just relax, pet." She realized her breathing had picked back up, the panic edging back in with his anger, and every memory of Marcus' hands or belt on her. "Your safety is my priority now, in everything we do. I promise I will keep you safe." James' palms slid down her thighs, massaging the aches and the tender skin there. His mouth placed a trail of soft kisses along the marks. In moments he was down her calves, and he sighed and got off the edge of the bed.

"Master?" She felt anxious when his touch left her, and she pushed herself up to look for him. He stepped back to the bed holding a small white box with a Red Cross label on the top. His green eyes found hers and she felt a blush flood up her chest and into her cheeks, heating her skin. He had a look of concern, but it faded as he took control again. She dropped her eyes to the box in his hand, a first aid kit.

"Thalia, I'm here. Lie down." Her heart rate slowed as she lay back down and she felt him untape the bandages on her feet. "I still cannot *believe* you broke his back door. You are a fighter."

"It was stupid, Master." She bit her lip and buried her face in the bedding, as she realized she'd spoken out of turn, contradicted him, and challenged him in a single sentence. She was afraid of what he'd do about her behavior. A cold swipe ran across the arch of her foot and she hissed through her teeth as it stung.

"Just antiseptic, pet, and while it *was* stupid considering your consequences... it takes a lot for someone to be brave like that with a person like Marcus in control of them." He gently took care of her feet as she let that sink in. She remembered the fear that had held her when she had broken the sliding glass door, and the complete terror when she'd heard him shout her name.

"Yes, Master." She said into the sheet, and she felt him place a kiss on the newly bandaged arch of each of her feet. He shifted to sit at her hip, his fingers brushing through her hair.

"No one has ever called me that before, Thalia, it's always been sir." His lips brushed along her neck as he pushed her hair out of his way. Her body hummed in response, her muscles relaxed and warm.

"Would you rather me call you sir?" She asked it quietly, wondering why he hadn't corrected her earlier if it bothered him. Her body arched as his hand slid down her side. That tingling heat starting to coil again between her thighs.

"It's always been sir, but..." he paused and she lifted her head to look up at him and like at the party their lips were barely an inch apart. This time he didn't pull back though he kissed her hard and she moaned against his mouth. His hand on her hip as he rolled her to her back until he was above her, she moaned and pressed her mouth to his but he held himself back and pulled away. Her head spun, *what had he been saying?*

"But?" She asked, her breaths coming harder as she looked up at him. His green eyes were darkened by arousal and she could see the tension in his shoulders as he kept himself away from her.

He leaned back from her more and chuckled bitterly, "I've never been in this situation before, I've never been the Dominant to someone like you, and I've definitely never *bought* someone."

"And?" She asked, wanting to pull him down over her after all of his gentle touches, his liquefying massage, and then his kiss which had ramped up the pulse of need between her thighs; taking her back to that moment in the car when he'd stared at her hungrily.

"It has to be your choice, pet. What will you call me — Sir or Master?" His voice was still low and direct, but it was a choice. He was giving her another choice, but this one made her stomach twist with anxiety. She didn't want to choose, she just wanted him to tell her what to say so she couldn't choose incorrectly. It felt like a test she could fail even though he seemed more focused on her mouth than her answer. And what if she failed? Would his whole demeanor change?

Anxiety and indecision made her shake a little as her body urged her to run. That futile fight or flight instinct that had caused so much trouble over the last week. She had to remind herself she was relatively safe, that James had not done anything without her permission, and she made herself think about his question. She kind of wanted to call him sir, because Master had been something Marcus forced out of her.

But that would mean Marcus was the only one she'd really called Master.

She couldn't handle that.

Just like she wanted to take 'chair' back from Anthony, she could take 'Master' back from Marcus.

"Master." She spoke her answer softly, and he groaned above her and then quickly gripped the back of her neck to pull her up to his lips. His tongue swept into her mouth and she moaned against him, pushing her hands into his hair again. His fist tightened in her hair at the back of her head, and he held her back when he lifted his head again.

"I didn't think that was the answer I wanted until I heard you say it." His eyes moved down her body greedily and she wanted to complain that his clothes were still on, that he wasn't against her. Her skin was humming and he'd barely touched her.

"Why, Master?" She murmured, and he groaned again. His hand slid between her legs and she bucked her hips and gasped loudly as his fingers moved over her clit and he found her soaking wet. Pleasure tightened around the base of her spine and tore her breath from her lungs.

"Because you're mine now, not his." James growled the words out as his fingers slid inside her and she arched off the bed as his thumb rolled over her clit, her voice shouting something unintelligible. "And I have never wanted someone twenty-four seven like Marcus demands, but I wanted *you*, and we will find a balance." Thalia twisted her hands in the sheets as he moved his fingers inside her again. "I promise, in time we'll find a balance."

"Okay... yes... okay, Master." She didn't know what balance he was talking about; she just wanted to feel him against her skin. Thalia had lifted her back and her hips off the bed, so her front was brushing against James' shirt and pants. He was torturing her by staying suspended above her. She didn't want to focus on the future, it was too much to absorb at once. What she wanted was him to help her lose herself after this insane day. "Please, Master..."

"Please, what, pet?" He grinned down at her. That wicked smile sneaking back across his lips, his thumb rolled her clit again and she whimpered. "Tell me."

She bit her lip sharply. His fingers moved inside her as she felt herself moving closer and closer to the edge, his thumb rolling her clit sending sharp shots of pleasure up her spine to rebound back down between her thighs. She let her hips fall back to the bed, squirming against his hand as he drove her need higher, and higher, until she finally caved. "Please... please fuck me, Master!"

He growled and kissed her hard, "Of course, whatever you want, pet." He was off the bed in a moment, and she stared openly as he unbuttoned his shirt and then tugged off his undershirt. His skin was even, a dusting of blond curls across his broad chest. He was fit, his arms looked strong, and her eyes fell to the V of his hips that disappeared below his belt line. She swallowed as he hooked his thumb into his pants and she looked up into a grin on his face. Her blush heated her cheeks, but he didn't call her out for staring. When his pants were off she was surprised at the size of the bulge in his boxers for a moment before his cock was out and his hand gripped it. Thick and already hard as steel, the head dark and shiny with precum.

Thalia had propped herself up on her elbows while he tore a foil packet and then slid the condom down. As he stepped back toward the bed she reached for his cock but he grabbed her wrist and she flinched. His touch immediately gentled, his thumb rubbing across the fine bones there. "While I would love to know what your touch would feel like, I'm afraid after everything this evening I know I couldn't handle it." He turned her hand over and placed a small kiss across her knuckles, as she realized he'd complimented her. "Especially if you still want me to fuck you."

She nodded and held her breath as he climbed onto the bed, his fingers tracing from her shoulders, down the sides of her breasts, across her ribs and down to her hipbones. His palms pressed her hips into the bed and his mouth closed over her nipple, and she cried out at the pleasurable tugging. The break in his touch hadn't mattered, it had shoved her right back to the edge and she whined as his hand moved over her pussy again, the wetness that had gathered had flooded her upper thighs and his fingers swept it up to smooth it over her lips and clit.

"Please…" She felt herself say it as his knees pushed hers farther apart. He slid his fingers from her and she felt the head of his cock press against her, and she tried to lift her hips but he held her still.

"Last chance, Thalia. Are you okay?" His own breathing was harsh, but he was still asking her. She didn't just want him, she needed this right now. She nodded, her hands lightly touching his sides as she was suddenly unsure of what she should do with them. He groaned, "Thank god." Then he pressed inside her, part of the way and waited as she adjusted. He stretched her and she moaned softly against his shoulder as his body lowered against hers. His elbows were braced close to her body, his arms under her shoulders so he could hold her there. He gripped her shoulders a little harder as he withdrew and thrust forward again. Her body arched against his as he filled her, and she heard him mumble a curse and he pressed her to the bed with his hips. One of his hands moved up into her hair to hold her still, and she obeyed the unspoken request to let him set the pace.

As much as she wanted just a little more, she waited for him to start moving. The pending orgasm sending her teetering closer to the edge as he really started to move inside her. Pulling back and thrusting hard. She moaned as she felt herself sliding ever nearer to that glorious abyss, his cock fueling her need, and she could feel his muscles tense and bunch beneath her hands. His hand gripped the back of her neck and she moaned louder. He shifted his hips and the new angle rubbed against that bundle of nerves inside her and she screamed out her request, "PLEASE, Master, please may I?" He groaned against her ear as his forehead pressed into the pillow.

"Wait. Breathe through it." The command made her whine, but she took a breath to push back the orgasm as it threatened to overwhelm her. His hand slid back into her hair and when he tugged, it almost sent her over. She screamed and bucked against him and he growled and stilled inside her. Their breaths were harsh as they mingled between them, and she was moments from begging him again to let her come. Then she slowly felt herself move a little back from the dangerous edge she'd been on, and he pulled back and thrust inside her slowly. She was wrong, the abyss was still there and he was stroking her deep inside to keep her there. Her hips lifted against his in time to his patient thrusts, her fingers clenched into his hips and he groaned. She was soon arching against him, twisting beneath him as he kept the pace just slow enough to keep her from shattering.

She gritted her teeth as another whine escaped her lips, "Please, please, please!" The orgasm had crested even higher now, the urge to fall over the edge uncomfortable in the tension in her lower belly. The pulse in her clit was intense, but he kept pushing her further. His steady movements inside her making her pant and whimper.

"Come for me, pet." His growling voice in her ear was almost enough to send her over on its own, but then he thrust hard inside her and she fell apart. Light burst behind her eyes and she screamed out her pleasure as the orgasm rebounded when she heard him groan and thrust deep inside her. She felt his cock swell and then jerk as he came, his fist tight in her hair as he pressed her into the bed.

"Thank you… thank you, Master." Thalia half-moaned it as her muscles shivered under him. She realized she had hooked her ankles behind his thighs and her fingers were pressed into his hips. Consciously she released her hold on him, but he sighed against her neck and placed a kiss there, inching his way back to her mouth. The heat in his kiss wasn't dimmed by the orgasm; he still kissed her like he wanted to take her again and again. She found herself moaning and she shifted her hips, but he broke the kiss and pressed her hips back to the bed.

"Thank you for trusting me, pet." He placed a soft kiss against her lips before sliding out of her while holding the condom in place. His hand brushed over her stomach before he slid off the bed and moved to the bathroom.

She sat up, surprised for a moment.

He'd never restrained her. Never pinned her. He'd even asked her if she was sure. Tears burned the edges of her eyes, but she swept them away not wanting to explain they were from relief — he wasn't like Marcus or Anthony. He was something new. He fell back onto the bed next to her, running his hand through her hair as he looked into her eyes. "Are you alright?" He asked with more than a touch of concern in his voice.

"What?" She shook her head and made herself look over at him confidently, "I mean, yes, Master, I'm alright." She lay back down and he pulled the sheets up over them both.

"You should sleep, pet. Today has been intense, and we leave tomorrow as soon as your documents arrive."

"Documents?" She asked, turning on her side to look into his green eyes, her eyes tracing the edge of light along his jaw that left part of his face in shadow.

"After Anthony receives the payment, he'll send over your license, your passport, et cetera." He said it clearly but it was a reminder of the situation she was in. She could only nod. "Then we leave."

"May I ask where, Master?" She whispered the question, and his hand reached across the inches between them to brush his fingers down her arm and hold her fingers in his. A smile tugged at his lips.

"London, pet. Home." Her eyes widened, she'd only had the passport for a weekend trip to Mexico once after she'd won a free two-night stay at some cheesy resort. She'd never traveled more than that. Deep inside she was excited. No matter what, she'd see more of the world starting tomorrow than she'd ever had a chance to before.

"I've never—" she started but he shushed her, holding her fingers a little tighter.

"Sleep, pet, I promise we'll talk more in the morning." His voice had regained the edge of a command and her head calmed down. She nodded and inched closer to him. He pressed a kiss on her lips. "Close your eyes." She did, and at some point she fell asleep feeling the soft exhale of his breath across her forehead.

Chapter Three
THALIA

Leaving the country had been an insane whirlwind. She'd flown first class for the only time in her entire life, and the plane had seats that basically became beds for the long transatlantic flight.

The airport before the flight had been… difficult. James watched her like she was wearing a giant 'FRAGILE' label across her forehead. He wheeled his suitcase and kept her hand in his as they had moved through the airport. They'd only been separated at security, and he'd had to pull her against him near a wall after she'd almost had a panic attack when a TSA agent had wanted to wave a wand over her. When the agent had pointed to the floor in front of him, James had to call her name to keep her from dropping into a kneel. Her reaction had made *James* nervous, she could tell, but he played it off. He'd held her until she'd stopped shaking, whispering over and over that it was okay, he wasn't upset with her, assuring her that no one had noticed.

He had given her a sleeping pill to take for the flight and kept her by the window so no one could reach her without moving by him. At one point on the flight she'd woken up drowsy and confused about where she was, panic rising fast and she had made some noise that had him gently covering her mouth and whispering soothing words to her. James had been sitting up working on his laptop but he leaned down by her, telling her it was okay, reminding her where she was, saying he was watching over her. He continued to talk until the effects of the pill took her back under.

The airport in London was massive and confusing, but they were out relatively quickly and in a car and on their way to James' apartment; except he called it a *flat*. It was surrounded by beautiful older buildings, near several parks, and his flat seemed to take up the entire floor it was on; he'd had to insert a key in the elevator control panel to even get floor four to light up.

Thalia had been awed by the size of it. It felt like the floorplan of a house, not an apartment, and it was inside the city and near everything. He had given her a tour and then put her in bed to sleep, blackout blinds blocking out the sunlight as she slipped back into unconsciousness.

Their first three weeks together were all about *trust*.

That's what James told her. He talked about what it meant to be Dominant or submissive. He explained limits and what they were and why they were important. He promised to never violate them, and then he helped her make their list. Her first was easy: No electricity. He had kissed her and promised it wouldn't happen. The others became easier after his assurance: he would never strike her face, he would endeavor to only leave marks she could easily cover and never any permanent marks, he would not draw blood, no bathroom play. She asked for him not to take pictures or video without permission. He'd agreed that if he wanted them, they'd discuss it. Then she'd asked him through tears not to sell her, and he had cursed, and told her it would *never* happen. Together they listed each of the limits and reread them. They agreed and he kissed her wrists where the faint green and yellow bruises were almost gone.

She asked about his rules in their first few days, and he had seemed surprised, casually listing a few about honesty and respect. Then mentioned that they'd discuss ones specific to their play when they had their first session. Thalia had panicked. She had too many questions, she didn't know what she could do and couldn't do. The openness of his design made her feel like the floor was sliding out from under her, the pending threat of some great and terrible error that she could make causing her anxiety to skyrocket. He could see it. Could hear it in her rapid breaths and her concerned whine as she asked for more clarification, more details, more rules. James had sighed and said that, for her, he would change the scope and was going to add rules to his normal list, but that they could change as they found the balance that worked for them. For their beginning, the rules would always be in place inside his flat. *Never* when they were outside of the flat; and he made her promise to act as normally as possible when they were out, and she had even though she wasn't quite sure what that meant anymore. Inside the flat she would kneel when he entered a room but would not crawl after him. She would always call him Master in the house, and she would use 'sir' or nothing outside of it. She would keep the flat clean, and herself fit in the small home gym he had for himself. When they had sex she would still ask permission to come, she would still obey him. She would always be respectful, but he reminded her that he *wanted* her to speak to him. Just expressing an opinion would not be punished. Things that would warrant discipline: dishonesty, disrespect, defiance, breaking a rule, or endangering herself by not using the safe word. Punishments could be paused using the safe word to address why she needed to use it, but it wouldn't cancel the punishment she'd earned.

And with that, she had clear boundaries. She had limits. She had a Dominant and a Master.

She had a framework to function inside. And where Marcus had never really stuck to his, James was consistent. Twice in their first week she had grown frustrated when he asked her questions that she wasn't sure how to answer and she had shouted at him that he should 'stop making her answer him.' Giving him a command? *Not a good idea.* He had clearly been irritated, but in full control. The spankings he'd given her both times had left her ass red and had her sleeping on her stomach for a night each. But after each punishment, she was forgiven completely.

No lingering anger, no threats, no fear.

She knew they were okay, and after the second punishment she realized she felt *better* that he'd addressed it instantly. It didn't hang over her as if he would suddenly bring it up again or hold it against her.

He was also never immune to her distress; he cared and he showed it. The nightmares started after the first week. She would wake up in the night unable to breathe, having dreamt of Marcus on top of her, of being unable to move while he hurt her and shouted at her, over and over. In the nightmares she couldn't speak. There was no safe word. There was no escape. The first time she'd woken up screaming James had reached to comfort her and she had screamed again and tried to push him away. Instead of pressing it he had moved to give her space and turned on the light so she could see where she was, and he had spoken softly to her reminding her of what had happened. After a few minutes he had opened his arms and she had curled against his side and cried until she was worn out and fell back to sleep.

Their first month was as 'vanilla' as he could manage, or so he said, because he wanted her healed before their first session. He still pulled her hair and made her ask permission to come, sometimes he pinned her — and the nights she earned discipline she could see his struggle not to do more. Even when she told him she was ready to submit with him, to go further, he would trace a fading bruise on her skin, or push her back to lift her feet and check the almost healed cuts there, before firmly telling her, "No."

It was the second month when he finally gave her the news she'd been waiting for.

"You're all healed, pet." He grinned down at her as he finished running his hands down her sides, and she smiled back. She was on her back on their bed as he looked for every mark he'd memorized from her time with Marcus. All gone now like they'd never happened. Except for the faint lines of healing skin on the soles of her feet and the tattoo that would never go away. None of that bothered her though, because they were just part of her history; a history that the tattoo would permanently remind her of. Something she could look at and remember that she had survived it. A rush of energy flooded her, her mind lighting up with ideas.

"A session?! Does that mean we'll have a session, Master?" The excitement in her voice may have come across as a little desperate. While he had absolutely fucked her wonderfully hard over and over in their first four weeks together, and she had come often and loudly, it wasn't a Dominant with his submissive — or at least based on what she *knew* it wasn't. Which, admittedly, wasn't much. She did know for sure that other than setting limits and following his rules they hadn't addressed what she supposedly was: sexually submissive. He had promised he would plan a session when she was healed, and when he could control the marks on her skin.

She'd spent hours running in his gym, moving through long memorized sun salutations, and thinking about what the idea of being submissive meant. What had it been about the things Marcus had done that she liked? Why had he called her responsive, and why had James had echoed that phrase? The memory of the belt on her skin, of being tied down, of the rope and the nipple clamps, of him keeping her on edge for hours until she begged and pleaded for him to fuck her, to help her come — all of it ran through her mind. When she thought of Marcus doing it she felt sick, but when she imagined James she was instantly wet.

She wanted to know what it was like with him. What it was like when she consented.

His mouth came down over hers and snapped her back as she listened to the low rumble of laughter in his chest. She moaned as he kissed her, her excitement building, wondering what he had planned for her. "Yes, pet, we will have a session, I promise you, but something else first." Her excitement soared, and then stuttered. She pulled her brows together as she looked up at him.

"What's first, Master?" Her voice came out with more whine than she meant it to. Weeks before he'd had them both tested at a local clinic and they were clean. She hadn't even thought of it with Marcus, and she was relieved James had taken care of it. So, with that out of the way what else could there be? She almost resorted to begging when he started talking.

"Most women wouldn't look so distressed about being taken shopping." He smiled at her but her jaw just dropped open.

"Master! Shopping?!" She asked a little loudly, exasperated and still solely focused on identifying what being a submissive meant. *That* was what she wanted to do, she wanted to figure out if Marcus had been right, if that was what she was, and James had promised to help her, to show her! She'd been waiting for weeks for him to agree she was healed. Each time he'd taken her to bed and he held her firmly, or he bit her nipple or her skin, or his hand wound in her hair she had felt her body respond. *That* is what she wanted to explore. She didn't want to go shopping.

"Yes, shopping, Thalia." His voice was stern and it instantly chastened her urge to beg. "You need clothes for when we go out and I've had to guess at what you'd like and your sizes because I couldn't very well take you somewhere where they might see you covered in his marks." James' voice had the edge of anger it always did whenever he referred to Marcus' hands on her.

"Yes, Master." She mumbled, but his fingers lifted her chin to bring her eyes back to his.

"And once we've gone shopping, then I can give you some marks of my own in a session, pet." A wicked smile tugged at his mouth and she grinned.

"Prom—"

"I promise." He interrupted her, and quickly leaned back, rolled her over and delivered a sharp swat to her ass that made her yelp in surprise. "Now stop questioning me and get dressed to go."

She smiled into the sheets but wiped it off her face as she sat up and responded, "Yes, Master." Then she rushed to get ready. The sooner the shopping was over, the sooner she could have her first session that would be, as he said, SSC — *safe, sane, and consensual.*

Three things that had never been true with Marcus.

Thalia always tried to look good when she went out with him. It had been rare so far, quick trips just to get her outside and around people, but he always looked so *nice*. It made her nervous just in deciding what to wear. She pulled on a blue blouse he liked and a white skirt that skimmed her knees. She slipped her feet into a pair of sandals and walked into the living room. She was about to slide into a kneel when his hand caught her elbow, "No, Thalia, don't ruin your skirt." He stepped around her and traced his thumb just below her lip, his voice gentle. "What are the rules when we go out?"

"I have to act normal." She said it flatly, bitterly. Because she never felt right when they were out and he knew it.

"Are you wanting to earn a punishment, pet?" His tone held an edge to it and there was no confusion that if she kept up the smart responses he'd make her regret it.

"No, Master. I'm sorry, Master." She took a breath, "I must refer to you as sir, or leave off the address completely. I must look at you, and others, normally. I am not to display submissive behavior that would draw attention. I'm supposed to act like myself." The last line he had told her so many times — but it just didn't work. She was hyper aware of herself now, of how she stood in relation to him and anyone else. Other times her mind was so focused on him that it became difficult to be aware of others. With the opportunity to observe him acting naturally, it's all she wanted to do. The way he talked to people, smooth and charismatic, his confidence drawing people like moths to a flame. She couldn't tear her eyes away. She was so distracted she could barely form a sentence around him at times.

If she was honest, Thalia had never been great at being *normal* before. She was fucking terrible at acting normal now.

"Good girl, Thalia. If you make it through today without causing any scenes, we'll have a session this evening." His voice was still strong and direct, but the end held a hint of his smile. Her spirits lifted instantly. She could buy a few outfits and be back soon to finally see what being with James, the Dominant, would be like.

Chapter Four
THALIA

Soon? She couldn't have been more wrong.

James spent the next six hours taking her to designer stores all over London. He bought her dresses, casual clothes, shoes and accessories. He basically let the people who worked at the shops dress her like a doll and then he said yes or no and swiped a card.

Thalia got in trouble with him early on in the day when she approached him outside a shop she was supposed to be in, and quietly asked him if he had planned the day around the movie Pretty Woman. He had gritted his teeth, reminded her very quietly that she was *not* a whore and that if she didn't want to earn a punishment as his submissive, she'd better go back inside and select some clothes. She had obeyed but couldn't keep herself from laughing at her own joke as she did. It was ridiculous not to see the connection. Handsome wealthy gentleman? Check. Female, purchased, sexual object totally out of her depth socially? Check. Very expensive shopping trip? Check. When she'd turned around in the shop she'd found him smiling to himself as he stared down at his phone outside the front window. James had agreed with her whether or not he wanted to admit it.

However, that was the last entertaining moment of the trip for her.

Only a few times did Thalia like something enough to mention it, but he always added it to the yes list. She'd never cared much about clothes, and the longer they spent shopping the more anxious she grew. But it made sense she needed more than the handful of items he'd previously bought for her. He had mentioned they'd be traveling for his work soon, so the shopping wasn't optional. It also made sense why he'd waited until the marks on her skin had faded, because the women working at the shops constantly 'peeked in' to see if an item fit, or if they liked it on her. It would have been a great way for James to be answering some awkward questions with the employees, or the police.

The women surrounded her and asked her so many questions about James every time he stepped out of the shops to take calls or send emails. Each time it happened, the panic would creep in. They'd surround her or tap on the changing room door, speaking brashly in giggling voices. How did they meet? Where in America was she from? Had they met here, there? Then they talked about how handsome he was, made comments and asked about how he was in bed — it all left Thalia tongue-tied and blushing and wanting to hide from them. She couldn't even explain it to James, couldn't form the words to beg him not to leave her alone in a store again. They mocked her for her inability to answer their questions, asking why she was being so modest, so shy, why wouldn't she talk with them, 'just with the girls.'

But James caught on after a few hours that she wasn't doing well.

She wouldn't eat lunch, and she finally started shaking at the last shop when one of the girls brazenly asked what she was willing to do in bed to nab a guy like him. He had come back in and seen she was about to cry so he finally ended the trip. He held her tightly in a hug for the briefest of moments outside the store and whispered that he was there for her, he wasn't going anywhere, and that they would head home immediately — and they did.

Once they had all of the boxes and bags inside, Thalia slid into a kneel and felt an easing to the tightness in her chest. The cool, quiet of his flat and being alone with him again did a lot to soothe her. She felt herself sliding into the calm of what he referred to as her submissive mindset. Any time he caught her relaxing into an aspect of submission, he had tried to make her aware of the change in herself. She was aware, she felt it, she enjoyed it. And she wondered if he'd notice now.

"Strip." James said as he walked past her to their bedroom. She took a step after him and he added, "Stay there." His voice was already different, his posture strong and confident. After the anxiety of the day, she was grateful for him giving her clear direction. Her body was wound so tight she couldn't even think straight as she slid the clothes off and folded them against the wall.

Naked and back in the kneel she was able to breathe better, her lungs filling more deeply.

Then her breath stopped completely when he walked back into the living room. Everything about him had changed like a switch had been flipped. He wore loose black pants low on his hips, revealing the incredible V inside his hipbones. Her eyes moved up his smooth stomach, over his chest and the clean lines of his collarbones. His arms were relaxed at his sides, but everything about him drew her attention. He seemed even taller than usual, and although she hadn't dared to look at his eyes yet, she could feel them on her like she had the night of the party. His glance brushed her skin and made her shiver. "Master?" Her voice wavered.

"Yes." His response both answered her and accepted the title. It sent a chill down her back. Even his voice was different. Low and steady and serious. He pointed at the floor in front of him, "Crawl to me, pet."

Her stomach did an excited little flip. This wasn't the James that teased her about coffee, or the James that gently kissed her when he woke her in the mornings. This was James the Dominant, her Master, the one she'd chosen to go with, and it seemed she'd finally be allowed to be his submissive. "Yes, Master." She crawled to him slowly, aware of the way her breasts swayed with each movement. When her knees were close to his feet she sat back into a kneel. His thumb traced her jaw line, and then he tilted her head back until she looked up at him.

His eyes were dark, bottle glass green, and there wasn't a hint of playfulness in his expression. "Tell me your safe word so I know you remember it."

"My safe word is chair, Master." Her voice was breathy quiet, her heart beat racing in her ears.

"Use it if you have to. I won't stop until the session is over for anything other than the safe word, but I will stop immediately and unbind you if you say it, do you understand?" He said it with an urgency to his voice.

"Yes, Master, I understand that I should say the safe word if I need to and that if I do you will stop and release me if I'm bound." Thalia repeated it so he would know she understood. She felt the need to add, "I'm submitting willingly, Master, I want this."

His firm grip on her chin relaxed and a smile flashed across his lips, "I want this too, pet, and I think we've been very patient. Are you ready?"

"Yes, Master." She said it excitedly. Butterflies filled her stomach and made her skin hum as his eyes scalded her with the heated look he gave her body.

"Then follow me, stay on your knees." He turned down the hall and stopped at the one door that had always been locked. It was maybe fifteen feet but in crawling after him she felt her whole body tensing in anticipation. He took a key out of his pocket and opened the door. It was a room similar to the one in Marcus' house but on a much smaller scale. She moved through the doorway and knelt just inside near the wall, her eyes wide as she looked around. Her mind was racing with what he had planned. What items in the room would he use? There was so much to look at. A large cabinet that she knew would hold a variety of toys, a large X installed against one wall. A table in one corner, a full-sized bed in the other, a wide padded bench at the foot of the bed. In the center of the room was something like a gymnastics horse, but he stepped in front of her and blocked her view of it. Out of reflex she almost looked up at him but caught herself.

"Thalia, our sessions will always begin when this door shuts, and end when I open it again. Understand?" His voice held that edge to it that sent thrilling shivers down her back. "The room is soundproofed on all sides, so in this space there is no need to be quiet, and I don't want you to be. You're free to scream if you need to." Her heart thundered in her ears, a heady mixture of fear at what he might do to make her scream, and excitement for the same reason, sent her head spinning.

"Yes, Master," she spoke in a shaky voice.

His finger touched under her chin and tilted her head back so she was looking at him. The expression on his face was dark and hungry, "You are mine, beautiful." His words left her mind blank, and she only nodded. He let go of her chin and the door slammed at the same time making her jump, her body surging with adrenaline that only served to put her more on edge.

Her first session was starting.

James walked to the center of the room and pushed the horse back toward the wall. His steps brought him back to her and his fingers slid under the thin collar around her neck to draw her to her feet. He didn't speak as he moved her to the middle of the room and turned her to face the door. His hands ran down her arms and then he slid a wide cuff around each wrist, tightening them firmly. With a quick movement he linked the cuffs together in front of her with a clink. Then he smoothly drew them over her head to connect the cuffs to a carabiner at the end of a chain that went into the large tiles that covered the ceiling and the walls and the floor. He stepped back from her and she felt a blush flood up her chest, as his eyes devoured her pale skin.

James moved to the cabinet and opened it. A variety of items were hanging from hooks, and several drawers were beneath them. He took out a long piece of dark metal with cuffs at either end and turned back to her, leaving the doors open. She realized she'd been holding her breath and she gasped slightly when he knelt down in front of her. His touch was gentle on her ankles as he wrapped the cuffs around each of them. When he spoke the edge in his voice ramped her tension higher, "This is called a spreader bar." Something clicked and the metal extended pushing her legs apart. He stopped when her feet were almost uncomfortably wide, and he didn't need to explain it further.

"Yes, Master." She said softly. His hands traced up the outsides of her legs, over her hips, her waist, until he cupped her breasts and rolled her nipples between his fingers. She moaned and pressed her chest forward into his hands. James turned back to the cabinet and opened a drawer then returned to her. His mouth closed over one nipple and the tugging had her arching toward him, then he bit down enough to make her cry out. The zing of pain shot down her spine and made her clit pulse, her hips bucked and then he released her nipple.

"Your body is incredible, pet. So responsive." He repeated his attentions on the other nipple and then held up two beautiful black clips with shiny dark beads dangling from each. "I'm going to decorate you. Be still for me." She recognized them as nipple clamps instantly and her mind fought to push back the memories of Marcus and the hours she'd spent with the rope — she bit her lip against the yelp as the first one bit down. Thalia shook her head a little and focused on James, his strong jaw line, the angle of his shoulders. His hands, they were *his* hands on her. The second one bit down and her cry was a little louder, but she trusted him and that meant she could let go. She wasn't afraid of him.

"Breathe, pet. Remember to breathe." His voice was soothing as his eyes locked onto the dark beads against the pale skin of her breasts. "You are so beautiful." He knelt again and she expected him to push her legs farther apart with the bar, but instead his tongue brushed up her slit. She moaned and clenched her fists. Stretched as she was she couldn't push her hips forward more than an inch or so, but he groaned against her core as she tried. His tongue swept slowly again from her perineum, between her lips, until he finally sucked her clit gently. Thalia whined as his gentle licking stoked the heat inside her, making her pull against the cuffs on her wrists to try and get more. It distracted her from the clamps until they became a dull background ache to the pounding pleasure between her thighs. He stood up suddenly and thrust two fingers inside her, before he tilted her head back with a fist in her hair. When he kissed her she tasted herself and she moaned loudly against his mouth. Her hips rolled in time with the thrusts of his fingers, and she felt that glorious edge rising to meet her. Her pulse racing, the muscles in her belly tightening, the moan rising in her throat.

Then he stopped.

She panted and jerked in the bindings as he stepped back from her and watched her whine and struggle against the cuffs. Other than the slight flush in his cheeks, she'd never know he was affected at all. He was stoic, his breathing even, his dark green eyes moving like heat across her skin. Her thighs were wet and her pussy clenched tightly against the absence of his fingers, "Please, Master?"

"Not yet, pet. You may not come without my permission, if you do you will earn a punishment, understand?" His voice was lower, and it had that delicious bite to it that made her legs weak, but he still spoke so evenly. How was he so much calmer than her?

"Yes, Master, I understand." It came out as a whine, but she tried to take a breath to push herself back from the edge he'd brought her to.

"Good. Let's begin."

Chapter Five
THALIA

He turned back to the cabinet and she was stunned, he hadn't started their session yet? What would starting be? What did he have planned? All questions she wanted to ask, but the words disappeared in her mouth as he took out something that looked like a many tailed, short whip from the cabinet.

"This is a flogger, Thalia." He held it in front of her so she could see it clearly. It was black with a braided handle and a lot of long strands hanging from it. "I'm going to use this on you, and it will sting and light your skin up beautifully. I want to see your skin turn pink under my hand. It will not hurt much at first but it will build on itself," he stepped close to her and his skin brushed against the nipple clamps making her moan. His free hand wrapped gently around her throat as he leaned her head back, "Be as loud as you need to, pet, I want you pink all over." Her pussy clenched at his words.

"Yes, Master." Her voice shook as she said it, her body taut as a bowstring after the stress of the day, the long wait for this moment, and then him bringing her right to the edge of orgasm. He placed a gentle kiss on her lips and released her throat to walk around her.

"Your skin is so pale, pet." The strands of the flogger flashed across her ribs with a thump, the tips lighting up in stings where they landed. She gasped at the first sensation. "Lovely." He almost whispered it, but it made her soar on the inside that he found so much pleasure in her skin. The strikes began to land steadily across her ribs, her back, and then started to trail down the round of her ass. The stings quickly faded into heat in her skin, and she felt fine for a while as the flogger moved down her thighs, and her calves. He stepped around to her front and she bit her lip as she saw the controlled expression on his face before she dropped her eyes. He made her feel beautiful, his comments on her skin changing her mindset from being the girl who couldn't tan to save her life, to her pale skin making her someone who was wanted, craved.

"Thank you, Master." She moaned at his first strike across the fronts of her thighs. A growl came out of his chest as the flogger wrapped around her hip and the tips struck the already sensitive skin of her ass. She yelped, and he repeated the strike on her other side. She arched in the restraints as the skin of her ass lit up again.

"Thalia." The flogger swept across her stomach and her pussy tightened, her clit aching. She twisted in the cuffs, the spreader bar keeping her legs from closing as she realized she was building toward an orgasm. "Who do you belong to?"

"You, Master." She almost shouted it, taking deep breaths as the flogger swept across her right breast and her clamped nipple made her cry out. He did it again on her left breast and she screamed and jerked in the cuffs as a quick pain shot down her spine.

"Say that you're mine." His voice was low and strained, and she wanted to look into his eyes but she kept them down. The next strike came between her legs, and she screamed again, biting down on her lip as his command sank in. The pain across her clit holding the orgasm at bay.

"I'm yours, Master!" she shouted, and the flogger came up between her legs again, her swollen clit aching. Tears were at the edges of her eyes but she took a shuddering breath.

"Yes, you are, pet. Now tell me why you're mine." He dropped the flogger on the floor in front of the cabinet and took out a black strip of leather that looked like a belt without the metal fixtures.

Her breath caught as she stared at it hanging at his side, his strong hand holding it in a loop. "Bec-because you bought me, Master."

James stood to her side, brought back the strap and laid it across her ass. She jerked forward in the restraints and instantly started crying as the sharp burst of pain faded to blend with the heat in her already over sensitive skin. His voice was steady and clear, "Wrong. Anyone could have bought you, pet. Buying you just took you from Marcus and Anthony. Think back, why are you mine specifically?"

She shook her head as she felt the tears streak her cheeks. *If that was the wrong answer, what did he want?* He didn't wait. He laid the strap across her ass again, a little below the last one and she bucked again and cried out.

"Answer me, pet. Refusing to answer is not an option." She twisted in the restraints and gritted her teeth against the whimpering sounds coming out of her mouth. Thalia made herself remember the auction, and the panic and the fear and how terrified she had been of what Marcus would do. How Marcus had reacted when James had said he'd take her, that he was going to buy her.

"Master, I'm yours. Please..." she begged, her skin was electric and too sensitive from the flogger. The strap hurt a lot more, and he brought it across her a third time and she screamed again. She jerked in the cuffs as frustration built in her. *What did he want?!*

"Think, Thalia. Why are you mine and not still with Marcus?" His voice was tinted with anger, like it always was when he spoke about Marcus. The same tone he'd had every time he'd reviewed her marks. It had become clear that he didn't just disagree with Marcus like he'd said that night, he hated him. A fourth lash of the strap had her screaming and begging.

"Please, Master, please, I'm yours, I'm yours, I'm yours—"

"Stop. Answer me why." He said it louder and she whimpered as she saw him appear on her other side with the strap. A fifth stripe went across the backs of her thighs and she sobbed.

"Because I chose you, Master! I wanted to go with you, please, Master, stop! I'm sorry!" She was shouting through her tears and she jumped when his warm palm started to rub across her ass and the backs of her thighs. The strong, soothing movements of his palm helped even out the stinging skin as he whispered against her ear.

"Shh, pet, shh. That's right, you're here with me because you chose it. I asked you if you wanted to come with me and you said yes. I asked you if you wanted to submit to me, and you said yes. And you're doing beautifully, you are perfect, Thalia, bloody perfect." His voice was warm and soothing, but she couldn't stop crying. His hand kept rubbing her skin, letting the heat of the welts absorb. "God your skin is gorgeous like this. All pink from the flogger with the red lines of the strap..." His voice slid into a growl as he continued, "and they're all mine."

"Ye—yes, Master. I'm yours." She said it through hitched breaths as she tried to calm down. His hand slid down her stomach, and his fingers parted the lips of her pussy and she gasped. The flogger had brought her blood to the surface making even the faintest touch between her legs so much stronger.

"I wish I could explain to you how lovely you look right now." His fingers thrust inside her to gather her wetness before bringing it back to her clit to circle it. "Flushed, marked by my flogger and my strap, the way the red stands out on your skin. The way your body looks stretched out and waiting for me, how your swollen pussy tells me you're enjoying everything I give you." His voice was right against her ear, his breath brushing over her neck as she whimpered. His fingers circled her clit in tight movements that spun her higher and higher.

"Master, please, may I come?" She asked him on a moan, her head dropping back against his shoulder, her thighs quivering as the pleasure started to overwhelm her.

"I want you slick when I enter you, so yes, pet, come for me." His other hand moved from behind her and two fingers thrust inside her pussy until she was moaning loudly. The sting of the welts, the bite of the clamps, the intensity of his touch on her clit, and his fingers working inside her — it snapped the tension that he'd wound so slowly through the session. Her orgasm crashed through her and she screamed her release, his chest pressing against her back as her muscles tightened and relaxed rhythmically. James kissed her temple and palmed her pussy as she continued to come against his hand. His palm providing gentle waves of pressure between her legs to drag out her orgasm.

She could feel how wet she was when he swept a finger up her slit. He stepped around in front of her and grinned as he slid his finger between his lips and slowly drew it out. "You are delicious, pet."

Her mouth was dry as she watched him taste her, "Thank you, Master." He knelt down and unlatched her ankles from the spreader bar quickly. When he stood up again he kissed her hard, one hand grabbing the back of her neck to pull her against his mouth.

"Hold on, pet." He tugged down his black hipsters and his boxers, his erection straining up hard against his stomach. His hands went under her thighs and he picked her up swiftly. Thalia's hands grabbed onto the chain that suspended her as she instinctively wrapped her legs around his hips. With a groan he shifted her and thrust inside her in one quick movement, she was over slick and he bottomed out inside her hard. His head was down, his breaths moving over the damp skin of her breasts. "You feel so incredible..." He groaned and lifted her hips, before thrusting hard again.

"Mmm, Master, please..." she couldn't think straight as she moaned. The welts along her ass stung, and her flushed, sensitive skin overloaded her senses. His hard body pressed against hers as he started to move. Each powerful thrust bouncing her against him. At first her body's exhaustion fought the tingling pleasure that pulsed between her thighs each time he brushed against her clit, but as his cock split her over and over, the head driving deep inside her with her hips split wide around him — another orgasm sparked like an electric current down her spine.

"Come for me, pet. I want to feel you come." His voice growled against her ear and he thrust a fist into her hair, yanking her head back so she had to tilt her hips forward to balance. His next thrust undid her, the thrumming energy in her spine exploded between her thighs and she screamed again, vaguely aware as lights danced behind her eyes of his cock growing and kicking inside her until she could feel the sticky heat of his seed flood her.

"Ahhhmmm..." she sighed, moaning against his broad chest. The muscles in her legs and arms were shaking, making her teeth chatter for a second. She heard him growl against her skin, and her arms were released from above her. His arms wrapped tightly around her as James eased them both to the floor, laying her out on her back in front of him as he slid from her.

"Thalia, pet, check in. Are you okay?" His voice had an edge of concern, as his strong, warm hands brushed over her arms, her body. She wanted to tell him she was just fine, that the orgasm had been intense and she just needed a minute — but her brain to mouth connection had a severe lag. He cupped her face and spoke more sternly, "Thalia." Her eyes snapped open to find his incredible sea green eyes poised above her, his yacht club features pinched in concern, his soft lips parted as he took quick breaths from his efforts. She managed to nod, murmuring what she hoped were reassuring noises. The edge of his mouth ticked up into a smile. "Did you enjoy yourself?"

Thalia felt the cat who got the canary grin spread across her face and she practically purred as she stretched out in front of him, nodding slowly, "Mmhmm...".

"Almost done, pet, take a breath for me." His voice had laughter in it and she felt her brows come together as he leaned over her. *What did he mean almost done?*

"Oh my — *fuck!*" She gasped and tried to sit up before his mouth covered the nipple he'd just taken the clamp from. The warm wetness of his mouth soothed the sharp ache as blood surged back into the dark red bud. When he released her nipple with a soft pop, he arched an eyebrow at her.

"Such language." He smiled though as he moved to her other breast. She squirmed and shook her head a little, pleading.

"No, no, no, Master!" The other clamp came off and her back arched, and his mouth closed over the offered breast as he soothed her with his tongue and lips, his palm continuing to rub her other breast gently. She collapsed back against the floor and squirmed as the welts across her backside lit up with each shift of her hips.

His hands slid up her arms and he took the cuffs off, leaving them on the floor as he held himself over her. He buried his face in the space between her neck and shoulder, his teeth nipping at her skin as he tasted her. She groaned as his chest rubbed against her sensitive nipples, but he continued to place little nipping kisses across her skin, tracing across her jaw line until he took her mouth with a searing kiss that cleared her head of all thoughts of her aches.

The man knew how to kiss. He knew how to do a lot of other things too, but god, he could *seriously* kiss.

When he broke away with a moan of his own, she almost pouted. He untangled their legs and pulled his pants into place before scooping her up against his chest.

Walking to the door he adjusted his hold on her to open the door and then stepped into the hallway. "How was your first session, pet?"

"Bloody perfect." She grinned at him and he laughed.

"Don't say that. Americans don't say that." He was laughing at her but she loved it, loved the way his eyes glinted as he slid her down his body so she could stand on her own. James never scared her, he was playful, and kind, and ridiculously hot. His loud laughs made her bite her cheek to stop from smiling.

"Fine then, it was only *incredible*, Master." She scrunched up her nose at him, feigning insult, but he tugged her hips back to him when she tried to step away.

"Just like you, pet, and you're all mine." Then he kissed her again, and she ran her fingers through his soft blond hair.

Now she knew for sure. She wanted this, she wanted him. She wanted this life.

Chapter Six
THALIA

Three Months After the Auction

Thalia stretched in the kitchen thinking about James' hands on her the night before. He'd been working long hours all week and it was finally the weekend. Which meant there was plenty of time for play — as the warm welts along her back and ass attested to. She smiled to herself remembering how he had wound her up with the flogger, waiting until she was begging for his attention before he touched her. And then, like always, she had come under his touch.

Over and over and over.

James was good to her. Really good to her. It had taken some convincing but he had even caved in to having a coffee maker in the house. It had required more convincing to get the one she wanted since it was the type that sounded like a small jet plane every morning as it ground fresh beans to make a pot. She laughed to herself as it turned on, the smell of fresh coffee beans filling the kitchen to her delight. The miserable whirring that accompanied it would surely wake him up, so she had to hurry if she wanted to drink a cup. As soon as she could pour herself some coffee, she did, grabbing the creamer from the fridge. James catering to her mild addiction to coffee was just one of the many things he'd done to make her happy in their first few months together.

She'd gone for a life raft and ended up safe on a ship. Looking around at his beautiful flat, it was more like she'd ended up on a luxury yacht.

She heard James mumbling about the coffee pot as he walked into the kitchen and she sat her mug down on the counter and slid into a kneel. Much more gracefully than she'd been able to manage a few months before. His hand moved into her hair and his nails traced over her scalp as he stepped past her to the pantry.

"Finish making your coffee, pet, but would you make me tea as well?" His voice was always lower in the morning, but regardless his English accent always made her a little giddy inside.

"Yes, Master." She said as she stood again. He brought bread to the counter and sliced off toast for them both while she put water on for tea. She lifted her coffee, but he was suddenly behind her. His hips pressed her forward against the counter and his hand pushed her mug back to the counter. "Let me say good morning before you drink that."

"Yes, Master." She smiled as his lips moved over her neck, and then he touched her chin and leaned her back so he could kiss her. Heat washed over her as his fingers wound in her hair to hold her head back, and he groaned a little against her mouth. Then his fingers tweaked a nipple and he nipped her bottom lip to end the kiss.

"Good morning." He smiled as he stepped back from her.

"Good morning, Master. May I have my coffee now?" She felt her lips curve into a smile. Every morning he was home with her they played this game. Him wanting to touch her before she had coffee. Sometimes teasing her until she gave up the coffee completely just to go back to bed with him.

He gave a slightly sour expression as he put the toast in the oven. "If you must." Then that wicked smile crossed his face, "I'll just have to wash your mouth out when you're done."

She held the mug between her hands and took a long, slow drink, moaning softly at how good it tasted just to draw his attention. "Totally worth it, Master." Thalia knew she was teasing him, and he liked her smart mouth up to a point. It always depended on his mood when he'd cut it off, and how he would.

She bit her cheek against the urge to smile over her coffee cup, and James arched an eyebrow at her. "I think you want me to wash your mouth out." His voice was playful, and heat blossomed between her thighs in anticipation.

"I'm sure you'll think of something better than coffee for me to have in my mouth, Master." She took another drink to hide her grin, her stomach fluttering with her brazen comment as he took the toast out of the oven. She sat her mug down when the kettle finished heating and she began steeping a small pot of tea for him. She was about to reach for her mug again when she heard him make a tsk'ing sound.

"On your knees, Thalia." His voice had the edge of command in it. The one that always made her want to be able to spy on him at work, to see how others reacted to that tone in his voice. For her, it always made her pulse pick up, and her pussy wet. It made her feel a delicious, nervous energy at the unknown of what he'd do next. And as she slid to her knees again she was wholly aware of just how wet he made her.

She was about to turn her face toward him when he placed one of his silken ties over her eyes and tied it firmly at the back of her head. Slips of light snuck around the edges, but his deft fingers adjusted it until she couldn't see enough to make anything out.

"I thought last night would have you somewhat tamer this morning, pet." His voice floated behind her and slightly to the right. It was always dizzying to lose her sight, it left her a little unsure of where she was in the room. His touch surprised her and her body arched forward as his warm fingertips traced over the faint welts she knew were scattered down her backside. It sent a shiver through her. His voice was sharper when he continued. "And yet, you wake me up with that damn coffee pot and then tease me?"

He spanked her hard across the welts and she yelped. It had surprised her more than it hurt, but the heat that suffused her skin made her even wetter. She bit her lip and then said, "I'm sorry, Master."

"Oh, pet…" His hand was in her hair and he tightened it until she moaned. "Your mouth often gets you into trouble, but right now it will be what gets you out of it as well." He bent her head back a little. "Hands behind your back. Release them and you won't be happy with the consequences. Understand?"

She nodded, clasping her hands behind her back. It pulled her shoulders back and lifted her breasts, which he didn't ignore. His palm cupped her breast and squeezed firmly, ending by pinching each nipple until she knew they stood erect in the cool air of the kitchen. "Open your mouth, pet." The head of his cock touched her lips and she slid her mouth around him, reveling in the way his breath caught and he let out a soft groan as she slid him deeper. His fist tightened in her hair and she moaned but he didn't direct her. He did it as a recognition that he liked what she was doing. He had learned quickly how much she liked having him pull her hair. The harder the better. She slid back and then let him deeper into her mouth, swallowing as he hit the back so he could dip into her throat. His groan above her filled her with a warm flush of satisfaction, and she grew even wetter.

Thalia had always enjoyed a blow job. Where else in the bedroom did she have so much control over someone so much stronger than her? Each flick of her tongue, each movement drew out such a powerful response. The feel of his velvety hard cock in her mouth, the way his body tensed and relaxed in waves only to lock up until the tension would snap, and his release would spill into her mouth and throat for her to swallow. An instant acknowledgment of her skill and his satisfaction.

His hips thrust against her suddenly and she heard him groan her name on an exhale, his hand twisting in her hair. She dug her nails into her hands to fight the urge to touch him, so she could push him over the edge with her hands. Instead she sucked him a little harder and let him push himself into her throat, holding her breath as he thrust again. Each swallowing constriction of her throat pushing him closer. She moaned as he slid back and cursed above her as he came in hard pulses in her mouth, his fist tightening in her hair to hold her still. Each swallow came with a soft moan from her and he let out small groans until his hand relaxed in her hair. She trailed her tongue along him as he slid from her mouth. She licked her bottom lip and knew her lips were swollen and wet. He was silent except for his breathing, and then he chuckled and pulled her up gently.

"Now I remember why I let you get the damn coffee pot." His thumb swiped her chin free of saliva and she could tell by his voice that he was smiling.

"Yes, Master." She smiled a little and he made her gasp as he picked her up suddenly. Her head spun in the void of the blindfold and then the cool top of the island in the kitchen was against her shoulders and arms. Her hands were still behind her, and it lifted the small of her back off the counter. He didn't tell her she could release them, and she wasn't going to ask for something so small.

"Spread your knees, pet." His voice came from between her legs and she almost moaned in anticipation as she obeyed.

His hands trailed down her thighs, pushing them farther apart. He started placing gentle, nipping kisses on the inside of her thigh, trailing closer and closer to her core.

Then his touch disappeared.

She floated in the darkness of the blindfold and bit her lip against the urge to complain. She couldn't hear him moving around the kitchen and the idea that he was just standing there staring at her exposed pussy still inspired a blush to rush up her chest no matter how often he'd done it.

Minutes passed and she let out a little whine, her hips lifting slightly as she adjusted her arms underneath her. She was wet, she could feel the air cool between her thighs, and her anxiety was making her skin tingle in anticipation of his touch.

Her mind was totally focused on when and where he'd finally touch her again.

When it eventually came, his touch was feather light, starting at her belly button and trailing down between her legs, brushing over her pussy. It may as well have been a bucket of water over her as loud as she gasped. Her hips lifted to his touch but he didn't increase the pressure. After his third trailing touch like that she arched off the island and groaned, "Master, please! I'm sorry!"

"Sorry about?" His voice held a little laughter in it and she wanted to scream in frustration.

"I'm sorry about waking you up with the coffee maker and teasing you when I drank it! Please, Master!" she begged, her hips lifting again as his hand rested over her pussy, pressing gently against her.

"Please what, pet?" Now she knew he was smiling, she could hear it in his voice. His rhythmic pressure on her clit was making her pant softly.

"Please make me come, Master." He laughed quietly and thrust two fingers inside her, immediately curving them around her pubic bone to press against the bundle of nerves inside her. She arched off the counter and he pressed her hips back down with his other hand. She moaned and squirmed under his hands as the absence of sight and spending so long waiting for his touch made her incredibly sensitive. His warm mouth surrounded her clit, his tongue flicking until she was crying out. He held her down against the island with more force as she edged closer and closer. She gasped in a breath and bit down on her lip, trying to focus enough to ask for permission. He relented on her clit for a moment so she could think enough to shout, "May I please come, Master?!"

He left little nipping kisses down her thigh, dragging out her ecstasy until she whimpered and he spoke. "Come for me, pet." His mouth found her clit again and he thrust his fingers inside her and she came hard, arching up against the pressure of his hand on her hip. Her pussy clenched against his thrusting fingers as he dragged out her orgasm until she was quaking. His fingers slid from her only to be replaced by his mouth as he lapped at her, his own quiet moan between her thighs making her squirm.

"Thank you, Master…" She breathed, as she tried to slow her heart rate down. His hand grabbed her behind her neck and pulled her up toward him where he kissed her hard. She tasted herself on him, moaning as she dug her nails into her palms to keep her hands behind her back and not thrust them into his hair to hold him to her. With a tug he pulled the tie off and she blinked against the light to find James smiling broadly at her.

"You make my day, pet." He kissed her again, biting gently at her lower lip as his hands cupped her face.

She couldn't help but smile back at him. "Ditto, Master. May I release my hands?"

"Yes, pet." She unclasped them and immediately pushed them into his hair, pulling him back to her mouth. Her hips moved to the edge of the island and she wrapped her legs around his waist. He let her kiss him for a moment until her hips began to grind against him.

He was grinning when he grabbed her shoulders and shoved her back down to the island hard. She moaned as he pressed her down, her hips lifting against him above her. His hips dropped against her as he took a breath. "Stop, pet. We're having breakfast, and then I need to work a little. We can play more later."

She pouted a bit, but she relaxed against the island with a sigh. James pulled her back up and tilted her head back by her hair. He arched his eyebrow at her and his fist tightened in her hair sharply as he waited for her response. "Yes, Master" she said and then he kissed her hard, and when he pulled back they were both smiling again.

"Drink your coffee." His voice had a satisfied growl to it that made her stomach flutter. She dumped out her cold coffee and remade her own cup and made him a fresh pot. As she finished making his tea, he made toast for them both and set two plates on the kitchen island. They each took their breakfasts into his office and he settled in at his desk while she knelt on the pillow on the floor next to him.

Chapter Seven
THALIA

The level of comfort they'd developed with their morning routines was something she would have never imagined in her life. She wouldn't have wanted it with any of her exes, and with Marcus? She fought back the urge to physically shudder — it wouldn't have been possible to be like this with him. Playful and smiling and laughing? Never.

Thalia grabbed the book she'd been reading and leaned her head against his thigh as his laptop whirred to life above her. His hand casually moved through her hair as she let herself get wrapped up in the story between bites of toast and sips of coffee. James spent over an hour typing above her and making various phone calls, one of them in French.

She just stared up at him as he spoke in another language, him smiling down at her when he noticed her staring before continuing. She remembered how she'd been surprised that the guard's brother, Anthony, had called him Dr. Hawkins. One of the first questions she'd asked had been about it. He had laughed and said that he wasn't a medical doctor, he *just* had a Ph. D. in business economics. He was an executive at a company based in London, but he traveled often. When he'd first taken her from Marcus she had thought her life would be trapped in a house forever, but it wasn't true at all. He always took her with him. She'd already seen Paris, Dubai, Morocco, and Barcelona. He would dress her in beautiful clothes for the trip, and then hungrily strip her whenever they got to their hotel.

That was usually her favorite part of the trip.

He also liked to take her out to eat, to go shopping, and to the movies. While their earliest outings had been fraught with her own confusion on how to act, she was getting a little better. As long as he was with her.

A heavy sigh came out of his mouth as James glared at the laptop in front of him, his jaw clenched tight above her. He was clearly irritated for a minute and then it faded and he just looked exhausted. He'd been playing with her hair the entire time he was reading the screen, and his fingers worked deeper into her tresses. Then he tightened his grip and tilted her head up to look at him, his green eyes scanning her face. Whatever he found must have made his decision for him, because he spoke. "I have something to share with you, Thalia."

"Yes, Master?" She knew when he used her name it was serious and she felt a little nauseous.

"I want you to know I won't be angry with you no matter how you respond." He unplugged the power cord from the thin laptop and handed it down to her. "Read the email."

She could feel her brow furrow as she took the warm laptop and rested it on her knees. The email on the screen was scrolled back to the top:

```
From: Marcus Williams

To: James Hawkins

James —

I already told you, there are no more girls. I
haven't taken another one since Thalia, and none of
the clients wanted Anthony's feed activated again. I
understand you never saw his methods, but if you had
you probably wouldn't judge me as harshly as you
have. He's furious with me right now for not training
another girl, and I don't care.

I'm telling you, I don't care, about him or any
of it.

I spent years perfecting my methods and I was proud
of what I could do with a girl. Proud that it took me
less than a month to make her a pliant little slave.
Now? I don't care if the business falls apart. It IS
falling apart. That's what you wanted, right? Now you
have it. Just give me Thalia back, or sell her back
to me. I'll pay you twice what you paid for her, and
I'll never take another girl. Three months with her
```

and a nice profit — a smart businessman like yourself wouldn't pass that up.

I promise you it will be different when she's back with me. I'll never let Anthony near her, I'll buy a new place wherever she wants to live. We'll have rules, and a safe word. All of that. I swear it.

You made a lot of good points in the conversation last year about my methods in acquiring and training the girls. I wasn't ready to hear it, but I've thought about it. About why she would have chosen you over me... after everything I showed her.

It doesn't matter now. I'll treat her well. I will. And I know you thought we should have been up front with the fact that the girls didn't come to us to enter the lifestyle voluntarily. Maybe we should have. But if I hadn't taken Thalia, neither of us would have found her. *You* wouldn't have her now.

I know I've asked too many times already to speak with her, but would you at least tell Thalia I want her back. At least give her the opportunity to answer for herself if she'd want to be with me. You were the one who lectured me about trust, and how important it is to treat a submissive well and for the relationship to be consensual. Well, if you believe all of that — then have the balls to find out if she would still choose you.

I knew who she was before she did, and I can give her a fulfilling life. She knows that.

Ask her if you're not a hypocrite.

— Marcus

She finished and slid the laptop off her thighs and onto the floor in front of her. Her stomach twisted and for a second she thought she might be sick as she suddenly became light headed. Marcus had not given up. He still wanted her back. Her mind summoned images from the nightmare of a week she had spent with him. Fear and confusion and ill-defined rules that he sometimes enforced and sometimes didn't. She remembered exactly what it had been like with him as her Master, and how drastically different it had been with James.

James interrupted her thoughts, tucking a strand of hair behind her ear. His voice was distant, "I've only asked you for six months, and we're halfway through that." He sighed and took his hand from her cheek. "If you want to leave at the end of that, even to go back to Marcus, you are free to do so."

Thalia felt a laugh bubble up inside her and it burst from her lips slightly hysterically, "You think I want to go back to him? After this?" She raised her hands to gesture around her, trying to encompass the entire life that James had given her and everything he did for her.

"You wouldn't be the first girl to want to stay with him."

She leaned forward and shut the laptop hard, staring at it while she spoke clearly, "Master, I will never go back to Marcus. I hope his whole world crashes down around him and his sadistic fuck of a brother. I hope he's never able to take another girl. He said he was going to break me, well, I hope I fucking broke *him* when I left." There was silence for a moment interrupted only by her rapid breathing as her anger filled her up.

"I think you did break him, pet." James said softly and grabbed her, pulling her up into his lap. He wrapped his arms around her and buried his face in her hair. His words sent a thrill of satisfaction through her, soothing the anger that had surged. Marcus had threatened to break her, but she'd survived. James had come for her, she had chosen to go with him and she had escaped. Her mind went back to the email and Marcus' references to a discussion.

"May I ask what your conversation with Marcus was? The one he referenced?" She asked it quietly and his breath blew out against her neck.

"I told you at the auction that I didn't agree with his methods, but I didn't originally know them when I was referred to their... *business*." He pressed his forehead against the side of her head, "Honestly, I think I willfully ignored it, so I wouldn't have to think about it. Feel guilty about it. As you know my tastes run... darker, but I genuinely thought the girls were all there willingly. At least at the start I did."

"Yes, Master." She whispered. His voice was a little lower when he spoke again and it sent a hum through her body.

"Their feed was an outlet for me, for those tastes. My last submissive and I had parted ways, and I've never found much pleasure in vanilla relationships." His fingers traced down her spine lightly. "Then I watched a party where a guest asked a question about if the girl fought back often. Marcus said he'd had to knock her out when he *took* her."

Thalia tensed, remembering the stairwell in her office building.

"I confronted Anthony about it first, and he didn't even attempt to deny it. He was very clear with me that if I attempted to cause issues for them they would take action."

"Action? Like what, Master?" Thalia tried to turn to see his face but his arms tightened so she stayed where she was, curled against him in his lap.

"Let's just say he'd implicate me badly enough that no company that had a morality clause would hire me. I'm sure he had more than enough to expose my preferences to family and friends and co-workers alike." James said it like he was tired. "Then, to ensure I remained complicit he said it would be in my best interest to maintain my account with them. It was simple: expose them, or stop paying, and I'd hang myself in the process." His voice was quiet against her hair, and her pulse pounded as she wondered how many people thought it was some elaborate charade. Just a bunch of girls like Anna who had volunteered. That there was some safe word that would stop it all.

And there wasn't. Marcus had never offered anything like that.

"And you went to talk to Marcus too?" She asked.

"He called me, actually. Anthony must have shared my concerns with him, and Marcus' call was much more," he paused, "physically threatening."

"And you—" She started but he kept talking.

"I told him he was a bastard," he said bluntly, and Thalia burst out laughing as she felt the rumble of a laugh in his chest. "I told him he wasn't a real Dominant, or a real Master, that he wouldn't know what that was like unless he made it a consensual agreement. He called me an idiot, I called him a rapist, and it devolved until he hung up on me."

His hand returned to trailing lightly up her back, then down again. Thalia bit her lip as she imagined the two of them arguing over the phone. Marcus passionate and loud, James confident and steady. Two alphas refusing to back down. Except Marcus had apparently been thinking about James' speech all this time.

"I didn't watch his feed at all for a long time. I think you should know that. I sought other outlets, but once or twice in the six months before you, I would cave and access it. Then I'd feel terrible about it and avoid it again." His confession made her feel — *strange*. It didn't surprise her really that he'd looked, she knew very well what he liked. She felt like she should be upset, but she wasn't really. The fact that he'd even told her the truth made her feel... trusted? That was the word. "I caved again the afternoon I accessed it and saw you wandering the room. Your beauty caught me off guard, and then you pounded on the door and screamed at him. So feisty. So brave. And then when he came to get you and you slapped him? I was more than impressed, I was enthralled. I wanted you away from him. I wanted you for myself. Unbroken."

"You have me," she said and pressed his arm tighter around her.

"And Marcus wants you back." His voice was rough as he spoke. "And he doesn't take 'no' very well, as you recall."

She remembered that clearly. The word had left her vocabulary fast when she was in his possession. But she was with James, an ocean away. She was safe.

"It doesn't matter, I'm with you. If I may ask… has he been emailing you for long, Master?" She made herself breathe evenly to calm down.

"Since a few weeks after I left with you." James sounded irritated, and it made her smile.

"And he's been asking for me back the whole time?"

"He's been asking to talk to you, to see you, for me to relay messages to you — and yes, for me to give you or sell you back."

"May I ask what you've been telling him, Master?" She wanted to see his expression, but he still wouldn't let her turn around in his lap.

"Mostly that hell would freeze over and there would be a duck in parliament before I'd ever do anything for him." He laughed and so did she. It made her feel protected; he didn't want to sell her. "But then I realized I was making a decision for you before you'd had the chance to even think about it." He intertwined their fingers and she leaned back against him again. "And you have the right to know all of your options when it's time for your decision."

"I already know my choice—"

"No." He interrupted quickly, his voice taking on the edge of a command.

"I know. You said I'm not allowed to make a decision before the six months is up. Which is ridiculous." She paused, irritation threading through her voice, and then added, "Master."

"No, pet. It's for your sake." He sighed, exasperated with her.

"Of course, Master." She pouted, sulking in her frustration. She'd tried over and over in the last few weeks to tell him she wanted to stay, she wanted to be his, but he adamantly refused to hear it. He even locked himself in the bedroom without her one night as a punishment for her trying to tell him she chose him. He'd told her to sleep on the couch but she'd slept on the floor outside his door as penance for upsetting him. She'd still woken up in his bed with his arm across her, because at some point he'd come out and got her.

Since then she'd kept her mouth shut because he adamantly refused to let her choose before the six months — but it was driving her crazy. And now he actually thought she'd view Marcus as an option? It made her angry again just to think about it.

"Don't be upset with me, pet, I'm making you wait for a good reason." His voice was bordering on stern, but she knew he was trying to stay calm and comfort her.

"I know you have my best interests in mind, Master, and I trust you. I only wish you trusted me and my choices as well. Unless I don't deserve that." The words were out before she'd thought them through. It was how she felt, but she could have said it more gently, more submissively. She bit her lip, knowing she'd likely overstepped the mark.

He slid her off his lap and her stomach sank. She'd gone too far.

Chapter Eight
THALIA

As she formed into a kneel on the pillow at his feet she felt his hand slide between her collar and her skin. He pulled back and the soft black leather tightened, causing the silk lining to put pressure on her throat. She could still breathe, but she knew he wouldn't let her move away if she tried.

"Thalia." His voice was low and serious behind her ear.

"Yes, Master?" Her heart rate picked up as he pulled the collar a fraction tighter. *Yes.* She'd overstepped.

"I can't trust you yet, Thalia. I do have your best interests in mind. I understand, and I am grateful, that you chose to come with me three months ago. But I don't trust your judgment yet. Your alternative to me was Marcus, and with him Anthony." His voice had an edge to it when he discussed them. "Time has to pass, Thalia, for you to decide if this is something you enjoy or if I was just a way out of a very bad situation. What you deserve is the time to make a good decision."

She started to open her mouth but he yanked the collar back to silence her.

"You could wake up in a month and realize you never enjoyed being submissive, that you did it out of a need to survive." His voice was clear and direct in her ear, and regardless of the point of his comments he was still turning her on. Which only made her want to scream that she chose him anyway.

She wanted him, she wanted this!

He wouldn't listen though. She leaned back into his pull so the collar wasn't so tight as she spoke. "And if in a month I did decide that I wasn't submissive? I'd still have two months left in our agreement, Master."

He released her collar instantly and sat back in his chair. "Then you could say your safe word every day until the six months were up."

She turned and looked up at him, surprised by how level his response had been. His green eyes were darker and she knew he was aroused, but he still offered her choices and safety. Her bottom lip was between her teeth as she dropped her eyes to his chest. He was serious. If she chose it, he'd let her say 'chair' ten times a day. She took a shaky breath. "You really mean that don't you, Master?"

He leaned forward and grabbed her hair hard, making her gasp before his lips covered hers and she moaned against his mouth. When he pulled back his voice sent shivers down her back. "I told you once before I don't want someone in my bed that doesn't want to be there. No matter what I'd like to do to them… and that includes you, Thalia. Paid for or not."

"Yes, Master," she said breathlessly, panting slightly. He pushed the chair back and stood.

"Get up." His voice was sharp and she stood in front of him, replying appropriately. He slid his hand into the back of her collar and pushed her forward, moving out of the office and down the hall. She already knew they were going to the playroom. As soon as they stepped inside he let go of her and she dropped to a kneel so he could shut the door.

She kept her eyes on the floor as he moved through the room in tense silence. A moment later he was in front of her, removing the thin collar that resembled a choker and replacing it with a thicker collar with rings on either side of her neck. Then he pulled her up again. As their conversation had progressed she had felt him sliding further and further into his dominant side. Each of her outbursts pushing him further until her final complaint had flipped him completely. He gripped behind her head and pulled her forward. There was no playful discussion as he brought her over to a wide padded bench.

"Lay on your back." His voice was sharp and direct, and it always made her jump a little when he talked to her in that tone. When she lay down he attached something to the collar on each side, which connected under the bench and held her head down. Narrow leather cuffs went around her wrists, and he pulled them over her head, latching them to the underside of the bench.

She opened her mouth to apologize for pressing the issue again but bit her lip against the urge. He was already upset with her, the best way to apologize was to accept the discipline he had planned. His hands pushed her thighs apart, and she moaned and lifted her hips as he traced a finger up her slit. Already gathered wetness making her slick. He didn't continue though, instead he fastened her ankles to the supporting legs of the bench leaving her open and restrained.

"You already have such pretty welts on your backside, pet, that I thought for this discussion we'd make the front match." Stepping to the side he returned with a riding crop, running it down between her breasts before flicking it sharply against her clit. The sting made her legs try to close instinctively but ineffectively.

She yelped tugging on the leather cuffs as she squirmed, but she nodded. "Yes, Master."

"You're asking me to trust your decision when you've only had thirteen weeks with me." The stinging crack of the crop across her thighs made her whimper and bite down hard on her lip before the heat of the welt spread out. "You want me to believe you can think for yourself, that Marcus' training didn't irreparably alter your way of thinking?"

"Master—" the crop struck at the sensitive skin just above her pussy and she cried out and tried to move, but she was bound too tightly.

"Don't speak." The crop trailed across her thigh and then snapped down so the edge curved to the inside of her right thigh. Her instinct was to close her legs but it just pulled the cuffs on her ankles. She made herself nod. "I can't trust you until you can admit to yourself that what happened affected you. Pet, you can't even go shopping without me there." His exasperation was evident.

She closed her eyes as she remembered when he'd told her three weeks before to drive to the local market, pick up a list of items, and come back. She had sat frozen in the locked car outside the store having some kind of panic attack. When she'd come home empty handed he hadn't yelled at her. He'd kissed her and then taken her to bed, and everything had felt better when he'd pinned her down and fucked her until she begged to come. She hadn't even asked for another chance because the idea of being alone, without him there, made her sick.

More than anything she hated that the point he was making about Marcus' effect on her was accurate.

"If this is what you want, you have to be able to balance life as a submissive, and life as yourself. Which means you have to be capable of *being yourself*." The snap of the crop on her other thigh left a matching welt on the inside of that leg. Heat blossomed as the sting faded and she twisted her wrists in the cuffs. She gritted her teeth against the urge to argue with him, to try and explain her panic with anything other than leftover trauma from Marcus. She wanted to be able to ignore that Marcus had shown her so many things that had frightened her, but also left her desperate for things like this. The crop snapped hard across both of her thighs again and she screamed before she shut her mouth against it.

"You have to be stronger, Thalia. Being with me is not about survival, it's about living, and that takes more than saying 'yes, Master.' I need you to show me the woman who fought, not the woman who started to call out for him. *Then* I'll be willing to hear your answer at the six-month mark." His voice was strong and even, and it didn't necessarily sound judgmental but shame washed over her anyway at the memory of crying out for Marcus. She tilted her head back as much as she could in the tethered collar, trying to not see him in her periphery. The crop struck hard across another part of her thighs and she hiccupped, and felt the tears burning the edges of her eyes before they spilled over.

"I don't want him, Master!" She half-shouted as the tears started. Another crack of the crop on her pussy made her whine and close her eyes tight as her legs strained to close against the cuffs on her ankles.

"I'm glad. But why do you think you want me, then? Be honest." His voice was so calm and she felt like she was falling apart. All the memories of Marcus were too close. A blush flooded up her chest as she realized she was so wet she could feel it under her on the bench. James knew, he knew she was this wet and he wanted her to explain why? She didn't KNOW why. James should ask Marcus why he'd picked her. What secret thing inside her made her like this, made her crave this? Every time James ordered her to do something, every time she obeyed him, every time he brought her into this room — she filled up with so much anticipation and excitement, her pussy gushed at the unknown of what he had planned. He did so many things similar to Marcus, so many things that took on a completely different life when James did them.

But there was no terror, and *that* was the difference.

"I'm not afraid with you!" She shouted it through her tears. Yanking hard on the cuffs around her wrists until she felt them ache. She turned her face away from the side he stood on. "I want you because you ARE like this, but I'm not afraid with you. I was always afraid with—" She hiccupped again as more tears spilled out, unable to say Marcus' name aloud. "And I don't know why I like this, I don't KNOW why!" She tugged hard at the cuffs on her wrists and ankles again and suddenly her wrists were loose, then her collar. She sat up and covered her face instantly, wiping tears off her cheeks.

"Pet..." He sighed and tilted her chin up, and she dropped her hands but still tried to turn her face out of his touch. His other hand quickly fisted in her hair to hold her head still. "Thalia. Look at me." His voice was instantly more demanding.

"Please." Her face was so hot from the blush and the crying, and she kept her eyes closed as tears ran down her cheeks. She still didn't understand exactly what was wrong with her that she liked this. James made it so easy, and she just wanted to be with him, to let go and be his for as long as he wanted her. She didn't want to think about *why*.

"No. Look at me, now." His voice was edging toward angry and she sniffled and opened her eyes, wiping under them before her hands rested in her lap. His sea glass green eyes were so much darker than normal. "You're going to listen to me, do you understand?"

"Yes, Master." She murmured as her breath hitched and she tried to calm down. His eyes bored into her and his fist tightened in her hair until she felt the pulse between her thighs — a well-timed reminder of her altered preferences. All of this was Marcus' thumbprint on her. A sob threatened to choke her again, and James shook her a little.

"There is nothing wrong with you, Thalia. Many, *many* women are natural submissives who find happiness in a Dominant or a Master." She tried to turn away and he craned her neck back until she had to look up at him standing next to her. "There is *nothing* wrong with liking this. I like it too, pet, and I feel very lucky to have found you." His fingers brushed over the welts on the tops of her thighs and she shivered.

"I—" She choked on the words she wanted to say. She felt tainted by what had happened to her, by who or what she was. "I feel like anywhere I go they will know. The way Ma— the way Marcus knew before anything had even happened. I'm worried I'll go somewhere and they will know what I am, and what I've done, and—" another hiccup "—and hate me for it."

"You don't have a scarlet letter, pet." He released her hair and his hands cupped her face until her eyes found their way back to his. "It seems obvious to *you* because you know yourself. Marcus trained himself to find women like you, but he is not the norm. No one is going to know, Thalia. You can be yourself. No matter who that is." His thumbs wiped her tears away, and she took her first steadying breath in minutes. Her tears slowed as she watched his eyes move down her body.

"And if you decide that part of you is submissive," a wicked smile tugged at his mouth, "then all the better for me and my interests." His hand slid between her thighs and her nails dug into her palms as his fingers rubbed over her clit. She arched backward and he let her lie down, but her ankles were still bound underneath the bench keeping her thighs far apart.

"Yes, Master." Her voice was pleading for more, her hips bucking against his hand as he slid two fingers inside her. She moaned and squirmed on the bench. When his thumb rolled her clit she almost sat up, but his other hand pressed her back down.

"You enjoy this, don't you pet?" His tone was low and his accent made her shudder. Each thrust of his fingers inside her brought her closer to the edge, and she nodded.

"Yes, yes, Master!" Her shout escalated as she arched her back off the bench.

"Do you want to come, pet?" She could hear the smile in his voice and she answered before he was done speaking.

"Yes, please, Master!" She begged and his fingers were back under the collar on her neck as his hand moved from between her legs. He unlatched the cuffs from her ankles and then pulled her up. There was a table against one wall and he moved her there by the collar and she flushed in anticipation as he slammed her forward onto it. She moaned as he stepped behind her, his fingers sliding inside her again and making her body quiver. One hand pressed her to the table when he removed his fingers and thrust his hard cock into her in one hard movement. He stretched her for a moment and she winced before her body adjusted. He pulled back and thrust again.

She gasped and heard him groan behind her as he filled her, the welts from the night before woke up and made her moan louder when his pace picked up. Everything was focused between her thighs as heat coiled at the base of her spine, and each stroke of his cock inside her increased it.

"Come for me, pet." His hand slid into her hair and yanked her head back. The sharp sting at her scalp always did it for her, and he thrust in hard as she came. Her pussy contracting around him as he joined her a few thrusts later, his fingers digging into her hip to hold her against him as he filled her with jets of his seed. She was limp against the table as her orgasm faded and her muscles shook slightly under him.

Mentally, emotionally and physically exhausted.

"Thank you, Master." She murmured against the table, and she heard him moan quietly as he withdrew from her. In a moment he had her gathered in his arms, her head leaning against his chest.

"I think we've had enough excitement this morning, pet, I'm taking us back to bed." He leaned down and kissed her as she felt them moving through the room. He only broke the kiss to open the door and then he was back, nipping her lip and then trailing the kisses across her jaw line to her ear. "You still have the cuffs on." He mumbled in her ear as he finally laid her down on their bed.

"Yes, Master." She stretched as he laid her down and she smiled at him. He grinned back, his eyes devouring her before he got on the bed next to her, leaning over her to kiss her again.

"I like the way they look on you, almost as much as I like the way these welts show." His fingers brushed the welts on her thighs, and she could feel the texture underneath his fingertips.

"Thank you, Master." She murmured and arched her back, lifting her hips into his touch. His mouth moved into her hair, down her neck where he bit her shoulder and she gasped.

"You know you make me very happy, pet." His voice was quiet against her skin, but the smile that spread across her face was impossible to hide. He laughed softly.

"Don't say anything, pet. Just nod if you're happy." She exaggerated the nod, and heard James laugh against her shoulder again. He lay down next to her and tugged her against him so his arm could coil around her waist and hold her there. She heard a beep and then a soft grinding sound and the room went dark as the blackout blinds slid over the windows. He tilted her head back and kissed her again, her mouth opening as he delved deeper. Then he groaned and broke the kiss, pressing his forehead to the back of her head. "Rest, pet. We can go out later. I think it's time we really start reintroducing you to the world and try to get you back to how you were before."

"Okay." She smiled, nuzzling closer to him in her languor.

His voice made butterflies dance in her stomach when he spoke again, "I think it's a given though that your submissive side is here to stay."

She nodded, her lips stretching into a grin, "Yes, Master." Thalia always felt safe when they were out together, she could work on being more normal in public. And she could wait three more months to tell him she wanted to stay. Just three months and she could be with James without this question looming between them. For Thalia there wasn't a question about who she wanted to be with, and Marcus would just have to let her go. Then she would just have to wait for James to accept her answer.

Three months was nothing.

Chapter Nine
MARCUS

Marcus woke up again and flipped to his stomach, which made him painfully aware of the throbbing erection he now pinned between his stomach and the mattress. He buried his face back into the pillow and tried to recapture the dream. Thalia, on her knees, her face pressed into the bed, his hands on her hips as he thrust inside her tight heat. He groaned as his cock throbbed in need.

Over three months and he was still fucking dreaming about her. Fantasizing about her.

He looked down at the pillow and realized it was one of the ones he'd stolen from the room she'd slept in. Her scent had long ago left it, but he refused to wash the pillowcase anyway. His eyes adjusted to the dark room as he flipped back over, stretching out and trying his best to ignore the tent of the sheet over his erection. There was no way he was getting back to sleep.

His hand slid under the sheet until he grabbed hold of his cock, squeezing and running his fist to the tip where precum was already dripping after the intense dream. He worked the wetness down, and up, pumping his cock as he remembered her mouth on him. Her wide hazel eyes looking up to seek his approval, his fist twining in her hair to hold her still as he thrust into her throat.

"Fuck." He muttered under his breath as he felt his hips kick up into his grip. It was Thalia he pictured kneeling between his thighs, her warm mouth sucking him in, her delicate hands cupping his balls, tracing her nails across the skin to send shivers of pleasure up his back to combine with her quick tongue. He groaned and worked his fist faster, his other hand throwing the sheet off him. The cool air made him hiss a breath between his teeth as he worked toward an orgasm.

It was Thalia tied to the whipping post, his belt marks down her back, her hips bucking against the wood as she cried out for him.

It was Thalia calling out in her sleep, saying 'Master' in that breathy, needy voice.

It was Thalia crawling behind him, sitting on her heels and spreading her thighs. Thighs that he could push apart to thrust inside her.

It was Thalia. Thalia. Thalia. Thalia.

He came with a barked cry, spurting against his fingers and his stomach, and leaving a huge fucking mess.

It should have been her mouth.

"God dammit." He groaned and tried his best to wipe up with his hand before he moved to the bathroom and wiped off with a towel from the floor. He took a piss and then walked back into the main bathroom, catching himself in the mirror. 'Scruffy' didn't even begin to cover it. A couple of weeks' beard growth had him looking more than dark and brooding. His hair had grown out enough in the last couple of months that it was actually affected by bed head. His eyes were bloodshot from his evening routine of drinking until he passed out.

He was a mess.

At least he didn't have to smell like one. He reached into the shower and turned on the hot water, stepping back into his bedroom to wait for it to warm up. The place looked like he'd been robbed. There were dirty clothes across the floor, stacks of papers overflowed his desk to the floor. He had taped photos across one wall, and while he had started originally grouping them, that had stopped.

Grouping didn't matter. They were all of Thalia.

The private investigator he was paying in London thought that Thalia was his cousin. He'd told him she had run off with a new boyfriend and everyone was concerned. The fucking PI kept reporting back that while she seemed anxious, and a little off being in a new country, she seemed to really like her boyfriend — Dr. James Hawkins.

The motherfucker who had taken Thalia from him.

Each of the pictures that had James in them Marcus cut them so that he was left with just the half of the photo with Thalia. The set of photos he'd received a couple of weeks before where they had been embracing, James' arms tight around her waist while waiting for a taxi? *Those* he had burned.

He tore his eyes from the wall and stepped back into the bathroom to shower. His rage was back full force. Marcus took thick breaths in the steam of the shower, leaning his hands against the wall before he let loose and roared out his frustration. His temples were pounding as his blood pressure skyrocketed. Marcus couldn't handle imagining him with her. It always brought back the day of the auction, his stolen touches when she'd knelt at his fucking feet. James' bravado in asking to touch her more, to taste her.

Who the fuck did he think he was?

And then Anthony, fucking Anthony telling him it was okay? Telling Marcus he had to let the customers spend time with her? Thalia belonged to HIM. Anthony should have never accepted the bid without his permission, there should have never been a fucking auction without his permission.

He slammed his fist into the tile, but the sharp ache was quickly in the background of his thoughts. All he could see was Thalia bent gloriously over that asshole's legs, James' hand between her thighs, her sweet moans and cries when he'd spanked her. The way her skin had flushed when she came.

And then she'd chosen him. He had commanded her to stay, and she had chosen James. The bastard who was born into money, who hadn't had to earn his way into that elite circle of privilege. Thalia had chosen the Oxford businessman over him. Marcus growled. That wasn't how it was supposed to go, and Thalia had to have realized that by now. Realized that she wanted a real man, one that knew how to control her the way she needed to be controlled. He'd been the one to show her she liked it. It had been his feet she'd knelt at first!

Marcus turned the water off and stepped out. He pushed his hands through his hair to get it to look decent when it dried and left the beard. No one was coming by anyway.

Anthony had tried to stay with him after the auction at first. He'd gone through the files on the list of potentials and tried to distract him from Thalia with another girl — but he didn't want another girl. He told Anthony that and his brother had fucking *mocked* him. It wasn't that he was in love with her, which was what Anthony kept saying. That wasn't it at all. Thalia *belonged* with him, Thalia was his property and she was meant to be with him. He could have made her happy. And Anthony had been the one to ruin everything. The last day Anthony was at the house Marcus had cracked him over the head with a bottle of vodka when he'd tried to actually *order* him to go get another girl.

As if he was some submissive bitch for Anthony.

The fucker had now resorted to just occasionally leaving an angry voicemail or forwarding customer request emails all of which seemed to just ask when they'd be online again. He ignored them all.

The only other guest he'd had was Thomas, who had brought Kaia a few times. Kaia had been a convenient distraction in the first few weeks, she'd always had a thing for him. She still had actually, but then she'd started crying when he'd called out Thalia's name, and Thomas had refused to bring her back. *He was so whipped.*

Screw them.

He didn't need any of them or their shit.

He dropped into the chair at his desk. The monitors had been converted back to normal screens because like hell he was running the cameras when it was just him walking around the house. More pictures of Thalia. More notes on where James had taken her, where she'd been, what she did — which wasn't much, and she was always with James.

He opened his email and was shocked to find a response from James. Probably more bullshit. The asshole flat out refused to let him speak to Thalia. He was obviously terrified that Thalia would want to come back to him, and then James' code of honor would require him to let her go.

Idiot.

Marcus clicked the email so it filled the screen and started to read.

From: James Hawkins

To: Marcus Williams

Subject: No Hypocrite

Marcus,

I am not a hypocrite, and I was more than happy to let Thalia read your email. She has, and always will have, the choice to be with me or not. Something you never offered her. But you know my stance, the rest of this email will be from Thalia herself.

— Dr. James Hawkins

...

I don't even know how to start this. Even as I'm typing I don't know what I want to say to you, I don't even know if I *want* to write to you. Maybe I'll write all of this out and delete it. I'm only responding because I feel like you have to hear this from me, because you'll never believe it from him. And I want you to leave us alone so I can forget you.

So here it is: I will never, ever want to be with you.

I hate you, Marcus. I hate you and your psychopath brother. There is nothing you could do that would make me forgive you. I can't believe you even think that's possible. I can't believe you would even compare yourself to him, to my Master, to the man I chose to leave with, to the man who gave me the choice to be with him. He takes care of me, he's good to me.

You raped, beat, and tortured me. I'm glad you haven't taken another girl, I'm glad you're not torturing someone like you did with me. I hope you and your brother never do this again.

You can offer all the money in the world. You can offer a safe word, and whatever other false promises you want to make. But I will never come back to you. I'm spending too much energy already trying to forget you.

So stop writing to him. Stop trying to reach me. The answer is no, and if anything in your email was true maybe you'll respect my answer this time.

— Thalia

Marcus felt the heat in his face build as he read through the email. She'd used his name, she'd called James her Master. The bitch had used his name. The bitch had the nerve to tell him what to do.

He roared and grabbed the monitor her email was on and ripped it off the desk. The screen exploded into plastic and smoking wires as he slammed it into the floor, effectively scattering piles of papers. All the papers were about her. *That fucking slut.*

He swept his hands across his desk sending papers tumbling into the air and across the floor. "You stupid cunt!" Marcus' shout tore out of his throat as he kicked another stack of papers and thrust his hands into his hair. She thought James was taking care of her? James was good to her?

How many times had she come for him? How many times had she begged for his cock? He had been the one to see her submissive nature, he had been the one to free her from her boring, miserable, vanilla life and show her what she was capable of. Every girl he'd trained had submitted perfectly, and if Anthony hadn't taken her so damn fast then Thalia would have been no exception. She would have been an obedient little cock slut who would have never dared to write his name, to write to him like that at all, and like hell she would have ever told him to do anything.

Stop writing to them? Stop trying to reach her?

If she were in his house he'd whip her bloody for giving commands like that. The fact that James allowed her to speak to another Master in that manner was all the evidence Marcus needed on his weakness.

He found himself in front of the wall of photos. Thalia's wide hazel eyes stared out at him, her light brown hair covering her face, then her pushing it back. Her smiling. Her in a dress going to dinner. Her long legs. The curve of her hips. Her delicate shoulders.

Marcus started tearing them all down. Ripping her traitorous image in half over and over and over.

He'd given her this life. He had made it possible. He didn't know how long it would take, but he'd get her back so he could finish her training. Then she'd never forget to show him respect again.

Chapter Ten
JAMES

Four Months After the Auction

James slammed the front door after Thalia walked inside ahead of him. The navy dress clung to her curves in ways that had heads turning all night. Her pale skin was glowing in the can lights in the living area and what he wanted more than anything was to bend her over the table in the kitchen and lose himself in her.

He couldn't do that though, he couldn't keep ignoring their issues. They were going to talk.

She turned and looked at him for a second. Wide, hazel eyes filled with anxiety, and positively radiating her urge to submit to him. But he didn't need the submissive Thalia right now, he needed the real her, he needed to talk to her and get real answers. She started to unzip the dress and dropped her eyes from his.

"Stop. Leave it on, Thalia." He wasn't going to think straight if she undressed.

"But... Master?" Her eyes were up again. Amazing; she could apparently look at him at home, but at dinner she'd been performing a deep investigation of the damn tablecloth. It only irritated him further.

"Take a seat, I'll be right back." He pointed at the sofa and walked away from her before she could respond. He knew her head had to be spinning at the number of rules he'd just told her to ignore. He'd told her to keep the dress on and told her to sit, which meant that if she knelt she was defying him. Testing her obedience was helping him as he walked to the bedroom, taking the edge off his anger. He knew Thalia wanted to sink into her submissive mindset to escape the tension from dinner, but he wasn't going to let her avoid the discussion they needed to have.

He stepped into the bedroom and shut the door, starting to pull off the suit he'd been in all day. James kept replaying the miserable dinner they'd had, another spectacular failure in a long string of attempts to have Thalia act normally with him in public. He had thought as she healed physically that she would heal mentally, that he'd finally get to know the feisty girl that had slapped Marcus, broken the back door, screamed and cursed at the bastard to let her go. He had been patient, really, he had been for four months. But he had never wanted a full-time sub and Thalia was so close to that — *too* close for him.

He groaned as he dropped the shirt onto the floor, stripping off the undershirt. Then he removed the belt and slid his pants over his uncomfortable erection. His cock clearly did not get the memo on his brain's plans for the evening. He adjusted himself and turned to the stash of comfortable, black, hip-hugging pants he preferred to be in for sessions. He knew it was sending a mixed signal, but he wanted Thalia to know which version of himself was asking the questions.

The Dominant was asking so she would give the answers, but it was James who needed to hear them because he cared about her. He wanted her, he really did, but he couldn't have a slave.

He growled to himself.

He wanted to kill Marcus. To beat him down for crushing whoever Thalia had been before he ripped her out of her life, and he wanted to shake Thalia until she stepped out of the submissive side for just one night out! One night where they could be a normal couple, one night where he could have her on his arm and treat her like a god damn princess.

He suppressed a frustrated shout as he thought of how after four months with him she could argue with him at the flat if it came to finishing a chapter in a book, or having her damn coffee in the morning, but if he took her out in public all that fire just went out like he'd dumped water over her.

He silently hoped that having her at home, keeping her dressed, and on even footing, would be the trick to finally understanding if they were compatible or not.

Better to rip off the band-aid sooner than later.

He stepped into the bathroom and noted the flush in his cheeks from his temper. He'd spent most of dinner filling the awkward silence and trying to talk to her. James had repeatedly watched her open her mouth to speak. Then he would watch the thoughts and the frustration and the anxiety flicker over her expressive face, and then she'd stay quiet. She'd managed a few watery smiles, but by the end of the meal his mood was stormy and it had only shut her down further. It didn't matter if they were at a dive, a nice restaurant, or a local favorite — the results were always the same.

He looked at himself in the mirror and took a deep, steadying breath. As irritated as he was with her, as much as he wanted to shout at her, he knew it wouldn't help. He had to let go of his anger so he could figure out why this kept happening. James felt the shift internally before he saw it reflected in the mirror.

Control. Rigid self-control.

Trademark of a Dom, and something he'd worked at and developed over the years. He'd never had to use it so much until he met Thalia. She submitted so completely, she wanted him to tell her everything, to give her guidance for every rule and every decision. And he'd done it, for her. He'd done it for months.

But he couldn't do it anymore.

With that resolve in mind he pushed his hand through his hair, blond strands angling across his forehead as it lay back down. He knew that it wasn't just his money, his family, or his job, that had women hitting on him at work, at events, and when he traveled. They found him attractive, and he did make the effort to be appealing. He worked out, he took care of himself, he dressed well. But those women didn't know what he was, what he wanted, what he *needed*. Thalia did. Thalia could be perfect for him, if he could just get her to find a balance within herself.

He pushed away from the bathroom counter and walked back to the living room. He found her perched on the very edge of the sofa, her hands gripping the cushion like it was a life raft. He could see the tension in her from the lines of her shoulders to the expanse of skin revealed by the open back of the dress that closed just above her waist.

"Thalia." He kept his voice low and direct, the tone that always made her snap to attention. Her face turned to him quickly, her honey brown waves tumbling back over her shoulder. Light caught the intricate platinum necklace that lay close to her neck, resting on the line of her collarbones. To anyone else when they were out it was just a beautiful necklace, but to Thalia it was her reminder that she belonged to him. She'd been the one to ask for something she could wear out with him, the thin leather one she had kept didn't work with every outfit. Instead of telling her to just leave it off, it was another thing he had relented on.

For the hundredth time he thought about taking it off her and telling her she was free, that he'd date her but he wasn't going to be her Master every minute of the damn day.

Screw the rest of the six months.

He almost laughed at the absurdity of that. The only way she was leaving was if she chose to leave at the end of the period. He was addicted to her, hopelessly addicted. As much as he thought about sending her off... he couldn't bring himself to actually do it. Even thinking of it brought up too many conflicting emotions — because he still wanted her, craved her every time he saw her. Even standing in front of her, resolved to have this discussion on her behavior in public, he imagined winding his hand in her silky hair and burying his cock in her sweet mouth. Where he could look down and watch her entire body tense as he thrust hard into her throat and held her there. Hear and feel her moan against his flesh, feel the way she always traced her hands down his thighs. Thalia was his — and that thought alone made him want to keep a collar on her, whether it was the platinum one or the soft, silk lined leather one. To mark her as his. And he'd never wanted that until Thalia.

Brilliant.

If he'd thought he was hard before, his little daydream had him aching, and it hadn't escaped Thalia's notice. Her eyes were locked at his hips, her cheeks flushed in arousal. The hardest part of this conversation was going to be not caving and fucking her. He drew on his control and pushed back his lust. This was about figuring out what they both needed.

"Master?" She breathed the word, moving her gaze up his body in a way that made him swallow a groan in his throat. She had no idea how incredibly sexy she was, how her wide eyes and her urge to please and her rare hints of sass undid him under the surface of his control.

Lock it down, James.

"What happened tonight?" He asked, not moving toward her. He studied her as she struggled to respond, her hands clenching harder on the cushion, her head bowing.

"I'm sor—"

"That's not an answer, Thalia. Answer me." He could see the effect his voice was having on her, her urge to please him colliding with whatever the hell was keeping her from acting normally.

"Master, pl—"

"Stop it. If I wanted you to beg me, I'd tell you to beg me. Answer me. What happened at the restaurant tonight?" The control slid over him like a favorite jumper. Warm, reassuring, comfortable. A shiver went through her and he knew he'd made the right choice. James wouldn't get the answers, her Dominant would though.

"I don't know, it just *happens*," she whispered. Finally, something he could work with.

"What is 'it,' Thalia?" he asked calmly. Her hands left the sofa and twisted in her lap, twining and gripping and untangling against the navy fabric that had risen high on her thighs. He didn't speak. He let the silence stretch. He'd already ordered her to answer him, and he knew she would eventually.

"It's... it's just this panic, Master. All the people, the intensity of being out, and I try so hard to act — to..." She whined, the tension in her voice revealing the difficulty of what she was trying to say. "To act right for you."

"What do you mean *to act right for me?*" He knew his brows were pulling together in confusion at her answer, and he tried to wipe the expression off his face.

She was crying when she looked up at him and it felt like a punch in the stomach and made his cock jump at the same time. She was beautiful as her nose turned red and her cheeks flushed, "I know you want me to be — to be normal — to act like myself. And I know I'm failing you, but I *am* trying."

He opened his mouth to talk and turned away from her to re-gather his thoughts. Maybe he'd been asking her to do something she didn't *want* to do. He steadied his voice so he wouldn't color the question with his opinion. "Thalia, does it make you happy to be a slave? Do you want to submit 24/7?"

Silence stretched again and he turned around to see her in distress, panic rising in her. He could see her breaths growing more rapid, her hands clenching at the hem of her dress and releasing. She was chewing her lower lip so hard he was surprised she hadn't drawn blood.

"Thalia. All I ever ask for is honesty, is that what you want? Do you want to be a full-time submissive?" His stomach twisted as he asked. James needed the answer. Even if it meant he lost her, and it became instantly clear that losing her would hurt a lot more than he originally thought. It was by sheer will power he stayed standing and didn't drop down in front of her to beg her to say no.

Tears slid down her cheeks as she looked up at him across the room, "Master, I—" Her eyes dropped, and she sounded so submissive again. "I like submitting to you. Please..."

He wasn't sure what that answer meant or what she was pleading for. "Answer me."

A little frustrated scream came out of her and he almost smiled — *almost*. That was the Thalia he needed, but that version slipped back under the surface of her submission. "If it's with you... if it's you..." She growled a little, balling her fists up next to her thighs, "You know I want to be with you, Master!"

"That's not an answer, Thalia." He took a few steps toward her, making sure to stand far enough back that his urge to touch her wasn't impossible to ignore. "Look at me."

Her hazel eyes met his, and he was so frustrated. All he could see in there was her overwhelming urge to please him. "Please..." She pleaded again and he could feel his temper underneath the control. He pushed it down again.

"Thalia... *bloody hell*, I have always been able to read my subs, to know what they want or need... but you're like a mirror!" He stepped back from her as her mouth dropped open. "You're trying so hard to want what I want that I can't even figure out what *you* need!" James' voice had started out so calm, but he'd raised it. He took a breath to calm down again.

"I just, I want you, Master. That's what I want!" She said it through the start of a sob, and he heard her breathing hitch as he turned away to regroup. He wanted her as well, he really did. But people didn't always get what they wanted.

"Then tell me. Do you want to be a full-time submissive?"

"Master—"

"Tell me." He turned to face her and the anxiety in her was reaching the level that always made him worry. Rapid breathing, flushed from the neckline of her dress to her cheekbones, her hands clenched tight into fists. She was going to hyperventilate if he wasn't careful.

"Please—"

James stepped up to her and she leaned back to look up at him. His hands landed on either side of her on the back of the sofa until his face was only a few inches from hers. She sank into the cushion, instantly submitting to him and he wanted to take her when she looked at him like that. Accepting, and trusting, even as her own mind was likely telling her to run, that he was a predator and she was his prey.

She never ran.

"Tell me your answer. Now." His voice held the edge of his anger, but he was in full control. A tremor went through her and he could see her pulse at her throat, and he wanted to put his mouth there, nip her skin and pin her down.

Answer first.

Her mouth opened, and his eyes traced her lips. He said a silent prayer, and then she spoke on a whisper, "I want to be with you, and I want to submit to you. And —" Her breathing was quick, and she bit down on her lip again. Before he thought about it he'd cupped her chin and pulled her lip from between her teeth with his thumb.

"And?"

"And I wish I could be normal for you!" The tears followed, and she hiccupped. He stared down at her, confused. His hand moved up and he caressed her cheek with his thumb, even as she turned her face to the side and closed her eyes.

"Thalia, pet, what do you mean? Do you mean you want to be a full-time sub?" His voice shook a little as he asked, his breath freezing in his lungs.

And then she shook her head. She shook her head violently, and he grabbed her face in disbelief.

"You don't? You don't want to be full time?" She shook her head again, her eyes clenched tight as the tears kept coming. He almost shouted in joy, but with her crying he thought that wouldn't go over well.

So he kissed her.

She was stiff for a second and then she melted against him, her lips parting and letting his tongue brush against hers. She moaned against him and her hands were in his hair, holding him to her. His hands dropped to her hips and he moved onto the couch, lifting her so that she straddled him in his lap. He pushed her against the back of the sofa, and she rolled her hips against his erection and he groaned into her mouth.

They finally took a breath, and Thalia murmured against his mouth, "Was that the right answer, Master?" The hint of humor in her voice was a balm to the fear that had crept inside him the first time he'd had the thought that she may not be able to come back from what Marcus had trained her to be.

"Pet, that was the answer I've wanted since I first met you." She smiled up at him, but he could still see the nerves. She was still panicked. "What's wrong?"

She shook her head a little and tried to kiss him again. He pulled back.

"What's wrong, baby?" He sat up and she stayed leaning back against the cushions.

"I know you want me to be normal, I know you do. And—" Dammit, she was crying again. "And I've been trying. I've been trying, but I keep failing you."

He ran his thumb over her lips and smiled reassuringly at her. "You haven't failed me, darling. You've been doing so much. Your yoga classes, your—"

She sobbed and pushed at his shoulders. "No, no, stop!"

She'd *never* pushed him away. *Never* refused him. It made him queasy to have her panic at his touch. He slid her off his lap and stood up to give her space, confusion at what he'd done warring inside him. Had he hurt her? Had he said something?

Chapter Eleven
THALIA

❦

Thalia felt like her ribs were going to cave in. She couldn't breathe, and James was just standing in front of her, a slight crease between his eyebrows revealing his confusion at her words, at the fact that she'd pushed him away. Gorgeous, shirtless, with his hard-on apparent underneath those black pants that hung off his hips. She wanted him against her again.

But she didn't deserve him.

She didn't deserve his patience. Four months of him waiting for her to be something she didn't think she could ever be again. Something was wrong with her. She felt the sob rising in her chest and she pulled her knees up and hugged them.

"Baby?" His voice was perfect. Caring and warm. She tried to memorize it... because it was probably the last time she'd hear it like that.

He was going to be so upset with her.

"Please don't be nice to me." She mumbled it against her knee, and he looked even more confused.

"What? Thalia, what happened? I'm happy you don't want to be full time. That's all I want, too!"

She shook her head violently. He was too good for her, she didn't deserve him. The confession leapt out of her mouth like it was desperate to be known, "I haven't gone to yoga."

"You said—" He started to talk again but she sobbed and he stopped.

"I know, I said I would. I just—"

"What about your classes, you said you were going to take classes online." His voice was losing its warmth.

She pushed herself off the couch, forgetting for a moment she was in heels and barely catching her balance as she moved past him to a closet. From inside she pulled out the unopened box for the laptop he'd bought her. She couldn't even lift her eyes as she slid it out of the closet.

"You promised me." His voice was back to the steady calm of his Dominant half, but she knew she'd disappointed him.

"I'm sorry, I—"

"You promised, Thalia!" He raised his voice and she watched him start pacing back and forth across the room. The urge to drop to her knees and beg was overwhelming. "What about going to the cafe, you said you'd been going to the cafe down the street?"

"Master... I've tried—" She was crying hard again, as the recognition of just how badly she'd failed him moved across his face.

"What the fuck have you been doing all day when I'm not here?!" He shouted as his hands thrust into his hair and he turned away from her. She'd broken his trust. She'd ruined everything. "All those times I asked you how your day had been and you said *good*? What were you referring to? Cleaning my flat? Is that why it's been so impeccably neat?!"

"Please..." She dropped to her knees as the guilt flooded her.

"You lied to me!" He snapped at her and she sobbed, trying to explain.

"Master, I know I promised, bu—but I never said I'd actually done it!" She'd been careful. Avoiding the conversations so she didn't have to admit it to him or directly lie, "I know I've failed you." Her head bowed, knowing this might be the last straw.

She had failed him miserably. Over and over.

She'd failed when she hadn't enrolled in school, all because the more she read about the required online participation in the pamphlet the more that tightening in her chest clamped down. Just like she had failed to do more than walk by the yoga studio she wanted to join. Just like her only trek to the cafe had been to stand in line and order a latte while she tried her best not to hyperventilate.

Thalia remembered that for a while after the auction she had wondered why she didn't just leave him. He never tied her up when he left, never locked her in. Hell, she had a credit card that she was pretty sure didn't have a limit, a key to every door in his flat, and a key to one of his cars that he never drove anyway. He had never told her she was trapped, he had never told her to stay.

He had asked her, and she had said yes.

Now... she no longer questioned why she stayed. Now, she actually couldn't stand the idea of leaving. She was lucky James was so *good*, that of all people to be purchased by, to be cared for by, to develop some form of agoraphobia with — at least it had been someone as wonderful as James.

She was also lucky it had taken four months for him to finally lose his patience with her.

She was even more lucky he hadn't kicked her out.

Yet.

That was probably next.

"Thalia. If you couldn't do these things, why the bloody hell didn't you tell me?" He was staring at her, a fierce look in his eyes as she looked up at him.

"I didn't want you to know. I kept thinking I could do it, one day I'd just—" A scream of frustration tore out of her as she imagined every day that she'd stood in the hallway outside his flat, halfway to the elevator before panic set in. "I thought one day it would just happen, that it would just *work*. And I wouldn't be sick at the idea of going out."

"So it's not just with me?"

"No!" She wiped the tears off her cheeks, "You make it so much better! You make everything so much better. It's just all so hard, and the panic is — it's worse when you're not there!" How could she explain something she didn't even understand?

"I believe you, Thalia, but..." he took a breath, "But I want someone I can take out to dinner, and talk with, and laugh with, and introduce to my co-workers and my vanilla friends." He was speaking in a level tone, but his words had the impact of a death knell. She felt tears rolling down her cheeks as he stared at her. She shook her head, silently asking him not to say more, but he kept speaking, "And right now, that's not you."

She sobbed, because his words were exactly what she'd been terrified of hearing. She looked up and she could see the pain on his face as he said them. This wasn't easy for either of them, but she wasn't giving up. She wouldn't give up, not until he dragged her out of his flat. She choked on the words as she tried to get them out fast enough to try and explain herself. "Pl—please..." She hiccupped in between loud sobs. "I'll be better, I'll... I... I just will, I will, it's just HARD! But I'm sorry, I *am* sorry!"

"Thalia..." His voice made her ache.

"No, no. I need…" She took a breath and for the first time actually said what she needed, "Pl—please punish me for breaking my promises. Pu—punish me so you can fo—forgive me, but please don't give up on me!" A keening whine came out of her throat and then he was in front of her. He knelt down and grabbed her shoulders.

"I should have seen this before now, I shouldn't have missed it. But I'm aware of it now, and I'll figure something out." He was pulling away from her. She could see the walls coming up inside him, distance coming between them, and she grabbed his hand. She'd never dared to touch him first, and it caught him by surprise as well.

"Please punish me for this." She begged, she needed the absolution.

"I'm not punishing you for being traumatized, Thalia." He tried to pull his hand out of her grip, and she only gripped him harder. She'd never argued with him when it came to their roles either.

Now is a great time to grow some balls, Thalia. Now that you may have ruined everything. Now that he's already said you're not what he wants, NOW you find a voice?

"I'm not asking you to punish me for being fucked in the head, I'm asking you to punish me because I kept it from you." She tried to keep her voice calm, but she was desperate. And she'd cursed, he hated when she cursed. He tried to pull away again, and she realized what to say, right before she yelled it, "I'M ASKING YOU TO PUNISH ME BECAUSE I PUT MYSELF AT RISK BY KEEPING IT FROM YOU!"

His green eyes flared as he looked back at her, and she didn't break eye contact even though her submissive side quailed as pure-Dominant James leaned over her. He hissed out a single command between his teeth. "Explain."

"I hid the anxiety, the panic. I knew I needed help, I knew something was wrong, and I didn't tell you. Because I wanted you to think I was strong. That Marcus—" James actually growled when she said his name. "—hadn't damaged me beyond repair. But maybe he has, and if he has I'll accept that, but this can't end like this. I need to at least earn your forgiveness."

"Thalia." His voice was edged with warning, and she let go of his hand and clasped hers together in earnest begging.

"Please punish me, so you can forgive me." She tilted her eyes up to him and found his green eyes dark with arousal as they searched her face. Thalia thought of how earnestly she wanted this, how all the guilt in the last few weeks, all the half-truths, the lying-by-omission had torn at her.

"You don't know what you're asking for, Thalia." His voice was low and direct again, a Dominant fully in control. He was probably trying to scare her, but she trusted him, and they both needed this.

"I'm begging you, Master, please punish me for putting myself at risk and for breaking my promises to you." Her voice was calmer with her resolve. Even her anxiety and panic moved to the edges of her mind. It was her submission, and her focus on not losing James, that filled her thoughts.

His hand was suddenly tight in her hair, bending her head back until she had to look at him. "Let's get one thing straight first. You *are* strong. This has nothing to do with the bravery or the strength it took you to survive what you went through. This punishment is for keeping things from me that affected my ability to keep you safe. Do you understand?"

She nodded, a crushing wave of relief moving over her, followed quickly by the heat of arousal as his fist tightened in her hair again.

"Say it, Thalia." James' voice made her stomach flutter.

"I understand, Master."

"What's your safe word?" He leaned even closer to her, and she felt her mouth go dry.

"Chair." She whispered.

"You will use it if you need to, you will *not* put yourself at risk again — if you need it, you will use it. And you may need it." That should have made her nervous, but it just made heat coil in her belly, her pussy growing wet at the promise of what was next. "If you use it, we will pause the punishment but it will not erase it. Understand?"

"Yes, Master. I will use my safe word if I have to, but it will not cancel my punishment. Thank you, Master, for this." She was breathless when he released her.

Chapter Twelve
THALIA

"Strip. Then meet me in the playroom." James didn't look back at her, he moved into the hallway past her and her heart pounded in her ears. As she took her clothes off, folding them neatly and leaving them on the arm of the sofa, she was already relieved. *He knew now.* He knew what was going on with her, and maybe he could fix it. Maybe he could help her get past this so she could be what he needed, and what she wanted to be.

When she stepped into the playroom she dropped to a kneel just inside the door and James shut it firmly without speaking to her. His fingers slid under the platinum collar and he unlatched it, taking it off, but he quickly replaced it with a wide, soft lined collar with rings on the outside. Looping a finger through the center ring he pulled her up and over to one of the walls. A nylon strap hung from a sturdy looking bracket embedded in the wall high above her head. James linked a carabiner from the end of the nylon strap to the center ring on the collar and stepped back.

He returned a moment later with wide leather cuffs. One went around each wrist and then the cuffs latched to rings on either side of her collar. It left her with her hands alongside her neck, in a submissive posture she'd held for him before without the aid of the cuffs. James stepped to her side so he could see her face, she took a deep breath and met his eyes so he could see she wasn't afraid — and she wasn't. She trusted James. She was determined to take this punishment and be forgiven. He must have seen whatever he needed because he nodded and tugged a part of the nylon strap and it shortened, yanking her closer to the wall. He repeated it, making small adjustments until she found herself close to the wall and up on the balls of her feet. From behind she could imagine she looked very vulnerable. Just an expanse of pale skin that he'd said before he loved so much.

His palm suddenly cracked against her ass, hard enough to make her jump, but he didn't give her a break. She stifled the moans as he spanked her, spreading out the strikes evenly across the skin of her ass and the backs of her thighs — but she knew this was just a warm up. James was always careful, he'd told her before he would prepare her body before he used stronger implements. When he stopped she swallowed, the heat suffusing her skin, her pussy already soaked from the spanking, and her mind raced at what he was getting from the cabinet behind her.

"You will count, no need to say Master. Just don't lose count." His voice was intense, and she nodded.

"Yes, Master." She heard a swish behind her and knew he had moved a cane through the air not only to get a feel for it, but also to warn her. Her fists clenched, but she made herself relax. He never talked much during a punishment, but he still cared enough to give her the heads up as to what kind of pain she'd receive. The cane hurt, a lot, but it didn't matter. It was because he cared that she knew she'd be safe, that she believed she could handle anything he gave her — and that he'd stop if she discovered she couldn't.

"Why are you being punished, Thalia?" His voice was measured and controlled, but there was still a hint of warmth in it.

"I kept my panic and anxiety from you, which meant you didn't know what you needed to know in order to keep me safe, Master."

"Correct."

Thalia heard the swish a moment before she felt the cane wrap across the flesh of her ass, leaving a line of fire in its wake. She groaned and breathed through it; after all they were just getting started, "One."

"Two." The second welt was just below, the first. "Three." The third came just above the first. "Four. Five!" They came almost on top of each other, moving down the swell of her ass. The fifth had her clenching her fists and fighting the urge to twist away. She deserved this, she'd earned this punishment by keeping things from him.

The cane strikes kept coming in even measures. She bit down against the urge to scream until he got to nine and the strike came on that sensitive place where her thighs met her ass. "Nine! God, Master, I'm sorry!" Heat was insanely coiling around the base of her spine, her pussy throbbing as each burning welt thrummed with the pulse at her clit. She wanted to beg for him to stop, and at the same time wanted him to keep going until she couldn't handle it.

Ten landed without him responding to her. By twelve she was screaming out each count, and crying between them, she had pressed her hips against the wall in front of her and her legs were shaking with the effort of holding her up, but her thighs were still damp. "Please... forgive me... I'm so sorry, Master... forgive me! THIRTEEN!" She squirmed against the wall as the next strike overlapped another welt, and the fiery pain had not had enough time to spread out and fade yet. She felt his hand on her shoulder, pressing her forward against the wall. His grip was warm and firm, and she felt it tighten just before another vicious line of fire striped across her ass. "FOURTEEN! Please, I'm so sorry, stop, Master, please, stop."

His grip on her shoulder stayed firm, but he waited longer between the strikes. James gave her plenty of time to breathe through her ragged sobs, to decide whether or not to use the safe word. She finally gulped down air and leaned her head forward in wordless resignation. His fingers tightened on her shoulder again and another strike landed, even harder than before. "FIFTEEN! Fifteen, fifteen..."

He let go of her shoulder and stepped back. She breathed slowly through her tears trying to see if she could calm down. The throbbing skin of her ass matched the pulse between her thighs and he had to know how wet she was.

"You made me five promises, Thalia. Your last five strokes are for breaking each of them." The hurt leaked into his voice, and she sobbed and nodded. To earn his forgiveness, she'd take ten more, fifteen more, whatever he decided. "Stay still, continue the count."

"Ye—yes, Master." She took a shuddering breath and resolved to keep still. Her brain was tempted to let go, to step into that mentality he called subspace where the pain bled across the border into sheer sensation that would start to build her toward an orgasm. But that wasn't for a punishment, she knew better. She stayed firmly present.

"You promised you'd enroll in school." A line of fire that made her back arch.

"Sixteen!" She shouted and pressed her thighs together and he waited until she returned to position.

"You promised you'd attend yoga classes." Another stroke.

"Seventeen!" she wailed and gritted her teeth against the urge to beg.

"You promised you'd visit the cafe to do class work." Another that almost made her legs buckle.

"Eighteen!" she screamed.

"You promised me you'd make friends so you weren't alone all week." His voice was pained, and his disappointment hurt almost as much as the lash of the cane.

"Nineteen! I'm sorry. I'm so sorry, I'm *so sorry*."

"And you promised me... you've promised me so many times that you'd never put yourself in jeopardy. That you'd never risk yourself. And you did." His voice was iron when he said it, and the lash landed right where her ass met her thighs and it made her legs buckle for an instant before she recovered enough to scream.

"TWENTY!" She sobbed and she heard the cane hit the floor before his hand rubbed gently over the welts, and his other arm wrapped around her to lift her and let her gain her footing. It soothed her in one way and made her shiver in another as sensation piled on sensation.

"I need you." His voice was raw against her ear and she nodded through her tears, widening her stance in time for his hand to slide over her hip and between her thighs. "Fuck, pet, how are you so wet after that?"

His fingers slid through her folds and he thrust two fingers inside her, she groaned and pushed her hips back against him. He eased the tension on the nylon strap connected to her collar so her legs could spread a little wider. "Master?"

"This is for my pleasure, not yours. Do not come unless I tell you to, understand?" His words growled against her ear, his fingers withdrew and she felt the head of his cock against her. She bit down on the moan and nodded as the coarse hair of his legs brushed against the welts.

Then he thrust hard inside her in one movement. His strong body pushed her forward against the wall and he ground his hips against her ass making her gasp and whimper as the welts sent aftershocks of pain through her. But then he withdrew and thrust hard again. His fingers dug into her hips, pulling her against him hard and she gasped in pleasure, her fists clenching. He ground against her again and she moaned.

"Do not come." He growled in her ear and thrust again, and she had to swallow the cry of pleasure. The pain and pleasure were rebounding so quickly her body couldn't differentiate. Her clit was throbbing with her pulse and she was one flick away from coming apart against him. She was sure he knew that, he knew her body. There was no point in begging for release. If he wanted her to have it, he would give it to her.

His pace picked up and Thalia's legs shook as he drove her against the wall, his fingers leaving his mark on her hips as he thrust deep. Stretching her, filling her, stoking the heat that coiled around her spine until she was shaking her head against the wall and whimpering as she fought her pending orgasm. "Master, oh god, please... please, I can't, I can't..."

"You're forgiven, pet." His voice was thick as he mumbled against her ear, his mouth kissing its way down her neck to her shoulder. "Come for me." He bit down on her shoulder, his fingers slid to her clit and he rubbed her in that rhythm he knew perfectly — and she shattered. Pleasure exploded on the other side of the pain and the guilt she'd felt, her mind shorting out with the intensity of it and the relief of his forgiveness. He caught her when her legs gave out, pinning her against him with an arm around her waist as he came inside her. He growled her name against her skin. His warm seed filling her as she mumbled incoherent thanks through the haze of her brilliant orgasm.

She heard a click and the tension of the nylon strap was gone and she just slumped against him. He released her wrists one at a time and sat down on the floor with her tucked in his lap. They were both sweating, and the welts along her backside were burning and aching with the forming bruises as his legs brushed against them but she didn't care. James wrapped his arms around her, and spoke against her neck, "I'm going to figure out how to help you, pet. I'm not giving up on you, but you can't give up on me either. You have to trust me with all of it, even the bad stuff. We either know all the good and all the bad, or we don't stand a chance."

Hope bloomed in her chest. Fragile and tentative.

"We still have a chance?" Her voice was shaking, but she'd finally stopped crying. Thalia felt like she'd cried for hours, and she was tired of it.

"I think we have a very good chance, but will you trust me? With all of it? No more half-truths?"

"Yes, Master. I'll always tell you the truth, I swear." She said it confidently, because she knew after facing the risk of losing him tonight she'd never take the chance again. He tilted her head back and kissed her, his mouth taking control. His teeth grazed her bottom lip and he moaned into her mouth, and she moaned back. She kissed him hard and murmured against his lips trying to voice how his caring, his touch, his dominance filled a place inside her. She thought his returned groans sounded just as satisfied.

She'd never risk this again. Ever.

Chapter Thirteen
JAMES

James was in awe of Thalia as he left her lying face down on the bed asleep. He'd rubbed her down with balm on the twenty lashes of the cane he'd marked her with from the top of her ass to the middle of the backs of her thighs. All of those welts were going to bruise, most of them already had. He'd watch them.

She had needed it. Needed to cleanse her guilt, and his Dominant side had needed to punish her for disobeying him about her safety, and for breaking her promises to him. And she had been amazing, still so incredibly responsive. Her juices had dripped down her thighs while he took the cane to her, and even when he thought she might safe word, she hadn't. She'd taken the punishment, and now it was in the past.

He went into his office to think, because while her actions were done with, her issues were still present. "What are you going to do, James?" He mumbled to himself as he leaned on the desk.

On one level he felt better addressing the issues with Thalia, but he still felt like shit for not recognizing WHY she hadn't been making a life for herself all these months. He hadn't even double-checked her in the last couple of weeks... probably because on some level he'd known she wasn't doing any of it. The nightmares had grown infrequent, but she wasn't better. The bruises and the welts had been the easy part to heal, and the least important. She was traumatized. Of course she was. What on earth had made him think he had anywhere near the expertise to help her through what had happened to her?

Arrogant bastard.

He should have known better. He wasn't some twenty-year-old new Dom. He should know the limits of his own abilities and know when to ask for help.

His eyes dropped to his phone. He knew whom he had to call. The same name and number he'd given out to new Doms he'd met who had questions, who wanted help and guidance. The phone was ringing against his ear before he realized he'd pulled up the contact.

A gruff voice came across the line, "Well now, James, this is a surprise." The serious tone broke out into loud laughter that gave James the first relaxed smile he'd had all night.

"Kalen, it's—" He sighed and sat back in his chair feeling some tension ease in his back. "—it's good to hear your voice."

"Ye sound, well to be honest, ye sound like utter shite, James. Ye need some help?" The rough brogue of his friend's voice, and his instant offer to help, with no questions asked, lifted a bit of the weight off James' shoulders that he hadn't even realized he'd been carrying. He'd met Kalen when they were both twenty-year-old idiots swaggering around pubs and BDSM clubs in Europe like the world was going to be theirs. James had been on a break from university, Kalen had just gone wandering, and they'd fallen in like long lost brothers over a bottle of whisky and a mutual interest in a blonde submissive five years older than them. He loved the bloke like family, and the man knew him well.

He was also the only one who had the experience and the resources to help him and Thalia.

"Yeah, I do. Specifically, I need your sister's brand of help." James should have called Kalen months ago, the guy had a way of dealing with life that made anything seem easier, and his sister was incredibly well informed on the lifestyle.

"Ye need to talk to Ailsa? Ye've known us sixteen years, over ten of those Ailsa has been a psychologist, and *now* ye ask to talk to her? Ye need to tell me what's going on." Kalen's voice had lost all of its humor.

"Lay your hackles down, Kalen, it's not for me." It was James' turn to laugh at his friend's immediate protectiveness. He was a good friend.

"Ah, got yerself a new sub then? I thought after Shannon you'd gone celibate. It's been over two years, James, I'm happy for ye!" Kalen's smile was back in his voice, and then he heard another voice in the background. "Yes, it's James, my sweet blessing. Oi—"

"James Thomas Hawkins, as I live and breathe, did I hear this right? Ye have a new girl?!" Maggie, Kalen's spirited wife, had apparently grabbed the phone. He couldn't stifle his laughter as he heard Kalen arguing with her in the background, and she shushed him. Actually told him to 'shh.' She was definitely getting a spanking for that; and a sharp twinge of jealousy surged inside him that reminded him exactly why he'd pulled away from Kalen. Listening to their perfectly balanced D/s relationship cut him like a knife.

"Yes, Maggie, her name is Thalia." James said it through laughter and another round of shushing from Maggie to Kalen. He heard Kalen's rough voice, a quick pop, and Maggie's squeal of delight before her voice came back to the phone laughing.

"That is a beautiful name, James, I can't wait to meet her." She said it quickly and then she squealed again.

"Give me the phone, dammit! I am going to bend ye over my knee the moment I'm done talking to him! Aren't ye in enough trouble from earlier?" Several more pops as Kalen spanked his wife, and her squeals came over the phone before she laughed and he heard her kiss him. "Off with ye!"

"I can let you go, Kalen, we can talk tomorrow." James was still smiling, but it was bitter. Listening to their banter made the gulf between what they had and his relationship with Thalia that much more obvious.

Wasn't that why he'd called him though?

"No, I'll settle the score with her in a bit. My palm was itching anyway!" He laughed loudly, and James realized how much he missed being around them, even though watching their interaction without having it himself was painful. "What Maggie said is true though, we want to meet her, and then Ailsa can talk to her too. Ye doubting the girl's submissive side?"

That question was a can of worms.

Like hell he was opening it before he was face to face with Kalen to explain Thalia's *unique* introduction to the BDSM lifestyle. What could he say right now without lying to Kalen — shit.

"No, um, opposite issue really. She's... coming from a 24/7 type, and—"

"That's not yer thing," Kalen interrupted.

"No. Never has been, as you know, and we've been trying as close to it as I can manage for a few months, but—"

"It's driving ye mad, and ye want Ailsa to determine what the girl actually wants? See if yer compatible?" Kalen interrupted him again, picking up what James himself had barely put together in the last few weeks in only a matter of minutes. He was an idiot for not calling his friend sooner. He heard Kalen sigh, and the distinct clink of ice in a glass. "Ye wouldn't be bothering to bring her to me if ye didn't care about this girl, James."

"Yes, you're right. As usual. On both points." James took a full breath, and it felt like the first one since he'd initially seen Thalia on Marcus' feed.

"Listen, it's a lot easier to take a sub from part time to full time than it is to bring them back. Her whole headspace has to change, are ye sure she's capable of that?" Kalen asked.

"She's strong, Kalen. Brave. Fierce when she wants something. She convinced me to buy a bloody coffee pot. One that grinds the beans in the morning and sounds like a fucking jet taking off in my kitchen." The memory made him smile, he loved how much she enjoyed it, and loved the banter it caused.

Kalen's laugh boomed across the phone and James found himself laughing again. "So this little full-time submissive has ye, *James*, the powerful, business executive, Dom of too many European sex clubs to count… wrapped around her little finger?"

"Fuck off." James was grinning as he said it, because it was true, and he really didn't care that Thalia had him so wrapped up in her. He was enjoying it.

"That's a yes if I've ever heard one! Of course ye can bring her, me and Maggie need to meet her, and Ailsa would love the challenge of talking to a full time sub who wants to suddenly go part time. Ye know she's written so many of those journal articles about the lifestyle." Kalen was the answer. Kalen could help them, both of them, and then at least James would know he had done everything he could to repair what Marcus had done.

He just wished he had thought of it earlier in their six months together.

"How long will it take, Kalen? In your experience."

"Hmm…" The sound of ice clinking in a glass filled the phone line. "It depends how strong she is, and if she even *wants* to be part time. She may not be right for ye, James. But let's say she wants it—"

"She's strong and she does. At least, she told me tonight she does. She even took a pretty severe punishment to prove that she'll do whatever it takes."

"Alllll right…" His response dragged out. More ice clinking. Kalen and his evening scotch. "Two or three weeks could get ye guys on the right track. Ye know I'll work with her for ye, but we've got people here, so it won't be private."

Kalen never stopped working, then again, as Master of his own submissive training school there wasn't much incentive to take a holiday. James knew he worked quite a bit as well, but his work wasn't as *rewarding* as Kalen's. Another thing to be jealous of the bastard for. He kept his voice light, "Busy time? I can wait if you need me to."

"There's always room for ye, James. But I've got five girls here, and three of their Doms. One girl is just staying with us while her boyfriend travels, and two of the girls belong to one Dom." Kalen laughed loudly, "That is one lucky idiot."

"Why is that?"

"He's lucky because those two girls can't keep their hands off each other, and he's an idiot because those two *really* can't keep their hands off each other! No matter the punishments!" They were both laughing now. "It's been entertaining trying to keep them in line. But, in addition to all of them, I've got two apprentices sent my way by Eryk in Amsterdam. So, as you can tell, it's a full house, but ye and yer sub will be welcome."

Kalen had just lit the light at the end of the proverbial tunnel. With his help there was a possibility they could both come out the other side of the six months with the possibility of more. "Her name is Thalia, Kalen."

"Great, I can't wait to meet the girl who has ye this dedicated." Kalen's voice was warm and sincere.

"We'll be there soon, I just have to make arrangements."

"Brilliant. We'll speak soon then." Kalen paused, "I'm very glad ye called, James. It's been too long."

"I am as well. Truly. See you and Maggie soon."

The phone clicked, and James was still smiling. With help, and guidance, and examples of more balanced submissives he knew Thalia was strong enough to find herself again. And James would be there with her to do it.

He walked back to the bedroom and slid into bed next to her, careful not to touch her welts before he brushed her hair out of her face and kissed her softly.

"We're going to be fine, baby, just fine." He interlaced their fingers as he laid his head down. She made a little murmur in her sleep and buried her face in the pillow. He was smiling just watching her sleep. *Yeah, he was in trouble.* His thumb traced over her fingers. "This time it's my promise to keep."

Chapter Fourteen
THALIA

Thalia woke up to nipping kisses down her neck and over her shoulder. James' arms were tight around her as he pulled her back against the front of his body and she squirmed against his morning hard-on until he groaned and gripped her hip hard.

"Good morning, baby." His voice buzzed against her skin and Thalia grinned into the pillow listening to it.

"Morning..." She stretched against him and he bit down on her shoulder, as his hand slid down her hip and between her legs. Her breath caught as his fingers slipped expertly between her lips, rolling over her clit until her hips bucked and she moaned.

"Still nervous about today?" He pressed his hard cock against her ass, his fingers distracting her while pleasure flooded her brain in waves as he alternately rubbed her clit and dipped his fingers into her soaking pussy. How on earth could she think of anything with his hands on her?

"I don't know, Master."

His chuckle made her bite her lip. "Why, pet? Is there a reason you can't answer me?"

She opened her mouth to respond and he thrust two fingers inside her and all that came out of her was a moan. "Oh god..."

"So eloquent this morning." He purred against her ear and she arched back, trying to grind herself into his hand.

So close.

She gasped and bit down on her lip hard, but he backed off on the intensity of his touches and her orgasm slipped out of reach. Her hips shifted against his touch and he groaned his approval against her skin, his mouth moving to that little place behind her ear that sent shivers down her spine.

Thalia knew exactly why he was doing this, and she was grateful. For four days she'd been on pins and needles.

The morning after her confession and her punishment, she had been sure she'd wake up to a Dom's version of a "Dear John" letter. *I like you a lot, but it's just not going to work out for us...* But that's not what happened. Instead he had woken her up with breakfast in bed, insisting she shouldn't be sitting on her welts yet, and he had fed her fresh fruit and the buttery things he called crumpets while explaining he was going to take her to see his friend Master Kalen at a submissive training school.

Not just a friend though, an *old* friend. James had seemed so excited at the idea of it, and Thalia's nerves had only skyrocketed. If she fucked up this introduction, they were through. It was the best friend test.

Master Kalen would either like her and approve of her, or not, and Thalia was very sure that if Kalen didn't give her the thumbs up, there was no *happily ever after* for them.

James redoubled his efforts, his touch spiraling her back to the edge fast enough to rip the air out of her lungs. Her body quivered against his, and he laughed — all male satisfaction.

"Oh GOD, please, Master, please let me come, please let me, Sir, please!" Her voice was begging, there was no point in being coy when her pussy was soaking wet and she was writhing in his arms. Even without the accompaniment of words, her need was obvious.

His hand was quickly removed from between her thighs and with a quick movement he was on top of her. His hands clasped her wrists and pinned them sharply above her head, his knees planted on the insides of her own as he slowly widened his stance on the bed. Each inch he pushed her knees apart brought him closer and closer to her. She squirmed, lifting her hips, feeling his cock brush against her, but he tightened his grip on her wrists. "Tut tut, pet. You're not in charge. Be still."

She nodded and whimpered, fighting her body's urge to feel him inside her. "Yes, Master, okay."

He placed the most chaste and gentle kiss against her lips, keeping his lips closed as he trailed tender kisses across her jaw line, and down her neck.

This was torture.

She wanted to squirm, to scream out her frustration, to beg him to fuck her until she was a warm puddle version of herself. But she wouldn't. James didn't want her begging right now and obeying him brought another form of pleasure she really didn't have a method of describing even after so many months. The control she exerted over her body to be still at his command, to push down the orgasm when his fingers plunged back inside her — that was submission, and *that* made her proud, so proud of herself when he smiled down at her in recognition of her struggle.

"Good girl." His voice almost undid her, she whimpered a moan out and his hips slid against hers, his cock brushing against her damp folds. It was some kind of miracle that she didn't lift her hips to try and get him inside her.

"Master…?" Her own voice was so breathy with need, so filled with sensuality that she surprised herself. He just smiled at her as he sat up.

"I have a plan for our morning if you're up to play?" His mischievous grin as he looked down at her made him incredibly hot. Ignore the aristocratic good looks, the blond hair, the green eyes, the fit musculature of his body — when he was playful with her, and when he smiled at her like that? There was basically nothing she'd refuse him.

"Yes, please, Master. I want to play." Desperate much? At least he laughed and didn't find her as pathetic as she sounded to herself.

"Lovely. Get up, and crawl to the playroom with me, pet." James slid off the bed, his erection barely restrained by the black pants he slid over his cock as he stood. Thalia's mouth was watering as she slid to the floor, momentarily eye-level with what she'd really prefer to be tasting at the moment. He knew exactly what she was thinking, and he tilted her chin up so she looked him in the eye. "Safe word?" His voice dragged out the question into a low growl. If begging to taste him, to suck him, would work — she'd be begging. But she knew it would all be on his terms this morning, so she answered on a whisper.

"Chair."

"Good." He beamed at her and started walking backward, the deep V of his hips rolling as he moved. "Crawl to me."

She started crawling toward him, instantly aware of the sway of her breasts, the shift of her shoulders, and the way his eyes followed all of it. Six months ago, she would have been impossibly embarrassed by this display, now she just reveled in the way his eyes showed his pleasure as she submitted with her body and followed his requests. His steps moved evenly backward until he came to the door of the playroom and pushed it open behind him. She followed him in and dropped her eyes to the floor to slip into a kneel.

He must have been up before her because everything was ready and waiting for them, all set out ready to play. He just stepped forward and shut the door. Then he tugged the soft lined leather collar at her neck until she stood. James guided her carefully to the middle of the room where the padded gymnastics horse sat.

"Lay down on your stomach." James ran his fingers down her spine as she lay atop the horse. He walked around her, his fingers massaging one globe of her ass before trailing up the other side of her, tweaking a nipple. Then he stopped in front of her. "Come forward a bit." She slid forward and he tilted her chin up, and her mouth was inches from his cock, separated only by his black athletic pants.

"May I—" Thalia started to ask to taste him, but he brushed his thumb across her lips to stop her.

"While I'd love to hear you beg for my cock this morning, pet, it's going to have to wait." His voice was full of humor and she nodded. In a moment he had her wrists bound with cuffs to the closer of the two bars underneath so she could still push her upper body away from the horse a bit. Her ankles, however, were bound to the widely spaced bottom bars.

She moaned loudly and jerked at the wrist cuffs when he slid his fingers back inside her, first one, then two, curving down to rub against her g-spot until she was writhing and nearing an orgasm again. He slid his fingers back and shoved forward again with a third that stretched her and made her whimper with the delicious ache and pleasure. She was soaked already, she could feel the air brushing the cooling evidence of her arousal as her juices coated her clit and moved over her mound. His fingers left her pussy, and he pressed a single finger against her ass. Thalia dropped her head forward and made herself relax, groaning as his finger pushed past her tight muscles and thrust inside her. She moaned as he continued, and he slid back and worked two fingers into her. The burning ache quickly giving way to a strange pleasure at being invaded by his touch.

He stepped away and returned, dripping lube against her ass. "Breathe for me, pet. I want to see this plug inside you this morning." Thalia pushed herself up enough that she could turn and see a moderately sized plug in his hand. Her body tensed at the idea of taking it inside her, it was larger than his two fingers for sure, but she had taken him inside her and she trusted him. She took a breath, lay back down, and relaxed.

"Yes, Master."

The tip pressed against her and she pushed back as much as she could, his fingers splayed across her lower back to hold her still as he worked the plug farther and farther in. It ached as it stretched her and his other hand moved soothingly across her lower back. A burning sensation made her gasp as the widest part of the plug pressed inside her, and then it filled her as it was seated. Her body tightened around the base and she squirmed against the feeling that already had her panting.

"You look so beautiful." His hand rubbed across her pale skin. All of the cane marks had faded in the last four days to thin lines, surrounded by pale bruises because her skin was so delicate. The smack of his hand landing made her jump as the plug moved inside her. She moaned as he spanked her again, and again, and again. Heat coiled inside her as the tension built. Thalia was dripping when he finally stopped, leaving her ass warm to the touch.

"Please, please, Master, please fuck me!" Thalia begged, wiggling against the horse as much as she could. He grabbed her hips from behind and she prayed a thank you as his cock brushed against her slit. She tried to push back but her legs were bound well and she didn't have that much room to shift herself.

"You want me?" he asked, the smile evident in his voice. He was playful this morning.

"God, yes! Master, please!" she begged and rocked her hips against the horse, trying to get some kind of friction.

"All you have to do is ask, pet." He was laughing as he said it, inching himself inside her so slowly. She moaned loudly as she felt him fill her, his cock and the plug grinding against the thin walls separating them. When he finally bottomed out, his pelvis only pressed the plug in deeper and she groaned in pleasure. He pulled back just as slowly and the heat coiling inside Thalia was torture, she jerked at her wrists, arching her back as much as possible trying to get friction to her clit. James continued to move slowly inside her, his hands pressing her hips down against the horse as he took his time.

She couldn't handle this slow pace, she wanted to come. Her wrists tugged at the cuffs hard and she squirmed again. "Please fuck me harder, please, Master!" Thalia begged and he laughed, before he rocked his hips back and slammed them forward. She cried out as he bottomed out, the plug slamming forward with the impact of his hips as he filled her ass and her pussy simultaneously. And then he did it again, and again. She was moaning loudly into the horse when she realized she was about to come and she tried to pull herself forward away from him. He leaned forward and grabbed her hair to yank her hard back against his cock, and she knew exactly why she had more freedom in her wrist cuffs. As he arched her back by her hair she screamed, "May I come? Master, please?!"

One. Two. Three hard thrusts and she was sure she was going to come without permission as his cock nailed her g-spot and the plug made her feel even fuller as he stretched her. "Come, pet, come as many times as you like."

As she let go and came hard, the heat shocked up her spine as it exploded into pleasure and her fists clenched. Her muscles locked as she clamped down on him and the plug, whimpering as quivers of pleasure moved through her. He continued to thrust slowly inside her as she moaned and knew he was nowhere near done. He never gave her permission to come as often as she liked unless he planned to make her beg him to stop. She babbled a thank you as he slid from her.

"Did you enjoy that?" His voice was at the cabinet. *Fuck.*

"Yes, Master, yes, thank you." She breathed shakily as she felt her body floating down from the height of her orgasm.

"Good, I'm glad. Feeling less nervous about today yet?" His hands slid something between her mound and the horse and she tried to look back, but all she could see in his hands was the huge vibrator he had brought from the cabinet. His question evaporated from her mind, there was no way he was getting that inside her.

"Umm, Master?" She mumbled, biting her lip as she gawked at the toy in his hands. His fingers slid inside her wetness and she whimpered.

"Is that a yes or a no on being nervous, Thalia?" His voice was direct and clear, and as he finished speaking she felt the head of that monstrosity press against her. She groaned and pulled away from it, but his other hand pressed the small of her back against the horse. "Answer me."

"Gah!" She groaned as he pressed the head of it inside her, working it forward and back, making her soaking pussy take a little more with each thrust. "Yes, I'm nervous — *oh God* — yes, Master!"

He chuckled and she felt a harder thrust that had her shaking again, bordering on a second orgasm as she stretched to accommodate it. Her ass was already so full that imagining accommodating what must have been a toy of ten inches with a girth that was currently making her whimper — it was too much. Which was exactly his plan. She could barely think about their plans for the day, the flight to Scotland, the long car ride, meeting James' friends of many years. He was doing all of this *for* her, to distract her.

"So, you're feeling anxious?" His voice was low behind her, and she twisted to see his eyes glittering with arousal as he watched her filled so completely. His eyes flicked up to meet hers and he grinned at her and shoved the vibrator in the rest of the way. Her second orgasm crashed over her and she cried out, the feeling of being so full and unable to move away from it was too much when combined with the look he'd given her. She was gasping and squirming when he flipped the vibrator on and her body immediately tumbled into a third orgasm, and he held her there by activating the vibrating little pad he had slid underneath her mound. Her clit sent a crippling wave of pleasure through her making her scream. Heat flushed her body and when the shivers of pleasure calmed down she knew she was coated in a thin sheen of sweat, and her body was shaking already.

"Oh God, oh God, Master…"

James was in front of her now, and his hand cupped her face and pushed her hair back until he wound it into a pony tail and fisted it at the back of her head. "If you're not feeling anxious at the moment, I have a better use for your mouth than pleading with me."

"Yes, please!" She'd wanted to taste him, and as the vibrations tormented her she needed to do something, she needed him in her mouth, in her throat, anything to take her focus as the vibrator stretched and tormented her and the pleasure rebounded against the plug inside her.

"Anything for you, pet." He grinned and pressed against her lips. She took him into her mouth and instantly swirled her tongue around his head, sucking as he pulled his hips back and thrust a little farther in. She braced herself on the bars underneath, and without the aid of her hands, barely able to rock back and forth, he was setting the pace.

His first few thrusts were shallow, letting her tongue play against him, his groans filling her with satisfaction. Then he started to thrust harder, and when his cock hit her throat she took a breath and swallowed so he could bury himself in her throat. James held himself there as the combination of the vibrator against her clit and the one inside her worked her higher and higher toward another orgasm. Each moan vibrated her throat against his flesh and his moans joined hers. He slid back and swung his hips forward and she caught on to the pattern so she knew when she could breathe. In a moment he was fucking her mouth hard, her throat aching and her lips feeling bruised. She was squirming against the horse as all of the sensations piled up and another orgasm slammed into her.

"Oh, fuck, Thalia!" Her moan against his cock as he thrust into her throat had him groaning loudly along with her, his fist tightening in her hair, before he continued to thrust inside her throat seeking his own pleasure. Her skin was electric from the fourth orgasm, her head was spinning as she tried to refocus her attentions on his cock thrusting in and out of her throat. Then the pleasure between her thighs switched in an instant from insanely satisfying to brutally overwhelming.

Thalia tried her best to lift off the vibrating pad against her clit, but her ankles were tethered and she could only make it less intense, not release it completely, and the fullness of the vibrator and the plug were relentless. She began to beg wordlessly for it to stop, but his thrusts into her throat were more effective than any ball gag. If she wanted she could snap her fingers three times, she knew that, but she didn't want to safe word. Even as a painfully pleasurable fifth orgasm crept up on her.

"Hold on, hold on." His words soothed her as he growled them between gritted teeth, he thrust hard and she held her breath as he buried himself in her throat and spilled his seed. His fist tightened in her hair as he came and commanded, "Come for me, pet!" Her orgasm slammed into her as he pulled back enough that she could taste him on her tongue. She stole a breath and then swallowed as light burst behind her eyes and the pleasure rose against the razor edge of pain. He slid from her mouth and she was gasping, raw and exhausted as her body quivered and she realized she was crying from the intensity. Everything was too sensitive, and her legs shook with the quivering effects of so many orgasms.

She begged. "Please, Master, please, take them! Take the vibrators away, please. I can't again, I can't!" Thalia's voice was cracking as he ran his hand down her back and flipped off the vibrator and the little clitoral stimulator pad before taking them away. He tugged at the plug and she pushed to help him remove it. His hand caressed her ass and she knew how wide open she looked from behind, and how much he liked to look at her.

"Shhh, it's alright. Deep breaths. You were perfect, baby." His soothing touch traced down her back, her sides, her legs, and he slowly eased her down from the over-sensitive edge she had been at. "How do you feel now?"

Thalia took an unsteady breath and evaluated herself. For the last few days the fear of meeting Master Kalen had left her wound up and miserably tense. Now, her muscles were so well-worked and relaxed that she couldn't feel any of that lingering stress. The haze of the orgasms had her mind warm and fuzzy, without a hint of the anxiety she'd felt. James had known just what she needed today. She smiled against the horse as he unclasped her ankles and massaged them, before doing the same with her wrists. "I feel much better, Master, much better."

"Good." He leaned her up and kissed her hard, his mouth making her moan again as he leaned her back. "Do you feel ready to meet Kalen?"

A distant part of her tensed at the idea still, but she just wasn't capable of feeling the anxiety at the moment and she was unendingly gratefully to James for that. "Yes, Master, actually, I do."

Chapter Fifteen
THALIA

After hours of planes, trains, and automobiles where James did his best to keep her calm, they were finally on the gravel road that led to his friend's property.

"You remember what's going to happen when we get there, yes?" James was holding her hand across the car as he glanced at her.

"Master Kalen will inspect me, he'll touch me. He has many other guests and it's possible they could be there too. I'll behave, I promise." Despite the incredible stress-relieving morning James had given her, her stomach was still in knots now that meeting Kalen was moments away.

"You know I wouldn't let anyone near you that I didn't trust implicitly. Don't you?" His voice was serious, and she knew it was true. She nodded and he squeezed her hand and returned his eyes to the road. Thalia also knew that anyone he'd been friends with for so many years would have to be a good man. She had no reason to be afraid, but logic didn't really have a place in her anxiety.

She saw the long line of stone before she noticed the gate. His property was bordered by high cobblestone walls. In the expanse of countryside around it, it seemed like a sudden fortress. There were no signs, no labels, nothing to identify the property. The gate itself was sturdy and James paused the car before it. Thalia noticed the camera just before the gate swung inward to allow James to move the car up the long drive. His hand tightened on hers as a grouping of houses and buildings came into view. Two houses dominated the end of the drive where it looped back on itself in a circle. They were beautiful old manses that were close enough to be sisters but not identical.

"Just remember to obey Kalen like you obey me." James pulled the car to a stop on the circle in front of the left-hand house.

"Yes, Master. I will." Her voice shook but it had nothing to do with a fear of Kalen himself, but of what he could do. She knew his opinion was important to James and she had one chance at a good first impression. She smiled at him and he smiled back and ran his thumb across her bottom lip before he kissed her. James' hand slid to the back of her neck and her lips parted for him as he deepened the kiss. His tongue swept into her mouth and she moaned while she leaned toward him across the car.

She didn't want to lose him.

He bit her lip softly before he sat back and smiled, and then his eyes moved past her to the entrance of the house and his face split into a grin she had never seen on him. Mischief and excitement. He opened the car door and shouted, "Kalen!"

"James!" The man who answered was huge. He must have also been over six feet except where James was lean and fit, this guy looked like he bench-pressed cars. Thalia had never been attracted to overly muscled men, but this guy — he had a thick beard and looked like he was about to bust out of his button down and look good doing it. His sleeves were rolled up and she watched as his powerful arms swung around James as they slapped each other on the back.

James looked like the picture of civility, still in a suit, still gorgeous, his hair perfect, and next to him was a man who looked... wild, and whose voice boomed across the lawn. "Let's get a look at her! Thalia, out with ye, girl!" He shouted and she fumbled with the door before she hopped out and moved toward him.

The little yellow dress clung to her in the breeze and she stumbled slightly in the black heels. Grace had never been her strong suit, it was why she'd started yoga. When she got near them she started to kneel and she heard Kalen's booming laugh, it made her jump. "No, no, no. Up, now lass, up!" James supported her elbow as she stood back up, he smiled at her but she was bewildered at what she was expected to do.

Don't screw this up.

"I'm sorry, Master Kalen, I—"

"No need to have ye kneeling out here, let's get inside." He smiled warmly at her and she made herself smile back before dropping her eyes. They walked inside the house to the left of the drive and Thalia was instantly in love. It was clearly a nice house, they were wealthy, but it was cozy and welcoming at the same time. The foyer opened into a wide living room with three couches facing into a broad, low table with a huge fireplace completing the square.

As soon as they were inside Kalen shut the door and Thalia dropped into a kneel, the hem of her dress riding up on her thighs. The men both continued into the room a little as they talked.

"It's been too long, James." Kalen's voice was booming even inside, apparently this was his normal volume.

"I know, I know. It's hard to get away sometimes." James spoke in his clear voice, but it was filled with warmth. They were obviously good friends. Old friends.

She didn't think she'd ever wanted someone to like her so much.

"Well, Maggie is making dinner, I knew ye'd be hungry by the time ye got here. So why don't we get the formalities done with so we can enjoy the meal." There was a pause and she felt their eyes on her. "Look at that, she's already kneeling!" Kalen's booming laugh made her jump.

"Ah, yes. Thalia, stand up." James' voice was reassuring as he walked over to her. She took his offered hand and stood, but he clasped their hands and didn't let hers go. She appreciated it more than words could express.

"Right. In here now." Kalen said as he moved into the living room where the low center table dominated the space. "Did James tell ye what happens when a sub first arrives at Purgatory?"

Purgatory?

"Ye—yes, Master Kalen. Inspection." Her voice was shaking more than she wanted it to, she wasn't afraid, she was just nervous. Really fucking nervous.

"Good girl. It's a pretty dress, lass, but I need ye to strip." His voice still rumbled, but it had shifted and she could hear the Dominant in him.

Thalia liked the yellow dress. It was a simple dress, chosen specifically for this purpose.

James released her hand and she pulled it off over her head in a single movement, folding it against her lap as she slid the shoes off. She stacked the shoes against the wall and laid the dress atop them. So many people had seen her naked, in person and on Marcus' feed, that it didn't faze her as much as she thought it would when she stripped off the cream-colored bra and underwear. Once she was done she relaxed her arms at her sides. James leaned back against the wall as Kalen held his hand out for her. Her eyes stayed on James for a second and then he nodded to her, his eyes darkening with arousal.

He wanted to watch her.

Her mouth was suddenly dry and she tried to swallow as she took Kalen's hand and he tugged her forward.

"Kneel up here." Kalen issued the command and pointed at the low table waiting until Thalia shifted onto it. He stood next to her and her breath caught as his fingers brushed down her arms. "Hands behind yer head." She interlaced her fingers, and Kalen leaned down in front of her and smiled. "Yer gorgeous, ye know that?"

Thalia opened her mouth to reply and found herself tongue-tied and blushing bright enough that she felt the heat flood up her chest and into her cheeks. Kalen brushed his thumb over her cheek and tilted her chin up. A shiver ran through her and he chuckled.

"Lovely. Thalia, be a good girl and be still for me." His voice was commanding, and she felt her pulse pick up and her breathing increase. His fingers traced down her side and she focused inward so she could keep herself from moving. "While yer here if I ask ye to 'present,' this is the position I want, understand?" His hand brushed the side of her breast before he cupped the weight of it and she bit her lip as she fought the urge to lean forward.

"Yes, Master Kalen." Thalia tried to speak evenly but she gasped when he pinched her nipple, he held it and then pinched sharper and she caught herself before she arched into his hand. Opening her eyes again she saw the flush in James' cheeks and heat flooded her, pounding between her thighs. His eyes were that dark green he always had in their playroom, sliding down her body in such a way that she could almost imagine the ghost of his touch.

Kalen released her nipple and brushed her bottom lip with his thumb before slipping it between her open lips. She closed her mouth around it on instinct, running her tongue over the pad of his thumb before sucking softly, keeping her eyes locked on James. "Wonderful..." Kalen mumbled as he pulled his thumb from her mouth and pinched her other nipple, making both pink buds erect.

This is so intense.

Thalia's mind was a whirlwind of sensation as Kalen released her and slid his hand behind her neck, pulling her forward so she bent at the waist.

"Down." His deep voice struck a chord inside her and she submitted as he guided her head to the table. "When ye hear that command, put yer arms out in front and yer head down. Good, now lay yer head to the side on yer cheek." She tilted her head and extended her arms in front of her. Kalen moved behind her and she kept her eyes on James against the wall, his erection was apparent and she swallowed the moan that rose inside her as she felt Kalen's touch slide over her ass. His hand moved between her thighs and she clenched her eyes shut as she felt his fingers slip between her lips to find her juices already flowing. He made a low sound in his chest — a mixture of surprise and amusement. "She's soaked, James."

"Thalia is incredibly responsive, aren't you, pet?" James' voice was thick with arousal and pride and it almost made her squirm — she wanted his hands on her, she wanted him in front of her so he could touch her too. Clenching her fists to regain control she took a steadying breath.

"Yes, Master." Thalia whimpered, and then Kalen slid a finger inside her and she tightened against him. He worked his finger in and out inside her slick heat and she found herself panting, then a second finger joined and she heard the whine escape her lips. She wanted more, and she pushed back against his touch.

"Stay still." He pulled his fingers back and spanked her sharply. She yelped and nodded against the table, taking steadying breaths as his hand returned between her thighs. One more torturous dip inside her pussy, where heat was coiling dangerously, and then his fingers slipped from her and rolled over her clit.

"Oh god…" She hissed between her teeth and reached for the edge of the table, gripping it to control her reactions as pleasure thrummed through her. Her eyes moved back to James to find his steady stare on her body, moving down the smooth slope of her back. Kalen continued to roll his fingers over her clit, and his other hand dipped two fingers inside her. She whimpered, the urge to push back, to rock her hips into his touch was almost irresistible. Shots of pleasure came from her clit and rebounded as his fingers curled down and brushed over that bundle of nerves inside her. A moan burst from between her lips and she bit down on it.

"Yer doing well, lass. Keep it up." Kalen removed his fingers from her pussy and he dragged her juices back to the rosebud of her ass. After James' attentions that morning she was ready as Kalen pushed against her and then slid his finger inside her tight ring of muscles. She moaned and tightened and his efforts redoubled over her clit until her legs were shaking in her efforts to stay still.

Too much. Too much sensation. Kalen's deft fingers, James' heated stare, the intensity of the judgment Kalen could make on her.

Everything built, the heat inside her raged and a tension coiled in her belly.

Oh no.

"May I please come, Master Kalen?" The question came out in a panicked rush as he pushed her further toward the edge. The powerful thrumming of pleasure he was creating with each roll of his fingers over her clit and his insistent push inside her ass made her whimper.

"No, Thalia." He removed his hands instantly and she relaxed against the table. Half-regretting that he hadn't continued, but internally proud of herself for not embarrassing James in front of his friend. "Present."

It took her brain a second to process the command and remember what it meant, but she remembered. She pushed herself back up and interlaced her fingers behind her head again. Kalen was smiling at her as he grabbed her hips and turned her to face him at the edge of the table and he slid to his knees in front of her. Thalia's breath caught as he leaned forward, his breath brushing over her mound. He was going to—

Kalen stopped suddenly and his whole body jerked back. The look on his face was terrifying, full of rage. *What happened?!* He growled, his face reddening and his voice booming as he stood quickly and turned toward James. His voice was on the edge of shouting, "James, ye know I respect ye a lot. Always have. For who ye are as a man, and a Dom, and for how ye've always treated yer subs, but if ye don't feking explain why this girl has the Williams brothers' mark in the next ten seconds, I'm going to kick yer head in."

Thalia's heart stopped. *Kalen didn't know?* Her eyes moved sharply to James who seemed calm as he raised his hands, holding them out in front of him. "Kalen, I can explain."

"Explain? What the bloody hell, James?!" Kalen was shouting now.

"Just listen to me. Yes, I bought her from them—"

"Stop. If this was legit, ye would have told me. Get out of my house, James." Kalen pointed at the door and Thalia felt like the floor dropped out from underneath her. *No, no, no!*

"How about we talk about this first? Just let me explain what happened, Kalen. Come on, you know me!" James stepped forward, clearly trying to keep the situation calm, but Kalen got in his face, fuming with barely contained rage.

"And ye know me! So how about ye NOT bring a *rape* victim into MY house and ask me to make her yer submissive!" Kalen roared as his arm swung back for a punch, and Thalia covered her mouth as he brought it forward swiftly.

"Kalen!" James shouted and brought his arm up to block Kalen's strike. He pushed him back in a quick movement, and Thalia was stunned by how fast James had moved. Since when did he fight anyone — ever?

"OUT!" Kalen roared and James shifted to his side, farther into the house.

"NO! Bloody listen to me!" James tried one last time to calm Kalen down — then all hell broke loose.

"Ye bought a girl from them!" Kalen tackled James and they hit the floor hard. Kalen was a bigger guy, but to Thalia's surprise James seemed to know what he was doing. There was a quick movement and James wasn't on his back anymore, but they were both trying to pin the other, delivering brutal sounding body shots that had Thalia panicking.

"Stop!" She pleaded, too quietly, clenching her fists in her lap.

They were exchanging grunts and curses, fists and knees. For a moment James had Kalen in a head lock and arched him back, telling Kalen to listen to him, but Kalen broke it and reared back to punch James again — and that was it.

"FUCKING STOP IT!" Thalia screamed at the top of her lungs. She stood shivering by the table and was surprised when they actually stopped. From their crumpled pile on the floor they both looked at her like she'd lost her mind. *Maybe she had.* She was shaking violently with the adrenaline flooding her system that came from the anxiety of being openly defiant but she continued to shout anyway, "He *saved* me, dammit! He *asked* me—" She realized she was sobbing as her gasp for air interrupted her shouts. "He asked to touch me, Master Kalen, he asked permission, he asked if I wanted to go with him, he asked if I wanted to submit to him. And I said yes! That's what this is all about right? My right to say yes or no? Well I said yes to him, and I'm failing him—"

"Thalia—" James pushed away from Kalen, his eyes focused completely on her and his expression illustrated how much her words affected him. She cut him off anyway.

"No matter what he says, I know it, I know I'm failing him, and—" She sobbed again. "I'll do anything to stay with him, because he saved me, he *fought* for me. He took me from Ma—Marcus. And I'm grateful. And he's wonderful. And whatever I have to do to understand this submissive part of me and still be me, I'll do it, for him. And for me."

"Listen here—" Kalen was standing a step behind James, both of them breathing heavily from their quick tussle, but she cut him off too, her desperation not to lose this last chance fueling her speech.

"Don't take away my only chance to show him I'm serious about being better! Please, Master Kalen — I can do this! I can, I just need to know *HOW*!" She was screaming by the end of it, and as if she had been buoyed up by her passion to defend James, as soon as she was done with her speech the bravery left her. She immediately dropped to her knees, hard, and she suddenly realized that she had just shouted at not one, but *two* Dominants, including her Master. She covered her mouth and could feel the heat of tears on her cheeks as an awkward silence fell.

Chapter Sixteen
THALIA

James and Kalen's eyes were both a little wide as they turned and looked at each other for a moment without saying a word.

Kalen broke the silence first, "I thought ye said she was too submissive, James?"

"She has her moments." James' eyes were glinting as he stared across the room at her, and she knew she had likely earned a punishment for speaking to them that way — but it was worth it. His mouth ticked up at the edge like he was fighting a smile though, and it warmed her on the inside. He wasn't really mad. He continued speaking to Kalen, "What I need your help with is getting the girl you just saw, and the submissive you first met, to balance out. She deserves to be that person regardless of how I met her."

Thalia was breathing heavily as they talked about her like she wasn't there, her skin had broken out in a sheen of sweat as her anger left her and anxiety poured in.

What would happen if Kalen really did kick them out like he said? Would James give up on her?

"I see." Kalen's voice was stoic.

At the other end of the room appeared a redhead in an extremely short green dress. She walked across the room confidently, concern etched across her features. "What on Earth is happening in here? I just heard more shouting in here than I did for the last World Cup game!" Her voice was rich, and she actually sounded annoyed as she walked up to them. Kalen looked at her indulgently — it must be Maggie, his wife. She was also his submissive, according to James, but she definitely didn't act like one, at all. And other than the fact that her dress was so short that Thalia could see the pert curves of her buttocks below the hem, she would have never guessed she was anything other than an irritated wife.

"Ah, blessing, well…" He smiled bitterly, "It seems James bought Thalia from the Williams brothers." Kalen said it smoothly, without the rage that had been present just a few moments before. But before anyone could react Maggie turned on her heel and slapped James across the face. Hard.

"Ye right bastard!" Maggie screamed at him, and Kalen grabbed her arm and yanked her back.

"Stop!" Thalia jumped back to her feet as James brushed his hand over his cheek and looked first at Thalia to hold up his other hand, pausing her, and then he turned back to Kalen and Maggie.

Maggie's eyes went wide and she covered her mouth as if her actions had shocked herself. James didn't seem bothered at all, despite the red spot on his cheek. "I'm sor—"

"I know, Maggie. I know. It's okay. Will you both let me explain? If neither of you forgive me after that, we'll leave. I swear it."

Kalen leaned forward and whispered in Maggie's ear and she nodded. "That was wrong of me, sir. I should not have struck ye, I'll accept whatever punishment ye decide." Maggie smoothly dropped to her knees, and as the fever in the room calmed Thalia slid to her knees as well.

I am so out of my depth.

"Kalen, it's fine. Maggie doesn't need to be punished, I deserved it." James spoke in that clear, direct voice that she loved so much. He looked over at her again, and it was almost as reassuring as if he had touched her.

"Okay, James. I'll listen, *only* because I have known ye for years and ye have never been this feking stupid — but Maggie will still be punished. She knows the consequences for breaking rules. How do ye want to handle Thalia's little outburst? That was some… colorful language." Kalen looked over at her and she quailed. Anxiety flooded her again and she felt her lungs locking up — what if he hated her now because she had been so disrespectful?

"I'll handle it myself tonight." James spoke evenly, and Thalia couldn't tell how much trouble she was in.

"Sir?" Maggie spoke and both of them dropped their eyes to her mop of red hair, bound in a loose bun. "I will, of course, accept whatever punishment ye decide. But dinner is going to burn if I'm not back in the kitchen soon." Then she looked up at Kalen and smiled brightly — and he smiled back at her, not even a hint of anger left on his face.

"Then back in the kitchen with ye." He tugged her to her feet and slapped her on the ass as she walked toward the kitchen with a big grin. Maggie winked at her as she passed by and Thalia was stunned. Why wasn't Maggie more worried? Why wasn't Kalen more upset?

"Thalia, join us in my office." Kalen pointed through a doorway and he and James walked through it. Thinking that more submission was better than less after her speech, she crawled after them and knelt just inside the doorway. When she lifted her eyes a bit she found Kalen staring at her with his arms folded across his barrel chest. "Is she like this all the time?"

"Yes, except she knows she has explicit permission to walk around my flat." James sighed as he dropped into a comfortable looking leather chair, "Baby, come here please."

"Yes, Master." Fumbling to her feet Thalia walked the few steps to James before she knelt down again next to him and immediately rested her head on his thigh. She didn't care how pathetic it was, after all the shouting, her outburst, the violence — she needed his reassurance, and he gave it to her. His fingers slipped into her hair and he trailed his nails over her scalp in little circles.

Thalia zoned out under his touch as James outlined the fact that he had caved to his urges to watch the feed after he was blackmailed into maintaining his account, that he had seen her, forced the earlier auction, and since buying her done his best to help her.

"But I was a bloody idiot to think she'd just move past it." James was looking down at her and when she looked up at the pain in his eyes she wanted to hold him, comfort him.

"Yes, ye were. Ye were a bloody idiot to try and call them on it as well. Was it just Marcus or did Anthony get his hands on her?"

"Thalia?" James was asking her. He'd never made her talk about that week — he'd seen enough.

It wasn't necessary to be so detailed about the things that had happened when the cameras were off. Her stomach turned just remembering the brothers.

Her voice sounded hollow when she talked about it, "It was always Marcus, but Anthony ran the chair, and he came for me, but Marcus stopped him before—"

"It's alright, lass, I get the picture. When I first heard about the Williams brothers I signed up thinking they were running a training program in the states — *feking butchers*." Kalen growled. "They are traffickers, scum, and ye *knew* that James, I can't believe ye would ever—"

"Kalen, I know, and I hate myself for being so weak. It's just hard to hate myself completely when she's in my life because of it." James' voice was low, and her stomach fluttered.

"Master, you shouldn't hate yourself at all, please don't, please don't…" Thalia begged and they both looked at her. James was concerned, and Kalen looked skeptical.

"She can start meeting with Ailsa tomorrow, she comes to Purgatory three days a week." Kalen said.

"Purgatory?" For a moment Thalia didn't realize she'd whispered the question out loud.

"Ah, I didn't tell her the name of your school."

Kalen grinned, "I called it Purgatory as part joke, and partly to honor Maggie and mine's Catholic upbringing."

"He likes to say the school is just like Purgatory, because after ye attend here yer either in or yer out of the lifestyle. The main difference is *we* don't let people stay forever before a decision is made." Maggie laughed and leaned against the doorway, her eyes twinkling with humor. Kalen grinned when he saw her and stalked across the room toward her. They came together like lovers separated for years instead of minutes. Maggie was pressed hard against the doorframe as Kalen's body covered hers, and they both moaned as they kissed each other. Thalia found herself kneeling at attention and looked up to see James leaning forward and smiling at them.

When Thalia looked back again Maggie's legs were wrapped around his hips. She had never seen such an open display before, and she was instantly wet watching them. James' hand tightened in her hair and a soft moan escaped her lips.

"Kalen?" James' voice was rough with arousal, and she wanted to whisper that she wasn't really opposed to mimicking Kalen and Maggie at the moment. She'd never finished during Kalen's inspection after all. But Kalen slid Maggie to the floor and kissed her gently on the forehead.

She leaned around him, flushed and smiling, "Dinner is on the table, that's what I came to tell ye, but we can talk about Purgatory as well."

They sat down to eat and Kalen spoke first, "Tonight ye are both our guests, so ye will stay in our home, but tomorrow it's normal procedure, James. That means over to the dormitory."

James nodded, "I expected nothing else, and thank you for helping us and letting us stay."

"While I offered this originally for ye, James, I'm keeping my offer for Thalia's sake. She needs Ailsa, and she needs to be deprogrammed. The kind of full time the brothers required—"

Deprogrammed? That sounded ominous.

"Enough serious talk, sir." Maggie interrupted Kalen, took a bite of food, and winked at him.

"Yer already at two today, my blessing, plus the incident with James. Want to keep pushing it?" Kalen was smiling as he said it.

"What's my punishment this evening?" Maggie lifted her eyes to him, she was practically taunting him.

"I'm still *deciding*, sweet blessing." He taunted right back, and Thalia was shocked that he wasn't upset at Maggie's belligerent behavior.

"Ah, then I'll mind my tongue." Maggie popped a forkful of green beans in her mouth and sat back smiling to herself.

"May I ask why you call her 'blessing,' Master Kalen?" Thalia let her curiosity run her mouth and then she tensed and stared at the table. *Stupid*, asking intrusive questions was not how to win him over. She was still naked, but that didn't bother her. Not knowing her limits around James' friend? Now, that was terrifying.

There was tense silence for a moment, and Thalia almost asked for forgiveness when she glanced up and saw Kalen holding Maggie's hand across the corner of the table, his thumb brushing across the pattern of freckles there. "Because she is a blessing. We both grew up in the church, being condemned for our thoughts and feelings at confession. I was sure God hated me, that the Devil had for some reason chosen me for these dark feelings." Kalen sighed and Maggie got up to grab a bottle of whisky, pouring glasses for each of them as Kalen talked. "Decided if I was doomed to Hell I might as well act on my urges and left. Met up with James while I was in that self-destructive phase, he was doing his own self-destruct under the pressures of being the good boy to keep up his parents' sterling reputations. That's when we found the lifestyle, and I found the brother I'd never had. He has been a brother to me for years."

"We are still brothers, I'll fix this. I promise." James took a long draught of the whisky in front of him, "Kalen here taught me how to fight, and how to let go. I mostly funded our shenanigans and we kept in touch when I went back to university and Kalen went back to... wandering." They both laughed, and Maggie was grinning to herself, staring into her drink before taking a sip.

"I came back to Scotland, because I missed it. Missed the people. Didn't miss the church though. There was a sex club in Edinburgh, would pop up a few nights a week, never in the same place. Had to know someone who had the address to get the invite and trailing after that party became my life while James was off becoming Master of the Universe." Kalen paused, his tawny eyes raking over Maggie like he wanted to devour her, "But that's where I met Maggie. Leather clad, smart mouthed, and begging to be bent over my knee."

"Ha!" Maggie laughed loudly and leaned forward, her cleavage on full display. "I was quiet, and demure."

Now James laughed, and Maggie glared at him, "Maggie, you've been a lot of things, but quiet or demure have never been on the list."

She stood up, hands on her hips, her cheeks flushed. "Well, *sir*," she made the title sarcastic as she looked down at Kalen who leaned his large body back in his chair, totally relaxed, "I believe *I* was the one who invited ye to play."

"And I liked that quite a bit," Kalen growled.

"Ye've always liked my mouth," she retorted, her lips twitching into a smile despite her best efforts to look angry. Kalen moved fast, grabbing Maggie's hips and lifting her to straddle him on his lap. She let out a bawdy laugh before grinding against him.

"Yes, blessing, I have." He kissed her hard, his hands clutching at the back of her head, and then he twisted in the chair so she no longer blocked his view of Thalia and James. "Maggie here convinced me I wasn't sinful, that my priest had been misled, and that she was as Catholic as the day she was baptized — and still definitely wanted to be dominated in the bedroom. We were married in the church, we go to Mass every Sunday, and I'm pretty sure we burn the ears of our priest at confession every week. But she's been with me eight brilliant years, and we accept each other fully… so why wouldn't I call her my blessing?"

"Oh Kalen…" This time when Maggie kissed him it was long and slow. James broke Thalia's blatant voyeurism with a stroke of his hand down her cheek, but he was smiling at her in a bittersweet way.

"Let's leave them to it, pet. Time for bed," James said quietly, but Kalen and Maggie broke apart anyway.

"Don't worry about the table, I've got it." Maggie smiled brightly at them both, and surreptitiously ground her hips against Kalen. He groaned and grabbed her at the waist.

"Ah. Take yer usual room, James. Talk in the morning, right?" Kalen's voice was low and by the end of his question his eyes were fully on his wife — his submissive — and it seemed like he wanted to worship her. For a moment she wondered if James would ever look at her like that.

James ran out to the car and brought up the overnight bag, leaving the rest in the car since apparently they'd move to the dormitory tomorrow — which must have been the other house.

When they had both cleaned up in the bathroom, Thalia knelt by the bed and James paused in his adjustment of the covers to stand over her. "Thalia. Do you have something to say?" Dom voice. It sent shivers down her back that exploded into heat between her thighs.

"I'm sorry for my outburst earlier, Master."

"Hmmm." She heard him adjust the sheets again and a drawer of the armoire slid open and back. "Lay face up on this side — come on. Quick now, we both need sleep." Thalia hurried to obey and found herself on a comfortable mattress and soft, cool sheets.

"Master, I know this is Master Kalen's property and therefore I should have never raised my voice, I just wanted him to understand you did nothing wrong — you saved me." Thalia babbled as he leaned over her, his blond hair angling forward and his green eyes dancing in the light of the lamps.

"First, this is Maggie's property. She's the one with the money, and she gave Purgatory to him as a wedding gift seven years ago." His hands pulled hers above her head and she felt the familiar tightness of leather cuffs, which he linked to the headboard through some conveniently placed carvings.

Maggie owns this place?

"Second, while you should not have yelled, or cursed, at either of us — I appreciate you finding your tongue when it came to defending me." James leaned down and kissed her hard, his hand sliding down to tweak her nipple until she moaned against him. Then his hand trailed further, his nails leaving thin pink lines on her skin as he dipped over her hip and between her legs. She instantly bucked when he found her soaking wet.

"You never fail to impress me, pet. You performed so well at the inspection, and — It. Was. Very. Hot." The last few words he punctuated with thrusts of his fingers inside her, and then his thumb swirled over her clit in an electric surge of pleasure that had her shivering with need.

"But, third, I need you to understand that what I did — watching Marcus' feed, supporting them financially, even buying you — was wrong, and directly against everything Kalen stands for." She opened her mouth to argue and James shook his head, pressing a finger of his other hand over her lips. "Oh no, pet, you don't get to argue about that, and you've reminded me — you lost your speaking privileges for the night."

His grin was wicked, but his eyes were playful as he dug in the pocket of the overnight bag and pulled out a small ball gag. Even though his touch had left her, Thalia found herself even wetter. Her arms subconsciously tugged on the wrist

259

cuffs, but she was very secure. James cupped her face gently, kissing her softly before whispering against her lips.

"Open." And she did. He pressed it between her teeth and gently lifted her head to latch it behind her. "Beautiful."

Thalia lifted her hips and groaned against the gag, wordlessly begging him to touch her. It wasn't large enough to bother her, but she knew it wouldn't be comfortable by morning. James was watching her as she squirmed. He ran his tongue over his bottom lip in what may have been the hottest expression she'd seen on his face, and he trailed his hand slowly down her stomach. After a moment he began lightly touching her again, her body responding immediately to his expert swipes between her lips, spreading her open. She shifted her knees farther apart, and he leaned down and licked her dripping pussy, his mouth flooding her with pleasure, and she moaned loudly against the gag. He sat up and spanked her pussy hard, and she yelped behind the gag.

"Fourth thing." His fingers returned to thrusting inside her, rolling his thumb over her clit until she was panting and delirious from the waves of pleasure building inside her. It was hard to focus on his words, or on his intense stare as he watched her rise higher and higher. "Here at Purgatory…" He thrust his fingers inside her hard and she squirmed, lifting her hips for just a little more.

Just a little more!

"Subs don't get to come unless it's part of their training, and only with permission from Master Kalen." His touch left her completely, and she writhed trying to reach him again. She jerked at the wrist bindings and begged wordlessly against the gag. He grinned down at her, wiping a little drool from her chin, "You don't want to mess up your training already, do you, baby?"

With a whimper and as much of a pout as Thalia could muster while flushed with arousal, on the edge of a glorious orgasm, and gagged, she shook her head.

"Good girl." James flipped off the lamp and climbed into bed next to her. His hand torturously slid up her side and cupped her breast, tweaking her nipple, which sent pulses directly to her clit until she started to beg again. He chuckled and pressed a kiss into her hair, "Sleep well, I'll release you in the morning." Then he rolled over and Thalia tried to focus on anything other than the burning wetness between her thighs and the ghostly echoes of James' touch all over her body.

Sleep well? That was impossible.

Only Kalen could give her permission?

Fuck.

What had she signed up for?

Chapter Seventeen
THALIA

Thalia couldn't quite remember actually falling asleep. At one point she had been squirming in bed, her thighs sawing together in the aftermath of James' touch, and then she had tried to distract herself from the pulse between her thighs. Her mind had been racing between nerve-wracking predictions of what Kalen's training would be like, and tense doomsday prophecies involving James kicking her out, declaring she was too messed up for him to deal with.

Her mind had spun until she was exhausted enough to let her physical tension and her nervous brain go.

Then, there were touches in the dark.

James' face floated over hers. That wicked grin tugging at the edge of his mouth before he kissed her. His hand aggressively wound in her hair, tightening until she moaned. Thalia's hands gripped his shoulders and she reveled in the sheer power of his kiss, lifting her hips into the open air above her in silent invitation. In an instant she felt hands pushing her thighs apart — but they couldn't be James,' his hands were at her hair. Panic filled her for a moment and she turned her head until he broke the kiss and shushed her. James grinned and looked down the plane of her body to look at Kalen, his broad smile showing white teeth inside his beard just before he buried his mouth against her soaked pussy just as he almost had that evening.

She cried out as pleasure surged, his tongue delving between her lips to plunge inside her. His fingers slid through her lips to tease her clit into a hard bud that made her clench her teeth and hiss in pleasure.

"Oh fuck!" Thalia groaned as James' mouth latched on to a nipple, his teeth grazing it before he sucked hard on her flesh, sending pulses of pleasure to meet Kalen's touch between her thighs. The combination of their mouths had her whimpering in pleasure, her body arching and squirming as their strong hands held her down to the bed to keep her fully at their mercy. The effect was all encompassing, and powerful as it hurtled her toward an orgasm. Without a word being spoken James propped a pillow behind her head and stroked himself. Thalia's mouth opened in her urge to taste him and he straddled her, teasing her lips with the head of his cock. She greedily sucked it in and as James' groan echoed in the dark of the room, Kalen thrust two fingers inside her. Her own moans vibrated against his flesh, the velvety hardness jerking against her tongue as his breath picked up. James started to move in her throat, pushing further in as Thalia sucked and swirled her tongue against him. Grabbing gasps of air on the backs of moans whenever possible.

Her hips lifted sharply when Kalen slid a third finger inside her and his tongue laved clit, before sucking the hard little nub at her center into his mouth again and sending her reeling. She moaned and James cut off her voice with a deep thrust into her throat which made her choke, but the tears that sprang up were ignored in the waves of pleasure pulsing from between her legs. Then Kalen's touch disappeared and Thalia pressed her heels into the bed, lifting her hips to seek him. James smiled down at her, his hand cupping the back of her head as he shoved hard into her mouth again and she winced, but she wanted to beg him to continue. His eyes were so dark she could barely see the green tint, and his grin was all mischief.

Then she felt broad hands at her hips, lifting them until she felt knees underneath her lifting her more. *Oh god he was going to...* The incredible pressure of Kalen's cock pressing inside her made her moan, and she looked up to see James slightly twisted at the shoulders so he could watch his friend enter her.

Thalia almost came right then.

Kalen was thick, but he took his time to work inside her. Each gentle rocking of his hips had her moaning loudly against James' cock. His eyes were back on her now, his hand stroking her jaw, her neck, as he pushed deeper and withdrew in a slow, strong rhythm. Kalen was following James' pattern at first until he pressed into her completely and his balls rested against her ass. She heard him groan as he slid back and slammed into her hard. Thalia cried out against the thickness in her mouth and throat, her body clenching around Kalen and sucking James deeper. James' hand reached back and twisted a nipple until Thalia's hips bucked and Kalen ramped up the sensation by rolling his thumb over her clit.

Both of them. Both of them were—

The orgasm hit her before she knew it was rising inside her. The intensity of it had her shivering and James slid from her mouth and away from her so she could gasp, and cry out, her hands clenched into the sheets at her sides. The world spun and she realized Kalen had rolled onto his back and brought her with him, his hips working like a smooth piston inside her, which kept her shivering on the edge. James' touch traced her spine, and she felt the slippery cool of lube worked between her cheeks against her ass.

There wasn't even a veiled attempt at coquettishness. Thalia shifted her knees farther outside of Kalen's to offer herself to James, and he grabbed her hips to steady her, his hand overlapping Kalen's own tight grip on her skin. Then she felt James slip a finger inside her, and then another. She could only make a whimpering groan as Kalen's thrusts slowed to almost nothing and the tension of waiting had Thalia begging in moments, "Please fuck me, Master, please…" His fingers were removed and his hard cock pressed against her ass, pushing until he finally thrust inside her. The steady groan as he pushed until he bottomed out was mirrored by Kalen beneath her while she became even tighter as she was filled.

Then they started to move, occasionally they were alternating, and then they would sync again, and she would be terrifically filled and moaning and shaking as pleasure pounded between her thighs with each delicious thrust of them inside her. She had never imagined that she would want this or that she could handle it, but Kalen and James worked her body in perfect harmony. Their low moans and heavy groans filling her ears until she wound higher and higher, their thrusts growing more urgent until—

Thalia tried to gasp only to find the uncomfortable ache of a ball gag in her mouth. She was hopelessly twisted in the sheets, but her bound wrists only clattered against the headboard as she tried to move. As realization set in she pressed her thighs together hard, finding them sticky with the evidence of her damning arousal. A harsh blush raced up her chest as memories racked her of Kalen between her thighs, his cock buried inside her as he rolled her and positioned her ass for James to take. She groaned in frustration and turned to find a sleepy James looking at her with one brow neatly raised.

"Well, good morning, beautiful. Why do you look so guilty?" Even though James was the antithesis of a morning person, his eyes lit up as he traced down her sweat-dampened skin, before zeroing in on the soaked flesh of her thighs. Even from this angle Thalia could see her labia swollen with arousal, her juices shining in the dim light of the morning, the sheets tangled around her legs. James reached behind her head and with a flick unlatched the gag and eased it from her sore jaws. The ache was miserable and bringing her teeth back together took more effort than it should have.

She almost complained until she noticed James slipping between her thighs, his hands pushing her knees farther apart — just like Kalen had in her dream. She shivered with need as James' satisfied groan rose up.

"Baby, you smell incredible." James took a deep breath and then dragged his tongue up her inner thigh sending chills down her back. His voice growled against her skin. "And here I was wondering if I'd get breakfast in bed."

"Oh god... please?" Thalia couldn't even formulate the request as his tongue started to clean the evidence of her wicked dream from her thighs. Each swipe of his tongue bringing him ever closer to her pussy, her hips lifting in a plea for him to really taste her.

"What were you dreaming about, pet?" His voice was low and rumbling as he nibbled the place where her thighs met her mound. She tried to shut her legs when he asked and he dug his fingers in to push her legs apart. "Come on, tell me baby."

The blush deepened and heat suffused her skin from pussy to cheekbones. He just laughed and dragged his tongue slowly and carefully between the lips of her pussy. His fingers spread her open and he lapped against her, each time stopping short of her pulsing clit.

"I'd love to know what has you soaked." His tongue thrust deep inside her, and her thighs shook as she whimpered. Biting her lip, she writhed against his mouth, his fingers clamping down on her hips, pressing her thighs over his shoulders so she could no longer wiggle. "Tell me."

It was his Dom voice that undid her. His complete control as he tongued her to the edge again and again with no concern of her tumbling into an orgasm without his permission. She was his, wholly and completely, and that meant honesty and sharing fantasies — even ones about his best friend.

"It was you and—" She wasn't sure that it was possible to blush harder, but the embarrassment that flooded her made her clench her eyes tight against his dark green gaze.

"And?" Humor filled his voice before he cracked out another direct command, "Open your eyes and tell me." His mouth buried between her thighs, instantly distracting her from her bashfulness as her eyes snapped open. His mouth worked magic on her, little sparks of heat rising up inside her to make her shiver.

"Oh god, yes! It was, I dreamed of you, of you and, and — *oh fuck* — and MASTER KALEN!!" She shouted the last part to get it out before she lost her nerve again. He paused between her legs a moment, leaving her achingly on the edge, and then slid up her body slowly.

"Oh really?" His voice was low and unreadable and her stomach dropped.

"Yes? I'm sorry, I'm really sorry, Master." Thalia quailed under his intense stare, and then she felt his erection pressed firmly against her through his pants.

"Don't be, pet." His hips rocked against her core, and she knew she was soaking the cloth as he thrust against her. A low laugh rumbled out of him, "Kalen and I share very well. So does Maggie, actually." James' teeth grazed her jaw line as Thalia's brain fought to wrap around the words he'd said. For a moment, Maggie's perfectly shaped ass appeared in her mind and she wondered what it would be like to touch another woman like that. His teeth bit down onto her shoulder and she gasped and bucked against his hips, but he only pressed her into the bed more firmly.

"I—" She was breathless. Her body tensely coiled with thrums of pleasure pulsing through her with each grind of his hard cock against her core.

Had he really said all of that? Was she still dreaming?

"Would you like that?" His cock ground against her and she found herself trying her best to find completion by rubbing against him. His voice was a fierce growl against her ear, his warm breath making her shudder. "Would you like Kalen and I to fuck you, baby?"

"YES!" she cried out, her confession racking her with flashbacks of her dream as his body leaned her tenuously over the edge of completion. With a sudden move he pushed up and off her, grinning wildly down at her. In the absence of his touch she screamed in frustration and yanked hard on the wrist cuffs.

"Then you need to pass Kalen's program, baby. He won't touch you until he's sure you're alright." His hand slid between her thighs and he pushed two fingers into her dripping pussy, the liquid sound of his touch all the assurance she needed of just how much the dream and the entire idea had turned her on. "But I want you to know, that knowing you dreamt about it is going to be driving me mad for weeks. You are perfect, and delectable, and impossibly sexy."

His lips found hers and she groaned against him as his kiss made her see stars despite the fact that he carefully kept his hips from hers. Her mind was still spinning that James wasn't just okay with her dreaming of Kalen but seemed even more excited than she was by her dream. Maybe she hadn't misinterpreted those looks yesterday, James loved watching Kalen touch her, and if they wanted it?

She had even more incentive to pass whatever tests Kalen would throw at her.

Chapter Eighteen
THALIA

Thalia hadn't come that morning, at least not while she was conscious. James had unlatched her arms and massaged her shoulders, arms, and wrists until their ache subsided. A hot, lonely shower later and James was handing her a pale gray dress embroidered with delicate flowers near the hem which barely came to her mid-thigh. A pair of lace, pale pink panties and a matching bra were hidden beneath it. He explained that the other subs weren't as comfortable being naked yet so Kalen's dress code was just enough to make them comfortable.

By the time they wandered downstairs Thalia could smell breakfast and her stomach growled. Kalen called out to James from in his office and Thalia flushed at the sight of him in the doorway, the memory of her dream and his hands on her made her pulse pick up.

"Baby, why don't you go see if you can help Maggie in the kitchen? I'm going to talk with Kalen." His grin spoke volumes, he loved how she was squirming just being in the same room with the two of them.

"Yes, Master, I will." She blushed brightly and took the opportunity to escape Kalen's dark stare before she was more obvious.

Maggie was in a similar short dress, except hers was a diamond patterned blue that matched her eyes. She gave a warm smile when she saw Thalia. "Morning! Are ye hungry?"

"Yes, ma'am, thank you. Can I help?" Thalia crossed her arms over her waist and moved next to Maggie by the stove. There were fat sausages in a pan next to eggs, and a pot of what looked like oatmeal.

"I'm not a ma'am, just call me Maggie. And there's not much else to do for it." Maggie was smirking at her, one hip popped out as she rolled the sausages again then stirred the oatmeal. "Should I call ye Thalia?"

"Oh, yes, ma'am — Maggie. Um, so…" Thalia leaned back against the fridge as Maggie slid eggs onto a plate and added more to finish. "My Master told me you own this place, I mean, Purgatory?"

"Hmm. Well, it's true I bought it with my family's money, which is a delicious irony, I promise ye. But I gave it to Kalen as a wedding present, and it is his. He runs it, recruits for it, trains the subs. All of it." She rang the spoon against the side of the pot to knock off the oatmeal. "And, trust me, lass, I get what I want out of it."

"Oh?" Thalia leaned forward, and Maggie turned back to her with a broad smile. Her energy was kind of contagious, and she seemed totally comfortable with the fact that they had met the night before while Thalia was naked. Maggie's obvious comfort and acceptance made it easier to breathe and kept the usual panic at bay. It was also likely because Maggie knew what she was, she didn't have to hide here, or worry about messing up and revealing her relationship with James. But, what could Maggie get from the school other than the obvious of making Kalen happy?

"Would ye like to know what I get?" Maggie's grin was positively gleeful as she seemed to read her mind, and Thalia just nodded in response. "Everyone asks that! I… get to watch. And I *love* to watch Kalen work."

"Work? You mean — oh!" Thalia covered her face to smother the blush in her cheeks, and Maggie let out a loud peal of laughter. It was bawdy, but friendly, and genuinely happy. Thalia felt her own mouth curve into a smile, helpless in the face of Maggie's uninhibited joy with her life.

"Yer quite pretty when ye blush, but yes, if ye haven't seen a Dom work with a sub yet — *hmm* — let's just say ye might end up with a similar appreciation!" More loud laughter that brought Kalen smiling to the doorway of the kitchen, his eyes moved over her and he winked.

Had James told him?!

At this rate Thalia would never stop blushing! She dropped smoothly to her knees and was surprised when Maggie stayed standing at the stove. Their eyes followed her and a quiet pause filled the room, halting the laughter.

"If nothing else yer going to be a great example to the other girls, Thalia. Let's eat so we can go meet them. Up with ye now!" Kalen's hand brushed her arm to help her up, but he quickly turned his attentions to Maggie. Thalia slipped back into the dining room needing some room to breathe and cool down.

With the full light of the morning flooding in, everything was easier to see. Beautiful carpets, framed photos of trips and smiling faces of friends and family. Above the front door were letters in different shapes and styles that read 'HeaVeN.' Thalia was staring at it when Maggie and Kalen brought out breakfast to the table, the clatter of it being set out still couldn't distract her from the little display.

A hand wrapped around her hip and she knew it was James because he smelled like clean, fresh laundry and warm skin from the shower, and underneath it all that undeniable scent that was him.

"They call their house 'Heaven,' even though the rest of the property is 'Purgatory.'" James spoke quietly in her ear, answering the question she hadn't even asked. She leaned back a little against his chest, soaking in the warm comfort of his body against hers.

"That… makes sense," she murmured.

James twisted her by the hips so she could see Maggie and Kalen at the table. He was standing behind her, with Maggie bent over the table adjusting the plates. Kalen pressed himself against her and Maggie let him push her to the table with a grin. He followed forward and kissed across her shoulder blades, mumbling something that made Maggie laugh and lean up suddenly. Kalen laughed too and delivered a sharp swat to her ass before letting her up. Then they kissed, and kissed again, before grabbing seats and looking over at her and James as if nothing sexual had happened at all. Two incredibly happy, loving people.

Thalia wasn't surprised that people who came to Purgatory with tendencies toward dominance or submission looked at Maggie and Kalen and wished for a partner like that. Wished to find a similar balance. It did look like heaven to be that comfortable with someone else, to be accepted completely for who you are; kinks and all.

Acceptance. Isn't that what everyone wants?

After breakfast the four of them walked over to the sister house which Kalen just called 'the dormitory.' It was two stories, and huge. A soft gray stone on the front and a beautifully manicured landscape leading to the entrance. Thalia looked across the large expanse of green lawn that led out into the distance where the tall walls formed the boundary. When she looked back Kalen held the huge, dark front door open so everyone could go inside and he pointed to the left.

"Everyone will be in the drawing room. Just go through the double doors there." Thalia tucked herself behind James as casually as possible and he reached back to grab her hand and squeeze it before they stepped through the doorway.

There were three distinct groups in the large, sunlit room. Two young men leaning against the back wall who bounced to attention the moment they saw people in the doorway. Three men closer to Kalen and James' age sitting in chairs drinking out of tea cups, talking in easy, relaxed voices. The most rambunctious group was absolutely the five women on the couches tucked to the right. Two of the girls were giggling and talking loudly, another was grinning at them and joined in the laughter. One was quiet, with a rosy color filling her tanned cheeks — Thalia could sympathize with the blushing. The fifth girl was long legged and beautiful, her dark hair was wound into a high ponytail that dropped between her shoulders. A tight white dress made her look elegant and gorgeous as she leaned forward at the very end of a couch in silence, staring out the windows that let sunlight pour in.

"Attention!" Kalen's voice boomed but the two girls continued to giggle a moment, one of them clearly whispering something in the other's ear to send them into renewed peals of laughter. "Ach, Brad, ye know I'm going to make them run for me, right?"

One of the men in the chairs had twisted to look at the two girls who had finally noticed Kalen and were now staring wide eyed at him as they covered their mouths to hide their smiles. One girl had beautiful dark skin, black hair, and almond eyes — the other had softer tones, olive skin, earthen brown hair, and a wicked gleam in her eyes. "Chloe! Lauren!" Brad sighed and stood up. "Girls, we talked about Master Kalen's rules just this morning."

Thalia slipped to her knees next to James, as everyone's heads swiveled to the two girls on the couch. She couldn't help but watch as their mouths dropped open in complaint, their brows pulling together in concern almost in unison before they stood and turned toward Kalen.

"Master Kalen we didn't see you and—"

"—have been so good, we haven't touched each other at all!"

"It's been *over a day*, Master Kalen!"

"We are trying!"

The girls talked over each other, pleading as they stood up, the darker of the two clasping her hands together.

"Girls, sit down, and be quiet. We'll handle yer punishments later, and ye can update me on how yer keeping yer hands to yerselves." Kalen used his Dom voice and both Chloe and Lauren dropped back on to the couch with a pout. "We have a new sub at Purgatory today, everyone. This is Master James, and—" Kalen paused and Thalia suddenly felt the weight of the room's attention. "—and this is Thalia."

"Seriously? She's kneeling on the floor by his feet?" The female voice had the hint of a Spanish accent and rang out across the room full of irritation.

"Thalia is a submissive, Marisol. She has been full time and is determining whether part time will work for her." Kalen's voice was perfectly controlled.

"She obviously doesn't need *training* like the rest of us. She looks as obedient as a show dog. Is THAT what you want from us? To be little obedient dogs?" Her voice was shrill, and Thalia peeked up to see the woman in the white dress twisted around glaring daggers at her. Moments before she had seemed so elegant and beautiful, but with her face contorted in anger she looked ugly. Thalia's eyes instantly dropped and her stomach turned. That was the reaction she'd feared since her first time in public after Marcus — that someone would see her submissiveness, and instantly hate her for it. James ran the back of his hand against her cheek and she glanced up at him to see him shaking his head, with a reassuring smile. He didn't see her as some show dog. That's not what he wanted from her, and that's not what she was. Submission was always a choice with James.

Thalia made herself take a shuddering breath as she reminded herself of those things.

"Marisol, as we have discussed, if ye disagree with this lifestyle ye can leave anytime ye'd like. No one is keeping ye here, Ethan isn't keeping ye here. As myself and Ailsa have explained, it is yer choice to explore this relationship with Ethan." Kalen's voice was tired, and Thalia could see why. Marisol was bristling with anger and the man that seemed to be looking at her across the room just looked sad. Tension crackled through the room and Thalia felt like she was witnessing something big. For a tenuous minute everyone was looking at Marisol in silence.

Then the woman looked across at the man, probably Ethan, and her features softened, collapsing until she was crying prettily, "I'm sorry, I'm sorry again. I'm just not used to this, but I love you, Ethan! I love you more than anything!" The tension dropped out of the air as he crossed the room and wrapped her in a bracing hug. Thalia caught the slight headshake from James, and the pointed look between him and Kalen.

Then, the drama was over.

Chloe and Lauren were chatting close together again, and the third girl talking with them stood and approached Kalen with her eyes down. "Um, Master Kalen? Should Thalia come sit with us? I can talk with her if you like?" The girl sounded sweet, her blonde hair was pulled back into a messy braid, and she was a tiny thing that barely came to Kalen's massive shoulders. But Kalen smiled broadly at her.

"Thank ye, Julie. Yes." His gaze turned to Thalia, and James smiled down at her offering his hand to help her up. She took it and realized she was several inches taller than Julie, but Julie just cheered and — hugged her. Thalia stiffened instantly, but Julie didn't give up.

"Ignore Marisol and you'll have so much fun here." When she pulled back her eyes twinkled. She bounced a bit before turning toward the couches the girls were on, and tugging Thalia forward. "Come on!"

Thalia followed, looking back over her shoulder to see James smile at her. "I'll be back soon, baby," he called after her. Thalia felt butterflies swirl in her stomach at the idea of facing all the girls. But he was smiling at her, and this is what she was here for. She took a deep breath and nodded at him as she continued to the couch.

The blonde immediately started on a chipper little speech with a light English accent. "So, I'm Julie, my boyfriend Antonio travels on business to Pakistan sometimes and he lets me come to Purgatory so I'm not bored out of my mind. I came here for training *years* ago!" The girl babbled at a hundred words a minute as she started pointing around the room like a hostess at a party. "This is Chloe and Lauren, they are *together* with their Dom, Brad." She giggled, and the two girls leaned against each other with big grins. "This is Analiese, she's super quiet, and over there is her Dom, Nick. He's quiet too; they're a perfect fit. *Seriously*." Analiese gave her a shy smile and a little wave, which Thalia returned. Julie sighed and rolled her eyes a little, "And you already saw Marisol and Ethan — I'll fill you in on *that* mess later."

"Shut up, Julie." Marisol hissed. Ethan had returned to the chairs with the other Doms who were now all getting up and crossing over to Kalen and talking in low voices, as they were joined by the two younger men from the wall. "So, Thalia, how did James get you to come here?" Marisol's question was laced with venom.

"Um..." Thalia sat down next to Julie, her mouth open as she tried to absorb the flurry of information she'd just been bombarded by. Her eyes bounced around the room where everyone seemed comfortable, except obviously Marisol.

Why was she even here?

"You're so rude, Marisol. Thalia will tell us what she wants to, when she wants to." Chloe, the girl with the mocha skin, gave her a big smile.

"Girls, ye all know the rules. Stay in here until the morning briefing is over. Physical training is this afternoon, so if ye want to warm up, follow Julie's lead. Otherwise practice on your current training focus." Kalen spoke clearly and then all the men left the room, shutting the door firmly. Thalia waited to hear the heavy click of a lock, but it never came.

No one is here against their will. Thalia reminded herself and forced a breath.

Julie grabbed her hand and Thalia swung her eyes back to her, "It's okay, they'll be back soon, they just meet to update on everyone's progress and choose the next steps in the training. That's all!" She grinned, "So... Master James is cute. Right?"

Thalia blushed a little but felt the warmth of acceptance from the loud little group around her. Chloe and Lauren leaned forward, and even Analiese raised her eyes. Taking Julie's advice and blocking out Marisol as best as she could she leaned forward too, tucking her hair behind her ears. "Yeah, he's... he's amazing."

Chapter Nineteen
JAMES

James dropped into a chair around the long dining table that dominated the space. It was both the dormitory dining room and the official meeting room for Purgatory with seating for twenty; more than enough room for the collected group. Ailsa had arrived about ten minutes after the morning meeting had started, her long red hair dropping down her back, a trim skirt suit making her look feminine but professional. She wasn't submissive at all but loved her brother and was sincerely fascinated with people who participated in BDSM.

Kalen was in his element, updating each Dom on their sub's progress with a mixture of kindness and stern advice. The subs never saw it, but Kalen could crack the proverbial whip with his expectations of the Doms as well. He accepted nothing less than respectful, caring, well-informed Doms at Purgatory — and he had no trouble guiding willing new Doms to achieve that goal, or shutting down and then kicking out the assholes.

Ailsa was a force of nature in and of herself, anyone could see that they were siblings. When she spoke, she transformed the clinical speech she was capable of into easy to understand comments that helped Kalen make his decisions about next steps. The full update took about thirty minutes, and then Kalen turned to the new Doms who had come to learn from him.

"Lars, Sven, ye'll be helping me with training today. Grab the therapy schedule from Ailsa and make sure the girls go — especially Marisol. If she refuses her therapy session again, come to me." Kalen glanced at Ethan who rubbed a hand across his cheek with a sigh. "Sven, would ye make another batch of tea, and some coffee, for the girls? Lars, make sure they're actually practicing and not just gossiping and hounding Thalia for her life story?"

The two young Doms-to-be jumped out of their chairs quickly and agreed, rushing toward the door to take action. The other Doms excused themselves to go work, make calls, or relax — whatever was on their menu. In a matter of moments it was just Ailsa, Kalen, and him near one end of the table.

"Yer turn, James. Let's talk about Thalia." Kalen's demeanor was a little different, but he didn't drop his Master of the House style of speech. He was in charge at Purgatory, and James accepted that. He'd come here for his help after all. Even though that meant giving up some of his own control so his friend could help him fix this.

"Absolutely, I want to get started." James sat up and clasped his hands on the table like he always did in meetings at the office. Calm and ready.

"First, I want to know why ye never told me about the blackmail shite. Ye told me all about when ye figured out what the Williams brothers really did, and then — what? Ye decided I wouldn't have yer back when they twisted yer arm like that?" Kalen was deadly serious, he had gone straight to it — this was what lay between them. He'd kept the whole story from the man he called brother, who knew all of his other dark secrets.

"That wasn't it at all, Kalen. I absolutely knew you would have my back, I knew you'd want to take them down and…" James blew out a breath. "I couldn't risk you ruining your life on my behalf, and, honestly, I couldn't risk them somehow exposing my tastes and ruining my life as well."

"But ye still watched?" Kalen's cheeks were ruddy, and James knew his friend well enough to recognize the anger simmering there.

"Rarely. After Shannon I tried to go vanilla and it — it wasn't enough. I was always fighting who I am, and that was exhausting. So, as horrible as it is, yes, I brought the feed up a few times even after I knew." James felt sick saying it out loud. It was worse than when he'd said the words to Thalia. She had been so accepting, not shocked in the least. After all, she had already known he had watched her.

He hated himself for it, or he at least hated the weak part of him that had caved to temptation. Where was his stellar self-control when it really mattered?

Kalen was silent longer than he had expected. His friend's dark eyes bored into him across the table, but he didn't look away. He wasn't hiding from his mistakes. As much as this trip was for Thalia, Kalen was clearly not ignoring the correction that needed to occur with James either. "If I hadn't already hit ye, James, I'd hit ye again. I just—" He sighed and took a deep breath. "I still love ye like a brother, but I am angry with ye. For watching after ye knew, and for buying her, and then not bringing her for help immediately, and for bringing the lass here without telling me! Dammit! Ye feking great dipstick!" Kalen slapped the table in front of him and leaned back.

"I know—"

"I don't think ye do, but..." Kalen looked over at Ailsa who had her expression schooled into a flat, unreadable one. "For now, let's just say that how we are at the end of this is going to largely depend on how Thalia ends up. Right?"

James swallowed and finally turned his eyes to the wood grain of the table. He'd known bringing Thalia to Purgatory would make him face consequences, and he deserved them, but it didn't mean his stomach wasn't trying to upend itself at the idea of losing Kalen's friendship.

It's not like you wouldn't deserve it.

And that was true. He hadn't experienced anything but the benefits of his bad choices. He'd never been exposed, he got Thalia from Marcus, and he'd had Thalia with him for four months.

His happiness after his mistake was a huge portion of his guilt.

James realized suddenly that he had reached out to Kalen to cleanse himself as well as help Thalia. Admitting his failure to the person closest to him on the planet meant he had to face it, and the consequences, himself. And he was prepared for it.

"I understand, Kalen. Whatever you decide, I won't fight you on it."

"I just want ye to know, that Kalen doesn't speak for both of us." Ailsa leaned across the table until James looked her in the eyes. "Based on what he's told me this girl has needed help for months, and ye are going to fill me in on everything, right now, and then I'm going to try and help her, and THEN I'll decide how I feel about ye, ye bloody dumpling!"

James tried to hide his smile at Ailsa being riled up at him and listening to her use an insult with him that she'd used on Kalen countless times let him know she hadn't given up on him completely. "Alright, I can accept that. I brought the file on her, let me get it out of the boot and we can talk." He stood up and both Kalen and Ailsa leaned back. She was two years younger than Kalen but their mannerisms were so similar. It made James miss his little sister too, but she was busy with her own life and had no place near this mess.

When James returned from grabbing a few bags from the car, he dropped them at the edge of the room and dug out the file Anthony had provided him that detailed Thalia's history. Medical, personal, everything. When he sat down he gripped it tightly, trailing his fingers over it. He felt like he was exposing her, revealing her history to strangers, and it felt wrong after everything she'd already been through. But he also knew it was necessary, so James made his hands slide the file across the table to Ailsa. Thalia had been so alone, for so long, and he never wanted her to feel that way again. They could help her.

Sven knocked at the doorframe as Ailsa was flipping through the folder, occasionally pointing out things to Kalen and speaking to him softly. James had been checking email on his phone when the young man entered. "Tea?"

"Yeh, bring it over, Sven. Thanks." Kalen murmured as the young Dom from one of the largest BDSM clubs in Amsterdam poured tea for each of them. Eryk, the owner of the Vermaak Club, was close friends with Kalen and often referred both subs and Doms to him. Lars and Sven were just the two most recent. Once Sven had left, Ailsa slid the folder in front of Kalen so he could continue looking through it.

"Right. Tell me what happened and be honest with me. I haven't got the chance to slap ye yet, so if ye sugarcoat this, I happily will." Ailsa leaned back in the chair and waited.

James sighed, steeling himself to provide as brief a summary as possible of Thalia's suffering.

"Marcus, of the Williams Brothers, kidnapped Thalia a little over four months ago. He—" James gritted his teeth and felt his muscles lock up as he forced the next words out. "He raped her, and — and he quite *literally* whipped and beat her into submission under the twisted guise of training her. It was brutal. Then—"

Ailsa interrupted him, "I said don't sugarcoat it, James. How am I supposed to know what to ask her about if I don't know details? What did he do to her?"

James swallowed, the images from the feed filling his head and turning his stomach with guilt again. "You have to understand, Thalia is... responsive. To pain and pleasure, and he *used* that to get her to submit to him. He tied her up and whipped her with a belt, raped her many times, he edged her until she begged for him, and then he made her call him Master to get relief. He made her ask for him, over and over — and she did." James felt sick, because the lines in his own head blurred between their own times together and what he remembered on the feed.

"How violent did the punishments get? Did she have any kind of safe word in this?" Ailsa sounded clinical, which helped. She wasn't gasping in shock or glaring him down. If she had to know this shit, he'd tell her no matter how much it tore him apart to think about it.

"No, he hurt her whenever she tried to refuse him. He never gave her a safe word, she didn't even know what that was until I told her. It got pretty bad. She tried to escape out of a glass door once, she smashed it, cut her feet up trying to get out. He caught her, beat her for it, and let his brother Anthony play with electrocuting her until she passed out from the pain." James' voice was flat.

"Anything else?" Ailsa asked.

"Not that I know of." *Wasn't that enough?*

"So, this was all nonconsensual." Ailsa had pulled out a notepad and was scribbling furiously across it.

"Yes."

"And what about with ye?" Ailsa paused her pen and looked up at him.

"It has *always* been consensual." James felt his temper spike and he made himself speak evenly through gritted teeth. Losing it on Ailsa would make Kalen's hits the night before feel like feather pillows compared to what he'd do to him if James yelled at his little sister. Especially when she was trying to help. Ailsa tilted her head and watched his response as he schooled his breathing into even measures.

"If I may, I do believe that it was consensual, Ailsa. Thalia was pretty vocal about that point last night." Kalen spoke up, glancing between the two of them before looking back at the file and leaving Ailsa to continue her interrogation.

"Ye did say that Thalia was protective of him." She made more notes and James immediately realized why so many people hated going to therapists. *What the bloody hell was she writing?*

"What else do you want to know, Ailsa?" He was making himself stay calm despite the hint of doubt in her voice about Thalia's consent.

"Why did ye decide to bring her here?" Ailsa's dark eyes lifted up from the pad.

Finally, questions he wanted to answer. "Thalia can't be herself, she just can't act normally. We've developed a more relaxed style at home, although she's still incredibly submissive, but out in public? I'm lucky if I can get her to talk. She told me she wanted to start building a life for herself, that she wants to be normal. We had agreed to some things she should do to work toward that, but—" James groaned remembering their argument, the pain in his chest when he realized she hadn't done any of it. The guilt he'd felt that he'd ignored her distress so blatantly.

"But?" Ailsa prompted.

"But she finally confessed that something is wrong. She's not able to be who she wants to be."

"I'll have to wait until I talk to Thalia to identify what *she* wants to be. So, in the meantime, tell me… what do ye want, James? At the end of all this." Ailsa was writing again, but her eyes were on him.

"I want a girlfriend. I want Thalia to choose to submit to me sometimes, because we both enjoy it — not because she's terrified of punishment thanks to Marcus. I don't want her to be scared of failing me, as if I'd actually hurt her beyond our play. She knows she has a safe word with me, I ask her every time—"

"Has she ever used the safe word?" Ailsa interrupted.

"No, she hasn't, but I've never seen her lose it in a session either. No hyperventilating or anything like that." James spoke but his mind was stuck on the fact that Thalia had never tested her safe word. Had he ever pushed her too far?

"Do you think she'd use it, James? Or do you think she's afraid to?" Ailsa had paused her pen again.

"I don't know, Ailsa. And... honestly? Part of me still worries that she still just views me as the best alternative to Marcus." James said it and felt the twist of the knife inside him as he finally voiced that fear.

"That might be true. But ye trying to have a normal BDSM relationship with this girl who has no other experience except one filled with terror and violence?" Ailsa scoffed, dropping her professional persona as she slammed her pen down. "Ye ballsed this up. Three or four months of relentless fuck ups from ye, James. Let's hope she's willing to work to fix herself and work through this shite. If not, I don't know what I could do for ye."

"If we can't fix this, I don't know if I want you to try and do anything for me." James muttered, staring at the table between his hands.

"That a boy, James. Yer not hopeless yet." Kalen was half smiling when he looked up at him. "A few more things before we go back."

Kalen's smile dropped, he had shut the file and he was staring seriously across the table.

"Alright." James waited.

"This is my place, right?"

"Of course." James was a little confused as to why Kalen would clarify that. He had never challenged him about Purgatory.

"Then ye understand by coming here, by bringing Thalia, ye are choosing to follow my rules. Whatever I decide they are." Kalen slid the file back to Ailsa who started to pack up while she listened to her brother.

"I haven't argued any of this, Kalen. Wha—"

"I'm not done, James." Kalen's short response grated his nerves, but he made himself listen. "A few things. While ye two are here, neither of ye come without my permission. Ever. That rule doesn't just apply to Thalia, that means no fucking yer pretty little sub, and no handling the business yerself, understand?" Kalen had one hand splayed flat on the table as he spoke, and James felt the urge rise in him to challenge Kalen, to tell him off for setting down rules for him — but James yanked his own leash internally. He'd come here for Thalia, and he'd do whatever it took. He swallowed his pride for her sake alone.

"Fine." James spoke it through gritted teeth and Kalen bared his teeth in something resembling a smile.

Dealing with other Doms was always a bitch.

"In addition to a very generous donation to Purgatory that I think ye'll be making before the end of the day, Thalia is mine to make decisions with until she leaves here. I'll keep ye informed, but ye are not in charge of her time here. Understand?" Kalen was deadly serious, and James pushed back from the table but didn't stand.

Thalia was *his*, and no one else's. James could share with Kalen, fuck knows they'd done it often enough before. But to not have the same standing as the other Doms? To not make decisions? The heat of anger rose up inside him and he felt his cheeks flush. He was about to tell Kalen to shove off.

"Think carefully before ye respond." Ailsa's cool, clinical voice dispersed the rising tide of rage and it fizzled out like foam on the shore. James felt his shoulders relax a bit as he forced a breath. Kalen wasn't some psychopath. If he was asking to be in control of Thalia's training it was because he thought it best. He had come here purely for Kalen's expertise. James just had to remember that, without ripping his friend's head off.

"Yes. I understand. I would have made a donation anyway, and—" James growled a bit. "And I fucking trust you, Kalen. I trust you a lot to even let you near her, so yes, I'll let you run her training, but I won't pull punches if you hurt her or if *you* fuck up." James leveled his gaze at Kalen who returned it steadily.

"Glad to hear it, and I agree to it." Kalen took a breath, in and out. "Last thing — at the end of this I'll decide if ye get to leave with Thalia."

James slammed his hand down on the table, his anger spiraling back so quickly it shocked him. She was the only topic that had ever wound him up so fast. "That is *her* bloody choice, Kalen! Not yours, not Ailsa's, and not mine. Hers."

"I'm glad to hear ye say that, but I'll still do everything I can to keep her safe, even if that means from ye, James. Brother and friend or not. That sub won't leave with ye until I say she's ready." Kalen's eyes finally softened and James took a steadying breath as he tried to imagine not coming home to Thalia for a time, or maybe ever. Her smile, her light brown hair, those hazel eyes sparkling with excitement at seeing him. If he never heard that damn coffee pot again it would kill him.

"Then I guess I better do everything I can to help her succeed." James spoke quietly, and Kalen nodded.

"Ye do that, and I will too." He pushed up and Ailsa stood as well, sliding her bag onto her shoulder. James stood to join them feeling like a heavy weight had settled on his heart. "Let's go see yer girl, alright?"

Now that was something James absolutely wanted.

Chapter Twenty
THALIA

These girls were ridiculous.

Thalia hadn't been able to stop blushing, or laughing, since Julie and Chloe and Lauren had tricked her into admitting just how incredible James was with his mouth. Just the visual of his blond hair between her thighs, his wicked grin when he nipped her, or the way he'd dig his fingers into her hips to stop her wiggling — it had her soaking wet.

"I knew he had to be fantastic! Makes me miss Antonio even more." Julie sighed dramatically as she flopped back against the soft cushions. The way Julie talked about him it was clear she was hopelessly in love with him. "What I wouldn't give to climb on his face for just a few minutes!" She kicked her feet in frustration as they all dissolved into giggles again at her brazen comment. Even Analiese was laughing quietly, it was just Marisol's awkward, glaring silence that dampened their fun.

"Well, Lauren is the best I've ever had." Chloe purred as she ran her nose down Lauren's neck, sending a visible shiver through the girl.

"Chloe..." Lauren's voice was breathy with need and the smile that lit up Chloe's face was unmistakably mischievous. Chloe's hand slid up beneath the hem of Lauren's dress just before Lauren grabbed Chloe's face and yanked her into a kiss that was worthy of a music crescendo, and a close up, and — *holy hell* — Thalia really needed a glass of water and some fresh air and a change of panties.

"Chloe! Lauren! Master Kalen is going to—" Julie started but was cut off when the doors swung open as if his name had summoned him. Kalen stood in the doorway with his hands dropping to his hips and Chloe and Lauren snapped apart like they had suddenly demagnetized. Their eyes were wide as they settled on him, and everyone was waiting for his reaction.

"Thalia, stand up." His voice rumbled through the room, and for a moment she was so surprised to hear her own name instead of the two girls' — who were literally caught in the act — that she didn't move. He tilted his head a bit and she realized she was just staring at him.

"Oh! Sorry, Master Kalen!" Thalia jumped up as Kalen approached her in swift strides. She was overwhelmed by the pulse of arousal between her legs from the conversation with the girls and the sudden flush of memory from her dream as his powerful presence overwhelmed her. His dark eyes swept over her and then he slid his hand into her hair and gripped firmly, tilting her head back. Her mouth was suddenly dry as she looked up at him, his rough features blended together into a warrior's beauty that made her want to curse herself for her dream.

"Thalia." His other hand slid under her skirt and she must have jumped straight up as she felt his fingers swipe the very damp panties against the core of her. "Ye've agreed to submit to me while ye are here, correct?"

"Yes, sir." She shivered as his fingers slid back and forth.

"Good girl. I need ye to tell me something, and I need an honest answer."

"Yes, Master Kalen?" She felt the tension in her belly increase as his touch slid across her pussy, her eyes drifting toward James.

"Only pay attention to me." His fingers moved in rhythmic pulses against her clit, and she felt her hips jerk with each movement. She bit down on her lip to stifle a whimper of pleasure as her eyes met his.

"Uh huh? Yes, sir?" Thalia was quickly rising to the edge. His grip on her hair, his sharp control, the dream, James edging her last night and this morning, and now Kalen touching her… it didn't matter that everyone was staring she was about to shatter.

"In yer own words, why are ye here?" He didn't let up, instead his hand slipped underneath her useless panties and she let out a cry of pleasure as she arched forward into his touch, her legs threatening to buckle.

Just a little more.

"I want to be right for him, Master Kalen." Her voice was so breathy, the need changing her voice until she was almost begging.

"Be specific, Thalia." Two fingers dipped inside her and she arched up, but he slammed her heels back to the floor with a tug on her hair.

"God! I—I want to find a balance between staying his submissive and — *Jesus Christ!* — and being normal! Having a life! Being able to go outside! PLEASE let me come, Master Kalen!" She was so close, her entire focus was in the heat between her legs, the coiling tension around the base of her spine. She'd been waiting and waiting for release. The presence of anyone else in the room had faded and she was almost—

"No." His hands left her and she swayed violently toward him, but he caught her shoulder easily and held on until she steadied. His eyes were compassionate, but he wasn't going to let her come.

Thalia almost cried over that.

"But I'm glad ye feel that way, we just talked and that's what we all want for ye too." Over Kalen's shoulder was James and she felt her lips part to call out for him, but he just smiled a little at her. Although he looked tense, he wasn't angry that she had begged for Kalen, and that calmed her despite the unclaimed orgasm that had the muscles of her lower belly tight with need. Next to James was a beautiful redhead in a skirt suit who was watching her carefully. Thalia's staring was cut short when Kalen's voice boomed again. "Kneel!"

Thalia slid to her knees on reflex, and she realized she was almost directly in front of Kalen. "Yer already doing so well, Thalia. I don't want ye to fret. Just keep it up." He brushed his two fingers against her lips and then as she opened her mouth he slid them over her tongue so she could clean her taste from him. Thalia whimpered with the reminder of her impending pleasure that had been yanked back at the last second. He ran his fingers across her mouth as he took his hand away.

"Good girl." His hand brushed her cheek before he stepped to the side. "See how smooth that was, girls? She didn't just drop to the floor. Yer turns. Kneel, all of ye."

Julie and Analiese slid from the couches with grace. Chloe and Lauren were practically a comedy of errors as they tried so hard not to touch each other that they ended up almost entangled each time they went to kneel in the narrow space between the couches. They finally managed just as Marisol dramatically uncrossed one leg and stood. She took several long strides past the other girls, ending directly next to Thalia. She could feel her eyes staring down at her and Thalia had an urge to trip her; but she didn't get the chance.

Marisol went down on one knee first, letting her dress expose her completely before dropping her other knee into a kneel. Before that, Thalia would have thought there was no way to kneel before someone *rudely*, but Marisol had managed it. And judging by the lecture on submission and how ease and grace play into it, Kalen wasn't ignorant of Marisol's little ploys.

The afternoon flew by with them changing into workout gear to run laps around the huge lawn, followed by high intensity cardio led by Julie. Her chipper voice encouraging and laughing through round after round of exhausting moves. Thalia would have said she was in pretty good shape until Julie had them doing sprints with cardio bursts of various exercises.

Dinner was full of laughter, everyone was spaced around the long table and food appeared from the side from an unseen kitchen. Julie and Maggie laughed and told explicit stories from times Julie had been at Purgatory. Kalen occasionally piped up with his booming voice, and although James had been tense most of the day he started to relax and laugh too. He would lean over occasionally and kiss her neck, or whisper commentary on Kalen's history that had her giggling through dinner. It was the first time she'd been out to eat with him where she didn't feel panic. She couldn't make herself talk loud enough to be heard, but neither did Analiese. She sat in Nick's lap throughout the meal and they whispered to each other, kissing and teasing. Thalia wanted to get time to talk to the quiet girl she had found out was from Germany. Chloe and Lauren sat on either side of Brad who was as loud and boisterous as the two of them. He obviously needed the energy to keep up with the girls. Near the other end of the group were Marisol and Ethan. Marisol wasn't eating, and Ethan looked like he was attempting to bore holes in the table with his stare. The level of uncomfortable silence between them was leeching across the room by the time dinner was drawn to a close.

Kalen's rule of no orgasms without permission meant sleeping was a nightmare. James would always kiss her before bed, making her knees weak and a moan slip out before yanking himself back. His self-control was going to drive her crazy. Especially, since Thalia's mind summoned up everything imaginable to torment her once she was asleep — leaving her wound up and her thighs sticky each morning. And she didn't get any more early morning touches from James.

Two days passed of rinse and repeat. Morning gossip with the girls, practicing holding positions, discussing proper responses, watching Kalen deliver punishments — primarily to Chloe and Lauren, who had no self-control. Their pretty gasps and pleading apologies had her squirming and she absolutely understood what Maggie had meant about watching.

By contrast, Thalia was pretty sure that Julie and Analiese were incapable of messing up — and somehow, they could both still laugh and joke and act like normal people. Thalia envied them both for the ease with which they acted.

Marisol was horrible, and Kalen didn't punish her with a belt like he had Chloe and Lauren, but she had earned a particularly devious punishment by mouthing off *again*. With her hands bound she had to kneel on a mat made of large beads. At first it hadn't seemed to bother her, her chin defiantly in the air. Quickly the pressure on her knees and shins had her begging to be allowed up. Kalen had ignored her while talking with the rest of the group and their Doms about open communication — that is until she had sincerely started crying and shouted "Red! Red!". Ethan and Kalen had immediately helped her up, Marisol had collapsed into Ethan's arms, and Julie had mumbled under her breath.

Julie was convinced that Marisol was only with Ethan for his money, and Chloe, Lauren, and even Analiese agreed. The more she watched her, the more she agreed with them.

Marisol was defiant, aggressive, and disrespectful. She didn't accept her punishments no matter how well deserved and had called out her safe word in almost no time at all. Thalia was angry with herself for judging the other girl, though. Who was she to say what Marisol's threshold for pain was? Marisol may be rude, and probably a gold digger, but Thalia couldn't fault her for using her safe word. Although it only took one glance around the room to see that Julie, for sure, didn't believe she'd needed it.

Chapter Twenty-One
THALIA

On the third day it was finally Thalia's turn for therapy. Lars had waved her down while she was running laps with Analiese — who was insanely quick and was still able to talk while Thalia was pretty sure she may drop into a dead faint trying to keep pace. Thalia could run a long time at a decent gait, Analiese was just fast. She'd never been more grateful to see the young Dom-to-be as when she got to go back into the dormitory and follow Lars down a hallway while catching her breath.

One of the bedrooms on the first floor had long ago apparently been converted into Ailsa's on-site office. Complete with waiting chairs outside the door. Lars smiled at her and turned to walk off, but he stopped. "I have advice for you, if that's okay?" His accent was thick, Julie had told her he spoke Dutch, but Thalia couldn't have picked that language out of a line up at all. Thalia nodded and smiled at him. He gave a half smile back, his eyes looking her over as he spoke, "I have not been at Purgatory long, but... be honest with Ailsa, she can help. It's always bad if you lie to her, okay? Nothing will go good if you lie."

"Yes, sir. I won't lie, I promise." Thalia smiled at him again and he nodded and turned to go back down the hall. Probably doing whatever Kalen had on his to-do list next. She sat down on the floor to stretch and then stayed there as she waited, tucking her legs underneath her as she brought her heart rate down.

"THEY'RE ALL CRAZY!" Marisol's Spanish accent rang out through the door, making Thalia jump. Soft murmurs came in response, but she couldn't make them out.

"I refuse to be some trained pet!" There she went again on that rant. If Ethan was anything like James, he didn't want that. And if she hated this so much, why didn't she just leave? No one would miss her.

"Why would Ethan want this? I thought he loved me! Have you asked him? Have any of you even asked him whether or not he loves me more than this bullshit?!" Marisol's voice was grating, and her words were prideful and manipulative. A better question might be: Why was she with someone who was dominant if she didn't want who they were?

What a bitch.

There were more murmurs and then a screech of frustration. After a few days around Marisol, Thalia could imagine her stomping her foot and throwing her hands up.

The door opened and Ailsa's soft voice came through, "I really want ye to think this through, Marisol. Ye do not seem open to this or happy with it at all."

Marisol huffed and stomped out in her workout clothes that looked like they were made by some designer. Black running pants hugged every inch of her long legs, clinging close down to her ankle. A light, airy top barely hid the t-back black sports bra underneath. Her dark eyes landed on Thalia who immediately dropped her gaze to the floor hoping to avoid her.

It didn't work.

"Happy?! How could I be happy like that?!" Marisol must have gestured toward her and it made Thalia flinch. "She's just kneeling on the floor waiting for her *Master*," she sneered the word that Thalia held with such care. "Waiting for someone to tell her what to do! I'm NOT weak like that, Ailsa. I'm no one's slave."

Weak?

"For the last time, Ethan does not want a full-time slave." Ailsa spoke calmly and evenly.

"But—" Marisol started, and Ailsa immediately stopped her.

"I've heard enough today, Marisol. Yer time is up, please return to physical training, we'll talk again in a few days."

Marisol burst out with a little frustrated scream and then started muttering in Spanish as she stomped down the hallway. Thalia stayed kneeling, but as the silence stretched she tilted her head up to find Ailsa leaning against the doorframe watching her. She made a quiet sound as her dark eyes moved over her, analyzing and calm. "Tell me, how long would ye kneel there if no one told ye to get up?" Her accent was thick, like Kalen's, but she sounded curious, interested — not judging or demanding.

"I don't know?" Thalia's voice cracked when she answered. The bitter taste that Marisol's words had left in her mouth crashed against the undeniable physical representation of her submission. Kneeling for no reason next to a row of waiting chairs. Great start to therapy. She wanted to get up, and correct it, but Lars' words rebounded in her head. The truth was Thalia didn't know how long she would have knelt in front of Ailsa, and she rarely sat on chairs anymore without direction. Thalia knew that was weird, wasn't that why she was here?

"Thalia, come inside, let's talk." Ailsa just walked back in the room, and after a moment Thalia rose and followed her in. Ailsa sat down in a chair next to a desk, and she sat down on the love seat Ailsa indicated across from her. Kalen's sister spoke again immediately, "I want to talk about Marcus."

Thalia flinched and she looked up to see Ailsa analyzing her again.

"Does it bother ye for me to say his name?"

"No." Thalia licked her lips and grabbed a pillow on the couch, tucking it into her lap. "I've said his — *Marcus'* — name. I'm fine."

"That's good." Ailsa made notes in a journal she had balanced on the arm of the chair. "I'm glad ye can discuss him because we need to."

"Yes, ma'am." Thalia took a breath trying not to get sucked into the memories Marcus' name brought up.

"Call me Ailsa, please. I'm not a Domme, I'm just a therapist, and I'm here for ye. Not Kalen, not James. Alright?"

"Alright." Thalia felt her hands tightening on the edge of the pillow, and Ailsa looked up at her. "Ailsa, I understand."

"Wonderful. So, tell me about Marcus, what happened?" Her voice was calm, interested, open.

"He took me to his house, and he—" Thalia stumbled over how to describe everything Marcus had done. "And Marcus, he trained me to be a slave, so he could sell me."

"That's it?"

"Yeah." Thalia's knuckles turned white as she gripped the pillow, her voice was tense and she really wanted to leave. This was not how she imagined therapy, shouldn't there be a warm up? A discussion of her mother's death? Her neglectful father? Her lack of ambition? Anything but diving head first into the worst week of her entire life?

"Thalia." Ailsa was leaning forward, it clearly wasn't the first time she'd said her name. "Breathe, Thalia."

Thalia gasped a breath and realized she hadn't been breathing, and once she started the rapid, shallow breaths wouldn't stop.

"Thalia, with me." Ailsa started to breathe slowly and evenly, and she made herself mimic her while trying to calm down. A few minutes later she was breathing slower and steadier and Ailsa was writing in the journal.

"Does that happen often?" Ailsa glanced up at her.

No lies, right? "Yes. It happens."

"When you discuss Marcus?" Ailsa asked it, and Thalia felt her muscles tense.

"No, but it happens a lot." Thalia hated it. It happened all the time. It was why she was useless outside of the flat, it was why James had brought her here.

"Hmm. I see." More notes in her journal. "I have a relatively good idea of what happened with Marcus, I won't make ye detail it for me unless there is a specific event ye want to discuss." Ailsa looked up at her, "Ye understand that none of what happened with him was consensual, right?"

Thalia was silent, biting on her thumbnail and staring at the floor. Memories were flickering through her mind at rapid speed.

"Thalia, do you understand that ye never consented to it? That yer not responsible in any way?" Ailsa was using therapist voice. Scottish accent or not, therapists always sounded the same when they asked questions.

Thalia clenched her eyes shut and pressed the heels of her palms against them. "You don't understand."

"What don't I understand?" More therapist voice.

How can you explain something so horrible? Confess to the worst things you've ever done?

But James had told her to work with Ailsa, Lars had told her she had to be honest for it to work, so she would. No matter how terrible.

"I did consent, Ailsa." Thalia bit her lip against the urge to scream or throw up. "I didn't just consent, I *begged* him."

"Under what circumstances, Thalia? Tell me about a time when ye gave him consent." How could Ailsa be so blasé after such a confession? Maybe being a therapist made you good at hiding your disgust.

"There were a lot of times." Thalia mumbled, dropping her hands back to the pillow in her lap to stare at them.

"Tell me one? I want to help ye, so please tell me."

Thalia looked up at Ailsa and saw such a gentle expression on her face that she found herself answering. "The second day there he had me tied to a bed. And he had, he left me there with a vibrator, you know, in me. And he left me there for hours until I begged for him to come back, until I called him Master. I begged for him to come back and I knew what he'd do."

"So, what was the alternative?"

"What?" Thalia felt the heat of a blush after her confession, but confusion overwhelmed her embarrassment.

"What would have happened if ye had refused to call for him? To 'beg for him' as ye said?"

"I guess he would have left me there?"

"Anything else?"

Thalia thought back to the day and remembered that he had also withheld lunch; she had been hungry. "He wouldn't have fed me."

"So yer options were to stay tied to a bed, being sexually tormented, and starving — or call out for him, and be fed, and be taken care of?"

"I could have refused him. I could have fought him. I could have—" Thalia realized she was crying and forcefully brushed the tears off her cheeks, burying her reddening face in her hands.

"What?"

"Nothing." Thalia dug her fingernails into her palms. *Stop crying, dammit.*

"Thalia, this doesn't work if ye don't talk to me." Ailsa leaned forward in her chair, setting the folder aside. "Come on, talk to me. What do ye think ye could have done?"

"I could have not come for him!" Thalia shouted and hated herself for crying, for hearing her breath catch.

"Really? Ye think ye could have avoided a very natural biological response to stimuli?"

"I didn't come for Anthony!" Thalia was surprised when she shouted at Ailsa, but Ailsa didn't even flinch.

"Anthony didn't condition ye, Thalia. Marcus did." She spoke so calmly. Thalia just stared at her, not knowing what she meant. "Tell me, what happened when ye disobeyed Marcus?"

"He punished me."

"Rather harshly if what I've been told is true. And what happened when ye obeyed him? When ye did what he wanted?" Ailsa's pen was poised over the journal.

"He was... nice." Thalia felt nauseous and shook her head. "No, that's not the right word. Not nice, but he kind of was, it's just—"

"It's alright to use whatever language fits. So, if ye obeyed, he was nice." She was writing again. "He gave ye orgasms, right?"

Thalia blushed furiously and couldn't bring herself to answer, but Ailsa didn't seem to need it.

"He brainwashed ye, Thalia, with the simplest of biological urges — pleasure and pain. He programmed ye to react the way he needed ye to. Obedience resulted in a chemical high from orgasm, a rush of endorphins, pleasure, kindness, food. Disobedience resulted in pain, punishment, and violence. And ye wonder why ye didn't fight him? It was survival, Thalia, and ye survived. But now ye have to recognize that those harsh alternatives aren't yer reality anymore."

The words sank in. All of it was true, but the crippling guilt over coming for Marcus, for calling out for him, was still there. Did it really matter *why* she'd begged for him?

"Thalia? Talk to me." Ailsa set her pen in the middle of the journal and leaned forward. "Does James use these same methods?"

"What the fuck?" Thalia stared at Ailsa like she had grown a second head, and for once she saw a slight response in her facial expression. "What is it with you and Ka—Master Kalen? Master told me you were his friends, that you've known him for years, and both of you — BOTH of you — have accused him of being like Marcus!"

"Thalia—"

"Stop it! Marcus was—" She gritted her teeth. "He was fucking terrifying. I never knew what I could do, or couldn't do, and he changed the fucking rules all the time. My Master is consistent, and he never just hurts me, he's never scared me, and he cares about me. Don't compare them! Don't fucking compare them!"

"Alright, alright, I'm not." Ailsa was trying to soothe her, her voice calm and steady.

"Good." Thalia sat back and wiped her cheeks again.

"One more question and I'll be done for today... if yer not afraid of James, if he is so different, then why are ye so afraid of being yourself, of maybe screwing up around him, that ye won't even try to be more than his submissive?"

Thalia opened her mouth to answer sharply, and then closed it.

She wasn't afraid. *Was she?*

Chapter Twenty-Two
JAMES

James was frustrated because Thalia had seemed off since her first therapy session with Ailsa, but she wouldn't tell him what was bothering her. She'd said she'd had to talk about Marcus, about what he'd done, but she wouldn't say anything else and *something* had happened to upset her.

James wanted to tell her she never had to talk to Ailsa again, that it was alright, and that they could just leave. Maybe in the middle of the night.

Like right now.

Because he really wasn't sure how much longer he could deal with letting Kalen run the show, experience and expertise or not.

Moving carefully on the bed James pushed himself up until he was leaning back against the headboard. Thalia was curled on her side into a little ball, her light brown hair spread out on the pillow above and behind her head, and her soft lips were parted with the slow, steady breaths of sleep.

God. He really wanted to fuck her.

He wanted to hear her gasp and moan in his ear, feel her body go tight under him as he brought her to orgasm, pin her down to make her come again when she thought she couldn't handle another one. His cock *absolutely* agreed with that line of thinking, and it throbbed inside his pants, rigid and impossible. He gripped it through the fabric and immediately regretted it as his stomach tightened with the instinct to thrust against his hand.

She made a sound in her sleep, and although his eyes had trailed down the outline of her body, his gaze snapped back to her face to see if she was okay. He had flashbacks to when she'd first come home with him, and she'd had nightmares almost every night. She was fine though, and back to breathing evenly. Beautiful, and smart, and strong, and absolutely fine — but it didn't suppress James' sudden urge to metaphorically wrap her in bubble wrap and do everything in his power to keep her from feeling upset ever again.

What the bloody hell had Ailsa said to her? And why hadn't Kalen let her, and him, get off in the six days they'd been at Purgatory?

His head wouldn't let it go so he grabbed his phone to find that it was after four in the morning. Pointless to try and sleep now since today was the day Ailsa and Kalen wanted to test Thalia's sense of self-preservation. And if James was honest with himself, there was a part of him worried that Thalia wouldn't protect herself in the session. Especially after she kept the panic attacks hidden.

Thalia rolled onto her back and the whisper of fabric over skin as the sheet slid down to her waist had his full attention. His cock jumped against his hand, and he gripped himself harder. So much perfect, milky skin. Before he could think about it James was running his fingertips across the slice of her collarbone, brushing the hollow under her neck and trailing down between her breasts. She arched slightly into his touch, and he gritted his teeth against a groan as he watched her body roll up toward his hand. He brushed his thumb over her nipple and the pink bud tightened under his touch. He wanted to taste her skin, to pull that bud into his mouth and hear her cry out. He moved his hand farther down instead. Her stomach was soft and smooth as he trailed his fingers to where the sheet cut a diagonal line toward the swell of her hip.

James wanted to repeat that path with his tongue, wanted to push her thighs apart and bury himself inside her to wake her up. Feel her nails dig into his arms, his shoulders, his back, where she could leave little half-moon marks as she rocked her hips, meeting him thrust for thrust. His balls ached and he growled as he tugged her sheet up, instead of down.

He had to get away from Thalia or he was going to break his promise to Kalen and potentially ruin everything.

A moment later he was in the shower and he flipped the water to cold and bit down on a curse as he was pelted with water a few degrees away from forming ice. He leaned his head against the wall and started to run through topics he had to cover in his unavoidable meetings at work the following week, statistics and fiscal reports. Anything to block out the beautiful, and very naked, submissive lying in the other room. It was foolish to think of Thalia again, because he wanted to touch her, taste her, spank her, fuck her — but as he thought about the next week his lust wavered. Thinking of being away from her for five days while he was back in London instantly had him miserable. An effective deterrent to his ever-present sex drive. Just as he started to shiver from the cold water, his cock finally gave up.

When he flipped the water back to warm so he could shower he blew out a breath.

James knew he was in deep with Thalia. That she had found some unknown place inside him that was making her impossible to remove if she left him, and he'd give anything to stay with her, to be worthy of staying with her, because he—

Well, shit, the 'L' word already?

He had to talk to Kalen.

Before he left for London.

And in that discussion he'd have to remind Kalen that he cared about her, more than he was even admitting to himself. He'd also remind him of just who Thalia belonged to, because this second-rate Dom bullshit wasn't going to work.

Yes, he and Kalen needed to talk.

Their morning routine went relatively smoothly. When the phone alarm went off James woke up Thalia with a kiss, and she pressed against him, tugging at the shirt he'd put on until he had to pin her arms before he gave in to her sweet pleas and fucked her until this half of the dormitory could serve as auditory witnesses for James' lack of self-control. "Get up, pet, and get ready." His voice was rough.

"Master…" She pouted prettily, begging him to touch her with a roll of her hips.

Vixen.

"Up." James sent her to the shower with a spank, trying to ignore the way the light of the bathroom outlined her curves. The way she smiled at him and looked over her shoulder before she stepped through the doorway, had his cock making suggestions. He spent the next fifteen minutes reading the most boring emails he could find, while imagining everything he'd like to do with Thalia once they were back home and all this was done. He was definitely going to bind her, light her skin up with a flogger, and then make her come until she begged him to stop — after that? He'd get creative.

The morning meeting was focused on Ethan again, with Kalen explaining calmly that Marisol was not interested in being a submissive. Ethan kept replying that Marisol wanted to try the lifestyle. If that guy couldn't see through Marisol's bullshit then it wasn't James' place to enlighten him. Kalen was working on the situation, but the poor guy said he loved her, that he was even thinking of trying it vanilla for a while. Ailsa asked good questions about whether that would satisfy Ethan's needs, and he'd stayed silent. James had seen Doms like him try to make it work and it always fell apart — but no one was going to make Ethan see that until he was ready. No matter how many credit card bills he got in the meantime.

Then they had spent time talking about the plan for Thalia, to 'test her ability to protect herself.' If she failed Kalen and Ailsa's test, it would damage Kalen's perception of their relationship, and it would color every session James'd had with her over the past few months.

He was sick over it.

The opportunity to grab Kalen and talk with him one-on-one before the session with Thalia never came. By the time James had made it over to him, Kalen was late for a training session with Brad, Chloe and Lauren and he didn't have a minute. Kalen gripped his shoulder and said they'd catch up later, but he didn't see him again until it was time.

James was even more sick when Sven came to grab him and brought him out to the front lawn where the girls had been doing a warm up run and some cardio. Thalia was laughing with Analiese as they finished a lap, and he couldn't believe how comfortable she looked, or how her smile could make him feel warm from two hundred yards away. The sun was filtering through the overcast sky, occasionally lighting up the honey strands of her hair. She didn't even understand how beautiful she was. Her ass looked incredible in the running pants, and once he'd noticed *that* he completely lost track of whatever Kalen was saying. She was perfection. James watched as Thalia started to walk over to him, broad smile, that excited twinkle in her eyes — but Kalen didn't let that happen and James had to root himself to the spot to keep from touching her or contradicting Kalen in front of everyone.

It grated on his nerves like nothing else. James was her Dom, dammit.

"Thalia, come here." Kalen's voice snapped across the lawn, and she paused a second before turning back to kneel by the other girls — disappointment evident on her face.

Yeah, baby, I feel the same way.

"Chloe, yer meeting with Ailsa. Lauren ye will *not* just sit outside Ailsa's office, go with Julie for a review on patience and quiet. Ye could use it. Analiese could help with that I'm sure." The German girl couldn't stifle her smile or the side glance she cast at Lauren who was blushing and almost opened her mouth to speak — but quickly thought better of proving Kalen's point. "Marisol, ye will go with Sven to meet up with Ethan for practice. Thalia, yer staying here. Alright ladies, go on." There was a flurry of activity. Julie hugged Thalia tightly before bounding off toward the house with the other girls, and then they were alone on the wide lawn.

"Thalia, we're about to run yer first session here at Purgatory." Kalen spoke clearly as he stood in front of her, and Thalia's eyebrows pulled together in confusion. Kalen picked up on it, "We're outside because based on yer history we've decided to do this a little differently."

"Yes, Master Kalen." Her voice was perfect submission, hazel eyes on the ground.

"All ye have to do is obey, understand?" Kalen was using his Dom voice, and he was always a little louder than necessary, but it had Thalia nodding. "Tell us yer safe word."

"Chair." She spoke it clearly and James could only pray silently that she used it.

"Thalia, look at me." Kalen gentled his voice a bit, but it still held bite. She lifted her head and James smiled when her eyes found him first, and then corrected back to Kalen.

That's my girl.

"Yer going to do burpees for us, just like ye have done with Julie. But we want them done perfectly. That means jumping, both feet off the ground, dropping down, jumping yer feet back to a push-up position, and then bringing them back, and jumping again. That counts as one. Do ye remember how to do it?" Kalen finished, and James could have laughed. Thalia did them all the time at the flat, she had her own little routine that James took great pleasure in watching while he ran the treadmill. It wasn't a question of *if* she could do them properly, but for *how long* she could do them.

"Yes, Master Kalen. I know how." Thalia held his gaze with confidence and James was proud of her. Her legs were slightly spread in the kneel, her palms resting on her thighs, back straight, light brown hair pulled back into a bun to stay out of her face for her morning run. The dark running pants hugged her legs, and the pale purple tank top made her chest stand out. He liked it better when he watched her do them in just a sports bra and underwear, but it was cool outside so he'd enjoy this view just fine.

"Well, get started, pet." James had spoken before he realized it, and her gaze flicked to him instantly. Kalen looked at him too and he felt the tension between them strain. Thalia stood up to do her first one, and he spoke again, "Face the left so we can make sure you stay in form."

Another ratchet of tension from Kalen, he could see his friend's shoulders tighten, but he didn't care. Thalia was his submissive and if anyone was going to push her to her safe word, it was going to be him.

"Go on." Kalen added, and it grated with James. He'd always been good at sharing with Kalen in the past, but right now he wanted to push his friend back from Thalia and stake a claim.

She's mine.

"Yes, Master." Thalia responded only to him and a swell of pride filled his chest. She bounced on her running shoes, dropped smoothly to a crouch, kicked her feet back and landed in a perfect plank position. His eyes traced the line of her back to the swell of her ass and bit his cheek to keep from smiling. She held the plank for a moment, and then jumped her feet forward and bounced up.

"Perfect. Again." James spoke before Kalen had the chance and his friend took a half step back to stand shoulder to shoulder with him. Thalia continued, her breaths still smooth and even, repeating the moves again and again.

"James, what are ye doing?" Kalen whispered so that Thalia couldn't hear over the sounds of her own movements.

"Doing what you asked, Kalen." James muttered in response, trying his best to keep the irritation out of his tone. She'd already done so many perfectly, and James was impressed. He was normally focused on things other than proper form when he watched her, but she was strong and showing it now.

"I told ye, I'm in charge while she's here." Kalen spoke quietly again, his words covered by her soft grunt as she jumped her feet forward.

"If she's going to safe word for anyone, Kalen. It will be me. She's my sub." James said it in such a way that made it clear to his friend that it wasn't open to discussion. Previous agreements or not, James couldn't handle Kalen running this. *Not this.*

"I'm staying, James." Kalen crossed his arms and James shrugged. As long as he kept his mouth shut, he could watch. James tracked her as she jumped back and her hips dipped toward the ground as her core began to tire.

"Lift your hips, flat back." James felt the control come back and the frustration that had been fraying his nerves over the past week faded. Watching Thalia instantly correct from his command was like a fix of his favorite drug, and he only wanted more.

Again, and again, she completed the moves. The muted bounce of her chest when she jumped up made his cock pay attention. Every curve of her body as she moved had him imagining his hands, his mouth, all over her. Her hips dipped again.

"Hips up, Thalia," he corrected, and she groaned.

Chapter Twenty-Three
THALIA

She lifted her hips until she felt her back straighten again, but she was quickly regretting trying to keep pace with Analiese that morning. The girl was sweet, but was really only talkative during a run, and so Thalia always pushed herself to keep up with her. Jumping forward she forced her legs to bounce her feet off the ground as she reached for the sky, and she could feel James and Kalen's eyes waiting for her next error. She just kept going, over and over.

How many of these was she going to have to do? She hadn't even been counting.

As more passed she could feel her legs getting weak, her knees aching to give her some respite by dropping to the ground.

"Legs straight!" James' voice caught her before she'd even started to drop her knees, at least, she thought she'd had them straight.

Who did burpees like this? No one. That's who. And why didn't they do it? Because it's ridiculous. This is ridiculous! She dropped again and felt her arms shaking to hold her in the plank position. As she tried to catch her breath the shaking spread down her body until she could feel her whole core vibrating with the effort of holding position.

"Thalia, straighten out. You know better." The admonishment made her gritted her teeth and push through. Rinse and repeat. Over and over. Her breathing was getting ragged, the shaking growing more intense with each plank. He caught her just after she had jumped back to hold the push-up position, her body quaking under the strain.

"Hold it there." James' voice had that wicked edge of amusement, he knew exactly what he was doing. She knew if she could see his eyes they'd be turning that dark green that always made her wet in anticipation. "Hold it. Back straight. Lift your hips." She did. The shaking grew more intense and she whimpered, fighting the urge to drop her knees, or just hit the ground. "Good girl. Up. Again."

With a grunt of effort, she brought her feet forward and bounced up.

"Both feet off the ground. Jump again."

Seriously?

She jumped again, pushing harder to clear the ground for a nanosecond before dropping back to a crouch, plank again, and up. *How long were they going to make her do this?*

A handful later and the frustration was getting to her as exhaustion set in, her muscles were giving out and every cycle was an endless list of corrections from James. "Did I say you could rest? Get in plank. Hips up. Legs straight. Straight back. Don't step forward, jump your feet to your hands. Jump higher. You know you're supposed to clear the ground. Up. Again."

A little scream of frustration ripped out of her, as she did yet another. Her body was shaking from the strain, getting back to a standing position took an exhaustive amount of effort and left her whimpering.

"Again." James' voice was clear and steady, and she wanted to scream at him that she couldn't do another. But she tried. Her arms almost collapsed when her weight dropped onto them to get into push-up position. Tears gathered in her eyes as she felt her hips drop, her knees angling toward the ground. "Straight back, Thalia." She pushed until her body shook hard.

"Please, Master. Please may I stop?" She begged between her loud breaths, and she couldn't lift her head to see his expression, all she heard was—

"No. Again."

Frustrated tears ran down her cheeks as she pushed harder to get to her feet again. She stood for longer than she knew was okay, but she just couldn't do another. She couldn't. "Please, Master?"

"Thalia, jump." James' voice hadn't changed and she wanted to scream, she wanted to beg him, she wanted to drop to her knees in front of him and ask him what the hell this was supposed to prove. Why wasn't this enough?!

She dropped to plank again and her arms gave out, but she caught herself on an elbow before she hit the grass. "Master—"

Instead of comforting her, James' voice snapped above her, "Up. On your hands."

That's when she started crying. She was exhausted, she couldn't do anymore. She couldn't. Couldn't he see that?

"Thalia! Up!" His command had her responding, and she pushed up even though her muscles burned and her body argued.

She knew it was terrible form, but she moved through one more cycle, James' voice running commentary on every tiny error she made. Every little way she was failing him, in front of Kalen. Who knew how many she had completed? Fifty? A hundred? Two? How could he ask for more than she was capable? Couldn't he see she was done? That her body couldn't take any more?

She snapped.

Thalia had been standing but she collapsed to a kneel, dropping her head down as she heaved a ragged breath, tears streaking her cheeks as she finally gave up. "Chair! Chair, I can't! I can't anymore! Chair, please, Master, please." She planted her hands on the ground in front of her as she tried to catch her breath, her fingers digging into the blades of grass. She was shaking from the strain she'd put herself through, and then she felt cool hands on her cheeks lifting her head up.

"You did amazing, baby. Amazing. You are incredible." James kissed her, his fingers pressing against the back of her neck, but he pulled back so she could continue catching her breath. His thumbs wiped her cheeks, and now that she could see his face, his dark green eyes had her swimming. "I'm so proud of you." Pride flared in her chest at those words.

"Ye did very well, Thalia. Maybe we should have ye running the physical training instead of Julie." Kalen was smiling warmly at her.

"She can keep it, Master Kalen. I prefer yoga for a reason." They both laughed and James kissed her again.

"For a minute there I was worried you wouldn't use your safe word. You pushed way past what I thought you could handle, baby." James' expression was tense with concern, and she glanced at Kalen to see him evaluating her in a look so similar to Ailsa she almost laughed.

"That was the purpose of this? To make me safe word?" Thalia looked back at James, a little spark of irritation lighting inside her. She had thought there was a number, that they'd stop it when they saw her physical exhaustion. She had felt ridiculous saying her safe word for what was basically an intense workout.

"We had to know that ye would, it was Ailsa's primary concern. James told us ye had never used it." Kalen was still dissecting her with his gaze.

"I've never needed it." Thalia turned back to James, "Master, I swear, I've never needed it." The edge of his mouth lifted, and the hunger in his eyes softened for a second.

"I believe you. We just needed to know you'd recognize your own limits, that you'd keep yourself safe if you needed to." James' voice was gentle, the edge it held through the session had faded. The hunger returned to his gaze though as he slid his hands to her shoulders, his mouth finding hers just before he bit her lip. "Let's go back to our room so I can make you feel better." A wicked grin slid across his face, and Thalia was instantly wet. Six days of teasing and tension — she wanted him more than anything. She wanted him to take her hard, however he wanted her, again and aga—

"We should discuss the session with Ailsa." Kalen's voice held an edge, and it made Thalia trip over her very pleasant thoughts. James stood up and faced Kalen. In a second the whole mood of the space shifted, Thalia watched silently as they locked their eyes in a stare down.

"I'm taking her upstairs, Kalen." James' voice had a growl to it, and her stomach dropped. Why would Kalen argue with James? She'd passed, hadn't she? Was she in trouble for something?

"That was not our agreement, James." Kalen was speaking through his teeth, and she felt their anger spike.

"What the bloody hell do you want from her? Are you looking for something specific, or is this just a power thing with you?" James raised his voice, facing off with Kalen properly and leaving Thalia on her knees to his right.

"Everything I'm doing is *for* her! Just because it's not what ye want, doesn't mean it's not the right feking choice!" Kalen raised his voice too which went from booming, to uncomfortably loud. Thalia was waiting for people to come out of the dormitory to see what was happening. A blush spread across her cheeks that had nothing to do with her workout.

"She is *my* sub, not yours. Fuck your special rules, Kalen, I deserve at least the same respect you give the other Doms here!"

"Really? Ye *deserve* respect?" Kalen laughed bitterly, "After how ye got, Thalia? After ye lied to me? After ye betrayed everything we have ever stood for and walked into *my* training school, and dared to pretend to be the same man I've called BROTHER?" Kalen was shouting, and Thalia could only watch with a sinking feeling in her stomach as the two Doms cleared the air.

"I am the same man, Kalen! Jesus, I came to you! As soon as I realized she needed more than I could provide, I came to you!" James shoved his hand through his blond hair, holding it back from his forehead a moment as color hit his cheekbones. "Would you rather me have left her with them? Rather me have not harassed the fuck out of Anthony to move up the auction so I could get her out faster? Bloody hell, I would do anything for her! I will NOT apologize for having her in my life. I — I care about her!" Thalia's heart was racing, and the tears in her eyes were all about how hard James had fought for her. They had *both* fought to get here. Why couldn't Kalen see that?

"Ye know we are all glad she's here and safe. That is not the issue." Kalen's voice calmed a bit.

"I knew you'd be pissed, but I trusted we could weather this after everything we've been through together. I trusted you to know my intentions better than this! I didn't think you'd abuse the bloody situation or try and pull me away from her!"

Pull her away? What?!

Panic gripped Thalia's chest as the same fear from the night of their argument swelled. She couldn't imagine not having James. She wouldn't leave him, not unless he kicked her out — and that would leave her hollow. Marcus hadn't broken her but losing James might do it.

"Dammit, James." Kalen turned away and walked a few steps with his fists clenched. He turned around and his eyes landed on Thalia, and she jerked back with the intensity of his gaze. "I don't want to pull her away from ye. I want ye to be happy, we were all worried the last couple of years, and I think Thalia makes ye happy." Kalen's eyes moved back to James and she felt like she could breathe again. "But ye brought her here to get better, and we are all working on that. And part of that is talking about this session with Ailsa."

The tension eased and James looked down at her, his dark green eyes moved over her in a way that had her heart hammering a tattoo in her chest. "I want to take her upstairs, then she can see Ailsa."

"My God…" he sighed, exasperated, "Thalia? What do ye want?" Kalen was looking at her again and having the undivided attention of two very intense Doms made her mouth dry. She wanted to disappear into the ground for a moment, but the tilt to James' head as his eyes roamed over her pulled her back.

She'd been begging for days for what she wanted, what she always wanted — every minute of every day.

"Please, Master Kalen, I would really like to go upstairs. Please?" Her voice sounded so soft in comparison to the angry voices that had thundered across the expanse of the lawn moments before, but Kalen just laughed and looked at James.

"She does beg so prettily." Kalen's voice rumbled, and James' wicked grin was back.

"Yes, she does, and I think I want to hear more of it." His voice dropped and liquid heat pooled between her thighs.

"Not on my lawn, please. Fine. Get upstairs. Then she sees Ailsa." Kalen sounded stern, but his eyes were dancing as James tugged her to her feet and swept her over his shoulder in a fireman's carry. She squealed and he brought his hand down sharply on her ass, making her squirm against him.

"Gladly."

The door to the bedroom slammed and her world flipped again, but she never touched the ground. James slid her down his front and pinned her against the door with his body. He kissed her like he was starving, and she returned it — because they *were* starving for each other. It had been too long.

Her legs wrapped around his waist and she moaned into his mouth as she felt his hard length grind against her core. She pushed her hands into his hair to hold him to her and she rocked her hips against him, and he let her. He nipped her lip and she gasped, rolling her hips against him again as electricity sparked down her spine. She was *finally* starting to work toward release.

"I can't be gentle right now." James growled against the skin of her shoulder.

"I don't want you to be gentle." Thalia breathed and he bit down on the skin of her shoulder as he drove his hips hard against hers with a groan. The full length of her back pressed against the unforgiving door, and she moaned against his skin. One of his hands slid up under her tank top while the other wrenched the hair tie from her hair, the sting making her hiss before her waves dropped around her shoulders. His hand found her breast and he pinched her nipple through the sports bra. Not enough!

Stupid clothes.

She rubbed against him again, his own groan matching hers and then his fist tightened in her hair. "Go on. Take it. Make yourself come." He ground his hips into hers, the hardest part of him giving a delicious friction that had her arching away from the door. He wasn't having it, his body slammed her back against the door hard and he rocked his hips again, and she met him. Again and again, her pleasure spiking as he gathered her wrists and held them above her head. Her mouth was open, moans and whimpers of pleasure were all she was able to articulate as she tumbled headlong toward her orgasm. His mouth was on her neck, her shoulder, tracing her jaw and then he captured her mouth and pressed against her so she could finally come. She used him, rubbing her core against him in rapid rocking movements that had her mind overloading.

Her body tightened, her lungs caught, and lightning pulsed into liquid heat between her thighs as she shattered. She cried out, knocking her head back against the door as she squirmed against him, but he held her firm. Every line of his body still taut with tension as he let her coast down from her orgasm. "Thank you, thank you, thank you…" she was babbling and she didn't care. He groaned in her ear and left a trail of nipping kisses down her throat.

"You are so hot." His hips bucked against hers again and she was intimately aware of just how much he wanted her.

"Please, Master," she pleaded, arching against him again, and tugging at his grip on her wrists.

"Please what?" His voice was rough, and she hissed as he tilted his head down and bit her nipple through the layers of fabric.

"Please fuck me!" She jerked at his grip again and he tightened his hold on her wrists and in her hair until she moaned. She'd missed this, she needed this. When his head came back up there was only a thin rim of green around the black of his pupils, and she knew her own need reflected back at him.

"Anything for you." His hands dropped to support her against him and he walked to the bed and pushed her back onto it. His fingers instantly delved under the waist of her running pants and her panties, and he pulled them off with such force her hips came off the bed. Then his mouth was nipping, kissing up the inside of her thighs and her fingers found his hair again, driving her hips up toward his mouth.

He didn't disappoint her. He growled as his tongue swiped between the lips of her pussy, gathering the evidence of her first orgasm and sending her arching off the bed with a moan that ripped out of her at surprising volume. His fingers dug into her hips as she moved against him, his tongue swiping ever closer to her clit. She was whimpering, begging in incoherent streams, her hands alternatively in her hair, and then the sheets, and then back into his hair to try and bring him closer to what she needed.

"Oh God! Please! I can't! I can't!" She was half-screaming, and he lifted his head with a grin, leaving her tenuously at the edge.

"You can. I know you can, baby." And with a delicate swipe of his tongue he thrust two fingers inside her, leaving her clit untouched as she squirmed. She tried to rock her hips harder, so close to another orgasm, but he eased his touch back, keeping her completion just out of reach. His mouth trailed bites and kisses over her hips, the outside of her thighs, his tongue moving across her lower stomach, inches from where she craved it. She was losing it, too much teasing over the last week, her body was tense, her back arching sharply so she was looking at the opposite wall.

"Oh fuck, oh fuck…" She twined her hands in the sheets by her head and he bit down on her thigh, making her gasp.

"Language, pet." His mouth edged closer to her core just as his fingers curved to hit that bundle of nerves inside her that had her lifting off the bed in whimpers. "Beg me."

"Master, oh fu— umm, please, please make me come! I want to come for you, please, please, I'll do anything, just *please* let me come!" Her voice was rising, each word punctuated by gasps and little cries — and then his mouth found her. Heat thrummed over her clit, and before she could think another orgasm crashed over her like a wave, drowning her in the aftershocks as she screamed and writhed in front of him.

"Thalia... you are perfect." One more devilish lick that had her shuddering and he stood up. "Take your top off." His own fingers were deftly sliding down the front of his shirt undoing each button and revealing his hard chest. She tore off the tank top, and the sports bra and felt the cool air of the room harden her nipples even further. His pants dropped, and her mouth opened at the sight of him. She wanted to taste him, reaching forward he grabbed her wrist, and shook his head.

"But—"

"No." His voice slammed into her, zeroing in on her submissive nature, and she found herself speechless, heart still racing as his cock leaked precum that she wanted to taste. Leaning forward he grabbed her hair and lifted her toward him, his lips finding hers in a bruising kiss that told her exactly how much he needed her too. Her hands found his waist and her nails dug in, and she felt him jerk his body forward, his cock seeking. He pulled back a fraction so he could see her face. "You're mine."

"Yes." Thalia breathed it and he kissed her again, hard, the ferocity of it ripping the air from her lungs as he wound his fingers into her hair, bowing her back. Then he tore his lips away and grabbed her legs and flipped her, yanking her back toward him until she felt his cock against her pussy. She wiggled, clenching her hands in the sheets a moment before he thrust forward. He groaned, and she moaned into the bed as he filled her. He slid back once, and slammed forward hard, burying himself inside her completely and she felt her body stretch around him. Her toes braced on the frame of the bed as his fingers dug into her hips to hold her in place.

Then he really started to move. As tense as she had been in the past six days, every hard thrust, every bruising grip of his hands at her hips, every bite he trailed down her ribs, spoke that the time hadn't been easy for him either. She came once as he continued to thrust into her, and he pulled her back by her hair until her screaming moans turned back into whimpers of pleasure. One hand slid under her to cup a breast and pinch a nipple sharply, which had her bucking back against him in breathless need. When his hands returned to her hips and she felt him pressing her down into the bed she knew he was close, and she tightened around him as he shouted, "Thalia! Fuck!" She felt him spill inside her, his body taut against hers, and then his forehead pressed against her back and there was nothing but the mixture of their harsh breathing.

"Language." She mumbled into the bed and he delivered a sharp spank as he slid from her that made her jump and laugh. He crawled onto the bed and jerked her against his front, his arms wrapping tightly around her. After a few minutes as their breathing started to calm, his fingers traced the random red spots across her side and hip. He laid his hand over one, and placed a kiss into her hair, breathing deep against her neck.

"I'm pretty sure you're going to be covered in marks." His tone held a little humor, and she grinned like a kid at Christmas. She'd wanted him for days, and this is exactly what they'd both needed.

"Mmmm, good keepsakes," she murmured. He propped himself up on his elbow and kissed her again. Soft, nibbling kisses that had her moaning against his mouth.

"Agreed. I like seeing my marks on you." He kissed her again.

"I wish we'd come here sooner." Thalia hadn't meant to say it out loud, and she almost backpedaled when she saw the furrow appear between James' blond brows. His voice was soft when he spoke.

"I'm sorry I didn't *bring* you here sooner, baby. I am. I'm sorry that I was so arrogant that I thought I could help you all on my own." He kissed her forehead, her cheeks, her chin, her nose, and then her mouth. "I wish I'd brought you here months ago, because I can already see how much being around everyone has relaxed you, and you should have had that before now."

"They do relax me." She ran her fingers over the arm that laid across her waist. "The girls, they just, they understand me. What I want to be anyway."

"And you think you can…?" James asked, sincerity threading heavily through his voice.

"They make it seem easy, and it's easier to copy them than it has been to try to figure it out on my own." She bit her lip for a second, "I think that's what I mean, I just wish I'd had someone to observe before now, to know what I could do, that wouldn't—" A lightbulb went off in her head and she almost sat up straight. She needed to tell Ailsa.

"Wouldn't?" James prompted.

"Wouldn't make me look like an idiot around you." She smiled, but there was more. More. She just needed to say it to Ailsa, to make sure she was right.

"You are much too smart to ever be an idiot, baby." He grinned. "And, while I'd much rather spend the afternoon like this, Kalen will absolutely come up here. Do you want to shower before you go see Ailsa?" His eyes were locked on her mouth, his thumb tracing her bottom lip.

"Five more minutes?" She pouted a little and he smiled down at her.

"Ten. And then we'll shower."

She grinned and he kissed her again.

Chapter Twenty-Four
THALIA

Shower, dress, make out session, and promises that they'd be together one more time before James left for London the next day, and Thalia was at Ailsa's door.

She knocked and heard her call out, "Come in, Thalia!"

Easing the door open, Thalia couldn't wipe the happy grin off her face. She was blushing the second she sat down across from Ailsa who flipped open her journal and studied her with those dark eyes. Anyone could tell Kalen and Ailsa were siblings, they both had the evaluation stare down perfectly. It sort of made Thalia feel like she should be on a witness stand, or a doctor's table — or, *well*, a therapist's couch.

Ugh. At least she wanted to be here right now.

"Before you say anything, can I answer your question from last time?" Thalia stammered over the words, riding the high of her orgasms, her time with James, and the confidence of her new revelation.

Ailsa's eyebrows lifted, "Absolutely. If ye have an answer."

"I think I do, it came to me when I was talking to Master about how glad I was that he brought me here."

"He should have brought ye here sooner, Thalia." Ailsa interrupted with a little more snark than Thalia expected, but she quickly schooled herself back to professional neutrality.

"He said that too, he already apologized about it." She remembered the way his green eyes had been filled with guilt when he'd admitted his mistake, and she knew that hadn't been easy for him.

"Did he?" Ailsa made a note in her journal, and Thalia leaned forward.

"Wait, that's not what I want to talk about. You asked me why I haven't been more than just his submissive, since I said I wasn't afraid of him? Right?" Thalia barreled forward, not wanting to get distracted before she forgot what she wanted to say. James' kisses and touches in the shower had been distracting enough.

"Yes, I'd still like the answer." Ailsa leaned back in the chair, the stone gray of her dress making her red hair blaze.

"I think I know. I'm not afraid of my Master, he would never hurt me like Marcus did." Her stomach still tightened at the thought of him, but she ignored it, "I've just always been afraid of ruining it with him. Of doing the wrong thing in public, and somehow revealing our relationship. I don't know if he told you, but—" Thalia grabbed a breath as she rattled out her answer, "but Anthony and Marcus blackmailed him, he tried to confront them, he did, and they blackmailed him to keep their secret. If he revealed them, they revealed him, and that idea is the worst possible outcome to him."

"Okay..." Ailsa was writing and listening.

"Don't you get it?" Thalia held her hands out like it should be obvious, and Ailsa just stared at her, waiting. "I was afraid to ruin his life! By screwing up, by calling him Master in public, or doing something so submissive that everyone would *know*! I was so afraid that I might do that, and then he'd have to leave me, or kick me out, or — or maybe he would stay with me but I would have ruined *everything*. I was terrified to do that, and I just can't be without him. I can't."

"Why do you think you can't be without him, Thalia?" Ailsa was calm. She wasn't excited at all that Thalia had finally figured it out. She finally knew what had been wrong for so many months! Tears came up in her eyes as Ailsa ruined the high she'd been riding when she'd walked in the room.

"Don't ask me that, Ailsa."

"That's the million-dollar question, Thalia, I need ye to answer it." Ailsa wasn't going to budge, and now Thalia regretted coming into her office with such hope. She thought her realization would resolve everything, make everyone *understand* what had been wrong with her.

"I only want to be with him, Ailsa." Thalia said it through gritted teeth.

"Why?" Her face was open, curious, like that was a valid question.

It wasn't a valid fucking question.

"Why? You're really asking me why I only want him?" Thalia laughed, pushing her damp hair back from her face. "He knows *everything*. Everything. My entire fucked up history, and he still looks me in the eyes, Ailsa, he still cares about me. It's not like you, or Master Kalen, or anyone else who has only *heard* about Marcus... he fucking saw it. He heard me beg him, he *watched* me beg him. He knows every horrible thing, and he still looks at me and he, he *smiles*."

Her heart hurt as she spoke, and she could feel the heat in her face as the tears came again.

"He still wants to take me to dinner, wants me to meet his friends. His fancy, high-class friends and co-workers. He still wants to touch me, and he doesn't judge me that in all that horror I realized I fucking liked it. That I wanted to be a submissive — not to Marcus — but I liked it, I fucking liked it. Who else would know all that, could have seen all that, and still want me in their bed? Still want me as their girlfriend? Still want me as their *submissive*? Still want to introduce me to everyone he knows and be excited to do that?

"It's why I'm HERE, because he really BELIEVES in me, he believes I deserve to be seen with him, that I'm *worth* that. He wants to have me with him so much he admitted his own mistakes to his best fucking friend and risked everything for ME. Damaged, and fucked up — me. And you're asking me why I'm afraid to lose that? You're really asking me that?"

Ailsa sighed heavily, set her pen down, and clasped her hands. Thalia's heart pounded in her chest as she waited for Ailsa to try and argue. "I *am* asking ye that, Thalia. Do ye think that no one else could want ye? Really? Yer a beautiful girl, a natural submissive, who is strong and a survivor, and clearly has the ability to be vocal when ye want to be. If ye decided not to be with James, Kalen and I could absolutely help ye find someone, and they would be very lucky."

"I want him," Thalia answered flatly.

"Thalia." It was Ailsa's turn to hold her hands out, as if she were making any kind of sense. "Ye have PTSD, that much is obvious. Panic attacks, hyperventilating, agoraphobia, trouble with crowds. And all of that is understandable, it's expected. But ye have James on such a pedestal that ye can't even see his faults, his mistakes, *his* issues. I don't think ye are in a place mentally or emotionally to make a decision like that. It's why I am so bloody angry that just because ye used yer safe word Kalen let ye go to bed with James again, ye—"

"Fuck you," Thalia growled, and Ailsa's open mouth and her shocked look said it all. "Fuck you and Kalen! Marcus took me and took away everything, every choice. I was supposed to be a blank slate, his slave, or the slave of whoever bought me. I was going to have no choice in that. And now YOU, you and Kalen are trying to tell me I can't have sex with my Master if I want to? That I can't choose to be with him? How are you any different than Marcus? The only person here who is willing to let me make my own choices is my Master! How ridiculous is that?!" She was shouting, anyone nearby would be able to hear her, hell, people not nearby could probably hear her screaming.

"Thalia that is not what we—"

"That is exactly what you're doing! Telling us we can't be together? Telling me I can't choose him? That I'm not capable? Well when am I supposed to be capable?! Am I supposed to need guidance for the rest of my fucking life because of what Marcus did?"

"No. No, yer not." Ailsa was trying to calm her, speaking softly, her dark eyes radiating concern. "We just want what's best for ye."

"Then how about you all let me fucking decide what's best for me? I still have almost two months until my Master will let me tell him my decision, and I have chosen to submit to him, so I will accept his timeline. But if this is your plan to help me, you're doing a shit job and it's not working!"

Ailsa went silent, her gaze evaluating her again. Thalia was breathing heavily, and she realized that this was the loudest, and most angry, she'd ever been. She'd just screamed, and cursed, and insulted Kalen's sister, but every word of it was true, and Thalia didn't care what magical list of Dominants Kalen or Ailsa had access to, the only person she wanted was James — and nothing they did or said would change that.

"I think it is working, Thalia. Quite well, actually. That's the best glimpse of ye that I think anyone involved has had."

"But you still want me to let you run my life, or keep me from him?"

"That's not what we want at all." Ailsa sighed. "All I really want is for ye to admit that James isn't perfect. Ye want a relationship with him, like he wants with ye? Those types of relationships don't happen when one person thinks the other is infallible."

Thalia let out a frustrated scream, and then forced herself to take a breath. James' voice played in her head, "I'm not an idiot, Ailsa. I am very aware that what he did was wrong. He watched the feed even after he knew what Marcus was doing, but I *also* know he hates himself for his weakness. But what would have happened to me if he hadn't been weak? If he didn't have faults? If he was perfect... where the fuck would I be?"

"I'm not sure, Thalia." Ailsa spoke solemnly.

"Neither am I, but I bet I wouldn't be here, surrounded by people who are at least trying to help me — even in some misguided ways. I'd — I'd probably be in some brothel in some horrible place, begging for death. That's what Marcus had promised me." Thalia closed her eyes, remembering the party, the auction. How

James had instantly called her over, how after he had her with him he had kept everyone away, had even stopped Anthony. *That* person was a good person. "I know he's not perfect, but he's who I want, and I can't tell him that for a while yet, but I can say it to you." Thalia looked Ailsa in the eyes so she could see and hear her sincerity. "I want him, mistakes and all, and unless he suddenly decides he doesn't want me, I'm going to remain his submissive, and his girlfriend, no matter what you or Kalen say."

"Okay." Ailsa nodded.

"Okay?" Thalia was caught off guard by the sudden acquiescence.

"Okay." Ailsa shut her journal and shrugged. "I'm comfortable telling Kalen, and James, that ye know exactly what ye want, and that although ye still need help, and more therapy, to deal with what's happened to ye… I think ye are in a place where ye can have a healthy relationship with James."

Thalia laughed out of shock. "You're going to tell them I'm okay?"

"That is *not* what I said. Ye still need therapy, Thalia. I can recommend someone in London, or we can speak over the phone, but I do think that ye have at least evaluated yer circumstances with a level head, and I feel comfortable telling them that we can trust yer judgment where James is concerned."

"Can I tell him?" Thalia was thrumming with excitement, and she could feel her pulse racing as she stood up, wanting to leave and find James right now, show off her brand new 'not crazy' sticker, and then kiss him and drag him back to their room if he'd let her.

Ailsa smiled at her, a warm smile that made her look more like someone she could be friends with instead of an adversary. "Let's go tell James and Kalen together. Alright?"

Chapter Twenty-Five
THALIA

Thalia was sick of crying, but absolutely cried saying goodbye to James on the circle drive. He held her tight and kissed her until her lips felt bruised, whispering in her ear, "It's only five days, pet. I'll be back before you know it."

"Promise?" she asked, her voice breaking no matter how strong she tried to be.

"I promise. I will come back as soon as I can." Another bruising kiss, but it wasn't enough. Nothing would be enough, and she was sure they both knew that, which was why he grabbed her arms and pulled himself away. "Listen to Kalen and Ailsa for me, okay?"

All Thalia could do was nod, sniffling as she tried to hold back her tears.

"It won't feel too long, I swear." James pulled her into another quick hug, embracing her tightly, and she squeezed him back just as hard until he finally forced them apart again. "I have to go, pet."

"I know. I don't want you late for your flight."

"I'll call you every day," he promised, and then he made himself get in the car and drive away.

She didn't want to go back inside.

Long after the blue rental car had disappeared down the drive she stood there sniffling and wiping her cheeks. Maggie was the one who eventually wrapped her arms around her. "I know this is tough, but he'll be back soon. Ye won't be apart for long."

"Five days," Thalia repeated, feeling hollow and cold without James nearby.

"Right, it's just five days. Ye should come inside though, James wouldn't be happy with ye if he knew ye were just standing out here," Maggie said, patting her side as she took a few steps toward the house. "Come along. I've got wine for ye if ye follow me?"

It was tempting to stand there and watch the drive, imagining James canceling his trip back to London to stay with her, but she knew it was foolish. He had to work, and she couldn't live on this patch of gravel. It took more effort than she imagined, but she finally walked inside and found all of the girls in the drawing room — no Doms in sight.

Must be the morning meeting.

"Oh, Thalia." Julie jumped up and hugged her, and Thalia found herself crying again. "Sweetheart, I do the same thing every time Antonio leaves."

"And every time, I always open wine." Maggie shut the doors to the room and wandered over to a bar tucked in the corner with a bottle of wine in her hand and another under her arm. "It's after noon, so Kalen can't complain about it." She grinned as she popped the cork of one bottle. "And if he does, send him my way. I'll take the credit, *and* the punishment." Her eyes twinkled as she poured glasses, and she let out that bawdy laugh as Julie joined her. Despite herself, Thalia felt her mouth turning up at the edges.

"Don't be sad, Thalia. He'll be back in a few days." Lauren kissed her on the cheek as she walked over to the bar to grab a glass of the wine, and Thalia dropped to the couch.

"Yeah, before you even know it! Although if I'd been screaming like you were yesterday and earlier today, I'd be in mourning too." Chloe grinned at her and Thalia felt a blush flood her cheeks.

Ah, so everyone *had* heard them.

"You act like Brad doesn't have you melting into a puddle every time, and I know for a fact that I make you come hard enough to wake a few neighbors," Lauren said and laughed across the room.

Chloe grinned and winked at her as Lauren came back with a glass of wine for Thalia. She accepted it and took a sip, and then a much larger drink. Red, and dark, and delicious, it was exactly what she needed to dull the sharp edges of her sadness.

A chirruping sound filled the room and Maggie pulled a small cell phone from her dress and answered it as she walked out of the room with a smile and a wave over her shoulder.

Thalia jumped when she felt fingers dig down the neck of her shirt and tug the fabric back.

"I knew it was Valentino." Marisol's voice floated behind her before she came into Thalia's line of sight as she headed toward the wine. "From your other clothes I thought you had no taste." She shrugged one delicate shoulder as she took a sip of wine. "Guess I was wrong. It's a relief *someone* here cares about looking decent. At least sometimes, anyway."

"No one wants to hear it, Marisol." Julie rolled her eyes.

Thalia didn't even know who had made the shirt, it was another of James' purchases for her, just something in the closet to choose from. It was a simple, white blouse, and the name Valentino vaguely registered in Thalia's mind as a designer. Maybe she'd heard it on TV?

"Or, Julie, it might be that Thalia *does* want to hear from me, unless that shirt belongs to another of James' lovers?" Marisol glared across the room at Julie, and Thalia almost choked.

"Marisol, please stop. Can't you see she's upset? He just left." Analiese was so quiet, but the girl could talk when she wanted to, and the fact that she spoke up for Thalia made her feel brave enough to respond too.

"He's only with me, Marisol, and I didn't know who made my clothes. My Master bought them." Thalia took a generous drink from her wine glass to quell her nerves, and Marisol scoffed.

"Well, for a minute I thought you had one redeeming quality. That at least someone here could value fashion. But, no, it is your 'Master' James that has the taste and the money for it. Maybe he can educate you about designers while you're licking his shoes." Marisol walked back to a couch with her wine and coiled at the edge to stare at the small group.

"Not everyone is as interested in material shit as you, Marisol," Julie snapped.

"Like you all stumbled on these men by accident? You find men who just happen to have the money to come to this place? *Ridículo*." Marisol rolled her eyes this time, and Thalia felt her temper spiking behind the wave of sadness still rolling through her after James' departure.

"I can't wait for the day Ethan figures out what a gold digging bitch you are." Lauren was normally bubbly, and she still said the biting statement with a gleeful tone, but the tension of the room increased with her caustic — albeit accurate — assessment.

"He loves me, he *worships* me, and he does what I ask. He won't leave me, and he'll give up on this little fantasy of his soon enough. Then we get back to our life." Marisol was so prideful.

"You mean you can get back to his money," Julie mumbled, but Marisol heard it.

"If you want to crawl around on your knees, saying 'yes, sir' or 'no, sir,' go ahead. I'm worth more than that, and I get what I'm worth." She drank more of her wine, and Thalia wished she could record this bullshit for Kalen to play for Ethan.

The man deserved to know the truth about the woman he was seeing, and if he was anything like James, she knew that the reality of who Marisol was would upset him.

Maggie came back in with another bottle of wine, and Marisol instantly went quiet. Analiese was shaking her head, and Chloe and Lauren had dropped into a chair together to whisper quietly.

"Yer going to be just fine, lass." Maggie topped off Thalia's glass before grabbing the seat next to Julie. "He'll be back soon, and we will keep ye busy. James mentioned ye do yoga? Maybe ye could show us some things?"

Julie perked up at the mention of that. "You do yoga? Have you ever taught it?"

"Not really," Thalia admitted.

"But you know how, right?" Chloe piled on, leaning forward.

"Well, yeah…"

"Then why not?" Lauren pressed. "I could always benefit from a little more flexibility."

"You're already very flexible," Chloe purred, and Maggie sighed, snapping her fingers at the two of them.

"If ye two get caught on top o' each other again, I'll be getting a lashing right beside ye, and I like to earn my own punishments, so hands off." Maggie sighed before turning back to look at Thalia. "I do think it's a good idea, though."

"Well…" Thalia thought it over. She had missed yoga, and she had filled in for instructors before in an unofficial way.

Teaching the other girls some basic sun salutations could be a nice distraction, and she'd done those often enough to have them memorized.

"Please?" Analiese added quietly, and Thalia shrugged.

"Okay, yeah. If Julie would be okay with me using some physical training time, I think— I mean, I'd love to lead yoga."

"Sounds great. So, here's the really important question, girls, does Valentino make yoga pants?" Julie dissolved into laughter at her own joke, and Maggie laughed even though she didn't know why it was funny. Soon, the whole group was giggling and Marisol had stormed into the corner to refill her wine.

It was going to be a long week, but at least she'd stopped crying — and right now she had wine, and several people who were quickly becoming friends, and a way to contribute to the group.

A week alone in Purgatory was manageable. She could do it.

Not like she had a choice.

Chapter Twenty-Six
THALIA

"This is torture," Thalia whined into the phone and she heard James' soft laugh from the other end of the line.

"Agreed, baby. I'd give anything to be there with you instead of here." His low groan filled the line and she bit her lip as she imagined his jaw tightening, his eyes darkening.

"Come back early then?" She was close to begging even though she knew he had to be at work this week, something about a review of the company's quarter, and James *had* to be there for it. Three days without him after four months of seeing him every night? She'd take a week of canings before she'd voluntarily go through this again.

Dammit.

Now all she could think about was James and a belt and screaming and coming for him. Over and over. She squirmed in the chair by the phone and fought the urge to slip her hand between her legs while she could hear his voice.

"I'll be back as soon as possible I promise." He paused and she heard him chuckle. "Thalia. What are you doing?"

Her nails were gliding along her thigh and she hadn't even realized that she'd pulled the hem of her dress up, her breathing changing as she imagined his hands on her. She was soaked. "Um, nothing." Thalia pulled her hand back and pushed it through her hair, forcing a shaky breath.

"Hmmm." His voice dropped to a whisper, and she pictured him leaning forward in his office with that wicked grin. "Are you wet for me, pet?"

She groaned quietly. "Yes, Master."

His chuckle filled the line again, all male satisfaction. "You should ask Kalen if you can relieve some of that tension. Maybe if you ask *very* nicely—"

She blushed furiously and buried her face in her hand. "Oh God, I can't ask Master Kalen that!"

"Can't ask me what?" The deep booming voice came from her left and her blush spread like wildfire. Kalen was standing a little down the hall, a dark t-shirt stretched across his chest, and jeans hanging off his hips. Thalia's mouth dropped open in wordless shock.

"Is Kalen there, pet?" James' question purred across the line and she couldn't even respond. Kalen's dark eyes had her stuck. "Give him the phone." James' command had her holding the phone out toward him.

"It's my Master." She barely whispered the words, but Kalen smiled and walked over to her, his heavy steps thumping over the floor before he took the receiver from her hand.

"James." Kalen's voice was deeper, and his eyes didn't move as he stared down at her. "Ah, I see." His smile widened, and he tilted his head a bit as she heard the murmur of James' voice from the phone. "I think I can arrange that. Yes. We'll see ye in a couple of days, brother."

Kalen held the phone down to her and she took it back, cupping the phone to her ear.

"Thalia?" James' voice was back in her ear.

"Yes, Master?" The breathless tone in her voice matched the sudden pounding staccato of her heart in her chest.

"Kalen is going to help you out with some stress relief. I want you to obey him," he commanded, and her breath caught, but he continued without pause. "Don't worry, you're not going to bed with him, at least not until we discuss your dream some more and then I will *absolutely* be there for that." He groaned as if the visual aroused him as much as it did her. "I need you to do something for me though. I want you to describe everything that happens in vivid detail for me when we speak again. Understood?"

"Yes, Master." Thalia couldn't breathe. Kalen was standing over her, and she suddenly felt dizzy with the rush of heat that pulsed between her legs.

"Good girl. I have to go. We'll speak soon." James sighed. "I really miss you, baby. Now go on, hang up."

"Yes, Master. I really miss you too."

Kalen took the phone from her hand and set it in the cradle, and she stared up at him. "Wait here."

His command settled over her and all she could do was nod. Turning on his heel, he left her in the chair, her thighs pressed together firmly against the gathering wetness. Minutes passed as a hundred scenarios rushed through her mind. What had James said to him? What had they planned? What was going to happen?

When Kalen returned he was holding a small white plate, and he smiled. "Stand up."

She did and he held the plate out toward her. Taking it in a shaking hand, she held her breath again to try and slow it.

"Drop it." Kalen locked his eyes to hers and her mouth went dry. Her fingers slid over the smooth edge of the plate, and she was confused by the command.

He wanted her to—

His voice deepened, his Dom voice making her jump. "Drop the plate."

Thalia let it slide between her fingers and the loud crash of it shattering at her feet made her gasp. His hand snapped forward into her hair, angling her head back as he stepped closer to her. "Now, look what ye did? Ye broke one of my plates. That's not very nice," he said with a playful smile, and far from fear, a whimper of anticipation slipped out of her.

He pushed her back, his shoes crunching on a piece of plate before he used her hair to guide her around the remnants. "I'm — I'm sorry, Master Kalen."

"Well, I think I know how to punish subs who break things so carelessly. Follow me." The edge of his mouth tilted up and her knees went weak.

James had known exactly what she craved without her even voicing it, and now she was going to be punished. By Kalen.

His hand left her hair and he turned down the hall, leaving her standing there for a moment as her head spun. When he was almost ten feet ahead of her she rushed forward to keep up with his long stride. Then he stopped at a door, but he didn't open it yet. "Tell me yer safe word, Thalia."

"It's chair, Master Kalen," she whispered softly.

He grinned at her. "And I know ye know how to use it." His hand slid to the back of her neck where he held her and pushed her ahead of him into the room as he opened the door.

Inside, Thalia immediately saw Analiese and Nick to the side, and Analiese was already naked and on her knees, her forearms wrapped in coils of rope that seemed to be braided together. It was... beautiful. Kalen applied more pressure to her neck so she was forced to look away from them. Maggie sat on the floor in a corner, her legs folded to the side and her blue eyes locked on Thalia, her eyebrows lifted slightly.

"Sir?" Maggie's voice floated in the silence, and Thalia's pulse was too loud in her ears as she stood there. Kalen let go of her and took a step toward his wife, who was also, absolutely, his submissive at the moment.

He paused mid-step and glanced back at her. "Thalia, strip." Then he continued to Maggie and tugged her off the floor to kiss her fiercely. Thalia's hands shook as she unzipped the dress, and Maggie moaned against Kalen's mouth.

"I figured an example would help Analiese, and since Thalia decided to break a plate..." He kissed Maggie again and she nodded with a little smile and slipped back to the floor. "She's due a punishment."

The dress pooled around her feet and her hands went to the bra, it dropped, and then she slid her panties down. Naked in front of four people, Thalia's stomach was all butterflies and liquid heat as Kalen moved toward her like a predator. His hand went back to her neck and he nudged her forward toward Analiese and Nick. That's when she saw Lars sitting in a chair in a corner where the dim light of the room barely reached.

Correction. Five. Five people. Holy shit.

Thalia almost tripped over her feet on the plush carpet, but Kalen's other hand was there at her shoulder to steady her. Nick was shirtless, in black jeans, and he was lean but fit. Normally, he reminded Thalia of a laureate, all quiet intellect with a brooding stare. But standing over his submissive bound in elegant lines of rope, he oozed a casual power that made Thalia want to have a very detailed conversation with Analiese. Kalen stopped her in front of the girl who had yet to lift her eyes, "Kneel."

She slid down, mirroring Analiese's form and dropped her eyes from the girl's taut body. She couldn't take a full breath in the anticipation.

"Nick, I didn't get to watch ye bind Analiese. I'd like to see ye work yer magic with Thalia. Do ye have more rope?" Kalen was speaking above her.

"Of course." Nick's feet moved past them, and returned a moment later with loops of smooth, beige rope hanging at his side. Thalia's mouth was dry in her excitement, and she bit her lip as Nick crouched in front of her and picked up her arm, his dark eyes capturing hers. "You will tell me if it pinches even a little, because it will hurt a lot more once you're pulling. Understand?" His voice was soft, but it sent a thrill down her back. She nodded.

It seemed to take forever as he coiled rope, alternating arms and braiding in between until her forearms were linked together as intricately as Analiese's. Kalen asked questions and watched carefully as Nick worked. It was like art, and it felt comfortable, and with each coil she grew more excited as a hundred ideas ran through her head.

"Does it feel alright?" Nick's voice shook her out of the quiet meditation she'd fallen into. Analiese had barely moved the entire time, completely quiet.

"Yes, sir." Thalia nodded, and she fought the urge to squeeze her thighs together as the realization of how firmly she was bound settled over her and turned up the heat in her lower belly.

"Then let's get started." Kalen grinned and helped Thalia stand while Nick helped Analiese to her feet. They kept their hands on each of the subs as they led them to what looked like thick wooden beams embedded in the wall. They would have been decorative except for the series of dark metal circles installed above her head. Kalen and Nick moved almost in unison, hooking carabiners through the loops of rope at the end of the braid and lifting the girls' arms above their heads to attach them to the metal circles. Thalia had a little more give in her reach than Analiese, but neither girl could move back.

Thalia stole a glance to her right to find Analiese's honey brown eyes looking back at her. The girl gave a little smile and then trained her eyes forward. Her excitement was evident as well.

This was exactly what she needed.

Chapter Twenty-Seven
THALIA

❦

"Thalia, why are ye being punished?" Kalen's tone was low and without humor, which was the only reason Thalia didn't mention that she'd only broken the plate on his order. Not that she regretted it.

"I broke a plate, Master Kalen," Thalia said and dropped her chin as she balanced on her feet.

"Why, yes, ye did. How clumsy." Now she could hear the humor in his voice, and she knew how much James would have loved to hear those comments, so she swore to remember all of it to tell him.

"Analiese." Nick's voice was sinful as he said her name, full of promise, and she could see Analiese's chest rise and fall in her peripheral vision. "Why are you here today?"

"To work on being more vocal during our sessions, sir." Analiese's voice was ridiculously quiet when she responded.

"See, Analiese's last Dom preferred silence, and Nick wants to hear reactions. I think Thalia will be a great example of that, won't ye?" Kalen's hand moved down her spine, his thumb tracing each vertebra, and she arched forward at the sudden contact.

"Yes, Master Kalen." She blushed as Kalen revealed knowledge about her that only James could have told him.

"I know yer already comfortable with floggers. Let's try the crop today, okay Nick?" Kalen was moving behind them, and Thalia clenched her hands and tested her range of motion. Not much. But at least she was able to see the intricate rope work up close. Her pulse was racing again now that the session was moments away, and she suddenly remembered that Lars and Maggie were also both present — and she was infinitely grateful she was facing the wall.

"Start with a few warm up strokes and be sure the tip doesn't wrap around the sides. Keep it on her ass and upper thighs." Kalen must be working with Nick as well as Lars. "Watch."

The crop landed across the middle of Thalia's backside, making her jump in surprise, but it hadn't been very hard. Several more strokes moved down the round of her ass until he landed one right where her thighs started. To her right, she heard Nick's strokes start landing on Analiese. Kalen trailed several more down her thighs that stung lightly, and heated her skin, and then he waited. When Nick stopped, Thalia could hear the smile in Kalen's voice.

"Yer both so quiet, and yer not being a good example for Analiese, Thalia. I guess ye can definitely handle more." The next stroke made her gasp as it lit up her skin, another followed like a line of fire, and they kept coming. She was squirming and whimpering by the time he stopped halfway down her thighs, and she was so wet. When she heard the strokes landing on Analiese she bit down on her own whimpers to listen to her. The pop of the crop against Analiese's skin was barely echoed by a small gasp each time.

A sharp swat from Kalen had her crying out, tears springing to her eyes, and then pressing herself against the wood beam as the line of pain spread out. "That's better. When ye vocalize, it lets yer Dom judge how yer doing. Silence makes it more difficult to judge when ye get close to yer limit."

A loud pop to her right was followed by a feminine squeak from Analiese.

"Again."

Nick listened to Kalen and delivered another, Analiese gasped and whimpered a little louder than before. Thalia could see her wiggling, her forehead pressed against the wood.

Another sharp line across her ass, and another and Thalia was crying. The heat that followed on the heels of the pain of each lash was coiling between her thighs, her wetness spreading as she pressed her hips forward against the wood. If she could just get some friction! Kalen's mouth was quiet against her ear, the heat of his body radiating against her back, "Come now, Thalia. We all heard how much noise ye can make. Do ye want it harder?"

Thalia's breath came on a shudder before she bit down on her lip — and then she nodded. He chuckled against her ear and placed a light kiss in her hair. "Alright, be still for me."

They must have communicated somehow because soon Nick and Kalen were alternating strokes and Thalia found herself pressed against the wood in front of her and crying out with each stroke that blazed across her skin and left her panting in anticipation of the next. She was crying, but she could feel that sweet precipice rising up and her voice rose too. "Master Kalen! Please, please, please!" She let out a little frustrated scream as he brought another stroke down across her thighs. Her body wasn't really registering the sting of the crop anymore, it was sensation, pure sensation as her body thrummed.

"Please what, Thalia?" Kalen was smiling, she could hear it. And she had no idea what she was begging for, her breath was coming so fast, her pulse pounding between her thighs, and her entire backside was aching with heat that wound at the base of her spine. But she needed something more, she tugged at the rope holding her to the wall and whimpered.

He trailed the crop over her hyper sensitive skin and she couldn't even articulate what she needed, if it were James she'd beg him to fuck her.

Thinking of James was a bad idea, the pulse between her thighs grew urgent and the lazy passes of the crop over her back, her ass, her thighs were winding her tighter and tighter. Suddenly, Analiese burst into speech beside her. Her soft cries dissolving into pretty pleas, "Sir! Sir, please, *bitte, bitte*—" A swat cut her off and she cried out. It was definitely the loudest she'd ever heard Analiese, and her soft sounds were only adding to Thalia's own need.

Kalen pulled Thalia's head up with a fist in her hair that sent shots of pleasure directly to her clit without him even touching it, she moaned, and bit down to cut off the cry when he delivered another rapid series of strokes that suddenly had her at the edge of an orgasm. She gasped and cried out, "Oh God! Master Kalen, please?" She arched her back as he moved the crop over her welts.

"Come, Thalia." The command was punctuated with a strike that blew past the pain and into pleasure and she hummed with it as she shattered, her body tightening and her arms lifting her onto her tiptoes. Her head was swimming as she trembled against the wood, and she could hear Nick speaking to Analiese as she gasped and moaned, closer and closer to her own edge. Then she tumbled over and there were soft moans and whimpers and heavy breaths, and Thalia felt like she was floating. She was really hanging by the metal ring above her now, and she glanced to the right to see Nick's arms wrapped around Analiese. One hand buried between her thighs as she pressed herself back against him, her mouth open as he drew out every quaking moment of pleasure he could.

Kalen's body pressed against hers as he wrapped an arm around her waist to hold her up and unhook the carabiner. Then he scooped her up into his arms. He sat down on a small couch near Maggie and held Thalia in his lap. His hands were sure as he brushed her hair back, saying something that sounded soothing but she couldn't make it out. Her whole body was buzzing. He leaned her against his chest as he began to reverse the coils of rope around her arms, but they came off much quicker than they went on. Her arms were pink, and the imprint of the rope was present, but she doubted she'd have any lasting marks from it.

"Thalia?" Kalen's voice broke through, and she felt dreamy as she made a questioning sound in response. "Thalia, can ye nod for me if yer feeling alright?"

Thalia nodded and smiled. She was aching where her skin rubbed against Kalen's jeans, and she was very aware that he was hard, but every inch of her body was relaxed and warm. He chuckled and leaned her head back against his shoulder.

"That was impressive to watch, Thalia, ye entered subspace and responded beautifully." He took a breath and she felt his chest rise and fall. When he spoke again his voice was very quiet, which was out of character for him, "I want ye to know that I'm very glad ye and James have each other. That I'm glad he went and got ye, and I do believe he deserves to be happy — and based on what he's told me, ye make him *very* happy." Kalen spoke softly, and she opened her eyes as joy suffused her. She wanted to respond and say thank you, but she was distracted by Maggie standing in front of her, blue eyes alternating between her and Kalen.

"Sir, may I—"

"No, Maggie. Thalia's done very well, but this visit is about her and James. Maybe another time we can all play." The crestfallen look on Maggie's face made Thalia blush furiously. So James *had* told Kalen. She thought she'd be more upset to hear it, but it was exciting to think that they were interested in her, and that in the future some version of her dream could become a reality.

Right now? Thalia wanted to curl into a ball and sleep.

Which Kalen noticed.

"Lars?" Kalen called out. The young Dom seemed to appear, and his cheeks were flushed. "Make sure Thalia gets to her room, take care of those welts, and then go check the schedule. House rules are still in place. Understand?"

"Of course, Master Kalen." He turned away and Kalen slid Thalia to her feet, helping her stand up. In an instant Lars was back with her clothes, holding out the dress for her. She slipped it on, he zipped it for her, and then they were leaving the room. Glancing back, she saw Maggie on her knees in front of Kalen, and she noticed that Analiese and Nick had already disappeared.

The walk upstairs was shaky, but Lars watched her carefully. When she came to her room, he had her lay down and began to sweep the cold, soothing cream across her welts. The young Dom cleared his throat. "Master Kalen is good with the crop, you might have some bruises, but it will heal fast."

She nodded sleepily. "Mmhmm, he's very good." Lars chuckled and put the cream on the night stand.

"Sleep well." He pulled the sheet over her, and she heard him leave. She laid there for a few moments and then curled up on the side James had slept on, breathing in that clean, masculine scent that made her feel like she was home.

And with him she was home, she just needed him back with her.

"Thalia!" A voice snapped her out of sleep and she sat up with a jerk, her heart pounding. "I need ye to get up. Now."

Kalen.

Kalen was standing over her, next to her bed, in her room.

"Huh?" She pushed a hand through her hair. The room was dark, it was the middle of the night, and she was naked. What the hell? "Um, Master Kalen, I—"

"Get dressed, we need to leave." He turned the lamp on next to the bed and she flinched against the light. When her eyes finally adjusted she saw he was already dressed, he even had shoes on. Kalen's face was tense and he was pulling at his hair.

"What's wrong?" She pushed herself out of bed as he walked away from her to open the closet and started grabbing things off hangers. "Master Kalen, please tell me what's going on?" He threw clothes onto the bed and went to the small dresser, opening and shutting drawers until he found her underwear. What the hell was he doing? "Sir!" She caught the underwear and bra as he tossed them to her.

When he faced her again she saw how pale he looked. Oh no, something bad. This was bad.

"Thalia, I need ye to get dressed. We can talk—"

Something bad had definitely happened. A pit opened in her stomach.

"No! Tell me now!" she shouted at him and surprised herself, her body was humming with fear.

What is it? Please, don't let it be—

"It's James, he's been in a car accident. I need ye to—"

Her knees just gave out and she hit the floor, her heart had been racing but she was pretty sure it had stopped, it had to have stopped because she couldn't feel it pounding in her chest. James? She shook her head, and bit down on her lip. Not James, nope, this was a nightmare. She pinched her thigh.

Wake up. Wake up. Wake up.

She pinched harder, and then Kalen grabbed her by the shoulders firmly and lifted her from the floor, his fingers digging in. "Thalia! Ye have to get dressed! Right now!" He made it a command and shook her a bit, but her brain wouldn't work, couldn't work, not with those words. Not with words that said James was hurt, or—

No. No. No. Those words didn't make sense.

Kalen made her sit on the bed and grabbed her face in his large hands. "Thalia. The hospital he's at is over a half-hour away, we need to leave now. They just called me, and they couldn't tell me his status, we need to go. Ye can do this. Now. Get. Dressed."

Her hands moved mechanically as she put on whatever he handed her, he put her shoes and socks on for her while she sat numbly on the bed, her brain refusing to process the words he had said. His strong hands pulled the laces tight as she stared through him. She didn't even know what she was wearing as he led her out of the Dormitory in the pitch black and across the gravel drive to his garage.

Kalen buckled her into his car, still trying to talk to her, but she couldn't hear him. Her head was full of cotton and fog. He must have given up talking because he was staring out the windshield when they left, the car turning toward the gate, the endless sky above them.

Not James.

Please, not James. Not after everything. Not after she was finally figuring out how to make it all work. Not now that a life with him seemed possible, realistic.

Thalia turned to look at the tense line of Kalen's jaw, the tight grip of his hands on the steering wheel, his shoulders hunched as he drove carefully along the narrow road. He was worried too, and that made everything all the more real.

Please let him be okay.

THE END

End Notes

Thank you for reading Book 2 of Thalia's story! I know this is a difficult place to stop, but I had to choose a place to break for Book 3 and this worked best. Fortunately, 'Salvaged by Love' is ready and waiting for you to read the next part of Thalia's story!

It's a wild ride with beautiful highs and dark lows, but it's worth it in the end.

Keep reading in Salvaged by Love!

Jennifer Bene

A DARK ROMANCE

SALVAGED BY LOVE

BOOK THREE OF THE THALIA SERIES

USA TODAY BESTSELLING AUTHOR
JENNIFER BENE

Text copyright © 2015 Jennifer Bene

All Rights Reserved.

No part of this book may be reproduced in any form or by any electronic or mechanical means including information storage and retrieval systems, without permission in writing from the author. The only exception is by a reviewer, who may quote short excerpts in a review.

This book is a work of fiction. Names, characters, places, and incidents either are products of the author's imagination or are used fictitiously. Any resemblance to actual persons, living or dead, events, or locales is entirely coincidental.

ISBN (e-book): 978-1-946722-13-3

ISBN (paperback): 978-1-946722-25-6

Cover design by Laura Hidalgo, https://www.spellbindingdesign.com/

"The past beats inside me like a second heart."
— John Banville

This story was an adventure to write, and it was an adventure I never could have gone on without all of the support of the amazing readers and other authors on Literotica. This book is all about the decisions that shape our lives and the choices we have to make to get away from the darkness in our pasts. That inevitable choice to be a survivor or a victim. Everyone has a history, and everyone has to choose who they want to be and fight for it. That is what I tried to explore in this book.

As usual, major thanks to my many author friends and real life friends who supported my insanity in publishing this. I also want to thank all the authors in The Erotic Collective for supporting me as I wrote Thalia's story, especially for naming this book when I couldn't decide on a title.

This is a rollercoaster with lovely highs and dark lows, but I hope you enjoy the ride, lovelies.

Chapter One
THALIA

Four and a Half Months After the Auction

Time is weird.

When you want to savor something, it seems to end too quickly. While horrible things seem to take an eternity to end. When you can't wait for something to happen, time stretches and elongates, taunting you by making the seconds drag. And when you really need time to pull yourself together, to prepare for news you don't want to hear, or face, or handle — suddenly time folds in on itself and the moment arrives with no warning. As if no time passed at all.

That was what happened when Kalen pulled up in front of the small hospital in the Scottish countryside after he had yanked Thalia out of a deep sleep with the news that James had been in a car accident. It was all too soon, too fast. A red cross blazed next to the word 'Emergency' and Thalia found her lungs couldn't work, that her body was somewhere disconnected from her mind. Kalen was talking again, his voice rough as he leaned across the car.

"Thalia, I'm here with ye. Okay? But we need to go inside, I need ye to get out of the car." He was asking too much. She didn't need to go in there. She couldn't go in there. He growled and got out of the driver's side and was quickly opening her door. "Look at me. Look at me, Thalia."

Her head swiveled at the order and his hands undid the seat belt across her. His eyes were dark, and under them were bruise-like smudges as if he hadn't slept.

What time was it anyway?

"I'm right here. Come on. Come with me." He took her hand and pulled her out of the car, shutting it before dragging her toward the too-bright entrance.

She wanted to run, but his grip was tight on her hand, and the rush of air from inside the hospital hit her with the scent of antiseptic. Thalia was sure she was going to throw up.

"I'm looking for Hawkins. James Thomas Hawkins. My name is Kalen Reid, someone called to tell me he'd been in an accident?" Kalen was talking to a nurse at the desk, she could hear the concern in his voice, the fear, and he hadn't let go of her hand. She felt dazed, dream-like. Big, no-nonsense Kalen was worried. About his best friend. About James.

How could any of this be real?

It was a nightmare. The clatter of the nurse typing into the computer, the ringing of a phone at the other end of the desk, the dull hum of voices and machines working across the sterile emergency room — all of it was slowly breaking down the careful numbness that had cocooned her on the drive over.

Twenty-seven minutes.

Kalen had made the drive in twenty-seven minutes. The little clock on the radio had changed, minute by minute, number by number, as they had moved closer and closer to this small hospital. For a moment Thalia became aware that none of her usual panic was present. The shock of Kalen's words had inoculated her against it, made it impossible to feel anything other than the pending emptiness if she was alone. If James was… No. Those words wouldn't even form in her mind. Just like at the dormitory, she couldn't stand the idea even existing inside her. Kalen was frustrated next to her. His grip firm on her hand, his other hand pushing into his hair as the nurse seemed to take an eternity to find the files.

Thalia's eyes roamed the emergency area, and it was more crowded than she had imagined. There were people sitting on chairs, curtains hanging from the ceiling to section off areas. So many people for the middle of the night. People in beds, people on chairs, people just wandering around, one that looked just like —

"JAMES!" Thalia screamed and ripped her hand from Kalen as she took off toward him. Tall, blond haired, light blue button down, dark slacks, one arm in a sling. Perfect sea green eyes that locked onto hers, widening in surprise.

James.

She collided with him and he hugged her to him with his free arm. Thalia pulled back and ran her hands over him as her heart thundered back to life in her chest. He had a bandage near his right temple, the sling on his arm. But no blood. No blood. "You're okay? You're okay?!" She was sobbing, her heartbeat was pounding in her chest at double-time as he shushed her. He pulled her against him again, his mouth against her ear — and his warmth, the scent on his clothes, all of it was there, and real.

"Yes, baby, yes, I'm fine. Just a bump on the head and an injured shoulder. Doctor is already done." Oh God, his voice, it sent her crying harder. She had thought he was gone.

She thought she had lost him, lost everything.

Thalia suddenly leaned back and shoved him, and he looked surprised and confused. "What the fuck? I can't believe you're okay! Kalen said you were in a car accident!" She pushed her hands into her hair as she tried to breathe through the hiccups her crying had brought on.

"Yes, I was, but it wasn't serious, baby. I fell asleep at the wheel, ended up in a ditch, but it's okay." He tilted his head a bit, smiling down at her, "I had changed my flight to the red-eye so I could get back—"

"Idiot!" Thalia shoved his chest again. "You asshole! You colossal, complete—" She screamed in frustration when she couldn't find a word that encompassed just how pissed she was with him as her relief at seeing him alive segued into anger. "You fell asleep at the wheel?! You CRASHED your car? How could you do that? How could you risk yourself like that? Are you fucking kidding me?!"

"Baby…" He looked so shocked, his mouth forming apologies she couldn't even listen to right now. She cut him off again.

"Did you even sleep?! Tell me! Did you actually get up at five AM, go to the office all day, and then fly to Scotland and try to fucking drive to Kalen's?!" She was shouting and a nurse to the right was watching them with a smirk.

"Come here." James touched her shoulder and tried to get her to move, but she shook him off.

"No! You tell me!" She grabbed fistfuls of his shirt as another wave of tears took her over. "You tell me if you were that stupid, to risk everything, to risk leaving me without you—"

He grabbed her and pulled her into his chest, hugging her tightly with one arm as he kissed the top of her head. "Yes. Yes, I was that stupid, and I'm sorry. I'm so sorry I put you through that, baby. I'm very sorry, I don't know why the nurse didn't tell you both I was fine, but I am, I'm okay, I am, and I swear I'll never do it again."

"Ever," she added, burying her face against his chest, and he kissed her temple, her cheek, and tilted her face up.

"Ever, I swear it." James kissed her, and she melted. There was nothing in the world that she wanted more than this. To have his hands on her, his body against hers, and for him to even be there for her to be angry at.

But the anger was fading, and the relief had returned. He was okay.

James chuckled and she leaned back to look at him. She didn't see anything funny about this. "So, baby, what did you call me a moment ago?"

She blushed and swallowed. *Oh.* "Um, an idiot? An asshole?" Her mind immediately leapt to the punishment he might have in store for that language, and she pressed her thighs together at the thought.

His grin increased, but he shook his head. "Well, yes, you called me those names too. Before that though, what did you call me?"

Her mind raced until she realized what she'd shouted across the emergency room — she'd shouted his name. His *first* name. The one she'd only ever said in her head. She covered her mouth, her blush burning her cheeks, but he tugged her hand away from her face.

"Say it again." His eyes were dark, bottle glass green as he stared down at her. Easing his body close to hers.

"James," she whispered and she could feel the groan in his chest. She bit her lip and he used his thumb to pull it from between her teeth.

"Again." The way he looked at her could have easily combusted her clothing.

"James," she said it a bit louder, and suddenly he was kissing her again, his hand sliding to the back of her neck to hold her there, her mouth opening to his as his tongue swept into her mouth. She moaned into the kiss, and the force of it rocked her back slightly. When he stopped, her head was swimming.

"I like the way that sounds coming out of your beautiful mouth," he whispered against her lips, and her breath caught in her chest.

"I've never, um, you're not… upset?" Thalia's voice shook, and James grinned.

"Not at all. I love—" He grinned again and took a breath. "I love that you said it. Say it any time you like, baby." He pressed a kiss to her lips, and she suddenly knew what it felt like to swoon under someone's touch. She'd call him anything if it meant he'd look at her like that and kiss her like this. Kalen cleared his throat from a few steps away and it jarred them both out of their private moment.

"So glad yer alive, James, but maybe ye two could continue this in my car?" Kalen was grinning as they separated, and Thalia blushed furiously as she saw the audience their encounter had gathered.

Okay, so, not so private a moment.

James released Thalia and stepped over to clap Kalen on the back with his good arm, and Kalen slapped him on the back as well. The second time Kalen cleared his throat, his eyes didn't quite make it back to look at either of them. "I'm glad I'm okay too, Kalen." James' voice was rough, and he didn't look at Kalen either.

Men. Ignoring emotions for centuries.

"Right. Let's get back. Ye have everything ye need?" Kalen asked as he ran a hand across his beard.

"Doctor gave me some pills for the headache and the shoulder, my mobile is toast though. It's why the nurse called you." James went to shrug and winced when he moved his injured shoulder. Thalia wanted to smack him for hurting himself.

"We can get ye another phone later, ye need to rest. Let's go on, I'll have to call Maggie on the way back so she stops worrying over ye," Kalen mumbled and started to march back toward the exit. James went to follow but turned and held his hand out to Thalia, which she gladly took.

His warm skin against hers was everything.

As they walked toward the exit a voice called out to them. "Oy! A lass that mad at ye for makin' her worry, and will still kiss ye like that? That is one ta keep! Trust me on that, lad." An older man sitting on one of the waiting chairs had spoken up, the whole time laughing to himself.

James looked back at her, the edge of his mouth tilting up in a smile. "Yes, I know. Thank you." He squeezed her hand and moved forward toward the exit.

Thalia smiled at the old man, her heart still fluttering from finding James safe, but it had done triple-time when he had looked her in the eye and said to the man, with complete sincerity, that he knew he should keep her.

The few tears that slipped out as they were getting in the car weren't from panic, or frustration, or fear, or sadness, or pain, or anything else that had pushed her to cry over the last few months — it was joy, plain and simple, and it filled her up like a balloon. Crushing out all the little doubts and fears that had inched their way into her head, and it sealed her decision completely as his fingers twined with hers in the backseat.

Nothing would keep her from telling him at the six-month mark that he was all she wanted. For as long as he'd have her. Nothing.

Once they were back at Purgatory Thalia had hovered over James in worry until he'd snapped at her to get into bed and lay down. He kept insisting he was fine, and he was sorry he'd made her worry, but that she didn't need to stare at him like he was a ticking bomb. However, her brain wouldn't let go of the memory of her panicked wake up just a couple of hours before. After another grouchy complaint from James she finally lay next to him on his uninjured side and curled her body against his. He instantly relaxed, pressing a kiss into her hair. The lack of sleep and the pain meds made quick work of him after that and she took the opportunity to run her fingers over his bare chest. His firm pecks, the way his skin stretched over his ribs with each breath, the way when he shifted the muscles of his stomach tightened all the way to the deep V between his hips — it all mesmerized her.

To think for a moment she might have lost him. She had no idea what she would have done, it would have been like ripping her heart out. No one would even need to shout *Kali ma* Indiana Jones style to make it happen. No, Thalia was pretty sure if James had died her pulse wouldn't have returned like thunder in the ER, it would have stayed silent forever.

Thalia trailed her gaze up until she was looking at his face. His strong jaw had a haze of scruff across it and she wanted to trace her tongue across the roughness there. Wanted to bury her face against his neck and straddle his hips and — and James needed his rest. She brushed a strand of hair away from his eyes and focused on his mouth. His lips were parted, slow, patient breaths easing in and out.

He had been so stupid to rush back like that, to not take the flight he'd booked for this morning. But the reason he had done it made her smile. He'd said he wanted to be back with her, and it filled her with a warmth, and a light, that eased the tension of the night away.

She loved him.

Holy shit. Her breath caught.

She loved James...

She had actually said that, in her head, and meant it.

Thalia bit down on her lip as the magnitude of that revelation settled inside her. James wouldn't even accept her confession of wanting to stay with him until the six months were up, he definitely wouldn't be willing to hear this.

Not yet.

Her eyes traced his features again, all soft in sleep. She wouldn't push. She didn't need to push. They had all the time in the world, and she could hold those three words inside, keep them somewhere safe, until she could say them out loud.

And that's what she would do.

She tucked her newfound realization down deep and focused on just how grateful she was to feel the rise and fall of his chest under her cheek, to hear the soft thud of his heart against his ribs. Then she fell asleep.

Chapter Two
JAMES

James woke up sometime later in a haze. His head ached, and his shoulder throbbed, but his cock was — *fuck, yes* — his cock was wrapped in warm heat. Thalia's nails trailed down his thighs lightly and his hips lifted as her tongue traced the underside of him. He was hard, and the gentle suction as she drew back and then bobbed her head forward had him hissing through his teeth. She moaned against him and swallowed him deeper.

"Baby, that is—" He groaned as she pulled him into her throat and held there as her muscles swallowed against him and sent his hips straining. Her mouth was glorious. He tried to move the wrong arm first and was rewarded with a sharp ache when his shoulder fought him, he bit down on the pain and corrected. Burying his other hand in her hair he let her pull back, and he felt her draw a breath before she pulled him into her mouth again. "Fuck."

Her murmurs against his cock only added to the intensity of her wake-up call. He lifted his hips into her mouth and she didn't try to pull back when she gagged a bit. Instead, she swallowed against the head of him and he was once again in her throat. His balls ached with the sweet torture of her movements. Wet heat surrounding every inch of him as those muscles tightened, and released, and tightened. He couldn't bite back the satisfied groan, and when she slid back again working him with her tongue, her hand gently squeezing his balls, he almost came.

Not yet.

When she slid forward her moan vibrated against his hard flesh, and he wanted more than anything to drag her up and fuck her, but he definitely didn't want to kill this moment because of his stupid shoulder. She slid up and down, her tongue focused on the underside of his sensitive head, and then the flat of her tongue ran down him. Then she repeated it. Over and over until he was groaning, and she was echoing her own pleasure at hearing his. When he looked down to see her pressing her thighs together, her pert little ass dancing in the air behind her as she swallowed him, and those hazel eyes locking on his seeking approval — this was perfection. Her mouth drew down and he caught her hair as his balls tightened, his spine firing heat as he came with a shout.

Thalia's name was on his lips as he emptied himself into her mouth, and she swallowed every drop of him. Gently tracing her tongue across his too sensitive flesh before she released him and sat up between his knees. She was flushed from her efforts, her chin wet with saliva, her eyes damp with tears from the times she had gagged, and her beautiful mouth red.

How the bloody hell had he ever been so lucky to find her?

"Come here." He held his hand toward her and she smiled and slid down next to him, her smooth hand tracing over his stomach as he pulled her into a kiss. Her mouth was still so wet, and she moaned against his lips. He leaned his head back a little and smiled at her, "Thank you, baby."

"How are you feeling?" Her eyes were locked on his, her face filled with nervous expectation. He was still mad at himself for the idiot, lovesick decision he'd made to try and drive to Kalen's in the middle of the night. He really could have hurt himself, in fact, the doctor had told him that falling asleep had likely saved him from more serious injury. Hard to tense up in a crash when you're not awake for it. He sighed.

"After that? I feel fantastic." He grinned at her and she smiled with self-satisfaction. He loved the pride she showed when she pleased him, that excited little shimmy of her body against his as he praised her.

"Other than that. Your head? Your shoulder?" She smiled when she said it, but he could see the worried tension in her face, pulling her brows together.

"A little sore, but I'll be fine, baby." He pressed a kiss to Thalia's forehead and she relaxed against him, her body fitting to his like it was made for it. Every soft edge of hers melting against his rough lines until there wasn't a breath that could pass between them. He couldn't wait to be home with her again when they could lie like this for a whole Saturday. Nowhere to be, no one to see, except each other.

"If you're feeling up to it, I heard voices a bit ago and I think they're having lunch now?" She leaned up to look at him and her stomach growled. She blushed and he laughed.

"I believe your stomach has already voted that we go downstairs. Are you hungry, pet?"

"Yeah. A little?" She bit her lip and he laughed again. If she was hungry enough to admit it to him with them naked in bed, he hoped Kalen had saved them food or James would be harassing the kitchen until she was fed.

"Then up, baby. Let's get dressed." He smiled at her as he said it and she rolled away from him and slid off the bed. Her naked skin in the daylight was fantastic, and his eyes traced the handful of pale bruises across her ass from Kalen's crop. Remembering the way she had moaned and whimpered on the phone when she'd recounted the little punishment he and Kalen had devised made his cock start to wake up again. Before his lower half could start making plans of its own he pushed away that delicious memory and eased out of bed to find clothes.

Thalia had almost convinced him to go shirtless when he tried to get his injured shoulder to cooperate, but he'd settled for letting her nimble fingers slide the shirt on him and quickly do up the buttons. The little smile at the edge of her mouth, and the excitement in the tension of her muscles as she dressed him, gave him a lot of ideas for the future.

When his head wasn't throbbing that is.

Thalia was radiant with her hair thrown up in an artful bun at the back of her head and a moss green dress that flared at her hips and stopped high on her thighs. He couldn't resist lifting the back of it to check out the black lace panties she was wearing when they got to the stairs. She had laughed and grabbed his hand, and his chest swelled with the look she gave him.

At the bottom of the staircase he tugged her toward him and kissed her, he wanted to wrap both of his arms around her but settled for feeling her squeeze him to her. James wasn't sure if it was Ailsa, the others at Purgatory, or the accident, but Thalia had become so much more confident with her affection. She wasn't the least bit timid with reaching for him, or returning his touches, and the sheer normalcy of it was the best shock he'd had in years. Thalia grinned at him and gently tugged him forward for lunch, yes, she was hungry. He almost laughed at her hurry when he heard a sharp voice around the corner that led to the dining room.

"Everything is *fine*, Ethan! Why do you keep asking me?" Marisol's voice. James caught Thalia before she turned the corner and pressed her against the wall. He did not want them running into Marisol and Ethan's drama. Thalia's wide, hazel eyes looked up at him, and he realized he was pressing his hips against her. It felt way better than it should at the moment, but he pressed his hand lightly to her mouth to keep her quiet.

"I keep asking you because you're obviously not happy here, Marisol." Ethan's voice was tired, like it had been since their first week here. Thalia squirmed against James and he pressed her harder against the wall. The memory of her wake-up blowjob combined with that little dress and the mischief in her eyes made his cock harden in his pants. She smiled under the fingers he'd pressed over her lips and he smiled back.

"I'm fine, Ethan. I don't want to go!" Marisol whined. Yes, they were eavesdropping, and yes, he was enjoying the way Thalia's shifting body rubbed against him. But they couldn't take action right here, and he really wanted to know what they were talking about.

"Princess, you tried. You came here after I explained what I liked, you tried it, but it's not working. Let's just go." Ethan was speaking in a soothing voice, but Marisol let out an unattractive little screech. Thalia rolled her eyes and James grinned down at her. He loved that Thalia never acted like a brat and wasn't at all entertained by Marisol's antics.

"What about what you said! You wanted this, and I said I would if—" Marisol screeched again, her voice dissolving into a string of mumbled Spanish that James couldn't catch.

"Are you really bringing up the car? The stupid Porsche?" Ethan asked, irritation threading through his voice.

"Porsche *Boxster*, the sport one." Her voice was back to whining. "It's not stupid."

"The car. The fucking car? That's why you kept saying you wanted to stay?" Ethan's tone was edging on anger, and Thalia's wide eyes likely mirrored his own. This was way more than they should be hearing. James looked down the hall to see if there was a place they could easily slip away to.

"No, baby, no." Marisol was crying, he could hear it in her voice. "I want to do this for you, I can be like this, this submissive thing. I'm not wanting to break up our agreement."

"Agreement?" Ethan sounded disgusted.

"No! *Por favor*, Ethan, not what I meant." She was definitely crying.

'Come on, Ethan. See through it,' James pleaded with the guy in his head.

"What do you mean then, Marisol?" Ethan was calmer, but clearly still upset.

"I mean I don't want to go home. I promised! Just give me one more chance, just one!"

"I don't even know if Master Kalen will let you—"

"*Por favor, Querido*, one more chance. I know I have not been nice, I have not tried, but I will. For you, because I love you." Marisol was sugary venom, and Ethan was obviously addicted to her. He could hear them kissing and Thalia scrunched up her nose as she heard it too. James sighed and ran his thumb over her mouth, and then bit back a groan as she rubbed against his still hard cock. He pulled his hips away from her so he could breathe, and her devilish grin had him smiling despite himself.

"Okay. Okay, Princess. I'll talk to Master Kalen again, but no promises. This is his place and he can ask anyone to leave," Ethan said quietly.

"Thank you! Oh, thank you, Ethan, I won't do bad again. Promise!" Her voice was chipper and he heard her heels clicking toward the dining room and Ethan's response was lost as they moved down the hall.

Thalia's eyes were locked on his and her hands were slipping toward the button of his pants. *Minx.* He lifted her hand to his mouth and nipped her knuckle before kissing it. "If only you weren't so hungry, pet, we could go straight back to bed." He grinned when her mouth dropped open and then formed into a pout.

"I'm not that hun—"

James pulled her forward from the wall and shook his head. "Your stomach already spoke for you, baby, and we need to face Kalen and Maggie. I'm sure Maggie has a few choice words for me, maybe even some you didn't think up last night."

Thalia blushed, and the way she looked up at him made it an act of pure willpower to start down the hall with her. "What do you think Maggie will call you?" She was walking with him and when he glanced back at her he saw the smile. He laughed, he loved Thalia like this. Playful, feisty, brave.

"Probably nothing I don't deserve, pet."

Chapter Three
THALIA

"You have to keep in touch with me, Analiese. Swear it! Pinky promise!" Julie's hyper voice rang through the room as she embraced the quiet brunette for the tenth time.

Thalia couldn't help but bite her thumb to keep from laughing. She was sitting in James' lap, leaning on his good shoulder, and she was just so fucking happy to be with him, to feel his hand brush up and down her arm at random as he talked to Kalen, or Nick, or Brad.

"Thalia?" Analiese was talking to her now, and James helped push her up off his lap as she stood to say goodbye to the girl.

"I'm going to miss you, Analiese. I think we still have lots to talk about." Thalia smiled and Analiese blushed. For once Thalia wasn't the bashful one.

"Ah, yes. I'll call you, what's your number?" Analiese asked and Thalia almost rattled off her old cell phone number before she remembered that phone was long gone in the wreckage of her old life. She shrugged and pointed at James who was tilting his head to listen to them.

"You can call James, it's—"

"Uh, Thalia," James interrupted and she flushed, it was the second time she'd used his name that day. The other time had been during the chaos of lunch when everyone was grilling them over the accident, and Maggie had called James a very creative name that had made him laugh. When she looked at him though, he wasn't upset about her using his name. "Where is *your* mobile?"

"At home," Thalia replied.

"Then why can't Analiese call you when we get back?" James arched an eyebrow at her neatly and Thalia crossed her arms with a sigh.

"I..." She looked away from James to avoid his judgment. "I never activated it."

Analiese smiled at her but hid it quickly with her hand. Nick stepped up behind Analiese and rested his chin on her shoulder as he watched Thalia squirm with a hint of a smile.

"Hmmm, I think that deserves a punishment, don't you, pet?" James' voice was heated and filled with laughter, and he might as well have turned her to putty when she turned around and saw his dark green eyes. "When we're back home that is."

"Yes, Master." She smiled at him and pressed her thighs together when Analiese hugged her. She shifted in the girl's embrace to return the hug and sighed. "I promise we'll talk, and I'll call you from my cell as soon as it's *activated*."

"Thank you. London is just a train ride away, and I'd like to see you again, maybe you could keep teaching me yoga?" Analiese's sweet question made Thalia smile.

"Yeah, I'd like that."

Friends. These girls were her friends.

How weirdly normal.

Thalia stepped back to stand by Julie who nudged her with her shoulder and grinned. Chloe and Lauren took their chance to overwhelm Analiese with hugs and cheek kisses and questions. All giggles as they talked about visiting them. Analiese wasn't even able to get a word in with their babbling, but she smiled at them both.

Nick eventually wrapped his arms tightly around Analiese and spun her away from the energetic girls as if he could sense her unease. He spoke up, "Ladies, Ana and I have a flight to catch. She has your contact information, and I'm sure she'll contact you." His quiet voice seemed to tame Chloe and Lauren like they were hypnotized. That was a trick Brad could use for sure. Kalen walked up to Nick and they shook hands firmly while Nick kept his other hand twined with Analiese's.

Everyone walked out with them to their rental car, and Maggie was the last to hug Analiese and Nick. She reminded them they could come back any time, and then they got in. Nick gave one of the bigger smiles she'd seen from him when Analiese kissed him in the car, and the affection Thalia saw there made her feel warm inside.

They were going to last. She could feel it inside, like their future was already a well-laid path and now Analiese and Nick just had to walk it. When she looked up at James and he smiled down at her, she could feel the pieces of their path shifting together, grinding a bit in places as the rough edges wore away — fitting a little slower than she'd like, but still fitting together.

James placed a kiss in her hair and she felt a calm wash over her. They just needed time, time to let their world settle, time to figure each other out outside of the playroom and his flat, time to go to dinners and movies. Time to be normal together. They needed time for the pieces to fit, and they had plenty of that.

JAMES

"Yer really feelin' alright?" Kalen handed him a glass of scotch and James laughed.

"It's barely one o'clock, Kalen." He watched as Kalen dropped onto the dark leather chair across from him. Analiese and Nick had left the day before and Purgatory was already back to normal. Lars and Sven were monitoring physical training, and Kalen had grabbed James to talk. They were in a secluded little office on the first floor of the dormitory, the curtains drawn tight and the light dim.

Kalen chuckled to himself and took a drink of his own glass. "Shut up, James. Yer definitely not driving anywhere today."

Touché.

James took a drink and let the burn carry down his chest and into his stomach. The scotch was smoky and smooth. "I'm good, Kalen. Really."

"Hmmm." Kalen made a noise that expressed little, but acknowledged he wasn't convinced. He ran a hand across his beard, taking a breath as he balanced the glass on his knee. After a moment he lifted his eyes to James.' "Ye remember that brunette in Amsterdam, the year ye went for yer doctorate?"

James' head spun at the change of conversation, but, after he thought about it, yes, he remembered their month-long binge in Amsterdam, before James had gone back to school. He remembered the girl too, dark eyes, dark hair, olive skin — "Yes, um, Gina? Jana? I remember her."

"Jana. Yeh, that was her name." Kalen took another drink and James shifted his weight under his stare. Kalen leaned back in the chair. "She was a lot of fun."

"Yes." James took a drink and tilted his head. Kalen's features were shadowed in the dim light, and he wasn't giving anything away. *Why bring up some girl from years ago?* "I don't understand, Kalen. Did you see her again or something?"

"No, haven't seen her since we left that year." Kalen just stared at him.

What. The. Fuck.

"What's going on, Kalen?" James pushed out a breath on a laugh and shifted again to lean forward slightly. "Whatever you want to say, just spit it out."

"All right." Kalen tipped his glass up and finished the scotch in a swallow. "Ye told me back then that ye loved that girl, that Jana was yer future."

"That's what this is about?" James was confused, surprised that he even remembered her. Kalen shrugged and nodded. "Jesus, Kalen, I was twenty-three. I was half-drunk most of the time and she was gorgeous and submissive and a great escape from thinking about the pressure I was under." James tilted up his scotch and finished it, setting the glass on the table by him before pushing his hand into his hair. "I haven't thought about her in years, why are you bringing her up?"

"Because—" Kalen pointed a finger at James' chest and leaned forward. "—ye told me before ye left that ye love Thalia, are *in love* with Thalia. And in sixteen years there are only two women ye have said that about, and one ye left behind in Amsterdam as soon as yer father called ye home."

James gritted his teeth and fought the urge to throw some of the stupid shit Kalen had done in his face. Hundreds of nights, and almost as many women, when they'd trekked across Europe each holiday. Any time James had a break from his responsibilities. Had all that idiocy stopped Kalen from finding and falling in love with Maggie? *No.* So why was he treating him differently?

"That's low, Kalen. I thought we were past this, I thought you understood."

"Give me yer glass." Kalen stood and held out his hand. James handed it over and Kalen walked to the bar against the wall and refilled both of their glasses with more than a few fingers of scotch. When he came back they both took a hefty drink. "I'm not trying to be cruel, James. I want ye to talk to me about why yer saying it this time, about Thalia."

James grimaced as he took another drink and watched Kalen settle across from him. "I do love her, Kalen. I don't know what else you want me to say."

"How do ye know ye love her?" Kalen asked.

James started to respond and stopped. Thalia's smile popped into his head, the one she only gave him. He thought of the way her eyes always found his in a room and lit up. He thought of how the sound of her even breaths when she slept were the best antidote to his insomnia he'd ever had. He thought of her mouth, and the way she kissed him, sometimes tentatively, and sometimes hungrily. The way her cheeks flooded with a blush, the way she arched into his touch, and how she always trusted him with every inch of her.

There weren't enough words for that. Weren't enough words to describe the way he wanted to dress her up to show off how beautiful and brave and incredible she was, and still strip her naked to lay her out for him to taste and touch and savor.

How could he put that in words?

"Kalen..." James took a drink and tried to roll his sore shoulder, which only made him wince. "I just know. I just *know* that I love her, it's so much a part of me now that I can't separate it. I love everything about her, I don't know what else you want me to say."

"I want ye to tell me that yer not going to say it to her until yer beyond sure about her," Kalen replied with a serious tone, and James started to respond that he *was* sure, but Kalen talked over him. "That girl has ripped herself apart here to prove to ye, and to me, and to Ailsa, that she wants ye. She went through hell, and instead of wallowing in self-pity she's fighting for ye."

There was an ache in James' chest as Thalia's history flooded him. He knew it was hard for her to face all the shit with Marcus, but she had — and it only made him love her more. "I know. That's one of the reasons I love her, Kalen. She's strong."

"Then ye need to respect that and not abuse it. She's strong, but ye could crush her, because everyone can see that she's in love with ye, even if she hasn't said it." Kalen took another drink and ran his hand over his mouth. "She doesn't deserve to have her heart broken after everything. So, if there's even a chance ye will leave her, if there's even a chance ye'd let yer father yank yer leash again... don't tell her."

"I wouldn't do that, they don't have any sway over me anymore. And... I can't tell her yet." James sighed as the weight of Kalen's words rattled around inside him. Part of him soared at the chance that Thalia could feel as strongly as he did, and flashes of a future with her tumbled through his head on fast-forward. The other part shook him with why he needed to wait, why he couldn't rush those words out of his mouth.

"Why's that?" Kalen asked.

"I promised her six months. When I took her from Marcus I promised her six months of my best, of showing her what a D/s relationship could be. Away from that nightmare. I asked if she would give me that long to show her so she could decide if she wanted it. If she wanted *me*."

"It hasn't been six months." Kalen said it like he understood.

"No." James shook his head. "It hasn't. And I won't fuck with her head by dropping an 'I love you' into this. She has to decide what she wants first."

"She wants ye, James." Kalen leaned back.

James felt his mouth tick up into a smile. "I think she does. *She* thinks she does. God knows how many times she's tried to tell me that. But our time here has been the most comfortable and natural we've ever been together. She said my fucking *name*, Kalen." James took a harsh drink of the scotch, and almost coughed as he shook his head. "No way would she have ever said that before we were here. I mean, she yelled at me, in public, she cursed at me because she was so fucking worried about me."

"Thalia loves ye, James. What did ye expect her to do when I dragged her out of here in the middle of the night and told her ye were in an accident?"

"The Thalia before this would have had a panic attack at the entrance to the hospital and been unable to speak." James felt the grin on his lips as he remembered her pulling back, anger flushing her cheeks as she shoved him. So small, and cute, and feisty. He'd wanted to kiss her mid-sentence, but at the same time had reveled in listening to her berate him for making her worry.

"The Thalia at the hospital? That was my girlfriend, not my submissive. That was the girl who twisted my arm to get her a coffee pot, and who gets so much delight in waking me up with it. And I love both halves of her, I love having both halves of her now. And I won't tell her I love her yet, but I'm going to show her every day so that when my six-month promise is up, she'll choose to stay with me."

"It's all about choices, brother. We give them choices, and enjoy the results whatever they are, because we love them." Kalen was smiling and James knew he was thinking of Maggie. "I knew ye were still a good man."

"When I decided to come I had hoped you would remember that," James said quietly and they both drank.

Chapter Four
JAMES

The scotch was humming in his blood, softening the edges of his pain, and somehow their conversation shifted to a rugby match that would be on television in the afternoon when Thalia was visiting Ailsa.

James and Kalen were in the middle of trading laughing insults on the other's *supposed* knowledge of rugby when a knock came at the door. Kalen leaned to the side and called out, "Come in."

The door cracked and James twisted in his chair to see Brad poke his head in. "Hey, um… never mind." Brad waved a hand and moved to shut the door.

"Brad! What do ye need? James and I are just talking about his ignorance of the game later." Kalen grinned and James rolled his eyes. Brad pushed the door open and leaned on the doorframe, his hand rubbing the back of his neck.

"Ah, it's the girls. If you've got a minute I'd love some suggestions." Brad chuckled to himself and held his hands out with a shrug. "They're a handful."

Kalen looked to James and grinned. "Why don't we see if we can help Brad out? Eh, James?"

"All right." James grinned back and stood. Chloe and Lauren had fast developed a reputation around Purgatory for being untamable. Brad had been the only Dom in Leeds willing to even take on the pair. Kalen had told him that Chloe and Lauren had toured local clubs and events for over a year as a pair. They were both subs, but their only rule was anyone taking them on had to take them both. No preference, no favorites. Their time together had made them bolder than they already were, and as high energy as the two were he was amazed Brad kept up with them at all.

James could hear the two girls shouting and laughing as they approached the double doors that led to Kalen's main playroom at the Dormitory. Over the years Kalen had held a lot of events in that fully-stocked room that had things day-to-day Doms could only dream of. Most people just didn't have the space.

Brad was grinning when he got to the door and opened it to reveal Chloe and Lauren chasing each other around the room in some very nice lingerie. Chloe had a flogger in her hand and Lauren was squealing as she put a spanking bench between the two of them with a wild smile on her face.

"Girls." Brad stepped into the room as Kalen and James followed him, and his voice was threaded with humor. Brad didn't have a hint of temper in him, he was always in a good mood, which matched the chaos that was Lauren and Chloe perfectly.

"Sir! Help me!" Lauren laughed loudly and vaulted the spanking bench, sprinting to tackle Brad to the ground. He caught her and dropped to the floor with her. Lauren ended up straddling him and wiggling on his hips just as Chloe caught up and snapped the flogger across Lauren's backside. Brad leaned up and grabbed the hand Chloe held the flogger in and tugged her down. She didn't argue and knelt with her knees wide next to him as she kissed him with a brazen laugh. James' eyebrows were up as he watched the display and he glanced at Kalen who was trying his best not to laugh.

"Thought ye were running a practice session with them, Brad?" Kalen couldn't keep the laughter from his voice. Brad detached from Chloe's lips and looked up at James and Kalen with a grin. Lauren was rocking on Brad's hips as she tugged at his waistband, and he moved his hands to her hips to stop her.

"Ah, yeah, that's why I came to get you. My girls are wild," his eyes flicked between Chloe and Lauren, "aren't you, girls?"

They cackled and Chloe tackled Lauren backward off Brad's hips. In a moment they were kissing, Lauren grasping Chloe's face to hers and James shifted his growing cock in his pants. Kalen seemed to be having the same difficulty as the girls slipped out soft moans between giggles. Hard to ignore the display they made, and his cock wasn't consulting him on appropriate reactions. Brad pushed himself up to a seated position and just tilted his head as he watched them.

"Ach, Brad." Kalen laughed openly, "I told ye that ye were in for trouble."

Brad shrugged, keeping his eyes on them as Lauren slipped her hand between Chloe's thighs. "Totally worth the trouble, and *you* are supposed to be helping us." Brad finally took his eyes from the girls and looked up, his cocky, satisfied grin still plastered on his face.

"That I am." Kalen shifted and James noted the change in his stance. "Girls! Present!" His voice cracked across the room and effectively short-circuited the little tryst unfolding before them. It took Lauren and Chloe a moment to separate and move into kneels, their hands clasping behind their heads as their breathing calmed. Both were still grinning and glancing at each other occasionally, their lips swollen and red from their efforts.

"Hi, Master Kalen." Lauren spoke up with a smile.

"Quiet, Lauren." Kalen's loud voice silenced her. "Chloe, explain to me why ye two are not obeying Brad."

"We are obeying—"

"Master Kalen, we're trying to—"

"Hush!" Kalen snapped and both girls bit down on their lips. "Ye two chose Brad, right? Just nod." They both did. "Ye two are submissive in nature, but both of ye are doing a shit job of obeying yer Dom. Submission is a gift ye give him, it's something ye have to choose, and work on. We have been training ye both on how to do this, and yet—" Kalen gestured toward them, their eyes looking sad suddenly, "—this is what ye give him?"

"We're sorry, Master Kalen." Lauren spoke softly.

"Yeah, we like Brad, we don't mean to—" Chloe started.

"Be disrespectful?" Kalen clapped his hands together and then crossed his arms, the picture of stern control. "Well, ye are."

Brad stood smoothly, and both girls looked at him. He had an indulgent look on his face. Kalen had been right that Brad was a lucky idiot, the girls were delicious to watch but an absolute mess as subs.

"Sir, I'm so sorry—" Chloe spoke directly to Brad.

"I never meant to disrespect you, sir!" Lauren sounded upset at the idea of it.

"Girls," he shrugged, "I just want us to have fun. I know you like our play, but you have to give up the control like Kalen has explained." Brad stepped forward and brushed his thumb across Chloe's mocha toned cheek. "You two can't top from the bottom and expect me to be an effective Dom. After all, I am outnumbered." He grinned and chuckled.

"We'll listen, I promise." Chloe leaned her head against his hand.

"Promise." Lauren added, her eyes on Brad's face.

"So, what was yer plan today, Brad?" Kalen made a point of deferring to Brad in front of the girls, further solidifying who was really in charge regardless of Kalen's coaching. James had always respected his friend's ability to do that, and he was glad they had moved past the awkwardness of Kalen wanting to run Thalia's training.

"Ah. That." Brad's grin turned mischievous. "The girls have been so excited by some of the things you offer in this playroom, that I thought we could take advantage of some things I don't have back home."

Kalen grinned and they all looked around the room at the possibilities. Doms in Kalen's playroom might as well be kids in a candy shop. Almost hard to decide *what* to use, because you wanted to use all of it. "What are ye thinking?"

"Lauren hasn't been able to keep her eyes off your Sybian." Brad's voice edged on sinister, Lauren's little gasp of breath had James smiling.

"I'm sure. And Chloe?" Kalen was running a hand across his beard as they watched the girls' breathing increase as their excitement spiked.

"Chloe likes to have control over Lauren in our sessions, I'd like to balance the scales a bit and give Lauren some control over her." Chloe gaped at him, and Brad continued, tilting Chloe's head back by her hair. "Lauren's challenge is going to be *not* coming on the Sybian. For Chloe, I'll have her bound across my lap in your spanking chair. As long as Lauren holds out, Chloe gets pleasure, if Lauren comes Chloe gets spanked. Harder than the last each time Lauren comes."

"Lovely." James was grinning as he imagined the control Lauren would have to exert to hold back her orgasm, a devious plan since both girls struggled with self-control.

"One more thing." Brad tilted Lauren's chin up so she looked at him, her face flushed in her arousal, her eyes losing focus as her pulse increased, "Lauren, doll, you aren't allowed off the Sybian until Chloe comes. Only fair, right?"

Both girls were stunned into silence, their arousal blatant as their knees pulled together and they squirmed at Brad's feet. Maybe James had underestimated him; Brad seemed more than capable of handling both girls at once. Evenly, fairly.

"Want some help?" Kalen was smiling, and a whimper slipped out of Chloe's mouth as she looked up at Kalen.

"I'd love some. Let's get them sorted." Brad walked past the girls to a cabinet on the wall.

"Strip." Kalen ordered and the girls stood to take the lingerie off. In a matter of minutes Brad had grabbed the items he wanted and with Kalen's help had set up the Sybian with an impressive dildo toward the front and a smaller one just behind. James slid leather cuffs on Chloe's wrists, ensuring they weren't too tight, and he guided her to kneel by the spanking chair that Brad had moved in front of the Sybian.

Both girls were a bundle of nerves, taking shallow breaths as they waited for Brad to take control. The addition of two other Doms in the room probably wasn't helping their tension. James could read the anticipation in Brad's shoulders, and in the nervous tic of Kalen running a hand across his beard over and over. When Brad had Lauren stand by the Sybian she shifted her weight from foot to foot, "Sir, I don't think I can handle—"

"Hush, doll. You have your safe word if it's too much, but I want you to try this for me." Brad was the most in control that James had ever seen, and he was impressed with this side of the young, fun-loving guy. He held on to Lauren as she climbed on after he had applied some liberal lube to both dildos. At first her thighs shook, but Brad pressed his lips to her ear and James could hear him talking to her as she started to ease down, the shaft slowly disappearing into her pussy. Brad held her there for a moment, and she moaned as he slid his hand over her ass before pressing a finger against the tight ring of muscles and then dipping it inside, slowly warming her up. Lauren arched, beautiful to look at as she held on to Brad's arm across her chest. After a minute or two he removed his fingers and Lauren eased down further, taking the second shaft in with a groan that had Chloe moaning softly next to him.

"You'll have your turn soon." James smiled down at Chloe, brushing hair behind her ear. Her pupils were dilated and she swallowed before returning her gaze to Lauren. The look of focus on Lauren's face as she rocked down slowly, had all of them holding their breath. Her harsh breaths and moans filling the quiet of the room.

"That's my girl, come on, doll, just a little more." Brad was running his hand down Lauren's back as she finally gasped prettily and her flesh pressed against the Sybian. She rocked her hips again and moaned, gasping already at the sensation. James chuckled to himself because Brad hadn't even turned it on yet. "Perfect, Lauren, just perfect. Give me your hands."

Brad stepped away and brought over leather cuffs, Lauren was already tense atop the Sybian, her breathing rapid in her excitement. Reaching above her Brad linked a nylon strap to the end of a chain hanging from the high ceiling. In a moment he had the cuffs on Lauren and her arms bound above her head. She wasn't taut though, and she could lean forward or back easily, but it meant it would be very difficult to dismount without assistance.

Brad was very fucking creative.

The look on his face when he turned to Chloe had small moans slipping from between her lips. He stopped in front of her and tilted her chin up sharply, "Ready, darling?" Chloe nodded with a whimper and Brad chuckled. "Good girl. Up for me." He held his hand out and she stood gracefully.

Brad dropped into the spanking chair and tugged Chloe across his lap, adjusting her until her ass was turned up for his hand. He nudged her thighs apart and the scent of her arousal was evident. James took a step back to stand by Kalen. With a clink of metal Chloe's hands were bound to the chair, and she moaned again.

"Ready girls?" Brad was running his hand over Chloe's back, and the round of her ass, and she was already squirming. Their tension was incredible, every shift of Lauren's body had her groaning and tensing her arms against the cuffs. "Girls!" Brad's voice was sharp for once and the shiver that went through both girls was satisfying for all the Doms in the room.

"Yes, sir." They moaned almost simultaneously.

"Brilliant." Brad smiled at Kalen, who stepped forward and handed the Sybian remote to him. The cry released from Lauren as the machine started moving inside her, and vibrating against her clit, was all the notice anyone needed to know the game was on. Her moans and whimpers were escalating quickly as her nerves ramped up her sensitivity. Even from James' angle he could tell that Brad was barely teasing Chloe, his fingers dipping between her lips, brushing lightly over her clit, and making her plead.

"Please, sir, please touch me. More? Please touch me more?" Chloe's soft pleas made James' cock twitch and he wanted to find Thalia. Right now.

"The name of this game is patience, darling." Brad slid a finger inside her and Chloe moaned, pushing back against him as much as she could. James' attention had been distracted from Lauren who suddenly released a loud cry; her head dropping back as her muscles tensed and she came hard. She was biting her lip as she shivered and her eyes snapped to Chloe and Brad. Brad was grinning. "Tsk, tsk, Lauren. Look at that, already a punishment for Chloe." His hand came back and landed sharply on Chloe's beautiful skin. She yelped, and he did it four more times until she was wiggling and tugging on the cuffs. Lauren was gasping as she watched Chloe get punished, a hint of need in her own eyes.

Ah, submissives, no other women could compare.

Lauren was rocking again, the spanking clearly exciting her which made her grind down on the Sybian. Brad's gentle touches returned between Chloe's thighs, but this time he slid two fingers inside her. Lazily stroking her as she begged over and over for more. Kalen nudged James' shoulder, his cheeks ruddy as he grinned. He nodded at the door and James nodded back. Brad winked at them before turning his eyes back to the writhing Lauren.

As James and Kalen slipped from the room they could hear Lauren moaning, "Oh God, not yet, not yet, not yet!" Then her voice rose sharply, and a series of spanks followed like thunder after a lightning strike.

"Ahem, well," James rocked back on his heels as Kalen shut the door and stopped, "I think Brad may have a handle on them now."

"Yeh." Kalen laughed. "I think the girls are learning the benefits of obeying. On that note, I think I'm going to track down Maggie."

"I'm grabbing Thalia before she meets with Ailsa." James checked his watch and groaned as his cock strained in his pants. Not long enough for too much fun, but he needed her. Fucking craved her.

"See ye later." Kalen grinned wickedly and walked away, and James turned the other way to find Thalia.

Chapter Five
THALIA

Thalia was deliciously sore as everyone sat down for dinner. She was smiling and laughing with Julie and it felt easy, natural, *normal*. The most normal she had felt since her life consisted of a dead-end contract job, a douchebag boss, and an empty apartment and social life. Her mind was wrapping around how drastically her life had changed when she felt James' hand against hers. The babble of voices effectively hid his words as he leaned over and whispered in her ear, "I want you to know I'm nowhere near done with you for the night, pet."

Her pussy flooded with heat, her panties dampening instantly at the anticipation of what he was planning. His devilish smile flashed before he turned his head to respond to something Brad had said, but he linked his fingers with hers on her thigh.

Thalia licked her lips as she remembered his fierce need for her earlier in the afternoon. The way he had grabbed her from the bathroom where she was drying her hair. Pushed her to her knees in front of him where he barely let her taste him before tugging her onto his lap in a chair. She'd ridden him until they both found their pleasure, and Thalia had muttered a curse realizing she was late for her therapy session.

Ailsa had only laughed when she'd arrived almost ten minutes late, her cheeks still flushed from their efforts, and a silly grin plastered across her face. They had talked about James' accident, how Thalia had felt, and then Ailsa had openly asked if she loved James. If she was *in love* with James. It had surprised her. But then it had been exhilarating to admit it out loud, and in a very untherapist-like way, Ailsa had leaned forward before moving her book to the side. With a conspiratorial grin, like a long-lost girlfriend, she had urged Thalia to tell her everything.

And Thalia had.

Which was why now, at dinner, Thalia couldn't hide the blush or the way her pulse picked up at James' promise. She was tempted to make an excuse to leave when Julie grabbed her other hand and brought her back to reality.

"You've got that dreamy look on your face again." Julie tilted her head, her voice all-knowing.

"Ah, I do?" Thalia laughed, and Julie grinned back at her.

"Mmhmm, you do. What did James say?" Julie had dropped her voice to a whisper.

"Just that he has *plans* for us this evening." Thalia couldn't keep eye contact with her as she felt her blush burn in her cheeks. Julie cackled and clapped her hands together.

"That's brill! I'm so jealous, Thalia. There isn't enough phone sex in the universe to match just one night with Antonio." She groaned and dropped her head back, and Thalia felt terrible for her.

A month away from James would be misery, and apparently it happened a few times a year for Julie. The Middle East wasn't as friendly to women as Antonio would like, and especially not with an exuberant, highly sexual girl like Julie. So, she spent that time at Purgatory with Kalen and Maggie so she wasn't lonely or bored. And Thalia was pretty sure that Antonio sent along suggestions to Kalen just like James had.

"I'm sorry, Julie, really." Thalia felt guilty about the blatant displays of affection that Julie was surrounded by at dinner. James' suggestive comments, Chloe and Lauren's overt flirtations with Brad, Maggie and Kalen's sweet whispers and kisses. It must be torture.

"No, no! I'm used to it, I swear. And he'll be back soon!" Julie laughed again, her bright smile back, "Plus, the 'I've missed you' sex is phenomenal!"

Thalia laughed as well and James leaned over to place a kiss behind her ear. His teeth nipped at her skin and she found her back arching, her breath catching. His grip tightened on hers and she turned into his mouth. James kissed her and it didn't matter that she could feel everyone looking at them. She wanted to kiss him. She always wanted to kiss him, no matter where they were. James pulled back a bit and smiled against her lips.

"Oh, now, don't stop on our accounts! Please continue!" Kalen's voice boomed across the table and a few chuckles shuffled across the room. When Thalia looked up, Maggie's eyes were twinkling and Kalen was grinning through his beard.

"Hmm, maybe later, Master Kalen." Thalia grinned and Kalen looked surprised for a moment before he let out a loud laugh. Julie's mouth was in a perfect 'O' as she stared at Thalia in shock.

Had she just said that out loud?

"Maybe you should consult me before you offer things like that, pet," James purred in her ear, and she blushed furiously, but he chuckled and pressed a kiss to her hair.

"Look how cheeky ye are!" Maggie cackled.

"Quite right!" Kalen slapped the table and some sly smiles spread across the room. Kalen's voice gentled, "I have to admit I've never been quite so glad to hear someone be cheeky. Ye've come quite a long way, Thalia."

James tightened his grip on her hand and she smiled. "Thank you, Master Kalen. And"—Thalia took a breath—"and thanks for letting us stay, it means everything to me."

"To us." James added, running his thumb in a hypnotizing pattern over the back of her hand.

"Ah, yes, I'm glad ye stayed too. Both of ye." Kalen's voice was sincere for a moment, and then he laughed again. "And!" He raised his glass and nodded toward Brad, "We've got another success story at the table, don't we Brad?"

"Absolutely. Chloe and Lauren had some fantastic realizations today." Brad smiled and Lauren and Chloe looked at each other.

"Do tell?" Kalen leaned back in his chair, taking a drink of his scotch. Maggie was toying with her own glass of it, and everyone was waiting for Chloe and Lauren to answer.

"We need to listen to Brad, to have self-control, to be obedient!" Lauren piped up with a grin.

"It's much *better* when we are." Chloe added with a gentle correction.

"More fun for sure." Lauren winked and everyone laughed.

"I think my girls enjoyed their session this afternoon." Brad grinned.

"We did. It was—" Lauren sighed dreamily. "—amazing."

Chloe bit her lip for a moment, shrugging as she leaned against Brad's shoulder, "Brad is amazing to put up with us."

It was Brad's turn to laugh, "I'm bloody lucky, because both of you girls are my kind of crazy."

Everyone laughed, but the side conversations soon took over again. The trio was talking quietly to each other and Lauren crawled into Brad's lap so she was closer to Chloe as well.

Kalen kissed Maggie and left the room on his cell phone, leaving Maggie alone at the end of the table on her phone. But she seemed content as she sipped from her glass and scrolled through something.

After a few minutes Chloe and Lauren were giggling and it made Thalia smile. They were ridiculous. But from the corner of her eye she caught Marisol rolling her eyes at them. *Bitch.* Thalia had to bite her tongue to keep from calling her out on it. Luckily, Julie took that moment to pick up their conversation.

"So, Thalia, I know you and James are leaving in a few days... are you going to keep teaching yoga back home?" Julie asked the question while toying with a fork she hadn't used.

"Ailsa and I *have* talked about it. About ways I can build a life, and, yeah, I'm planning to join the local studio back home." Thalia shrugged, trying to suppress the excitement that bubbled up inside of her at the idea of it. "And if they have a teacher certification program, I'm going to sign up."

"Is that right?" James' mouth was against her ear, and Julie did a terrible job of hiding her smile. She had known he was listening.

"Um, yes?" Thalia shifted so she could see James' expression and his eyes were full of warmth. He was happy. They were both so unbelievably happy. And they had friends. Thalia's eyes roamed the room. Julie, Chloe, Lauren, Brad, Maggie and Kalen. Analiese and Nick had insisted they'd visit. Even Ethan was funny when he let himself not be so serious.

"That sounds perfect, baby." James ran his thumb over her cheek, and the edge of his mouth curved into a smile.

"Even... if I'm not planning on taking college courses?" Thalia had talked about it a lot with Ailsa, about what she actually wanted to do, and it didn't require a degree. She'd always been terrible at studying anyway, but she hadn't even brought it up with James.

"As long as you're happy, I would never ask for anything else." His smile went full-watt bright, and she practically gaped at how gorgeous he looked when he grinned like that. She'd always compared him to some yacht club ad, but no magazine model had ever made her stomach flutter like James did.

He kissed her. Then he kissed her again, and she felt his hand sliding up her thigh. Somewhere at the back of her mind was the inkling that Julie was within arm's reach, that the entire room was likely staring at them, and that the ideas that Thalia's brain was suggesting were about to give the group one hell of a show.

Then Julie screamed.

Thalia and James jerked apart, and she watched as Julie sprinted across the room and leapt onto a very tan, dark haired man who caught her with ease. Julie's legs were wrapped around him, her arms so tight around his neck that Thalia was a little concerned for the man's air supply. It could only be Antonio.

"Angel! Angel!" His rough voice sounded American as he wrapped his arms around Julie and squeezed her. "Love, I've missed you, but you're going to choke me."

"Shut up!" Julie squealed and squeezed him tighter until Antonio made a gurgling sound. His hands reached back to pry her grip from him, and he forced out a laugh.

"Angel, please?" Antonio leaned her back and she finally relented, relaxing her grip and tilting back on his hips so she could look at him.

"Antonio, you didn't even tell me you were coming! You always tell me!" Julie pouted but he pulled her against him and kissed her. They both groaned and Antonio lifted her higher, his hands wrapping around her thighs.

The entire room was staring and Thalia had a pretty good idea of what hers and James' audience had been like. Maggie was covering her mouth, and Kalen walked over to wrap his arms around her as they watched Julie and Antonio come home to each other.

"I love you, angel. I can't even tell you how miserable every damn day has been without you to wake up to." Antonio was gruff as he turned and pressed Julie to the wall of the dining room.

"I love you, too. So much. I'm so glad you're back." Julie kissed him again and Maggie almost talked but Kalen covered her mouth, tucking her against him.

What's going on?

"Jules, Julie... slow down, I wanted to tell you something, or ask, well—" Antonio slid her down his front and pushed himself back from her, taking a breath.

Then he dropped to one knee.

Every girl in the room let out the same surprised squeal-gasp, and Julie started crying when Antonio slid a box from his pocket.

"Antonio..." Julie whispered and he took a deep breath.

"Angel, you are everything I've ever wanted. You are my sunlight, my joy, the warmth in my life that makes me feel whole, and when I'm not with you I feel empty. Alone, even if I'm surrounded by people. Cold in places that can't be warmed without you there. You are — you're perfect to me." Antonio took another breath and looked up at Julie whose blonde hair was bouncing as she tried to stifle her tears. "I feel like you deserve so much more than me, but I'm a selfish bastard, and... and I'd really like it if you'd agree to marry me."

"YES!" Julie cried and half-tackled Antonio. He caught himself on one hand, laughing, but she silenced him with a kiss. He eventually pushed her back and smiled, dark scruff on his tanned cheeks made his white teeth stand out.

"Don't you even want to see the ring?" Antonio held the box between them and Julie wrapped her hand around it and kissed him again. He slid a hand into her hair and bowed her back, taking charge as his tongue explored her mouth and she moaned against his lips. He pulled back and held her away from him by her hair. "Look at the damn ring, Jules." His grin was full of nerves and anticipation.

She sighed with exasperation, but she obeyed and opened the box. Julie's eyes lit up, and Antonio's low rumbled laugh filled the silence. Julie's voice rose up, "It's beautiful, I love it, I love you! You really want to marry me?"

"I actually thought I might have to beg, so thank you for saving my pride. Because I would have." Antonio smiled. Julie slapped his shoulder and he rolled her under him to pin her. He sat up, straddling her hips as he tugged the ring from the box. Antonio took her left hand and kissed it before slipping the ring on, and Thalia leaned forward to see. James squeezed her hand as the yellow diamond caught the light.

"Antonio!" Kalen's voice boomed, followed by the thunder of his laugh. "Are ye going to let yer new fiancé up so we can congratulate the two of ye? Or do ye want the room to yerselves?"

Julie giggled, seeming to be perfectly happy under Antonio's weight. He groaned and kissed her hard, and Julie arched prettily against him. But he slid off her and stood, pulling her up with him. James tugged Thalia to her feet as everyone stood to surround them.

"Congratulations! You are perfect together."

"The ring is gorgeous—"

"—happy for ye, man—"

"—get an invite?"

"What a story—"

"—so happy for you—"

Julie and Antonio were overwhelmed with back slaps and hugs and oohs and aahs over the gorgeous yellow teardrop diamond that looked like frozen sunlight.

When Thalia finally stepped forward she hugged Julie tight and spoke into her ear, "You'll have to tell me if fiancé sex is as good as 'I've missed you' sex."

Julie cackled and blushed, and Antonio glanced at her with a look that made Julie seem like the only person in the world he knew existed. Ethan was shaking his hand, but it was as if he wasn't aware once his eyes were on her. In a moment they were back in each other's arms and everyone else was just watching them.

"Oh! Kalen!" Maggie spoke up, scrambling back to the table. "We have to celebrate and I have the *perfect* way!" She returned to their little group with her phone grasped in her hand and a grin on her face. Her blue eyes were radiant as she almost vibrated in her excitement.

"Yes, blessing?" Kalen seemed wary, but he wasn't fighting the smile on his lips very well.

"Crucible." Maggie said it with a dark tone, and Kalen held up his hand, but Maggie kept talking. "I have the address, the password, and come on, we have to celebrate this. Please?"

"Maggie..." Kalen sighed.

"Sir. Pretty please?" Maggie pouted and it was fun to watch Kalen melt with a groan.

"Just the four of us?" He asked, and Thalia almost opened her mouth to ask what Crucible was and why she and James weren't invited.

"Everyone should be invited! It's a party!" Maggie paused and glanced over at Marisol, "Everyone that wants to come anyway."

"Hell, Kalen, what's Crucible and why are you being all secretive about it?" Antonio cut straight to it and it made Thalia smile. He was just as brash as Julie.

"Crucible is a very exclusive, very hard to find, and even more difficult to gain entrance to, sex club in Edinburgh." James' voice purred next to Thalia's ear and she shivered. "It's where Kalen and Maggie met."

"True. Though at this point we are almost benefactors. Maggie and I do our part to keep it going." Kalen tugged Maggie forward so that she tripped into his arms. He grabbed the cell phone and pinned her against him with the other arm. He calmly read through the texts, sent a response with a quiet beep, and then looked down at the squirming mop of red hair.

"Kalen! Don't erase the answer to tonight's question!" Maggie fussed at him as he tucked the phone into his pocket. With a grin he brought his hand back and landed a loud pop on Maggie's backside.

"First, blessing, that's three for ye today, and second, since we're going to Crucible tonight... I'll pay out all three sets in front of a crowd." Kalen was suddenly all Dom. Loud voice, immoveable and solid as a crag. Maggie turned breathless in his arms, nodding against his broad chest.

"We're going, sir?" Maggie asked quietly, her smile peeking out at Julie from beneath her hair.

"Yeh, blessing. I think everyone here will find that Crucible helps them solidify their decisions." Kalen's mouth hovered over Maggie's and she tried to lean forward to kiss him, but he pulled back. "After all, it worked for us, right?"

"Like magic." Maggie whispered, and Kalen kissed her hard.

Chapter Six
THALIA

Crucible.

Thalia hadn't known what to expect when Maggie had suggested it. She'd asked James about it and he'd only kissed her and told her it was a 'wait-and-see' kind of place. Of all the ideas that had floated through her head, she could have never imagined what they found when they got to Crucible's location for the night.

After parking on a busy street in the middle of Edinburgh and climbing out of Kalen's car to wait for the others to grab spaces, Thalia's mind was racing. James had hugged her close to keep her warm in the cold air since the very tight, and very short, little black dress she wore did nothing against the chill. He had picked it though, and the way he'd grinned when she put it on was worth the temporary shivers. Julie and Antonio had arrived next. She was wearing a dress the color of mist and it made her hair glow like a halo around her head in the streetlights. Antonio's dark hair and dusky skin were a sharp contrast. They stayed to the side, whispering to each other and kissing occasionally with big smiles. It made Thalia feel warm to watch them.

James pulled her attention away when he turned her in his arms so she looked up at him, "Well, baby, how are you feeling?" His thumb traced her bottom lip and she smiled. He looked so serious, and all Thalia could feel was the thrumming nervous excitement beating through her veins. None of her usual panic or anxiety.

"I'm fine, I promise. I'm actually excited to see it... You know, Analiese said she used to go to clubs like this all the time." Thalia felt heat in her cheeks as she heard Chloe and Lauren's laughter approaching, "She said I'd probably like them, like getting to see others like me, that I'd like getting to be myself where no one would judge me."

James chuckled and pulled her closer to the heat of his body, and she slid her arms under his jacket, soaking it in. Thalia pressed her cheek to his chest, breathing deep the smell of clean soap, warm skin, and spice that was intrinsically James. "No one is going to judge you at Crucible, pet, trust me."

"I do trust you. Completely. So..." She fought the urge to bury her face in his shirt and ruin her make-up. "What's going to happen when we get there?" Thalia voiced her only question for him, and he leaned back to look down at her, concern etching his forehead again.

"Nothing you don't want, baby." James brushed her hair over her ear before he cupped her cheek. "In fact, let's agree right now that if you want to leave, you don't even have to say your safe word. All you need to do is tap me three times. Anything makes you uncomfortable, or if you are simply done for the night? Tap three times. Alright?"

"Thalia!" Lauren was waving at her, and Thalia waved and smiled at her before looking back at James' concerned face. He always gave her an escape route, it was always a choice, and she loved him for that. And everything else.

"I promise if I want to leave I'll tap three times, but I don't think I'll need it." Thalia spoke softly, "Plus... you said earlier you weren't done with me for the night."

James laughed a little and grinned down at her, his eyes turning bottle glass green in the street lights. "No, pet. I'm nowhere near done with you."

"That's good to know, Master." Thalia watched as the title made James shift closer to her, his grip tightening around her. He'd liked it since their first night together, and she still loved to say it. His fingertips traced her curves and a shiver ran across her skin, promising more.

"Come on!" Maggie shouted and grabbed Kalen's hand as Ethan and Marisol approached. Her shout unfortunately interrupted wherever James' hands had been going. They led the group down a quiet side street, marked with charming old-style street lamps, before stopping without warning in front of a weathered old stone building. It was tall, and it was clear at one time it had been well cared for. Important in the area, but the whole section of the city seemed to have been forgotten by time.

A broad-shouldered man stepped out of the shadow of a doorway and smiled warmly at them. "Well, this is a surprise, Kalen."

"Sorry we did nae reach out to ye in advance, Michael." Kalen stepped away from Maggie and shook his hand.

"Ye and Maggie are always welcome." Michael laughed, his shaggy hair falling in his eyes before he pushed it back. "So are yer friends as long as ye can give the right response for the night. Can nae break the rules for ye."

Maggie bounced on her toes and leaned up to whisper in Kalen's ear. He chuckled and slid his arms around her to hold her in front of him. "Alright. Go ahead, Michael."

Michael crossed his arms, shrugged a shoulder, and spoke clearly. "They condemn what they do not understand."

Huh?

Kalen chuckled to himself and mumbled, "Clever." With a nudge from Maggie he looked up at Michael and spoke his answer. "Pontius Pilate."

Thalia felt her forehead crease at the Latin sounding words, and James chuckled. She had definitely missed a joke of some kind.

Michael grinned. "Welcome to Crucible. Enjoy yer evening." He pushed the door open with some effort and the heavy pulse of music from inside flowed into the night. The man's eyes traced over each of them as they moved inside, and Thalia felt like she was about to skydive, or sing on stage, or swim with sharks. Her heart was racing, her stomach filling with fluttering butterflies that beat a rapid tempo inside her and made it difficult to breathe.

The weird code word exchange should have been the strangest part of Crucible — but it wasn't. It was *where* Crucible was for the night.

Thalia tightened her grip on James' hand as they stepped forward into the dark interior. It swallowed them whole, and no one made noise even as the door swung shut behind them. Continuing forward they emerged from a short hallway and the ceiling suddenly rose high above them. Thalia felt her lips part in awe. There were burnished gold arches disappearing into the gloom at their peaks where the dim light of the space couldn't reach. Intricate designs were carved into them with old paintings almost invisible on the ceiling spaces between them. The room was lit as if a club had been installed in the old building. Which, after staring around her, was obviously an old museum or gallery of some kind. An endless smooth floor reflected the flashing lights that cut through the dark, and the movement of people seemed to fill the space. Some sitting on chairs or couches, others obviously kneeling on the floor. Others tied in place on the walls, where the sounds of a dozen sessions compounded with the music. Thalia felt her stomach tighten with nerves and excitement, her heart crashing into her ribs as she tried to watch everything at once.

Even Lauren and Chloe were quiet for once.

"Still okay?" James' lips were against her ear and Thalia forced herself to swallow even though her mouth was dry. Not fifteen feet away there was a naked girl on her knees between the legs of her Dom. The man's head was dropped back on the chair, his fist buried in her hair as she sucked him. Heat pooled between Thalia's legs, but a sharp tug from James brought her back from staring.

"Yes, Master." Thalia breathed and he chuckled, his hand sweeping down to brush over her thigh and send a shiver through her.

"Let's sit. James, would ye find space? I have something to arrange." Kalen grinned and something passed between James and Kalen unspoken. Thalia was glad they had mended what her arrival and her situation had damaged. A friendship that old, and that important, couldn't be lost. Kalen turned and walked off into the dark like he knew the place, and James took Thalia's hand and pulled her forward.

People. People everywhere.

Not just *people*.

Submissives.

Doms.

There was a very handsome young man in a pair of leather pants kneeling with his hair in his eyes at the booted feet of a woman. The woman's eyes locked onto Thalia's as she passed and on instinct she dropped her gaze. The woman's laugh followed her, but Thalia wasn't worried. She was brimming with questions. Were female Doms common? Were male submissives? Did places like this really exist? Thalia had only met everyone at Purgatory! Her brain was a blur as they passed a girl being spanked in turns by two couples with paddles. Her cries and moans rose over the music. A man's shirtless back moved in front of her, coated in sweat, and Thalia had to jump to the side to not run into him.

By the time James sat down and pulled Thalia possessively into his lap, her cheeks were burning. Her eyes were devouring everything with abandon and even though she knew she *shouldn't* look, she was. A lot. And she couldn't stop. Heat pulsed between her thighs, her clit throbbing to be touched, and she found herself squirming on James' lap. His laugh buzzed across her skin as if he'd stroked her. "Like anything you see, pet?"

Thalia nodded, biting her lower lip as she stared across the room at a girl bound by her wrists to the wall. Her body was stretched up, her feet on tip toes. She had obviously arrived in a corset and skirt, but the corset was mostly unlaced, and the skirt was bunched at her waist. Bright red lines marked down her backside, and the man next to her was speaking against her ear. Even from so far away Thalia could see the tremble move through her. She knew that feeling. She loved that feeling.

Anticipation. Nerves. Excitement. Tension.

"Talk to me." James' hand slid up her thigh, pushing the hem of the dress up. Thalia parted her legs slightly and his fingers took advantage, dipping to stroke the inside of her thigh, but no higher.

"Her." Thalia's mouth was so dry. She knew she should be talking to Julie, celebrating with her, or at least chatting with Chloe or Lauren — but she couldn't tear her eyes away as the man swished the cane through the air.

"Remembering your punishment?" James' lips were against her neck, running warm, soft kisses down to meet her shoulder.

"Yes, Master." She arched as his teeth nipped her skin, an involuntary moan slipping from between her lips.

"What's going on in your head, pet. Tell me." His voice slid quickly into that clear edge of command and she felt any internal barriers that she normally maintained in public buckle under the onslaught of sounds and visuals and his voice.

"I've missed you. I've missed that." Thalia said it just as the man brought another lash of the cane across the girl's backside. Her cry of pain, her shivering dance on her tiptoes, made Thalia's breath catch. "I—I want to do that again?"

"Anything for you. Let's make a list." James shifted her back farther into his lap so that the heat of his chest bled through the back of her dress. "What else would you like to try?"

Thalia felt like she had when he'd taken her shopping. Only now she wanted to shop. Her eyes skipped over the ecstatic Julie who was sitting in Antonio's lap and leaning forward to chat with Lauren, while Chloe was straddling Brad and kissing him — she was telling him something, and he was laughing. Thalia pulled her eyes from them too, ignoring the sullen Marisol who forced a smile at Ethan before staring off into nothing again.

"The girl, the one with the people with the paddle." Thalia pointed back down the gallery, and where once there were paintings now there were people.

"What do you like about it?" James' voice was level against her skin. His warm breath moving across her collar bone made her whine, and his damned hand hadn't moved an inch higher.

"I just like it. Please, Master, touch me?" Her voice was pleading, but he didn't relent.

"Answer me, pet. Is it the fact that strangers are doing it?" His voice didn't hold an ounce of judgment, but she shook her head. That wasn't it. In her head she could only picture James standing behind her, and maybe Kalen if she was honest with herself. "Hmm. Is it that she's bound? The other girl who caught your eye was bound as well."

Thalia felt her body shiver, her thighs tightening and pressing together as her pussy flooded with heat. Memories of James pinning her, cuffing her, keeping her bound so he could touch her, it overwhelmed her. "Yes." It was the only word Thalia could form as James' hands pulled her thighs apart.

"Hmmm." His mouth was against her neck again, the heat of his breath making her whimper with need. "Is it also the paddle?"

Thalia's mouth opened and she moaned softly. "Mmhmm," she murmured the affirmative as his fingers slid higher up the inside of her thigh. She wanted him. She wanted him badly and based on the hard press of his cock against her ass, he wanted her too.

"See anything else you want, pet?" he growled against her ear, and she felt the first incredible stroke of his fingers against her soaked panties.

"You, Master, please, Master?" Thalia didn't care who could hear her begging, or who was watching, or what was happening. Her world shrank to just her and James. His hand between her thighs, the warmth of his body at her back, his mouth against her neck, the sharpness of his erection under her echoing her own need and amplifying it.

"Patience. Part of coming to these clubs is watching, and learning." His other hand slid up her side and cupped her breast for a moment, before moving up her neck to force her head to lift. "And you have to watch to learn."

The lights across the space dimmed, the electric flashes that had seemed to be timed with the music calmed. The pounding bass and dreamlike vocals swelled for a moment, and then softened so that the last few gasps and cries in the dark seemed so much louder.

A warm light bloomed against the back wall, highlighting the gold arches that formed the incredible ceiling of the place. There was no grand announcement as Kalen helped Antonio strap Julie to a large wooden X. But all attention was focused toward them. Thalia hadn't even noticed them slip away. The blonde was naked and so tiny against the tall beams of wood. It made her seem all the more fragile as Antonio almost blocked her completely from view when he stepped behind her to speak with her. Thalia could see Julie's hair bounce when she nodded and Antonio stepped back and turned to the room.

"Tonight is a celebration for me and my friends!" Antonio's voice seemed amplified in the space, or maybe it was the softer music, or the sudden absence of the small chorus of cries and moans. "This incredible, beautiful, smart, funny woman agreed to be my wife tonight." A short round of applause accompanied by murmurs of congratulations followed his announcement. He continued, "But that's not all. I didn't fall in love with Jules because she's beautiful. Or because she's smart, which she is. Or because she makes me laugh, or because she has a heart way too big for a girl that's only five feet tall." Laughter bounced across the groups in the room. "I fell in love with Julie because we found in each other someone who accepted, and balanced, the core of who we are. I can be myself, and so can she, and we are unapologetically ourselves when we are together. So earlier this evening we toasted the fact that she agreed to be my wife, and now we will celebrate the way we really like to celebrate." His grin spoke volumes. "Isn't that right, Julie?"

"Yes, sir! Please!" Julie was tugging on the cuffs, her small, fit body reminding Thalia of a gymnast as she begged. She knew Julie was wound tight after a month away from Antonio and since the girl didn't have a shy bone in her body, this was perfect for her.

"Be a good girl, angel, and wait to beg until you really need it?" Antonio's voice hummed with promise, and Thalia shifted on James' lap in anticipation.

"Yes, sir." Julie responded and Antonio stepped out of the pool of warm light, leaving Julie's pale skin bathed in that golden glow, her hair hiding her face from view as she rested against the St. Andrew's cross.

Antonio returned and raised his arm, uncoiling a single tailed whip for the crowd. Energy pulsed through the room as a collective shudder of anticipation concentrated attention forward. "Have you missed me, angel?" His voice sounded deadly serious, and the quiver in Julie's voice meant she had an idea of what was coming.

"Yes, sir. Every day, sir." Julie turned her head a bit, but she couldn't see the whip in Antonio's hand from where he stood.

Antonio moved closer to her, his voice staying loud enough to be heard. "What did you ask me for last week?"

"Punishment, sir." Julie said it lightly, almost laughing, but her fists were clenching and releasing in the cuffs. Preparing. Waiting.

"Yes, angel, and I promised I'd make tonight memorable." Antonio trailed the leather handle of the whip down the line of her spine and Julie's back arched. He stepped away confidently and with a quick movement of his arm the whip cracked harmlessly in the air to her right. Julie, and half the room, gasped. Thalia jumped and James slipped his hand into her hair, which pooled heat in her belly. She needed him as much as Julie needed this.

"Kalen wouldn't let Antonio touch a whip around a sub if he didn't know how to use it, baby." *James thought she was afraid.* That wasn't it. Thalia was trembling with excitement and need. Her hand traced over James' and she tried to press his touch more firmly against her clit to get some relief. He chuckled and tightened his grip on her hair and she clenched her fists on her thighs to keep them still. "Watch."

The room was hushed as Antonio stepped to the side, "Don't forget to breathe, angel."

Julie's ribs expanded and the whip cracked across her skin. She cried out, her body tensing before she relaxed. A moan of thanks rising out of her. Thalia had to remind herself to breathe too as she watched the red mark blossom on her skin. As another whip lash landed, Thalia felt James spread her thighs until her knees draped over the outside of his. Her legs spread wider in the dark as he leaned her back against him, and his hand trailed up her thigh until his fingers finally found their mark. She cried out in unison with Julie and dug her nails into her palms trying to hold still. Trying to pay attention, to watch as he'd commanded, but, fuck, his fingers were slipping under her panties. Parting her lips to drag his touch lazily up to graze her clit, and then he dipped his fingers lower. She was so wet she was slick, and James' groan in her ear as he felt it only made her want him more.

"You really are enjoying this, aren't you?" James' voice growled in her ear, and she pressed harder against him.

"Yes, Master." She moaned it, just as Julie let out a scream when another lash landed. Her eyes were glued to them as Antonio moved to her side, whispering to her. A smile tugged at his lips and his hand disappeared between her thighs. Julie jerked and moaned, her cries instantly flipping to pleasurable whimpers, begging for more.

"Please, sir, please, I've missed you, I've missed you—" Julie's sweet voice carried up into the open air of the ceiling, rebounding back and across the gathered group. Other sighs and moans filtered through the dark, as if they were answering, or pleading for her, or with her.

"Please?" Thalia joined, her hips rolling to press more firmly into James' touch, and he responded. The hand in her hair slid to wrap gently around her neck, holding her tightly back against him so he could look down the plane of her body. The steady beat of his heart countermanded the rapid staccato of her own, until he thrust two fingers inside her. She moaned, louder than before, and she knew that the dark wasn't hiding them completely. She knew the beautiful distraction that Julie made wouldn't make her invisible in James' lap — but she felt fine. There was no panic, no fear, just a rising heat that coiled around her spine and begged for more.

"Eyes open, pet." James crooned in her ear, his command had her body responding before she realized her eyes had closed. But there was Julie again, her skin glowing in the warm lights, bright lines across her skin, and Antonio drawing back.

"Oh fuck!" Thalia gasped as James rocked his hand against her clit, alternating the thrusting of his fingers with a torturous pressure on that bundle of nerves. Her hips bucked, her breath hissed between her teeth and she leaned back to brace her hands on either side of James. His touch on her throat tightened a little and it filled her with a buzzing lightness that made her whimper.

"Language, pet." His words came low against her ear, his lips moving against her skin and she writhed on his lap. Another snap of the whip, and Julie's scream collapsed into a quiet sob. It yanked Thalia's attention forward again. Her body was wound so tight. A week away from James, the accident, their relatively gentle touches since he'd come back — it had all neglected this side of her. The side of her that James had helped her accept. The side that made her pulse pound between her thighs at the sight of a whip, at the sound of Julie's cries. The side that made her want to be in Julie's place, that wanted James to create that perfect balance of pleasure and pain with her.

"Jules? Check in, angel." Antonio was talking to her, his voice warm with concern and affection.

"Hmmm..." Julie sounded dreamy, her head lifting, her muscles tightening and relaxing under her skin as she shifted. "A little more, sir?"

Antonio's grin could have matched Julie's sunshine any day. It was pride, and love, and desire — and his hand adjusted his grip on the whip. "I fucking love you."

A soft laugh came from Julie, but it was cut short when she gasped and cried out as the whip landed again. Her body was taut, and Thalia was fighting the urge to arch off James' lap completely as his fingers rolled over her clit. He spiraled her higher and then slid them back inside her, stoking the heat at her core. When his other hand trailed down inside the top of her dress and found her breast she jumped in his lap. Another lash for Julie. Another sinful bend of James' fingers that had her rolling her hips to meet his hand again and again. He pinched her nipple until she cried out, and then rolled it between his fingers to soothe the pain.

Over and over. Rising and falling waves of pleasure spiking with crests of pain that James handled with every inch of knowledge he had about her body.

Another lash. Julie's scream and sob.

James biting down on her shoulder to muffle a groan that sent a shock of pleasure down her spine.

Antonio dropping the whip. His hands finding Julie's body, and instantly drawing out moans as he returned his hand between her thighs.

"Please, please, Master. I'm so—" Thalia was begging, but a sharp pinch to her nipple cut her off. James knew she was close, she could feel her body trembling as that tension reached a brutal level. Heat wrapping around her spine, increasing with every roll of his fingers over her clit. His touch speeding up to match her need.

Julie's cries rose as well, "Sir! Oh God, yes, please!" And the room seemed to follow. Groans and sighs and moans and the sound of skin echoed, and rebounded, and built.

Until it snapped.

Julie screamed her release, a babble of thank yous, and laughing sighs. Thalia arched sharply when James snapped her head back by her hair, and his command against her ear pushed her over the edge. "Come for me."

Sparks exploded behind her eyes, the sounds of the others in the room blurred into the thrum of the music and the rocking of her hips as James slowed his touch to help her ride out the wave. Her legs were shivering, her breath shaky as she felt the tingling buzz across her skin as the orgasm began to ebb.

"Beautiful. You are beautiful and perfect, Thalia, bloody perfect." James tilted her head back and he kissed her. Whatever breath was left in her lungs was instantly stripped away in the heat of his kiss. His lips claimed hers, his tongue sweeping in to taste her. He groaned against her mouth, his hand digging into her thigh as she tried to control her shivers in his lap. When he finally pulled back, Thalia felt dazed. Her mind was fuzzy and blissfully unaware of everything outside of her and James. Nothing else needed to exist.

She had him. And in him, even if he didn't know it yet, she had love. And acceptance. And fun. And joy. And really, *really* great sex.

Chapter Seven
THALIA

Thalia giggled and James arched an eyebrow at her, his dark green eyes catching hers for a moment before a smile split his lips as well. "Mmm... thank you." She mumbled and leaned forward, placing a kiss on his lips. He kissed back before he smiled and broke it.

"I'm sorry, pet. Do you think we're done for the night?" His voice was all mischief, and she laughed.

"Give me five minutes to stop shaking like a leaf?" Thalia smiled at him and he laughed.

"Anything for you." James let her slip off his lap, and she felt her legs fold until she found herself sitting on the marble. Her knees drawn under her as she laid her head on his thigh. Warm comfort rolled over her as James' hand instantly slid into her hair, his nails grazing her scalp, his fingers moving through her hair in a rhythm they had developed over months.

It was something she hadn't been able to do at Purgatory as much as she wanted. Kneeling next to him, sated and comfortable. And she still wanted it. She felt cherished as James looked down at her, the edge of his mouth tilted in an unconscious smile, while she bathed in the afterglow of her pleasure.

Thalia's eyes tracked to Antonio as he released Julie and he sat down with her in front of the large cross. She fit in his lap perfectly, her head tucked under his chin, his tanned arms wrapped around her protectively. Julie was coming out of subspace, and Thalia could see it in her soft gaze, and the way she melted against Antonio.

Angry murmurs pulled her attention away from the newly engaged couple, and Thalia looked over to see Marisol standing up next to Ethan. She had her arms crossed, her eyes wild as she hissed something else and Ethan tried to tug her so she would sit back down on the couch. Marisol suddenly looked over and locked eyes with Thalia, her anger snapping Thalia out of her glow in an instant.

"Fuck this!" Marisol shouted, and the buzz of the room stuttered.

"Sit. Down." Ethan's voice was all command, but Marisol didn't even recognize it.

"Really, Ethan? I am not a dog!" Marisol slammed her heel onto the marble. "You like this? This bullshit?"

"Stop, Marisol." Ethan growled it and stood up, but she took a step back from him and waved her arm across the room.

"These people are crazy! You said you wanted to treat me like a princess! But you want to be like them? You want to hit women for fun like some — like some abusive motherfucker?!" Marisol was screaming, and there wasn't a person in the old museum that wasn't staring at her as she raged. "I was fine when you wanted fuzzy handcuffs and to be wild a little, but this? You are wrong. You are all wrong! This is — this is just a bullshit excuse for violence against women! And you!" Marisol pivoted and pointed at Julie and Antonio. "Julie, you agree to marry him? You, *all* you girls, you need HELP!"

"Shut the fuck up, Marisol!" Thalia hadn't even realized she'd stood up, but she had. Something shifted inside her when Marisol's vitriol was aimed at Julie, tainting the moment she had built with Antonio. Enough was enough.

"What?!" Marisol faced her, her beautiful face all twisted in disgust and shock.

"I told you to shut the fuck up, Marisol." Thalia threw her hands up, "An excuse for violence against women? *Really*, Marisol? What the fuck do you know? Did anyone do *anything* without your consent? Didn't you always have a safe word to stop it? Every. Fucking. Time. You did. You have no idea what it's like not to have that! You have no idea what's it's like to have someone actually hurt you and have no way to stop it! You don't know what that's like, but I do! I do, and this, ALL of this, is *nothing* like that!"

"That's—" Marisol's face was shocked. Maybe from the words that Thalia had said before she'd even thought them through. Maybe from the fact that it was probably the most words Marisol had heard from Thalia at once — ever. But it didn't matter, because Ethan didn't let her finish.

"Get out, Marisol." Ethan's voice was level, his expression cold, when Marisol's head whipped around to stare at him.

"You are telling me to leave?" The disbelief was apparent in her voice.

"Yes."

"And what? You are not leaving with me?" Marisol laughed.

"No, Marisol." Ethan's words cut off her laugh sharply.

"Seriously? You are choosing this *chorrada* over *me*?"

"We are done. I'll pay for your ticket home, then you can get your things out of my house, and never deal with this *chorrada* ever again." Ethan was cold. He didn't even flinch when she slammed her foot down and screamed.

"You cannot do this!" she screeched.

"It's over, Marisol. Go to the airport. Go home." Ethan crossed his arms across his chest, his brown hair and his dark eyes making him look more serious and more in control than she'd ever seen him.

"Fine. I leave. You can't make me a dog. And I'm keeping the clothes, Ethan! And the jewelry!" she shouted at him as she started stomping toward the exit.

"Too bad you didn't keep up the lies long enough for the car, eh Marisol?" he called after her and she screamed something in Spanish that made him laugh as she stormed out the door.

Thalia was willing to bet she and James were the only ones who knew why that last comment was so damning.

At some point someone had cut off the music, and now the room was quiet enough to hear the creak of leather seats as people shifted uncomfortably. Ethan sighed and rubbed his hands over his face, and Kalen disentangled himself from a half-dressed Maggie to stand and drop a hand on his shoulder.

"Well, everyone, it looks like I made the right choice to bring a few bottles of whisky along, eh!" Kalen's voice boomed out, cheerfully dragging attention away from Ethan. "No matter what ye want to drink to tonight, for good or bad, the drinks are on me!"

Several cheers went up and the man from the door, Michael, brought in a box where the distinct clinking of bottles could be heard. The music thumped back to life as glasses were filled behind a makeshift bar in the back corner that Thalia hadn't noticed. As she stayed standing and the club resumed as if someone had hit play, she felt James' hand slip across her shoulder to rest behind her neck.

"Yer girlfriend has quite the flair for angry speeches." Kalen was grinning as he looked at her, and Thalia felt the heat in her chest and face. Why did she keep losing control of her mouth like that? And why had she mentioned anything about her past? She'd definitely have to say *something* to the girls now.

"I thought she was amazing." The pride in James' voice made the fizzy warmth spring back to life inside her, and it pushed away her nerves.

"That she is." Kalen took a step to the side and grabbed two glasses off a tray passing by. "Here, before they drink all the good bottles and we're left with shite."

Thalia took one and so did James, and in an instant Kalen was pulled aside by someone he knew. A half-dressed man with a large tattoo of a tree coiling up his side started laughing with him. The naked woman next to him had Japanese orchids tattooed over her entire left side down to her knee — it was beautiful. James tugged Thalia's arm so she turned to face him and he moved them a few steps away from the crowd gathering near Kalen and Antonio and Julie.

"Are you okay, baby?" James cupped her cheek, his thumb tracing over her cheekbone as he leaned down to look in her eyes. The lines that formed between his eyebrows as they pulled together made her smile.

"I'm okay. I promise, Master." She smiled and he sighed.

"Not James?" One of his eyebrows ticked up.

"I'm not sure that's proper etiquette inside Crucible, sir." Thalia grinned and James laughed, pulling her against him by her hip.

"Well, as your master, I want you to say my name, just for now."

"James." Thalia half-whispered it and she heard the soft groan in his chest.

"Thank you, baby. Now, did you really mean what you said to Marisol? About this being nothing like—" he paused and she watched his shoulders tense and then relax. He blew out a breath and continued, "About us, all of this, being nothing like Marcus?"

The sincere worry in his voice was like a punch in the stomach. Had he ever thought that? Had he ever thought they were similar? Actions are all about intent. You can yell at someone and intend to hurt them or intend to help them. When Marcus had punished her, it had been to create fear, to force submission from her. When James gave her pain it was controlled, calculated to give her pleasure in perfect balance. And she wanted it. He watched, he was careful, and she could always end it. She could stop him with a word, just like he'd promised the day they'd met.

"James." Thalia's voice was steady, and his eyes widened at hearing his name from her mouth without an ounce of shyness or nerves. She interlaced her fingers with his free hand. "I trust you. Completely. You have kept every promise you've ever made to me. You have helped me understand a side of myself I didn't know existed six months ago, and you have helped me enjoy that side of myself. And I *can* enjoy that side of myself with you because I can let go, I can let go and trust that if I needed you to stop, you would."

"Always." James interlocked their fingers more tightly and squeezed her hand.

"I know. And I know you care about me, I know you want the best for me, and I'm really looking forward to going out with you, in public, without the panic attacks. Maybe to more places like this?" Thalia grinned and James laughed.

"I think normal dates are what we need, baby."

"But we should have special dates like this, too. We could alternate!" Thalia smiled, and James almost choked on the drink he was taking.

"Maybe not alternate, but a couple of times a month I think a special date would be very fun." He grinned at her, but she tilted her head countering his offer.

"Hmm, maybe two normal dates, then a special date?"

"Are you trying to bargain with me?" James feigned irritation and Thalia only rolled her eyes.

"It's a good deal."

"Hmmm. Five normal dates, then a special date. After all, I have quite a few places I would like to take you now that you will look at something other than the table." His cocky grin almost made her swoon and lose track of her goal, but she held on. Probably only by the grace of the incredible orgasm he'd given her earlier.

"*Three* normal dates, and I'm also looking forward to what normal dates will be like." She smiled, but he just grinned wickedly at her.

"Four normal dates. One special, and if you don't agree I'll tie you up like you want me to so badly, pet, but we'll play the frustration game for the rest of the night." James ran his fingertips slowly across her collarbone, between her breasts, and down her stomach until he cupped her pussy through her dress.

Her resolve crumbled.

"Four. Deal." Her breath caught as he started to rub her through the dress, and he moved her until her back collided with a cool wall.

"Have I mentioned I adore how smart you are as well?" James' mouth was on her neck, his fingers tugging her dress up so he could slide his touch under her panties again. Her hips bucked against his seeking fingers and she whimpered. She still wanted him, needed him, craved him.

"God, I want you." His words melted her and ignited a blaze inside her. He grabbed their glasses and set them aside before he pressed against her again.

"Yes, yes, please." Thalia was working on his belt when he grabbed her hands and pinned them sharply above her head.

"No. We are not having sex in open space, at Crucible, on your first visit to a club." His voice was growling, commanding, and edged with desire.

"Come on..." she whined and tugged at his grip on her wrists, but he simply gripped tighter until it hurt a little. Which only served to turn her on further, and she pressed her thighs together for self-control.

"I'm thinking, pet, and *you* still need to work on patience."

Chapter Eight
THALIA

His smile was wicked as he turned her around so she faced the wall. "Hands on the wall, bend at your hips."

A cheer went off in her head, but she stayed silent as she followed his commands. Palms flat on the wall she bent forward and she felt his hand move over the round of her ass. Then his hands slid up her thighs, pushing the hem of her dress ahead of them until it pooled around her waist. When he slid her panties down and had her step out of them she was sure he had relented and was going to fuck her. In the middle of Crucible. Her pussy squeezed around nothing as she imagined him driving into her from behind — and then she felt the stinging pop of his hand across her ass. She jumped and almost stood up, but his other hand rested on the small of her back to remind her to stay in position.

"Oh, pet, you are so very tempting." His voice was a growl above her as he landed two more swats across her skin, the places where his palm landed heating up.

"Maybe you could give in, Master?" Thalia bit her cheek to try and stop herself from smiling even though her hair curtained her face. A series of sharper swats across her ass had her shifting her weight from side to side, biting her lip as she waited for the stings to subside. James' hand moved up her back and into her hair, tightening his grip to hold her in place and stop her wiggling.

"Making suggestions, pet? Maybe I should leave you be for the night so you gain an appreciation for what I do give you?" James' Dom voice sent shivers over her, but she knew he was teasing. At least she *hoped* he was teasing. It was still impossible for her to ignore, especially when his other hand slid between her thighs and brushed her slick folds.

"I'm sorry, Master, please keep going," Thalia begged, "I want you, whatever you want." Her fingers pressed into the cool wall, the heat of her skin rapidly warming the stone beneath her hands. A sharp spank made her bite down on a moan. She'd missed this.

"Then hush." James brought his hand down on her skin in a steady rhythm, occasionally pausing to rub away the stinging sensation that was building with the heat in her skin. He continued and she found herself moaning with each strike of his hand. Her body was humming, her mind fuzzy with desire, her pussy growing more wet with each set of spankings. Each set punctuated by the gentle rubbing of his hand to soothe the sting.

Her body jerked when his fingers suddenly slid inside her, and she moaned and whimpered, fighting the urge to push back. Fighting the urge to take her hands from the wall. Her lips parted to beg again and she gritted her teeth to stop herself. He'd told her to hush. His touch teased her, and she shook as the heat in her skin seemed to concentrate at her core. His fingers curled down to brush against the bundle of nerves inside her and it had her gasping, her fists clenching against the wall. She whimpered, tilting her hips to meet his touch. He groaned above her and pressed a third finger inside, pumping them in and out as she stifled moans and whimpers and pleas. Just as she thought she would fall over the edge James removed his fingers and tightened his fist in her hair. He pulled her up, breaking her position so he could take her mouth. His body pressed her to the wall, his mouth conquering hers. The firm pressure of his erection pressed against her through his pants and she held on to his shirt while her head spun.

"Fuck it. Come with me." James took her hand and pulled her forward. He took long strides through Crucible, the blur of people around her couldn't distract her from the tense lines of his shoulders. He stepped down a side hall until he slammed a door open and pushed her inside. They were in an elegant bathroom, and James reached behind her to flip the lock. Then he grabbed her and his arms were around her, his hands tugging the dress up until the tight fit stopped its movement. "Bloody dress," he cursed, the frustration clear in his voice as he deftly yanked the zipper down.

"You did pick it, Master." She smiled and murmured as he ripped the dress over her head leaving her in just her bra.

"And it looks lovely on you, but I want it off." James grinned, the dark green of his eyes obvious in the soft light of the bathroom. Thalia reached out for the buttons of his shirt and he caught her hand and tugged her against him. His hands slid over her skin, following the curve of her waist, and then her bra was coming off. He groaned and took her mouth again, his hands cupping her breasts, his fingers brushing her nipples until they hardened into pink buds. With his hands distracted she worked on the bottom buttons of his shirt, sliding her hands across his stomach. He pulled back and pointed at the counter, "Up. At the edge."

She hopped up and the counter felt ice cold against the heated skin of her ass, she yelped and he chuckled. His fingers finished the work she'd started and his shirt dropped to the floor. Thalia stared hungrily at the skin he revealed. The deep V of his hips as he undid his belt. His hands stopped.

"Enjoying the view?" James was grinning when her eyes found his again. She blushed, but she didn't back down.

"Yes, Master." She answered and he stepped between her legs to kiss her again, his hands cupping her face to his. In a moment his touch switched from sweet to dominating. His hand twined in her hair and craned her head back as he broke the kiss. She was breathless as she looked up at him, his body angled over hers as she braced herself against the counter. His eyes devoured her, sliding down her body, and then his mouth followed. Her fingers found his hair as he slipped between her thighs, but he caught her wrist. "Both hands on the counter and do not come without permission."

"Yes, Master," she whimpered, knowing before she even felt his mouth on her that his command would be difficult to obey. Her body was taut as a bowstring, and when his tongue split her, dragging through her wetness slowly, she shuddered and moaned. He gave her no mercy, his tongue delved inside her making her rock her hips to meet him. When his mouth closed over her clit she cried out and almost lifted her hands. Strong hands pushed her thighs apart, and she lifted her hips to meet his mouth. He groaned against her flesh and she dropped her head back against the mirror. Each stroke of his tongue flooded her pussy with heat and she was slick with her juices. Her hips rolled and he pushed them back to the counter as another wave of pleasure sparked up her spine when he drew her clit into his mouth and sucked hard. "Oh God! Master! Please, I'm going to—"

"No. Hold it back." His mouth returned to her without mercy and she was shaking her head, biting her lip as she pushed back the crest of her orgasm. There was no way. His tongue found her clit again and she screamed and tried to push away but he tugged her hips forward again.

"Oh no, I can't, please?" She was begging, she couldn't even form coherent sentences as the tension built inside her, her heart racing, her fists clenching. Just as she was sure she would tumble into oblivion without permission — he stopped. Her eyes opened to find him pulling her up toward him. His mouth was wet with her when he kissed her and she could taste herself as he moaned against her mouth. She wrapped her arms around his neck, pulling him closer and his tongue warred with hers. Then he grabbed her arms from around his neck and pulled her off the counter. In an instant he had flipped her and pushed her chest down onto the marbled top. His hand held her arm behind her back and she heard a distinctive *tsk tsk* behind her.

"Didn't I say to keep your hands on the counter, pet?" His voice sent a thrill through her, as did the tinkling sound of the metal fixtures on his belt as he slid it out.

"Yes, Master." She wiggled in anticipation and he pressed her down on the counter by her arm. The belt came down hard and fast, stripes of fire overlapping the sting of the spankings on her cooled skin. She bit down on the cries, her cheek laid against the counter. Pain and pleasure thrummed inside her, the stings heating her skin and rebounding inside her. He stopped as quickly as he'd started and the belt clattered to the floor. An instant later he thrust his cock inside her.

She came instantly.

The way he filled her, the ache of her skin, his grip on her arm as he held her down all combined to shatter the heat inside her. Her scream of pleasure rebounded off the tiles in the room, and James groaned behind her. She shook under him, lifting onto her toes as he pressed her harder against the counter, letting the fluttering of her internal muscles grip him before he started to move. He slid back and thrust hard, the counter bruising the front of her thighs and she didn't care. Her body was tingling, his thrusts stretching out her pleasure until she couldn't identify the end of her orgasm from the beginning of the next. Soon, Thalia was meeting him thrust for thrust again, pushing her hips back to meet him only to be pressed sharply against the counter again. The sting of the welts on her ass made her cry out louder, made each thrum of pleasure inside her that much more intense. She arched up as he pushed her pleasure to the edge again, heat spiraled down her spine, the tension building as his thrusts increased. She bit her lip trying to hold back, trying not to come without permission again, but he knew her. He shifted his angle and thrust hard so that he brushed directly against the bundle of nerves that exploded pleasure inside her. Thalia cried out and his moans joined hers. She felt his cock jump inside her, his warm seed filling her. Then there were just their mingled breaths and the dull thud of the music through the wall. Her whole body was humming, and warm, and her brain sparked with aftershocks of pleasure. He slid from her and gently pulled her up from the counter. Thalia caught a view of herself in the mirror. The fronts of her thighs were red from the countertop, her chest and face were flushed, her lips swollen from their kisses and her bites. When he turned her in his arms she got a peek at the red lines across her ass, but he distracted her with a kiss, and then that's all she could think about.

"You make me lose control, pet." He smiled down at her so she knew he wasn't upset, but his confession confused her.

"You seemed very in control to me tonight." Her voice was breathy, still strained from her cries and their exertion. James laughed.

"Ah, maybe. But don't think I'm forgetting that you came without permission." He held up two fingers, "Twice."

"I never imagined you'd forget, Master." She grinned and he kissed her hard, before pulling back on a laugh.

"Just so you know, I had no plans to fuck you here. I was going to do *that* back at the Dormitory." His arms wrapped around her and banished the cool of the room, "But I'm pretty sure that idea was out when you were writhing on my lap." He smiled and she felt his hand trace a few of the welts across her ass. "Are you okay?"

"I'm fantastic. That was... amazing." She smiled and he kissed her again, warm hands pulling her tight against him where she felt sated and happy.

"Agreed. And as long as you're alright, we should go back, everyone will be looking for us." He grinned and snagged her bra and dress from the floor and she took them.

"They will be... James, I—" *love you.* She stopped herself before she said it aloud and used the excuse of tugging her dress on to hide the pause.

Not yet.

"What, baby?" He was pulling his shirt on and she took the opportunity to drink him in, that smile still plastered across her face.

"I'm just so lucky to be with you." She said and he took a step forward to kiss her again and helped zip up her dress. He handed her panties to her with a devilish grin and then reached for his belt on the floor.

"I'm the lucky one, Thalia, I promise." He kissed her quickly before checking himself in the mirror and she did the same.

They had to return to their friends. Everyone who had become so important to her so quickly. They needed to finish celebrating with Julie. Then they'd head back to Purgatory and leave in just a couple of days. And then?

Then it was back home. *Home.* With James, and their life, and their dates, and their future. And two more months until she could say the words she wanted to say.

She couldn't wait.

Chapter Nine
MARCUS

"Where the fuck is she?" Marcus growled into the phone. Three weeks with no updates, no photos, nothing.

"She's still in Scotland, Mr. Williams. At the same property she's been at this whole time. I told you I'd contact you when she left." The irritation in the private investigator's voice put Marcus' teeth on edge. This loser had been feeding him the same line for weeks.

Large property. Surrounded by walls. No visual possible.

What if he had missed her leaving? What if she was back in London already?

"This is unacceptable," Marcus spat. He had to focus to relax his grip on his phone and force a deep breath.

"Listen, they're obviously on some kind of vacation. Dr. Hawkins went back to London for a week, but he returned. I updated you on that." Another sigh from the motherfucker who wasn't earning his pay.

"Yeah, you told me the asshole wrecked his car and ended up in the ER. But you said the nurse at the hospital told you he was fine. That would have been a worthy update if you'd told me he fucking died!" Marcus knew he was borderline yelling, but he didn't give a shit. This PI hadn't been worth the investment, and his funds weren't infinite.

"Thalia seems very happy with him, Mr. Williams. As I've said before, I don't think you or your family has anything to worry about."

"Did I ask for your fucking opinion?!" Marcus snapped. He turned and kicked the empty trashcan next to his desk — the resulting crash as it banged into the wall barely took the edge off his rage.

Another sigh came over the phone and Marcus almost lost it on the guy. He was paying him, *very* well, to snap photos and follow Thalia around. He wasn't allowed to fucking *sigh* at him. If he were in front of him, Marcus would show him who he was talking to. He'd show him exactly what he was capable of when someone didn't uphold their end of a deal. The PI's voice sounded exhausted. "What do you want me to do, Mr. Williams?"

"I WANT YOU TO BRING HER BACK TO ME!" Marcus yelled so loudly he heard his own voice rebounding in his room. His harsh breathing almost masked the surprised response.

"What?" Honest shock in the man's voice. "I don't do that. I'm not taking anyone against their will, and as I've said she's very happy—"

"She would be *happier* with me," Marcus growled, before he remembered to add, "And our family. She doesn't know what she wants. She's young, and we need to keep her safe."

"I have only observed Dr. Hawkins treating her with care. He treats her very well, and she has never shown any signs that she's afraid of him." The guy was trying to be reasonable, but all his words did was bring up an image of Thalia at his feet. Wide hazel eyes looking up, her breaths shallow and fast, her fists clenched as she awaited his command.

He needed her back.

"Just find me someone who will bring her back then." Marcus paced across his room, stepping over papers, and remnants of photos, and dirty clothes.

"No."

"No?" Marcus felt his rage pounding in his temples. "You work for me. You don't fucking tell me no."

"I'm not going to be involved in this, and as of now I don't work for you anymore, Mr. Williams." The guy was talking to him like *he* was in charge. "One last word of advice, free of charge, leave your cousin alone. She's happy, she's fine. Just let it go. Reach out to her and maybe she'll come visit."

"You fucking—"

"Goodbye, Mr. Williams." *Silence.*

Marcus looked down at his phone and saw that the call had ended, and then promptly threw his cell against the door. The smart phone broke. The screen shattered, spider webbing across, the case cracked.

He didn't give a fuck.

His fists were clenching and unclenching as he looked around the room for something else to destroy.

Thalia.

Thalia's face was everywhere. On every surface. The walls were a collage of her perfect mouth, her shoulders peeking out of dresses, the swell of her hips and ass.

Marcus stalked over to the largest photo he had of her, his hands landing on the wall on either side of it. He'd blown it up because it was an expression he'd never seen. Her eyes were looking just left of the camera lens, focused intently on something. *'Or someone...'* his mind reminded him. She was tucking a strand of hair behind her ear, and the barest hint of a smile curved her lips. She wore a yellow blouse, dark jeans that hugged her thighs. She looked —

'Beautiful,' his head filled in.

But that wasn't it. He knew that look, had seen it before on other women. She wanted the person she was looking at. The flush in her cheeks, the way she angled her hips toward them.

That is what he wanted.

He wanted Thalia to look at him like that, and in time he could make her. He could make her want him, need him, crave him. He just hadn't had enough time. There hadn't been enough time.

"You'll be mine again." He traced the outline of her face in the photograph, trailing his fingertips over her lips, over that smile. The sense of calm that appeared with his focused intent overwhelmed him for one brief, peaceful moment.

Then reality flooded back.

Thalia wasn't with him yet. She was in Scotland, on some lavish estate, with *him*. Just one thought of Thalia underneath James and Marcus' rage was howling back. Shooting like fire up his spine, tightening his muscles, and making him want to destroy everything. Everyone.

He pushed himself back from the wall of her pictures, tearing his eyes away and practically running for the door. He threw it open and stomped down the hall. Down the hall where he had taught Thalia to crawl. In a moment he was at another door, he unlocked it and kicked it open.

Soft crying could already be heard from the girl tied to the post. She was shaking, her head hanging down so all he could see was light brown hair, almost obscuring the view of her breasts.

"Finish your call?" Anthony asked nonchalantly. His brother was sitting in a chair off to the side, watching the girl struggle and cry. For a minute he wondered what Anthony had done in his absence. His eyes tracked back to the girl to look for obvious damage, but he couldn't find any.

"Yes. I did." Marcus tried to mimic his brother's placid calm, but he was too angry. His pulse was a machine gun behind his eyes, and his breathing wouldn't slow.

"Anything you'd like to share with the class?" Anthony tucked something to the side and then folded his hands like he was waiting patiently.

"Fuck off. Why are you here?" Marcus crossed his arms, fingers twitching with his urge to check and make sure he hadn't touched the girl when he wasn't there. She was *his*.

"I get worried when you don't answer my calls. Then I arrive and find this lovely little present, all tied up and packaged." Anthony tilted his head and his eyes moved over the girl. "Since you didn't know I was coming, I'm guessing she isn't a welcome gift?"

"No." Marcus was fighting to control his temper.

"Pity." Anthony turned his dead eyes back to him. "Willing to share? It's been a while."

"Find your own."

Anthony did his imitation of a laugh, which had never sounded right. Not even when they were kids. It had always sounded like Anthony was mimicking what *other* people sounded like. But Anthony was hollow, devoid of all emotion. And emotionless people don't laugh. "If that's how we're playing now, okay. I'm just glad you're back to work. I'll update the clients."

"I—" Marcus started to tell him not to, but Anthony kept talking.

"I'll turn the cameras back on tomorrow. Make sure she's in decent shape for her debut, all right?" Anthony stood carefully and walked over to him, and Marcus had to fight the physical urge to step back or hit him. "I'm so happy I don't have to monitor you anymore. I knew you'd move past your little obsession eventually."

Marcus gritted his teeth, heart pounding in his ears, and he was seeing red as his urge to rip his brother apart surged. Thalia wasn't an obsession, she was a possession. A stolen possession. Stolen by Anthony's party, by James' pretty lies, by Thalia's refusal to see what she really needed.

"I'll call later in the week for an update. *Have fun.*" Anthony revealed the belt he had been holding at his side and pressed it against Marcus' palm. With that dark-toned suggestion, Anthony was out the door. Marcus finally focused his attention on the girl and approached her. As soon as he walked toward her, she started shaking harder. Whimpering.

"Please, please, let me go, pl—"

Marcus' hand shot forward and wrapped around her throat to shut her up. Her voice was *wrong*. Too high to be Thalia's, too whiny. "Don't speak," he commanded, moving his hand to push her hair out of her face. Light brown, but still not the right shade. And a little too short, it barely came past the girl's shoulders. "Open your eyes, Thalia."

The girl's eyes snapped open, full of fear and terror, but too close to green. Thalia's eyes were more hazel, a perfect mix of brown, and green, and even gray in places. He let go of the girl and stepped back with a growl, hand thrusting into his hair to pull at it. She wasn't *right*.

"M—my name is Vicky. Victoria. I'm not who you're looking for! I'm not Thalia! Please, please just let me go. Let me go, I won't tell anyone!" Her sobs were making her hard to understand. "I wo—won't s—s—say anything."

He backhanded her before he had actually thought about it. Her head snapped to the side, and she started sobbing harder. Even the way she cried was wrong. So whiny, shrill with fear. "Shut up!" he shouted. "If you talk again, you'll regret it."

In response she only shook, her fists clenched in tight little balls on the other side of the cuffs. Marcus reached forward and pulled her head up by her hair. "You think you can just leave? Walk out on me? Without permission?"

The girl's imperfect hazel eyes widened, but she didn't speak. Marcus' fist tightened around the leather of the belt, the perfect loop begging him to let his rage out.

No, she wasn't Thalia, but she would do.

Chapter Ten
THALIA

Five Months After the Auction

"Do we really have to go to this party?" Thalia heard a bit of a whine in her voice, but she couldn't help it. She was nervous.

"It's a gala, baby, and yes. I skipped the last one and have not heard the end of it at work." James stepped into the bathroom where she was staring at herself in the mirror.

"What's it for again?" she asked.

"We did well in the last quarter and have expanded our reach into Northern Africa. So, tonight is to celebrate and to raise money for an organization providing aid there. Giving back and all that." He tilted his head at her and she made herself meet his eyes, perfectly green like sea glass.

"Who would you normally have brought to this?" Thalia felt the insecurity rise up in her. The deep blue dress was worth a fortune, and even in the mirror she looked like some kind of imposter.

"Normally?" James' forehead creased, his hands pausing as he adjusted the tie at his neck.

"Before... me." Her eyes couldn't stay at his, his questioning stare was too intense. She looked down at the bodice of the dress and forced a deep breath that strained the fabric. All their dates to local places had gone so smoothly. She had barely felt an inkling of the old fear, the old panic. Even when they'd dressed up for a nicer restaurant she'd been fine. Perfectly content to talk with James, to call him James, while out and about. And all of it had been perfect, *normal*. The dates had been fantastic. Their first foray into a 'special' date had been at a loud, dark club in London, and it had been exhilarating. On her knees, the music pounding, his hand in her hair as she tasted him. The sex they'd had when they got home — hard, fast, intense. It was perfect. It was so perfect. So why did he want to go to this gala? Now? With her?

James had turned to lean back against the counter, forcing her to look at him again. He gripped the counter edge lightly as he spoke, "If I required a date to attend a function like this one, I usually gave in to whomever had been pestering me for one."

Of course women had pestered him. James was gorgeous. Broad shoulders, blond hair that sometimes fell in his eyes when he was focused. The tux he was in made him look like some kind of movie star. How the hell could she compare? To him? To these women he knew?

"What were they like?" she mumbled, trying to ignore her reflection in the mirror.

"Irritating. Snobby, aristocratic—"

"Rich?" she interrupted.

James sighed, pushing a hand through his hair. "Yes, they usually came from money." Thalia laughed, throwing her hands up.

"And now you're bringing an uneducated, middle-class, American, ex-data entry employee to this?!" Thalia's voice was bordering on hysterical. Why he thought she would even remotely fit in she couldn't understand. "I'm just a yoga instructor... *in training!* I don't fit in with these people! I'll just embarrass you!" The concern jumped out of her mouth before she could stop it.

"They already offered you the position when you finish the certification in two weeks, didn't they?" James was unfazed by her rant, he just tilted his head as he stared at her.

"Well, yes, but—"

"And didn't Kalen write you a very nice recommendation letter so you had a resume to provide them?" His voice was warm, a hint of a smile on his lips as he spoke.

"Oh yeah, *yoga instructor at a Scottish couples' retreat.*" Thalia rolled her eyes. "God forbid anyone asks me questions about *that*." Kalen had written it a couple of weeks after they got back when Thalia started the instructor training. The letter had made her blush like crazy.

James laughed. "You'll handle it beautifully, baby."

"You have too much faith in me. In this, and in this party. *Gala*," she corrected. Thalia's eyes found herself in the mirror again. She'd curled her hair, applied makeup like Julie had taught her to, and she was wearing the obnoxiously expensive gown that looked like she should be on a red carpet. What the fuck was she about to do?

"Thalia." James' voice was serious as he took her hand and tugged her toward him. "I want to show off my sexy, soon-to-be yoga instructor, American, girlfriend. Is that so wrong?" His grin should be illegal. It was overwhelming, and enticing, and — she had to admit — it quelled her nerves a bit.

"You're so smooth." She laughed and he grabbed her tight and pulled her against him, the fabric of the dress crumpling a little.

"You like it." James grinned and kissed her, and for a moment everything melted away. The worry over the celebration gala where she'd finally meet his work friends, and other important people in the city. The awkwardness of being in a dress that probably cost more than her old monthly salary. The tension of James being so comfortable in this world, and it being so alien to her. None of it mattered. None of it mattered when his hands landed on her hips, and his tongue moved against hers. She wanted to strip them both out of these fancy clothes and spend the evening in bed, or in the playroom. Anywhere but the gala. He broke the kiss and smiled at her, and she brushed an errant lock of his hair back in place.

"I still can't believe what you paid for this dress. It's way too much." Thalia's eyes tracked back to her reflection, and James moved behind her, his arms wrapping around her waist. He looked the picture of elegance. Aristocratic perfection. And she was — brutally normal.

"Baby, just think of the dress as your armor. Ignore the designer—" *who was the designer again?* "—ignore the cost, and just focus on how beautiful you look in it, and how very excited I am to have you with me. I definitely won't be bored for once with you there." He trailed kisses down her neck until he nipped her shoulder.

"You'd be bored without me there?" Thalia leaned back against him and he murmured against her skin, his lips next to the fancy sapphire necklace he'd borrowed from some store. *Who knew you could even do that?* Then he leaned back up, locking eyes with her in the mirror.

"Miserably." James' fingers touched her chin and leaned her head back until his lips could capture hers. Another distracting kiss. It ripped her mind away from everything, and she wanted to tell him what he did for her. Wanted to tell him how much she loved him, and how he made her feel. But he broke the kiss with a grin and continued adjusting his tie.

"We need to go, baby. Are you ready?" James looked over at her and she shrugged. She was dressed for a nice party, a *gala*, and she would get to walk in on James' arm, and come home with him after.

She could do this.

"Yes, Master, I am." She used the term because it symbolized more than being just his girlfriend and it brought her comfort.

"You should call me James for tonight, pet." His grin turned mischievous, and he stepped toward the doorway and held out his hand. "And the car is downstairs. If we leave now we could have some fun on the way?"

"For that, *James*, I'm ready to leave immediately." They both laughed as he took her hand and moved to the door.

"You said car. This is a limo." Thalia looked around the spacious interior as they pulled away from the flat, and James just chuckled.

"All the better to have some privacy, pet." His hand was already nudging the hem of the dress higher, his body close to hers on the seat. "And everyone will be arriving in one, it would look odd if we didn't."

"So, you used to ride in limos often?" Her breath caught as his fingertips brushed across the lace of her panties and she lifted her hips on a whimper.

"Only for events like this." His touch slid under the lace and brushed her pussy, already wet in expectation of what he'd promised. "Now, pet, stop thinking about it. It's just a party—" His fingers found her clit and she moaned quietly. "—and you look delectable."

"Yes, Master." She dropped her head back on the seat, her hands clenched at her sides as he worked his magic between her thighs. Heat pooling, static-like tingles rolling over her skin as she bit down on her lip.

"Good girl." His voice growled against her skin as he slid two fingers inside her, and she bucked and spread her thighs farther. She turned her head to kiss him, and he took her mouth, muffling her moans as she squirmed. Each movement of his fingers had her whimpering against his lips, the soft whisper of the dress shifting the only other sound above the dull road noise. Then James broke the kiss, "Stay quiet, pet. We wouldn't want to distract our driver, now would we?" His grin was mischief and promise as his fingers slid from her and he pressed her shoulders back until she leaned against the end of the seat.

"No, we wouldn't." She shook her head as he bunched her dress around her hips and nudged her knees farther apart.

"Let's see how quiet you can be." His fingers pulled her panties down her legs, and she gasped in anticipation. Then his blonde hair disappeared between her thighs and she felt the first incredible brush of his tongue. A moan burst from her lips and she covered her mouth, stifling it as the warm swipe of his tongue over her clit had her arching off the seat. His fingers returned to her and she shook her head.

No way could she stay quiet, he was way too good at this. He knew every inch of her. "Master, please!" She cried out too loudly and covered her mouth again before she moaned.

"Hush, pet." His breath brushed over her pussy lips and he thrust his fingers a little harder inside her, sending her head reeling. Sparks of pleasure were spiraling inside her like embers from a fire. Heating her, erasing her nerves, destroying the tension she'd carried all day. He sucked her clit back into his mouth and she cried out against her hand, the fingers of her other hand digging into the seat to brace herself. She was already trembling, the knowledge that the windows were blacked out barely registering as she stared up at the streetlights of a main thoroughfare. This was sweet torture. Her hips rolling against his mouth, his tongue tormenting her, his fingers thrusting inside her to curl to that place that had her muffling cries of pleasure against her hand. A crackle of pure pleasure pulsed down her spine and her hips bucked, but his other hand was there to firmly press her back against the leather. She was rising higher with each sinful lick of his tongue, her moans a steady thrum against the skin of her palm as she started to shiver. Her muscles tightened, and he drew on her clit again, his teeth grazing her to thrust her over the edge and into the glorious abyss of orgasm. She shattered. Her head slamming back into the space by the door as she shook, and he drew out every wave of sensation that rocked her until her mind was nothing but a warm, relaxed liquid puddle.

"Jesus Christ..." She mumbled against her hand as he leaned up and over her.

"Feel better, pet?" His mouth was wet with her.

"Do you even need to ask?" She laughed softly and he kissed her. Thalia could taste herself on his lips, and she moaned against him, her hands finding his hair to hold him to her, but they couldn't continue. James leaned back from her, tracing her mouth with his fingers.

"We're almost there. Clean up." His grin was sinful as she sucked his fingers into her mouth, cleaning her taste from them, and she loved how his eyes had turned bottle glass green in his arousal. He was so perfect.

His fingers popped free of her lips and he wiped his mouth, still grinning as the limo slowed. "We're here, baby." James handed her the panties he'd stripped from her and she pulled them on. In a few quick shifts of clothing everything was back in place and a moment later the limo stopped.

The door opened and he turned to her again before he stepped out, "You know you're the only person I want to be here with, right?" If the orgasm hadn't melted her nerves completely, that did the trick.

"I do now." She smiled and he returned it before he stepped out, reaching back in to offer her his hand and help her out.

They were in front of a gigantic hotel, obviously a five star one, and it resembled one they had stayed at in Paris a week before for one of his work overnight trips. An actual red carpet was lining the steps and she almost laughed aloud at it.

How on earth was she even there?

"Then, if you'd be so kind Thalia, are you ready to make our entrance?" James' warm tone filled her up and she nodded, letting him lead her toward the front doors that were lit in bright, golden light, and into the party.

Chapter Eleven
THALIA

The gala was much more sedate than she'd expected. There were a series of boring speeches that she didn't quite follow because they were talking about the success of the recent business ventures in Algeria and Libya. She applauded politely at the end of each speech, and then finally the actual party started.

A live band struck up and a few couples found the dance floor, a silent auction lined one wall filled with art and luxurious trips and expensive bottles of wine and basket arrangements of delicacies. Then there was the food table, half as long as the silent auction and brimming with a hundred things she wanted to try, which James seemed to adore. But why wouldn't she eat? Ignoring all that food would be stupid. Every time she snuck back to it, he gave her a real smile. The one that told her he didn't have any ulterior motives at the moment, he was simply happy to watch her enjoy herself. After her fourth cheese poof thing, James and a group of others stepped over to her.

"Thalia, this is Andrew and Tom and Alice. I work with them. Everyone, this is my girlfriend Thalia." She smiled at them as they all burst into speech at once.

"So good to meet you."

"— love your dress—"

"— never seen James this happy!"

Thalia blushed and took a sip of the wine she'd been holding. She really didn't want to mess this up. "Thank you, I'm glad to meet all of you too!"

"American? Why, James, when did you have time to find this beautiful girl?" Tom grinned at her and laughed, "Or have you been keeping her a secret?"

"Can you blame him? She's bloody gorgeous! I'd keep her locked away too!" Andrew laughed and took another drink of the glass in his hand. His nose was already ruddy with how much he'd had, and her own blush just grew worse.

"Ignore them, darling. I, for one, am glad to see James actually interested in someone for once. I've been telling him for years that being the lone bachelor isn't in style anymore!" Alice's laugh was like tinkling bells, and before Thalia could try and sink into the floor to avoid more discussion, James rescued her.

"You're all quite right, and I'm sure you will enjoy telling me so, but for now, I'd like to ask Thalia to dance." He smiled at her and she nodded, taking the opportunity to escape the intense scrutiny of his co-workers. They were already almost at the dance floor when Thalia regained the ability to speak.

"I don't really know how to dance like this, James." She looked up at him, ignoring the spiraling couples on the dance floor, once again a bundle of nerves — but he just smiled.

"Really? You've always been so good at responding to the directions my body gives you." He grinned and set her wine down on a table. "All you have to do is follow my lead."

"But—" Her argument was cut off as he pulled her out onto the floor and tucked her against his chest. Turning once and forcing her to keep step with him. One hand was at her waist, his other holding hers aloft, and she left her free hand against his chest as he moved her backward across the dance floor to the rhythm of the band. Who knew James could dance so well?

Who knew she could?

With James' gentle nudges she found it easy to react as he led her. During a shift in the tempo he spun her away from him, and then pulled her back and she actually didn't trip over her own feet. It was the kind of thing girls dream about. But it was real. And James was real and smiling at her as they moved across the floor in sync with the other dancers. The song drew to a close with a swell, and they froze in place. Her hips tucked tight to his, her hand gripping his for dear life, and he leaned down to kiss her.

Prince Charming had nothing on James.

He had made mistakes, made bad choices, but he'd made one really amazing one — he'd saved her. And he kept saving her. Every day that he gave her was new and special and powerful as she built a new life out of the ashes of the old one. She leaned back from his lips to breathe, and he pressed his forehead against hers. "Thank you, baby."

"For what?"

"For making my entire life more vibrant." He pressed another kiss against her lips before she could ask for clarification, and then he led her toward an empty table. "I'm going to grab us some drinks, alright? One of the waiters took your wine. I'll be right back."

"Okay." She nodded and he slipped away from her into the crowd of beautiful dresses and tuxes.

For a moment Thalia let herself just watch. The couples twirling to the music, the laughter, the serious conversations, the flirting obviously lubricated by a few too many drinks. It was a great party, and she was there with the only person who could have ever made it possible for her to even remotely feel comfortable.

James.

He reappeared through the crowd with a smile, and she felt her lips curving to match his as he handed her a fresh glass of wine. "Apparently my co-workers adore you. They are furious I didn't have you meet them earlier."

"What did you tell them?" She asked as she took a sip, the white wine sending a chill into her stomach as she suddenly realized how warm it was inside.

"That we've only been together five months and I didn't feel like throwing you into a shark tank of the rich and powerful of London before I was sure it wouldn't scare you off." He grinned for a moment, but it slipped off his face as he looked past her. Thalia turned to see what had distracted him and locked eyes with a tall brunette in a black dress as she approached them.

"Good evening, James." The woman's voice was frigid with aristocratic airs.

"Gwen." James replied, his voice empty of all the humor from a moment before.

"I must say... after all the times I've offered to attend with you, and you've refused — to see you now bring this random girl as flagrant arm candy?" she scoffed, "Quite a step down, James."

Thalia felt her cheeks heat and tightened her fingers on the wine glass to quell the shiver the woman's words sent through her.

"Thalia is my girlfriend, Gwen, and who I choose to spend my time with is no business of yours." James' voice was colder than she'd ever heard it as he took her hand and tried to brush past the woman.

Gwen twisted and moved in front of them both, her anger cracking the frigid exterior she'd had at her approach. "What does *she* have that I don't?" The woman sneered and raked her eyes down Thalia's dress. She felt James' grip tighten on hers and he turned toward Gwen. His jaw was tense, his temper rising. But Thalia stepped forward and spoke first, sudden bravery giving her a voice.

"Tact, if you must know." Thalia took a breath and met the woman's furious glare, "One thing I have that you obviously don't? I have tact."

Gwen gawked at her, and James seemed stunned into silence. When Gwen turned her shocked look to James, as if looking for his defense, he only shrugged. The woman's face turned bright red in fury, and she spun on her heel and disappeared back into the crowd. For a moment Thalia felt the same way she always did after an outburst — self-conscious, anxious, worried she had overstepped.

"I'm sorry, James. I shouldn't have interfered. She just—"

James touched her chin so she looked at him. His eyes were warm, and his lips were curving into a smile, "That was perfect, baby. Gwen needed to be taken down a peg."

"Really?" Thalia turned to scan the room to see if the angry woman was still hovering. "I felt like I overstepped, I just couldn't stand her. She's—"

"Irritating, right?" He laughed, and she nodded. "Now do you see why I feel so lucky to be here with you instead?"

"Those are the women you used to bring with you?"

"She's the worst of them. Haughty, obnoxious, and rude. Which is why I've never agreed to escort her." He shrugged and took a drink, commandeering a table once again for them to sit at. "But, yes, the women I was exposed to by my family, and by this career, are a lot like Gwen."

"Yikes. Remind me to avoid all of them." She laughed and tried to cover the truth of that statement by taking a large drink of wine.

"Don't worry, baby. There's only one gala a quarter, and they always end. At least that's what I always tell myself." He smiled at her and she smiled back. The fact that he even mentioned she might be at the next one had butterflies zinging through her stomach, and the wine going straight to her head.

"Ah, James? I assume you're the reason Gwen just grabbed her coat and stormed out?" Tom dropped into a seat at the table and grinned. Andrew and Alice took chairs as well.

"Actually." James leaned back in his seat and tilted his glass toward Thalia. "That would be Thalia who caused that."

"I didn't mean—" She immediately floundered to defend herself, but Andrew laughed loudly and interrupted her.

"Oh really? Ha!" Andrew leaned forward, obviously intoxicated, "I would have happily paid to see that! What on earth did you say to her?"

"She probably just pointed out what a miserable bitch Gwen is all the time." Alice chimed in, smiling politely as if she hadn't just insulted someone. The entire group laughed and Thalia tried to control the blush flooding her cheeks.

"Oh come on, tell us what happened. Everyone will be talking about Gwen storming out on Monday!" Tom leaned forward conspiratorially, pointing at James with the hand holding his drink. "You owe us for holding out on Thalia, and for outright lying when we asked if you were seeing anyone last month!"

"Especially since it's been painfully obvious *someone* has been making you so happy." Alice took a sip of champagne. "Personally, I'm chuffed to bits you're with someone who can also stand up to Gwen!"

"I already apologized, let it rest!" James laughed and held up his hands in defeat. "Gwen said some nasty things about Thalia and asked what she had that Gwen didn't, and Thalia told her."

"Well?" Tom lifted an eyebrow.

"What did you say?" Andrew prodded.

"I told her I have tact?" Thalia spoke quietly, unsure of herself until the whole table broke into laughs again.

"Brilliant! Bloody brilliant!" Alice cheered at her, "Even better than if you'd told her right off! No way Gwen will be able to talk about it!"

"And you were worried she wouldn't play well in the shark tank, James?" Tom was still chuckling to himself, "It looks like she could teach us a few things!"

The group purred with laughter and murmurs of conversation around her as James turned toward her, "I think you're just what we need, baby."

"Hear, hear!" Tom cried, and everyone echoed it as they toasted her. Thalia raised her own glass and sipped it as her blush died down, and then James kissed her. He kept it tame compared to the limo, but she still felt her body respond to his touch. The cheers from his co-workers at his public display returned the blush, and James broke the kiss to look at them.

"I am a very lucky man." He spoke and Andrew clapped him on the shoulder, but his eyes told her it was the truth. That he really felt fortunate to have her there with him. Truly, for the first time, in his world. A world of privilege, and affluence, and aristocratic entitlement. In James' eyes she belonged.

And that was all that really mattered to her.

Chapter Twelve
THALIA

Six Months After the Auction

Thalia's phone beeped and it made her jump. She'd been so deep in thought thinking about their six-month anniversary the next day that she hadn't heard a word of the news. James glanced over at her from the chair and smiled. When she returned it, she knew her own was weak, watery.

She had too much on her mind.

The text message was from Analiese asking for verification, *again*, about the girls only weekend Julie was trying to plan in London. The plan was for everyone — Julie, Analiese, Chloe, Lauren, and Maggie — to attend one or two of Thalia's yoga classes and then spend two nights in a huge penthouse suite enjoying massages and room service and chick flicks. She wanted to tell them yes. She wanted to be excited about it and chat about it with James like she would any other topic.

But the weekend was two weeks away, and that meant it was on the other side of The Decision.

Thalia had begun thinking of the day in capital letters. She had no reason to think that James would want to break things off. He seemed to spend all his time making sure she knew how much he liked being with her — but logic holds no power over the heart. And Thalia's heart was aching at the remote possibility that tomorrow James could tell her he wanted her to move on. She'd already spent too many hours wondering where she'd live. Her paychecks from the yoga studio couldn't possibly pay for a flat in this part of the city, which meant moving far from the studio she worked at. Which meant taking the tube to work instead of walking a few blocks. Or she could go back to the states, try and find a new place to start a new life —

Thalia wanted to throw up just thinking about it. Why wouldn't her head just shut up?! She knew she was going to tell James she wanted to stay, and she was ninety percent sure he wanted the same.

Maybe eighty-five. Eighty?

She groaned and yanked her mind away from the doom and gloom and tapped out a response to Analiese that felt like a rock settling in her stomach: *I'll know for sure tomorrow. I'll text as soon as I can! Promise!* She dropped the phone into her lap and sighed. None of the girls, except Maggie, knew about her deal with James. They knew she'd had a bad Dom before him, which was an understatement to say the least. They knew that James had helped her get away from him — but she wasn't going to burden them with the whole nightmare. Which meant it was pretty much impossible to bring up the odd deal she had with James.

"What's wrong, baby?" James' voice pulled her out of another bitter reverie.

"Huh? It's — um, it's nothing." She shrugged and turned back to the television, internally hoping he'd drop it. But that wasn't going to happen.

"Thalia." His voice had that edge, the one that sent shivers down her spine and made her want to drop to her knees. "What's our rule about honesty?"

Dammit.

"I'm just thinking about tomorrow. That's it." Her hands were twisting in her lap as she stole a glance at him. "Don't worry, I'm not trying to say anything today, but it is on my mind."

"It's on mine too, pet." He clicked the television off and stood, moving over to the couch to tower over her. When she looked up at him she felt better, when he brushed her hair back from her face and cupped her cheeks she finally felt the painful tension in her chest ease for a moment. He was still there for now, no use ruining today over what *might* happen tomorrow. His voice was dark with promise when he spoke again, "I have two options for this evening, and you have to choose. I will not choose for you."

He knew her too well. She nodded against his hands, "Alright."

"First option, we can watch a movie, drink a bottle of wine, and go to bed where I will give you a massage and then we can pass the time by seeing how many times I can make you come before you beg me to stop." He smiled down at her, his thumb tracing her bottom lip.

So far, so good, that sounded like a *very* nice evening.

"Or, second option, we can go to the playroom where I'll work your body in a very different way, but we'll still play the game of how many times I can make you come until you beg me to stop." That turned his smile molten, his eyes were that dark, bottle glass green that sent a wave of heat to her core. She was instantly wet under the panties she wore, her hard nipples pressing against the cami top. James could do the romance thing like a pro. He could, *and had many times*, make her feel like she was in an impossible fairy tale. But that's not what her favorite part of their relationship was, it's not what made her body shiver just at the sight of him, and her choice was clear.

"I'd like the second one, please." Thalia was breathless as she felt his eyes scorch down her body.

"You're going to feel it tomorrow, pet." His voice had an edge of warning to it, a definitive heads up for what he had planned for her. It did nothing to deter her, in fact her body heated up and did everything but set off fireworks of affirmation at the promise.

"That's what I was hoping, Master." She smirked as her eyes traced his lips. She wanted to kiss him.

His eyes came back to hers and the edge of his mouth tilted up. His voice was clear and intense. "Good. Then strip. When you're ready meet me in the playroom, pet."

James brushed her cheek before he stood back up, immediately turning to head down the hall to their bedroom.

At least this would effectively, gloriously, distract her until morning.

Her hands shook a bit as she stood up from the couch and slid her panties down. The cool air against her pussy told her better than anything how wet she already was. Tugging the camisole over her head she put both items on the couch before walking to the playroom. The door was open, but the room was empty, so she stepped inside and knelt by the door. The peace of submission washed over her as she dropped her eyes to the floor and waited. She lived for this.

In the quiet of the flat she couldn't tell how many minutes passed as she steadied her breathing from the excitement his options had brought her. She tried not to guess at what he had planned. Spanking? The belt? Would he bind her? Did he have some new toy he wanted to try? Her mouth was dry as she heard the padding of his bare feet approach the room, and then the door closed.

Their last session before The Decision was starting.

James didn't speak as he moved past her into the room. She heard the cabinet open, a rustle of a drawer and something else, and then it shut. He returned to her empty handed. "Stand up."

When she did his eyes devoured her, sending shivers across her skin that hardened her nipples further and sent heat between her legs. He touched her elbow and moved her to the middle of the room, where he tapped the insides of her feet and she knew to spread her feet apart. Then he drew her arms up behind her head and let her interlace them. Her heart rate was picking up, her nerves a symphony of excited tension as he left her standing there. She wanted to look around, to take a peek at what he had in store for her, but not knowing had its own benefits.

"So you said that you want to feel this session tomorrow, pet?" James' voice was a purr behind her and she tried to hide the tremor of need that it caused in her muscles.

"Yes, Master."

His chest brushed against her back and she leaned back slightly, keeping the position he'd put her in but still pushing for more contact. His lips pressed to her shoulder in a warm kiss, his hands gliding up her waist, her ribs, and then up her arms. "I want you to feel me tomorrow as well."

A soft moan slipped past her lips as his hands trailed down her arms and over her front. Cupping her breasts, his fingers pinching her nipples until she was pushing her chest forward into his hands. She felt his groan against her skin as her body reacted to his touch. Just as his pinches bordered the line between pleasure and pain he released them and trailed his hands down over her hips. Her skin was lighting up under his ministrations, desire unfurling slowly inside her, and she found she wanted to beg him already for more.

But it was way too early in the night for that.

James pulled her back against him by her hip, his mouth drawing on the skin of her shoulder in small sucks and bites that she knew would leave marks. It sent a pulse to her core to know he was choosing to mark her, and his hand slid between her thighs to answer it. His fingers swept up the cleft of her pussy, already soaked in anticipation, but he was teasingly gentle. Thalia's hips tilted forward, seeking more.

Then he let go of her completely, her body rocking back on her heels at the absence of his chest, his hands. She had to tighten her grip behind her head to avoid breaking position. "Master!" Her voice was a plea, but James only chuckled.

"If you wanted the easy path, pet, you could have chosen option one."

Thalia groaned and forced a breath, trying to calm the tension in her body that James seemed in no rush to ease. "Yes, Master."

"Good girl." His voice was smooth but edged with humor as he approached her side. He had moved something behind her, but she couldn't focus as his hand returned between her thighs. His fingers brushed across her clit and she moaned, biting down on her lip as she pushed forward again. James teased her clit for a moment before he moved in front of her and crouched. She felt the flush in her cheeks from her arousal as he moved a wide based stand between her thighs.

Ah, so he *did* have a new toy.

A metal pole extended up from the base, and at the top of the pole was a dildo pointing straight at her pussy. He grinned at her, his excitement at getting to use his new toy overriding his usual calm and collected expression. "I think you're going to enjoy this quite a bit, pet. This is going inside you, and it's your job to keep it there." With a click the pole extended and she moaned and looked up at the ceiling as she felt him push the dildo up inside her. Her pussy stretched around the smooth head, and she groaned as he slid it deeper until it filled her completely. When he locked the pole at its new height she opened her mouth to breathe and James captured her lips in a kiss, his hand around the back of her neck. Her hands itched to touch him, to rock on the dildo as his tongue moved against hers. Just the idea of it had her moaning against his lips, her grip behind her head loosening. But he broke the kiss before she moved.

"Now, no matter what I do to you, you will hold this position, and if you break position, or move off the pole, or come without permission, you'll earn a punishment. Do you understand, pet?" His voice was all dark excitement, and she couldn't resist it. Her pussy tightened around the dildo and she whimpered at the promise of his plans.

"Yes, Master." A quick nod and he rewarded her with a smile before he disappeared behind her again. The first smack of his hand against her ass caused her to jerk forward, and the pole moved with her, dangerously tilting until she shifted her feet back into place. The movement had caused the dildo to rub inside her and her legs shivered at the sensation.

Ah. That would be the game of the evening then. No restraints, no bondage — nothing to help her hold position except for her own willpower.

Fuck. She was terrible at this game.

The next set of spankings had her gripping her fingers tightly behind her head as the sting in her skin caused tingles to rush over her. Heat blossomed on her ass as he warmed her up. Each time his palm landed her body shifted and the dildo rocked inside her, rubbing against her slick walls in a torturous tease that had her whimpering. At twenty he stopped and she grabbed a deep breath. Her ass was glowing with heat, her pussy clenching around the dildo buried inside her, making it impossible to ignore the rising need between her thighs.

"Your skin is beautiful, pet. All pink and ready. How is the pole?" His voice was a mocking tease.

"It's *wonderful*, Master. Thank you." Thalia made her voice one of perfect submission, and her lips curved up at the sound of his quiet chuckle behind her.

"I'm not sure you'd be so cheeky if you knew what I had in my hand, pet." He moved closer to her and she felt the movement of leather strands across her ass, trailing up her back until he pulled the flogger away. Over their months together Thalia had learned that James collected floggers like other people collected art or memorabilia. With a fervor and excitement that completely belonged to his Dominant side. Various types of leather, designed in a myriad of ways to cause a hundred different sensations when wielded in different ways. Would the one in his hand be heavy and feel like dense thuds across her skin making her body shake under each blow? Or would it be designed so that the tip of each leather strand felt like a swarm of stings landing on her skin? Lighting her up and making her gasp and whimper. "Breathe, pet."

Thalia drew in air she hadn't even realized she'd been holding, and then sparks of pain lit up her backside. She cried out just as a matching strike landed on her other side. *Thin strands, maybe oiled leather as sharp as the sting was.* Another burst of sharp stings and she lifted onto her toes, the shifting of the dildo inside her distracting her for a moment. James picked up a rhythm, the falls of the flogger stroking across her back and ass and thighs in a crisscrossing pattern that left an electric network of fading stings across her skin. Tears pricked her eyes, but a moan burst from her lips.

She loved this.

He moved in front of her, and she drank in the sight of him. Strong shoulders, firm chest, toned arms, his hand holding the balanced handle of a red and black flogger with a silver ring on the end. He pressed the handle to her lips and she kissed it, and he rewarded her with another smile that ratcheted up the heat inside her another degree. When he stepped back his hips shifted and her eyes dropped to the V that disappeared under the edge of his pants. And beneath that? The very evident bulge of his erection that made her whimper.

God, she wanted him.

"Not yet, pet. Ready for more?" How he had so much restraint she had never figured out.

She nodded, ignoring the stinging along her backside and the dripping wetness between her thighs. James adjusted his grip on the flogger and she tightened her hands behind her head. "Yes, Master."

The first lash came across her stomach, and her body jerked backward. The pole pressed the dildo hard back inside her when she moved forward and she squirmed, gritting her teeth against the moan. James quickly picked up the same rhythm as before, only now the flogger landed across her breasts, her stomach, her pussy and upper thighs. She clenched her fists in her hair to hold them there, her hips rocking forward and back on the dildo. Heat suffused her skin under the stings, her body singing, and she knew she was moaning steadily. She bit down on her lip, and then he landed the tips of the flogger across her pussy again. Electric sensation pulsed through her, and the orgasm she hadn't been aware had been building crashed over her. She was shuddering. Pleasure echoing back inside her on the tails of the pain from the flogger. Thalia had folded forward, her arms wrapped around her head as she breathed through the wave of pleasure, willing her legs not to buckle as they shook.

"Oh, pet. That was lovely to watch, but you really should have asked permission." James' voice was a delicious taunt that pulled her back to their session.

Thalia made herself stand back up, presenting the way he'd told her, but her body was a shivering mess in the aftershocks. The heat of the flogger covered her, front and back, from chest to thighs. The dildo was shifting in time with her wavering legs, teasing her body.

James had set the flogger aside and stepped back in front of her with the strap. Her lips parted on a whine, an inarticulate plea for mercy that made him step closer to her. "Have something you want to say, pet?"

His fingers found her clit and they moved against her, making her legs shake. She bit down on her lip and shook her head. He was pushing her back to the edge and she hadn't even taken the punishment for her first orgasm.

"You know if you come when I'm using the strap, you'll earn another punishment." His Dominant voice had her whimpering again. It had happened before, especially when he wound her up like he had.

And she knew by the tone of his voice he'd push her there again.

"Yes, Master." Her voice was breathy with need again already. His fingers continued rolling her clit as he kissed her, her moan trapped between their lips, his tongue finding hers. She wanted to move her hands, she wanted to touch him. But she held position, reveling in the incredible feeling of his mouth on hers. When he pulled back he left her gasping. She was soaked, the dildo hard inside her as she clenched around it.

"Ready?" His eyes were molten as he lifted the strap up and she kissed it too. She could tell he was fighting a smile this time, and pride filled her up, made her stand a little straighter when he moved behind her.

"Yes, Master. Thank you!" The last words came out as a cry when the first lash of the strap landed. The fiery line across her ass seemed to have a direct line to her clit, sending a pulse of pleasure through her when the sting faded. Two, three, four. She was going to lose it. Her body tightened around the dildo inside her until she was whimpering, begging. Irrational words tumbling from her lips that she couldn't stop. "AH! I'm sorry, I'm sorry I came! Please, please!" Another lash that had her dancing forward, the pole between her legs leaning dangerously until she came back to herself enough to shift back, readying for the next blow and keeping it inside her. "Master, I'm sorry! Please, stop!"

Another.

The fire in her skin was impossible to ignore, her body teetering on the edge of a glorious tingling abyss. No way could she stop, and she didn't really want him to even as she begged. Not with the way he got so turned on watching her squirm, the way he told her she was doing *so well*, his voice making her shiver until the next lash landed. Her voice an aching cry that dissolved into a moan even as tears rolled down her cheeks. Her fists tightened in her hair again, but it only pushed her further, and she fell with the next stroke of the strap. Dissolving into the endless pulse of pleasure that came from between her thighs and washed up her body.

A second orgasm. Without permission.

She came back to herself slowly, the dizzying fade out of her awareness leaving her in subspace. Her skin a network of tingling nerves that sent confusing signals of pleasure and pain. It was still overwhelming even as the shivers faded. She had stumbled forward when her legs started to give out, and she was on her knees, her hands planted firmly on the soundproofed floor. The pole somewhere behind her.

"Pet." His voice was dark above her, and another shiver shook her. The leather of the strap dragged up and over her ass, along her spine, her nerve endings buzzing to the beat of her rapid pulse. She whimpered as the strap fell to the floor beside her. His fingers traced her spine, and she knew he could feel the tremors in her. "So many broken rules." His hand moved into her hair and tightened, pulling her up into a kneel with a firm grip.

"Master, I—"

"Oh, no. You knew the rules, I was clear. You were not to come without permission, you were to keep the dildo inside you, and you were to keep your hands behind your head. I didn't think that was too much to ask." His voice was clear, direct, and with that tone of dominance that melted her into a puddle. But he knew exactly what he'd done, and this was all a part of the plan for the night. The plan she was starting to understand in its entirety.

Oh yes, she would *definitely* be feeling this tomorrow. Probably into next week.

And he wasn't even finished.

Her reply was something of a mewling whimper, her brain too fuzzy to form anything else.

"Up." He commanded, tugging her hair until she rose on shaky legs. He moved her ahead of him until her legs met the edge of the padded table he kept in the room. The one covered in straps. He bent her forward and began strapping her arms down in front of her, keeping her fully prone. "Since you're having so much trouble following my instructions, I'll make sure you can't break position for your punishment."

Her body was a soaked, quaking, liquid, mess. She pressed her forehead into the soft top of the table, her ass presented perfectly as he crouched behind her and cuffed her ankles to the legs.

"Since you broke three rules at once, we'll finish off your punishment with the cane."

A cry burst out of her. Her ass already felt impossibly sore, heated lines scoring her skin until she couldn't take a breath without being hyper aware of every handprint, every fall from the flogger, each line from the strap. "Please, please, Master, please..."

"I know you can take it, pet. Just breathe for me." His voice came from the wall where the canes were lined up. She heard it swish through the air once as he returned to position behind her. Her hands clenched into fists on the other side of the cuffs as she braced. "There will be five, and they will not be easy. Breathe now."

"MASTER!" She cried out as the first vicious line laid across her skin, but her mind had ridden the place between pleasure and pain for too long so that the second one was a cacophony of sensation. Tingles filled her body up like bubbles, her mind sliding off into subspace where the third lash had her moaning through the tears on her cheeks. Some part of her knew a punishment shouldn't let her do this, but when the third had come she was buzzing, the vicious pain melting quickly into pure sensation. Four rocked her body forward, and her muscles locked up briefly before she melted against the padded top of the table. Five came shortly after, and Thalia knew he was speaking to her, but it was static in her ears. His fingers slid inside her from behind and her body hummed in pleasure.

Then she felt his cock against her. Blissfully, gloriously filling her until her entire world consisted of nothing more than the burn in her skin, and the force of his thrusts inside her. On some level she knew he was leaning over her, bracing a hand on the table near her hip as his other came to her front to find her clit. Her hips bucked back against his thrusts, and through the haze of pleasure, and the sting of the welts, she heard his voice against her ear, "Let go, pet, come for me."

A thrust, a roll of her clit, and her body answered in trembling shocks of pure bliss. She lost count of the number of times her body tensed against the waves of pleasure before she was whimpering and pleading incoherently against the soft leather top of the table. He finally joined her, his cock thrusting deep, almost painfully so, before the warm pulses of his seed filled her up.

The releasing of the cuffs, his lifting of her trembling body into his arms, them both dropping into the small bed inside the playroom. It was like a dream. One that ended with her head on his chest, his arms wrapped tight around her as he spoke soothingly about how beautiful she was, how incredible, how sexy, how strong, how perfect.

She could only nuzzle against his chest, feeling his fingers run along her arm, his kisses in her hair. Then there was sleep. Exhausted, sated, dreamless, sleep.

Chapter Thirteen
THALIA

Morning came on the heels of her body alerting her to one obvious fact: *everything* ached.

"Fuck." Thalia groaned, and tried to roll over but she found that she was firmly encased in James' arms, and he was still sleeping peacefully. Tilting her head up she saw his features soft in sleep, his lips parted as he breathed slow and deep. The rise and fall of his chest moving her slightly.

With a wince she forced herself to nestle back against him, soaking in his warmth, breathing in the masculine scent of his skin, the faintest hint of his cologne still clinging to him. Her entire backside felt like one solid welt, but she reveled in it. Feeling the evidence of his passion for her was the most important thing to her today.

Because it was D-Day. Decision Day.

Happy six-month anniversary, she thought as she trailed her hand over his stomach. The muscles jumped under her touch and he murmured in his sleep.

With a grin she slid her hand lower, underneath the waist of his pants to grip him. His hips lifted into her hand, his cock stirring under her touch. She ran her thumb over the head, her fingers tracing the sensitive underside as he began to swell under her palm. He shifted under her and she lifted her head from his chest, gently stroking him as he woke up. His hips thrust against her hand and she heard his breathing change, a rumble in his chest as he became consciously aware of her.

"Mmmm, baby? What are you doing?" His voice was low with sleep, his eyes cracking open to look down at her.

"Saying good morning?" She spoke softly, but he grabbed her wrist and pulled her hand away from him and up to his mouth to kiss it.

"You should be resting." James had let his head drop back against the bed, his eyes closing again. He was *not* a morning person.

"I'm wide awake." She bit her lip, ignoring the twisting in her stomach and continuing before her nerves got the best of her. "I want to tell you my choice."

His breath stopped. Her nerves clanged inside her, and then he seemed to force his chest to expand with breath. With a gentle nudge he moved her off his chest and she worked to hide the wince as she rolled to her side and the welts woke up with a fury. James sat up, not looking at her as he rubbed his hands over his face before pushing a hand through his hair. "Can we have breakfast first?"

"James—"

"Baby, please?" His voice sounded pained, and she couldn't deny him anything when he sounded like that.

"Okay. Breakfast."

He peeked at her and for once she couldn't read the expression on his face. His hand reached forward to tuck her hair behind her ear, and then he seemed to shift focus. "Oh, bloody hell. Your back, how are you?"

"Sore, but I promise I'm fine." She bit her lip again. "Can I please just—"

"Not in here, Thalia. Not in the playroom, come on." James slid off the bed and held out his hand for her.

Sitting up was a revelation in just how painful the morning after could be. Her body screamed at her as she put pressure on the welts, and she whimpered when she slid forward on the bed for him to pull her up.

"Baby..." His hands cupped her face and he kissed her gently. The tenderness of it almost brought tears to her eyes. Why wouldn't he just let her tell him?! She just wanted to know everything was okay! She wanted to know that this, every moment of it, wasn't going to abruptly end in some catastrophic fireball! He pulled back and kissed her cheeks, her eyelids, her forehead, and then he carefully hugged her to him, keeping his arms high on her back. "Come on."

He took her hand and led her out of the playroom. Her eyes moved over the abandoned toys across the floor. Memories of her body responding to each of them assailing her as they stepped out into the hallway. Instead of turning toward the kitchen he pulled her to the bedroom.

"Lay on your stomach, baby. On the bed." His voice sounded quiet, reserved. Panic was moving in from the edges of her brain. She had the strangest urge to cry, which had nothing to do with the welts down her backside.

When she didn't move toward the bed James stopped at one of their chest of drawers and turned back. Thalia heard her voice break as she spoke again, "Do you not want me to—"

"Wait. Please, just wait." James held up his hand and he leaned back against the chest of drawers as if it was taking it out of him to just talk to her. "I just want to rub something on your welts, and I want us both dressed, and fed, before we talk. Okay?"

She nodded even though her chest was aching. The hollow feeling hurt worse than the welts. She'd take the cane again if he'd just let her tell him she wanted to stay with him, that she loved him, that she never wanted to be apart. She'd take the cane a hundred times if he'd say it all back to her. Instead of pushing the issue she walked over to their plush bed and gingerly climbed on top of it, laying on her stomach. James was there a moment later, a cool swipe of cream making her hiss breath between her teeth. His hands were confident as they rubbed over her skin.

"I'm sorry I didn't do this last night baby, that was completely stupid of me." His voice sounded almost sad and it amped up the panic in her chest. Before she could stop it, tears were slipping out from between her lashes. She forced even breaths, keeping the hitches in her breath silent as he worked his way down her thighs.

Why the fuck did this feel like a goodbye?

She felt like her ribs were cracking under the strain of keeping quiet as she cried into the bedding. Did James not want her? For the first time that seemed like a possibility, and she didn't understand it. She didn't understand any of it. If he wanted her, why wouldn't he just SAY it?!

"Thalia?" James' hands froze and she buried her face in her arms further. He leaned back from her and she heard him breathe slowly. "Grab some clothes, I'm going to make us breakfast."

She heard him open the door of their closet — or *his* closet? Then his steps took him out of the room. She sat up and the sensation of her pulse in her skin was distant. She couldn't even feel the ache of the welts under the cooling cream. It was nothing compared to the bottomless pit that had opened in her chest. Thalia mindlessly found soft yoga pants, a bra, and a green top that she knew he liked. She stepped into the bathroom and brushed her teeth, tearing the brush through her hair and washing her face so it wasn't as obvious she had been crying. Her eyes looked sad and empty, and she felt like her world was crashing. Like all her worst fears were coming true.

"Don't cry. You're not going to cry, no matter what happens," she whispered at her reflection, steeling herself for whatever he had planned. "You'll survive. You will." When her face looked more neutral she turned and left their bedroom and walked toward the kitchen. The smell of eggs and toast filled the hall. Just as she turned the corner she heard the grinding racket of her coffee pot turning on. Her lips almost ticked up into a smile.

He *hated* that coffee pot.

"Hey," she mumbled and James turned around from the stove. He was gorgeous. Gray t-shirt that fit to his strong frame, dark jeans, his blond hair still a complete mess from sleep. And he looked more nervous than she'd ever seen him.

She probably didn't look any better.

"Hey, baby. Grab a seat, I'll have plates for us in a second." His voice was low and solemn, and she wanted to scream her choice at him. She wanted his answer. She didn't want breakfast, she didn't want to sit at the kitchen island like it was any other day.

But she did, and she hissed between her teeth as she settled on the chair. She looked up at James to see the hint of a smile on his lips.

"I did tell you that you'd feel it today." He was trying for lightness, but it fizzled in the tone of the air between them.

"I chose that option for a reason..." *Because I love it, and I love what we do, and I love you, dammit!* She didn't say it out loud, she just buried her face in her hands. Her stomach growled when he slid a plate in front of her, next to a cup of coffee made just how she liked it. He set his own plate down across from her with a mug of tea.

"I'll be right back. Eat." The last word came out as a command and she looked up at him, but he tilted his head, his expression soft. "Please."

She grabbed the toast, egg in a basket, her favorite, and took a bite. It was like ashes in her mouth. *Why was he dragging this out?* A minute later James came back to the island with a small stack of manila folders. Her eyes couldn't tear away from them. He took a bite of his own toast and then sighed.

"Baby—"

"James, please. Can I just give you my answer?" she interrupted him, because she couldn't wait anymore. He sighed and sat back, grabbing his mug from the granite top.

"All right." He ran a hand over his face. "I just have to say one thing before you do. No matter what you choose, and you can choose whatever you have planned, I won't stop you. I would never—" He paused and took a steadying breath. "I'm not him, Thalia. I'm not Marcus, and I meant what I said, what I *promised*. If you want to go, you can."

His eyes had left her face while he talked and now he was boring holes into the island. Thalia groaned. "You can't possibly be that stupid."

"What?" His sea green eyes snapped up to hers.

"I've been trying to tell you for MONTHS that I want to be with you!" Thalia half-shouted as she stood up and stepped away from the island. "James, I don't want to leave! I want to stay with you! I've been terrified for weeks you'd tell me to leave, and if that's what *you* want, then I won't fight it. But I fucking love you, James. I *love* you!" She was facing him, disbelief written on his face as her voice calmed. But she'd said it, it was out there, and her chest ached as she waited for his response.

Chapter Fourteen
THALIA

"You love me?" James stood up slowly, moving around the island toward her.

"I thought that was pretty obvious." She whispered as he approached her. His hand brushed her cheek, and a smile touched his lips.

"Since when?" His smile widened and she felt an easing in her chest. This was going well, very well. Smiles were good.

Smiles were fucking great.

"Um, Purgatory? After your accident, I knew. I knew I loved you and that I never wanted to be away from you again." Thalia spoke quietly, but then he grabbed her face and kissed her. It was exactly what she needed. Passionate and warm and inside she felt a piece of herself fall into place. His hands held her hard against his mouth, his tongue seeking hers until a soft moan rose out of her. He leaned back and his grin was infectious, she felt a giddy fizzy feeling inside her.

"Baby, I have to tell you, you were late to the party. I fell in love with you first." His voice was playful, but his words sent her head spinning.

"What?" She laughed. There was no way. No way he loved her first. Not with all his huffing and puffing about their six-month time clock, not with his refusal to listen to her every time she tried to tell him.

"Before I left to come back for work, I realized it. You were just — you *are* — just so perfect for me, and I'm so unbelievably lucky." James pulled her against him, his arms wrapping around her and she felt like she was at home. She was too happy, she had to be radioactive with it. Of all the ways she had imagined today going, this had never even registered. Not only did he want her to stay, but he loved her too? He had loved her *first*?

"If you really believe you're the lucky one, you're wrong. My life could have ended the day of the party — the auction. Literally and figuratively. And instead it started. Instead I really started living, instead of just going through the motions, and that's all because of you! Because you saved me! And I know you're not proud of how you knew I was there, and I know you're not proud of your choices, but all of those things brought you to me, and you've given me a life, made me really *live* my life, and I couldn't love you more for all of it." Thalia wrapped her arms around him, "So, I am definitely the lucky one." She kissed him, and he kissed her back, and it was sweet, and soothing, and it smoothed all the rough edges inside her. She could feel their path clicking into place and she had never thought this kind of happiness, this kind of radioactive joy, would have ever been a possibility.

"You have no idea how worried I've been." He shook his head, "I mean, you're so strong, and you've become this incredible woman. You rebuilt your life and I didn't know if you'd want me to be a part of it. Not with me as a constant reminder of how you got here."

"James." She reached up and held his face, his eyes looked pained as she listened to what were apparently his deepest fears. "You aren't a bad memory for me, you're my favorite memory. If you thought for even a minute I'd want to leave you, to leave *us* behind... you really can be an idiot sometimes." She smiled and he smiled back.

"Yes. Yes, I can." His grin grew wider, "Can I give you my six-month anniversary gift now?" He was suddenly all boyish excitement, and he grabbed her hand and pulled her to the island. "Here, sit."

"Okay... but, I don't have anything for you?" Thalia sat down gingerly and James grabbed the chair next to her.

"Baby, you already gave me the only gift I wanted today." James reached across the island and pulled over the manila folders. "I wanted to be sure that whatever you chose you knew I supported it, so I planned ahead."

"Of course you did." She smiled, taking a sip of her coffee as she looked at her organized, type-A, executive, Dominant, boyfriend. If there was a possibility, he had planned for it, and it sort of felt like Christmas morning as she stared at the folders.

He took the one in the middle and flipped it open. "This isn't just from me, it's from Kalen and Maggie too. I know you've been official at the yoga studio for about a month, but I thought you might like to open your own." He nudged the folder in front of her and she was staring down at a thick packet of legal looking papers.

"What is this?" She started flipping through it and saw an address down the street, square footage, and her name all over it.

"Your own studio. Analiese did some marketing research and said this is a great location, she is also volunteering her time to set up your brand, and Julie really wants to help you do the interior design." James looked a little nervous in his excitement.

"You bought me a yoga studio?" Thalia's voice was disbelief.

"Half of one, like I said, Kalen and Maggie wanted to help. And it's not a yoga studio yet, it's an empty space, but you will be able to build it out however you like."

"Did *everyone* know about this but me?" She laughed and looked up at him.

"Sort of. I wanted to make sure you'd like it." His fingers wrapped around her hand, "Do you?"

"I don't even know how to run a business! But, I mean, yes. Yes! I do like it, I love it, it's just a lot?" Thalia's head was spinning again. She was going to end up with vertigo at this rate.

"I'm pretty good with business, I think I can help, and this way you'll be able to do whatever you want, hire whomever you want. It will be completely yours." His thumb traced over the back of her hand and she sat back in shock.

"Wow. That's a hell of a gift." She jumped, "I can't just leave Marie! She just hired me!"

James chuckled, "It will take a few months to get it situated and register the business. You won't leave suddenly, but I know how much the yoga thing has made you happy — and I just want you happy, baby."

"*You* make me happy." She leaned over and kissed him before glancing back at the other folders. "What are those?"

James looked at them too and grabbed the top one, "This was if you had said you wanted to go. I rented you an apartment, set up a bank account in your name, and there's still the copy of the property information for the studio. No matter what, I wanted to make sure you were well taken care of. Even if it wouldn't be by me anymore."

"You were still going to give me the yoga studio?"

"I have to admit all of that was a little selfish. I thought if you stayed in London, if you felt like you didn't *have* to be with me, that maybe I could convince you to date me." James blushed a little. Actually fucking blushed.

That was a first.

"So, your plan was to still try and woo me? After giving me—" Her eyes bugged out of her head when she saw the figure in the bank account. "Holy shit, James!"

"Language." He chided with a smile. "And you can keep that separately if you want, or I can close it. It doesn't matter to me."

"That's so much money! What were you thinking?!"

"That I promised you if you decided at the six months you wanted to leave that I'd help you rebuild your life after he took everything. I wasn't going to go back on that." He shrugged. "And it's not that much money."

"To you!" She gasped and closed the folder on the obscene number.

"Yes, pet, to me." He grinned again. "But it doesn't matter because you want to stay, and everything that's mine is yours anyway."

"You're insane." She laughed but he gripped her hand, his eyes tracing her face, her mouth. Then he kissed her again, and he almost succeeded in distracting her from the third folder. The largest of the three. "Wait, what's in the last folder?"

James' expression changed as he reached for it. Instantly solemn again, the giddy joy that had been theirs for a few moments dulled. "Ah. Well, *this* I was offering you regardless." He pulled the folder in front of them, pushing the others back across the island. "Do you remember when I showed you the email from Marcus? Do you remember what you said?"

Thalia nodded, her stomach tightening at the mention of his name.

"You told me you hoped their world crashed down around them. That they never hurt another girl. That you hoped they burned for what they'd done." His eyes were on the folder, his fingers gripping the edge of it just a little too tightly.

"I remember."

"I couldn't think of a better anniversary gift, a better way to end our six-month agreement, than to give you a way to do exactly that." He laid his hand flat on the top of it. "I've had a team of people digging up every scrap of evidence on the Williams brothers. Hacking their servers, their accounts, their website. There's enough information in here, and on a set of digital drives, to completely destroy them — but it's up to you, baby."

Her head was spinning again, only now it was making her nauseous. "What's up to me?"

"There's a few options here. We don't have to do anything with this. We can leave all of it alone, never think about either of them again. We can just live our lives."

"Okay."

"We can ask the people who have been working on all of this to just bring it all down. Delete everything, destroy their finances, scatter all their ill-begotten money across the world. Maybe funneling it into some needy organizations. Make it so it will be very difficult for them to rebuild anything." James was staring at the folder, and so was she.

"And the last option?"

"The last option is we destroy them. Turn it all over to INTERPOL and let the police drag them out into the open. Take them down. Make them pay for everything they've done." James' voice had an edge to it as he spoke, and she felt her own pulse increase. "Now no matter what, every trace of you and I are gone. Every mention of my name, of your time there, all of it. Gone. We won't be involved in any of it. So, baby, what—"

"Destroy them." Her eyes came up to his, ignoring the thick folder of their crimes that she didn't want to even look at. "Turn them over to the police. They deserve to pay. To rot in jail forever for what they've done."

"Done." James pushed the folder away and grabbed her face in his hands. "Done. I swear it. They'll burn for what they have done… and I have to say that was the one I had hoped you would choose."

He was kissing her again, pulling her away from the island. Away from all of the wonderful things signaling that they were staying together, and the darkness in the last folder. His arms were around her, and then his hands were behind her thighs and he was lifting her so she wrapped her legs around him. He was hard and she rubbed herself against him, his groan buzzing in their mouths. She felt them moving, but she didn't care. Her hands were in his hair, holding his mouth to hers. James was kissing her. James wanted her to stay. James loved her.

The world was radiant, and glowing, and — he dropped her on the bed. His mouth was on hers again as he pulled at her top. "Remind me to call Kalen after this, they wanted to know when you said yes."

Thalia laughed as he ripped the green top over her head and she pulled at his shirt. "*When* I said yes?"

"They had no doubts. Kalen was the one who told me he knew you loved me." James' lips pressed against hers again before he leaned up to pull off his shirt. "I thought it was too good to be true."

Thalia unhooked her bra and threw it off the bed, reaching for the button of his jeans as soon as her hands were free. He grabbed her wrists and pinned them to her sides, making her moan as he pressed himself between her thighs.

"And Alice and her husband want to go to dinner with us." His lips were trailing kisses over her ribs, his teeth nipping at her until she was groaning. His voice hummed against her skin. "I didn't want to give them an answer before today."

"Ah!" She cried out as his warm mouth found her nipple and drew it in, her back arching. "Julie is planning a girls' weekend in two weeks! AH! Same thing, didn't want to say yes—" he kissed her again, his erection rubbing against her through their clothes, his warm chest against hers. She was moaning against his lips.

"You should have just said yes, pet. You could have gone either way." His hands released her wrists and then he was pulling her pants off. Once freed her fingers returned to his button, popping it and sliding his zipper down until she could reach inside and grab his cock. His body stilled and his hips jerked against her, a growl rumbling in his chest. He slid off her to kick his clothes away, and she did the same. Then he was on top of her again, his hips between hers, his fingers seeking and finding her soaking. She was slippery as he thrust two fingers inside her.

"Oh God!" She groaned and arched her back, "Please?" She was begging and she didn't care. This was her boyfriend, her Dom, and they had a lot of time, but she wanted him *now*.

"Tell me you love me again?" His hand slid from between her thighs, his touch trailing up her waist until he interlaced their fingers and he was pinning her again.

"James, I love you. Now please, pretty please, fuck me." Her voice was breathy with need, and his answering grin made that fizzy joy return to join the need coiling inside her.

"I love you too, Thalia. More than I can even say." His voice dropped to a growl as he thrust inside her and their cries came out as one. He filled her, and when he started to move her body lifted against his again and again. This was what she wanted, what she needed, and she had it.

She had James. She had everything.

Chapter Fifteen
THALIA

Ten and a Half Months after the Auction

If Thalia had thought her first trans-Atlantic flight had been interesting, flying back to the states to meet James' sister was a new level of everything. She had no idea if James had upgraded to the ridiculously luxurious first-class cabin of the Boeing 777 as a kind of atonement for taking her to meet Katherine, or if this was just how he normally made the trip. While it was nice to be in her own little bubble, with a seat that had become a bed once they were out over the ocean, she still wished he was right next to her instead of across the aisle.

During their first flight across the Atlantic she'd probably been in shock, at least that's what Ailsa would call it. The auction, James, the whirlwind of leaving Marcus on the front steps of his house, the hotel, the never-ending panic that had hummed just under her skin. The flight had been difficult, she'd been exhausted, but every time she had fallen asleep there had been nightmares. It had only been because James was right next to her that she hadn't had a total freak out and been taken down by some transatlantic air marshal.

Thalia huffed out a breath and tried again to get comfortable, to sleep, because she needed it. There was no reason this flight was any different than the many she had been on since that first flight with James. They'd flown all over Europe. He'd taken her to Venice one weekend just because he'd mentioned the city and she'd commented that she'd never been to Italy.

Oh, you've never been to Italy? We'll just go.

Those were the kinds of ridiculous things your boyfriend did for you when money had no meaning to him. Thalia didn't even care about the money, or the trips, or the fact that he'd bought her a yoga studio *just because*.

Well, that last part was a lie.

She didn't care about the other stuff, but she *really* liked the yoga studio. The studio was gorgeous. Julie had made sure of that. On the second floor, on a very nice street lined with upscale shops. Three rooms for classes, a front desk space that made it look like a warm and inviting spa. It had taken her weeks of interviews but she had found great people to run Nirvana with her. Becca had been her first hire, and she was hilarious and vibrant and had one of the dirtiest mouths Thalia had encountered in London. On top of that she was a very talented yoga instructor and had been doing it for years. It made her fantastic to work with. Their grand opening had been a few weeks before. All the girls from Purgatory had shown up, along with a lot of James' work friends, and *that* had not been the easiest party to referee. But it had gone off without a hitch, clients had poured in after the over-the-top advertising campaign James had constructed with Analiese, and they were already slated to more than cover their own expenses the first month.

For the hundredth time guilt gnawed at Thalia that she had left the studio in Becca's hands to fly to America and meet James' sister, but according to James it was either meet her *now* or she was coming to London to cause a scene and rope in James' parents on top of everything.

They had originally planned to meet James' parents at their huge Christmas party, before his parents cancelled the party and went to Morocco, — that would have been easier. Tons of people. Not much pressure to be perfect, or much time to be grilled on her life story. James' plan had been to introduce her as the girl he was dating, wish them a happy Christmas, and then disappear back home to drink until her nerves wound down.

Ah, and that was just one more thing weighing on her mind.

James really wanted his family to know her, she knew he did. She could see how much he wanted it, but every time he talked about it this cloud of concern fogged his features. He tiptoed around the subject as if she might bolt from the room — which wasn't *actually* that far from how she felt about it. In the first couple of months they had been together James had taken her shopping and she had made a joke about the movie Pretty Woman that he had not found very funny. But the comparison had never faded from her mind, and just imagine how awkward it would have been had they added in to the movie Richard Gere's character introducing Julia Roberts to his parents? The poor, classless American girl being introduced to the upper crust of society? Cue judgment, polite smiles, uncomfortable silence, and disappointment.

Would Edward really have given up his family to stay with Vivian? *Not fucking likely.*

Maggie had said his parents were nice. That Katherine was flighty and spoiled and ridiculous, but nice. James had echoed Maggie's opinion, mentioning Katherine's disconnect with normal people, citing that she'd never had a real job. That she'd finished a degree in business only to appease their parents and spent most of her time in luxurious communities in the northeast of the United States just to keep an ocean between her and their parents' wishes that she'd *do something with her life.* At least that was a parental line that bridged most of the tax brackets.

So, what if Katherine hated her? Would that be a nail in the coffin of their relationship? When she finally did meet his parents, which likely wouldn't be far behind this trip, what if they hated her? What if they thought James was too good for her? Because, in reality, James *was* too good for her. They never would have crossed paths without her being kidnapped and James' dark side rearing its head. Which they definitely could *not* explain to either Katherine or his parents. What happened then? What happened if after all of their incredible luck over the last six months, since Purgatory, everything fell apart? Did he, *could* he, love her as much as she loved him? Enough to survive the condemnation of the most important people in his life?

Fuck. Fuck. Fuck. Fuck. Fuck.

Way too much on her mind. A new business which she had effectively ditched for a week just as it was getting its footing. *Genius move.* Flying through the air at a million miles an hour toward her boyfriend's sister so she could judge her worthy or not. *Terrifying.* The pending meeting of his parents on the horizon. *There had to be a stronger word than terrifying for that, petrifying? Mind obliterating?*

Dammit.

Sitting up in the quiet cabin she looked across the aisle to see James working on his laptop. For a moment her pounding heartbeat faded, the buzzing in her ears of all her thoughts whirring by quieted, and she just felt — good. His blond hair was almost in his eyes, he needed a haircut, and he was running his thumb across his bottom lip like he did whenever he was deep in work. If they'd been at home she would have grabbed a book, or her own laptop, and sat on the floor by him just so she could occasionally lean against his leg, and he could brush his fingers through her hair. It was a habit she refused to give up regardless of how overtly submissive it was. She liked it, it made her feel centered and calm. She liked to watch him work and just feel that comfortable closeness of not having to talk, but still being near each other. And she really needed that feeling right now. James must have felt her staring because he paused his work to look up at her from the blue glow of his screen. He arched an eyebrow and sighed.

Baby, you should try and sleep," he whispered across the aisle, "it's a very long flight, and you do not want to be exhausted when we get there."

"I can't sleep." She whispered back, crossing her legs to sit in the middle of the seat-bed so she could see him clearly.

"Why not?" He tilted his head, giving her his full attention, his eyes evaluating her from head to toe in an instant as he tried to figure out what was wrong before she answered. That was the Dom half of her boyfriend, always on high alert for her safety and well-being. Finely tuned instincts dissecting her body language, tone, facial expression, and probably a lot of other things that he used all the time to read her like a book. Sometimes his questions were more rhetorical than anything, just a request for her to speak what he'd already figured out.

Thalia wasn't that good at it, and that meant she couldn't tell if he was sincerely asking or if he already knew the insane doom and gloom spiral her brain had just taken her on while she was trying to fall asleep. Either way, she had to answer. "Honestly, my brain won't shut up. I'm thinking about—" She breathed. "—*everything* at once."

James closed his laptop and slid it into his bag before he opened his arms. Thalia was across the aisle and in his lap between one heartbeat and the next, her whole body melting against his. "Is it because I bribed you into taking this trip to meet Katherine?" His words were quiet against her hair.

"You didn't bribe me, I agreed to go." Thalia took a deep breath, inhaling the warm masculine scents of his skin and his cologne that were clinging to the comfortable sweater he was wearing. He was still rocking the yacht club look effortlessly, and a smile tugged at her lips as the comparison popped back up in her head.

This trip was bringing up a lot of old thoughts.

"Baby, I hired you an executive assistant for the week we're gone to make sure not a thing would be missed at Nirvana, I booked a vacation next month for you and the girls in Provence and got us tickets to every Broadway play you even blinked at for the days we're in New York City." James tilted her chin up and kissed her through the smile on his lips, "I absolutely bribed you."

"You also booked us first class in this ridiculous plane." Thalia smiled back and James chuckled softly.

"See? I bribed you." James kissed her again and it was like his touch alone could replace all of the cortisol in her system with endorphins. Stress melting away into fizzy pleasure. "Want to talk about it?"

"Not really. It's just me over-thinking everything." She leaned into him and murmured against his chest, "I love you." His arms tightened around her, and she loved how warm he was. Would the flight attendants throw a fit if they found her coiled up in his lap asleep?

"I love you too, baby. So much." He sighed, the fingers of one of his hands intertwining with hers, his thumb tracing circles across her skin as they sat quietly. The steady staccato of his heart was her favorite lullaby, but her nerves and her brain wouldn't shut up enough for her to fall asleep. "You are not going to sleep, are you?"

There he went reading her like a book again.

"I'm trying." She mumbled, her frustration leaking into her voice.

"Alright. Get up and go into the toilet by the bar. Be very quiet and leave the door unlocked. Now." James' voice was clear and direct even in the hushed tones he was speaking. Dom voice. A shiver rushed over her skin as she leaned back to look up at him. His eyes were dark green and promised so much if she took the challenge he offered.

The grin that covered her face caused his lips to twitch up as she slid off his lap and moved quickly. When she pressed the door to the bathroom closed a moment later her heart was pounding so hard in her ears she was sure someone would hear it. They had been in the air a couple of hours so people were likely not paying close attention, but she had already been on edge and the tense excitement of what he had planned only ramped it up further. The door opened and her breath caught.

James filled the space as he pressed the door closed behind him and slid the lock into place. Everything about him overwhelmed her. When he reached forward to pull her lips against his, the kiss ripped the last of the air from her lungs. His mouth moved against hers with the kind of heat he rarely displayed outside of the flat, and she felt the moan in her throat as she held on to the front of his sweater like she was seeking an anchor. He was hard against her as he pushed her back until her knees met the toilet and she was forced to sit on the seat. James pulled back until there was barely an inch between their lips. "There is only one thing I want you thinking about right now, pet, and that is how you're going to please me."

Thalia's lips felt swollen from the kiss and she managed to nod against his hands as the sweet calm of submission moved over her like a fogbank. One of James' hands slid to the back of her head and twined in her hair, tightening his grip until tiny fireworks burst inside her as arousal swept her up and she was wet and warm and waiting for his command.

There is nothing better than this.

"Hands behind your back. Move them and I'll punish you, pet. Understand?" James was all firm control as he stood over her, watching her closely as she obeyed and clasped her hands behind her.

"Yes, Master." Thalia whispered the words, her urge to be touched or to touch him was all she could think about. Everything else faded into the ether as James released her hair, unbuckled his belt and shifted his jeans down his hips. Then his boxers came down, and finally he had his cock in his hand. Hard, velvet covered steel and her mouth watered like she could already taste him. Thalia leaned forward but James caught her by her hair to hold her back.

"Is this what you want, pet?" James' voice was a soft growl, his own arousal darkening his tone as he slowly stroked himself. It was a torturous tease that had her lips parting as she nodded, her breath coming in short pants. "You want me to use your mouth? Fuck your throat?"

Thalia moaned at his words, her pussy growing wet as he let her move a little closer before jerking her head back again. His fist tightened in her hair as he waited for her response. "Yes, Master, please, use my mouth, fuck my throat, whatever you want."

James held her an inch or so from the head of his cock, precum forming on the tip that tempted her to flick her tongue out to taste it. But if she did he might very well send her back to her seat with nothing. "What are you thinking about right now? The truth."

"How much I want to taste you. Please let me taste you." Thalia was begging, as quietly as she could with the whine in her voice, but it seemed to have been the answer he wanted.

"Open. You don't need to do anything but take it, pet." The head of his cock brushed her lips and she opened them to let him in. She moaned against the hard flesh, wishing she could touch the wetness pooling between her thighs as he moved against her tongue. He started with slow, shallow thrusts, guiding her head with his grip in her hair, and all of her focus stayed on keeping her lips tightly sealed against his skin so she could suck him in with each forward thrust. To give him as much pleasure as possible even as he worked to take it from her. He pushed against her throat and she swallowed to let him in, and he held there while her body fought the initial panic. The intense submission of relaxing against his grip, of trusting him, let the feeling of suffocation pass just before he pulled back enough for her to steal a breath. His hand tightened in her hair and he thrust harder, back into her throat, then out to skate the head of his cock over her tongue.

Thalia pulled in air before he released the hold on his control and he began to fuck her throat in earnest. Saliva pooled in her mouth, overflowing when he drew back to coat her chin, making wet sounds as he thrust hard, bruising her throat. His groans slipped past his lips when he pulled in a breath before gritting his teeth as he tried to stay quiet. A swell of excitement washed over her that she was the reason for his straining self-control. She felt his cock push into her throat again and James braced a hand on the wall, harsh breaths above her as she struggled to ignore her own urge to draw in air. He slid completely from her mouth, strands of saliva connecting them for a moment before he pulled her upright by her hair. James ran his tongue over his lip as he wiped his thumb across hers.

"You look incredibly hot like this, pet." His lips twitched into a smile as his eyes devoured her, his hand inching down her body. Cupping her breast, pinching her nipple through the bra, following the curve of her waist — and then deftly unbuttoning the top of her jeans. "Drop your jeans and your underwear and face the wall. I'm going to fuck you, and you can come as long as you're very quiet. Understand, pet?"

"Yes, Master, thank you, yes, I'll be quiet." Thalia's pussy clenched against the promise of having him inside her, and she scrambled to obey until her clothes were pooled around her ankles and James was bending her forward. He traced a finger up her slit and she shivered.

"So wet. Did you like me fucking your throat, pet?" There was laughter in his voice. This was one of those rhetorical questions.

"Yes, Master." She spoke softly, biting her cheek to try and stifle the grin on her lips. Instead she wiggled her hips and he squeezed her ass in response, his fingers digging in sharply.

"*Tease*. Bite down on something if you can't be quiet, pet. All the fun stops if you make too much noise." James brushed against her pussy and she fought the urge to push back. He was in charge and if she moved he'd drag it out, he'd tease her until she was pleading. She'd beg now if he'd only ask her too, the heat between her thighs was pulsing with the rapid pounding of her heart. Just when she thought he might have opted for the teasing path, he thrust hard inside her. Thalia clapped her hand over her mouth and tried to swallow the moan that rose up, James' groan was likely louder than he had meant it to be as well and he froze inside her as they both gained control.

Her body trembled waiting for him to move inside her again, to fill and stretch her again and again until she fell apart. "James..." she whimpered and he answered her with a thrust, his hands at her hips to pull her back against him hard. Then he really started to move and she kept her hand over her lips, her teeth clenched tightly to try and stay quiet as their gasps filled the small space. Pleasure bounced off her nerve endings until it was a steady thrum inside her, increasing in frequency until she felt like she was stretched tight in her own skin. Reaching for the edge she bit down on her hand and James pushed her over as his fingers found her clit and rubbed her in quick circles. The tension snapped with a release like fireworks inside her head, their embers fading to leave behind an empty euphoria that left no room for worries or concerns, and James joined her. His cock kicking deep inside her, his seed filling her in pulses, and as they both came down from their highs, floating back to themselves, their heavy breaths were all she could hear.

Thalia's legs were shaking when she felt James press a kiss between her shoulder blades as he slid from her. "Good girl. You did wonderfully." His hand slid over her ass again to squeeze her flesh. "Ready to sleep now, baby?"

"Mmhmm…" she murmured, listening to the tinkling sound of metal as James put himself away. He chuckled as he helped her tug her clothes back on, turning her to press her against the wall with a deep kiss as he zipped and buttoned her jeans. She was melting against him, the buzz of her orgasm still strumming merrily under her skin. James grinned at her and opened the door, moving her out ahead of him. A flicker of concern that a flight attendant might be waiting for them surfaced in her head, but there was no one. The cabin was dim and quiet, and theirs were the first seats. He tucked her into the seat-bed, laying the blanket out over her as she made contact with the tiny pillow.

"Sleep well, baby. I love you." A soft kiss on her temple was the last thing she was really aware of as her body finally gave up its hold on consciousness and she dropped into dreamless, sated sleep.

Chapter Sixteen
THALIA

"Well, how was the flight?" Katherine smiled at them as they stepped inside the restaurant to find her waiting. They had landed at JFK, gone to the hotel for a few hours, and then taken a car to meet her for dinner. She was beautiful. Long blonde hair like her brother's, shocking green eyes, and she was in some kind of wool dress that Thalia was pretty sure was designer.

Thalia blushed, thinking of what they had done on the plane, but fortunately James wasn't so flustered. He stepped forward and they kissed each other on the cheek, "It was just fine, Katherine." He half turned to look back at Thalia and smiled, "Katherine, this is Thalia. My girlfriend."

"You are lovely! Why would he keep you a secret?!" Katherine laughed and stepped forward, kissing Thalia on the cheek before she could react. "He can be completely daft, but I am sure you know that. Let's sit down so we can chat. I want to know positively *everything* about you."

"Katherine..." James groaned, but his sister ignored him, hooking her arm through Thalia's to lead them to the hostess who smiled politely and nodded, taking them to a small table in the upscale restaurant. Once again, Thalia felt the class divide like a wound she couldn't stop picking at. They ordered wine and a selection of food called the chef's tasting menu, and then Katherine's eyes were back on her.

"Alright, tell me all of it. How did you two meet? How serious is this? Are you a gold digging slut just trying to catch my dear brother with that innocent, pretty face of yours?" Katherine had a pristine smile on her face, like a beauty queen who had just said she would choose to end world hunger. But Thalia's heart was in her throat, her stomach wanting desperately to upend the bag of pretzels she had eaten at the hotel. Her mouth was too dry as she tried to think of a way to answer that wouldn't ruin everything before the trip had even truly begun.

"Katherine! Bloody hell—" James hissed across the table at her but Katherine waved a hand at him.

"It's a valid question and I want to hear *her* answer, James. Hush." Katherine was looking at her again, still smiling. From the outside it probably looked like a calm, friendly dinner. Inside Thalia felt like the earth was slipping out from under her feet.

"I — um, I'm not... I—" Thalia stumbled as she tried to answer and Katherine's eyes flickered with amusement.

"Let's start with this. Did you know my brother came from money when you met?" Katherine picked up her wine and took a sip, waiting for her answer. Thalia thought back to being on her knees in Marcus' living room, those green eyes staring at her until she could feel his gaze like a physical touch. Everyone in that room had to have had money, including James. They couldn't have been there without enough to at least be a contender for buying her.

"Enough, Katherine. You do not get to speak to her like that, I *love* her. I brought her here so you could meet her, not attack her! If this is how you're going to act, we're leaving. Come on, baby." He pushed his chair back and stood up and Thalia shook her head. She couldn't, she *wouldn't*, be a wedge between the two of them.

"James, wait!" Katherine reached across the table, a nervous energy in her voice.

"It's okay, James, I'll answer her. Please, let's just stay? If she doesn't like my answer, then we can go." His eyes were screaming apologies at her as he dropped back into his chair and stopped a waiter to ask for Scotch whisky, clearly needing more than a glass of wine to deal with Katherine. Thalia was tempted to upend her glass, but she didn't want Katherine to think she was avoiding the question.

"You'll answer?" Katherine was looking at her, appraising, and Thalia nodded trying to think of how to phrase their unique meeting in simple terms.

"I did have an idea, about James. When — *where* we met, it was an exclusive party. I think most of the people there had money. But that's not why I love him, I swear, the money has nothing to do with it." Thalia was talking with her hands and she forced herself to keep them in her lap.

"I pursued *her*, Katherine, not the other way around. I am not a fool. I know when I'm being hunted for my money and my connections." James was glaring at Katherine while trying to maintain a calm demeanor in the restaurant. If they had been anywhere else Thalia was sure he would have yelled.

"Of course, brother, men always know when a woman is only after them for their money. They are never distracted by a nice ass." Katherine tilted her head with a smile back to Thalia, "And yes, darling, you look quite lovely in the dress. I can see why he pursued you."

"Katherine, stop it." James snapped at her but Katherine was completely unfazed.

"Wait, just wait, please." Thalia sighed and they both looked at her again. James looked tense and concerned, Katherine held her mask of polite civility, her smile never wavering. "Katherine, when I met James I wasn't even sure it would last. *Any* kind of relationship. I thought *maybe* six months." James made a sound under his breath as the waiter brought his whisky. Katherine didn't understand the significance of that timeline, but it was the truth. All of this was the truth, just with the edges blurred. "I wasn't sure *because* of his money, and the fact that I came from such a different world, and I wasn't exactly in the best place mentally."

Understatement of the century.

"But I love James. I know he has faults, I know I have faults, I know that we're different, and I know that our relationship is probably not something he had expected, but we balance each other. I'd love him just the same if we spent every night eating take-away food in a tiny flat, because it's not anything else that makes me want to be with him — it's *him*."

Katherine stared at her, sipping her wine as her eyes moved over Thalia's face. This was the judgment, the evaluation, and Thalia felt like her heartbeat paused as she waited. Finally, Katherine drew a breath. "Well, I have to admit I had not expected to actually believe you. When Maggie told me James had been seeing someone again, and that he was *in love*, I thought for sure if I brought it up with him he'd refuse to let me meet you." She sighed and relaxed back against her seat, that plastic smile fading for the first time since they'd arrived at the restaurant.

"You have to understand, James has never let me meet any of his girlfriends. The fact that he even agreed to let me meet you set off alarm bells, and if he was willing to fly to America — I knew it was serious. I thought that if you were just after him for his money that if I could only scare you enough, you would run. *And* since you mentioned you do not come from money, let me tell you a secret. When you are raised like we were, people start circling you from childhood. I whole-heartedly accept this fact. I know that the pretty playboys that show up at the parties I attend just want to be a part of my world, they want to feel what it's like to have anything they want. Most of them think they are playing me, but honestly, I just want to get laid, and they are very pretty to look at. I am *also* not a fool, and if that means I buy them a few things while we spend time together," she shrugged elegantly, a wicked grin slipping over her lips that was so much like James it surprised Thalia, "Then I do. When I get bored with them, I kick them out of my bed and find a new plaything."

Thalia reached for her wine and took a large drink, hoping it would take the edge off her nerves as Katherine boldly talked about her sex life as if it was nothing. James was gritting his teeth between drinks, obviously forcing himself into silence.

"You know what I never do with my playthings, Thalia?" Katherine asked her with a real smile, all playful and mischievous.

"What?" Thalia breathed, holding her wine glass like a life raft.

"I don't introduce them to my best friends, tell them I love them, or agree to let them meet my family." With that comment, Katherine turned back to James, "Which seems to be exactly what my dear brother has done, which means one of two things — first, you are not a plaything at all and he sincerely cares for you, and you two are all kinds of cute and lovely, or second, most of that is true except you are a gold digging slut who will sincerely regret choosing my brother as her target."

"I—" Thalia started and Katherine grinned and leaned forward slightly.

"But, since I believe, for now, that you are *not* after my brother for his money. I have a bit of advice, as he clearly cares for you. Do not hurt him. Because if you hurt him, I will use my lots and lots of money to tear your little life apart until you'll wish you had died when you broke his heart." The plastic smile was back, and Thalia swallowed.

"It's not your money, Katherine, it's our father's money." James growled and Katherine just laughed.

"As if they would not completely support me tearing her to pieces if she hurt you? Don't be ridiculous, James." Katherine shrugged and took another drink of her wine as the first dishes were placed on the table.

"Katherine." Thalia felt her mouth tick up at the edge in a bitter smile, "Let me be clear as well. I have no plans to leave James. Ever. The only way this ends badly is if he chooses to leave me, and I'll be the heartbroken one. I can't even picture a life without him in it, so of all things for you to worry about as you're working to protect him, that should be at the bottom of your list."

Katherine grinned so wide that it surprised Thalia, "You want to be with James *forever*, hmm? Why, to me, that sounds like wedding bells." She turned on James in an instant, her body tense in excitement and his eyes widened a bit, "Is that why you agreed to bring her? Is that the other secret Maggie wouldn't tell me? Are you two getting married?!"

"Oh my God, I didn't—" Thalia tried to stop her but James just smiled.

"We have not discussed that, Katherine, but you will be one of the first to know if that happens. As far as Maggie's secret, I think you should call her and pester *her* about that. Now, if you're done attacking my girlfriend, I'd appreciate if we could have some civilized conversation?" Clear, calm, direct. It was how he sounded on business calls, usually when someone wasn't doing what they needed to. He hadn't told Katherine that it was going to happen, but he hadn't said no.

James didn't say no at all. The idea of a future with James unrolled in her head like a carpet she'd been keeping a leash on for months. A wedding? A little boy with a messy mop of James' blond hair, or a little girl with long blonde hair and hazel eyes? She could picture James scooping up a kid with that radiant smile he brought out when he was really happy. She remembered the smile on his face when they'd found out about Kalen and Maggie's pregnancy. The pang of want that clanged inside her was surprisingly strong. She wanted all of it.

"Fine!" Katherine yanked her out of her daydream with a laugh, "I was just looking out for you. I know for a fact if I ever brought a man to you, you would be much more frightening. You would probably have him pissing himself before the drinks even arrived." Katherine grinned and James smiled at her over his glass.

"Probably. But any man wanting to spend more than a week or two in your bed *should* be afraid of me, Katherine." James' voice sent a shiver through Thalia, but Katherine only laughed. Thalia couldn't imagine growing up around a personality as intense as James.' No wonder Katherine was fearless and completely unaffected by him. Katherine remembered him as a kid — which made Thalia wonder what he'd looked like.

"You are ridiculous, James. Anyway, do you work, Thalia?" She smiled and grabbed a bite of food, "I promise I'm not interrogating you anymore, now I sincerely just want to know more about you."

"I do, I teach yoga in London." Thalia blushed, hoping that she wouldn't have to mention that James had *bought* her the yoga studio she was teaching in. That might set them back a few paces. Katherine cackled loudly enough to attract the attention of other tables.

"Oh my God, James. You're dating a yoga instructor? Could you be any more cliché?" She took a drink before leaning over to pat Thalia's arm, "No offense meant, I just cannot believe he is! Imagine it in the society pages!"

Her blush was burning her cheeks as Thalia stammered out a response, "I, um, I was actually in data entry before I met James. He encouraged me to get certified in yoga because I enjoyed it."

"Look at her blush, James." Katherine laughed again, "I feel like a total bitch for being so aggressive earlier. You seem like a sweet girl, and I can see why James went after you. We need girl time, just you and me. Then you can tell me all of the secrets James has been keeping from me, and as his little sister it *is* my responsibility to know everything that can embarrass him. Is it true you don't like to shop?"

"I'm not very good at it? James knows so much more than I do, and he has great taste, so I usually just trust whatever he suggests." Thalia stole a bite of something that was rich and tart at the same time, which made her realize just how hungry she was.

"You are too cute. We will fix that, we can go shopping tomorrow before we see whatever Broadway thing James picked. I'm sure James wants to work so he can keep pretending he has to." Katherine was a totally different person when she wasn't grilling her about her intentions. She was loud and always on the edge of laughing at something. Her brazen admissions about her sex life made her seem wild and carefree and unapologetic.

"I enjoy working, Katherine. It's called being a responsible adult." James sighed, but his face revealed that he wasn't actually irritated with Katherine anymore. Thalia could tell he loved his sister, and she felt a pang of guilt that he hadn't seen her in a year — probably because of her presence.

"It's called martyring yourself so you don't feel so guilty about not actually needing to work. You and dad, always wanting to prove that you are just like everyone else, even though you absolutely are *not*." Katherine rolled her eyes, leaning over to speak conspiratorially to Thalia, "James feels guilty about all the money. He won't even use his trust fund! Has to make his own money, and he lives in that little flat in London when he could easily afford *anything* else."

"I like my flat." James commented.

"It's really not small?" Thalia added, thinking about how the flat was easily three times the square footage of the apartment she had been in.

"Jesus Christ, you two are meant for each other. Alright, enough about how sweet and down to earth you both are. I'm going to be sick if we keep chatting away about it. Instead, let's talk about how we want to spend the next few days in the city before we go to my house!"

Chapter Seventeen
THALIA

The four days they had spent in New York City had been incredible. Stores and shows and food and being total tourists.

Shopping with Katherine had been a hurricane of clothes, shoes, and elegant dresses. She'd learned that Katherine hated the aristocratic lifestyle she had to adhere to when she was in London. It was the whole reason she had moved to the states. When it was a seven-hour flight and a five-hour time difference, her parents couldn't expect her to show up at every event they attended. She couldn't be their show pony if she wasn't there to show off. Especially when all she actually wanted to do was enjoy her life.

One thing Katherine and James had in common was an urge to see the world. If she wanted to go to a party in Ibiza for a weekend, she just did it. Katherine had places rented or outright purchased in New York, Los Angeles, Milan, Barcelona, and London. She was unabashed about the kind of money she had access to, and the more Katherine talked about it, the more Thalia realized just how conservative James actually was. Thalia had known he had money, but the kind of wealth Katherine described was the kind of old money that it would be practically impossible to spend in a single lifetime. This was generations of money, and according to Katherine, James wasn't even using his share of it. All of the extravagances that had Thalia flustered and counting pennies were from his salary, and not his family. Adding in this trust fund Katherine kept referencing and Thalia felt light headed at the scope of their wealth.

Every day she let Katherine play dress-up with her before they went out at night. It made Katherine happy. The clothes Thalia had packed for the trip sat in the closet of their suite at the hotel, because Katherine sent her back with an outfit each day begging her to wear it out that night. James assured her that this meant Katherine approved of her. Katherine showed her affection with gifts, and the fact that it made Thalia so uncomfortable only made Katherine want to do it more. Especially since it was further cementing for his sister that Thalia wasn't a gold digger. The sheer number of packages that were being shipped back to their flat in London had her head spinning.

Fortunately, the one purchase Thalia had requested had been a yoga mat and some extra yoga clothes so she could find her center in the mornings and the evenings. It helped to keep her class routines fresh in her mind, and the yoga made her feel more like herself. In clothes that cost a few hundred dollars instead of thousands. Katherine had been astonished that Thalia did yoga every day, and thus bought herself an entire yoga wardrobe and a nice mat to join in.

That was how, now that they were at Katherine's huge house about twenty miles outside of the city, Thalia ended up walking James' sister through sun salutations before dinner and in the mornings. She'd even agreed to join Thalia for a run *outside* in *February* when she normally just used the treadmill in her private gym. They had spent most of their days catching up, or meeting Katherine's friends from the wealthy community she was surrounded by. Others who understood what it was like to grow up rich and who didn't gawk at the house, or the cars, or the private chef, or the extravagant spending patterns. But a day with Katherine was exhausting. Spending almost a week with her was like running a marathon on no sleep. She never stopped moving around — or *talking*. Being back in the room with James at night was a veritable oasis.

"So, Katherine is in love with you. I'm pretty sure if I had not already told her you were happy in London she would have convinced you to stay here with her just for her own entertainment." James smiled at her before he continued brushing his teeth. Thalia paused with her own toothbrush in her mouth, so relieved that it all wasn't just a show, that Katherine had actually given James her approval in private.

"She wants to go for a run with me in the morning. In the snow. I couldn't believe it when she told me after our yoga session this afternoon." Thalia shook her head, still surprised by the excitement in Katherine's voice when she'd announced it after their cool down.

"I told you, she loves you. Which I'm not surprised by at all." James winked at her, and she blew out a breath.

"You know, I was terrified she was going to hate me. It was one of the things I couldn't stop thinking about on the plane. And then the things she said at dinner when we got here? I was sure she was going to demand you find someone else." Thalia rinsed her mouth out and laughed quietly. "Now that Katherine is okay with me, I just have to survive your *parents*."

"First, Katherine had no right to speak to you that way, and second, she would have no say in our relationship anyway. Same with my parents. I barely see either of them, we're always busy. You just need to remember that we chose each other, and nothing is going to change that. Alright?" He glanced over at her as he finished up.

"Alright. She's just intense, and extremely protective of you. Which is a good thing, I just hadn't expected *that*." Thalia shrugged, and James leaned forward to kiss her. All mint and warmth. She smiled against his lips, and he smiled back.

"I know. It's why I wasn't in a rush to push you to meet any of them. They don't exactly live in reality and growing up around them is why I live the way I do. Why I went to school for all those years and worked hard to have the career I have." James stepped away from her and ran a hand through his hair as he leaned back against the counter. "I don't think we have talked about it before, but my father offered me a job in his company when I was still at university. He wanted to groom me to take over, but I didn't want that. I never wanted to just have a future handed to me. Not to mention all of the strings that would have been attached to that offer. Even when I was having my wild years with Kalen I was always working toward what I have now. Independence. My own money without the nagging sense that I have to obey my parents' every whim out of gratitude."

"You and Katherine are definitely... different." Thalia gave him an encouraging smile and he smiled back.

"I'll take that as a compliment, baby."

"I meant it as one. Not that Katherine isn't fantastic, she is, I just think I like things a little more low key." She made a face, hoping that hadn't been insulting, but James chuckled.

"I do too, I absolutely do." He tugged her against him, the thin top she was wearing letting the heat of his bare chest warm her in the cool air of the bathroom. "You know, Katherine wants you as her sister-in-law."

Thalia tensed in his arms, stammering a response in her surprise. "She — you talked about — I mean—"

"She just mentioned that if anyone was going to marry into the family, she'd be grateful if it was you and not some society bitch that Katherine would have to spend the next thirty years verbally sparring with." He chuckled, "Her words, not mine."

"James—" Thalia couldn't figure out what to say. That beautiful future she'd envisioned was like some fragile sparkling mirage that she was worried would shatter if she said the wrong words in this moment. Had they been together long enough to even talk about this? They had surely been through more than most couples went through in a lifetime, and they had proven over and over that all they wanted was the others' happiness. That was a solid foundation, wasn't it? Regardless of the strange circumstances of their meeting? Despite needing the help of an actual psychologist for her to function as a normal girlfriend?

"Thalia, breathe, baby. We don't have to talk about this right now, but I wanted you to know that I have been thinking about it since Katherine brought it up at dinner." He tilted her chin up, his green eyes like sea glass, "And I know you said you don't ever want to be without me, but I want you to know that I feel the same way. I don't see a life without you in it either."

"I love you," she said quietly. That was safe enough to say, and it was true. In response he gave her that radiant smile that seemed to fill her to the brim with light.

"I love you too, Thalia. Now..." James' smile shifted into a mischievous grin as he leaned down suddenly and threw her over his shoulder. She squealed and he squeezed her ass as he walked into the bedroom and tossed her onto the bed. Thalia landed in a fit of laughter and he wasted no time in grabbing her pajama pants and tugging them off her hips to sweep them down her legs. James lifted her foot after he'd dropped her pants to the floor placing a kiss on her arch, and she squirmed when it tickled. He grinned and began to trail soft kisses up her ankle, and her calf, speaking between each one. "I. Plan. To. Kiss. Every. Inch. Of. You."

"I like this plan..." she purred as his hands pushed her thighs apart and he kissed up the inside of her thigh, stopping just short of her panties, which made her groan and lift her hips. He chuckled and picked up her other foot, repeating the trail of kisses on the other side. For a moment his mouth hovered over her mound, and he looked up at her with a wicked grin — and placed a kiss just above her panties. Her stomach tightened and she whimpered as she grew wet, but his mouth trailed kisses over the curve of her waist, her rib cage, pushing up the thin top as he moved up her body.

"James..." she groaned as his mouth grazed the underside of her breast before diverting back to the center of her chest. His soft laugh against her skin made her squirm under him, his weight making her want to feel him against her more firmly. His lips traced her collarbone, her shoulder, before gliding down her arm. He kissed the tender skin of her wrist, her palm, and then the pad of each finger. James ran his hand back up that arm as his mouth repeated the trail on her other arm. Her nerves were lighting up, sending quiet shivers through her, which made her hyper aware of how taut her nipples were in the cool air. Her top bunched above her bared breasts, her panties soaked with how wet she was and there was no relief in pressing her thighs together, arching her back or lifting her hips against the air. Soft moans slipped out of her as he kissed up each side of her neck, his lips against the pulse at her throat, gliding along her jaw line, her cheeks, her eyes, her forehead.

"You are absolutely beautiful." His voice was a warm whisper and then his lips met hers. Softly, even as he opened her mouth, his tongue delving in to meet hers. Her fingers moved into his hair to hold him there but he took her hands, interlacing their fingers to press her hands back to the bed. It was a delirious, slow kiss. Each time he grazed her lip with his teeth he soothed it with a flick of his tongue, before kissing her again. She was moaning against his mouth, pulling gently at the pressure of his hands on hers, wanting to touch him, to pull his body down on hers. He continued anyway, ignoring her soft pleading moans against his lips, building the heat inside her slowly.

When he finally pulled back he slid his hands down her arms and carefully pulled her top over her head, he smiled and rolled her onto her front by her shoulders. She submitted, resting her head on the duvet as he brushed her hair out of the way to place a kiss on the back of her neck, and then he traced her spine with warm kisses. His tongue dancing out against her skin to make her writhe under him in delirious tension. Every touch was too soft, too gentle and she was winding up to a catastrophic crescendo where she would break apart if he didn't—

James slid his fingers beneath the edge of her underwear and started to drag them down her legs, his lips tracing over the round of her ass. She wanted to feel his touch between her thighs but instead he just dragged her panties off and rolled her back over. He straddled her thighs and she lifted her hips, but he ignored her completely. Thalia knew this version of James, he had a plan, and any attempt at begging or cajoling or trying to touch him would be met with gentle restraint to keep her exactly where he wanted her. The only thing to do was submit and wait for what he would give her.

With a grin he leaned over her, hovering his mouth above her breast, his warm breath brushing her nipple until she was biting her lip with the effort of staying still. "Please..." The word came out on a whimper, and he relented. He drew her nipple into his mouth, warm and wet with a delicious tugging that had her back arching and her eyes shutting tight. James cupped her other breast, his thumb rolling over the hard nub until she was gasping and shifting under him. Inching closer to that precipice that would shatter all of the tension he was playing with so carefully. His teeth grazed her and she moaned louder, encouraging, begging wordlessly for more. Instead of giving more he just switched sides, teasing the other nipple into an urgent bundle of nerves that plied small cries from her with every movement of his tongue.

With a low rumble in his chest he shifted back and pushed her legs apart, dropping his knees between them. The tops of the insides of her thighs were soaked, her body tense as his thumbs spread her pussy open. The softest graze over her clit had her shivering. He repeated the movement with his tongue, hot and wet and impossibly perfect as she arched off the bed sharply, her fists clenching in the bedding as he delved deeper with his tongue, setting off a buzzing in her ears.

"I love the way you taste..." he growled, before returning his mouth to her pussy, his thumb rolling her clit until she was shaking, rising up and falling in a burst of pleasure that filled her with a fizzy euphoria — and every lick, every movement of his thumb over her clit dragged it out impossibly long. Shivers took her over, her hips twitching, her body rolling as the waves washed over her again and again. It felt like forever when he finally looked up at her, his mouth wet and his eyes dark with arousal.

Thalia sat up as the gentle tremors started to subside, and he shifted to sit on the bed. They stared at each other, heavy breaths between them, her head so delirious with pleasure she couldn't focus enough to form words. James didn't seem interested in talking though, so she did the only thing she could at the moment to signal her submission to whatever he needed from her. She held her arms out between them, crossed at the wrist, and he bit his lip a moment before he moved toward her. His hand was in her hair, twisting her to the side so when he pushed her back she was laid out on the bed properly. His grip tightened and she arched sharply, his mouth taking advantage of her lifted breasts to draw a nipple into her mouth, biting and sucking until a whole new tension was building inside her. James shifted his pants down and pushed her thighs apart with his knees, capturing her mouth as he thrust hard, filling her in an instant.

It wasn't slow or gentle, but it was a perfect balance. All that delirious, fuzzy pleasure had her head cloudy, but each nip of his teeth, the way his fingers dug into her hip sharply, the pounding thrusts that stretched her — all of it had her rising toward an incredible clarity. James growled against her lips and moved his mouth to her shoulder to bite down. Thalia hissed between her teeth, her hands moving to his hair, but he captured them quickly and pinned them above her head. He felt powerful above her, his grip tight on her skin, his thrusts filling her and pushing her closer and closer toward a new edge. One that wouldn't let her fall gently but would toss her over into an electric storm of sensation.

Her body tightened, tensing under him as his next thrust snapped the tension inside her and she screamed a moan, arching against his chest as lights flickered behind her eyes and her body pulsed with pleasure. James pressed her harder into the bed, his final thrusts sharp until his cock jerked inside her, filling her with the warm wetness of his seed and his weight dropped over her to blanket her in heat. She tugged at the grip on her wrists, leaning her head to the side so she could place a kiss against his cheek as he caught his breath. Her hips rolled and he growled, tightening his hand on her waist until she stilled.

"That was fucking amazing." Thalia moaned quietly as another aftershock shivered through her muscles, sparking up her spine to send a chill over her skin.

"Yes." He pushed out the word on a short laugh and finally released her wrists, lifting his weight off. James slid from her and rolled to his back, both of them panting harshly, staring up into the dim light of the room. He patted the bed between them until he found her hand and interlocked their fingers again. It was a simple touch after so much contact, but it was powerful. They lay like that for a few minutes, catching their breath, the shivers in her muscles quieting until she yawned. "Come on, baby, under the covers." Grabbing the sheets, James tugged them up until they were both covered and he reached for her again, pulling her back against his chest.

"Love you..." Thalia murmured as the warm cocoon James had created with the bedding and his arms lulled her exhausted body into sleep.

Just before dreams washed over her, his words mumbled against the top of her head. "I love you more than anything, baby."

She fell asleep smiling.

Chapter Eighteen
THALIA

"Holy *shit*! It is positively freezing! We can't run in this!" Katherine must have been in five layers as they walked down her driveway to the sidewalk that ran through her peaceful, upscale community. Snow crunched under their shoes and Thalia had to admit that the chill in the air was biting, but after the first mile she'd be just fine. Katherine, on the other hand, would be burning up and wanting to strip off layers with nowhere to put them.

"You don't have to come with me, you know. I'm just going for a few miles, I'll be back in forty-five minutes or so, then we can do yoga." She smiled at Katherine who bristled like she'd insulted her.

"I'm not backing out, Thalia. I just cannot believe you run in this! Plus it rains in London constantly, you're telling me you run in the rain too?" Katherine rubbed her hands together, blowing warm air into her gloves.

"Once we're moving you won't even feel it, you'll be grateful for the cool air. Plus, it's sunny! It's rarely sunny in London." She grinned and walked backward a few steps, taking a deep breath of the cold air as they reached the end of the driveway. "Come on, I'll keep to whatever pace you want to set."

"You are insane, you know that? I'm going to tell James just in case he hasn't noticed. No one likes to run this much." Katherine grumbled and Thalia shrugged. She would much rather be doing yoga, but cardio was important as well, and even though running was one of her least favorites it was also one of the most effective. Julie had made that painfully clear during her first few days at Purgatory, and now it was just easier to keep up with it than to try and start over after a month off.

"Up to you, Katherine. I'm not twisting your arm." Thalia grinned, bouncing on her toes and stretching once more now that her muscles had met the chill. Katherine mimicked her, stretching out their calves and hamstrings before putting their arms over their heads and stretching that way. After a few dramatic stomps int he snow, Katherine finally sighed exaggeratedly.

"Alright. Let's just go."

"You sure?" Thalia teased, earning an eye roll from James' sister.

"Yes, I'm bloody sure!" Katherine bounced on her toes for a second, and then started up the snow-covered sidewalk.

The powder crunched steadily under their feet, but it wasn't very deep closer to the street. Most of the drifts were up on the expansive lawns and so it didn't slow them down much. For a while they just kept pace and Thalia counted in her head, using the impact of each foot into the snow to meter her breathing. Katherine knew how to run, taking air in slowly through her nose, then releasing it out through her mouth. Surprisingly, she kept up with Thalia pretty easily, but the other woman's longer legs probably had something to do with that.

Still, it was a beautiful morning. Clear blue sky, an endless expanse of white stretching up the large lawns on the other side of wrought iron fences.

When they took their first turn to begin the long curve back toward Katherine's house, Thalia smiled at her. "I'm glad I got to meet you. I know we're leaving in a couple of days, but I wanted you to know that I really have enjoyed being here."

"I'm glad you came to visit as well. I'm sorry I was such a bitch the first night, I really had no idea what to expect. Honestly, I wish I had believed Maggie when she said you were lovely, because you are." Katherine was pushing out short sentences while they ran, and she glanced over at her as they ruined the smooth snow with their footprints. "So, do you think you and my brother will get married?"

"What!"

"Not soon," Katherine said, waving a hand at her and rolling her eyes again. "And I'm not being pushy, I was just curious."

Thalia laughed, drawing in a deeper breath as they passed the intersection that marked the first mile. "I don't know, Katherine, and that's the truth. I know neither of us are planning on going anywhere, and that's all the commitment I'm asking for at the moment."

Katherine made a noise that expressed her opinion of that comment. "Thalia. Really? Take a note from Beyonce's playbook — if he likes it, he should put a ring on it. And I'm very aware of how much money my frugal brother has access to, so he can put a *very* nice ring on your cute little finger."

"I can't believe you just quoted Beyonce at me!" They both cackled at that, the cold air making Thalia cough as she glanced over at Katherine who had a big grin on her face, like they were sharing some secret together.

"Pop star or not, she's right."

"There is plenty of time for that," Thalia said, shaking her head as she realized that after James had agreed to stay with her, she hadn't even thought about getting married. It just wasn't a priority. She was happy with him, and he was happy with her — nothing else really mattered. "Neither of us are in a rush, and I'm really not sitting around just waiting for him to 'put a ring on it,' I swear."

"He does like it though. I can tell."

"Katherine!" Thalia felt heat in her cheeks that had nothing to do with the run.

"Oh, come on! My brother is absolutely drooling over you every time you're not looking directly at him."

Groaning under her breath, Thalia shook her head. "Oh my God, I *cannot* talk to you about this!"

"Why not? I'll tell you about Chad, and what he likes to do with his—"

"KATHERINE!" Thalia laughed and stopped running, only bouncing in place to keep her heart rate up. "You're James' sister, this is too weird."

"We're friends as well now, right?" Katherine tilted her head, grinning at her.

"Yes, of course we're friends."

"Well, *good* girl friends talk about these things. I don't want details. Please, God, do not give me details, but I guess I just want to know that you two are happy." She was grinning, but a more serious tone took over her voice as she faced her, shrugging one shoulder. "You don't know what James has been like before all this... or I guess before *you*. He used to be so stiff, so focused on business that he was almost robotic. The man making jokes and smiling at dinner is a version of my brother I haven't seen in many years. *Decades*," Katherine added.

"I think I make him happy. At least, I try to make him happy," she answered, feeling a warm glow in her chest.

"And does he make you happy too?" Katherine asked, lifting her eyebrows in a wicked expression that absolutely hinted at some things that Thalia would not be discussing with James' sister, but after a moment she relented with a roll of her eyes.

"I assure you, we are very happy. *Both* of us." Thalia was still laughing softly when Katherine looked past her to watch an SUV slowing and stopping behind them.

They both turned to see a light-haired guy get out of the driver's side, waving at them.

"Does he need help?" Katherine shielded her eyes and took a step toward the man. He was smiling at them as he shut the door and called out, leaving the car idling.

"Hi there! Sorry to bother you, do you know where Elmbrook Drive is?" He was in a thick coat, his phone held out in his gloved hands. "I swear Google maps keeps taking me to the wrong place. You live here, right?"

"I do! Let me see." Katherine held her hand out and he stepped up to them with an apologetic smile, giving her his phone so she could look at the map. The guy pushed his hands into his coat pockets and glanced back over his shoulder at the SUV.

Thalia cleared her throat aiming to fill the silence. "I'm surprised you're out in this weather, I'm sure the roads aren't easy to drive on this early." Thalia was trying to be friendly, but he seemed distracted. His eyes were glued to the SUV like he was looking for someone, except when Thalia turned she couldn't see anyone else in it. Was he worried someone was going to steal it? In this area? In all this snow?

"Roads are fine once you hit the highway," he muttered under his breath and his eyes flicked to hers, shifting from one foot to another like he was anxious to leave. Thalia looked back at the SUV and for a second it seemed like there might have been movement in between the front seats but the glare on the windshield made it hard to tell.

"Is someone else in your—" Thalia started to ask, but Katherine made a frustrated noise and talked over her.

"Wait, this isn't even my neighborhood. I don't think you're in the right place." She shrugged and held the phone back out to the guy, but he didn't move to take it.

"You weren't supposed to be here. She was supposed to be running alone," he mumbled, and Thalia's heart stuttered.

What the fuck did he just say?

"I'm sorry," he said a bit louder and alarms went off in her head.

Before Thalia could react the guy suddenly turned on her with something in his hand, and she felt a sharp pain in her side as the air crackled with electricity. Her whole body screamed with it, and she was vaguely aware of hitting the snow hard, of Katherine's shout of her name cut short by an agonized cry.

The world was a too-bright blur when Thalia tried to force her eyes open a moment later. She couldn't see anything with the sun reflecting off the snow, and her throat wouldn't work. Her muscles were ignoring her orders to get up. Get up. Get away. Get help.

What had he hit her with?

She heard the sound of running footsteps in the snow growing closer. *Help. Someone was going to help her.* Male voices above her, too quiet to understand through the buzzing in her ears. They hadn't seen a car all morning, there hadn't been a single fucking car on the road. The roads had been pristine, not even a tire track. Why had she just stood there? Why the fuck had they even talked to him?

Someone touched her, moving her hair aside, but she couldn't see. The light was too bright, and when she opened her mouth to ask for help no sound came out. A sudden piercing ache in the side of her neck was her answer.

No help. This wasn't help.

She managed to make a noise, but all she heard was a shushing against her ear, and then there was nothing as a thick gray fog filled her and dragged her under.

Down, down, down into the empty abyss of sleep.

Chapter Nineteen
THALIA

Thalia's head was pounding, and she could feel the draw toward consciousness beckoning her like warning bells — but it seemed far away. It was like she was trapped in quicksand, her brain and her body seemed too slow to respond. Unable to pull her out of the thick depths of sleep. She thought she heard a voice above her, saying her name, but it was gone, and so was she. Back under, away from the sound, down, down, down.

What had happened?

Trying to think was like trying to get a car in gear without using the clutch.

She had been running. With Katherine. Then — fuck, what had happened? An accident? She remembered a scream. Was someone hurt?

Her body rang like a gong. All the internal alarms going off at once, and she finally broke the surface of her consciousness.

She immediately regretted it.

She was nauseous. Her head felt like it was stuffed with sawdust and cotton. Her throat was dry and she tried to swallow but there was nothing there. Someone was touching her, brushing her hair out of her face. *James?* She forced her eyes open even though they felt glued shut.

Dark hair, blue-gray eyes, a serious mouth.

No. Oh God, oh God, oh God.

"Marcus?" Thalia croaked out his name and clenched her eyes shut, trying to turn her head away from his touch. Even that small movement made the pounding in her temples worse.

"Hi, Thalia." His voice. Fuck, it was actually his voice. Nightmare. Must be a nightmare.

Fear was coiling in her stomach, making the nausea worse. He cupped her cheek in his hand and she tried to swat his hand away, but her body's response had a lag and he simply ignored the weak attempt.

"Wake up. Come on, you've been asleep all day." His voice was closer, and she could sense him leaning over her. She hadn't had a nightmare like this in months, and she'd never had one where she could barely move. Thalia felt him kiss her forehead and she jerked back from him, the barest hint of motor skills returning as adrenaline started to flow. He even smelled like Marcus. How the fuck did she even remember what he smelled like? When she pried her eyes open again his expression was thunderous and she felt panic seize her chest. "Thalia." It was him. It was actually him. She shoved herself away awkwardly, which made the room spin and she thought she might be sick. That was when she realized she was on a bed. Naked. She was fucking naked, with Marcus, on a bed.

How the fuck did this happen?

Thalia whimpered, wanting to blink away the image of him sitting next to her. When he reached for her she lunged off the bed and managed to land gracelessly on a concrete floor on her knees. Her legs wouldn't obey her brain's command to stand up, and the floor seemed to be moving like ocean waves under her. She crawled forward, but she heard the bed creak as he stood up and she turned so she could see him. She couldn't take her eyes off him as she slid back on shaky arms and legs, pushing herself backward. If he wasn't going to disappear like the nightmare he was supposed to be, she needed to know where he was.

"That looked like it hurt." Marcus took a step toward her, sighing like someone might when dealing with a petulant child.

"Do—" Her voice cracked, her mouth was so dry. Why was everything so fucking hard? Her mouth, her voice, her brain, her muscles — nothing was responding right. "Don't come near me." Her throat was making every word raspy, and he ignored her and reached for her.

Adrenaline flooded her and she somehow got to her feet, swaying violently back from his hand until she stumbled backward into a wall. Her eyes scanned the room. Concrete walls, concrete floor, tiles in the ceiling.

But, there was a door.

She went for it, but he was on her as soon as her hand brushed the industrial metal. His arms wrapped tight around her and she lost it. She screamed and kicked, finally nailing his shin sharply with her heel. He grunted and then he had his hand in her hair. "Stop it! Stop it right now, Thalia. Don't make me hurt you." His voice was rough in her ear, and she felt the tears hot on her cheeks. It couldn't be Marcus, it couldn't be. Marcus was history, Marcus was just a nightmare now. One she didn't even have as often anymore. He was the bogeyman. He couldn't be real. Couldn't be here. Couldn't be touching her. His arms relaxed slightly and one of his hands trailed down her side, his face burying into her neck as he spoke, "Good girl. God, Thalia... you feel so good in my arms."

Thalia had stilled in his grip, and she could feel his bare chest against her back. He was hard, his erection pressing through his military style pants, the same ones he'd worn around her before. All pockets and black on black hardware. "Let go of me." Even with her voice cracking she put all her strength behind the demand — it came out like a plea anyway.

"I want us to talk. Will you behave?" Marcus' voice was poisoned honey. He could pretend to be nice, he'd always been good at *pretending* to be nice. But he wasn't nice, he was a psychopath. All the hours Thalia had spent talking to Ailsa flooded her, and she could feel herself rising toward panic. She needed his hands off her. He raised his voice, "Thalia! Will you behave?"

A quick nod and he let go. She stumbled forward without the support of his arms, catching herself on the wall because her legs were like Bambi's, unsteady and wobbling.

"The drugs should be wearing off soon. Can we sit down? You're not good enough to stand yet." Marcus was gesturing toward the bed like some gracious fucking host.

"You drugged me?" Thalia crossed her arms over her chest, pressing her thighs together to try and hide herself. She tried to remember what had happened, but it was blank. Nothing after the steady crunch of frost as they ran, the early morning light bouncing off the snow — there was nothing. Disbelief shook her, tears stinging her eyes as her situation began to sink in. "You fucking kidnapped me? Again?!"

"Thalia." He said her name and she pushed a hand into her hair, clenching her fist as she tried to maintain control over the horrible tide of panic inside her. She started shaking her head, tears streaking her cheeks as he sighed from a few steps away.

"Oh my God! What the FUCK, Marcus?!" She screeched the words at him, glancing at him before the sight of him became too much. His dark hair was longer now. Messy. He looked thinner, but it made the sharp contours of his muscles stand out in relief. Her memory of what he looked like had blurred over time and she hated that he was still so fucking attractive. It was a mask. The worst kind of mask that hid the truth of who he was, that made people look at him differently. The mask that had made *her* trust him, to not think twice those times he had walked her to her car at work. Nausea washed over her again and she felt faint for a second.

"You're going to hurt yourself trying to walk around. Come sit down and we will talk." Marcus continued pointing at the bed, and when Thalia didn't move she watched his anger spike and then recede as he took a deep, slow breath.

"We're not talking. We're not doing anything. Let me go, Marcus. Right now. Let me out of here." Thalia looked at the door again, the gears in her brain slowly coming online.

"No. Now come over—"

"LET ME OUT, MARCUS!" Thalia screamed and Marcus was suddenly in her face. His fists tight at his sides as he gritted his teeth. She flinched, expecting him to hit her, but it didn't come. He dropped his eyes from her and she could see him holding himself back. It was almost scarier than him actually touching her.

"It's okay, Thalia. I get it. I know you'll take some time to adjust, but that's fine. You're back with me now, and everything is going to be fine." He was crazy. Marcus was fucking crazy. Thalia felt a hysterical whimper rise in her chest as she looked at him again.

"Everything is not fine, and it's not going to be fine, Marcus. Take me back! I don't know what sick fucking fantasy you have about this but I am not going to be—" He backhanded her mid-rant and pain burst in white light across her cheekbone.

There was a beat of silence and then Marcus shouted, "FUCK. God dammit, Thalia! Stop it, just stop *pushing* me!" His voice was razor edged, and she took a few shaky steps back from him. Taking a deep breath, she held onto her strength through her wobbling legs and her fuzzy head, she wasn't going to cry even though it hurt. She wasn't that weak, terrified girl that Marcus had ripped out of a stairwell. He was standing a few feet away from her, rubbing his hands over his face, "Look, I'm sorry, I didn't mean to hit you, Thalia. You just have to stop pushing me. Please come sit down so you don't fall over."

"I don't want to sit down. Just take me back, Marcus. Please. I have a life! I have a *life*, a good life, you can't do this to me again! You got what you wanted, he paid you for me, I'm not yours to—" Thalia was trying to speak calmly, to reach some logical side of him, but it didn't work. He slammed his fist into the door and she jumped, pressing herself into the corner as he growled and paced back toward the metal framed bed — the only piece of furniture in the small room.

"God dammit! I love you, Thalia, can't you fucking see that? I've been miserable without you. I should have never let you go. I should have never let Anthony even arrange the fucking party!" He let out a yell of frustration and looked at her with a tormented expression. If it had been anyone else on the planet she might have felt something like pity, or concern, but it wasn't possible with him.

"This isn't love, Marcus." She shook her head slowly, speaking quietly as if it could keep his rage in check.

"This *is* love. This is the kind of love that asshole could never show you. I would give you *anything*, Thalia. I can make you happy, I can." Marcus groaned, taking a half-step toward her before he stopped himself.

"Then give me my freedom." Thalia pointed at the door, "Let me go. You want to prove you love me? Then let me out of here."

"I can't give you that! Anything else, ask me for anything else. But you have to remember — I need you to remember what we had. If you'll just fucking remember you'll understand! I need you to fucking understand!" Marcus was bordering on hysteria when he finally stopped talking, his arms held wide like what he was saying was an obvious fact.

There was no brimming realization inside her, no sudden discovery at being in his presence. How could he even expect those things? There was only anger simmering inside her. This was unfair. No. More than unfair, this was evil. What could she have possibly done to deserve this? Just as her life was falling in to place, her whole world rounding out with James, and friends, and a great job, and a future — for the universe to let Marcus find her? In fucking New York? On the other side of the fucking country from where he'd kept her? She felt cursed.

"Please, just try to remember, to understand why we're meant for each other." Marcus' voice was a quiet rumble, and she snapped.

"THERE'S NOTHING TO UNDERSTAND MARCUS!" She slid down the wall, choking back the urge to sob. "Don't you see that? Don't you see that there is no happy ending?! People like you don't get a happy ending! You don't!"

"We can have one if you'll just fucking listen to me!" He shouted at her.

"I don't want to listen to you! I don't want to even look at you! I want to go home to James, dammit! I love HIM! I am never going to fucking love you, Marcus!" The second the words were out of her mouth she knew she'd gone too far. He was across the space between them in an instant, dragging her up from the floor to slam her back against the wall.

"Shut up, Thalia!" His fingers wrapped around her throat and squeezed. She dug her nails into his wrists as panic squeezed her rapidly emptying lungs. "You are MINE and you're ruining *everything*." Marcus shouted inches from her face, his fingers were bruising her throat as he pulled her forward and slammed her head back hard enough to make lights flash behind her eyes. He was angry, that was obvious, but the strange tone in his voice could have been some other desperate emotion.

She didn't care.

Thalia felt her nails break skin, and she pressed harder. This time she wasn't afraid to fight him, but her vision was fuzzing on the edges, spots dancing. He growled and released her throat, breaking her grip on his wrists with no effort. She immediately tried to shove him back, coughing on her breaths as she moved to bring her knee up between his legs, but he was quick and her movements were still sluggish. In an instant she was flipped chest first against the wall, her bare skin chilled by the concrete. She tried to push back from the wall but he wouldn't let her. His hands pinned her wrists painfully above her head and he pressed himself against her, his weight holding her there.

The reminder of the first time he'd hurt her in the stairwell wasn't lost on her as she screamed in frustration. Hating herself for her weakness, for the complete uselessness of her fight. He growled and started shouting in her ear.

"All I wanted was to talk, Thalia! Just to fucking talk, but you don't even have the courtesy to give me that. Even after all I did to get you back! After the money I've spent, the time I've spent so that I wouldn't lose you. I never gave up, Thalia, not in all this time! Not on what we could be." His mouth was against her neck, and he inhaled deeply against her hair.

Was he seriously smelling her? A shudder moved through her and she tugged hard against his grip on her wrists but he only squeezed them harder.

With a groan he yelled at her again. "Why are you fighting me?! We had something, something real. We did. Why won't you just admit it?!" He took a shaky breath as if forcing himself to calm down. "It's okay, I'm just going to have to remind you of why we were perfect together, of why you need me." Marcus' voice rumbled in her ear and she pressed her thighs together as she felt his knee trying to push her legs apart.

"I do not need you, Marcus! I'm never going to need you! I'm NOT yours!" She spat out the words, even as a sour fear filled her stomach.

He grabbed her hair and dragged her back from the wall, her weak legs stumbling. "Yes. You are and you do, Thalia. You just need a reminder." Marcus pulled her toward the bed and fear washed over her like an ice bath.

"Don't! PLEASE! Don't do this, Marcus!" She shoved at his chest as he pushed her onto the bed, and he shushed her. He leaned over her and she tried to slap him but he caught her wrist easily. Too fast she was pinned beneath him, her wrists gathered above her head as he held her thighs apart by digging his knees in. She could feel his weight bruising her as he worked at his pants.

"You need me. You always did. I showed you what you liked. I was the only one who knew what you liked, and I can remind you again. Just relax, stop fighting me, and you'll see what I mean. You'll understand." Marcus kept one hand on her wrists as he shifted his pants down his hips.

She released a frustrated scream, before babbling, "Please! *Please*, don't do this. You don't have to do this, we can talk. We can fucking talk! I'll talk to you! I'll talk to you about anything, just please…" Thalia was begging, arching her back to try and free her hands. Her thighs were aching from the pressure of his weight on them, his knees pushing them wider until tears choked her.

"Shh, it's okay. You'll remember what we have. Stop fighting so hard." Marcus was insane. He pushed his boxers out of the way and she watched his cock spring up between them. Panic grabbed her — she couldn't let this happen, not again.

"NO! No, Marcus, no!" she screamed, shaking her head before she forced her eyes above her to the metal bars at the head of the bed. His fingers swept up her cleft and she was relieved that she wasn't wet. It didn't deter him though, he forced a finger inside her and she whimpered, biting her lip hard.

"I know the drugs are messing with you, Thalia. It's okay…" He sounded like he was talking to someone else, someone not begging him to stop, someone not fighting him. His thumb rolled over her clit and her hips bucked involuntarily as he plucked the bundle of nerves. After a few minutes she could feel the wetness gathering, his shallow thrusts joined by a second finger as he brushed kisses across her shoulder.

"Don't do this. Please don't do this. Dammit, I'm begging you!" Thalia's voice was weak as her body betrayed her. Ailsa had told her over and over that it was biology, well, *fuck biology*.

"That's it, Thalia," he groaned above her as he slid his fingers in deep a few times, her pussy responding regardless of her pleas. The heat was a distant sensation inside her, the tension of his tight circles on her clit pushed away from her mind. Finally, he removed his fingers and she sighed in relief for a moment until she saw him slip them into his mouth and groan. "I have missed you so much," he whispered, and Thalia tried to twist away when she felt him lower his hips, but he held her thighs open for him.

"No, no, no, Marcus—" She whimpered as he thrust inside her. It hurt, and his moan above her made her stomach flip. He drew back and pushed forward further, and she felt the tears slipping out, pooling at her temples as they found her hair.

How had he even found her? It had been almost a year. Why did he even still care? How could this even be happening?

He thrust hard, and her hips twitched with the urge to respond. "God, Thalia, you're perfect." He dropped his weight over her, hips swinging back and slamming forward hard enough to rock the bed against the wall behind her. He stretched her, filled her, and her body betrayed her because it wanted more. Her body reacted to being restrained, to the heavy weight above her, to the hard cock inside her, and the ache in her thighs and her wrists. She had to stop this. But she couldn't move, his fingers were digging painfully into her wrists to hold them down, and each thrust was a dangerous ember inside her, looking for the first opportunity to catch fire.

"Please stop," she whispered against his shoulder. Thalia wasn't even sure he could hear her over his grunts, the sound of his hips slamming into hers, the rocking creak of the bed. His body weight shifted and so did his angle, and when he slammed forward again he brushed against that bundle of nerves inside her that made her gasp and silence a moan. She gritted her teeth.

Like hell was she going to moan for him.

"Come on, you're going to come for me. You always come for me." He repeated that thrust and her back arched as she fought to change the angle back.

"No! I won't! I won't, just stop!" She hated how pathetic she sounded, her voice breaking as she really started crying. Because heat was coiling in her lower belly, her spine tightening as he slammed into her, forcing pleasure from her as his strength worked against her.

"I know you. You will." Marcus bit down on her shoulder and she cried out, a moan slipping out as he chose that moment to thrust hard again. Heat flooded her cheeks, because he was right. Her hips were subtly rocking to meet his as much as she tried to hold still, and each brush of his cock inside her was winding her tighter.

"No, no, no, no, no..." Thalia babbled as she tried to push back the orgasm, tried to breathe through it. To let the inklings of pleasure pass by, but her body was tense and just when she thought she'd be okay the pressure in her spine snapped and she locked up as she came. A flash of bliss, whiting out all the horror for a second, but then he chuckled in her ear and the gasping flood of pleasure fizzled fast.

She hated herself.

Weak. Fucking weak.

Marcus nuzzled into her neck, burying his face against her, pressing kisses to her skin. "I knew your body missed me. I just had to remind you of *this*, of what we had together."

She couldn't even respond as he picked up his pace, she was whimpering and he didn't even seem to notice. His grunts as he thrust hard grew rapid until he suddenly stilled and she felt his cock kick deep inside her. The warmth of his seed pulsing as his weight dropped over her.

He breathed her name and it shook her to her core. His breath hammering out by her ear.

"Get off me," Thalia mumbled, licking her lips to try and get her voice back. As his grip on her relaxed she pulled her arms down and shoved at his shoulders. Panic threaded her voice as his weight on her quickly became suffocating and terrible. "Get off me, Marcus! Get off me! GET. OFF. ME."

Marcus growled against her skin and his hand was suddenly around her throat again, tightening until she couldn't breathe. She twisted, grabbing onto his fingers to try and pry them away. "What the fuck did you say?" He relaxed his grip and she gasped for air, trying to push him off as he slid from her.

"I said — GET OFF ME, MARCUS!" she screamed as loud as her voice would make it. He growled and sat up between her legs and slapped her hard across the face. The pain shocked her, and she was crying again, trying to shield herself.

"Dammit, Thalia! You ungrateful cunt! Why won't you just behave?! Why won't you just BE with me?!" he shouted down at her. Twisting at the waist he dug in a pocket of his pants and pulled out handcuffs. Before she could react, he had one wrist trapped and was pushing her back on the bed while she screamed for him to stop. He looped the cuffs through a bar at the head of the bed and forced her other hand back until he could cuff it as well. "I've been so fucking patient with you. I let you sleep. I've let you use my name, and I have NEVER given you permission to use it. Now you're *telling* me what to do? That rich boy ruined all my work with you. He screwed with your head! You were perfect!"

Thalia was shaking, and when she tugged on the cuffs it only hurt. There was no way she was getting out of them.

"I'm obviously going to have to remind you of the consequences of being disobedient. I wanted things to be different for us, but YOU won't let them be. No, I have to get you in line again first… remind you of the rules." Marcus leaned over her, holding her face so her gaze met his, his eyes looking at her with some insane version of affection and concern. "Then we can build a relationship. Then we can be together. We just have to reestablish what you can and can't do. You'll be grateful."

He slid off the bed with one more touch down her thigh and tugged his pants back on. Standing over her for a moment as she twisted onto her side and scooted back as far as the cuffs allowed. Marcus cracked the knuckles on one hand as he watched her curl up, and then he suddenly turned and left the room.

Chapter Twenty
THALIA

Thalia started sobbing the second the door shut, jerking on the cuffs and turning farther to her side trying to curl up into a ball. She couldn't believe any of this had happened. Part of her kept waiting to wake up screaming and crying next to James, and then James would turn on the light and hold his arms out, never touching her first, but being there for her. Always there to wipe away the memory of Marcus' hands on her.

This wasn't just some memory though, and she had no idea where she was, and she really doubted he planned on letting her go this time. Her chest ached at the idea that she might never see James again, that he'd never be able to calm her down and tell her he loved her ever again. No more midnight snacks sitting at the kitchen island, waiting for her to calm down enough to sleep. And James never complained, even if he had work in the morning. He just held her, comforted her until the nightmare faded.

The door opened and slammed, the loud boom of it making Thalia jump. Marcus was looming near the door, tension etching the outline of him. There was a belt clamped in his fist.

Shit.

Thalia whimpered, shaking her head. "Please don't, please—"

"Quiet, Thalia. If you would have just been good, if you would just *behave* I wouldn't have to do this. It could be so different, it *will* be, you'll see. But I have to teach you a lesson first, I have to remind you of the rules or this won't work." Marcus walked toward her and she jerked hard on the cuffs, trying to push as far away from the edge of the bed as possible. He grabbed her thigh when he got to her and easily flipped her to her stomach, the cuffs painfully twisting as they crossed.

Her mouth opened to beg him not to, but he brought the belt down hard and the burst of pain stole the air from her lungs. His anger snapped through each lash. Five, six, seven strokes of the belt and she was sobbing again, screaming for him to stop, her skin on fire as he paused.

"What are you supposed to call me, Thalia?!" he shouted down at her, but she shook her head. *No.* She wouldn't do that. James was her Master, she had chosen James. Marcus had never earned that, he had stolen it, forced it. He growled above her and another flurry of lashes slashed down her ass and across the sensitive skin of her thighs.

Her fists clenched tight as she tried to breathe through the pain, to separate from it. Another too hard lash. A scream ripped out of her as the pain built into an inescapable wave that threatened to drown her. She'd never been hit this hard with a belt, Marcus was punishing out of anger. Never supposed to punish out of anger, but he didn't care. His entire twisted view of being her Master was wrong. Another lash had her screaming again, burying her face in her arms.

"THALIA! Say it! Tell me what you're supposed to call me!" Marcus shouted down at her and she tried to shift away from him. The belt striped across her lower back, and he growled and dragged her back toward him by her thigh. His fist wrenched into her hair and yanked her up, the strain on her throat making it impossible to swallow and hard to breathe. "Say it. Say it, Thalia!"

"NO!" Thalia screamed and he released her hair with a snort of disgust.

"I can't believe you let that asshole poison you against me! I showed you everything! ME!" He brought the belt down hard again and she yelped, her body trembling with fear and pain and probably a good amount of shock.

"You fucking raped me, Marcus! This isn't a god damn relationship!" she shouted into the mattress, preparing for more violence. Instead, he was still.

"I only had to force you the first time, Thalia, just so you would learn. And you came for me, you enjoyed it."

Thalia found herself laughing, and her tears stopped in the insanity of it. Maybe she was losing it, but on the other side of terror she found a kind of giddy relief that he wanted her to want him so badly. It didn't matter that her backside felt like a brutal web of fiery welts and deep, aching bruises. If he was so focused on her wanting him, on them being *together*, then he probably wouldn't kill her, or sell her to someone else, or some foreign hellhole. Those had been her fears the last time he had her, and they didn't even seem possible now. And if he kept her here, if he kept her alive, she had a chance to be found. Her laughter wound down and she spat out the next words. "You're fucking insane."

She jumped when she heard the belt clatter against the wall, his voice booming above her. "I'm the only one who knows what you really need, Thalia! The ONLY one. But I can wait, I can give you some time to think about how you want to speak to me." He walked away from her toward the door and she felt her body relax slightly. "In the mean time I'll just go talk with Katherine, see if she's more well-behaved than you've been."

Katherine. *Fuck. No.* He had Katherine too?

"She's not involved in this! You want me, not her!" Thalia turned so she could see him by the door.

"True, but making James' little sister call me Master? Making her beg for mercy? That's worth my time." He opened the door and slammed it behind him as he stormed out.

"NO! GOD DAMMIT! COME BACK!" Thalia screamed and felt the tears on her cheeks again. This was all her fault, all of it. Katherine wouldn't even be here if it wasn't for her.

The screams had lasted a while. She could hear them through the concrete walls, through the ceiling. Each time another had ripped through the space, Thalia had shuddered.

All my fault. All my fault.

When Katherine had finally stopped screaming, Thalia had tensed. Waiting for Marcus to return and gloat, threaten her, hurt her again — but there was only silence. It stretched and frayed her nerves. Guilt had settled like a stone in her stomach. How could she ever look Katherine in the eye again? Or James? Knowing her defiance had caused Marcus to hurt her? The realization that Katherine could be handcuffed and in pain like her, that he might have touched Katherine because of his obsession with her — it had Thalia crying again. The tears hollowing out the anger and defiance that had fueled her when he'd been in the room with her. At some point the pain and the guilt dragged her under, and she slept.

In her dreams she was back in the Conservatorium Hotel in Amsterdam. James had taken her there for a celebration weekend just a few weeks after The Decision. Her yoga studio was being built out and he had claimed they needed a vacation before her new job absorbed her. Everything about the trip had been unbelievable luxury. He'd borrowed his company's private jet and put them up in that gorgeous hotel that was such a magical mix of the old and the ultra-modern. Then he had taken her out to a dance club.

James could ballroom dance like Prince Charming because he'd been taught to, but his body definitely knew how to move in a club. Women had been staring her down all night, but he'd only had eyes for her, and they had danced until they were both drenched in sweat and their ears were ringing from the music. By the time they were back at the hotel, in the wee hours of the morning, they were both drunk, laughing, and half-taking each other's clothes off in the elevator. When they stumbled into their room, James had his hands behind her head, holding her lips in an urgent kiss. He'd mumbled into the kiss, "I want to fuck you."

A grin spread across her mouth, "I *need* you to fuck me after all that teasing on the dance floor." James was moving her backward toward the bed, alternately shedding items of his own clothing, and tugging at hers.

"You *were* teasing me quite a bit." His voice was a low purr as he watched her dress drop to the floor, and his hands tugged her panties down.

"Me? I wasn't the one sneaking a hand up my skirt!" Thalia laughed and he lifted her up against his chest, her legs wrapping around him as he walked them the rest of the way to the bed.

"You want to argue with me right now, pet?" He dropped her onto the bed but followed, climbing on top of her and keeping his body between her legs. Thalia groaned and rolled her hips, his cock brushing her soaking pussy lips to tease her need even further.

"No, I don't want to argue, I want you to fuck me! Please!" Thalia grabbed his shoulders and tried to pull him down on top of her, lifting her hips to stroke his cock against her. His low laugh rumbled into her neck before his hands ran up her arms and drew her wrists above her head, pinning them in place with one hand. His other hand slid between them, the first stroke of his fingers across her clit made her jump against him. "Please, baby! James, please, please, don't tease me!"

"James, hmm? Normally you call me Master when I have you like this." His voice hummed against the skin of her neck before he nipped the place above her collarbone. His fingers slid slowly inside her, stroking until she was crying out with each curve of his fingers.

"Oh God, Master, please, I'll say anything, I'll do anything, just *please* fuck me." Her voice was a whimper of need, and he pressed her harder into the bed as he kissed her. His tongue moved against hers and she felt the rumble of his groan as he lined up and thrust hard inside her. The kiss broke as they both moaned their relief at finally feeling the other. Thalia arched off the bed, her heels wrapping behind his ass to pull him harder into her, but he kept her wrists pinned. His mouth tracing bites and kisses along her skin, across her breasts, tormenting her nipples as he drove himself hard inside her over and over.

When they came it was bliss, the anxious tension finally relieved in her body and she whispered against his shoulder as he leaned over her, "I love you, James. I love you so much, so fucking much. Jesus..."

"I love you too, baby. You're perfect, even with the language that comes out of that mouth of yours, bloody perfect." He was smiling playfully, and then his lips were on hers again.

It was a perfect memory. Safe, and warm, and loving — and the polar opposite of her reality. It was a gift from her subconscious, and she wanted to stay in that luxurious bed in her memories. She wanted to stay wrapped in the arms of the man she loved, who loved her, and never wake up again.

Chapter Twenty-One
JAMES

"That's the most recent picture I have of her. It's a selfie she took with her friend Analiese back in London. She's the one with the light brown hair." James handed his phone over to the hired gun in front of him, his eyes not wanting to leave the photo on the phone.

Thalia's hair was catching the light, an incredibly bright smile on her face as she pressed her cheek to Analiese's. The two of them had done yoga in the morning, and then spent hours at brunch drinking mimosas and catching up. Thalia had sent him the picture to tell him she wouldn't be home for lunch, and he'd ended up sending a car for each of them as they'd had far too much to drink to trust them getting into, and directing, a taxi back to Analiese's hotel or their flat.

She had been so happy when she'd come home, babbling about their plans for the weekend, a trip in the summer where she wanted to meet up with Nick and Analiese. It had been so normal, and she was vibrant and alive and confident and so fucking sexy. He'd dragged her to bed as soon as she'd stopped chatting away, and he'd kept her mouth busy in other ways.

The reminder of her absence as the man took the phone from his hand felt like a knife to the gut.

"She's very pretty, it's a nice picture, but we already have a picture, Dr. Hawkins." The man was all business. What was his name again? The whole day had been a nightmare. The realization that Katherine and Thalia hadn't returned from running, the panicked search, the heavy realization that there was only one realistic reason for someone to attack them. He'd barely slept waiting for this man and his team to show up.

"I need you to find them. You have to get Thalia away from Marcus." James felt the dark hole in his stomach expand, filling him with anger and a bitter cold that was better than the helpless pain he'd felt all day and night.

"Sir, we don't even know if this Marcus person has her. The best way to tackle this is, unfortunately, to wait for the ransom demands. Then we have something to work with." Jake sighed and set James' phone on the edge of the desk he was using in the library. *That was his name — Jake.* "It's very likely he hasn't even done anything yet, a lot of times the people who kidnap high income targets are too afraid to—"

"It's too late for that. I need you to find them and get Thalia away from him as soon as possible. I don't care what it costs, or what you have to do. Just do it." James looked up and he saw the flash of exasperation on Jake's face before he masked it. His hands clenched into fists as he tried to control his temper — there was no use lashing out at the only person who could help him.

"Dr. Hawkins, I promise I know what I'm doing. You contacted me and my team because you know our reputation. We recover victims of kidnapping with a much higher success rate than the police, and I also know how these guys work. They're not going to damage the girl when they can still get a payday." Jake ran a hand behind his neck, obviously doing his best to sound comforting, but the man didn't know who he was dealing with. What kind of monster he was dealing with.

"It's already too late for that, and I already told you he won't ask for a ransom. He has more than enough money," James grumbled, feeling his temper rise up through the chill that had filled him. He had to stay numb, cold; this had to be business.

Because if he let himself feel anything he was going to lose it.

"You don't know that—"

James slammed his fist down on the desk, and the man's eyes widened. It brought him some small satisfaction to see the surprise on Jake's face that James usually caught across a negotiating table. James knew what the fuck he was doing, and he wished he didn't know *exactly* what Marcus had already done to Thalia. Instead of arguing with Jake, James just flipped his laptop open where the email he'd received was still waiting.

The email had been run through a hundred proxy servers across the globe, the return email was gibberish, there was no note, just the goddamn audio file. James clicked it and walked away from the desk. He fought the urge to cover his ears or scream and throw something like he had when he'd first heard it.

Thalia's voice bled out of the speakers, at first begging the bastard not to do it. Then *his* voice responding, her whimpers, the sound of a bed creaking as she struggled, his groan and her gasp when he started. The audio devolved into her crying, her pleading, mixed with his low moans, his twisted words.

Jake closed the lid of the laptop.

"It's not done. There's more." James felt hollow when he crossed his arms over his chest and turned to face the man who supposedly knew more about this than he did.

"Is this the only one you've received?" To be fair, Jake did seem shaken. He'd probably thought this was some money-fueled snatch and grab out of Katherine's million-dollar neighborhood. His expression told James he understood better now.

"Yes. It's the only one." *Cold. Stay cold, James.*

"And you're sure that's—"

"Thalia." Her name was like razor blades in his mouth. "And yes. I know what she sounds like." James let the weight of that comment sink in with Jake the mercenary.

For enough money you could buy just about anything. Cars. Buildings. People. Even teams of mercenaries to get the girl back who you bought from a psychopath and his sadistic brother when the same psychopath kidnapped her. Again.

"We'll move fast." The look in Jake's eyes told him that he might finally have a clue about what the fuck was happening here.

"You need to," James answered quietly. "I know her. She's going to fight him just like she fought him before. She's going to fight him because she's strong, and because she knows I was proud of how hard she fought him last time. And… and because she knows how much I hate him. She won't submit."

Panic was a dim presence somewhere in his mind, somewhere under the cold reason he needed to function. He forced the echoes of the audio and the flickering images from her first time with Marcus out of his mind, bringing his stare back to Jake.

"Money is not an issue. Understand? Fucking find them." James felt the earlier rage, the earlier agony threatening to rise up inside him again. He couldn't lose it right now. He had to find them, and when he did he was going to bury Marcus alive and stand on top of the fresh dirt until he heard the screaming stop.

Chapter Twenty-Two
THALIA

The door opening woke Thalia and filled her with dread, but as she pulled herself back to consciousness her body was too weak to react much. At least the fuzzy feeling of cotton in her head had faded, but her mouth was drier than ever, and her stomach ached with hunger. She'd forgotten that he only fed her when he was happy with her. Marcus walked toward her, the padding of his bare feet on the concrete drawing closer. "Thalia, I'm going to uncuff you. Don't do anything stupid."

He reached over her and with a ratcheting sound of metal her bruised wrists were free. She pushed herself up, drawing her legs close as she moved to the corner of the bed against the wall. The welts on her backside screamed at the contact, but she stayed against it. His eyes slid over her exposed skin, and she dug her nails into her arms to fight the urge to put more space between them, to burrow into the goddamn wall.

"Here. I'm sure you're thirsty." Marcus leaned down and picked up a plastic cup of water. He held it out to her. Her dry mouth screamed at her to take it, but she couldn't. He could have done any number of things to it. "Thalia. Take it."

"I'm fine." She tried to pull her legs tighter to her chest.

"I know the side effects of what I gave you. You need water, drink it and we can talk." His voice was level, and she wasn't sure how many hours had passed since he had left the room but his temper had cooled. How long had she been missing? "Don't make me force you."

She flinched and reached out to take the cup, her fingers brushed his and she jerked the cup back so quickly it spilled over the edge. The first sip was incredible, and in a moment she had drained the cup. Tainted or not, at least her throat didn't feel like sandpaper anymore.

"Good girl. I want to talk with you, can you behave?" His blue-gray eyes bored into her, and she reluctantly nodded. "I need you to accept that no one is going to find you here. You're *mine*. I went to a lot of trouble to get you back from him, and I *am* your Master."

"No." Thalia denied it on a whisper, and she flinched in preparation for him to hurt her. He growled instead.

"Thalia, just fucking behave! Do I need to teach you another lesson? Would you rather I have this talk with Katherine?" The mention of Katherine's name was like barbwire scratching her insides.

"Jesus! You have me here, isn't that enough?!" Thalia looked up at him and she saw him struggling with his temper, but he took a slow breath.

"I do have you here, and I'm not letting you go. It will take me a bit to get another house set up, but we can live anywhere you want. I know you like the west coast, do you want to move there? Do you want to live in Nevada again? I remember you were born there." He sat on the edge of the bed, leaving a few feet between them.

"I want to go home." She bit her lip and looked away from him.

He growled. "Stop saying that."

"I WANT TO GO HOME," she screamed, and he stood up and paced away from her. His frustration with her visible in the tension of his back, the way he shoved his hands into his hair to grip it at the roots. When he turned back to her she dug her nails into her arm to suppress the urge to scream at him again.

"Get off the bed. Get on your knees, Thalia." He moved next to the bed and she gritted her teeth against the urge to cry. For a moment she thought about just refusing, knowing he'd drag her off the bed if he had to. He popped the knuckles on one of his hands and she relented, scooting forward on the bed in tiny movements until her feet could touch the floor. He pointed at the floor where he wanted her and she slid into a kneel, the bruises on her knees lighting up. It created such strong flashbacks to the first time he'd had her that her heart rate doubled in an instant.

"Let me make your situation very clear, because nothing else is working. You have two options." He held up two fingers to make his point as he towered over her. "You can be respectful and obedient, and we can be together like we were supposed to be, and you *know* that I can make you enjoy it. I can make you happy."

She wanted to shake her head, but instead she just looked away from him. Not sure if she could handle another outburst of his rage. He continued talking, his voice infinitely colder.

"Or, you can continue to be an ungrateful little slut and I will still have you, I will still keep you, but I'll start your training over. I'll break you. And you'll still call me Master eventually. You'll still beg for me. So, what do you want to do, Thalia?"

Her heart sank. She knew that Marcus was serious, he'd never let her go willingly, and he'd already proven he still didn't care if he hurt her or not. She was ruined either way, but she wasn't the only one involved. Thalia forced herself to speak, "If—if I obey you, will you let Katherine go?"

"Why would I do that?" Marcus tilted his head as he looked down at her. She almost raised her eyes to his but caught herself.

Yes, she remembered his rules.

"Please..." She took a breath and swallowed her pride and any trace of hope inside her, and she called him what he wanted. "Master, please let Katherine go. You can send her back to James, you can have her tell him not to look for me, to leave me behind, whatever you want. I'll write a letter to him if that's what you want, just let Katherine go, don't hurt her again."

"That's right. You do like to write letters, don't you? Or, wait, would you rather send him an email?" His hand gripped her chin painfully, and he snapped her neck back so she looked up at him. "Yeah, I got your little email months ago. You used my name, told me to leave you alone." His fingers dug into her skin, and she winced. "But you're mine. Always have been. I found you, you were meant for me. Just me." He held her gaze for a moment and then he released her.

Thalia took a shuddering breath. She could survive Marcus. She had before, and she was better prepared now. Katherine? Pampered, spoiled, ridiculous Katherine? She was pretty sure she wouldn't recover. "Please. Let Katherine go and I'll tell James that. I'll tell him I'm—" She swallowed over the urge to throw up the water. "—yours."

"I'll think about it." Marcus glared down at her. "Let's see if you can behave first." He paced away from her, pushing both of his hands through his hair as he walked back and forth.

Like a caged animal, wild and unpredictable. *Dangerous.*

He let out a bitter laugh and faced her again. "You're just so ungrateful! Did you forget everything? I fucking protected you from Anthony! You don't even *know* what I protected you from. If you had seen what he did to other girls, girls just like you, you'd be begging at my feet to stay with me. You'd be thanking me on your fucking knees. You think Anthony controlling the chair long-distance was bad? It was *nothing*. And the only reason I let him do that was because you tried to fucking run! You broke my fucking door with a mixer!" His temper spiked, but he laughed again and walked back and forth across the other end of the room.

Thalia had her fists clenched in her lap, wishing she could disappear into the floor, or faint, or *anything* to not have to listen to him anymore. Could she will herself to pass out?

"You don't know what Anthony would have done to you. You have no *idea*, Thalia. He liked to suspend girls from the ceiling, have them bound so tight they couldn't move, and then he'd whip them, flog them, shock them with that electricity shit. Just to see how long they could take it before they blacked out. And, fuck, if you had seen Beth?" He laughed to himself and grabbed his hair again.

Thalia's head was spinning as she tried to process the words. Anthony had always terrified her more than Marcus, at least now she knew why. Anthony was a vicious sadist, a real monster, but Marcus wasn't far behind him. "Beth?" she whispered, simultaneously curious and afraid of his answer.

Marcus faced her. "Beth was the last girl Anthony and I trained together. She was this tiny little bronze skinned blonde. We grabbed her when we were working in California. I picked her, of course, I knew she was what the customers wanted, but she was feisty. Had a mouth on her just like you, but she fought a lot harder than you." Thalia felt herself bristle at the strange insult. Hadn't she been the only one to break the door? Hadn't she tried to run? Hadn't she fought him? Refused him? Left with James even when he commanded her not to?

And Beth had fought *harder* than her?

"We had her two weeks and she was still spitting at Anthony, calling him every name under the sun except Master."

Thalia couldn't breathe as Marcus walked toward her, towering over her as she imagined the girl fighting back against someone as terrifying as Anthony. Whoever Beth was, she was brave.

Marcus continued, "Anthony wouldn't let me take over, he wanted to be the one to break her. And so you know what Anthony did to her? After he did all his normal stuff? After he tied her down all day and all night with a blindfold and ear plugs so she went through sensory deprivation?"

She felt sick, shaking her head against the idea of Anthony's hands on that girl, of what he'd done. She didn't want to hear the rest of the story, she didn't want to hear what he'd already said. All she wanted was to curl into a ball and go back to the dream of her and James in the hotel. Even more, she wanted this to be some Inception-level bullshit and she'd wake up, in James' bed, and all of this would be a horrendous multi-layered nightmare.

Marcus grabbed her hair and bent her head back, snapping her eyes to him, hissing his next words at her. "He waterboarded her, Thalia. You know what that is?"

She knew, but she couldn't speak. She was crying again, horrified beyond words as he continued without her response.

"Anthony tied Beth down, covered her face with cloth and poured water over it so she felt like she was drowning. We used that shit on enemy combatants and they cracked easier! And each time he took the towel away he'd ask her how she should address him, but she never answered. She started off cussing at him… brave little bitch." He laughed. He actually laughed. Thalia's stomach dropped.

"Please stop. I don't want to hear—"

"*I* tried to get him to stop, I did, she was just screaming and crying, wasn't even begging him to stop anymore, but he wanted to hear her call him Master — and she wouldn't. So, Anthony didn't stop until she stopped screaming completely. Until all she did was cough out the water and gasp for air and stare. He's never liked it when they stop reacting." Marcus' eyes burned into hers, his intensity scaring her in a new way.

Thalia was crying, trying to turn away from him, but he just fisted her hair tighter. They were both evil. Both of them. Just different levels of hell. That girl. That poor girl. *They'd hurt so many girls.* "Please stop," she begged, but he kept talking.

"He didn't just break her, Thalia, he fucking shattered her. She was gone. Nothing he did after that got a reaction. She was empty, hollow. And he wanted to do that to you, he *told* me that he wanted to do that to you."

Thalia choked on a sob. Marcus terrified her, Anthony terrified her. The idea that Anthony had wanted to hurt her like that made her sick. Marcus' false protection was no better, but there wasn't enough in her stomach to even throw up.

"But I didn't let him do that, Thalia. I kept him away from you because he wanted to shatter you, just so that I wouldn't want to keep you. He wanted to destroy you because he knew we were meant to be together, and he wanted me to run his fucking business! And do you know why?!" he shouted, and she shook as her adrenaline urged her to run. Run, get away from him, flee — but there was nowhere to go.

"No, I don't," she mumbled, trying to avoid his blue-gray eyes.

He shook her by his grip in her hair. "Because, after Beth, no one trusted Anthony. We lost so many customers because it was obvious that she hadn't submitted. Was *never* going to submit. That's why I took over, because *all* of you submit to me in time. It just takes some convincing, it takes a firm hand and a knowledge of what you sluts need, and you..." Marcus laughed low and let go of her hair so her head dropped. "You didn't take much convincing at all."

Shame washed over her. She *had* fought, dammit! She had fought until he beat, and terrified her, and turned her over to Anthony. And she had fucking survived it! Ailsa had told her THAT was what was important! She wiped her cheeks, glaring up at him. "You *asshole*, you fucking asshole! I can't believe you'd—"

Marcus sharply cut her off. "I didn't do that to Beth, Anthony did."

"You were there, you let him—" The images in her head were shredding her.

"Shut up! *He* was in charge of her training, it was *his* choice!" Marcus sounded defensive, but she still pushed.

"THAT'S NOT TRAINING!" she shouted at him and he slapped her hard, snapping her head to the side. Her cheek burned, pulsing with her heartbeat, and she buried her face in her hands. Thinking of Kalen and Maggie at Purgatory. Guiding and fun and encouraging. The kind of training that let you become what you wanted to be, to push your limits in safety. Then the pounding of her bruising cheek made her whimper.

"God dammit! Be obedient, Thalia. Remember your choices!"

Chapter Twenty-Three
THALIA

He sighed above her. "It doesn't matter now anyway. Anthony tried to start things back up, but someone fucking talked and the cops showed up and took him and everything. The servers, computers, the accounts — everything."

Marcus leaned down, his voice cold and ominous. "They came for me too, you know, but I saw them coming. I was way ahead of them. I had a girl with me, but she wasn't *you*. She was never you. So, I moved my money, left her there, left the house in the woods, and disappeared."

"You took another girl? You said you wouldn't—" Thalia met his eyes and she saw the rage behind them simmering. Of course he'd lied in his email. Why would that have been the truth?

"I wanted YOU. If you hadn't left, I'd have never taken her. I wouldn't have needed anyone else!" Marcus was blaming her. He was actually fucking blaming her for his sick obsession?

"I can't believe this..." Thalia's head hurt with the effort of trying to think clearly through the adrenaline. The INTERPOL thing had actually worked? Anthony was in jail? Some poor girl Marcus had taken had been saved?

"I'm going to find out who fucking talked, and I'm going to kill them. I am glad Anthony is out of my way though. He would have never approved of me getting you back, but no one attacks me, no one comes after me and survives it." Marcus was pulling at his hair as his eyes jumped around the room, wild and unstable. "But you're mine now. You're mine, and I know how to stay hidden. No one is going to find you. *James* isn't going to find you. You need to accept that."

Thalia covered her ears, her chest aching with the weight of his words. He was insane, and he'd never let her go. He would either break her, or kill her, those were the only outcomes of this — and she wasn't sure which one she was hoping for. "Please, just stop."

"You know, I would have kept you. We could have been together this whole time, and you wouldn't have to be relearning the rules." Marcus sounded concerned for her, like he didn't *want* to hurt her. But it was fake, all of the nice shit was fake. He was a monster, just like Anthony, only brutal in different ways.

"Do you seriously not feel any guilt over the things you've done? Over the things you've both done?" Thalia didn't know why she'd asked it. It was stupid to taunt him.

Marcus grabbed her arm tight, digging his fingers in. "Anthony and I are very different." He actually sounded like he believed that. "And the police are using all of Anthony's files anyway to find our girls, since you're so concerned. And I've been keeping tabs, and they even found Beth. She's catatonic in some German hospital, but she's alive."

Alive. How many others had been found because of James' gift?

"But I don't give a shit about any of those sluts. Just you. I just want you." His fingers dug sharper into her skin. She tried to ignore the pinch of his grip, tried to stay focused on what he was saying. She and James had agreed after they sent everything anonymously to INTERPOL that they were done focusing on Marcus and Anthony. They'd taken enough of their time together, and so they had trusted the system. Left it alone. Not followed up. They should have at least made sure both of them were in jail. Hindsight is always twenty-twenty, but, apparently, they had still done *some* good.

"So, the police are rescuing them?" Her voice sounded hollow. Even as her own future became bleak, and dark, and hopeless — there was a light and she focused on it. Her and James' actions had maybe saved some of them.

"Rescuing?" Marcus laughed and crouched in front of her. "Thalia, you still don't get it. They're all sluts like you. They need this. You act as if you don't like this... but you do." He slid his hand between her legs and she whimpered and wrapped her hand around his wrist wishing she could push him away without him hurting her. He wrenched her hand off him and thrust two fingers inside her hard. She cried out, her nails digging into her palms to keep her hands away.

"No, please..." she pleaded. There was no doubt she was wet and she hated that he did this to her. His touch was rough, and she winced as he fingered her, but her body still responded. She hated herself. Before she could focus on what was wrong with her, his other hand was already pulling her up by her hair. His fingers slid from her and he held them out like evidence.

"You're already getting wet. Look at that, Thalia, you already want me again. I bet if I spanked you for all the times you've spoken out of turn you'd come like the little cock slut you are while across my lap." He moved her to the bed and forced her to sit, pressing her back so he could return to thrusting his fingers inside her. Leaning over her to watch her skin flush as she responded.

"Not again. Please? Please, just stop…" She swallowed against the lump in her throat as she forced out the last word. "Master."

"No. You like this, Thalia, I just have to keep reminding you. It's called conditioning, and you need it." Marcus pressed his lips to hers, and she tensed. He laughed softly when she didn't return it. "You know that traitorous slut Kaia wanted to stay with me. You remember her, don't you? She begged me at her party to keep her. Even after Thomas talked to her. She wanted this, what I'm offering you. *She* wanted to stay with me." His fingers curved and stroked the bundle of nerves deep inside that made her hips jerk in involuntary response.

"I don't want this!" Thalia insisted, pushing back the rising heat inside her.

"Just shut up and accept what your body is telling you. James turned your mind against me. Just like Thomas turned Kaia against me, and now they're both off happily testifying against my brother. Telling stories about me too, about how Thomas *saved* her." He growled, and her hips lifted against his touch and she despised herself for it, forcing them back to the bed as he rolled his thumb against her clit. "What Thomas doesn't know is that Kaia would be just as wet for me, she'd crawl to me on her knees if I told her to. She's been wanting the chance to be with me, to be mine again, for years."

"Then why not take KAIA?! Why not take Kaia and leave me alone?!" she screamed, her voice bordering on hysterical. Instant guilt at trying to sacrifice Kaia filled her. Marcus tightened his fist in her hair and angled her head back, and she hissed through her teeth at the strain. Digging her heels into the bed as she tried to push away from his touch.

"Because I want *you*, and you are meant to be mine. That cockslut isn't worthy of me." He removed his hands from her and began unbuttoning his pants. "Spread your legs, Thalia."

"No. No, please, please don't." Whimpering, she pressed her knees together firmly, her fists clenched in the sheet.

"Spread them, now." He grabbed her legs behind the knees and jerked her down the bed, laying her out. His fingers pried her thighs apart, and he commanded, "Farther."

Her legs eased apart a little more and she stared up at the ceiling. She was shocked when she suddenly felt his mouth on her, his tongue finding her core quickly, and her body's instant liquid heat was a terrible betrayal. Thalia covered her eyes with her arm, keeping her other hand in the sheets as she fought to ignore the pleasure of his mouth on her. His tongue delved between her lips, slowly and patiently, until he sucked her clit and she had to grit her teeth against the moan in her throat.

"Jesus, Thalia. You always respond for me. Do you see? This is what I mean." His tongue swiped her again and she silently cursed her body, cursed biology, cursed Marcus for her reactions. "If you would just accept this, we could be perfect together."

He licked at her lazily, thrumming constant pleasure through her while still keeping her miles from orgasm. It was like a promise of what he could give her. Then he suddenly bit down on her clit and she screamed, tears bursting from her eyes as pain shocked her system.

"But if you keep fighting me, I can and will do horrible things to you. And Katherine. Anthony isn't the only one with skills in that department. Understand?"

Thalia nodded, fear settling in her stomach as his tongue gently laved over her clit, soothing the sharp pain he had caused. She made herself stare at the ceiling so she couldn't see his dark hair between her thighs, his cold, blue-gray eyes watching her body flush and writhe for him as he increased the pleasure. He pinched her thigh sharply and she cried out.

"Say that you understand, Thalia."

"Yes, Master. I understand." She could hear in her voice that she was close to breaking down. He groaned and slid up her body, his hips pushing between her thighs.

"Say that you're mine." Marcus held himself above her, his cock brushing against her core. Thalia bit her lip, not wanting to say those words. Flashbacks of the last time he'd demanded it ringing inside her head. She just wanted James. She wanted her boyfriend, she wanted her Dom. She wanted the man she chose again and again. She didn't want Marcus.

"Please don't make me," Thalia pleaded. His cock pressed forward, her pussy already wet and waiting — *traitor*, her body was a traitor. He laid a hand over her throat, squeezing with the hint of a threat as she whimpered.

"Say that you're mine or fight me again and see what happens." His eyes were full of the kind of intense fervor usually reserved for the insane. Well, actually, Marcus *was* insane, and he had chosen her to focus on.

Lucky her.

The fear of what he might do if she refused again, of the ways he might act like Anthony, of the things he might do to Katherine to punish her, dissolved her will like flash paper. "I'm..." she mumbled, "I'm yours."

"Yes. You are." He thrust forward sharply and she couldn't cut off the moan that slipped out as he filled her.

Traitor.

Disgusting traitor.

She turned her head to the side, looking away so she could try and ignore the way Marcus breathed against her skin, but she couldn't escape herself. Her chest ached with the weight of her betrayal to James. She could be brave like Beth, refuse to obey him and let him do his worst. But Beth hadn't been responsible for someone else, and Thalia couldn't handle listening to Katherine scream again. So, she sent her mind elsewhere, ignoring the pleasure even as her body responded automatically, shutting out the sounds that slipped from her lips, and the words he hissed against her ear.

When he finished she knew he was waiting for her to yell at him. His weight pressed her into the bed as their harsh breaths mingled in the air, but she didn't have the energy to scream at him, to take his belt again, to listen to him punish Katherine for her transgressions. His lips brushed across her collarbone, and his hand traced her waist to hip as he slid from her. Thalia bit her lip and forced her hands to stay at her sides as he sat up between her legs.

"It's better when you don't fight, right?" His eyes moved down her body, and then back up to her face. Thalia turned away.

Yes.

"No," she answered quietly, and he growled and climbed off the bed, tucking himself away.

"You can't lie to me." Reaching under the bed, he pulled out a length of fabric. She winced, prepared for him to tie her already bruised wrists back to the bed, but he didn't. "Get up."

"What?" Thalia felt herself receding, pulling back from reality. Removing herself from the reality where Marcus had her again, where she was submitting to him again, where she called him Master. The reality where he'd just fucked her again. He grabbed her arm and tugged her to her feet, and she swayed against him.

"I'm taking you to the bathroom, and for a shower." Marcus placed the fabric over her eyes and tied it behind her head, his fingers adjusting it so she couldn't see. He twisted one of her arms behind her back and started to push her out of the room. Her bare feet padded across endless concrete and she could hear that the space around her was huge. She strained to listen for Katherine, but she heard nothing. She wanted to call out for her, but there was nothing to say, no comfort to provide her. So, she kept her mouth shut.

He pushed her backward until she sat on a toilet, and she heard him walk away into the large space. She was tempted to raise the blindfold but she had no idea if he could see her, so she didn't risk it. She let go, the relief of emptying her body letting her ignore the possibility of him watching her. Not like it mattered, not now. A moment later he handed her toilet paper and she winced as she knew for sure that he had watched her. The toilet flushed and he pulled her back up and moved her forward again. The metallic sound of a curtain being drawn back assaulted her and then she felt tile under her feet. Cold water hit her and she screeched and tried to back away from the stream. "Stop it, Thalia, don't make me handcuff you again."

She nodded and shivered under the freezing water, the blindfold getting soaked as he washed her. The scent of simple soap filling her nose, his fingers dipping inside her, which made her hiss between her teeth. She was sore, her back ached from the belt, and her throat felt bruised each time she swallowed. The cold water numbed her skin, easing all the aches and pains, but it left her teeth chattering. Once he was done washing her, he pushed her out of the stream against a cold tile wall.

"Stand here." He commanded. She shivered in the cool air, her teeth clacking together as he washed himself, the splash of the water against the tile echoing in her ears. Wherever he had her, the heat clearly didn't work, and it was fucking February. A few moments later, the scent of plain soap returned, the splash of the shower, and then he turned off the water. He dried her off first, and she wanted to hold the towel to her skin, but he took it back. She tried her best to wring out her hair, but it was still dripping when he stopped her. Then his hand gripped her arm again and he took her back to the room.

"Don't you have something to say, Thalia?" His voice was against her ear as the door shut behind him.

Her mind was somewhere else, anywhere else but here, and she didn't want to talk to him. "No."

Marcus pulled her head back by her damp hair, "I think the words you're looking for are 'Thank you, Master.' Why don't you try it?"

For what? She wanted to spit in his face.

Instead she mumbled, "Thank you, Master." He turned her in his arms and kissed her. Thalia whimpered, but he didn't stop until she opened her mouth to his. His arms held her tight to him and she felt panic rising up inside her that he'd hurt her again. But he didn't.

He finally left and took the blindfold with him. Her chest ached with a stifled sob, and she tried not to think about James. She tried to focus on Katherine. If she kept his attention, he wouldn't hurt Katherine. It was all about keeping her safe.

On the floor by the door were two wrapped protein bars, and she grabbed them. Immediately tearing into one to silence the gnawing hunger in her stomach. The bed only had a thin set of sheets but she crawled into it, trying to stifle the shivering from the cold air and her wet hair. The strange room she was in was slightly warmer than the vast open space she had been in, but still freezing. She tucked the second bar between the mattress and the frame and urged herself to sleep, to escape.

And she tried really hard not to think about James, about what he was doing, about how worried he must be.

She wished she could stop thinking at all.

Chapter Twenty-Four

MARCUS

Thalia.

Thalia was there. *Really* there this time. Not a dream, or a memory, or a drunken hallucination.

In the two days he'd had her, only one of which she'd been really conscious, he had tasted her, fucked her, made her come underneath him. She was coming around already. Already calling him Master again.

He hadn't wanted to hurt her. He had wanted their reunion to be easy. To be good. For her to remember how *good* it had been between them before Anthony and James ruined everything. His fists clenched as the idea of James' hands on her for almost a year drove him to the edge. He wanted to punish her for leaving him, for letting that rich asshole touch her. For putting an ocean between them that he couldn't cross without a lot of unwanted questions from authorities. He wanted to spank her for every smile she'd given James, every flirtatious look captured on camera. He wanted her to suffer like he had suffered.

No.

Marcus grabbed his head and leaned forward over his legs. "No, no, no." He groaned and ripped at his hair. He didn't want to hurt her. He wanted her to look at him like *that*. His eyes tracked to his favorite picture, so many times folded, the edges torn. That look. The look of her really wanting someone.

He wanted that.

As much as he reveled in her kneeling at his feet, crying and looking up at him in submission. He still wanted her to look at him with longing.

The way he looked at her.

Like that was so much to ask? After he'd plucked her from the obscurity of a miserable desk job that she hated? After he'd taken her away from all of those wandering eyes, those pointed comments, those whispered urges from her coworkers in the lobby to be the one to bang her?

He had saved her. He had saved her from that terrible, boring life — and he had shown her what she was capable of. He had shown her she was capable of so much more.

Him. *He* had done that. Not James. Not Anthony. No one else. He had delivered her into this new life that she claimed to love so much, and she couldn't even say thank you without fire in her eyes?

God, he loved and hated that fire. That incredible strength inside her. He wanted to subjugate it. He wanted her to be his completely. Mind, body, and soul. He wanted to restrain all of that fierceness in her and turn it into passion. For him. He wanted her to need him as badly as he needed her.

He needed the upper hand.

A whimper crackled out of the speaker on the table he'd set up. A rustle of sheets. A chatter of teeth.

Fuck. He should have dried her off more. Should have given her a blanket. It was February. In Pennsylvania. In an old warehouse. She had to be freezing with her hair still wet. But he hadn't bought a hair dryer. All of his fucking planning and he'd forgotten a god damned hair dryer. Well, actually, he'd had less than a week to plan *this* fucking location. Her sudden trip to the states had been a happy accident and saved him the cost of the people he was going to hire to bring her to him from London. And saved him the trouble of dispensing with them like he had with that first fucking PI, or the idiot who had agreed to help him grab her now.

Marcus leaned down and grabbed the thick blanket off his sleeping bag and marched toward the door. He slid the key in the lock and opened it. The light played across her form huddled under the thin sheet and he watched her shiver as another quake passed through her muscles. Then she stilled.

Still asleep. He knew her breathing well. He'd memorized every piece of footage he'd had on her before the police took it all. He'd spent six months memorizing her.

He shut the door quietly and moved to the bed, letting his eyes adjust to the dim light as he stared down at her. She was curled into a ball, her hair a flare above her head on the bed. Marcus shook out the blanket and then draped it over her.

Then he waited.

A moment later she shook in another wave of chills, her teeth clacking together, a groan slipping from her in her sleep. A good man would warm her up. A good man would hold her until she stopped shivering. And Marcus was more than happy to oblige. He removed his clothes in silence and carefully climbed onto the small bed behind her. Her forehead was almost against the wall, her knees braced against it, her legs folded over her core. Had there ever been a woman so fucking perfect?

His body touched hers and he almost jumped. She was freezing.

Stupid. Stupid fucking idiot. You want her to get sick?

Without another thought he pressed himself against her, bending his legs where hers bent until every inch of his warm skin that could possibly be touching hers finally was. He slid his arm around her and tugged her back to him, holding her tightly. But she still didn't wake, another wave of chills racked her body and he leaned up on his elbow to watch her. Her face pinched, her brows pulling together, and then she melted back against him. A puff of breath escaped her lips, and her muscles, at first rigid with the tension of her shivers, finally relaxed.

She was in his arms. Thalia was in his arms.

He watched as her breathing evened as his flesh took the chill out of hers. With one hand he carefully wound her hair away from her body, hoping it would dry on its own.

He was keeping her safe.

The thought filled him and pushed away all his earlier thoughts of revenge and punishment. All his anger at her shouts, the fire in her eyes. He wanted to shelter her, to be the one to keep her safe, to give her everything she needed.

His hand trailed down her stomach and she stirred. He stopped. He didn't want her awake, he didn't want her to wake up and fight this. Her body knew the truth. Her body knew what she needed, her body knew she needed him.

For the first time since she'd left he laid his head down behind hers, breathing her scent in. All wild sweetness, all female, all his. His arm tightened slightly to keep her firmly against him, against his warmth under the blanket. And for the first time in a long time he felt himself drifting off to sleep without half a bottle of liquor in his stomach.

She was what he needed. She was everything. And she'd realize soon that he was what she needed — or he didn't know what he'd do.

Chapter Twenty-Five
JAMES

"You haven't found them?!" James gripped the phone tighter as he listened to Jake's update.

"No, sir." It was clear Jake had not wanted to be the one to make this call.

"It's been five bloody days! How can you have no idea where they are? I thought you were following a lead. The abandoned SUV? You said that was what you were doing!" James shouted into the phone, suppressing the urge to throw the glass of whisky in his hand. Instead, he emptied it and returned to Katherine's wet bar to refill the glass. His whole world was a nightmare.

Two. More. Emails.

Full of her voice. Thalia pleading. And *his* voice. The fucked-up things he said to her. The things he made her say. Made her do.

James had tried not to listen to the last one, knowing the audio would only shred him, but it let him know she was alive. Even if it left him in such a state that he'd torn apart the room he slept in and the office he'd commandeered as his own hideaway. All he did every day was call every contact he could find that had any skill in tracking people or technology. His father had used an anti-corporate espionage team once to protect his business. It was just a high-class term for computer hackers, and James had used them before to try and take Marcus and Anthony down.

Not that it had worked like he had planned.

Apparently, the Americans had caught Anthony, and completely lost track of Marcus. The police had found that house empty except for the latest girl that he'd left behind — Victoria something. And now he had Thalia again, and Jake's team of mercenaries had nothing, the hackers had nothing. They couldn't find anything on the emails. No one could find anything, anywhere.

James should have had him killed. Morality be damned.

"Dr. Hawkins, I promise you we are doing everything we can. You said you received another email from him. Yesterday, correct?" Jake was speaking gently, trying not to set him off.

"Want to listen to it, Jake?" James asked, his voice frigid on the line.

"That's not necessary." He heard the man muffle the phone and return to it with a sigh. "At least we know he hasn't killed her."

"I'm sure she's so grateful for that fact, Jake." He knew the remark was cruel. He knew, at least some part of him knew, that Jake and his team had been hunting around the clock. Sleeping in shifts, looking at highway cameras, gas station cameras, anything they could as they tried to identify the vehicle Marcus had switched to.

How had no one seen him moving between vehicles? How was that even possible? It had been broad daylight.

"Sir, I assure you, we will not stop until we find them. We are pretty sure we know of a gas station he stopped at in an Expedition. He was moving southwest, either New Jersey or Pennsylvania." Jake talked to someone away from the phone before he came back. "I'll update you as soon as we verify anything."

"When you find them, you'll do what I asked?" James leaned his head against the window, looking out at the endless white of Katherine's backyard.

"Yes, sir. We'll restrain him until you can arrive. Then you can do what you want." Jake paused. "And if it's alright for me to say, most of the guys want to be there when you do it. We're all a little... invested at this point, sir."

James gritted his teeth, trying to breathe through the tension in his chest. At least they all understood. They finally understood, and James was going to make Marcus wish he had given up on Thalia the first time he'd told him to. "I honestly don't care who watches, Jake. Find them and you can start a betting pool on what I do first."

"I'll tell the guys that. And, sir? Try not to play the files anymore. He's sending them to get to you, that's all it is. It lets us know she's alive, but after that — destroy them." He sighed. "You're a good man, Dr. Hawkins. Don't let him ruin the person she wants to come home to."

James sighed and looked across the trashed office. The broken glass he hadn't let Katherine's maids clean up, the stacks of paper he'd printed to cross-reference when he was doing his own research on Marcus' movements. Going back through everything the hackers had found on him. "Right. Okay, Jake. Update me soon."

"I will. Goodbye, sir." Jake hung up and James dropped into the chair at the desk. His laptop was open to a map of the northeastern United States. His knowledge of the geography of the states was sketchy at best and he zoomed in on the area Jake had mentioned. The map made it look so small, so easy to search, but the scale of the US was impossibly large. Even zoomed in Marcus could have driven three hundred, even five hundred kilometers. James clicked the minus sign on the map and the details of the map disappeared to reveal more states, longer distances — an incredible vastness of space where they could be.

"How far did he take you?" James spoke quietly to himself before he shut the lid of the laptop hard. Forcing himself to look away from all the potential space.

Don't let him ruin the person she wants to come home to.

The words weighed heavy on him, and he tried to remember the last time he'd showered, eaten a meal, done anything other than obsess in this room and make angry phone calls. If Jake found them, this is what she'd see when she got back. A wrecked room, a wrecked boyfriend, and she would be the one who needed him.

And then there was Katherine.

How could he face his sister again like this? Half-drunk and shouting at her staff, breaking her things in fits of rage fueled anguish?

James shook his head and stood up, sliding the doors to the office apart as he headed back to his room. One of the maids was walking by and she froze, wide-eyed. *Fantastic, they were terrified of him.*

"It's alright. I'm sorry I shouted at you, you can tidy the office up. I'm going upstairs." He tried to speak softly, but his voice was raw with the emotion burning a hole through his chest. She nodded and moved toward the open doors. He turned toward her and she actually jumped. Guilt ate at him. "I truly am sorry, this — I'm not myself right now."

"I understand, sir. We just want to help. However we can." She was tense, nervous to be so close to him. Which was understandable since he was sure she had been the one that had tried to come in the room after the second email. He'd thrown an entire bottle of vodka across the room. Great. Now he was terrorizing women.

He nodded at her, "I know. I am going to clean up, and I was wondering if the chef could just leave something for me to eat."

"He's been making a plate for you at every meal just in case, sir, but I'll tell him." Her eyes were a dark brown, like melted chocolate, and they looked sad. For him. For all of them. He was such a prick for taking any of this out on her. And the whole staff was trying to help. He was shouting at them, and they were all trying to help.

"Thank you. I—" James cleared his throat, taking a step backward toward the stairs. "Just, thank you." He turned around and left her in the doorway.

When Jake found them, he was going to be someone worth coming home to.

Chapter Twenty-Six
THALIA

A bottle of water.

Thalia stayed still on the bed, keeping her breathing even, not wanting to make the bed creak as she stared at the bottle of water by the door.

He had come in the room again and she hadn't woken up. The bottle of water by the door was proof. It hadn't been there when she'd fallen asleep. Had he lain down with her again? Had she slept through him having his hands on her?

The memory of waking in his arms rose up again. It had been a few days, or was it a week, before. It didn't matter. What did matter was the way he'd known the moment she was awake, his body snapping into instant alertness. Then the quiet, sinister threat he'd whispered in her ear: *Think before you act, Thalia.*

He'd done it twice since.

Once while she slept. She had woken up when he got on the bed and she'd stayed still, but it hadn't worked; he had noticed the change in her breathing. He'd pulled her against him and talked to her about their *future*. When she hadn't responded the way he wanted, unable to fake even the smallest shred of excitement, he'd gotten angry. Screamed at her. She had screamed back, he'd backhanded her hard enough that her teeth cut the inside of her cheek and she'd spit blood onto the floor. That had made him leave the room, shouting again that she had to stop making him hurt her.

Wasn't that what all abusers said?

The other time had been after one of the times he'd fucked her. She had come again and again, and she'd just wanted to be away from him. She wanted to scream into the mattress, and curse herself, and cry because her body was so fucking stupid. He'd refused to leave, and he'd fallen asleep next to her, trapping her against the wall in his arms.

And now there was a bottle of water by the door. Like a flag staking a claim. He had been there. She hated that she was thirsty. The human body was such a weak machine. So many weaknesses. Thirst, hunger, pain, pleasure. It bent to all of them. He used all of them. When was the last time he'd brought her water? Even thinking about it made her throat itch.

But the sooner she got up, the sooner she moved on the bed, the sooner he would know she was awake. If she was awake, she was fair game. She couldn't listen to him hurt Katherine again, so she'd have to submit. To do her best not to fight back. The first time he'd hurt Katherine had been bad enough. The second time? The time after she'd told him she hated him? It had gone on and on until Thalia had covered her ears and screamed to drown it out. Her throat had been raw when it had finally stopped. What day had that been? How many days had she even been here? She could never tell how long she'd slept. And Marcus was too smart to tell her the truth. She'd read in a book once that it was a common technique to break someone down by confusing their understanding of time. Saying 'good morning' when it was the middle of the afternoon and they'd only slept a few hours, saying 'good night' when it was morning.

It was like before. No clocks. No windows. No one else. Just him.

Her whole world narrowed to just him. Interaction or no interaction. Food or no food. Water or no water.

Fuck, she was thirsty.

Maybe she could finish the water before he came in. The last time she'd upset him he'd taken the rest of a bottle of water with him. *Screw it.* She threw off the blanket and moved quickly to the door, grabbing the bottle of water before she moved back under the covers. Opening it she drank quickly, the cool rush hit her empty stomach and she shivered, but she kept drinking. She needed it. Thalia finally stopped, breathing deeply as she put the cap back on.

Still a third left, but it was more water than she'd had in a while. Lying on her side she traced the mountain on the label, her nail crinkling the plastic as she stared at the intricate little artwork of the logo. *North Mountain Water*. She was reading the label of a bottle of water because it was *something*. She'd already practically memorized the ingredients on the protein bar wrapper tucked under the mattress. This was at least kind of peaceful looking. A crystal blue lake formed the background for most of the text on the bottom of the label. Her stomach churned and she silently prayed to whatever deity was listening that she hadn't drank too much too fast. A shiver rushed through her and she sat up, breathing slowly to push back the wave of nausea.

A few deep breaths and the nausea faded, replaced by a light-headed tingling. It started in her lips and then spread steadily. She felt heat rush up her chest and neck in a blush, and the tingling got stronger. Like her skin was statically charged. She half-expected her hair to be standing up, but it wasn't. The feeling was inside her, spreading down her stomach, slipping between her thighs until her pussy was wet with the odd flickering, electric pulses. Her head was swimming, and she climbed off the bed because the sheets suddenly felt scratchy. Too much contact with her skin. They were itchy.

Except, when she got off the bed the itchy feeling didn't fade. Her arms, her legs, her stomach, it felt like someone was holding a balloon inches from her skin. That tense, hyper awareness just before the static shocked you. Thalia pushed her hands into her hair and heard the whine slip out of her mouth as she backed against the cool wall. Her skin was hot. The electric tension was making her skin hot, and the itchy frustration was pooling between her thighs. Her pussy was soaked, the tops of her thighs damp with it.

What the fuck?

She whined again, gritting her teeth as heat pulsed up her spine and her clit responded like an echo. It took effort not to moan, biting down on her knuckles. Thalia knew he could hear her in this room. He'd proven it. Repeating things she'd said aloud when she was talking to herself. She didn't talk to herself anymore, and she *couldn't* moan. She couldn't do anything to call him in here. Not when her body was—

"Fuck..." She slid to her knees as a wave of tense arousal made her breath hiss between her teeth. Her head was foggy, delirious with the overwhelming sensations. Every inch of her skin was tingling, and too hot — she was going to burn alive inside her own skin. Sweat broke out across her and she wanted to lie out on the concrete. Just for a minute, to cool down, to let the delirium pass.

The door opened and she lifted her head, aware on some level that she was on the floor, kneeling. Her knees spread wide, her hands on the floor between them.

"Let me help you, Thalia." Marcus let the door shut behind him and walked toward her. A flickering warning somewhere in her mind told her to run, but it was washed away in a wave of electric sensation. When he touched her arm, her body lit up like he'd set off a firework inside her nervous system. The shock of it made her buckle, but it hadn't hurt. It was too much. Too fast. Her breaths were hard and quick as she looked up at him, her mind a golden haze trying to process *everything*. The air, the light, the pulse under her skin, the movement of breath in her lungs. The world was too much. He crouched in front of her. "How do you feel?"

"I don't—" Just as she started to answer he reached forward to trace his touch across her breast and pleasure overwhelmed her like a riptide pulling her under.

She groaned, whimpering as her body tried to flinch away and move closer at the same time. He didn't stop. He cupped her breast and rolled her nipple gently, but her body shivered like she was approaching an orgasm. That same shaky tension, the toe-curling sensations that made her pussy clench. It wasn't until he grabbed her hand to stop her that she realized she'd been moving her fingers toward her clit. His blue-gray eyes were locked on hers as he held her wrist and returned to gently teasing her nipple. But nothing about the way her body was reacting was gentle. It was impossible. She pushed her chest forward against his hand, biting her lip as she sought just a little more. The edge of this golden fog in her head had to be close, she could feel it in the buzzing tension of her nerves. If she could only touch herself, just a little, she'd fall over. "Please..." she whispered, whimpering as she tugged against his grip on her wrist.

"What is it?" Marcus' lips were parted, and he was hard. She could see his erection straining the front of his pants. He leaned closer to her, making sure he had eye contact with her, his gaze watching her closely. Instead of fading, that golden buzzing in her head grew stronger. She just needed contact, she needed to push through the other side of this so it would all stop. The heat, the buzz, the itchy shivers that were focusing between her thighs to make her clit pound and drive her crazy. He was teasing the fog, intensifying it.

She knew how to make him stop teasing her.

He had her right hand trapped in his, but she grabbed the back of his head with the other and pulled him into a kiss. The heat doubled as he groaned against her mouth, his hands moving to cup her face and she returned the favor. Holding him in place as she climbed onto his lap, rocking herself against the front of his pants. She rolled her hips, grinding down against his erection until his fingers were digging into her waist, trying to pull her against him harder or lift her away — she couldn't tell. All that mattered was the driving pulse inside her, his lips against hers, his tongue delving in to push her for more. His fist tightened in her hair, and what normally just turned her on felt like electric light cascading down her spine in ribbons. He pulled her back from his lips, and she groaned and rolled her hips against his. Her clit seeking just a little more friction.

"Jesus, Thalia..." His eyes roved down her body, and she leaned back bracing her hands on the floor behind her so she could roll her hips against his. He licked his lips, and she moaned, her panting breaths growing shorter. Marcus slid his hand between her breasts, down her stomach, and began to slowly circle her clit with his thumb. It was what she needed. She needed to come. The buzzing was starting to hurt, the electric shock closer to her skin. It had to stop.

The orgasm hit her when he started to rub her in tight circles, but the golden haze in her head didn't fade at all. The sparkling crash of pleasure fed into it. It made her body hungry for more and she let out a frustrated scream when the aftershocks of the orgasm did nothing more than make her body tighten in need. "Please, please, make it stop!"

"Do you want to come again?" Marcus was breathing heavily, and he leaned forward to pull her up against his chest. Thalia spread her legs further, trying to increase the contact, but the fabric of his pants wasn't enough.

"I don't know! Just please make it stop…" She tugged at the button of his pants, the heat inside her wasn't going away. Marcus pushed her off his lap gently and undid his belt, pushing his pants out of the way. He was hard, his cock dark at the tip, and when he reached for her again she climbed onto his lap with urgency.

This. She needed this. It would make it stop.

He shifted her and then pulled her down on him, and she screamed, "Yes! Please. *Please*!" As he filled her it was a lightning storm inside her skin, and she wrapped her arms around his neck trying to hold herself together. His arms wrapped around her back and she rocked against him, his strength keeping her ribs from breaking apart with each breath she drew into the storm. Pushing the golden haze in her mind higher, letting the tingling buzz take her over, she rose and fell on top of him, driving him deeper. Her fingers wound in his hair, gripping tight to hold him, and he didn't fight her. Instead he dropped his hands to her hips and thrust hard inside her, and all of the power in her veins responded with a chorus of pleasure that had her moaning.

"Fuck. Yes. Just like that," he growled against her shoulder as she bounced on him, so close to another sparkling edge that she could feel it cutting through the haze like a knife. Just one more. One more and she'd be clear, and it would stop, it would all stop.

She shattered. Screaming with the orgasm, her hands tight in his hair. He groaned when she tightened around him in waves, and then he was kissing her. Rolling her to her back on the concrete and driving inside her again. She was held together by light. Electric arcs spanning her cells to keep her together, and each crash over the edge only landed her in the same place again and again. An infinite loop of spine snapping pleasure and aching urgency to find the next edge, to fall over, to find the end.

But it was an endless sky. A massive, gold, electrical storm that she had somehow been wrapped in. Gravity had let her go. Physics had released her.

There was only light.

Just light.

Chapter Twenty-Seven
THALIA

Yes.

Just light, so much light — until there wasn't.

Crashing back to earth had been waking up to an aching body, covered in bruises. It had been waking up to darkness, and pain, and a vicious nausea. The worst hangover she'd ever felt in her entire life. Everything hurt as she shoved herself off of the bed and crawled, shaking, to a corner to throw up. Except, nothing came up but bile. She had no food to reject, but her body wouldn't listen to that. It wanted her to keep trying. Dry heaving as memories ran her down like dogs on the hunt.

She had fucked Marcus. She had climbed on top of him, begged for him. He had done something to her. Thalia choked on a sob as her body tried to empty her already vacant stomach again.

The water. The fucking bottle of water.

Screaming into her hand, muffling it as best as she could, she bent over her knees to stifle the sobs that threatened to crack her ribs.

No. There was no way she could have done that. *Nothing* could make her — but she had. She pushed herself back against the wall and slammed her head back into the concrete. It hurt, but not enough. Not enough to atone for this.

She had begged him. She'd held him to her.

Thalia slammed her head back into the wall again, the aftershock making her dizzy as the ache spread across the back of her skull and into her teeth. Panic. She was having a panic attack. That strange wheezing sound was coming from her lungs. The shrinking feeling in the room was claustrophobia.

Ailsa would have so many fancy terms for this shit if only she were *fucking* here. But no one was here. No one was going to stop this. No one knew where she was, and she hadn't heard a peep from Katherine in so long.

Katherine was probably dead.

Her brain wasn't even working right anymore, and she had kissed him. She had kissed Marcus. And not out of fear, or obligation, she had reached for him. She had given herself to him. The pain of that realization tore out the last of her hope. Because why would she want to be saved? How could she ever look at James again? She'd gotten his sister killed. She'd submitted to Marcus, and then she'd given herself to him like a gift-wrapped whore.

There had been so much light. She'd been filled with it. And now there was nothing. All of that fake, glittering glory had been emptied out and all that was left was the shell of who she was now. And she wasn't worth anything.

She stumbled back to the bed and dropped to the floor next to it, leaning her head on the mattress, her hand tracing the metal edge. Reaching underneath she felt the rest of the frame, the metal underneath. Cold washed up out of the emptiness inside her and she stood and dragged the thin mattress off. Underneath was a metal lattice, cheap and rusted. It had to be why it always creaked. Why it creaked whenever she moved, whenever he was on top of her. Bile came up her throat again, but she pushed it down. There were so many perfect little squares — and one rectangle. A broken part in the metal.

Thalia leaned over it and saw the thin piece of metal leading back to where it connected to the frame. She pushed at it and it moved a bit. Climbing onto the metal lattice she reveled in the way it dug into her knees, the pain joining all the other aches inside her to fill the emptiness. Wrapping her hand around the thin metal she pulled and pushed at it, worrying the weak edge against the frame. She tried to be quiet, tried not to make the bed creak any louder.

Tink. Tink. Tink. Snap.

The thin strip of metal broke free and it was in her hand. One end had orange rust, the other end was still a dark brown. Easing off the lattice she sat on the edge of the mattress on the floor and traced the sharp edge across her fingertip. She toyed with it, pressing it into the pad of her thumb over and over. Then her eyes tracked to the fragile blue veins just under the thin skin of her wrist.

If you were serious it was vertical, right?

A scene from the movie 'The Craft' floated through her mind. She'd loved that movie when she was younger. There was a scene where one of the characters commented on another's suicide attempt. You're supposed to cut vertical instead of across if you're serious. And she was serious, right?

Thalia's hand was frozen, the point of the metal pressing into her wrist. How much pressure would it take? What if James was coming? What if he hated her for what she'd done? What if he never came and it was only Marcus? Only Marcus forever.

No one else. Just Marcus. No food without Marcus. No water without Marcus.

And sometimes the water would be filled with golden light that would burn her from the inside out until she begged and pleaded for him. And then the light would leave her and she would be like this.

He could do this over and over and over. It would break her.

She took a breath and dug the metal in and pulled toward her. Pain seared her and a scream escaped through gritted teeth. When she looked down there was blood, but not enough blood. Barely any. She'd survive that. She brought it back to the top, took a breath, and pressed harder. The pain was worse the second time, but she felt warmth trickling over her palm and onto her thigh. When she opened her eyes again there was more blood.

The sight of it, so vibrant, an unreal kind of red, made her feel light headed. She went with it, letting go of any of that fight or flight bullshit. It hadn't done her any good any way.

A minute later the door opened and she felt the edge of her mouth tick up in a smile as Marcus stepped in. His hair a mess of bedhead, his face confused when he first looked at the bed, and then he saw her on the floor. Saw the blood. It was like watching him in slow motion as he lunged for her, bending her hand back to yank the metal out of it, and then he clamped his hand over her wrist. She tried to fight him, tried to reach for the metal piece, to do more damage so he'd have to let her go. "What the fuck have you done? What the FUCK did you DO, Thalia?!"

He shook her and she tried to twist away from him, the pressure on her wrist hurt so much. "Stop. Just stop. I'm empty. Just let me go," she mumbled but he wasn't listening. He was panicked, muttering to himself as he lifted his hand and then pressed it even harder against her wrist. There was already so much red, that had to be a good sign. He couldn't take her to a hospital. No way to add more red back inside her.

"THALIA!" he shouted directly in her face and she winced. "Why, Thalia, why would you do this?!"

"I betrayed him," she muttered as an odd buzzing filled her ears.

"You — *James?* You did THIS over HIM?!" he screamed at her, but she just looked at him. There was nothing left inside her. He took his belt off and for a second she almost laughed. He was going to beat her for trying to kill herself? For mentioning James?

Sure, why not?

But instead of hitting her he coiled it at the top of her left arm and cinched it tight. He was saying something to her, but she shook her head and leaned back on the wall. He screamed as he stood above her, one knee of his pants was wet with her blood and she stared at it. A second later he rushed out of the room, and she was glad he was gone. She reached for the belt on her left arm and clumsily undid it. When she lifted her left hand she watched as the red created new trails across her pale skin. When he came back he was screaming again.

"The tourniquet has to stay on! Dammit, Thalia!" He grabbed the belt and cinched it even tighter on her arm, it hurt and she tried to push him off but it didn't even faze him. Reaching for her wrist again he cracked open a bottle of water and poured it over the wound. She screamed weakly but tried to remind herself it didn't matter. Then he was patting it dry and mumbling to himself. "...it's going to be okay, she's okay, just a lot of blood... not deep..."

She winced when she felt him pushing on her skin, the jagged edges of the cut pressed together, and he jerked her forward so he could brace her arm on his leg. She tried to pull back but she was light headed and weak. He did something that made the cut sting and then blew on her skin, holding her arm firmly so she wasn't able to move. She couldn't see anymore with his shoulder in the way, and she wasn't going to lean against him to look.

She'd never have to touch him again. All the empty darkness would swallow her up. She was taking his toy from him. It made her let out a little laugh, and he growled. Then she realized he was wrapping gauze around her wrist.

"Why the fuck are you laughing, Thalia?"

"Cause I'm leaving." She let out another little laugh, and he overlaid the gauze with duct tape to hold it in place.

"I'm not going to let you do that." He turned to her, but she saw spots in her vision. "Thalia, you have to stay awake! Fuck!"

He sounded far away and she felt her body slide sideways, black encroaching on the edges of her vision. Then she felt a thud on her thigh and she winced. Her heartbeat pounded in her ears, and instead of sinking further into the dark, she was rising, waking up. The fuzzy feeling fading. Marcus was shaking her shoulders and she shoved at him with her unbandaged arm. "Let me go! Just let me die!" she screamed, and then realized she *could* scream, and she screamed again in frustration.

"NO! I can't believe you did this!" He shook her shoulders again and she tried to push back from him.

"What did you do?!" She was crying. She was supposed to be dead. She was supposed to be gone. "I was dying! How did you—"

"God dammit, Thalia! Stop! I sealed the wound! You didn't get the vein. And when your blood pressure dropped and you started to pass out, I used the EpiPen from the first aid kit. I told you, I'm not letting you go. Now you need to rest while I clean up your fucking mess." He growled at her, his hands were streaked with her blood. She was too, and the sheet, and the floor.

How could there be so much outside of her? How could it not be enough? She started to cry again, hot tears running down her cheeks until she saw the metal piece under the frame of the bed and she lunged for it.

He grabbed her before she even got close to it and slammed her back onto the mattress. "WHAT THE FUCK, THALIA!"

"I HATE YOU! I FUCKING HATE YOU!" she screamed right back at him, her voice cracking halfway through from the strain of it.

"So you want to kill yourself?!" He stared down at her in disbelief, and she spit at him. His anger washed over his face, but he regained control and she kicked and fought as he flipped her to her stomach and dragged her hands behind her back. Grabbing the duct tape again he bound her wrists together, overlaying the tape already covering her gauze. Then he pinned her legs and did the same to her ankles, muttering and cursing as he did it. With her immobilized on the mattress he walked back out of the room and she screamed in frustration.

He came back with tools and started taking the bed apart, ignoring her as she cried and cursed at him, screaming that she hated him, that she wanted to die. Whatever she could think of, but he worked with a single-minded focus, throwing dismantled pieces of the bed out the door before returning to keep working. The small piece of metal that had almost been her salvation was tossed out too. Then he came back with a bucket and water. The blood, the corner where she'd been sick, all washed away.

The last time he came back with a granola bar and he sat on the side of the mattress not caked in drying blood. He opened it in front of her and broke off a piece, holding it in front of her lips. "Eat."

"Fuck you." She turned her head away from him, but he grabbed her hair and turned her back.

"Eat, Thalia." The anger was simmering beneath the surface but he was making himself be calm.

"No. You can shove that in my mouth, but if I don't chew it will just choke me and I'll die anyway. Unless you save me from that too." She glared at him and he let go of her hair and ate the piece himself.

"It's not drugged. See?"

"But the water was," she stated, and he looked up at the ceiling, taking a breath.

"Yes. I drugged the water. I just wanted you to see what it could be like if you'd just — *try*. I forgot about how hard it is to come down off that shit." He shook his head, laughing bitterly to himself as he broke off another piece of granola bar and offered it to her first. When she didn't even open her mouth, he ate it. "Do you even remember how amazing it was? With you not fighting me? We could have that all the time."

"You mean you could keep me high as a fucking kite all of the time so I can't even think straight? High enough to actually think submitting to you, fucking you, is a good idea? Go fuck yourself, *Master*. The first chance I get to kill myself, I'm taking it." She turned her head away again. When he bent her back by her hair she couldn't hide the wince. Every inch of her still ached.

"You will not kill yourself." He growled out the words and she didn't respond. "SAY IT. Say it, Thalia."

"No," she said softly and he let go of her hair. Reaching into his pants he pulled out a combat knife. A dark blade folded into its handle. When he opened it up it was almost six inches long. A sliver of fear ran through her because, no matter what, even a suicidal human brain is still hard-wired to react to knives. He reached behind her and she felt him tugging at her arms and then they were unbound. The duct tape tearing at her skin as he removed it. Her feet were next, and she pushed away from him and hugged her legs to her chest.

"You know what? It doesn't matter, there's nothing left in this room to kill yourself with." Marcus stood up, tucking the blade away and grabbing the granola bar.

"Do you really think if you keep this up long enough, that if you drug me enough times, make me come enough times, that I'll suddenly love you? Do you really think that I would ever give up on loving James? That I would ever want you over him?" she asked with an empty voice, but his jaw tightened and she watched him tense when she said the name out loud. So she said it again. "*James* loves me. And he doesn't just say it, he shows me. Every day. You're nothing like him."

"Stop it."

"I love James, Marcus." She kept going.

"Shut up, Thalia." He towered over her, his rage making him shake, but fear was something people who had hope felt.

"I love James for the way he cares about me. I love James for the way he fucks me. And I love James most of all because he got me away from *you*." She finished and he hit her. Pain exploded in her cheek as she realized he hadn't slapped her, his fist had been closed. Her head rang when she hit the floor and he straddled her, grabbing her face in a painful grip to make her look at him.

"Listen, you stupid slut. You want to play hard ball? You want to throw his name in my face? The man you whored yourself out to so you could go play house overseas with all his money?" She tried to twist out of his grip but he just angled her chin up and dug his fingers into her jaw. "I don't give a fuck what you think you have with him. But you *are* going to submit to me, and if you don't want to enjoy the process, fine. I'll break you. And I'll keep sharp objects out of your reach while I do it."

He climbed off her and she tried to sit up, but he hit her again. She caught herself on the floor and the tears came back. She was crying when the door slammed and the lights went out. Then there was nothing but the thin mattress, the pain in her cheek, the tinge of copper in the air, and his promise to break her.

Nothing. Nothing. Nothing.

Sleep came and went. Memories rose and fell in her head, taunting her and tormenting her.

She tried to pick at the duct tape wrapped around the gauze, but in the darkness she couldn't find the edge no matter how many times she traced her fingers up and down. Her teeth wouldn't cut the tape, and she eventually gave up.

Hunger gnawed at her as time stretched. She didn't know the last time she'd eaten. Had it been a sandwich? Another protein bar? For a moment she thought about calling out, offering to eat the granola bar, but maybe he'd let her starve.

Not how she'd want to go, but better than him breaking her. Better than more of that drug that filled her with poisonous light and emptied her out leaving only the poison behind.

The blackness was absolute. Not a hint of light from the doorframe. He'd always left half the lights in the room on for her. Industrial tubes set in the ceiling behind metal grates. She traced the door and tried the handle again. It turned, but nothing happened. The door didn't budge an inch.

Her ears strained for sound, her hands aching from the chill in the air until she tucked them between her thighs to warm them.

Had he left her? Was this his plan to break her? Solitary confinement?

Thalia crawled blindly across the floor until she felt the blanket and used it to get back on the mattress, slightly warmer than the concrete. She touched her cheek gently and winced. Bruised, swollen.

There were so many things she wanted to tell the people in her life. She wanted to tell James she was sorry, for ever getting him involved in her mess, for falling in love with him, for being such a fucking mess for over a third of the time they'd had together. It would have been better if she had never left Marcus in the first place. James would have been upset, but he wouldn't have lost his sister and his girlfriend. She wanted to tell Kalen and Maggie thank you for accepting her like a member of their circle, even in all her damage. To thank Ailsa for helping her put herself back together. For always answering her phone when Thalia needed to talk. She wanted to thank Julie and Analiese and Lauren and Chloe for being the best, and the weirdest, but still the best friends she'd ever had. She wanted to apologize to Becca and the others for bringing them on at the studio only to disappear.

For a second she even wanted to call her dad.

They'd rarely spoken since she'd been with James. He knew she was alive and living in London — but only because she'd called him. Marcus had been right that no one would have worried about her. Her dad hadn't even noticed the gap in time since her last call. But she still wanted to call him, to forgive him for falling off the deep end when her mother died. The cancer had eaten them both alive, only he hadn't died. He'd been a shell, but at least he'd kept food in the house, taught her to drive, let her see friends, let her try to go to college.

She realized she was crying and wiped her eyes, wondering where the water was even coming from at this point. She had to be dehydrated. No food. No water. No light.

Rolling to her stomach she grabbed the covers and curled up around them, building a nest on the mattress to try and stay warm. It seemed to take forever for the tightness in her muscles to relax, and then sleep took her again.

Her dreams were nothing more than shifting shadows in a huge gray room. No faces to look at or plead with, her voice gone. When she reached out for them her hand passed through them like smoke. She ended up curled into a ball trying to cover her ears against the sound of a wind that seemed to only touch her. Chilling her to the bone, ripping her hair into knots, and leaving the faceless shadows free to wander past her like she didn't exist. Like she was already forgotten.

Chapter Twenty-Eight
JAMES

"Please tell me—"

"We found him on a camera at a gas station in Pennsylvania. He's driving a truck with an enclosed bed. He bought a lot of supplies, spent almost twenty minutes in the store. A lot of food, a ton of water. He has to be close. Why else would he get it here?" Jake sounded confident and the sound of other men talking in the background made James sit up straight.

"Does the man know anything? Know where he might be?" He heard hope in his voice and tried not to let it grow. Seven days. Anything could have happened in seven days.

"He doesn't even remember him, but it's him for sure. He looked right at a hidden camera. We're scouring the area for secluded places — unfortunately, we're in farm country. There's a lot of space, but not a ton of buildings. I have one of my guys looking for abandoned properties or those recently for sale or purchased." Jake answered someone's question and came back to the phone, "We've got a chopper in the air looking for the truck as well. We will find them. I can feel it, we're close."

"Good." James nodded, leaning his head in his hand as he forced himself to breathe. To try and focus on the cup of tea in front of him.

"Have you — has he sent any more emails?" Jake's voice was quiet, like he didn't want his men to hear him asking, but the question cut into James.

"No. Nothing in three days." James took a drink of the tea and wished it was whisky. He'd have to call and update Kalen, but he couldn't handle anyone else. Text messages were coming across his phone from Thalia's friends, from Ailsa, from

Becca, all wanting to know what was going on. Where was she? Why hadn't she come back from the states yet?

The only ones that knew anything were Kalen and Maggie because they didn't keep secrets from each other. Ailsa probably knew by now as well, but he couldn't talk to anyone else, not when he didn't have answers. At least not answers he could say out loud. He only talked to the assistant he'd hired for Thalia to make sure Nirvana would be functioning if she got back. *When* she got back.

"Don't jump to conclusions, okay? We're going to find them. We are." Jake made himself sound more confident than James figured he actually was, but he appreciated it.

"Alright. Ring me when you do." James sighed and they said their goodbyes and hung up.

THALIA

Thalia shouted a cry into the cloth he'd shoved in her mouth, as he thrust inside her again. Without a bed frame he'd made do with taping her wrists behind her back again after he'd renewed her bandage, and by locking a spreader bar between her ankles. Bent forward on the mattress, she couldn't brace herself against each hard thrust, she just kept the side of her face that hurt the least on the sheet.

His hand came down on her ass and she winced. He'd spanked her the day before, counting out all of the rules she'd supposedly broken since he'd had her again. Over and over until she had begged him to stop. He had, but then he'd used the belt on her until she could recite the rules to him one after the other.

Crawl. Kneel. Eyes down. Call him Master. Thank him for punishments. Permission to come. I am his. I am his. I am his.

As if saying it out loud enough times would make her believe it. Punctuating each sentence with the vicious swipe of a belt lash. His version of re-education.

She was black and blue when he'd given up on any hope of her sounding sincere.

Now he was testing her, and she had already come twice without permission, because she had refused to ask. The third was rising up and she tensed, not wanting to have to ask, but knowing if she failed a third time he'd keep going. She wanted him off of her. Pleasure wound her spine tight, the orgasm threatening to hit fast and she begged through the cloth, a muffled version of 'Please let me come.' He thrust hard and deep and she moaned against her teeth, clenching her fists to push away from the slippery slope of her climax.

"Have something to say, slut?" Marcus leaned over her and ripped the cloth out of her mouth, and she dragged in air.

"Please. May I come. Master." She clipped the words out through gritted teeth, and he slowly thrust inside her, rotating his hips against her ass as he teased her.

"Beg me." A slow withdrawal, a sharp thrust that almost tumbled her over the edge. She bit down on her lip to distract herself, hard enough to resplit it and taste the copper tang of blood. He thrust hard again and she groaned and forced the words out.

"Please, Master. Please, may I come? Please?"

His hand slid over her hip to touch her clit and she screamed into the mattress. That was cheating. The tight circles over that bundle of nerves had her gasping and moaning, intense sensations knocking her defenses down. "Again." He ordered, his lips against her back.

"PLEASE!" Her voice whined as he pushed her higher, "Please, may I come? Master, may I come?" She dissolved into panting moans, pressing her forehead down into the mattress as he circled his hips behind her, tormenting her, dragging it out. Was he seriously not going to give her permission? Could he hold out for a fourth round of this twisted game?

"Fine. Come, slut." He pulled back and slammed hard, driving her forward with each powerful thrust and she let go and just let the pleasure wash over her. He filled her, and his fingers worked in tight circles over her clit as her breaths came shorter and shorter. Then all that incredible tension released and sparks crackled behind her eyes, and as she tightened on him he thrust deep and came inside her. When he pulled out of her he jerked her up by her hair until she balanced on her knees, stepping in front of her. "What do you say?"

"Thank you, Master." The words were empty, and he knew it. He could see it in her, but he still fisted her hair and pulled her mouth toward his cock.

"Clean me off. And remember, if you bite me, you're still bound with a spreader bar between your legs. You're not going anywhere." He was staring down at her, and she opened her mouth for him to push his cock between her lips. She tasted the mix of the two of them and fought the urge to bite down. To hurt him just a little bit like he hurt her. But she couldn't cut herself out of the duct tape, not with it wound almost to her elbows, even if she *could* find his knife on him and get it from him. She sucked him harder, wanting him to be done with her, to leave. Marcus hissed between his teeth and pulled from her mouth, she'd forgotten for a moment how sensitive he would be after he'd come. The ringing slap reminded her well enough and she sat back on her heels, clenching her eyes closed against the pounding ache in her cheek. "Are you misbehaving on purpose?" he asked as he tucked himself away.

"No, Master." She shook her head.

"Are you sure? You don't want another punishment? We could start making the front of you match the back." His voice was bitter, but she didn't care. The click of his knife opening made her tense, but she felt the relaxing tension in her arms as he cut the tape away and ripped it off her skin in stinging strips.

"No. Master. I do not want a punishment." She tried her best to keep the boiling hatred out of her voice. She wasn't very successful. He laughed low as he crouched behind her to unlock the spreader bar, the moment it was removed she eased her legs back together, ignoring the way her hips protested.

"Do you want me to give you a break?" He shoved her shoulder so she turned to face him. When her eyes stayed on the floor, like she was supposed to, he grabbed her chin to make her look at him. "Do you need a break, Thalia? Am I being too rough?" His grip tightened on her face until she winced, the mocking tone in his voice made her want to spit at him, bite his hand, kick him away from her.

"I'm just fine, *Master*." She growled the words out and he moved his hand to her throat, squeezing lightly.

"Aren't you a strong little whore. Have you decided to live long enough for me to break you?" Marcus leaned close to her.

"Since you won't let me die, I'll have to settle for *not* letting you break me." She tried to pull back from his grip on her throat, to get some space between them, but he shoved her back onto the mattress, straddling her waist before getting in her face again.

"Oh, Thalia. I haven't even started trying to break you. *This* has all been to re-train you." He pressed a kiss to her mouth, her lip stinging where she'd split it again. He smiled down at her when he leaned back. "Do you want me to start breaking you?"

"You. Won't. Break. Me." She lifted her head toward him, not taking her gaze from his cold blue eyes. He hated her defiance, she saw the anger in his eyes simmering underneath the shadow of control.

"Sure about that, Thalia?" He traced his thumb across her jawline and down her neck. She was about to shout how sure she was when his eyes came back to hers. "When I kill Katherine, all because you're having such a fun time defying me, ruining all of my hard work, my plans for us... you don't think that will break you? Even just a little bit?" Her heart stopped, skittered, her pulse all off kilter as her world went sideways.

"You already killed Katherine." Thalia believed it. He'd barely mentioned Katherine in so long, she hadn't heard her at all. Katherine was dead. Katherine was already dead. But Marcus tilted his head, his fingers running over her neck.

"Do you really believe I would have killed Katherine and not told you about it? What's the use in that?"

"Don't fucking touch her." Thalia tried to sit up but he pushed her back to the mattress with ease, his hand tightening on her throat.

"Look at you, disobedient again already." He squeezed until she couldn't breathe enough to do more than whimper, and then he kept continued. "As I was saying, I only kept her here because I thought you'd behave if you knew I'd hurt her. But you aren't behaving, and if I kill Katherine then the *next* girl I take you'll be more careful with her life — won't you?"

"Don't…" She tried to talk but he tightened his hold until she coughed. Tears forming as she reached for his wrist, not trying to fight him, but begging for him to stop.

"I just have to break you a little today, Thalia, once there's a crack you'll be at my feet soon. She dies, you'll know it's your fault for being such a disobedient little cock slut," he kissed her forehead and she tried to plead, to beg him not to, "and the next time I take a girl, you'll behave for me. Won't you?!" He didn't wait for her answer. He just stood up, grabbed the remnants of the tape and the bar and walked toward the door as she gasped for air.

"PLEASE!" Thalia lunged for the door, but he shut it and she heard it lock. She slammed her hand onto it and screamed against the metal. "PLEASE, MASTER! I'll be good! I'll be good, I swear I'll be good! KATHERINE! God, I'm so sorry! I'm sorry, I'm sorry…"

Chapter Twenty-Nine
THALIA

She collapsed to the floor, sobs wracking her until she was coughing against the lingering bruised feeling in her throat. Minutes ticked by, and the raw, tearing sensation in her chest was worse than all the bruises and welts and cuts. She stood and slapped her hand on the door again, yanking at the handle and then it suddenly gave and she stumbled back.

Marcus was on the other side, the knife in his hand dripping bright, red blood to the concrete. He took a step forward and she grabbed her hair as the impossible flashed in her head. "Oh my God, no, no, no!"

"This," he held the knife up, the blade edge wet, "is your fault." He moved forward, grabbing her by the hair to drag her back into the room. Something snapped inside her and she twisted and brought her knee up into his ribs as hard as she could. He let go of her hair in surprise and she went for his eyes, the knife clattering to the floor as he grabbed her wrists to hold her back.

"WHY?!" She screamed, trying to get to his eyes, to tear him apart, but with his hands distracted she brought her knee up hard between his legs. He shoved her and she fell back, but he dropped to his knees, growling. She landed hard, and screamed at him again, "She didn't do anything! She wasn't a part of this!"

"You. Did. This." He bit out the words between groans, and she got up and tried to kick him in the face, but he grabbed her foot and yanked her toward him. Her head cracked on the concrete when she fell and he was on top of her, choking her, her pulse pounding behind her eyes. "How many times did I tell you to behave?! How many times?! I am NEVER letting you go, Thalia. If I have to kill a girl every time you defy me to get you to finally submit to me, to finally accept what you're meant for? Then so be it. All that blood is on—"

Her hand had landed on the knife when she'd flailed, her fingers wrapped around the textured handle on instinct, but she had consciously chosen to drive it into his neck. The blade sunk in easily until she felt it grind against bone. The sensation made her shudder, and his eyes went wide. He choked, grabbing at his throat, his fingers finding the knife and he looked confused. Blood was everywhere, all over him, all over her, and spilling out of his neck at a rapid pace. For a moment he just looked down at her, time frozen as his brows pulled together, and then he slumped to the side. A horrible, choking, wet sound coming out of him as she pushed herself back from him. Her hand slipped in blood and she scrambled away and stood up, walking backward as he slowly stilled and the terrible noises stopped. Thalia jumped when her back hit the wall. Marcus was on the floor. He wasn't moving, the pool of blood spreading under him. She couldn't look at him anymore. Turning, she yanked the door open and slammed it behind her. The key was still inside the lock and she turned it and yanked it out, testing the door once to make sure it was locked.

Clenching the key in her palm she turned around and finally saw the space. It looked like a small warehouse, but it was empty. Windows lined the top, edged in frost, and she thought she could see her breath in the air. The doors weren't airtight and it couldn't be above freezing, but it didn't matter. She had to find Katherine. "Ka—" She cleared her throat. "KATHERINE!" A small office was on the other side of the space and she ran across. There was a sleeping bag on top of a cot, the toilet, the shower, a table covered in... pictures of her? Thalia picked one up and thought she might be sick. It was outside of the pub they went to in London. Her hands shook as she pushed more of them aside and looked through them. How did he have these? The possibilities tore at her before she snapped back to herself and walked back into the open space.

It was empty. It was so fucking empty.

Against the outside wall of the room she had been in was a table and she moved over to it, hoping there was another building, hoping she could get to Katherine in time. A laptop was set up with huge speakers attached, and she hit the space bar to wake it up. As the screen woke up she waited to see some clue on where he had Katherine, but she just found a desktop covered in video files. Double clicking one she saw a small room with a mattress. Her heart stopped when a dark-haired girl was tossed onto it, her hands up as she begged. The sound was off. Thalia pressed the volume up button and the girl's pleas blasted out of the speakers, begging the man that walked into view not to hurt her, to let her go. The man slapped her and she buckled, her short dark hair flaring out around her pixie like face. Thalia dragged the video tracker forward and the girl's screams ripped out of the speakers, and realization dawned on her as she rushed to pause it, to stop the screaming. The screaming she had heard. That had been the screaming.

"No!" Thalia grabbed her hair, the key digging into her palm as she backed away. It had been Katherine. It had to have been Katherine. Katherine had been screaming. She was about to turn away from the horrible laptop with the frozen image of the girl being whipped bloody, but then she saw something behind it, and she slammed the lid. There was a cell phone tethered to the laptop with a USB. Yanking it out, the screen lit up and she swiped the screen only to see the phone unlock without a code. The phone looked brand new. A few standard apps, no photos, no text messages, the contacts empty. She pulled up the keypad and prayed it could make international calls as she dialed in James' number. The phone was ringing and ringing and ringing — voicemail. She heard his incredible voice saying his name like he had the first night they'd met. *James*. She screamed and hung up.

"Dammit, James, please..." She whimpered as she started to shiver, but she couldn't go into the little office that was a shrine to his obsession with her, and the only other shelter was the strange storage room he'd kept her in. Where Marcus was. She dialed again — voicemail. Again — voicemail. Again—

"Who is this?!" James sounded exasperated, but the second she heard his real voice, and not the professional calm of his voicemail she started sobbing. Sliding down to the floor she curled forward, holding the phone tight as she tried to breathe. "Oh my God, Thalia? Baby? It's you. It's you, right? Baby, please, talk to me, please—"

"James, it was— he—" She couldn't talk through the choking emotion in her chest, on the other end of the line she could hear James shouting at someone, and then he came back to the phone.

"We know Marcus took you, we know. Baby, please, are you safe? Are you—" *all right?* The unspoken end to the sentence hung between them and she pressed her face into her hand, trying to talk. But that wasn't a question she could answer. Instead she grabbed onto the first panicked idea to make it to her lips.

"Katherine! James, it was Katherine! He hurt her, he said he hurt her, but I can't find her. I can't find Katherine anywhere, it's empty. It's so empty, and the screams were a video. They were a *fucking* video." She screamed through her teeth and rocked as she felt herself starting to break apart, but James' voice yanked her back.

"Thalia, Katherine is fine! He did hurt her, she was with a doctor, but she's here. He left her on the sidewalk! God, can you—" There was a voice near him, a man's voice, and then James' returned. His voice so full of shock and hope and surprised joy. "Wait, baby, stay on the phone with me. They're tracking the phone to where you are."

Katherine is fine.

The words sank down through her mind until her sobs calmed. *Katherine is fine.* Where had the blood on the knife come from? *Katherine is fine.* Marcus had lied to her? He had lied. To make her submit. To make her call him Master. To try and break her. *Katherine is fine.* "Katherine wasn't here? She was never here?" Disbelief made her voice sound hollow.

"No, baby. She's safe. I—" The strain of emotion in James' voice pulled her focus back to him. Away from the realization that her reality had been built around a lie since the moment she'd woken up in this nightmare. "Can you tell me what happened, baby? How did you get away?"

"I didn't. I can't leave. He's locked in the room though. I have the key." She turned and looked at the door, afraid any moment it would open and he would come out. "Can you please come get me? I need to leave, I need to get out, but there's snow and there's no clothes, and—" Panic clenched her chest tight until she couldn't breathe, air whistling into her lungs.

"Thalia! Thalia, baby, breathe. Please!" Voices around him again as he pleaded with her over the phone, concern etched in his tone. "They're not far from you, maybe twenty minutes. I'm coming, they are going to bring me to you, baby, please *breathe.*"

"James—" She choked out his name as she tried to do as he asked, but she couldn't get enough air to say everything she wanted to. To beg him to forgive her, to beg him not to hate her, to tell him she was sorry for being the reason for all of this — and to beg him to get here soon, to hold her and let her sleep in his arms, *to still love her.*

"Thalia, are you safe? Are you safe enough for the next twenty minutes until they can reach you?" He turned from the phone and shouted at someone. "*You can bloody wait, the helicopter isn't even here yet!*" His voice calmed when he came back to the phone, "Baby, I need to know you're safe. They need me to leave the phone line open so they can get to you as quickly as possible, which means we both have to set the phones down, and leave them on, but I'm getting on a helicopter to fly to you. Just tell me you are safe, it will be an hour, maybe, before I'm there. I just need to know—"

"I'm safe. Please, just hurry?" She forced the words out even as the chill set in her skin, and she heard him groan in frustration.

"I am. As fast as they can get me there, and you won't be alone. The people I hired to find you were close already, they should be there soon. The leader is Jake. They'll keep you safe until I can get there." A voice by him again and he muttered before speaking up, his voice gentle. "I have to set the phone down now, baby. You set yours down so it stays on the call. I love you. So much. I'm on my way."

"I love you too," she whispered through chattering teeth and held onto the phone a moment more as she strained to listen to the sounds of people shouting at other people. Then there was quiet for a moment — and someone picked up the phone. A man's voice, American, and she flinched away from it. "Ms. Reynolds? Thalia. Are you still there?" He paused, waiting, but she didn't want to talk to him. "It's okay. I can see the line's still open and that's good. You don't need to talk to me, we just need the line open to get as close as possible to your location. I wanted you to know they are about ten minutes away. So... can you tell me if you're injured?"

She huffed out a laugh, not wanting to even imagine how bad she looked. A chill shook her and her teeth chattered again as she curled up tighter on the floor, folding forward to try and conserve her body heat.

"I'm sorry, that was a stupid question. Are you—" He started to speak again and she sighed and set the phone down on the floor, pushing it away from her so she could wrap her arms around herself to stay warm. There were probably some of *his* clothes in the office area, but she couldn't stand to have anything of his near her, much less touching her. Her mind tortured her with every decision she might have made differently had she known Katherine was safe.

But what would the outcome have been? Could she have ever hoped to get as lucky as she had with the knife if she hadn't attacked him over the idea that he'd killed Katherine? If he hadn't had it out, in his hand, to show it to her?

Her body shook with the cold, her muscles jerking as the frigid temperatures got to her. That room had somehow been warmer, maybe because it was closed off? There hadn't been a scrap of light when he turned all the lights off. Thalia felt the exhaustion wash over her as the last of the adrenaline in her system faded.

She had dozed off when the sound of a door opening jerked her awake. Fear blanketed her and she sat up sharply as six men in black military gear poured through a door, guns in their hands as they rushed in. Thalia pushed herself to her feet and stumbled back.

"Holy shit." One of them froze, mid-step and they were all looking at her. The urge to run was strong, but James had said he sent them. Her stomach turned, and the cold made her shiver again.

"Thalia?" Another ripped a beanie off his head, sandy brown hair underneath as he held his hands up, keeping the gun loose in his hand as he scanned the room around her. When he took a step toward her she stepped back and he stopped. "You're Thalia, right? My name is Jake, your boyfriend James hired us to find you. You have a lot of blood on you, can you tell me where it's coming from?"

She shook and crossed her arms over her chest, glancing over at the room to make sure the door was still closed. Jake took another step toward her and she stepped back on instinct. She just wanted James.

"Okay, okay, Thalia. No one is going to move. Can you tell me where he is?" Jake glanced at the others who lowered their guns and stood still, several of them focusing on the floor, or the walls — anywhere but her.

"In the room. It's locked." She spoke and a shiver made her teeth chatter.

"Good, that's good. Then let's focus on you right now. Can I have one of my guys bring me a blanket for you? It's really cold in here. Maybe some water—"

"No water." The panic in her voice snapped out and she whined as a shiver took her again. "But a blanket, okay, a blanket."

Jake grabbed the arm of the guy next to him and spoke quietly, but his voice carried in the emptiness of the warehouse. "Get her a blanket, and whatever food and stuff we have in the car. Let her pick something." The guy ran back outside and Jake took a step toward her, putting his gun away and raising his hands up, "I'm not going to touch you unless you say I can, okay? I'm just going to move a little closer, alright?"

"As long as you don't touch me." She mumbled it as she watched the other man run back in with a gray blanket, the crinkling sound of wrappers inside it. When he got to Jake he stopped, and Jake nodded.

"I got this. Do a sweep of the building, make sure it's clear. Update Brendan that we're here." The guy nodded and left the bundle in Jake's arms before he whistled at the others who started moving around the walls. Jake took a few steps closer and Thalia fought the urge to back away, he sat down on the floor in front of her, about four feet away. Unwrapping the blanket there were snacks of various kinds, a few cans of soda. He slid those to the concrete and held out the blanket, when she didn't move to take it he reached as far forward as he could and set it on the floor. Thalia eased herself into a kneel and grabbed the blanket, wrapping herself up in it. The thick wool cut the chill dramatically and she burrowed into it.

"Thank you," she mumbled.

"You're welcome. Can you tell me, Thalia, is that your blood? I'm not seeing any fresh, so I'm starting to think it might not be." Jake opened a honeybun and bit into it before pushing the small pile of snacks into the neutral zone between them.

"I don't think it's mine." She muttered, leaning forward for a pack of Hostess SnoBalls. Bright pink with coconut and marshmallow, and she knew inside would be the chocolate cake. She hadn't eaten them in years.

"Good. Is it his?" Jake tilted his head, taking another bite of the honeybun and she tore the plastic on the snack cakes, nervous to eat anything. To drink anything. Even though a can of coke was glinting, vibrant red on its side. Thalia looked up at him and nodded, and he smiled and laughed a little. "Guess he underestimated you, didn't he?"

The edge of her mouth twitched, and she unclenched her hand around the key. "Here." She held it out and Jake reached for it, careful only to touch the key. He turned and whistled and one of his guys came for it at a run.

"Grab Mike and go in that room. Make sure he's restrained." Jake spoke quietly and Thalia watched intently as the men moved to the door of the room. She stared at it, comforted by the fact that their guns were drawn.

This was where the bad guy always came back from the dead in horror movies.

The two men stepped inside the room and a moment later one came to the door and shook his head, before staring at her. She turned away from his scrutiny as Jake just laughed to himself. "So you killed him? Want to tell me how you did it?"

"Happy accident." Thalia bit into the SnoBall and almost groaned with the pleasure of it. Fake, sugary, chemical sweetness and all the calories she'd been starved of for days. Jake laughed even louder and nudged a can of sprite toward her with his foot. She ignored the offered can and grabbed the coke. That only made him laugh again as he settled for the sprite.

"Alright, so we've established you're a badass. Would you let my medic look at you? Just to make sure all of the blood is his?" Jake wasn't pressuring her, his voice was calm, he was almost done with the honeybun, and his other hand was occupied with the soda can.

"I'm not a badass." The snap and hiss of the can opening was a deep relief, no damage to the can. It was safe. She drank, and drank, and drank.

"Benny!" he shouted over his shoulder, "Go see if there's another coke in the SUV!" One of the guys saluted and ran outside and Jake looked at her. "You're alive, after almost eight days with him. And you killed a guy probably twice your size. I'm going to stick with the badass label for now."

"Eight days?" Thalia was picking at the marshmallow coating on her SnoBall, eating it in pieces. How did it feel like so much longer? But at the same time not? She could clearly remember getting ready for the run with Katherine. That seemed like less than eight days ago. She could remember the last Broadway play they had seen. The way James had kissed her in the bathroom the night before they'd gone for the run.

Time was torturous.

"Yes. Almost." He set the soda aside and leaned on his knees, "Okay, Thalia. I'm going to be honest, you look like an extra in a zombie movie. You are covered in blood, and I don't think you want to give James the heart attack it will give him if he thinks it's yours. Am I right?"

She looked down and saw the blood on her arms, felt the itchy texture of it drying on her cheek, her neck, her chest. "I could take a shower. There's a shower in the office." She looked up at him, "He's really dead. Isn't he?"

"Definitely. You did a good thing, Thalia. He deserved to—"

"Stop." She cut him off. "I just wanted to make sure. If you think I feel guilty for killing him, I assure you I don't." She finished her coke and popped the rest of the snowball in her mouth. Hoping the sugar rush could carry her until she could find real food. When she stood up, he stood up with her, maintaining her bubble of space.

"Jake!" One of the men called out from a door in the back of the warehouse, "We've got a body out here." Thalia's heart hammered in her chest. *Katherine is fine.* Had that been a lie?

The man approached them and Jake watched her carefully as her tension increased, he waved the other man aside so he walked a wide path around her to approach him. Jake looked at him, "Tell me."

"White guy, been dead at least a few days, hard to tell since he's been lying in snow. Has she said anything about another—" The man stopped talking, his eyes glued to her and then he muttered a curse as he turned away.

"I'm pretty sure it's the one who attacked Katherine and me, when we were running. He helped Marcus take me." She looked at Jake who was obviously restraining his reaction to her words, trying to keep his expression neutral, "Marcus never planned on sharing me."

"Alright. We'll take care of the bodies, don't even think about it." Jake rubbed his hand through his hair. "Go shower, we'll grab you some extra gear. It'll be big on you, but it will be something. Dr. Hawkins should be here soon."

When her shower was done, she wrung out her hair as much as she could and tried to towel dry it. Jake tapped on the doorframe and she sighed as he stood outside. "You've already seen me naked, just give me the clothes."

"Jesus Christ." Jake hissed in a breath and when she turned back around she saw his cheeks flushed in rage, and she flinched. He cursed under his breath and set the clothes on top of the pictures of her before he raised his hands up and stepped back from her. "I'm sorry, I just— I hadn't seen your back. Will you let my medic look at you, please?"

"They're just welts, they'll heal. They did last time." Thalia grabbed a shirt and pulled it on to cover them, followed by pants that she had to hold up to keep on, thick socks, and boots a few sizes too big. It was just to keep something on her skin, and the hat was the best part anyway because it kept the cold away from her damp hair. She grabbed the jacket and held out her duct taped arm. "He can look at my arm if he wants. Just my arm."

"I saw the bandage before. What happened?" Jake looked at her with pain in his eyes. He was upset over the welts on her skin, the marks on her body, and she knew it had been the right decision to clean up the blood. James was going to be upset enough at the things she couldn't wash away when he got here.

"I tried to kill myself." Thalia brushed past him and left him coughing on his surprise as she moved to sit back by their picnic. The other guys had grabbed snacks but formed a wide semi-circle when she approached, giving her plenty of room.

Chapter Thirty
THALIA

It had been another twenty minutes of awkward staring, but at least now she was clothed and not naked or huddled in a blanket. Benny was their medic and he had peeled the duct tape and the gauze away and looked at her arm with clinical indifference. Thalia appreciated it. No gasping, no questions other than to ask what she had used to cut herself. Benny had reopened the wound, muttering about idiots using super glue on jagged edges, and then put in stitches. With the topical anesthetic though, it became one of the few places on her body that *didn't* hurt. He'd recommended a tetanus shot, a round of antibiotics, and to have the wound rechecked in a week.

Then he'd left her alone.

They were talking about her in hushed whispers, and it was starting to grate her nerves as she waited for James to arrive so she could leave the damn warehouse. If it wasn't freezing with snow on the ground, she'd be standing outside. "What the fuck are you all whispering about?" They went silent as six sets of eyes turned toward her. "Will one of you speak up?"

"I'm sorry, ma'am." One of them, Mike, wiped a hand down his face, "None of us want to upset you, we — fuck, we just didn't think we'd find you alive. All of us are kind of in shock over it."

"Let me try and explain… this is what we do. We find people who have been taken, and *none* of us have ever seen someone in your shape still alive, who also took out the guy who fucking grabbed them? I mean it's been more than a week!" Another of the guys spoke up, and they all nodded.

"I told you, Thalia, you're a badass." Jake shrugged, "Dr. Hawkins kept telling us how brave you were, that you were a fighter, but I'm not sure it sank in with any of us until we saw you."

She dropped her head into her hands, propping her elbows on her knees. They had no idea what they were talking about. They had no idea what she'd done, what she'd said, while Marcus had her. She had submitted more often than not. Her efforts at fighting him had been pitiful. Her killing him had been luck. Not skill, not strength — luck. An accident of action that could have just as easily ended up with him beating her again. Her body looked the way it did because she had lost every fight against him.

Except for the last one.

They were all staring at her but she didn't have a response for them. If they wanted to view her as some badass, one in a thousand, survival case — they could go ahead and do that. Maybe it would help them some day in the future to believe it was possible. Jake tilted his head and smiled a bit as he pointed up, "Your boyfriend is here." A moment later Thalia heard the strange heavy beating sound of the helicopter's blades.

She stood up, her body shaking as the sound grew louder and louder. *James.*

Guilt racked her again. She was torn between the impossible urge to have him hold her again, to feel safe in his arms again — and the intense fear that he wouldn't be able to move past it this time. She glanced at Jake, "So, how bad do I really look?"

"You look a lot better than you did when we first got here, and the worst of it is covered. But you have a pretty bad bruise on that cheek, it's swollen, and your lip is split. And there's the bruises on your neck." He cleared his throat and looked away from her.

"Great. James is going to freak out." Thalia clenched her fists at her side as her nerves took her over. The urge to cry was back again because she was so close to seeing him.

"Thalia, James would have freaked out when he saw you even if you'd looked just fine. Trust me on that. He's been sick with worry over you, and I have to tell you he can be pretty terrifying when he's like that." Jake looked at her seriously and the idea of it made her smile a bit. The sound of the helicopter winding down outside made her stomach turn over. She started to walk toward the door, but froze, not knowing what to do, what to expect. When the door finally opened James was framed in sunlight, but she knew the outline of him by heart, and his hair caught the winter sun like a halo.

"Thalia!" He rushed toward her and she felt her lips form his name, because just looking at him was like waking up from the nightmare she'd been trapped in. But

James stopped short of touching her, and she could see the restraint it took for him not to grab onto her. Some part of her appreciated it, and some part of her wished he'd just hold her. "Baby…" There was so much emotion in his voice, his green eyes showing it above the dark circles under them. He moved his arm slowly so she could see what he was doing, and he laid his hand against the side of her face not covered with a bruise. She leaned in to his touch, covering his hand with hers, and the tears came. It was a floodgate she shouldn't have opened, but it was too late. He stepped forward like he was going to hold her, but she slid to her knees before he could.

"I'm sorry, I'm sorry, I'm sorry…" she breathed harshly through the tears, her head dropping, and she was aware on some level that everyone was watching her.

"Thalia," James' voice was directly in front of her and he touched her chin lightly to make her look at him, on his knees in front of her. "You do not need to apologize. For anything." He dropped his hand from her chin, "Can I — can I please touch you?"

She forced herself to nod, and he pulled her against his chest. His warmth seeped into her and she buried her face against his shoulder, holding him tight and ignoring the ache of his grip across her bruised back. "Can you forgive me?" She whispered it and he stilled.

"There's nothing to forgive—" He started to speak soothingly to her, but she cut him off, whispering urgently.

"I submitted to him. I fought him too, it was useless, but I did. But I also submitted." Thalia grabbed his coat tightly, trying to confess so he knew everything. Like he'd known everything the last time. She needed it. She needed him to know all of it. "He drugged me, and I gave myself to him. It was — horrible, and when I woke up I tried to kill myself."

"Thalia!" He leaned back from her and cupped her face in his hands, his expression a twist of agony that she couldn't determine the source of. Had she hurt him with her words? Was that pity? Of all times she wanted to be able to read him as well as he could read her, now was the most important. "What did you do, baby?"

A bitter smile crossed her lips when she realized it was the same question Marcus had screamed at her when he'd found her. She moved her arm out of the jacket and tugged the sleeve of the shirt up to reveal Benny's bandages. James made a pained sound and bent over her arm, pressing kisses to the gauze, then he leaned up and grabbed her face and kissed her gently.

"I am so bloody sorry. I should have never trusted that the police would handle him, I should have had him killed. I should have killed him myself for what he did to you, but I'll fix that now." He pressed a kiss to her lips before she could respond, and he turned until he could see Jake. "Where is he?"

The men had moved toward the exit to give them their privacy, and they all looked at each other when James asked the question. Jake stepped forward, "He's dead, Dr. Hawkins."

James' shoulders tensed, his voice cold, "What did I ask—"

"I killed him, James." Thalia reached for his arm and he spun on her, his expression shifting from surprise to pain and then concern. "It was luck. He'd told me he'd killed Katherine, he wanted to break me, and I tried to hurt him. But I'm so weak, and he had me on the floor again, and he was screaming and I couldn't breathe — and then the knife was in my hand. And I — I stabbed him."

"God, Thalia..." James leaned forward and pulled her into his lap, his arms wrapping around her as a groan slipped out of him. "I hate this, I hate all of this. I wish I had been there to protect you, I should have fucking been there, but you are not weak, Thalia. You have never been weak. You have to know that. It was your strength, your fight, that drew me to you in the first place, you remember that?" His words came out hushed against her hair, and her heart ached with them.

"I love you."

"I love you so much, baby. I can't — My world fell apart without you. I wasn't a good person without you in it. If I had lost you, I don't think I ever would have recovered." He pressed a kiss to her temple. "Nothing that has happened changes how I feel about you, do you understand?"

It was impossible. No one could love someone that much, to not be colored or changed by a confession like she'd given him. "How can you? Last time... last time I wasn't yours, and you saw everything, but I wasn't yours yet. And — and I can't even *explain* everything this time. It's such a fucking blur, and I need to—" He stopped her speech with a brush of his thumb across her lips.

"I may not have had the video this time, Thalia, but Marcus sent me audio clips to make sure I knew exactly what he was doing. He wanted me to know." James' voice was tortured and she whined as she imagined the things he must have heard, must have heard her say. "And I am telling you, I love you. I love you the same. Actually, if it were possible for me to love you more, the idea of being left in a world without you in it made me love you more."

"Are you sure?" she whispered, and he shifted her in his lap so he could look at her. His sea green eyes blazing with a fierce energy.

"I am. And this time, whatever you need, whatever I can do for you — I will do it. The right way this time. Promise me that you will talk to me, that you will tell me what you're feeling so I don't let you suffer out of my own ignorance." He traced the bruise on her cheek, sympathetic pain flashing across his face. "Promise me honesty, please."

Tears slid down her cheeks, brushing his hand as she nodded. "Always. I will always be honest with you, it was why I told you everything. We have no secrets, right?"

"None." James kissed her, and she felt something inside her shift back into place, something that Marcus' violence had threatened, but not broken completely. Her arms went around his neck and he kissed her harder, a murmur rising up in her throat as he eased the kiss back. "I'm going to take you out of here. Katherine has a private doctor we used for her, will you let him look at you?"

"If you're there." She mumbled, and he held her against him gently, his mouth in her hair.

"You're not going to be more than a yard away from me for a while, baby. I can promise you that." His words made her smile. "I understand if you don't want to talk to me about all of it, but Kalen knows, and so I'm sure Ailsa will want to speak with you. Not today, but will you talk to her?"

She nodded. "I'll talk to you, James. I will. But, yes, I'll talk to Ailsa too." She winced as her back twinged. "If Katherine has been with you — does she, I mean... did you tell her?"

"Not everything. She doesn't need to know everything. I told her you'd had a stalker, and that's how I knew who took you. She's been torturing herself over what happened, hasn't even been able to speak to me. Not that I was very good company." He sighed and his voice was heavy when he whispered against her hair, "I am so very sorry, baby."

"I have you. I'm back with you, that's all that matters. No apologies needed, right?" She looked up at him and there was the ghost of a smile on his lips, but the pain in his eyes wasn't fading. She knew he'd look at her like that until she'd healed, maybe even after. But it was because he loved her.

"Right. You're right. Are you ready to leave, baby?"

"Yes, please. I really want to leave this place." She felt the desperate tide of panic rising in her, but she pushed it back. He helped her stand, and Jake approached them, shaking James' hand and making assurances that the bodies would disappear. No questions asked.

"Take care of yourself, alright, badass?" He looked at her, not even offering his hand, and the name made her mouth twitch into a smile again.

"Badass?" James asked, arching an eyebrow.

"Your girl is a badass," Jake reiterated, and James chuckled.

"Yes, she is." He kissed her hair again, and a hint of his normal mischievous grin played on his lips. "Baby, tell me, have you ever ridden in a helicopter?"

She laughed, and it was the first time that she felt any sense of normalcy since Marcus had taken her again. It was her weird kind of normal. The normal of her boyfriend's over the top comments and gestures. The impossible perfection of his love for her, and the new realization that all of her nervous fears of meeting his family were ridiculous. Nothing could break them.

They were unbreakable.

Chapter Thirty-One
THALIA

Fourteen Months After the Auction

Thalia stretched and shifted in the desk chair, her back popping with a satisfying crack that finally let her sigh and relax for a minute. She'd already been staring at the computer screen for an hour, typing and re-typing, deleting and re-typing again.

It didn't feel *right* yet.

Reaching for the spoon in her cereal bowl she groaned. Empty. She could refill the bowl with cereal, *or* just grab one of the cupcakes Becca had made for everyone at the studio. Turning the spoon over in the last of the milk she glanced over the words on the screen again. She wanted — no, she needed — them to be perfect.

And perfect required a fucking cupcake.

Grinning, Thalia took the bowl to the kitchen and abandoned it in the sink before popping open the little plastic container that Becca had handed her at the sunrise class that morning. "Red velvet. I fucking love you, Becca," she mumbled gratefully as she peeled the paper off and took a bite. It was heaven, and just as she was starting to savor it her cell started ringing in the office. Of course she'd be interrupted. With a groan she grabbed the container and ran to get the phone.

"Yeah, hi — hello?" Thalia rambled as she licked frosting off her fingertips, holding the cell phone against her shoulder as she regrettably tucked the rest of the cupcake back in with its two friends.

"Hello, Thalia." Ailsa sounded like she had something to *talk* to her about.

"Hi, Ailsa. What can I do for you this morning?" Thalia tried to sound peppy as she dropped into the chair, grabbing her coffee.

"I'm just checking in. How are ye today?" She had therapist voice on full blast. *Dammit.*

"I'm great! I taught a class early this morning, I was just about to eat a cupcake, and I'm working on the invitations to the forum."

"Hmm. And, how did ye sleep last night?" Ailsa's question wasn't innocent. *She knew.* James had called her. Glaring at her inbox, Thalia contemplated sending a not-so-nice email to him at work.

"James called you, didn't he." It wasn't even a question. James had told Ailsa about the nightmare.

"He said it was a bad night. So talk to me. How bad was it?" Ailsa sighed on the other end of the line when Thalia only groaned into the phone. "Thalia, ye promised me that ye would keep talking to me, that ye wouldn't shut me out. Ignoring it is not what makes you whole, working through it—"

"Alright!" Thalia cut her off. She'd heard Ailsa's speech on working through trauma over and over again as she'd worked at healing herself.

She had to admit, the first month after Marcus had been bad. Okay, *really* bad. Screaming in her sleep bad. She'd spent half her nights sleeping in the playroom with James so no one in the building would call the police. This time it hadn't been a fear of going anywhere, or a panic in public — it had been a fear of sleeping.

Because in her dreams Marcus wasn't dead.

Which eventually meant that Thalia had just refused to sleep. She had thrown herself into keeping Nirvana going from a distance since she couldn't teach yet, thrown herself into researching the girls INTERPOL was working to save, and then into Netflix marathons, and trying to learn to crochet. Night after night of blanketing herself in anything but sleep. Even if James lay down with her, held her, begged her to sleep — she just counted in her head to keep herself awake. Doing math to keep her brain busy until his breaths evened out and she could sit up without waking him.

Ailsa had shown up in London after Thalia reached three and a half days with no sleep whatsoever. James had called her out of desperation, and she had arrived — and then promptly tranquilized Thalia while she had screamed and begged for her not to do it. James had been the one to help hold her down.

She had slept for twenty-six dreamless hours straight.

James had not. While she was out cold James had stayed with her, refusing to leave her side, convinced she was trapped in a nightmare. He had been racked with guilt. And apparently, while she was sleeping, he had said some really terrible things to Ailsa. Kalen had flown in to take James out of the flat and Ailsa had stayed in the house with her. Even months later no one would actually tell her what he'd said, and James said he'd been so stressed he could barely remember shouting at her. It had been a mess.

The solution? Thalia had to speak with Ailsa three days a week, she had to talk through the nightmares, and she absolutely had to sleep.

So, Thalia had started sleeping. Even though the nightmares were waiting. Then, they had slowly started to spread out. Her injuries had mostly healed by the beginning of the second month and she had gone back to work with colorful arm socks on to cover the healing scar on her wrist. Becca had done an amazing job of keeping Nirvana running, and the executive assistant James had hired temporarily was now a permanent, and very necessary, member of the studio. Her name was Kimmy, and she was an organizing genius. But it had been *months* since that dark time. Thalia slept, and she was fine.

Pretty much.

Thalia groaned into the phone, "Okay, so I had a nightmare last night, but it's been seven days since the last one, Ailsa! SEVEN days. That counts for something!"

"Of course it counts, Thalia. Ye have been doing great, but that doesn't mean I don't want ye to talk to me about them anymore. James mentioned ye screamed and when he turned the light on ye were still asleep... like the ones in the beginning. He had to shake ye to get ye to wake up, and—"

"And then I freaked out. I know. I was there." Thalia rubbed her eyes and sighed. "James is fine, he's a lot faster at restraining me now."

Not like at first. Until Ailsa had told him it was okay to restrain her so she didn't hurt him, or herself, he refused to do anything to protect himself. One night he hadn't moved back in time and ended up with scratches on his neck before she remembered where she was. He was always gentle when he restrained her now though, grabbing her wrists and holding them in front of her so she could see him, and he was quick when he was awake. All the sparring he'd done with Kalen when they were younger finally coming in handy with his instinct to block. He liked to joke that she was keeping him sharp whenever she apologized about it — and he'd remind her that there were no apologies needed. No apologies for any of it. That was their rule.

Post-traumatic stress disorder is a bitch.

"I know that James is fine, how are *ye*, Thalia?" Ailsa repeated her earlier question, clearly expecting a more detailed answer.

"Ailsa, fuck, I'm always fine once I realize where I am! Once I remember that he's dead… it doesn't last. The fear, the panic — it's a flash in the pan. The one last night just felt real. So real. And in the dream he'd had me pinned under him and I just wanted him off me, and…" Thalia shrugged and drank more of her coffee, trying not to let the images back into her head. Instead she thought of the last image she had of Marcus. Just before they'd gone to the helicopter she had looked in the room and seen him in a pool of his own blood — exactly where she'd left him. Marcus was dead. That was the first thing she told herself after every nightmare.

The fact that it wasn't the first thing she told herself *every* morning was progress.

"And?" Ailsa prompted when Thalia didn't continue.

"And so I woke up fighting, and when James reacted I wasn't quite awake yet so I tried to kick him away from me," she smiled weakly. "He grabbed me and started talking to me. He talked about when I'd worn this green dress when we were in Barcelona, and that he still listens to *Travesuras* by Nicky Jam at work sometimes when he misses me." The memory made her smile more. She had gotten drunk at a little restaurant there and danced to it, singing the parts she'd memorized even though she didn't speak Spanish. It had been on the radio *a lot*.

"So that's working?" Ailsa asked calmly, and Thalia sighed. When she was having the nightmares more frequently Ailsa had been the one to suggest that James remind her of who he was, of where she was, by telling her a memory they shared. A good memory that would help to push back the nightmare.

"It always works, Ailsa. I told you, *everything is fine*. It was a bad night, but it's been seven days since the last one, and I didn't freak out that time. Before that it was four days. Before that, five days. I'm averaging just one a week!" Thalia felt exasperated.

"Ye know James only called me because he loves ye, and he wanted to make sure ye were alright. Ye are so focused on feeling normal that ye don't want to address the trauma anymore. And before ye interrupt me, I agree, ye are doing phenomenally well. It doesn't mean we ignore the lingering effects from your time with Marcus. It's only been a little over three months. Give yerself a break, Thalia!" Ah, Ailsa had dropped the therapist act. It was always easier to listen to her when she didn't sound like she was running a radio therapy line like some kind of female, Scottish, Frasier.

"I know. I know, Ailsa. I don't mean to be a bitch about it, and I'm sorry. I appreciate your help, I just hate feeling fragile."

"Ye are *not* fragile, Thalia, and we have discussed that as well. Ye survived him not once, but twice. A fragile person could not have done that." Ailsa had said it over and over in their talks. She had even repeatedly addressed that the suicide attempt was just an attempt at self-preservation, at avoiding the drugs again, at keeping herself away from Marcus. Ailsa had told her she had no concerns over a repeat attempt because it was situational, not psychological. That had helped some, and eased James' overprotectiveness a little. Although the security detail he'd hired still followed her everywhere. Ailsa sighed into the phone, "Alright, as long as ye assure me yer doing well, I won't bring it up again today. Go on, tell me where yer at with yer project."

That made Thalia smile, and she launched into an update on the number of girls located, on the number that had been rescued, on the tiny number who had found good men and happiness. On that very short list was Kaia. She had learned through court transcripts that Thomas had apparently been blackmailed as well, that Marcus had actually threatened Kaia to keep him involved. Kaia had never even known about the threats, which explained how her twisted affection for him could have ever continued. Even thinking of them reminded Thalia of the care in Thomas, the gentle way he'd touched Anna and Kaia at the house, the sad way he had looked at her, commented on her injuries. After everything came out, Thomas had cut a deal to stay out of jail for not reporting the crimes, for aiding Marcus with the tattoos, and for being involved in the trafficking of Kaia.

Thomas, Anna, and Kaia had moved to Colorado when Anthony's trial was over.

Marcus was still wanted by the FBI and INTERPOL, and a scrabble game's worth of other agencies. But Jake had assured James that there were no bodies to find. The warehouse had been cleaned. Like she had never even been there. His team had sent her flowers after she'd returned to London along with a care package filled with snowballs and Coca Cola. In the package had been a note: *For our favorite badass. Heal fast.* All of their names had been underneath. James had laughed and kissed her, saying she was the only girl in the world with a fan club made of mercenaries.

Ailsa let her ramble for a while about the security measures in place for her website, all of the technobabble that filled her inbox talking about VPN tunnels, proxy servers, and scattering IP signals. Then Ailsa had laughed and finally stopped her. "I am so proud of what ye are doing, Thalia. I think of anything, this is going to heal ye the most. And ye do promise me that ye are doing alright? The nightmares aren't affecting ye during the day?"

Thalia sighed and leaned back in the chair, thinking for a moment so she'd answer honestly. She went with most of the truth, knowing there were some things Ailsa couldn't help with. "Ailsa, I'm sleeping again. I go to bed with James every night, and I'd be lying if it didn't cross my mind before I closed my eyes that something horrible might come up while I'm dreaming. But I'm not trying to avoid sleep anymore, and I know when I wake up that James will be there and I'll remember that Marcus is dead. I don't even really think about it during the day, it just hits me when I lay my head down on the pillow."

"Alright. I believe ye. I have an appointment now, but we'll see each other soon." Ailsa sounded warm and kind, because she was, and an inkling of guilt threaded through Thalia but she pushed it away. She'd talk to James about the rest of it. They said their goodbyes and finally hung up. With a sigh Thalia grabbed the cupcake as she turned back to the letter on the screen. It was as perfect as it was going to be, but she reread it once more anyway.

```
Hello —

First, I am sorry for what happened to you. It
happened to me too, although our experiences were
likely still very different.

The man who took you was named Marcus Williams. He
had a brother named Anthony Williams. Anthony is in
jail for life, without the possibility of parole,
based on his involvement in the abduction, rape,
torture, and human trafficking of numerous others.
Marcus is dead. I promise you that this is true. I'm
writing to you because I hope that even if you ignore
the rest of this letter you will sleep better knowing
these things. I know I do.

Second, I also want to offer you the below log in
information for an anonymous forum. You were not the
only one they took. You were not the only one they
hurt. And no one understands like those who actually
experienced it, and no one will listen to your story
like those that went through it themselves. It's a
place for all of us to talk, to reach out to each
other. We are the only ones with access to this
forum.

It's your choice to log in, to speak with me, and
with anyone else that logs in — but I hope you do. It
helps to know that you're not alone. Maybe only a
little, but it does help.

I am TR0414, and I will be here when you're ready.
```

Thalia took a breath and pulled up the file of victims' names, current addresses, and the document with which brother had taken each of them. All she had to do was register them on the site to generate their username and password, adjust the letter to switch the brothers' names if needed, and then print them out. The letters would be sent through an anonymous mail service, accompanied by a tablet that came with a data plan so they wouldn't need access to the internet. Just a power supply. That had been James' idea, and he had happily told her which ones to order and how to order them anonymously.

From the moment Thalia had told James her plan, he had supported her. He'd stayed up at night talking with her about it, handed her the team of hackers who had originally found the information on the Williams brothers, and hired people to build the site she needed. He had also been making a series of anonymous, obscene donations to human trafficking organizations around the world. The last part was his own penance, and his own crusade, and she didn't pressure him to discuss the decision. It was a good thing, after all, and if it helped him ease his conscience — all the better.

Chapter Thirty-Two
THALIA

❦

Hours later and Thalia was staring at a stack of letters that was too tall to be real. Each one represented a life the Williams brothers had done their best to destroy. She bit her lip against the urge to cry as she flipped through them, and her hand stopped on the one that read 'Beth Doherty.' Not in Germany anymore, she was back in California with her family, but living in a facility. James had anonymously taken care of her bills, relieving the financial strain on her family, and she was awake now. She just didn't speak to anyone. Ever. Of every name on the list, the two she wanted to see log in most were Beth and Victoria. Beth, because Marcus had told her the girl's story — and Victoria, because she was the one who Marcus had taken to replace her. The resemblance between Thalia and Victoria had been disturbing to discover. They could be sisters.

She heard the front door open and wiped her eyes, setting the stack of letters on the desk where it slid to the side and fanned out. Thalia took a breath and called out to James, "Hey, I'm in the office!"

"Hi, baby." He walked in wearing a suit and she smiled at him. *She really did have the hottest boyfriend.* Leaning down he pressed a kiss to her lips and grinned against her mouth, his hand sliding down her side after a moment, but she grabbed it with a quick laugh.

"Oh no. Nuh-uh. You're in trouble." She looked up at him, and he arched an eyebrow at her. Then realization dawned on him.

"Ailsa." He sighed and crossed his arms.

"Ailsa," Thalia confirmed and crossed her arms as well, leaning back in the chair to look at him. "I told you this morning I was fine."

"Your attempt at body kicking me off the bed begs to differ." He shrugged. "You were due to call her anyway."

"Not the point." She stood up and pointed at him. "You do not get to tattle on me to my therapist!"

A wicked grin slid over his mouth and he reached for her hips, tugging her against him. "What if I promise to make it up to you?"

"I'm going to kick you while I'm fully conscious in a second." She bit her cheek so she wouldn't smile at him, but he didn't fall for it. His grin just widened and he slid his arms around her back.

"I don't think you will, pet."

"Why not?" She leaned back against his arms so she could see his face clearly. Sea green eyes sparkling with mischief, his blond hair still tousled like he'd been in the wind, and a grin that spoke volumes. He was up to something.

"Two reasons. First, I ran by the shop and got the ingredients for your favorite dinner. Second, I was able to move the evening with my parents so that you wouldn't miss the play with Analiese. I have been a *very* good boyfriend today." He leaned down and hovered his mouth in front of hers, and she relented and kissed him. He intensified it, bending her back so he could control the kiss and a soft moan slipped out of her. Then he stood them back up and his grin returned. "Are you sure you don't want me to make it up to you?"

Thalia rolled her eyes and reached between them to stroke his cock through his pants, the groan he made filled her with satisfaction. When his eyes returned to hers they were dark green, and his hands tightened on her hips. She felt her mouth curve in a slow smile, "Are you sure you don't want me to *let* you make it up to me?"

"Vixen." He growled as she stroked him, biting his lip until a rumble came from his chest. "That's it, dinner is going to wait." James grabbed her and lifted her up, and she wrapped her legs around him to hold on, laughing loudly. A second later she was against the wall of the office, his hardness rubbing against her as he took her mouth. Thalia pushed her hands into his hair, holding him against her as she rolled her hips, moaning softly.

"What will you do to make it up to me?" She gasped out the words as his mouth ran down her neck before halting by the tank top.

"Anything you want, baby." He smiled and tugged the top over her head, and she smiled back, foolhardy bravery filling her for a moment.

"I want the belt." She watched as his face fell and he leaned his head against hers, breathing out a sigh against her shoulder.

"Thalia…"

"Please? Pretty please?" She shifted on his hips, cradling his face to make him look at her again as she begged. "James, please?"

"I don't think—" His eyes flashed pain, and guilt ate at her. In the last two months they had played with almost everything… except the belt. The only implement Marcus had used with her. But she was not going to drop it this time. Ailsa's reminder that morning to address the issues and not ignore them was too fresh.

"Can we just try? I want it. I want you to use it. *You.*" Thalia bit her lip, and she watched indecision move over his face. She didn't want to say Marcus' name. She didn't want to bring up the fact that every time she saw a belt she thought of him. She needed to blur that connection, to mix it up. Just like she'd destroyed the power that the word *chair* had on her psyche, she had to take this back. And she had always liked the belt when James used it. She didn't want it to be some dark, mystical object in their playroom and in their closet. Filling her with uneasy tension and nightmarish memories.

"Now?" His voice ached, but she nodded and he let her slide out of his arms and she dropped onto her knees.

"Now. Please, Master?" Thalia made her voice quiet as he looked down at her, and then he took a breath and shifted. The indecision disappeared from his face like it hadn't been there, and a serious expression took it over.

"Thalia. You have to be certain. This could go—" *so wrong.* His eyes finished the sentence and she sighed and threw out the only alternative she had planned.

"I was going to ask Kalen," she said softly and watched his jaw tighten. *He hated that idea even more.* Thalia continued gently. "But I want it to be you. I just — I need to do it, James."

He closed his eyes for a second and lifted his face toward the ceiling like he was thinking. A deep breath rose and fell in his chest before he looked back down at her. "If you feel even the tiniest fraction of panic, you will safe word. I know you can handle pain, Thalia. That is not my main concern. Panic. Fear. Any of it, the smallest feeling, and you will safe word. I *cannot* have you afraid of me, so promise me. Promise me you will stop everything if you're afraid." As he spoke his hand slid over her cheek until his fingers cradled the back of her neck, keeping her gaze so she could see how serious he was.

She nodded quickly before he could take it back. "Yes, Master. I swear, I *promise.*"

"Okay. All right. Come with me, then." He leaned down and grabbed her hand, pulling her to her feet before leading her to the door of the playroom. "Strip. I'll be right back."

She was out of the rest of her clothes and kneeling inside the door in a matter of moments. James took longer, a lot longer, and she was beginning to worry he had changed his mind when she heard the tinkling sound of metal approaching. Her heart stuttered at the sound and she swallowed, taking a deep breath. He was in those soft black pants he loved and he crouched in front of her and laid out a ridiculous array of belts. Brown, black, shiny, matte, soft, and stiff. So many varieties. Razor-winged butterflies filled her on the inside as she looked up at him. He wouldn't meet her eyes, she didn't think he could, and for once she knew what he was asking before he spoke.

"Choose one." James' voice was stiff as he stood and walked away from her. *He knew.* He wanted her to choose the one closest to the one from her nightmares so she could work through it with him. He understood why she was asking. He understood what memory would be with them in this room, and he was still going to help her. Thalia forced a breath to push back the tears that burned the edges of her eyes and spread the belts out in front of her. Every time the metal fixtures moved the tension inside her increased. Finally, she saw one that was close enough, about the right width, a dull black. She folded it over in her hands and the sight of it struck home, her stomach tightening.

Yeah, it was close.

"Master?" she called softly, and he turned.

"Bring it to me."

Thalia moved to him and held it out, and his thumb traced the leather when he took it from her. With a careful movement he laid it on the table against the wall before turning back to her. She'd expected him to get it over with, to have her bent over the spanking bench, but instead he slid his hands to the back of her head and kissed her gently. Tenuous at first, and he walked her backward away from the table as his lips plied hers softly. The barest nip of his teeth over her lip, combined with his warm hands holding her to his mouth, had her relaxing and she found her hands landing at his waist to hold onto him.

It was the kind of *I love you* said with actions instead of words.

She backed into the wall and he opened her mouth under his, deepening their kiss. One of his hands trailed slowly down her side, no sudden movements, and she was infinitely grateful to be wet from their make-out session in the office. When his fingers traced her pussy she moaned in encouragement, her hips pressing forward. He didn't deny her, sliding his touch through her wetness, gathering it, before rubbing in tight circles over her clit. She dropped her head back against the wall and his mouth moved down her offered neck. "Oh God..." she breathed out on a moan.

James moved his kisses down her body, licking and nipping at her skin until he thrust two fingers inside her and his mouth covered her clit in a warm shock of pleasure. He lifted her thigh up, pressing it to the wall next to her and she balanced, lifting onto the toes of her other foot with panting moans. Her hands were in his hair, holding on as he pushed her higher, out of the stress of what she'd asked for and into bliss. It was a torturously slow climb, his fingers moving inside her to the rhythmic beat of his tongue's movements, and then he drew harder on her clit and she moaned louder. It encouraged him, and his touches grew bolder, her moans increasing until she was shivering, heat rushing inside her to pool between her legs.

"Please, please, may I come?" It came out as a rapid plea and ended on a gasping moan. He thrust his fingers harder inside her and pressed a kiss to her thigh.

"Yes, pet. Come for me. You don't need permission tonight." His words told her that this was all about her, and the realization washed over her, but when his mouth returned to the bundle of nerves her pussy quickly became the focus of her entire world. She was so close, but she needed more than gentle touches, more than soft kisses. He was being so careful with her. Too careful.

She moaned and tightened her hand in his hair sharply. He growled against her pussy, but she did it again, harder. Pressing his buttons. Pushing her thigh onto his shoulder he grabbed her wrist and pulled it away from his hair, pinning it to her thigh so he could return to licking her. She gasped and tugged at the grip on her wrist, and he tightened it on reflex. His thrusts inside her sharpened and she arched her back against the wall, pressing herself harder against his mouth. His teeth trailed over her clit and she cried out. Sparks crackled inside her and he curved his fingers, making her come hard against his mouth in a rush of heat that left her shaking as he drew out her orgasm. Mind blank, forgetting why they were in the playroom as pure bliss took her over in a wash of light and fire that speckled her skin with sweat. He continued with deviously gentle licks over her clit until she was whimpering and trying to close her thighs, to pull back from the edge he held her to with each movement of his tongue. "Ah! Master, please!"

With her plea he finally let her go and stood. His eyes were dark, bottle glass green and intently focused on hers, his jaw tight with barely restrained power. The look left her breathless, and when she reached to wipe the wetness from his chin he caught her wrist and pressed it to the wall beside her. "Thalia. On tonight of all bloody nights, are you trying to top from the bottom?" His voice was low and serious as he leaned forward.

"No, Master." She shook her head and his lips twitched up.

"I think you are, pet. If you want something — just say it. Tell me what you want." He gathered her wrists above her head and pinned them gently while the rest of his body stayed back from her. She wanted to argue with him, to deny it, but she'd played his responses on purpose. It was true.

"You don't need to treat me like I'm fragile," she whispered. The high of her orgasm still simmered under her skin, her breathing still shallow.

He tightened his grip on her wrists. "I know you're not fragile, pet." James' words were solemn as he leaned forward to kiss her softly, and she could taste herself on his lips. Then he had a hand in her hair, tightening his grip as he pulled her off the wall, and she gasped when he pushed her firmly to her knees. He towered over her when he moved in front of her, his voice a low rumble. "You were going to ask Kalen for this?"

His change of topic made her head spin, his voice cold and clear, with no hint of how he felt about her suggested alternative. She licked her lips and answered, "Yes, Master."

"Why?" He walked around her, and she hated not being able to see him, to see his expression when he spoke.

"I—" She bit her lip, trying to find the right words. "I didn't want to ask for something you didn't want to do."

His hand slid into her hair again, tightening until it ached and electric pleasure buzzed down her spine. She moaned and squirmed, the wetness of her orgasm coating the insides of her thighs. His mouth was by her ear when he spoke again. "Do you really think there is anything I would deny you, pet?"

"No, Master." The words rang true inside her. James would move heaven and earth for her. He practically *had*. There had never been a thing she'd asked for that he'd denied her. Not the small things like a coffee maker, or breakfast for dinner, or to watch a sappy romcom on a Saturday. And, more importantly, not the big things either. She'd wanted the Williams brothers' business destroyed — he'd done it. She had wanted to teach yoga — he had supported her to get certified and then bought her a fucking studio. And when she'd disappeared? He had hired a team of mercenaries without a second thought and thrown everything into finding her. What man in the world had done things like that, what man did *everything* for the woman he loved?

"Tell me you want it," he commanded, voice rumbling against her ear, and she forced a breath. After everything he'd done for her, after all they'd been through, now he was offering to do this. Even though she knew it would be as hard for him as it would be for her. Emotion threatened to choke her but she swallowed it, clearing her head before she answered.

"I want the belt, Master," she answered, and his grip tightened on her hair until she whimpered, a pulse of need aching between her thighs.

"Get up." He pulled her up and she moved with him until she was by the gymnastics horse in the center of the room. Then he let go of her and returned to the table. The metallic scrape of the belt across the surface made the butterflies swarm inside her, beating at her insides, making her heart race. James stretched out the belt in his hands, his head angled down to look at the leather, blond hair brushing his forehead. Her eyes were glued to it as he folded it over, and then he suddenly lifted his gaze to hers.

Thalia silently hoped her expression was neutral because it would be a lie to say she wasn't reacting to the belt. Her mind threatened to flood her with memories, to slam her back into that small room, onto that horrible bed. She shifted her eyes to James' and focused on him instead of the belt. That mask of control was over him from head to toe, a cold pool when her brain was overheating under the onslaught of her memories. When she stared into his eyes, her heart rate finally started to slow. It was James. His strong jaw line, the finest shadow of facial hair, his broad shoulders, his firm chest, and that delicious V between his hips — all of it reminded her of where she was. Of who she was with. And the feeling was safety, and security, and immeasurable love.

"Say it again, Thalia." James' hand tightened on the fixture of the belt, the leather sliding over his palm as he dropped it to his side and stepped closer to her.

"I need the belt, Master, and I need it to hurt." She barely finished speaking before he was kissing her hard. She felt the brush of the leather on her shoulder as he held her face to his.

"I love you," he whispered against her mouth, and the wave of emotion inside her almost broke free.

"I love you too. This is a gift, James, what you're doing for me, and I love you. Thank you." She spoke softly and he rested his forehead against hers for a moment, nodding and taking a slow breath. They stood there, connected physically and in ways that had no description. For a moment all they did was listen to each other breathe, and her mind went blissfully calm. Then, with a quick intake of air, James leaned up and pressed a firm kiss to her hair and she saw the control slide back over him. He stepped back from her, the muscles of his arms tensing and relaxing, his eyes devouring her.

"Is that how you address me in this room, pet?" Low and dark, his voice sent a shiver through her and her pussy responded with a flood of wetness that filled the room with the smell of her arousal.

"No, Master. I'm sorry, Master." Thalia dropped her eyes and said the words calmly, and she heard him huff out a laugh.

"Hands on the horse. Bend over and spread your legs, pet," he commanded and she obeyed. The soft texture of the surface caressing her palms as she shifted. James was next to her as he traced the leather belt down her spine, letting her adjust to its presence against her skin. "Why are you here tonight, pet?"

"I asked you to use the belt, Master."

"Are you being punished?" His question was clear and serious. He wanted to draw the lines before he started.

Thalia shook her head, her hair hanging in her face. "No, Master. This is my choice. You're doing this for me."

"Correct. This means that there is no number, I have no expectation for what you will take. When you have had enough, you will use your safe word. Do you understand?" James pulled her head back by her hair so he could see her eyes, and it increased the pleasurable tension coiling inside her. It helped to push back the fact that it was a belt in his other hand.

"I understand, Master. I will safe word." It was not an option. James would use the belt until she was done, until she'd had enough. Thalia bit her lip when he released her hair and her head dropped forward again. His muffled steps moved behind her and the sound of the metal on the belt made her dig her nails into the horse.

That sound was straight out of her nightmares. The warning before the strike.

"Don't forget to breathe." The words came out in that direct, cool tone of his Dom voice, and then the belt landed hard across her ass. She cried out as the sound cracked through the room. The second lash was echoed by an assault of memories, which were more painful than the sting of her flesh. Thalia gritted her teeth and swallowed the next cry. These weren't warm up lashes, they had power behind them, and she knew that had been a conscious decision. Marcus had never given her warm ups either, and she needed the catharsis of submitting, willingly, to the belt. To James. Her Dom, her boyfriend, her Master, her lover.

The lashes came in a constant stream, like lightning strikes under the storm clouds of her memory. Her body answered with the thunder of pain that spread across her ass and thighs, hot tears streaking her cheeks, but she needed more. He'd told her to tell him what she wanted. "Harder, please..."

There was a pause, an adjustment of the belt in his grip, and she was grateful to have the curtain of her hair to hide in. He would have never allowed it normally, but she was in control of this session. The next line of fire that went across her ass cheeks had her almost standing up, her hands coming off the horse for a fraction of a second as she screamed. He caught it and corrected her. "Hands on the horse. Now."

She dropped into position and her body lit up, pain zigzagging through her nerves as sobs tried to push out of her clenched teeth. Her memory played Marcus' voice, his twisted words, and she felt the ghost of his touch on her skin. A hard lash across her thighs almost made her knees buckle, and she screamed again.

James. It's James. It's James.

For a moment she could almost smell Marcus near her and she forced her eyes open so she could see the thick tiles on the floor of the room. She was home. It was the horse under her hands that she had memorized in her time with James. Lifting her eyes, she could see the bed she'd shared with James, *only James*. The spanking bench. Her breathing was rapid, a constant whine coming out of her as the lashes overlapped and pain became a constant, steady thrum inside her. "Please, please, please…"

Thalia couldn't tell if the next strike on her ass was actually harder, or if it was just the bruised skin sending sharper pain signals. She dropped to her knees in front of the horse, and she could hear James' heavy breaths behind her. Waiting. Waiting for her to safe word and stop it.

Marcus was in her head though, his breath against her ear as he called her a slut, told her she wanted it, told her she needed it, needed him. It was Marcus picking up the belt, the sound of metal fixtures dragging across concrete.

James' voice cut through her memories. "*Thalia.*"

He didn't say anything else as he waited for her to stop him, but she couldn't. *Not yet.*

Wiping her face, she stood again and shook her head to answer the question he hadn't said out loud. "Please, Master. More."

He was silent for a moment. She would have understood if he'd refused, she wouldn't have faulted him. He had already done more for her than she had any right to expect. Instead, he spoke clearly. "Hands behind your head. Hold your hair out of the way. Feet apart and Do. Not. Move."

Thalia obeyed, and a moment later felt the snap of the leather across the middle of her back. Back to normal effort, but the skin was so much more sensitive that it had the same effect. She wavered on her feet before pressing her heels back to the floor. James continued, lining up the strikes from her shoulders to the middle of her back, carefully avoiding her kidneys. Evening out the stinging lashes until her entire backside was a wicked pulse. Each flash of the belt over her skin made her cry harder and tighten her fingers in her hair. She danced forward after a lash and his voice cracked out.

"Do not move, pet," he growled softly, and she realized she had no idea the count. No idea of the number of times the belt had kissed her skin in a symphony of fire and pain. Leaving her flesh hot and bruising, the ache sinking down to her bones.

But she knew it was James, and there was no fear. There was the complete belief that one word would stop everything.

Chair. The word she had chosen the night he had saved her.

Another lash that made her arch her back and scream.

Chair.

Her lips almost formed it, and he brought the belt down hard over her skin, her brain tempting her toward the abyss of sub space, letting the pain become a buzzing in her skin. Letting her body renew the pounding between her thighs that made her want to drop forward and feel James fill her from behind, feel his cock split and stretch her. *James. James. James.*

"CHAIR!" she screamed and dropped her arms, stumbling forward to catch herself on the gymnastics horse as her next intake of air was ragged with a sob. The sound of the belt dropping to the floor and James' hard breaths behind her were all she had to hold on to as she tried to calm down. She waited to feel his hands on her, to hear his voice comfort her, but as she started to catch her breath he didn't come to her. Standing, she turned to see him, and her heart ached. His hands were in his hair, clenching into the mess of blond as his green eyes told her every emotion flipping through him. No mask of control left. His expression was concern, and pain, and it spoke of a terrible fear that he had done something horrible that he couldn't take back.

It was why he wasn't touching her.

Thalia pushed off the horse and stepped confidently forward until she collided with him, grabbing his face firmly to pull him down to her mouth. She kissed him hard and the force of her forward movement knocked him backward until he met the wall. He didn't stop her. She kissed him harder, her fingers digging into the back of his neck until he finally wrapped his arms around her. Her back lit up with pain, but she didn't care.

Every mark was his. And so was she.

"I need you." Thalia spoke harshly against his lips, her arousal filling her tone. "James, I love you, and I need you. Please."

He made a sound in his chest and grabbed her face in his hands. His eyes bored into hers, neither of them relaxing their firm grips on the other. She was about to beg again when he kissed her desperately and wrapped an arm around her waist, lifting her so she wrapped her legs around him again. He stalked toward the door of the playroom and threw it open hard enough for it to crack against the wall. She buried her face against his shoulder, breathing deep the lingering smell of his cologne, that scent of warm male skin that was so specifically James. In a moment they were in their bedroom, and he laid her carefully back on their bed. His pants were off a second later and she shifted back to give him room to climb up. When he did he kissed her hip, her stomach, the space between her breasts, her neck, and then he captured her mouth again. His fingers slid inside her, but she was soaked and the wet sound of his thrusts only verified further that her body had always responded to pain. When he moved his hand, he traced the wetness over her hip, and she lifted herself against him.

"Tell me again," James' plea was rough against her ear, his forehead pressed to the bed next to her, his hips between her thighs but refusing to move closer even as she pulled at his waist trying to bring his weight over her.

"I need you, James. I love you, and I want you, please fuck me," Thalia begged, one of her hands tangling in the hair at the back of his head. He lifted his head to look at her, and he looked tortured, his eyes a dark green storm cloud of emotion.

"You are so beautiful, you know that?" The edge of his mouth ticked up in the hint of a smile, and she melted. His hips lowered and he teased her, his cock brushing her pussy in slow, tantalizing movements that taunted her orgasm. She wiggled in frustration and he tightened his grip on her to hold her still. "You are so strong, and fierce, and feisty — and I love you more than I ever thought possible, Thalia."

"James—" She started to respond, but he pressed a kiss to her mouth and thrust inside her. She was slick, and he filled her instantly, their moans came out in unison and her body shivered under his as the orgasm threatened to overwhelm her already. The ache of the welts that lined the back of her answered each pleasurable thrust until she was moaning and digging her fingers into his sides to pull him down to her. Her hips met each pounding slap of his body against hers as heat blanketed her, electric tension coiling her tight and pushing her into the haze where the pain bled into pure sensation and she found herself babbling *'please'* over and over as she rose higher and higher.

It was a cacophony of sensation when her orgasm crashed over her like a tidal wave of pleasure and pain and love and closure. She was aware of screaming out his name as her body went taut under his, her muscles quivering as he thrust hard again and again and then stilled inside her to fill her with pulses of his seed.

Head to toe, inside and out, she was his, and he was hers.

James.

He kissed her again as they caught their breath, and he covered her with his body. Warm, and heavy, and welcome. It was perfect. After a moment he slid to the side and leaned up on his elbow, their legs still intertwined. He brushed her cheek with his thumb, cupping her face as he looked down at her. "Talk to me, baby."

"Thank you. Just... thank you." She shook her head, trying to figure out how to put anything else into words as her body shivered.

"You waited so long to safe word…" James started to say something and stopped himself, but the concern in his eyes hinted at the guilt he felt. Thalia grabbed his hand and saw the indention of the buckle in his palm. She traced it with her thumb and her brows came together as she made a sad sound and kissed it.

"James, your hand—"

He cut her off and pulled his hand away. "Forget my hand. What about your back, baby? You're going to be nothing but bruises from your shoulders to the backs of your knees. Why—" He stopped talking and she bit her cheek, reaching for his hand again so she could interlace their fingers. She hated that he had gripped the belt hard enough to make that dark imprint in his skin, but she knew her backside had to look bad. She had felt it. Which meant she had to explain. He had done what she'd asked for, what she needed. Now she had to explain.

"I couldn't even look at belts, James." She sighed and stared at their entwined fingers. "Every time I saw one, heard the sound of one being put on, or taken off — I was right back there. It was the only time the nightmares ever reached me during the day."

"Fuck, Thalia…" James winced and dropped his head back to the bed, but she leaned up on her elbow to look down at him, gripping his hand tighter in hers.

"Wait. I have always liked the belt. When *you* used it. You can't deny that, you've made me come using the belt alone before." She laid her hand on his cheek when he tried to look away from her. "James, I couldn't give it up. I couldn't let him exist in my head over something so simple, especially not something that is so good when it's between us. But he was in my head with it, and I know you understood that. You didn't bring me every belt in the fucking closet for nothing. You let me pick the one that would help me get rid of the connection, that would help me replace it in my head with something *good*."

"How was *that* good, Thalia?" There was emotion in James' voice and she kissed him, but he pulled away and kept talking. "I would have stopped long before you used your safe word tonight. But you asked for it to be harder, you asked for *more*."

"Because he was in my head when we started! All the memories tried to rush in, and I needed to get through them, I needed to burn them out. I needed to not have those things connected with the belt. And I kept asking for more because by the end of it I knew it was you without being able to see you. I knew if I said my safe word you would stop. I knew you were waiting to hear it. I *needed* that. And I waited until my body knew it too, until I was thinking about you fucking me when I called my safe word. Until you were all I could think about." Her words finished on a rush and he kissed her again, hard. It overwhelmed her, and she felt like he finally understood all of it. As if she'd asked the question out loud he nodded before resting his forehead against hers.

"I'm throwing that belt in the bin. If you want one you can pick a different one for our play. All right?" James' blond hair was feather soft under her hand as she brushed through it, and she nodded rapidly.

"Okay."

"Good. Now let me see you." He kissed her and then rolled her to her stomach, hissing through his teeth as he got another look at her back, but he didn't make another comment. He just rubbed her down with cream in smooth, confident strokes, until the ache dulled in her skin. When he was done he drew the sheets up and lay down next to her with her hand in his. She was dreamy with exhaustion, her body well-used, and sated, and calm.

James whispered his love for her, and she mumbled a return as she felt herself sliding into sleep — and for the first time in too long she let herself slip into dreams thinking of her future instead of her past.

She dreamt of two kids, a little blonde girl, and a light brown-haired boy, and James' laughter echoing across a rolling green lawn.

Chapter Thirty-Three
JAMES

One Week Later

"Absolutely. If that's the deal that has to be made to secure the new location, then do it." James stalked away from his desk, the wireless headset feeding the man's answer back to him. Another expansion, another opportunity to grow the company this quarter and keep the stock price rising. "Brilliant. Update me when it's done."

The call ended and James stared out at the London skyline. It was gray and misting, and while it was likely warm since it was June, standing in the air conditioning it just looked damp. For the tenth time that morning he worried about Thalia. Would she be walking around in this? She never brought an umbrella with her even though it rained often.

He loved it though.

Sometimes when she returned from teaching a class she would be like some wild, woodland nymph wandering back into the flat; damp from rain, her hair coming out of her ponytail from her run, her cheeks flushed and her eyes bright. If he said anything to her about it, if he asked her where her umbrella was, she'd just laugh and tell him he worried too much about her.

Worried? Worried was an understatement.

James grabbed his mobile from the desk and texted the head of the security team he had hired for her before they had even left the states for London. An instant later he had an update: *T is still at studio. Went to Café Illiad for lunch. Bought us all pastries.*

He groaned and sat back behind his desk. Thalia made it a point to acknowledge the men that followed her everywhere. James had told her to just live her life, to ignore them — and she had done the exact opposite. Thalia now knew all of their names, had insisted they eat lunch with her on numerous occasions, and had sent one of their children a birthday present and brought another's wife soup when she found out she was sick. One of the men had a teenage daughter who now had a free membership at the studio, courtesy of Thalia. In turn, the men were now incredibly dedicated to her, going well above and beyond their job description. A few weeks back, one had returned her jacket to her at the flat after she left it at the studio, another had started bringing fresh fruit every morning she had a class. It was Jake's team all over again. Everyone that met Thalia loved her.

But *that* James completely understood.

Their dedication didn't bother him. It meant that they were more committed to keeping her safe than they may have been for just a regular job. Peter, the head of the team, had insisted on knowing everything. James had given him the whole story and the man's eyes had said more than any words could have. That hard edge to his jaw settling in place as he absorbed the details and connected them to the bright, smiling woman he'd been following for over a month since she'd started leaving the flat again.

With Peter's team keeping track of her twenty-four hours a day, Thalia would never be at risk again.

James sighed and ran a hand over his face, making himself flip through the emails that came in faster than he could ever actually read them. It wasn't long until he ended up distracted from work again by the picture of the two of them on his desk. Julie had snuck the photo when they had been out at the pub with her and Antonio well before the trip to the states. James was whispering in Thalia's ear and she was about to laugh, her smile wide, her cheeks flushed from the alcohol and whatever he had told her. His own mouth was curved in a smile, and he often tried to remember exactly what he'd been saying to her. Had he been describing what he wanted to do to her that night? Had he been sharing a private joke with her?

Thinking about her meant all he really wanted to do was call her and hear her voice. Hear that edge of exasperation in her tone that he was calling her at work *again*. He wanted to hear her tease him that he must have nothing to do all day. And then he wanted to tell her he loved her more than anything.

She was his center. The pivot around which the rest of his life turned. She was the only person in the world who knew every facet of him. All of the darkness, and all of the light. And she loved him.

And he had almost lost her.

That terrible nagging feeling that she could slip away from him in an instant had not faded. Not in the three months since they'd been back in London. He had mentioned it to Ailsa once, casually, and she had told him it was natural, that it would take time until he felt confident in Thalia's safety again. Clearly, not enough time had passed.

Their road back to relative normalcy had been rough, but it seemed like they finally had it. A routine, like any couple would. Private jokes and habits and favorite spots on the couch.

James was suddenly overwhelmed with the memory of the night everything had started to turn for the better. It was early in their third week back at the flat, and it had been a few days since Ailsa had left, after she'd made Thalia sleep. In those early weeks James had been sick with worry every time they lay down in their bed. Never sure if he'd be ripped out of sleep by her screams or her sudden panicked movements as she tried to fight a nightmare.

He still couldn't remember when he'd actually fallen asleep, but he remembered waking up to Thalia's hands on him. Her mouth tracing a path across his chest, her hair tickling over his skin until he was completely awake but frozen, trying to decide if he was dreaming or not. His body reacted instantly to her, his cock surging until it was hard and aching, but he didn't reach for her. He couldn't reach for her. Her back was still a map of healing bruises, and he knew if he turned the light on he'd be able to see the yellowish shadow across her cheekbone.

She slid her hand down his stomach and under the waist of his pants to grip his erection firmly, a smooth stroke from base to tip where her thumb rolled over the head made him groan. The pleasure was a vicious tug on his self-control. He wanted to tell her to go back to sleep, to let him wrap his arms around her, but his body thrust his hips against her hand instead.

"Please?" Her voice was sinfully sweet and pleading in the dark of their room. James felt his jaw clench as he tried to regain enough composure to encourage her to wait, but then her hand was moving again, stroking him in confident movements that had his stomach tensing, his balls tingling, his hands clenching in the sheets so he wouldn't reach for her.

"Thalia, baby, you—"

"I had a dream." Her lips were against his throat, tracing up to his jaw, her warm body pressed against his side as she continued to slide her hand up and down his cock with agonizing skill. "It was a good dream. It was you."

James' chest ached, and he could see the intent expression on her face as she leaned over him, her lips so close to his. He bit back a moan as she slipped a leg between his and the wet heat of her pussy rubbed against his thigh.

Bloody hell. The devil himself could not have designed a greater test of his morality.

Thalia's lips met his and his hands were suddenly holding her to him before he remembered giving them permission to let go of the sheets. She moaned against his mouth and the buzz in his lips was perfection. Her breasts pressed against his chest, and she rocked herself against his leg. The shiver that ran through her had everything to do with the pleasure she was taking and nothing to do with the nightmares that had haunted them.

She lifted her mouth from his with the prettiest gasp, and then she pleaded softly, "Please don't push me away."

It cracked all of his defenses in half.

His arms moved around her and she slid up his body, her knees landing on either side of his hips as she kissed him again. Her hand gripped him and she slid down on his cock. Wet, tight, heat encased him and he groaned and yanked the reins on his self-control to fight the urge to thrust himself deeper. She used his shoulders to push herself up and she moved slowly. Rising and falling until with each drop of her hips he was buried inside her to the hilt. It was incredible as he felt every tightening wave of her pussy as she lifted herself, and the phenomenal slickness of each descent. The dim light of the alarm clock and the ambient light from the windows outlined her body. Her breasts rising and falling with each breath, her moans soft as she worked toward her orgasm at her own speed. Light brown hair spilled down the front of her shoulders, and he slid his hands slowly up her thighs, providing every opportunity for her to stop him. When she only rocked against him harder, he ran his hand down her belly until his thumb could stroke her clit.

With the first circle of pressure she buckled forward, her moan louder, and her nails dug into his chest. He instantly stopped and she whined, her hand finding his to press it harder against her. "Please keep going, James, *please*."

"Okay baby, move for me," he encouraged softly and she nodded and lifted her hips again. His thumb circled her clit in tight circles, and as he increased the speed her voice grew louder, her hips moving faster. His balls ached with the urge to come inside her, the tension in him pushing him to thrust, to take control and finish. But he'd had years of experience in holding that back, and he focused on her. On the tremors in her thighs as she got close, the little sounds she made as she found a rhythm that was going to take her over the edge. He wanted to follow her over, and he increased the pressure on her clit, strumming her faster until she tensed and trembled above him, and he felt her tighten and grind herself down. The tense pressure on his cock made his hips lift to thrust harder inside her. Then Thalia came with a moan and a curse, the walls of her pussy gripping him hard in waves and he let go and gritted his teeth against the shout of relief as he released the reins on his own pleasure and came hard inside her. An incredible fire shooting down his spine and spilling out of him to tumble him into the hazy bliss of orgasm as Thalia collapsed on his chest. He slid a hand into her hair to hold her against him, reveling in the feeling of her pounding heart on his skin. Of the sensation of her heat surrounding him, and her warm breaths on his shoulder as she nuzzled him.

"I love you... thank you," she whispered softly, and he hugged her tight for a long minute before he urged her hips off him. He instantly missed the feeling of her, and so he turned her slightly so he could pull her back against his chest. Her heat pressed to the front of his body, and the wetness on her thighs made him smile against her hair.

"I love you so much, Thalia. You are incredible, baby." It was the truth. She had always been incredible, and there were moments when her strength awed him.

That had been one of those glorious moments, and they had both fallen back asleep wrapped up in each other. Their first time since the abduction had been the first step toward bringing her out of the nightmares it had caused. It had been the first of three days she didn't have a bad night, an oasis in the storm of her recovery.

The loud tone of his phone signaling a call snapped him out of the memory and he shook his head to focus again. He had to stop daydreaming at work. James pressed the answer button on his headset. His assistant's voice came through, "Dr. Hawkins? I have Brian Schoeneke from the Montague Firm here to see you."

"Right, yes, send him in." James cleared his throat and ended the call, adjusting the erection in his pants as he made sure he was firmly behind the desk.

Yes, he definitely needed to stop daydreaming at work, and texting the security team twenty times a day, and calling Thalia just to hear her voice and make sure she was alright.

If Thalia could recover, if she could return to her life with a smile and a warmth unmatched by others — then James had no excuse. He wiped a hand over his face as he looked for the email that applied to the Montague Firm, and made himself think about work.

Chapter Thirty-Four
THALIA

Two Weeks Later

"Why are you in such a rush?!" Thalia laughed as James bundled her into the private car and dropped in next to her.

"We have reservations, baby, and you love Tozi. You don't want to miss it." He grinned at her and kissed her hard. It surprised her, and she moaned against his mouth as he leaned her back. Her whole world shrunk to the two of them; the road noise, the sounds of London evening traffic, everything fell away as his arms moved around her and his tongue met hers.

She was breathless and grinning when he finally pulled back and looked at her, his eyes bright and intense. "James, I do love Italian, but it's not urgent. I was just checking my email! Five minutes wouldn't have been the end of the world." He had pulled her out of the office like the room was on fire, and the blood in his cheeks had her laughing to herself.

"You are gorgeous tonight." He smiled back at her, and it filled her with a giddy flood of endorphins. James was so full of energy, so happy, and Thalia felt like it had to have something to do with the fact that since their night in the playroom with the belt there had only been one more nightmare. It had been over two weeks since that one. It was a milestone she wasn't sure she'd ever hit — but with James anything was possible.

"Thank you. *You* look incredibly hot in this suit, I think you in black-tie is my second favorite." She pressed a kiss to his lips as he sat up and grabbed her hands.

He laughed. "And your first?"

"Naked." She grinned and laughed.

"Minx. I feel the same way." He laughed harder and grinned, "You know that's not my favorite thing about you, right? Yes, you're beautiful... but you are so strong, baby. There are days I wake up and I cannot believe that I have you with me, that I can reach over and touch you. That I am lucky enough to have a woman like you in my life. Kind, and vibrant, and warm, and—" his hand trailed up her thigh, "—brilliantly wicked in bed."

The blush in her cheeks made her hot, and she bit her lip at the overwhelming compliments. "James... we've talked about this before, *I'm* lucky to have you. There's no contest here. You saved me, you gave me a life, you helped me rebuild myself. I couldn't repay that with a hundred lifetimes to try and do it."

He just shook his head and kissed her again, and she swooned. It was powerful, his lips moving over hers like he was staking a claim on her. Her pussy flooded and she wanted to climb on his lap, forget dinner, and have the driver turn around.

Instead, James broke the kiss and spoke again, "Thalia, bloody hell, you have no idea what you've done for me! I was such a dark person before you met me. All I did was work because I couldn't give in to my urges. Without Kalen around to keep me in line, I was always afraid of going too far with some vanilla relationship. My last submissive was... casual. There was no future with her, and she knew it, and she left because of it. I was dissatisfied because she was never enough. She was dissatisfied because she could tell."

His hands landed on either side of her head, and the serious expression on his face calmed her a bit. She remembered him talking about Shannon before, about how it hadn't been right for either of them, and about how thinking of that relationship made him know how perfect she was for him.

His lips ticked up in a smile again. "But, *you*... you, Thalia, fill me with light. I look forward to seeing you every day. I think of you when I'm at work. You are the first thing I think of when I wake up, and on the days you've already left for the studio — I miss you. And when you're on your knees in the playroom? I love and respect you so much for the trust you place in me, for the love you have for me, to let me be the one in control. To give me that."

"I—" Thalia tried to find the words to respond, but there was barely air in her lungs.

"I love you so much. There are not enough words to describe the million, brilliant ways you make me whole." James leaned back and ran his hands over his thighs before he reached into his jacket and pulled out a box. Thalia's world went sideways, shock emptying her mind of all thoughts, and she looked up at him to find his green eyes on hers. "I'd like to feel whole forever, Thalia. Will you marry me?"

The box was open in his hands, a sparkling, clear, diamond catching the street lights on a simple platinum band. She was vaguely aware that the car was slowing, but it felt like the whole world had slowed down. She was tongue-tied, afraid she was dreaming, and the urge to pinch herself through the navy dress overwhelmed her. James reached over and took her hand in his and the physical touch snapped her back.

Biting her lip for a moment she nodded rapidly before stumbling over her answer, "Y—yes. Yes! Of course, James! Are you serious?"

His body rocked forward as if he'd actually been anxious about her answer, and then he grabbed her and kissed her hard. "I am absolutely serious, baby. I want everything with you. I want to give you everything you've ever wanted."

Thalia laughed, joy filling her up as the grin on her lips made her cheeks ache. "You're all I want, James. If I have you, I don't need anything else."

She kissed him again and the rumble of his moan against her lips had her climbing onto his lap, her dress riding up her thighs, and she didn't care at all that the driver could easily see them if he tried. Her hips moved against his and he groaned before pressing her back.

With a boyish grin he slid the ring on her finger and then gallantly kissed the back of her hand.

The car stopped suddenly, and the door jerked open.

Thalia jumped and she caught a flash of blonde hair before she heard Julie's high-pitched scream, "SHE SAID YES!" A loud cheer rose up from outside of the car, and heat flooded Thalia's chest as she looked down at James, and he grinned.

"We may have a few people joining us for dinner." He chuckled and kissed her again as he moved her back to the seat.

Nervous excitement buzzed over her skin, and she couldn't stop smiling.

"Ready, baby?" James smiled back as he stepped out of the car before reaching in for her hand. When she stepped out there were camera flashes, and cheers, and the popping of confetti toys that spread the scent of gunpowder and colorful paper streamers around them.

It was a crowd of their friends. Julie was clapping and bouncing on her toes, Antonio smiling behind her.

"I am so happy for ye!" Maggie crashed into Thalia, her rounded belly pressing against her as she hugged her tight. After a firm hug Maggie stepped back with tears in her eyes, and Kalen leaned around her and kissed Thalia on the cheek.

"We could not be happier." His voice boomed, and he smiled broadly.

"Happy doesn't even cut it—"

"Oh my God, *another* wedding?!" Chloe and Lauren practically screamed over one another as they squeezed past Kalen and Maggie to press Thalia in a hug.

She tried to react, but they were babbling at a hundred miles an hour about Julie's upcoming wedding, and something about flowers, and colors, and bridesmaids.

Thalia was overwhelmed, and she searched for James' face and found him grinning broadly as Kalen hugged him. His eyes found hers in an instant and he reached forward to take her hand and pull her toward the doors of the small restaurant.

"Everyone! Let's go inside and celebrate!" James had never sounded happier. He'd never smiled this much, and the cheers that went up were a buoy of love and affection unmatched in Thalia's life. He tucked her against him as they moved inside to see the restaurant empty, and several waiters waiting to get the large party seated.

Thalia couldn't believe the number of people there. It was everyone that had made their relationship real and solid. Analiese was waving at her by Nick, as they sat down next to James' coworker Tom and his girlfriend. Kalen and Maggie and Ailsa sat next to James, while Julie grabbed the seat next to Thalia, with Antonio on her other side. Across from her Becca sat down, and she was quickly overwhelmed by the loud chatter from Lauren and Chloe who were leaning across Brad to keep up their discussion. Alice and her husband were on the other side of Becca, and Thalia smiled at them. They had double-dated after the gala and she loved Alice's brash humor. She loved *everyone* at the long table.

Kalen clapped his hands together as he stood and all of the girls from Purgatory dropped into silence immediately. A beat later and they were all laughing, much to the confusion of the part of the dinner party that had no idea why. Just as Kalen stopped grinning and raised a glass to speak, the door opened again and Katherine waltzed in the door, followed by James' parents.

"My fault! Sorry we're late!" Katherine called out as she tossed her hair over her shoulder. Thalia jumped to her feet, smiling at the three of them. Henry, James' father, was smiling quietly with his arm around Evelyn, James' mother. Henry looked so much like James it was startling, the same green eyes, but his hair was a soft brown and peppering at the temples with gray. James' blond had come from his mother, and tonight she wore it up in a bun. Evelyn smiled, her hands coming up to her mouth as they landed on Thalia.

"Oh, darling, please tell me you said yes?" Evelyn's voice was so filled with tentative excitement that Thalia almost burst into tears on the spot. To not only be accepted, but to be wanted by his family had once upon a time felt impossible.

The first meeting with them had been fraught with tension, Katherine had told them about the abduction, and James had barely been able to keep them at bay a few weeks until Thalia had healed enough to meet them at their lavish estate. The dinner had been nothing like Thalia had expected. Yes, a beautiful table in a beautiful home, but his parents had talked to her with genuine care and concern. Evelyn had gently chided James for not telling them about her sooner, and then they had spent the rest of the dinner politely ignoring the fading bruise on her cheek that she'd tried so hard to cover with makeup.

"Well?" Henry brought her back from her reverie and simply tilted his head, keeping his eyes on her as he waited for her answer.

"I did. Of course I said yes!" Thalia grinned and raised her hand to show the ring and Evelyn smiled and moved forward to lean past Becca and look.

"It's absolutely lovely! Good choice, James." She smiled at him and Thalia felt James slide his arm around her waist with a gentle pressure.

"Thank you, mum." The warmth in James' voice made Thalia's smile brighter. "Please, sit down."

There was a quick shuffling of seats as Becca and others moved to allow James' family to fill the seats directly across from the happy couple.

"Thank God it's you, Thalia. I was always terrified James would pick some mindless tramp!" Katherine laughed as she dropped into a chair, and Thalia watched their mother sigh indulgently and sit down in the chair Henry had pulled out for her.

"I believe what Katherine means, Thalia, is that we are all delighted you will be a member of the family." Henry's voice had a rumble of power in it that made it obvious to her where James had learned it. He smiled at them both and sat down, before nodding at Kalen who was still standing. "Kalen, it's good to see you again."

"Mr. and Mrs. Hawkins." Kalen grinned, and raised his glass again. "I was just about to toast James and Thalia."

"A toast? Wait, I need a drink!" Katherine glanced at a waiter who came to provide new glasses, and Kalen sighed at being interrupted again but waited. After a few moments everyone turned back to him, holding their glasses aloft, and he nodded.

"We are all here tonight for James and Thalia. I've known James for a long while, and in all those years he's become like a brother to me. He was the first person I wanted to introduce my blessing, Maggie, to, and he was the first person I called when I knew I loved her. And when he called me about Thalia, I had a feeling that this wasn't just any woman in his life. Then, when I saw them together, I knew. I like to think I knew before they did—"

"You did, Kalen." James grinned up at him, and he squeezed Thalia's hand under the table. She laughed, remembering Kalen's lecture about the two of them after the crop. About how glad he was that James had found her, that they had each other, and that he knew she made James happy.

"You *absolutely* did, Kalen." Thalia smiled too and he grinned down at them, tilting his head in acknowledgment before raising his glass higher.

"Their love for each other is the kind of love so few people find, but that I have had the fortune of finding myself, and as I look around this table I think many of ye know what I am talking about. James and Thalia balance each other. They acknowledge each other's strengths and weaknesses, and they are stronger together because of it. They fight for each other, and that's how I know that they will last." Kalen lowered his glass and dropped his free hand onto James' shoulder, "I love ye both. Congratulations."

"Congratulations!" The room echoed in a surge of voices and the clinking of glasses, and laughter, and cheers.

Julie leaned over to whisper in her ear, "You'll have to tell me what you think of fiancé sex." Their explosive laughter attracted the attention of everyone at the table, but when the two noticed the looks they were already laughing too hard to explain.

"I'm glad Antonio was able to make it, he's been away for a few weeks." Julie was still grinning as she sipped wine.

"Were you back at Purgatory? You know you could have stayed with me, Julie." Thalia laughed, turning to catch James and Kalen in the midst of a friendly debate. *Boys.*

"Of course I went back to Purgatory! It was a blast." Julie giggled and then her mouth formed into a perfect 'o' as she gasped. "Oh my God! I forgot to tell you. *Ethan* has a new girlfriend, an actual sub this time. Her name is Clair and she's so sweet, and gorgeous! Kalen and Maggie totally approve."

"Seriously?" Thalia smiled as she caught Nick and Analiese making out at one end of the table, and she heard Analiese's gasp and giggle over the white noise of everyone talking and laughing. Apparently she'd overcome being so quiet.

"They were only there two days after I got there, but yeah, they seemed really happy together, and she was sweet!" Julie leaned back on Antonio as he wrapped his arms around her.

"Wedding planning is insane, fair warning, Thalia." Antonio laughed when Julie elbowed him.

"Antonio is being dramatic, all he's done is pick out his favorite kind of cake. *I* will help you with everything, I swear it!"

"I'm going to need it, Julie, because I have no idea what to do." Thalia shrugged, about to say more but James turned her and kissed her fiercely. It was absolutely the most passionate he'd ever kissed her in public, and her face was hot with a blush when he pulled back and she had to turn and face his parents. They just smiled, and Katherine whistled before winking at her.

The evening became a whirlwind of conversation, of sweet words, and hilarious stories that were carefully tempered for the audience. Julie talked about helping with the wedding planning, and everyone pitched in ideas, but Thalia didn't mind that at all. Julie lived to decorate and plan, and she was damn good at it. The studio was an example of it.

Julie also made sure everyone knew she was still jealous that James and Thalia had been the first to learn about the baby.

Then the conversation had shifted until Maggie and Kalen were the focus. No, they didn't know the sex. Yes, they had ideas for names but they weren't ready to share. It was fun to watch Kalen pestering the waiters to keep Maggie's glass full of water, to watch him ask her ten times an hour if she needed anything. She just smiled and rolled her eyes, mumbling across James that he was only getting worse the bigger her belly got.

Becca had surprised Thalia by fitting in with the girls like she'd always been there, cracking jokes with Chloe and Lauren that for once had *them* blushing. Even Evelyn and Henry were smiling and laughing, and James' work friends melted into the group as the night progressed.

Until after good food, and a lot of good wine, there were no strangers to be found.

The night had been perfect. The kind of warm celebration that could only happen with real friends and loving family. A party full of acceptance and trust and shared histories and a commitment to be there for many more to come.

It was well past two when James and Thalia had finally made it home, and as James went to get undressed she stopped into the office and woke up her laptop. The light from the screen caught the diamond on her hand and she twirled the ring, still barely believing it was real and what it stood for.

A future. With James.

Her inbox updated and the soft beep of a new email made her look up. It was an alert from the forum, a new post. Thalia's heart thundered in her ears as she clicked the link to open it, and as she logged in she heard James call for her from the bedroom but she couldn't answer. There had been a few posts over the last week as the packages had started arriving all over the world. Tenuous little hellos, nervous posts asking if it was real. Thalia had replied, welcoming each of them.

The newest post was still bolded, unread, at the top. She clicked it and she had to fight the urge to cheer, or cry, or hug the laptop. James' hand landed on her shoulder, his voice etched with concern. "Baby? Is everything alright?"

She couldn't speak, she just tilted the laptop toward him as hope filled her up and pushed back the lingering scraps of darkness inside her. She had a future with James, she had a life, she had love, she had friends, and her project was working. It was actually working. The post on the screen was proof. He leaned past her to read, and her eyes traced the simple sentence once more:

```
I got the letter, and I know it says I'm BD0211, but
you all can call me Beth.
```

James' arms wrapped around her, pressing a kiss to her shoulder, and she leaned back against him as the last piece of their path clicked into place.

The End

"Temper us in fire, and we grow stronger.
When we suffer, we survive."
- Cassandra Clare

End Notes

This temporary pause in Thalia's story was in place for over two years, but I knew their story wasn't quite finished yet. After all, what would a wedding between these two be like? What would happen when you brought all the chaos of their friends from Purgatory together again? That is what I dove into when I wrote 'Tying the Knot' the last book in The Thalia Series.

I do hope you'll enjoy that book so that you can see their *happily ever after* with your own eyes!

Also, Beth has her own series now (but you definitely need to read Tying the Knot before you start it.) Still, if the curiosity is killing you, you can grab the books so they're waiting for you. Want to find out the dark & twisted truth of what happened to Beth when Anthony had her? *Start with Breaking Beth!* Want to skip the darkness and see what happens when Beth meets Jake and his team? *Start with Damaged Doll!*

As always, thank you for reading Thalia's story. This series is how I found so many amazing people who now fill my life with so much joy, and I cannot describe how lucky it makes me feel to know each and every one of you.

Jennifer Bene

A DARK ROMANCE

TYING THE KNOT

BOOK FOUR OF THE THALIA SERIES

USA TODAY BESTSELLING AUTHOR
JENNIFER BENE

Text copyright © 2017 Jennifer Bene

All Rights Reserved.

No part of this book may be reproduced in any form or by any electronic or mechanical means including information storage and retrieval systems, without permission in writing from the author. The only exception is by a reviewer, who may quote short excerpts in a review.

This book is a work of fiction. Names, characters, places, and incidents either are products of the author's imagination or are used fictitiously. Any resemblance to actual persons, living or dead, events, or locales is entirely coincidental.

ISBN (e-book): 978-1-946722-17-1

ISBN (paperback): 978-1-946722-18-8

Cover design by Laura Hidalgo, https://www.spellbindingdesign.com/

We have all been through such a ride with James and Thalia, haven't we, lovelies? I can't think of a more amazing group of people to dedicate this book to than all of the wonderful readers and authors who fell in love with Thalia's story right along with me. The incredible people who believed in the darkness and the light right along with me.

Each of you deserved this 'happily ever after' as much as Thalia.

I adore you all.

Chapter One
THALIA

Two Years, Three Months After the Auction

Most girls imagine their wedding at some point in their life, picturing the man who will stand beside them, in front of a sea of family and friends. Thalia had never really thought about it, never cut out pictures from magazines, or pinned centerpieces to boards online… but, then she got engaged.

To James Thomas Hawkins. Her *everything*.

And that meant flowers, and dresses, and cake samples, and centerpieces.

Twelve months filled to the brim with planning, and appointments… and now it was finally time.

If either Thalia or James had ever been religious, they would have held the wedding in a grand church inside London — although Saint James' Cathedral would have *never* happened for obvious reasons. There would have been a long train on a pristine white dress, prayers and hymns. It would have been a formal celebration for all in attendance.

Which Evelyn, James' mother, would have preferred.

Instead, they were at Hampton Court House in the countryside outside of London, with sprawling gardens, and a beautiful house with grand rooms, and, well…

Everything was mass fucking chaos.

"Where in the hell are my shoes?" Julie whined, turning in circles in the cramped dressing suite, which wouldn't have been cramped at all if it weren't filled with five bridesmaids all trying to put on complicated dresses, and one stunned bride-to-be.

"Here they are," Analiese answered, shuffling to grab the pale lavender heels hidden behind a pile of suitcases.

"Jesus… I can't see a bloody thing over my huge belly! I'm completely disgusting." Julie threw her hands up, sullenly staring down at the basketball shape sticking out of the pale purple gown.

"Oh, hush, ye look gorgeous," Maggie chided, laughing. "If I had looked half that pretty at seven months pregnant, I would have been counting my blessings."

"Maggie is right, Julie. You're still tiny!" Lauren stuck her tongue out when Julie turned and flipped her off.

"You're not the one exploding out of her bridesmaid dress, Maggie! I swear I should have had the woman give me an extra few inches." Julie shifted to stare at the open back of her dress in the floor-length mirror, reaching back to try and make the two halves meet. "I don't think it will even zip up. You're going to have to tape me into this fucking thing."

"If that's what it takes, Jules, we'll get you in." Chloe stood up from the floor, still clad only in underwear and no bra. "But, more importantly, has anyone found Thalia's veil?"

"I'm sure it's here somewhere," Thalia answered distractedly, sinking deeper into the chair as she stared out the window at the beautiful grounds surrounding Hampton Court House.

"Chloe! What the bloody hell? You took out my vodka?" Lauren stared at her girlfriend, irritation puckering her mouth.

"There's several bottles of champagne on the table, just open one! Lord knows we could all use some alcohol." Chloe waved a hand, but it had no effect.

"Exactly my point, I put the bottle in here to give us all a little pick-me-up before the ceremony."

"That wouldn't help me out much," Julie snarked, and Maggie laughed.

"Just wait until the little darling is born, then ye will be in for some real trouble!" Maggie turned around on the footstool to eye Thalia. "Are ye listening to this?"

Smiling despite the razor winged butterflies assaulting her insides, Thalia shrugged and looked over the insanity that always happened when the girls were together. "It sounds pretty normal to me."

"*This* sounds normal to ye?" Maggie turned around and snapped her fingers. "Julie, would ye just sit down and stop fussing? Yer not the bride!"

"Playing the switch today, Maggie?" Thalia grinned, and Maggie rolled her eyes.

"Don't ye start with me too, or I'll Domme the lot of ye!" Standing up, Maggie picked her way around the bags and scattered clothes so she could grab Julie by the shoulders and push her down onto the couch beside a still sulking Lauren. "Sit and breathe. Getting this worked up isn't good for ye or the wee one."

Julie took a slow breath, leaning back against the sofa where her bright blonde hair formed a fuzzy halo around her head. "I know that, and I know I'm not the bride. But I won't even be able to walk up the aisle to stand *beside* the bride at this rate. Jake is going to be dealing with a waddling mess who is sticking out of her dress like an overstuffed sausage."

"Jake is not going to care, Julie, I promise." Thalia turned in the chair to stare at her friend. "He handles guns for a living and deals with much more serious shit than a wedding."

"That's my point!" Throwing her hands up, Julie let them drop to her sides and went completely limp, her lower lip trembling. "You've got me paired with the commando hottie, and I look like a blimp. A big, gross blimp."

"Julie!" Maggie sighed as the tears started. "Would *someone* pop the champagne? I think we all need some."

"I'm on it! Alcohol fixes everything." Chloe jumped up, her breasts bouncing, and Thalia couldn't help but laugh because the woman's mocha toned back was striped with the lingering evidence of a flogger.

Well, at least my ass matches one of my bridesmaids.

Glancing back out the window with one more look of envy, Thalia shoved herself out of the chair. She was still in her yoga pants and tank top, the same ones she'd put on after James had given her the wedding day wake-up he'd promised.

A trio of floggers, an unknown number of orgasms, and then he'd fucked her until she'd begged him to just let her skip the wedding insanity and sleep.

That comment had earned her a swat from his hand that had tingled for half an hour.

Dropping to her knees in front of her friend, she caught Julie's tear-filled eyes. "Julie, come on, don't cry. What did Antonio tell you just before you came in here?"

"I don't remember." She sniffled, her nose turning red as her quiet crying continued. Pregnancy hormones and wedding day stress.

At least she was a distraction.

"Something about how you've never looked more beautiful than you do carrying his child? And that it was going to take him an effort not to punch Jake and take his place?" Thalia grinned when that drew a huff of a laugh from the normally vibrant woman, a smile tilting Julie's lips at the edges.

"That would be bloody stupid. I'm quite sure Jake is some kind of ninja."

"Exactly! At least you have the commando hottie, Julie. I have an aristocrat," Analiese mumbled as she started to peel the foil off a second champagne bottle. "If I make a mistake and say the wrong thing, I'm possibly outing James to his coworker and the rest of the London elite."

"You won't do that, Analiese." Thalia sighed. "First of all, you barely talk to people you don't know, and, second, Tom wouldn't care anyway. He's still stunned James asked him to be a part of the wedding party."

"I'm getting much better at speaking up and sharing what I'm thinking, which is *exactly* what I'm worried about." Rolling her eyes, Analiese popped the champagne bottle and handed it to Chloe. "Think a ball gag would clash with the bridesmaid dress?"

"Oh my God!" Julie cackled, and in an instant her tears disappeared, replaced with the wide grin that made her look so much more like herself. Soon, the whole room was laughing at the idea — but when Analiese pushed the champagne cork between her lips everyone lost it.

Thalia was laughing so hard her cheeks hurt, stomach aching as she sat down on the floor to try and catch her breath.

"I think Nick might appreciate an o-ring gag a little more!" Maggie shouted over the laughter, before erupting into boisterous cackles again.

"Just what we need, a little service under the tables during the Wedding Breakfast!" Chloe took a sip of her champagne, carrying two other glasses to the couch to pass them off to Thalia and Lauren. Both of them were flushed bright red and unable to stop laughing at the picture of Analiese wearing a full-on gag.

"Could you *imagine* the look on James' parent's faces? I would die! I would just fucking die." Thalia groaned, stifling herself so she could sneak a sip of the champagne. Delicious and expensive — a treat from Kalen and James for all of them. Swallowing the golden liquid, she let out a long breath. "We'd have to move to Canada just to escape the infamy."

"It would absolutely hit the society pages." Lauren winked at her when she glanced over, and Chloe simply grinned mischievously from her seat on the arm of the couch.

"Ye two promised Thalia ye wouldn't be naughty at the wedding." Tilting her glass at the two of them, Maggie raised her eyebrows. "That means no making out in front of the vanilla aristos. Today is for Thalia and James."

"Boo! You know James can't be the only kink-loving posh one." Leaning down, Chloe brushed her lips across Lauren's neck. "And I know for sure that *some* of the guests would like to hear the noises I can pull out of Lauren."

"Chloe…" The name came out on a breathy moan, Lauren's back arching, her knees parting as her girlfriend slid a hand between them, stroking over the silken underwear.

"Great, now I'm horny." Julie sighed dramatically and everyone groaned in agreement as Lauren and Chloe separated from their kiss.

"I'm sure there's a bathroom somewhere where *we* could burn off a little energy… just to make sure we behave." Lauren grinned, but Maggie snapped her fingers.

"Not a chance. Do I need to go get Brad for ye?"

"*That* sounds like even more fun!" Chloe giggled, tipping up her champagne to finish it.

"Oh, it does? Then how about I run and snag Kalen?" At the mention of the man who had trained each and every girl in the room, Chloe and Lauren quieted with pretty pouts.

"You wouldn't dare. He's James' best man, he's busy."

"Try me, girls. And don't forget, Chloe, yer paired with Sean for a reason." Winking, Maggie looked around the room and swallowed the last of her champagne. "All right… the wedding starts in less than two hours. We need to get into our dresses and get ready so we can all help Thalia into hers."

When no one moved an inch, Maggie set her glass down and clapped her hands together, smiling broadly when everyone sat up a little straighter.

Channeling all of Kalen's booming authority, Maggie raised her voice, "Right now, girls! Clock is ticking!"

"Yes, ma'am!" The others answered, still occasionally giggling, and Thalia returned to her chair by the window to get out of their way. Hanging from a rack in the corner was her dress, still in its clear garment bag. All ivory colored lace, with a voluminous petticoat that made the plastic bulge around it.

Just looking at it had her heart racing in her chest, tapping against her ribs as if to remind her that in a short time she'd be standing in front of over a hundred guests — and she'd have to speak. Swallowing hard, she reached down to tug the wad of papers from her purse that were *supposed* to be her finished vows. And they were kind of finished, *mostly* finished.

Fuck.

"Chloe, can I have some more champagne?" Thalia felt the shaky smile on her lips, and her friend read her like a book.

"Have the whole bottle, girl. You need to relax before it's your turn to get all fancy."

"Right… thanks." Tucking the bottle on the floor next to her, Thalia curled up in the chair and started to flip through the pages as she steadily sipped the champagne.

Everything is going to be fine, baby. The day will fly by.

James' words from that morning came back to her, and she rolled her eyes. Of course today was easy for him, he was used to society events. This was a piece of cake for someone raised in this world. He was probably sitting in the other dressing suite cracking jokes with his friends, relaxing without a single care in the world.

Chapter Two
JAMES

"Ye okay?" Kalen asked as James tossed back the whisky in his glass, the large cube of ice rattling against the sides.

"Of course, why wouldn't I be?" Reaching up, James tugged at his collar, undoing another button as a flush of heat made him start to sweat.

"Well, ye look like yer about to faint. Should I bring over a pillow for ye to swoon on?" With a grin, Kalen ignored the steady glare his old friend returned and simply poured another two fingers of whisky into the glass. "Talk to me."

"I'm fine," James insisted. Turning, he leaned back against the table to watch the other men running a game of poker. They were chatting quietly, circled around the coffee table in front of the sofa, random taunts and laughs cutting in and out of the buzz. He knew he should be sitting with them, playing cards as they waited for Thalia and the girls to be ready, but every time he sat down his entire body thrummed with the urge to move.

And drink.

Which, he promptly did.

Letting the gentle burn of the whisky Kalen had brought from Scotland settle in his stomach, he found himself fidgeting. Circling the ice in the glass, spinning it around, and around — until Kalen grabbed his arm.

The other man looked at him stolidly, releasing his arm to sigh. "I'd ask ye if ye were having second thoughts, but I'm pretty sure ye would hit me."

A frisson of anger pulsed through his veins. "You would be right about that."

"Then will ye just tell me what it is?" Kalen crossed his arms, stepping back toward the windows to force James to face him. "What do ye need, brother? Want to shout at me? Go for a walk? A fight to burn off some energy? I promise I won't hit yer pretty face."

"I do *not* want to fight you, Kalen, don't be a bastard." Stealing another drink, he shoved a hand through his hair and walked past the man to stare out the windows at the sprawling grounds. He felt, more than heard, his friend approach.

"Is it about the deal between you and Jake?" For once, Kalen managed to keep his voice hushed, and for that James was grateful, because he'd hit the nail on the head.

Setting his glass down on the table beside the radiator, he leaned on it, flattening his other palm to the surface just so he wouldn't clench his fist again. The dark, half-moon shapes he'd dug into his hands earlier couldn't be there when he was putting a ring on Thalia's finger.

He needed to get his bloody head on straight.

"No update?" Kalen asked.

"No update." Shaking his head, James growled low in his chest. "I finally agreed to let Peter and the damn security detail go after the wedding. She's been begging me for months, telling me she just wants to feel normal, and — *bloody hell* — I want that for her too."

"But?" Kalen prompted, keeping his eyes on the men playing cards.

"But the only reason I agreed was because Jake told me a *year* ago that he could handle it if I asked him to." James tapped the glass on the table before lifting it to his lips for another long drink. The beginning of a haze was forming in his brain, which was foolish. He had to be sober today of all days, but the ache in his chest was like a slowly twisting piece of shrapnel.

A keepsake from their history that he wanted gone.

"So, what will ye do if Jake's people can't come through?" The question hung in the air between them, and James felt the shrapnel dig a little deeper.

Glancing over at his friend's stoic profile, he knew Kalen wouldn't judge him if he backed out on the deal he had made with Thalia. Kalen would understand his need to know she was safe… but what kind of start was that for a marriage?

She had been overjoyed when he'd finally relented, and he had done it gladly. Partly because he was tired of the little arguments the subject caused, but mostly because he could see how miserable she was. How much she resented being followed everywhere, having to check-in like a child before she made a move, constantly having to explain her detail to friends and employees.

And, as she had said, it was a constant reminder for her.

"I can't break my promise." James finally spoke, chasing the bitter words with another drink.

"I agree." Kalen shrugged. "But ye can't keep brooding on yer wedding day. Let it go, brother. It will all work out."

"You're suggesting I ignore that I'm waiting for the update and just go and play cards with them? You *do* know that Sean runs a poker game every week at SW3, right?" Looking over at the man in question, the owner of one of the more elite BDSM clubs in London, he shook his head. "I really do not feel like losing money today, brother."

"That was not my suggestion." Kalen grinned broadly. "I do think ye should ignore what yer waiting for, and then ye should go check on yer bride… make sure she *remembers* yer relationship when she's walking down the aisle."

"Ah." James chuckled, looking over at the bag he'd packed just in case Thalia needed a little help to make it through the day. "*That* does sound like a good plan."

THALIA

The loud series of knocks on the door had Thalia turning, but Analiese jerked her back into place. "I can't get the draws tight if you're moving around."

"Sorry," Thalia answered, trying to turn only her head so she could see the door. Maggie had opened it and was standing in the narrow space between the jamb and the door, the lavender bridesmaid dress about three feet longer than anything she'd seen her in before.

"Almost done. Breathe out?" Analiese waited until she'd exhaled, and then the corset tightened a notch further.

Her ribs protested on her next inhale and Thalia groaned. "Fuck, am I supposed to be able to breathe in this thing?"

"No." Her friend answered, tying off the corset before she stepped around. "Oh, Thalia, that looks beautiful on you."

"Wow, it really does!" Lauren piped up, and Chloe nodded next to her.

Heat flushed her cheeks, and Thalia wasn't sure if it was the restricted blood flow or the sudden attention that was causing it, but she was distracted as Maggie raised her voice near the door, clearly irritated. "I said *no*," her friend hissed.

"Maggie, what is it?"

"It's *yer* husband-to-be. He wants to speak with ye."

Walking to the door, Thalia peered over Maggie's shoulder to see James smiling like prince charming in his bright white shirt. The instant flood of relief she felt at seeing him made up her mind for her as she pulled the door from Maggie's vice-like grip. "I'll only be a minute, I promise."

"We still have to get ye in yer dress!"

"Please?"

"Fine!" Throwing her hands up, Maggie turned into the room and grabbed Lauren's pale blue skirt from the floor. "If yer leaving the room, at least put something on bottom. I don't think the Hampton Court House is quite as friendly as Purgatory in having women walk around half-naked."

"Thanks," she replied hurriedly, tugging the skirt on even though bending made her ribs ache inside the corset. "I'll be right back."

"Ye better be!"

"We'll just be in the room next door, Maggie. I promise I will not whisk her away from our own wedding." James grinned, but Maggie was in no mood to be submissive — the look she gave him would have earned her a spanking at the minimum from Kalen.

With one more smile at the girls, Thalia stepped outside the door and James immediately wrapped her in his arms. It was like coming home, all of the tension melting out of her as she inhaled the scent of his cologne, the scent of *him*. "I've missed you, Master."

"Has the day really been so terrible?" He chuckled against her ear, brushing his lips down her neck to send a shiver over her skin.

"It's been chaos."

"Well, let me give you a brief respite." James took her hand and pulled her to the next door in the hall, pushing it open to find what looked like a storage room for chairs and extra furniture. "Quickly now, we don't want Maggie angry."

Thalia laughed as she walked in, turning around to face him. "Technically, I don't think you're supposed to see the bride before the wedding."

"I think that's about the dress, and you are still delightfully undressed." His voice held a growl as he shut the door tight and prowled toward her.

Standing there in Lauren's tiny skirt, the stockings and garter belt, and the corset — she had to admit the heat in his gaze steadied the lingering nerves in her stomach. Making all of that energy simmer into something much more pleasant, which settled *much* lower. "I still think it's supposedly bad luck."

"Hmm…" James made a noise low in his throat as he pulled her into a kiss, one hand at the back of her head, the other pressing her waist against him. The first sweep of his tongue against hers made her remember just how little air she had with the corset tightened, and she finally understand how women used to swoon so easily. He could have knocked her over with a feather if he had tried.

Instead, he held her against him. The firm, lean muscle of his chest, his strong arm wrapped around her back so that she was exactly where he wanted her. Finally, James nipped her bottom lip and lifted his head.

"I have been dreaming about doing that since we got separated this morning."

"I—" Thalia had to clear her throat, and her head, before she could speak. "I'm glad you did that in here, and not during the wedding."

His quiet laugh sent butterflies swirling in her stomach, which were only amplified by the thumb he dragged across her lip. "Worried about scandalizing the guests?"

Catching his hand, Thalia groaned. "Mostly worried about embarrassing your parents."

"They'd survive."

"That is not comforting." She pouted, and he smiled at her. A warmer, more comfortable version of the first smile he'd ever given her. The one that had made her imagine him as some male model on a yacht, but Marcus' living room seemed blissfully far away in this perfect moment.

"Are you really still nervous about today? It's a rather small guest list."

"One hundred and twenty-eight people is *small?*" Thalia laughed. "I have no idea what I'm doing."

"You've met almost everyone here, baby. Except for some obscure relatives of mine that will *only* be wondering how I nabbed a beautiful, kind, American yoga instructor for a wife." His wicked grin actually made her smile, but despite the blush she still shook her head.

"Like they'd doubt you're capable of that."

"Oh, they'll be astonished. They think I never leave the office." He grinned and leaned close enough to have his voice a sinful growl against the shell of her ear. "They think I'm positively boring."

"Boring?" The word made a smile tug at her lips as he leaned back, smiling down at her again. James was anything but boring. He was her hero, her Master, her partner, her lover. He was the other half of her life, the weight on the other end of the scales that kept her balanced even when things felt out of control — and just like when they played, when he said he knew she was capable of something... she always was. "You are anything but boring, and I'll be okay, Master. I promise."

"I know, pet. You're the bravest woman I've ever met." With that, he kissed her again. Warm, soft, sweet. His lips pressed against hers in an unspoken vow that made her stomach do little somersaults as she clutched at his crisp white shirt. When he lifted his mouth his eyes were that dark, bottle glass green that telegraphed his arousal better than anything. Well, better than anything *except* for the growing erection against her stomach. "How was that?"

"What?" she asked, confused.

"For the wedding, is it alright if I kiss you like that?" The wicked tilt to his lips had her laughing.

"That will be bloody perfect."

With a loud laugh he picked her up at the waist and set her on the covered table behind her. "What have I told you about using British slang?"

"I think I've lived here long enough to get to use it."

"Is that right?" he asked, an edge of humor creeping into his tone.

"Quite right," Thalia replied in her best attempt at a British accent, and James groaned.

"Keep that up and I'll spank you before I let you see the surprise I brought you."

"Promise?" Just as her smile spread across her mouth, she saw his eyes flash with lust and that heady aura of dominance descended over him. An instant later she was flipped to her stomach on the table, Lauren's skirt pushed up her back, and the first swat of his hand landed on her ass. Thalia gasped, bracing her hands on the table as the steel bones of her corset dug in.

James didn't pause, delivering a series of stinging swats over the lingering marks from the floggers that morning. Even through the overlapping pains, the muted yelps, Thalia felt her mind go quiet — easing into that beautiful place she only ever found with James.

No fear. No anxiety. No doubt that he would always keep her safe, treat her well, love her unconditionally. *Forever.*

It's why they were here, after all.

As her backside heated up, each swat took on a sharper tone. Burning just a little more, sending that thrilling rush over her skin that urged her to pull away, and beckoned her to stay — to hold on, to wait for the moment when her brain would turn all of the aches, the bright spikes of pain, into something deliciously languid. A quiet, heated pool to sink into and disappear.

Just as she felt herself tipping into subspace, James stopped, and she whined. "Please, Master?"

"Tsk, tsk, pet… we can't have you all dazed when I take you back to Maggie. She'd kill me." The laughter in his voice helped to pull her back from the abyss, but she wanted to linger a little longer. As if he sensed it, James slid a hand between her thighs, pulling her underwear to the side to stroke the slick folds of her pussy. "Want to know what surprise I brought you?"

"Yes, please? Please…" So used to begging him now that it felt second nature, she was barely aware of him holding her underwear out of the way, but there was no mistaking the cool metal that slid inside her wetness. It was short, wide, and it barely took an instant to recognize it. "Master?" she asked with what little air she had left in her lungs.

"I just want to make sure you remember this part of our relationship when you walk down the aisle, pet." Pulling the little plug from her pussy, she felt him run it around the entrance to her ass, occasionally applying a little pressure. "Ready?"

Fuck.

Chapter Three
THALIA

He wanted her to have a plug in when she walked down the aisle? It was almost surprising how much the idea turned her on, a rush of heat flooding between her legs, and she found herself nodding.

"You are absolutely perfect, baby…" James' voice walked that edge of dominance that melted her, tinged with enough arousal that she knew just how much he wanted her. One hand resting on her lower back, he started to work the plug in little by little. Stretching her, pushing her, until the pressure started to ache at the widest point. When she whimpered into the table, he instantly soothed her with soft words. "You've got it, pet. Just push back and take it for me. I want to know you have this plug in your ass when I'm lucky enough to have you as my wife."

Those words almost pushed her into an orgasm as the plug slipped past her tight ring of muscles and seated itself inside her. The weight of it was familiar, her body gripping it as if to remind her that she'd accepted it. Quick, soft breaths echoed back against her face, making her aware of just how much she was panting, just how needy she was. "Master? I want…"

"Yes, pet?" He was almost chuckling as his hand slid down to find her clit, instantly zeroing in on the bundle of nerves that had her biting her lip against the urge to cry out. "Is this what you want?"

She whimpered as she nodded, her hands balling into fists as James summoned lightning from her core and sent it skittering across her nerves like some spectacular storm. "Please, please!"

"Stay quiet, baby, or I'll have to leave you wanting." As terrifying as the idea was, she could hear the lust in his voice and knew that as long as she pressed her lips together to muffle the steady moans and sighs — he would take her over the edge into oblivion.

Her hips shifted in time with his fingers, toes pressed into the lush carpet under her feet trying to angle herself back just a little further, to gain just a little bit more as the urgent need inside spiraled her higher and higher.

James slid his other hand down her back, brushing over the heated skin of her ass, pinching the aching flesh so that she moaned into the table. Desperate, wanton, and completely uncaring.

She belonged to him as much as he was meant for her.

When his thumb found the end of the plug and pressed it deeper, she almost came, and when he did it again she couldn't bite back the high-pitched whine that escaped through her teeth. Each pulse of the plug inside her ass compounded the delirious pleasure of his fingers working her clit, and her ears were buzzing with the need to come. She was babbling something, an incoherent ramble of pleas, and James finally spoke the words her agonizingly tense muscles had been waiting for.

"Come for me, pet."

A gasped thank you, another hard press of the plug inside her, and pleasure exploded low in her belly like a brilliant shower of sparks. Her muscles drawn tight, caught rigid in the flood of ecstasy that erased every other useless thought from her mind.

She was nothing but glorious light, every inch of darkness pressed to the absolute limits of her mind, as her Master, her soon-to-be husband, stroked her pussy, slipping two fingers, and then three, deep inside. Another crash filled her ears with white noise as James found her g-spot with unfathomable skill and sent her tumbling before she'd even come up for air.

Breathless, dizzy, and swimming in pure bliss — Thalia had absolutely no urge to move.

Not even when she felt him adjust her underwear over her soaked lips, and the hidden plug. The tugging of Lauren's skirt over the still warm, aching skin of her ass, only made her murmur quietly against the table... and then she felt James press himself to her. His erection driving the plug in deeper as he mimed a thrust.

"Please fuck me?" It was the quietest of whispers, but the low growl released told her he'd heard quite clearly.

"Oh, pet, if only I could... but Maggie is going to positively kill me already." Still, he continued to grind himself against her ass, torturing the both of them as his hands gripped her hips to pull her back harder and harder.

"May I taste you? I swear I'll be good, Master."

"Baby..." his answer was a desperate sound, all of that perfect self-control holding on by a rapidly unraveling thread. With a hand in her hair, James ripped her off the table and spun her so that he could claim her mouth, parting her lips without the gentleness of before. This was raw, frenzied, hungry. His fist tightened at the base of her skull, renewing the tingling storm in her nerves that had never truly quieted.

Moaning into his mouth, Thalia reached between them to stroke the outline of his hard cock, squeezing until his hips jerked against her. She smiled, and he broke the kiss to run his lips down her neck, letting her focus enough to work at his sleek belt one-handed.

Tap. Tap. Tap.

Somewhere underneath the haze of her lust, she'd heard the quiet series of knocks, but it was James who pulled his hips away from her, muttering a curse as he tried to catch his breath. "Didn't I tell you that Maggie was going to kill me?"

"She can wait," Thalia whined, reaching for his belt again, but he caught her hand and lifted it to his lips to press a kiss to her ring finger.

"Unfortunately, she can't. The wedding is in about an hour, but as soon as the Wedding Breakfast is done I have quite a bit planned for our first night as husband and wife." James let that wicked smile spread as he fixed his belt, adjusting his elegant shirt, before pushing a hand through his hair.

TAP. TAP. TAP.

A fresh series of knocks made her groan as Thalia worked to right her clothes, feeling the plug shift with each wiggle of her hips, which was *not* helping her calm down from the orgasms or the tease of play. "I still think Wedding Breakfast is a stupid phrase, it's happening mid-afternoon."

"It's tradition, baby." James winked as he walked to the door, speaking louder. "I hear you, Maggie! I promise she's —"

Thalia was finger combing her hair when James tugged the door open and froze, the light from the hall clearly showing the surprise on his face before he erased it with a smile.

"Mum, I didn't expect you. Is everything all right?" Somehow, James managed to sound calm, even as Thalia's heart leapt into her throat. Evelyn's quiet response was impossible to determine over the rapid sound of her pulse in her ears, but she desperately tugged the skirt lower on her thighs, hoping that there were no errant bruises from their play that morning showing below the hem.

Unfortunately, there was nothing to be done about the way her breasts were lifted by the corset top, or the burning blush she felt in her cheeks, or the rest of her state of dress.

"Thalia, mum wants to chat for a few minutes. I'll go tell Maggie so she doesn't worry, alright baby?" With a careful glance over her, James grinned and gave a quick shrug before he pushed the door open.

"Thanks," she answered, trying to smile normally as Evelyn Hawkins walked into the room, elegantly dressed in a beautiful gown the rich color of eggplant.

"You can leave us now, darling. This is a chat just for Thalia and I." There was a warm note to her voice as James leaned down to press a kiss to his mother's cheek.

"Of course, mum." Lifting his eyes over the pale blonde, he smiled wickedly at Thalia. "See you soon, baby. I love you."

"I love you too," she answered, and this time the smile was much easier… only then James pulled the door closed behind him and Thalia was left half-dressed, soaking wet, and wearing a plug while in the same room as the woman who was about to *officially* be her mother-in-law. "I, um, I'm sorry about my clothes. I was in the middle of getting dressed when James wanted to talk, and —"

"Don't trouble yourself, dear." Evelyn waved a hand, eyes sparkling as she smiled at her. "We have all the same things, and I know you will look absolutely lovely in the dress you chose."

"Right, thank you again for connecting me with your designer friend, I had no idea where to go. I probably would have just done a web search for dress shops!" Letting out a nervous laugh, she almost choked when Evelyn took a seat in one of the uncovered chairs and patted the one beside her.

"I was glad to help. Now, please, sit with me a moment?"

Thalia felt her smile waver as she walked over and eased herself onto the chair, fighting against the urge to gasp when the plug seated itself deeper. "Was there, um, something you wanted to talk about?"

Her heart wouldn't slow down, beating like the wings of some caged bird seeking release, and all Thalia could imagine was that Evelyn was going to bring up the fact that James had refused a prenuptial agreement. *That* drama had lasted for weeks, with the Hawkins' family law firm harassing James to have one drawn up. But he had been the one to refuse, even though she would have signed instantly.

"I have something for you." Evelyn's soft smile drew Thalia's attention to the small box in the woman's delicate fingers. "I had always planned for Katherine to wear these at her wedding, but, as she so brashly reminded me last week, she does not ever plan to get married."

"Oh, I'm sure she'll find someone someday."

"Well, perhaps. However, she has also told Henry and I that if she ever does get married it will be in Las Vegas and presided over by Elvis." Lifting a shoulder in a graceful shrug, Evelyn seemed more amused by Katherine's antics than irritated. "To be honest, dear, I was always much more worried about James finding someone to spend his life with. You did not know him when he was young, but he was always so serious… so focused. Even when he had a girlfriend, we were lucky to even know her name. Meeting her was an utterly ridiculous idea."

"Really?" Thalia asked, leaning forward as Evelyn laughed softly.

"Quite. It was as if he thought we would frighten the girls away!" Evelyn smiled warmly at the memories, and then she reached for Thalia's hand, squeezing. "And then he found you… and almost lost you… but you came back to him, to us, so that we could finally meet you."

Tears stung the edges of her eyes, but Thalia blinked them away, squeezing Evelyn's hand gently in return. "Meeting James was the luckiest day of my life," she replied, knowing it was an impossible understatement, but they had long ago agreed on the version of the story James' family would know.

"I feel it is we who are the lucky ones, dear. I always knew it would take a very special woman to capture James' attention, and keep it long enough for him to be willing to share her with us." Evelyn delicately cleared her throat as she released Thalia's hand, lifting the small black box in her hands. "And you are everything I could have hoped for him to have, Thalia."

"Evelyn…" Her voice broke as she tried to speak the level of gratitude she felt at being so whole-heartedly accepted by James' parents, but she couldn't find the words.

Brushing a quick hand under her eye, Evelyn offered the box. "It is why I would very much like to see you wear these today. I wore them when I married Henry, and my mother wore them when she married my father."

Taking the tiny jewelry case, Thalia opened the lid to find two beautiful, antique earrings. Each had an oval diamond nestled in the center of a circle of intricate, lace-like metal work. Smaller diamonds were tucked into the design, with a round diamond at the top that formed the base for the drop. Speechless, Thalia simply lifted her eyes to Evelyn who covered her mouth for a moment before wiping her eyes.

"Oh, I can see how much you like them and that makes me endlessly happy." Gesturing to the little box, Evelyn was more animated than she'd almost ever seen her. "I'd love to put them on you, would you mind?"

"Of course! I… I don't know what to say." Shifting in the seat, Thalia bit her cheek as the plug moved, but she ignored it as Evelyn plucked one of the earrings free and brushed her hair back to work the drop through, working the hinged clasp at the back that held it in place.

"You don't need to say a thing, dear. This makes me happier than I can express. Other side now." Evelyn turned her head, putting the other earring in place with a soft, satisfied sigh. "Just look at you, absolutely beautiful."

"Thank you so much." Thalia managed to speak just before Evelyn pulled her into a hug, the small woman's arms squeezing her with more strength than Thalia would have guessed.

"I am so glad to have you as my daughter, and Henry is too. He wanted to come up and tell you himself, but I insisted it was inappropriate." Releasing her, Evelyn let out a conspiratorial little laugh. "And I must say, I was correct. He would have been burning to his ears to see you in this beautiful corset."

"Right." Feeling her *own* blush burning all the way to the crown of her head, Thalia was relieved when Evelyn stood so that she could as well. "Please tell Henry how grateful I am to both of you for accepting me."

"Accepting?" Evelyn's gentle laugh came again. "Dear, I was *praying* for you, you were simply a blessing to us. Now, Katherine? She was your real challenge, but you won her over easily."

"She was intense…" Thalia laughed. "But I love her too."

"Oh, we all do. She's just a wild spirit." Evelyn shook her head as she rested a hand on the doorknob, smiling as she spoke about her children. "It seems Katherine got every bit of Henry's mischievous side, and every bit of my wild youth."

"You?" Thalia asked before she could stop herself, but Evelyn's eyes sparkled as she lifted her shoulder in another graceful shrug.

"We were all young once, dear. But it was James who inherited all of our seriousness. Henry's drive and work ethic, and my quiet thoughtfulness. You bring out the joy in him, Thalia, and the one thing he has always needed in his life is a little levity." Evelyn leaned forward to press a gentle kiss to Thalia's cheek. "I truly do not think James understood fun until he met you."

"I, um…" Blushing brightly enough that Thalia could feel the heat in her cheeks, she fumbled over a response — because explaining to James' mother about exactly how he used to have his *fun* in BDSM clubs across Europe was absolutely not an option. Instead, she managed to squeak out a noncommittal, "I'm sure he had his fun… but I'm very glad that we found each other."

"We all are." Evelyn lifted her hands in the air, letting out a little sigh. "All right, dear, I've taken enough of your time. Go on and get dressed, we'll be in the front row waiting to cheer the moment you say *I do*."

"Thank you, Evelyn." Holding the door as the small woman stepped outside, Thalia was looking forward to catching her breath, but then Ailsa was smiling from the hallway. A laugh burst past her lips as Thalia leaned out of the doorway to glance around, catching sight of Evelyn walking away, but no one else. "Is there a receiving line I'm not aware of?"

"What can I say, yer a popular girl today. Do ye have a minute? I promise, this is something ye will definitely want before the wedding kicks off in proper fashion." Ailsa was almost antsy with energy, her grin growing as she stood there, a leather portfolio tucked in her arms.

"Hell, why not? Maggie hasn't pulled the fire alarm tracking me down yet." Gesturing inside, Thalia watched as Ailsa quickly stepped into the room with a secretive smile. When she moved to sit down, Thalia groaned inwardly, the plug shifting as she twisted to close the door. "If it wouldn't bother you too much, would you mind if I stand while we chat?"

Chapter Four
THALIA

"All right, what do *you* have for me, Ailsa?" Thalia smiled at her friend, and therapist, as the woman settled onto the chair Evelyn had just vacated.

Fidgeting with the edges of the leather portfolio in her lap, Ailsa spoke softly, "I knew how much ye wanted this today, but I know ye mentioned at the rehearsal dinner last night that James had said no…"

Eyes widening, Thalia took a half-step toward the other woman. "You don't mean—"

"I do." With a flourish, Ailsa pulled the tablet free of her portfolio and held it out. "This is purely a medical decision, completely covered by doctor-patient confidentiality."

The seriousness in her friend's tone just made Thalia smile wider as she reached out to pluck it from her fingers, holding it to her chest as emotion swelled inside her again. Different than the warmth that Evelyn had summoned with her kind words, but just as vital. Just as important to making today what it needed to be. Speaking past the lump of emotion in her throat, Thalia mumbled, "Is this what I think it is?"

"Do ye mean is it the tablet that James is unaware Kalen stole from yer flat this morning? The one with access to the private site for ye and the others?" Ailsa shrugged. "It might be."

"Oh my God!" Thalia let out a laugh as she leaned the device back enough to tap the power button. Her background flared to life, a photo she had taken on a trip to Barcelona with James a few months before. "I can't believe you guys did this."

"Just be quick about it, okay?" Standing, Ailsa closed the space between them to squeeze Thalia's forearm. "And when yer done give it to Maggie so Kalen can sneak it back into place. My brother has always been light fingered when needed."

"Thank you for this. I didn't even know how much I wanted to talk to them today." Emotion made the last few words tight, strained, but Ailsa always understood.

With another gentle squeeze she moved toward the door, pulling it open. "Ye might want to find another spot to work on it, Maggie does know *exactly* where ye are."

Ailsa left without another word, leaving the door cracked, and Thalia glanced down at her minimal dress wondering where she could hide for a few minutes that wouldn't be inappropriate. Sneaking into the hall she walked to the very end, finally finding an open door that seemed to be a storage closet. Industrial sized tubs of cleaning supplies, vacuums, brooms, and a myriad of other things that lent their soapy, chemical odor to the air — but Thalia didn't care at all as she pulled the door shut and sat down on the floor with a slight adjustment when the plug reminded her of its presence.

Logging in with the speed of a habit long-formed, she found her way to the site and saw the posts with new comments bolded near the top of their private forum. The one that held her interest was the one where she'd told all of the others about the wedding. It had taken days to write it, to temper her own joy with the bitter pain of the stories she'd come to know too well.

So much suffering.

So much pain. Torture. Loneliness.

A black hole of despair that had swallowed so many of those screen names — ones that were mostly now connected to *real* names. Real women. Scattered across the globe in various states of recovery… and she was talking about getting married to the man who had saved her. Twice.

With a slow breath of the chemical-sweet air around her, Thalia tapped her post and waited for it to load. Some of the replies she'd already read, but the ones she hadn't were still highlighted for easy recognition.

```
Couldn't be happier for you, TR0414. Maybe I'll find
someone someday. — AW0612

You deserve this, Thalia. Don't let anyone ruin your
day. We're all grateful for you and JH. — SC1109

He's dead. You're alive. You set us free, and this is
the rest of your life we're talking about. The way
```

> *you talk about JH makes me think that eventually someone will be able to deal with all of my shit. All of the shit Marcus did. Go marry your prince charming, TR, and get your happily ever after for all of us and share some fucking pictures! — VE0914*

There was an ache blooming behind her ribs, and Thalia rubbed at her sternum as she read Vicky's comment. The girl Marcus had taken to replace her, to be some kind of sick, twisted surrogate… the one who had yet to reveal even a tenth of the things he'd done to her.

Victoria Evans had survived two months with Marcus, while Thalia had barely survived two and a half weeks. She was impossibly strong, even if she hadn't moved out of her parent's house since she'd made it home.

Every one of these girls had suffered unspeakable things at the hands of the Williams brothers, and others, and as Thalia continued to scroll through their kind messages she felt the sharp twinge in her chest growing worse. It was only when a drop landed on the screen that she realized she'd started crying, but there was no stopping it. These other women were the only ones that understood. Connected by the most terrible moments of their lives.

When she finally reached the end of the recent comments she tapped out her own:

> *Thank you all for the sweet words, I can't express how much they mean to me. To know that you forgive me for being happy with JH. It may sound strange, but you're all with me today. In my mind and in my heart. The things that tie us together may be horrible, but I wouldn't trade this connection for anything. I'll post some pics, I swear, and I know that each of us will find the right person to love us for who we are. Damaged goods and all. —TR0414*

It was pointless to fight the tears, so Thalia let them flow as she posted and moved back to the homepage, where the bright red circle of a message waiting in her inbox drew her attention. Tapping it, she felt a twist deep in her belly once more.

There was one unread private message waiting, and it was from Beth.

BD0211. Beth. Elizabeth Doherty.

The girl who had lived through the closest version of hell that Thalia could imagine. First, Anthony's unimaginable torture, then being sold to the kind of foreign nightmare that Marcus had only threatened when she'd enraged him. Beth only mentioned her experiences there in off-hand comments on the site, casual mentions of surfacing to find herself under strange men, chained to strange beds — until she'd stopped surfacing completely. Years of her life lost, which may have been for the best.

And, yet, somehow in all that horror, all that perfectly terrible darkness... Beth began almost every private message the same way.

> *Thank you for today, Thalia. Today I watched my nephews chase each other in my parent's backyard, pushing each other and rolling around in the mud with this completely innocent joy. They made everyone laugh and forget about the huge fucking mess in the way that only little boys can. I laughed too. I felt happy, and it felt good.*
>
> *I hope you laugh today, TR. I hope you went through with removing their mark so it's not with you, because I don't want today to be a bad day for either of us. I want you and JH to make your wedding day perfect, and it should be. No fucked up nightmares, no tattoos, no scars, no painful memories.*
>
> *It's a new start.*
>
> *You know you won't be TR anymore? You'll be TH, but I figure you'll keep the screen name. I know they bother some of the other girls, but I like them. The timeline of it all, winding down to just you, then VE0914, and you once more. The last of us. The one of us that stopped it all.*
>
> *It all comes back to you, and I want to be like you someday. Strong and living and capable of being with someone. I'm getting closer. I've had four good days in a row thanks to you.*
>
> *You know that you deserve to have as many good days in a row as you can manage, right? You don't need to keep apologizing for them. You deserve to be happy, Thalia. So enjoy your wedding day, tell us every blissful fucking part of it. Let us soak in the possibilities, the hope, the love and the joy. Let us absorb it. Don't be so afraid to tell us how good life can be again because all it does is remind us we can find it too. You're not rubbing it in, you're lighting the way.*

> *Can't wait to hear all about it.*
>
> *— Beth*

Thalia's breath shuddered as she tried her best to avoid breaking down into sobs. Another series of *thank you* comments from Beth, another snapshot of her reclaiming her life piece by splintered piece, coupled with so much love and support.

The last of us.

No one had quite put it that way, not in all the time on the site, but it was the truth. If she let herself, Thalia could still remember the sticky sensation of Marcus' blood drying on her skin, and there had been times when she had summoned that memory like a shield. A shield against nightmares that happened so infrequently now that she almost felt free of them.

Almost.

Leaning back against the rack behind her she ran a thumb over the piece of corset that covered her hip, deftly hiding the gauze beneath that protected what had once been the Williams brothers' symbol — but now it was something so much more. So much better.

Tapping the reply button, Thalia wiped her cheeks, drawing on the strength that Beth seemed confident she held inside.

> *Beth,*
>
> *I don't know how many times I have to ask you to stop thanking me. Every time I see you post is thanks enough, it's more than I ever expected. You talk about me being strong, but it's you that talks with so many of the others about the things they could never write outside of here.*
>
> *It's like you always say... some things are meant for family and friends, some things for therapists and doctors, and the rest of the shit goes in here.*
>
> *I think we'd all be crazy, or crazier, if you weren't always around to respond and tell us that you feel it too.*
>
> *As far as the mark, it's gone! I'm still in a state of disbelief over it, but JH did exactly what I asked. He gave me a brand to burn away the ink forever, and it's beautiful — or it will be when it*

finishes healing. For a while I was sure he didn't believe that it was what I wanted, or that he hated the idea of permanently marking me after everything, but he did it. For me.

I'm pretty sure my therapist had something to do with it, you know AR can be pretty feisty when it comes to repeating the same damn words I've said to JH a hundred times. But you're always saying how WE can say it, but until a doctor agrees it's like we're not speaking at all. Fucking annoying, but in this case it worked.

While that's getting better with JH in general, on this one I definitely needed AR on my side. The way we did it was beautiful too, and it hurt, but less than I thought it would. I'll have to tell you the whole story in another message.

Today feels surreal. There are so many people I love here, but I still don't feel like I deserve it. Not when so many of you are still in so much pain. It feels like I've cheated somehow, taken a shortcut through the trauma, and I'm leaving all of you behind.

I'm happy, really seriously happy — but at the same time there's a part of me that isn't. And I think that's okay. It feels right to remember where I could have been without JH on the day I marry him, because it makes me love him even more.

Thanks for the message, Beth. I was thinking about you especially.

— Thalia

Sending the message made her even more aware of the strange little hollow spot behind her ribs. The spot that worried about the other girls, that got anxious when someone hadn't checked in. The page titled *Fighters* had a list of every girl that had been lost. Those that had died before she and James had ever turned over the evidence to INTERPOL, and those that had still been unable to cope when they were found. It wasn't a long list, but it was a powerful one, and the bottom of the page had a simple line:

WE REMEMBER ALL OF YOU. YOU WILL NOT BE FORGOTTEN.

Chapter Five
THALIA

The corset was digging painfully into her ribs, the plug prodding her with the memory of James' incredible hands on her, and she felt the tug of a smile at her lips. James, the one the girls all knew only as *JH*, was a hero. *Her* hero, and she now wore the brand of his initials instead of the tattoo Marcus had embedded in her skin. The small heart shape on the brand had obliterated every shred of the ink the Williams brothers had placed there.

She belonged to James, body and soul, and soon it would be official in the eyes of everyone they knew, legalized with papers, registered forever.

Thalia Hawkins.

It had a nice ring to it.

Smiling, she had started scrolling through the other posts about therapy appointments, nightmares, stories the other girls had shared — and then the red dot appeared next to her inbox again. This time when she opened it and saw Beth's message, she smiled, but the smile quickly turned to panic when the short message appeared:

> Shouldn't you be getting married right now? — BD0211

Heart racing, Thalia closed out of the browser and saw the time. "FUCK!" she shouted, yanking herself off the floor with help from the rack.

Pushing the closet open she stumbled into the hall to find her bridesmaids milling around outside of their dressing suite. Analiese was on the phone, one hand tangled in her hair as she paced, Maggie was shouting at Chloe and Lauren to go downstairs to find *her*.

Walking toward them with the tablet clutched to her chest, it was Julie who saw her first. "Where the bloody hell have you been?" her voice was high pitched, screeching, and five pairs of eyes landed on her, just before the rest of them exploded.

"The wedding starts in twenty minutes!" Maggie ran toward her, lifting the long lavender dress away from her heels. "Get yer ass in here so we can get ye ready!"

"Where were you?" Chloe asked, holding the door open as all the girls funneled her back inside.

"I was, um, there were people that wanted to talk to me. First James, and then Evelyn. She gave me these earrings?" Thalia tucked her hair over one ear, offering the beautiful jewelry up as some sort of excuse. "See?"

It was Maggie who ripped the tablet from her arms, holding it out, her cheeks flushing bright red. "Those earrings are lovely, but I talked to Kalen! I know exactly what ye were doing, and ye dinnae have time for this!"

"Please be careful with it!" Reaching for the device, Thalia whined as Maggie tucked the tablet under her arm and huffed.

"Of course I will be careful." Maggie rolled her eyes before she pointed at Thalia. "But Kalen knows ye went off hiding, and he knows *Ailsa* told ye to. She's in her own kind of trouble with him, but while he's been keeping James in the dark for ye, he told me to tell ye that ye have a date with his paddle after the honeymoon."

Lauren and Chloe giggled by her dress where they were carefully checking it over. "At least it's not us in trouble for once."

"Just ye wait, I haven't spoken to Brad yet, and Master Sean hasn't met ye either Chloe. I'm sure ye will make *quite* an impression." Grumbling, Maggie stormed over to her bag to tuck the tablet away, and then she planted her hands on her hips. "Girls, we have ten minutes to get Thalia in this dress and her hair and makeup done."

"Curling iron is still hot!" Analiese answered.

"I've done makeup in less time," Julie added, and Thalia noticed her friend had managed to squeeze into the dress, although it comically looked like she'd stuffed a basketball in the front of it.

"Skirt off!" Lauren called, and Thalia turned just in time to see her and Chloe coming toward her. The pale blue skirt was ripped down her legs, her calf swatted by one of them to make her step out, and then came the petticoat. The weight of it settling on her hips as Lauren stepped behind to tie it closed.

BAM. BAM. BAM.

Heavy-fisted knocks landed on the door and Analiese ran for it, yanking it open. High-pitched squeals preceded Kalen's booming voice, a toddler under each arm. "Blessing, I cannae keep them entertained and look for — Thalia?" Her name became a question as his eyes landed on her, and the moment he sat the twins down they bolted into the room.

Thalia raised a hand, nervously waving as Chloe put her in the ivory heels. The kids were loose, crashing over everything with the grace of newborn deer learning to walk. Red headed tornadoes, Noah was in the most precious tiny version of a tuxedo, and his twin sister Ava was in a fluffy lavender dress with the biggest tutu and a huge bow buried in her curls.

"Ye brought them HERE?" Maggie shouted, turning to snag Noah's arm as he ran past her carrying someone's underwear.

"What did ye want me to do? Yer mother is dealing with the caterer with Henry, and I couldn't very well drag them all over Hampton Court House trying to find one errant submissive!" Kalen's voice was booming as he stomped into the room, somehow missing every bit of clothing on the floor as he scooped up a squealing, giggling Ava. Tucking the toddler on his hip, his eyes landed on Thalia. "Ye are due one hell of a punishment. Ye know that?"

Wide-eyed, Thalia tried to catch her breath. "What did you tell James?"

"NOTHING!" he shouted in answer, and Chloe and Lauren chose that moment to carry over the huge ivory gown.

"Arms up," Chloe said, ignoring the chaos around them, and just as the ivory silk and lace descended over her head, Thalia heard Ava's high-pitched cry start.

"Ach, princess, yer Da isn't mad at ye. Look at me, are ye not the prettiest lass here? Aye, of course ye are! Dinnae cry, Ava. Please?" Kalen's voice had become soft and gentle, cooing to his baby girl as he tried to calm her, and as Thalia's head came free of the bodice of the dress, she saw him bouncing her. The little girl tucked against his barrel chest, wrapped in his huge arms, that mop of red curls tucked under his chin. Quietly, he started to hum some lullaby, and Thalia found herself smiling.

"Don't go smiling at me now, Thalia. I didn't tell James because it's *his* wedding day too, and I won't be the one to make him panic wondering where in the bloody hell ye are." Kalen shook his head, rubbing Ava's back with one massive hand. "Ye don't have a clue how much he worries about ye, how much it bothers him to let the security team go, and then ye go and hide on yer feking wedding day?"

"KALEN!" Maggie snapped, covering Noah's ears.

"Sorry, yer *damn* wedding day."

"Not better," Maggie hissed.

Growling, Kalen muttered under his breath, but Thalia interrupted before anyone else could speak. "I'm really sorry, I had no idea how late it was. I should have been more responsible. Thank you for not worrying James, it would have ruined the day."

"Yer d—" Glancing at his wife, Kalen sighed. "Yer right, it would have. So now ye need to get ready and get downstairs so he's not waiting at the altar wondering if Jake needs to call in helicopters."

For a moment Thalia almost laughed, but then she realized that was exactly what would have happened if she'd disappeared. With Peter and his detail on the premises, along with Jake, there was not a doubt in her mind that if Kalen had let James know no one could find her that she would have heard helicopters overhead and seen brawny men in tuxedos searching the building in no time. "I'm sorry," she said again, her voice jumping as Lauren and Chloe worked to close the back of the dress.

"Good." Taking a long slow breath, Kalen held his hand out for Noah's who grabbed onto one of his dad's fingers, arm stretched high above his little head. "Ye look beautiful, I'll go tell the men that ye ladies need just a few more minutes."

"Thank you, Kalen!" Thalia shouted as Analiese brushed out her hair.

Maggie kissed her husband quickly before pressing another to the forehead of each twin, and then she hustled them outside. Kicking the door shut, she stood with arms crossed, a furious blush still high on her cheeks. "See?"

"I know I messed up, and when have I ever argued a punishment?" Thalia tried to stay still as the girls moved around her. Chloe and Lauren fluffing the dress, tugging at the petticoat underneath. Analiese stood to her right curling her hair, while Julie starting laying out makeup on a nearby table.

"I think ye should be grateful there's two weeks between now and that punishment, because I think if he had the paddle with him today ye'd be unable to sit for the Wedding Breakfast." The wicked little smile on her lips had Thalia smiling in return, but at the mention of the breakfast she paused.

"Wait, did Kalen say your mom was working on an issue with the catering?"

"They got a flat tire on the road. Pretty much anyone with a car had to drive out to help get the food here." Julie stood from the chair by the little vanity table, one hand resting on her belly. "Maggie's mum has a rental car here so she offered to help. From what I understand it was quite a caravan."

"Oh my God!" Thalia groaned and Analiese swatted her shoulder.

"Be still or I'll burn you."

"Wouldn't be the first time this week!" Lauren laughed, and Maggie lifted her eyes from texting her phone.

"Bloody hell. The catering is fine, I've been talking to mum, they're setting up outside, but how is yer brand? I forgot to check it earlier." Concern drew Maggie's brows together, but Thalia shrugged.

"A little sore, but fine. We changed the dressing this morning."

"Good. Analiese, can ye do Thalia's hair with her in the chair so Julie can do her makeup? We really need to hurry up."

"Of course." They helped her find her seat, but she ended up with a mountain of lace and silk in front of her. The girls scrambled to find enough cloth to cover the expensive dress and protect it from the makeup, and then Julie started working.

Hair tugged one way with the curling iron, chin tilted another by Julie, Thalia just relaxed and let them do what they wanted.

After all, the only thing that really mattered was that she was marrying James, and she hadn't ruined the wedding day by hiding in a supply closet.

If she could just make it through the ceremony, it would be so much easier — *oh God*. The ceremony. Thalia's heart was instantly racing again, trying to push Julie's hand away from her lips so she could speak. Finally, her friend grumbled and let go.

"I'm trying to get you ready for your wedding! What the bloody hell is so important?" Julie snapped.

"My freaking vows!"

Chapter Six
THALIA

"What about the vows?" Analiese asked, tucking the comb for the veil into her hair, and Thalia tried to turn but both girls stopped her.

Groaning in frustration, Thalia waited for Julie to stop applying lipstick, but when she finished and Thalia opened her mouth to speak, a tissue was shoved between her lips.

"Press," Julie commanded, and she did, blotting them against the tissue with a growl.

"My vows, I didn't get to finish putting them together!" Thalia raised her voice, pointing blindly behind her. "I think they're still in the chair. James came while I was working on them, they're not done!"

Maggie appeared in her line of vision, smiling as she clapped her hands together in a perfect mimic of Kalen calling attention at Purgatory. "Thalia, yer just going to have to speak from the heart then, because yer all ready."

"But—" Thalia started to argue as everyone was helping her get upright. Tossing the random fabric that had protected the dress on the floor, they fluffed her petticoat, adjusted her hair, and suddenly her head swam.

She was about to walk down the aisle.

She was about to stand in front of one hundred and twenty-eight people… and she had absolutely no fucking idea what she was going to say.

They started to guide her out the door and she had the urge to dig her heels into the floor to stop them, as if she could freeze time long enough to think straight, to put together the right words for everything James was to her.

"We've got to go," Analiese had her elbow, tugging her into the hall, and Julie took her hand on the other side, showing the radiant smile that had been missing most of the day.

"Trust me, it will fly by. Just look straight at James, lock eyes with him, and the rest of the room will disappear." Tilting her head, Julie seemed to think for a moment. "It's kind of like playing in public, actually. Focus on your Dom, not the onlookers."

Chloe laughed, her mocha skin glowing against the soft lavender dress, dark curls in a voluminous, beautiful array around face. "Yeah, Thalia, just don't drop to your knees at the front, okay?"

"That's another one on the list," Maggie chided, flicking Chloe on the arm. Then Thalia's Matron of Honor locked those vibrant blue eyes on her. "Ye have loved James for a long time now, right?"

"Yes," Thalia whispered, trying to fight the earliest inklings of a panic attack that had her lungs feeling even tighter behind the corset.

"And ye know that James loves ye more than anything in this world, right?"

Nodding, Thalia found herself bracing her hands on her hips, digging her fingers into the brand hidden under layers of clothes just to feel the spike of pain from the healing flesh surrounding it. The dull ache spread as Lauren rubbed her back, and the whine of air entering and exiting her lungs had hushed everyone. Each of the girls stood quietly, eyes soft as they watched her.

"Sweetheart? We really need to get ye downstairs." Maggie was closer, leaning forward to pry Thalia's fingers off her hip. The rush as the dull pain in her hip pulsed had her lips tingling… or maybe she was about to faint. "Do ye really think James will care what ye say today? He won't, he probably won't even remember it. He's been head over heels for ye since I first saw the two of ye together, and all today is about is letting everyone celebrate ye."

"But what if—" *I ruin everything.* Thalia felt that age-old panic creeping in, the one that had brought her to Purgatory in the first place. The fear that she'd say the wrong thing, do the wrong thing, and out James to the world. Ruin his life, just because he loved her.

"What-ifs will kill you, Thalia. This is real life, and sometimes that just means jumping in with both feet even though you don't know if anything is going to catch you." Julie caught her hand again, squeezing. "But I have a feeling James will always catch you."

"Totally," Lauren said, smiling.

"You know he'd go to the ends of the earth for you, why would today change that?" Analiese asked, and Thalia smiled a little. Just minutes before she'd been absolutely certain that James would have called in helicopters and mercenaries and bodyguards to find her — and even though she had no idea what would happen in the grand hall during the ceremony, she at least knew James would be there. And she had the best, and kinkiest, friends any girl could ask for surrounding her.

Glancing back at Julie, Thalia let out a slow, shaky breath. "I just look at him, right?"

"Just look at him, and those sexy green eyes you like so much." Squeezing her hand one more time, Julie tilted her head toward the hall. "He's waiting for you, you ready to go see him?"

"Yeah."

A collective sigh of relief echoed around her, and she almost laughed as they started to hurry her down the hall. Maggie kept pace to their right, rapidly texting, most likely to Kalen.

No code reds, no runaway brides, no *missing* brides, and Thalia was relieved that the only people waiting outside the doors to the grand hall were the groomsmen, and a pair of very excited toddlers who were lying on the floor in their formal wear.

"Really, yer going to let them get all filthy right before the ceremony?" Maggie huffed, walking over to help the twins stand, dusting them off with her hands.

"At least on the floor they were in one place, Jake's been chasing them up and down the hall!" Kalen crouched down to fix the bow on Ava's head, sighing.

"Ma?" Noah asked, reaching for Maggie, and she pressed a kiss to his hair.

"Remember, ye have to walk with yer sister. All the way to Mister James." Maggie was trying to talk to them, but everyone knew neither kid was paying attention.

"I'm counting chasing the little ones as my cardio for today." Jake winked and walked over to Julie, offering his arm. "And I've been informed that your husband will be watching my hands very carefully when we walk."

"He did not *actually* say that to you!" Julie was gawking, no longer looking even a little self-conscious as Jake nodded with a serious expression. It sent her into a fit of giggles, and Thalia found herself smiling as the rest of the group paired up.

Tom approached Analiese, standing in awkward silence beside her, while Analiese bit down on her lip, avoiding eye contact like she had during the rehearsal. Lauren approached Adam, a longtime family friend of James' who lived in France. He was calm quiet to Lauren's bawdy brashness, and she leaned against him when he offered his elbow, turning the man's cheeks a little pink.

Sean, or *Master Sean* as she knew him better, walked up to Thalia first, taking her hand and kissing her knuckles. "How's the brand?" he whispered softly.

"Just fine, thank you, sir," she whispered back just as quietly, smiling at the breach of protocol not to discuss the *other* side of their lives around the vanilla crowd.

"Well, you look positively lovely." Releasing her hand, Sean glanced to the side where Chloe stood, a slight smirk waiting on her lips. "Is she as much trouble as I've been told?"

"More." Thalia grinned, and Sean laughed quietly.

"I think she'll earn a trip to SW3 before the end of the night. Brad came by the room earlier and we had a… chat." His smile was all Dom-with-a-plan as he turned and walked over to her. Thalia watched as he kissed Chloe's hand with all the gentlemanly grace he had used with her, but then he tugged the girl closer, leaning down to whisper in her ear. Chloe grinned for a moment, and then her eyes went wide.

Trouble. But Chloe had always enjoyed trouble.

The girls gathered their bouquets from the table beside the entrance, small bundles of white hydrangeas and garden roses, tucked in with lilac and dainty hints of green. Picking flowers had been one wedding task Thalia had enjoyed, and the flowers looked beautiful. Maggie brought over her bouquet when she didn't move to get it. A flourish of white hydrangeas and roses with the rambunctious ivy that Julie had first thought was crazy, until the florist had turned it into a cascading bouquet that now rested against the front of her dress.

Pressing a kiss to her cheek, Maggie whispered in her ear, "I couldn't be happier to be here for this. Whatever ye say will be perfect, even if ye just tell him ye love him."

As she stepped back, Kalen took her place, smiling warmly, turning all of his rough features into that warrior's beauty that had first stunned her at the entrance to Purgatory. It felt like a lifetime ago, and at the same time it felt like yesterday. Kalen gently caught her chin, lifting her eyes to his and holding her there. A wave of quiet submission rolled through her, pressing back the anxiety, and she took a slow, calming breath inside the peace. "Are ye sure ye don't want me to walk with ye? It would be my honor."

Thalia laid her hand on his wrist, speaking softly, "Thank you, but this is important to me. Walk with Maggie and Noah and Ava. I promise I won't disappear."

Kalen's eyes creased at the edges, and he tweaked her chin as he let go. "Alright then, we'll be waiting for ye." He turned away to take his place beside Maggie, resting a hand on Noah's head to keep the boy in place, and then he rapped his knuckles softly on the beautifully carved wood in front of him.

From inside, the string quartet quieted and the rest of the party lined up at the doors. The twins in front of their parents, each with a basket of flower petals. Maggie and Kalen, looking at each other warmly before he gave her a quick, *and slightly inappropriate,* kiss. Then there was Julie and Jake, both still giggling and chuckling, even though her belly almost reached the back of Maggie's dress.

Analiese and Tom were next, and she at least wore a smile now, her arm through his, but as pale as Tom looked it was unlikely he'd be pressing Analiese for information down the aisle. Chloe and Master Sean came after, and as quiet as Chloe was Thalia had no doubt that Sean had shared some of Brad's ideas with her.

Last were Lauren and Adam, and as usual, Lauren's unabashed openness had cracked the man's stoic disposition already. He was grinning, clearly trying not to laugh his way down the aisle, but Lauren was still whispering out the side of her mouth occasionally.

It was when the first notes of Bach's '*Jesu, Joy of Man's Desiring*' began to play inside that the group tightened up. The doors opened and the sound of the guests inside shifting in their seats was nerve-wracking even though Thalia couldn't see. For a moment neither twin would move, but Kalen leaned down and said something and they both took off squealing like banshees down the aisle. Laughter floated out of the hall, and Kalen and Maggie just grinned as they began the processional.

Chapter Seven
THALIA

Each of her friends smiled at her, whispering kind things just before they stepped inside, until it was only her waiting outside. She paced for a moment, trying to get her nerves under control, to stop her hands from shaking, and then she caught her reflection in a mirror.

For a second Thalia almost didn't recognize herself.

Julie had been light with the makeup, simply erasing the imperfections with her skills. The palest pink on her cheeks and lips, mascara but no bold liner, no intense eyeshadow. Even the gentle curls Analiese had put in her hair seemed natural. The ivory lace of the strapless dress seemed to make her skin glow and complemented the earrings Evelyn had given her. It had been Evelyn's designer friend who had customized the dress, ensuring the bodice tucked close to her curves before it swelled at her hips, flowing into a short elegant train.

She looked bright, and summery. She looked *alive*.

Most of all, she looked happy.

Taking her position at the edge of the entryway, the man at the door caught her eye and tilted his head like he was asking her a question. With one more breath she smiled and nodded.

This time when the strings hushed, they picked up again quickly. Pachelbel's '*Canon in D*' building slowly as she stepped between the doors. Everyone stood, the room filled with sunlight from the windows along the back wall — and there was James. Smiling like prince charming in his tuxedo, grinning broader when Kalen reached up to squeeze his shoulder.

Thalia took the first step and knew she'd made the right choice to walk by herself.

She'd been alone, lonely, unaware of how sad she was when Marcus had taken what little she *did* have and set it aflame. Torn her out of the life she was barely living anyway and destroyed what was left. When she'd first seen James, from her knees, naked and afraid — she'd truly had nothing.

So, it mattered to walk the aisle alone.

To acknowledge that her father walking her down the aisle would have been a lie, because he had never been there for her like that. To admit that while there were many good men in her life who had offered, from Peter to Jake to Kalen, wouldn't have been right either. Even James' father Henry had mentioned it to James, but that was wrong too. Thalia had spent years being invisible. She'd spent the last two as a victim, and now she was becoming someone new.

She was someone who *could* walk the aisle alone, head up, eyes on the man she loved, and not have a single urge to hide, or bow her head. Even with the knowledge, and sensation, that she wore James' pre-wedding gift hidden under all the bridal trappings.

And what a view she would have missed had she kept her eyes to the floor…

All of her friends lining the edges of the aisle that had clumps of flower petals on it, and one lost flower basket someone had pulled to the side. The girls at the front with their huge smiles, Julie practically bouncing in her shoes with her excitement. Evelyn's teary stare from the front row, Henry's wave, Katherine's sly wink, Ailsa's grin — and James' steady eyes seeing only her, backlit by the bright sunshine outside and the rolling green of the lawn.

When she stepped up to him, Thalia couldn't pull her eyes from his, her heart almost aching to think of just how lucky she had been to find him. "I've missed you," she whispered.

"I've missed you too, baby. You ready?" James couldn't stop smiling, and it made her warm through and through. Maggie had been right, it wouldn't matter what she said standing up here, because they'd both be walking back down the aisle together.

"Absolutely." Turning, Thalia handed off her bouquet to Maggie, and then she faced James to place her hands in his. Brushing his thumb over the back of her hand, they both looked at the officiant and he smiled at them. A kind looking older man, he opened the ceremony welcoming everyone, and the bustle of everyone taking their seats barely registered with James' reassuring touch on her hands.

The blur of the man speaking wasn't quite forming into real words in her head, but they'd reviewed the language so many times she knew it by heart. Not a religious ceremony, but more of an acknowledgment of the decision they were making. To be together, partners in all things, to support each other, lift each other up, and when the man looked at them she felt ready.

"Please, face each other." The man smiled at her as she turned to meet James' eyes, listening to the gentle baritone, aided by the microphone at his collar that spread his voice across the grand room. "Will you, James, promise to lift Thalia up when she is low, care for her when she is in need, and love her even when times are hard?"

"I will," James smiled.

"And Thalia, will you promise to lift James up when he is low, care for him when he is in need, and love him even when times are hard?"

"I will." She nodded, fighting the emotion rising in her chest.

"In a marriage you are vowing to do all of these things and more. You vow to stand beside each other, to weather the storms of life together, to keep each other close, and, ultimately to always be there for each other." He gestured toward the two of them, his hands almost touching their shoulders. "In addition to these, it is my understanding that each of you would like to exchange your own vows. James, please make your vows to Thalia." The officiant clasped his hands, and Thalia smiled a little wider to see James' throat work as he swallowed, eyes dropping from hers for a moment as he took a breath.

When he lifted them again he smiled at her, beaming and perfect. "Thalia, I honestly never thought I would be here, holding the hands of the woman I love more than anything. I thought it was simply not meant to be for me, but… then I found you." He pressed their hands a little harder, and if it were possible she loved him even more in that moment for the nervous way his mouth twitched in a bittersweet smile. "I have to believe that it was fate, destiny, that I was lucky enough to find you, because you are so strong, and fierce, and *feisty*."

Laughter thrummed through the room, and he swallowed again, his eyes moving over her face before settling once more.

"I love you more than I ever thought it possible to love another person. And I will not just stand beside you as your husband, your partner, I will move heaven and earth for you, because you are heaven *on* earth to me, Thalia. There are not enough words to describe the million brilliant ways you make me whole, and I promise to spend the rest of my life trying to make you as happy as you have already made me."

A chorus of sounds went through the guests, and Thalia bit her lip trying to keep herself from crying and judging by the sniffling in the audience she wasn't the only one. "I love you, James," she whispered, and he mouthed the words back as the officiant began again.

"Thalia, please make your vows to James."

Her stomach was filled with butterflies, her heart so full that it ached, and surrounded by the golden light of the afternoon she felt like it was actually flowing through her. Keeping her eyes on his, she did what Maggie suggested and just started talking, "James, I think I wrote ten versions of my vows, maybe fifteen."

A soft round of laughter echoed around her, and James let out a quiet chuckle as he brushed his thumbs over the backs of her hands in small, soothing circles.

"But they were never good enough. Nothing was good enough to describe how you make me feel every single day… precious, important, loved." Shaking her head, Thalia stumbled over her words. "Before you my world was dull and lifeless. I didn't know it, but I was lonely, I had just accepted it for so long that it felt like it was right — and then? Then there was you. Vibrant, and brave, and endlessly patient with me. You loved me before I even knew how to describe love. You showed it to me in every action, in every breath, and before I knew it I loved you too."

Biting down on her lip, James grinned and reached up, tugging her lip free with his thumb like he had a thousand times before. Brushing her cheek with his fingers, he returned his hand to hers, and nodded at her.

"I feel like we've already weathered enough storms together, we already know we will stand beside each other. You care for me and lift me up without even thinking about it, because it is who you are, James. You do more than simply keep me close, you chose to bring me into your life, to share your friends with me, your family — and because of that my world filled with color. Because of you I know I will never feel lonely again, and my life will *never* be dull." More soft laughter from the crowd that made her smile up at the man who was everything to her. "What could I vow that would be enough for that? I don't think there's enough in the entire universe, and in the end I can only offer myself. I can promise that I will always be honest with you, that I will keep no secrets, because you already know all of my darkness, and you have given me so much light. I love you James, and since I have this official occasion to do it, I would like to say that *I* am the lucky one."

The guests laughed, and James lifted an eyebrow at her, unable to look serious or stern with the wide grin on his face, but he did turn to the audience, raising a hand as he spoke loudly, "We all know I'm the lucky one, so hush up now."

Thalia laughed and he turned back to her, shaking his head through his own chuckles as the guests grew louder for a moment.

"You are in trouble for that one, pet," he whispered so quietly she almost couldn't hear him, but the words only brought a frisson of excitement through her.

"It was worth it," she whispered back.

They stood straight again as the officiant smiled at them, his own laughter making the creases at the corners of his eyes deeper. "Laughter is a gift that every marriage should have, it makes it easier to get through hard times together, but a strong community makes this even easier. Would all who came here today in support of James and Thalia please stand."

The sound of one hundred and twenty-eight people standing was louder than she expected, but Thalia barely even noticed. She was surrounded by light, and love, so filled with it she could have been levitating.

"James and Thalia invited all of you here today to witness these declarations of their love. They have demonstrated their commitment to each other, and there will come a time when they will need more than just themselves to succeed. Do you, their family and friends, promise to be there to love and support them when they need it? To stand as the community around them to help them be strong? If so, say *we do*."

It seemed they were both remembering Purgatory, and the family of support they had already built as they heard the guests loudly proclaim, "WE DO!" The brush of Maggie's hand against her back was just further confirmation, that even without the pledge, she and James already had a strong community at their backs.

"Thank you, you may be seated." The officiant waited a moment, and then spread his arms wide. "For thousands of years rings have been viewed as a symbol of eternity, with no beginning and no end, and today James and Thalia have chosen to follow this tradition by exchanging rings with each other."

Kalen and Maggie each stepped forward, placing the rings in James and Thalia's hands with the synchronicity that the four of them had formed.

"James, please take Thalia's hand and make your declaration."

Brushing his thumb against the delicate engagement ring she already wore, James hovered the wedding band at the end of her finger, his eyes finding hers as he spoke, "Thalia, I give you this ring as a symbol of my love and commitment to you, now and forever."

The ring slid home, fitting perfectly, and inside she felt whole, bruised and scarred in places, but unbroken. No more pieces out of place. Then the voice of the officiant broke into her thoughts, "Thalia, please take James' hand and make your declaration."

Feeling slightly giddy, her hands shook as she took his hand and held the ring in place. "James, I give you this ring as a symbol of my love and commitment to you, now and forever." Nudging the ring forward she settled it in place, and he immediately clasped her hand, the bright band glinting in the light.

I am yours, and you are mine.

"James and Thalia, you have shown today your great love for each other. Your family and friends have committed to supporting you, so now I just have one more question for each of you." The older man smiled, and when he turned to James there was not a hint of the fear that Thalia had worried about before, she knew exactly what James' answer would be. "James, do you take Thalia to be your wife, now and forever?"

"I do," James' voice was the perfect blend of how he sounded on Sunday mornings, aroused and playful, and the way he sounded when he was telling her something important, something he was passionate about. And she had all of him, every side, the serious and the fun, the darkness and the light.

"And Thalia, do you take James to be your husband, now and forever?"

"I do," she answered, almost shaking as she waited for the next words.

"Then I now pronounce you husband and wife. James you may —" Before the man had even finished the line, James had pulled Thalia toward him, one arm behind her back as he kissed her. Dipping her backward to the sounds of cheers from the guests and the roar of clapping. It was warm and soft, but he nipped her lip just once, enough of an edge to promise her so much more. From somewhere above them, the officiant finished amidst his own laughter, "— kiss the bride."

Chapter Eight
THALIA

What does perfection feel like?

Sitting in a chair beside James with the soft, green grass brushing the soles of her feet, Thalia had no doubt that this was it. The pinnacle moment of perfection in her life. Loved, cherished, surrounded by friends, and a family that accepted her completely. It used to seem too ridiculous to even dream, because… who really falls in love anymore?

Who actually gets swept off their feet, or *rescued?*

Things like this only happened in fairy tales.

Well, in fairy tales, and around James.

Her prince, her knight in *slightly scuffed* armor, her lover, her Master, her husband.

Their fingers were intertwined under the tablecloth, the party dress much easier to breathe in than the wedding dress, but he still managed to take her breath away. Every smile, every flash of his green eyes, every stolen kiss that was cheered by the guests who caught it — *this* was perfection.

"I love you," she whispered against his lips when he pulled back from another kiss, tasting of champagne and chocolate cake.

He tightened his hold on her hand, pulling her just a little closer to him until she thought she might just tip out of the chair and into his lap, but she knew he would catch her. James always did. "I love you more than anything, Thalia. *My beautiful wife,*" he added quietly, that smile coming back so full of joy that she felt it like a hum on her skin.

"Still happy you went through with it?" The laugh was so close it made her bite her lip to keep it in, but James didn't bother. He laughed and then released their hands to pinch her thigh through the dress, her body jumping as she lost the battle and laughed too.

"You're stuck with me forever, pet. Remember that tonight when I tie you to the bed and make you beg." James' voice was a growl, and suddenly her mouth went dry as the tilt of his lips turned wicked. Winking, he nodded toward the guests spread out before them. "Focus on them for now, baby, everyone is here to see you."

"*Us*," she corrected, still unsteady with visions of his possible plans running through her head.

"Oh no, they're all here to see you. I told you earlier today none of them think I ever leave the office." Pressing another quick kiss to her lips, he turned to answer something Kalen said, the two of them laughing at whatever she'd missed.

Trying to shake the thoughts of rope, and floggers, and his hands on her, she looked out at the party that was just getting started now that they were clearing the food away. The *Wedding Breakfast*, which was actually more of a late lunch, had been as wonderful as the wedding itself. Outside in the balmy weather, the slightest of breezes ruffled the white tablecloths, and for once England was without grey skies. Pale clouds drifted across a blue sky, and the sun shone as if the world were celebrating with them.

Thalia ran her feet over the grass under the table, sitting much more comfortably after removing James' pre-wedding gift, but now she noticed the plug's absence. The tickling buzz between her thighs that his promises had summoned making her antsy in the chair, unsure of what to do next.

"You're thinking too much, I can tell. It's your wedding day!" Julie nudged her with an elbow, leaning away from Antonio to smile at her. "Enjoy it!"

"I just can't believe I'm married." Staring down at the wedding band, she twirled it with her thumb, watching as the late afternoon light played over the metal. "It doesn't feel real, does that make sense?"

"Totally." Julie laughed, running her hand over her belly before she held up her own wedding ring. "It was a few months before it felt real I think. I suddenly woke up and it hit me that we were really married. Together *forever*."

"Did you have other plans?" Antonio asked, his voice comfortingly American to her ears, but Julie just grinned at him.

"Maybe I did."

Huffing, Antonio braced his hand on the back of her neck, his fingers twining into Julie's golden up-do before he tightened them and she gasped prettily. "And *that* is yet another reason I'm so glad I knocked you up. You're all mine, angel. You, and the little one." With all the gentleness that his grip in her hair lacked, he ran his other hand over her belly in a caring sweep. "My family."

Julie's cheeks were flushed, and she whimpered as she laid her hand over his. "I was only joking. Please don't tease me, sir. It will be *hours* before—"

"Oh, I know, angel. But you teased me first, and now you're just going to have to sit there needy, and wet, and absolutely beautiful until I get to take you back to the hotel and fuck you." Antonio's voice was so quiet that Thalia was sure she and Julie had been the only ones to hear it, but the moan the blonde released was *not* as quiet.

Heads turned along the table, but Antonio just pulled her toward him and kissed her with an intensity that had Thalia pressing her thighs together with a groan.

Dammit.

How soon was it acceptable to leave your own wedding reception, or breakfast, or whatever?

Turning toward James she ran her hand along his thigh and she couldn't help but smile. He was as carefree as she'd ever seen him, still laughing when he turned toward her, one eyebrow lifting. So hot, so absolutely wonderful, and she just wanted a few minutes alone to ease the ache growing between her legs.

"Master, can we—"

"It's time!" Kalen interrupted her from James' other side, and her new husband's bottle glass green eyes widened a moment before he turned his head.

"You wouldn't dare," James hissed at Kalen, but when their friend stood tall, clanging his knife against the side of his glass, he just gave a devious look down to the two of them. Groaning, James grabbed her hand under the table, pulling it from his thigh as he leaned close. "If I hit him to shut him up, I hope you won't judge me."

"It depends on what he says," Thalia whispered back, smiling against his lips when James snuck another quick kiss that did nothing to ease the need coiling down low in her belly.

"*Toast! Toast! Toast!*" The chant started and soon multiple people were clanging their silverware against champagne flutes and other assorted glasses as silence spread through the tables scattered over the lawn.

"Thank ye!" Kalen's voice boomed, the grin on his face making her a little nervous as she caught Evelyn and Henry's eyes at the nearest table.

What on earth did Kalen have planned that had James tense enough to be squeezing her hand this hard?

"As ye might have noticed, I'm the Best Man today, and that means I get to give a speech… no matter what James has to say 'bout it."

Laughter shuffled through everyone as more people turned in their seats to listen, the string quartet pausing the music off to the side.

"I don't know all of ye, but I was lucky enough to meet James sixteen years ago when we were both on holiday. Well, I should say that *James* was on holiday, and I was just roving around Paris because it seemed like a good place to be — and I was out of money." Another round of laughs as Kalen smiled down at James, and then he winked at her before continuing. "So, one night in Paris I'm drinking away the last few quid in my pocket when I see this lad at a pub, proper dressed, watching a rugby match. Of course, he knew as little about rugby then as he does now—"

"What!" James laughed, and Kalen held up a hand as the guests chuckled.

"No matter what he tells ye, just know that I taught him what little he *does* know about the game!" Kalen took a breath, shrugging his broad shoulders. "And, in exchange for the help, he bought me a pint. And then another, and another until we were *rather* drunk. If ye had asked me that night, I would nae have thought I'd spend another day with this *Sassenach* that didn't even know the better team in the match… but we actually spent the next two months wandering side by side across Europe. More oft than not getting into trouble, or *finding* trouble if it didn't find us."

"Oh bloody hell, Kalen," James muttered, but he was grinning, and Thalia couldn't help the smile that was so broad it made her cheeks ache.

"Ye know it's true, James. And as we moved from city to city, country to country, there were a few brawls — *sorry Evelyn*," Kalen raised his glass toward James' mother, and she just laughed. "But I taught James how to fight, and we learned pretty quickly that we much preferred to be the ones leaving the welts instead of taking them."

"Bastard," James cursed under his breath on a laugh, shaking his head, and a blush flooded Thalia's cheeks as her eyes went wide at Kalen's dangerous choice of words.

He wouldn't dare.

"I knew before the holiday was half-over that James was the kind of lad to always have yer back. The kind of mate that would share absolutely *everything* he had with ye, and we shared…" Kalen paused, grinning at the two of them, and then he continued like he had just wanted to look at the newly married couple. "…plenty of good times."

James was cursing while trying to keep his chuckles quiet, Thalia's cheeks were burning as she glanced at Evelyn and Henry and Katherine to see if *any* of it was sinking in, but they were both smiling calmly. No visible reaction from her new in-laws, while Julie sputtered to her right, trying so desperately to hold in her laughter that she was choking on her water.

"By the end of the summer we'd enjoyed the highest of highs, and been through the darkest dungeons together—"

The tittering giggles of Chloe and Lauren at one of the tables near the front made Thalia lean close to James' ear to whisper, "Okay, you can hit him now."

"— and I knew I had a brother for life." Kalen finished, grinning devilishly. Flashing white teeth through his beard as he rested his hand on James' shoulder.

"I cannot believe you," James hissed through his teeth as he smiled, but Kalen was unfazed.

"Brother, we used to say that we might never find the right women for us. That none of them would put up with us, but I found my Maggie, and I knew the day I met yer Thalia that she was *the one* for ye. James, ye light up when yer with her, more alive than I ever saw ye even in that first summer, and I'm just glad ye didn't balls this relationship up, because she is everything ye ever dreamed of. And, as much as we like her, if ye had messed it up we might have kept Thalia around instead of ye!" Laughter broke out again as James stood and Kalen pulled him into a hug, clapping him on the back with a few resounding slaps. Leaning back from him, Kalen raised his glass high, "TO JAMES AND THALIA!"

"TO JAMES AND THALIA!" The guests echoed back, and Thalia lifted her glass high into the air before finishing her glass of champagne.

As the boys settled back into their chairs, she heard James chuckling as he spoke low, "I will get you back for that, brother."

"Sure ye will." Kalen's laugh was booming, another resounding slap landing on James' back. "Good feking luck, brother."

James shook his head, grinning as he tapped his glass against Kalen's with another laugh. The wait staff was quick to refill glasses as Maggie stood from her chair, moving around to stand beside Thalia, and she grabbed for the champagne like a life raft.

"Oh, hell," Thalia whispered under her breath, and Julie grinned from her chair as she made room for Maggie to stand between them.

"Don't worry, I won't embarrass ye like that. Boys are boys, even at weddings." Maggie smiled at her, and Thalia nodded, begging with her eyes as her friend cackled.

"This will be good…" Julie muttered and Thalia groaned as her Matron of Honor began.

"If ye don't already know, I'm Kalen's wife and those two wild ones rolling around in the grass are ours." Maggie smiled as the twins stumbled and chased each other, darting after the fireflies that were starting to twinkle as the sun started to drop below the treeline. "I've known James for a long time, but in all those years I never really saw him happy in life. I saw him entertained, I saw him proud of his work, and I have listened to more boyish arguments about rugby than I care to remember."

People laughed, and Thalia reached for James' hand as she kept her eyes on Maggie, catching another glimpse of the James she'd never met through her words.

"But I always wondered what made him hold back, what made him stay just a *bit* apart from the rest of us… and then I met ye, Thalia." Maggie's blue eyes found hers, and she felt her heart start to race. "When he brought ye to visit, I already knew something was different. I'd never heard his voice like that before, and just the smile on his face was something completely new. There! *That* smile!"

Everyone looked at James and when Thalia turned she indeed found him smiling, just before he kissed her. The whistles that ran through the crowd made Thalia's cheeks burn, but James kept it *just* appropriate enough to be acceptable, while still being intense enough to send a shiver up her spine.

"Alright, alright, we get it." Maggie's boisterous laugh interrupted them and the cheers died down as they looked back at her. "I'm sure all of ye have seen it in him before today, or ye saw it during the wedding, and now ye know exactly what I mean. Thalia carries a light within her, and it blazes so fiercely that nothing can dim it. It was strong enough to pull James halfway around the world to be near it, and it was strong enough to ignite that light inside him too."

There was a strange ache in Thalia's chest as Maggie spoke, a tension that made her eyes burn like she was about to cry. James sensed it, or saw it in the way that he could always read her like a book, and his arm draped over the back of her chair, his fingers brushing her arm in small, looping circles that let her take in a deeper breath.

Maggie looked down at her, tears threatening in her eyes as well. "It would have been enough for me to know how happy ye make James, Thalia, but yer heart is so good, so open, that ye became my friend too. One of my best friends, one of my *favorite* houseguests…" She winked, and Thalia laughed, the tension easing in her chest just a little. "Ye made James better, and I can't imagine our lives without ye in it. That is why I am so glad to be able to say that today ye are Mrs. Thalia Hawkins, and that Kalen and I will always be here for the both of ye."

"Oh, Maggie," Thalia whispered, the tears came slipping down her cheeks, and her friend wiped at her own face to raise her glass.

"TO THALIA AND JAMES!" Maggie cheered loudly.

"TO THALIA AND JAMES!" The guests cheered, and then the lights came on across the lawn. Summoning a fairytale glow as people shouted their well wishes, and guests stood to applaud, many making their way toward them.

Before Maggie could slip away, she caught her hand. "Thank you so much, Maggie. I love you and Kalen both, you know that, right?"

"I know ye do, Thalia, and we love ye too. It's why we were both so proud to stand beside ye today." Leaning over, Maggie pressed a kiss to her hair before standing again. "Ye ready to get the party started?"

"Hasn't it already?" Thalia asked, looking out over the guests who were beginning to line up in front of her and James, but Maggie just laughed again.

"Oh, no… they haven't even opened the whisky yet!"

With that, Maggie escaped back to Kalen, her husband sweeping her into a kiss that made Thalia smile and roll her eyes. Those two were breaking their own rules about *public displays in front of the vanilla crowd*, especially as Kalen's large hand roved downward to cup Maggie's ass through the dress.

"I *think* that could have gone worse, what do you think?" James asked quietly, and Thalia laughed.

"As long as no one picked up on their comments, I guess we're safe."

Stealing one more kiss, James smiled. "I still might hit him later."

"I think a fight would entertain Master Kalen too much," she whispered, and James laughed just before he was distracted by someone from his side of the family reaching over to shake his hand. James stood, and Thalia stood as well, ready to greet the guests.

There were a few random people in the line that she smiled politely at, said all the appropriate *thank you's* and *so glad you could come* phrases that were required, and then Katherine stood on the other side of the table, smirking with a devious tilt to her lips that reminded her of James plotting something. "Hey, Katherine," Thalia said, laughing a little.

"I'm your sister now, and that means we tell each other everything." Leaning across the table, she lowered her voice. "Such as just *how close* are you two and Kalen and Maggie?"

Crimson heat filling her cheeks, Thalia pulled back, and Katherine's trilling laugh made her gawk as she stumbled over her answer. "We— we're great friends."

Winking, Katherine planted her hands on the table and leaned further forward, beckoning Thalia toward her. When she complied, her new sister spoke directly into her ear, "It's alright. I have *great* friends I like to play with too, just don't tell James. He gets *so* overprotective."

Thalia was dumbfounded. Not shocked by Katherine's behavior in *her* personal life, just surprised she had picked up on what should have been a series of inside jokes. Somehow, she managed to smile as she whispered, "Dear God, please don't tell James you noticed."

"Talk to my *brother* about *that?*" Katherine waved her hand as she stood upright again, keeping her voice low. "Absolutely not. But…" The blonde turned her head toward Kalen, her green eyes roaming slowly over the man's broad, muscular shape under the tux. "You can always share details about *other* things with your new sister, right?"

"You are going to get me in so much trouble!" Thalia hissed, but she was laughing, and Katherine was too. The woman who had terrified her on their first meeting in New York smiled like she was in on a secret with her.

"Not if you don't say anything, because I definitely won't. Sisters don't repeat what they say, right?" The bright smile on her lips was something Thalia would have given anything to see at one point, and now it was so common that it made her chest ache. A sister, a family, a husband, and friends that loved her completely.

How did she end up so lucky?

Smiling, Thalia leaned over the table and pulled Katherine into a hug, pressing a kiss to her cheek. "I will always keep your secrets as you keep mine, and because you helped us book the honeymoon I'll call you when we get back and we can… chat."

Pulling back, Katherine's sea glass green eyes were wickedly bright. "About *him?*" Her head tilted toward Kalen, and even though Thalia blushed, she nodded.

"Only if you swear to keep it secret."

"Sisters, right?" Lifting her pinky finger between them, Katherine grinned.

Linking their little fingers, Thalia nodded. "Sisters." Just as Katherine moved to step out of the receiving line, Thalia held on. "Wait! Thank you for accepting me, Katherine. I want you to know how much I appreciate it."

"You're lovely, Thalia. More than I could have hoped for James." She tightened the grip on their pinkies for a moment, and then let go. "I'll see you later, sister!"

"See you later!" she called after her, smiling to herself. She wouldn't tell Katherine *everything*. Not the BDSM for sure, definitely nothing about Purgatory, and not the exact details of the fun the four of them had together, but she'd give her a taste.

And she'd *definitely* warn Maggie that Katherine might offer to join. The mere idea of Maggie's cackle had Thalia laughing as the next guest approached, and she returned to hand shaking and platitudes, wondering when she'd get some time alone with James in all the festivities.

Chapter Nine
JAMES

Having his arms around Thalia felt like coming home. It always did, every single time he got to hold her, but the foreign weight of a wedding band on his finger made it… different.

Made it *better*.

As soon as the music had come on, the guests had poured onto the dance floor, and even though they were outside the speakers managed to make it loud enough to envelop them, pulsing with energy. No more string quartet, no more tuxedo jacket. James had the sleeves on his shirt rolled up and Thalia tucked against his front as they moved to the music.

He could watch her like this forever.

Eyes closed, a soft smile on her pink lips, completely happy and free as she shifted in perfect time to the beat. Moving his hands to her hips he tugged her closer to his front, ignoring the twitching of his cock that urged him to end the bloody party early and finish the plans he'd started thinking of earlier in the day.

Nothing better for stress relief than planning a scene… except actually *doing* it.

Which would happen tonight.

The thought made him smile as Thalia wrapped her delicate fingers around his hand, holding him to her skin as she rolled to the music, and he pressed his lips against her hair, breathing the scent of her shampoo, her perfume — *her*.

Absolutely intoxicating, and she was finally completely his, woven into every aspect of life.

Married.

Since when had that been a word he'd looked forward to? Before Thalia 'marriage' had felt like a death knell, like a cataclysmic life event that would ruin everything he enjoyed about life, or at least everything he'd *allowed* himself to enjoy about life.

But, then he'd seen her. Fallen for her bravery on that fucked up video stream, and he'd wanted her. His first urge had never had a thing to do with marriage, it had always been just to have her. To save her before they ruined her. To touch the fire inside her that blazed fierce enough to survive against the Williams brothers… but then he'd met her, and she had been so much more than he'd ever expected.

Bloody hell.

He had completely cocked up his vows, skipped half of what he'd wanted to tell her. She was so much more than her fierceness, her bravery. So much more than the memory of an angry, naked girl on a video stream. She was kind, generous, strong enough to submit and still be her. Her submission was a gift he wouldn't have had words for, even if they had been appropriate to say during the ceremony. James had been completely unable to articulate it even at the branding ceremony, but just the knowledge that she wore his ring *and* his initials branded into the flesh of her hip — obliterating the Williams brothers' mark — it made him want her even more. Want to possess her completely, and as the beat changed in the music he dug his fingers into her hips, knowing just where the brand was.

Thalia's soft gasp, followed by her sweet laugh, was bloody torture. She rubbed herself against him in time with the music, and James finally lifted his eyes from her to look at the dance floor around them. Gorgeous, massive tiles between two of the buildings of the Hampton Court House, and just in front of them Chloe and Lauren were sandwiching Brad on the dance floor.

A perfect distraction.

With those two girls dancing, no one was investigating exactly how hard he gripped Thalia's hips, or the way he lowered his head to taste her skin. Grazing his teeth over the place where her neck met her shoulder, he smiled when she shivered, her hand tightening over his. "I am going to fuck you so hard, pet," he growled just below her ear, and her whimper was music to his ears.

"Promise?" she asked, breathy, desperate, and he couldn't hold back the devilish chuckle.

"After I make you beg, and plead, and scream… absolutely."

"Master," she sighed, her head dropping in front of him as she ground her ass against him in a devious tease that had him glancing around again to check on just exactly which table his parents had chosen — but he was shocked to find them on the dance floor. Arms around each other, swaying to the beat like they were at an elegant gala, and he couldn't help the brief flash of envy.

Someday, he had to hope that he and Thalia would still be leaning against each other like that. Still in love enough to *want* to sway to whatever music existed in another forty years.

The music changed and the digital beeps of the song he'd requested came over the speakers. He felt Thalia go rigid in front of him, her recognition making him grin.

"James, did you—?" she started to ask the question, radiant joy in her voice as she spun around in his arms.

"Yes?" He couldn't help but smile as she cheered and reached for Analiese, grabbing onto her friend just before she started reciting the lyrics to *Travesuras* by Nicky Jam. The Spanish rolled off her tongue with the ease of too much practice. It was bittersweet to see her and Analiese dancing to it, and he shrugged at Nick as their women abandoned them for a moment on the dance floor.

It was the song that had helped to pull her out of too many nightmares, a single memory of their time in Barcelona that had somehow become important to the both of them. A silly thing at the time, when he had been there for work and the song had been on the radio *constantly*. Thalia had fallen in love with it, stood up in a bar to sing it when they were having drinks, and that single shining moment had become a lifeline for the both of them.

When he worried about her, the song made him remember her smile, her wild and carefree laughter. And she always said it reminded her of feeling loved, feeling safe.

Judging by the way she danced and smiled, it had been right to ask Antonio to request the song from the DJ. She was having fun, not even paying attention to the guests watching her Analiese. Not a single hint of her old anxieties, and *that* had James smiling, unable to pull his eyes from her. Finally, Thalia turned toward him, rushing back to wrap her arms around him, hugging him tight to her as she sang in Spanish about being unable to contain herself, her attraction. When she spun and rocked her hips to the beat, grinding against him, James loved the song even more than before.

"I think I like you in this dress even more than the green one, baby." He leaned down to say it directly into her ear, and she laughed and leaned back to kiss him. Holding her carefully, he deepened the kiss, parting her lips with his tongue so he could taste her, a cruel temptation of what waited for them after the party was over and they could leave the guests without being rude.

Even though all he wanted to do was throw her over his shoulder and walk to the nearest car, steal it, and leave. *Or* just find another empty room inside the house — at this point, he wasn't feeling very picky, he just wanted her. To hear her sighs, to have her begging again like she had earlier in the day, to make her come and watch her body rise and fall for him.

Submissives were addictive, and Thalia was the perfect drug for him.

Tailor made. Bespoke.

His.

Yet, it was their wedding day, and that required meeting certain societal expectations. Jumping through the hoops of civility so he didn't have to be civil later tonight. Thalia chose that moment to break the kiss, her urgency to finish the last lyrics of the song making her sing them almost breathlessly as she found the beat again with effortless ease. It was only because of his grip on her hips that he managed to get back in rhythm with her, laughing at the way Thalia pulled people in with her sheer enthusiasm for the song.

Because all around them were their chosen family, smiling and laughing right along with them as their song ended and the music changed again.

Kalen and Maggie were tightly pressed together to their left, Analiese and Nick dancing as if they were not on the grounds of Hampton Court House, and Lauren and Chloe? The way *they* danced was bordering pornographic, and Brad had the same boyish grin he always did when the girls misbehaved and he was enjoying the results.

The fact that no one had stepped in, no matter how many lingering touches the three shared, spoke volumes of either the tolerance, or rigid formality, of the guests from his side of the list.

Scanning around them, he saw that Antonio had both hands on Julie's stomach as he leaned close to kiss her, and in a flash James could see Thalia glowing and perfect, round belly carrying their child — and it made him pull her closer. Not just his submissive, more than his lover, she was his everything. His future. His entire life in a beautiful, smiling, radiant package. She laughed and leaned against him, the next song just as energetic, making her shift in the most delightful ways against the growing ridge of his cock. Of course, she noticed, and she took full advantage as she swiveled her hips, grinning at him over her shoulder.

"Minx," he growled, leaning down to nip her ear. "Maybe I should have left the plug in to remind you who's in charge."

"That wouldn't have helped with how wet I am, Master." Thalia kept the words in a hushed tone, but she may as well have had a live wire threaded into his pants. The mere thought of her tight heat squeezing him and he was grinding against her like a teenager… but he *somehow* managed to stay on beat.

She laughed, bright and airy, and he wrapped his arms around her waist to hug her closer, even though it ruined their dancing. "Have I mentioned just how much I love you?" he asked, directly against her ear.

"A few times today," she answered, obviously smiling. "And you know I love you too, more than anything."

"More than everything," James answered, and then he felt a tap at his shoulder that reluctantly pulled his head away from the intoxicating scent of her skin. He was irritated for only a moment, before he realized it was Jake standing beside him, a flash of something in his smile that made James stand to attention.

"I need to talk to you," Jake spoke just loud enough to be heard over the music, and then he glanced at Thalia with a questioning look, but James simply nodded as his heart rate picked up considerably.

"Let's talk, all of us." Adjusting his grip, and mentally focusing on telling his libido to stand down, he reached for her hand. "Come on baby, this is important."

Chapter Ten
THALIA

The music faded in her ears as she turned to find Jake and James facing each other with serious expressions, and something deep inside twitched to see the two of them like that. It brought back uncomfortable memories, thoughts that were unwelcome today. But then James smiled at her, reassuring and loving, and even Jake managed a grin — so Thalia made herself follow them off the dance floor. They walked as a small group, nodding at guests that smiled and congratulated them as they walked out onto the grass, near one of the tables that had been abandoned by its occupants.

"So?" James asked as soon as they were alone, his hold on her hand tightening slightly.

Jake's smile went wide, stretching his cheeks. "It's done."

"Bloody finally! Are you sure?" Releasing her hand, James shoved his fingers into his hair, breathing out a huff as he moved a half-step closer to Jake.

"I swear. I wasn't going to interrupt until I was sure. This was too important for any kind of error." The mercenary who had been present on one of the worst days of her life smiled at her, winking before he returned his eyes to James.

"What are you two talking about?" she asked as the men moved closer together.

"Show me the proof," James demanded, and Thalia's head spun.

What the fuck is going on?

"I should have visuals in the morning, but for now I've got this." Shoulder to shoulder, the two men closed her out, huddling around Jake's phone as she stood there. Glancing back at the dance floor, she saw Maggie and Kalen at the edge of the tiles, holding hands as they watched them.

"Is someone going to tell me what's happening?" Thalia asked, her irritation increasing with every moment the two men kept their heads together, mostly ignoring her. "Jake!"

His head lifted, and then they both turned to her, although James was now holding the phone, still looking at something on it. Jake opened his mouth to speak, but he stopped, glancing at James as if seeking permission, which James did not provide.

"You're not his employee tonight, Jake, talk to me." Crossing her arms, Thalia stared him down, and Jake ran a hand along the back of his neck, blowing out a breath.

"Actually, I am." He held his hands out in front of him when her temper spiked, almost exploding on them both, but she waited for him to continue. "*Not* as being one of his groomsman, I was honored he asked me, and I was absolutely here to support the both of you today. That's just not *all* I was doing today."

"For the last week and a half," James mumbled, eyes still glued to the screen, and Thalia clenched her fists at her sides.

"*James.*" As soon as she said his name, those perfect sea glass green eyes lifted to meet hers above the device in his hands. "What is this all about?"

"A wedding gift," he answered cryptically, a smile tweaking the edge of his lips as he moved a little closer, holding the phone where she could see it. The screen was filled with text, and she pulled it from his hands to read.

Starting at the top she was confused for a moment, and then she saw the name: *Anthony Williams.* Her heart stumbled over itself, forgetting to beat for a moment before it beat triple time to make up for it, battering her ribs from the inside as if the panic she felt at that name made it wish to escape. Only, the other words in the document seemed to steady her pulse into a rhythm more appropriate for a *moderate* cardiac arrest situation.

Violent incident.

Handmade weapon involved.

Prisoner found dead on arrival.

Thalia tried to process the words, scrolling through the details about locations and cell blocks and guards' names and none of it was sinking in, except the one possibility that seemed too dark to actually hope for. Lifting her eyes to the two men who seemed to be waiting for her reaction, she felt frozen. Jake's jaw twitched, and so she looked at him first, "Anthony is dead?"

"Thalia…" James' voice was soft, gentle, and when he reached for her she stepped back because she needed the space, the physical breathing room to process. As always, he respected it, lowering his hands to his sides. The men made eye contact for a moment before James looked at her again. "Yes, he's dead."

"How?"

Jake cleared his throat, shifting foot to foot, clearly trying his best to suppress the smile fighting to take over his face. "We, uh —" Glancing at James again, Jake paused, but at his nod the man continued. "Well, my team and our contacts had him… handled. At James' request."

"What?" Thalia shouted it before she gained control of her voice, lowering it as she remembered the wedding guests on the dance floor. "You had them… *handle* him?" she hissed, staring at James, but he barely reacted.

"Of course I did."

"I — I don't even…" Stumbling over her words she tried to run her fingers through her hair, but it was still stiff with hairspray, so she clenched her fist instead, digging her nails into her palm as James moved close.

"Did you really think I'd let any threat to you linger out there?" His voice was deadly calm, and she felt the frisson of his self-control buzzing around him. There wasn't an ounce of regret in him, and she met his eyes as all of her warring thoughts fought for mental space.

Anthony was dead.

Sadistic, evil, fucking nightmare chair Anthony was dead.

Thalia searched in the chaos of her thoughts for anything resembling pity over the news, and she found none. Nothing. What clashed inside her were the memories of his words on the screen, his control of the chair. The flickering panic Marcus had displayed when he'd been sure his sick fuck of a brother had killed her or damaged her beyond salvation. That terrifying moment when Anthony had arrived at the house and come for her. The first time he'd touched her.

The constant impending threat he posed just by existing.

Not just to her, but to every woman he had ever touched. Tortured. Sold.

To every username on the website she and James had so painstakingly constructed to keep every victim safe — from him. Or anyone he might sell his knowledge of them to.

"Anthony is dead," she repeated herself, but this time it felt more like a fact as it fell from her lips, and James nodded. Looking down at the phone in her hand she skimmed the document once more, searching it for any doubt, any possibility.

This time she raised her eyes to Jake's, and felt the steel in her voice, "Swear to me this is true."

"I swear." Jake seemed like he was about to reach for her, but his hand stopped in the air between them, flashbacks to their first meeting clattering in her mind amidst the rest of the horror show. "I would have never even said a word if I doubted, I've only been waiting for confirmation."

"*We* have been waiting for confirmation." As James spoke she turned her eyes to him and she could see the concern. Not for what he'd done, but for what she thought of him because of it, and so she did the only thing she could — she grabbed his shirt and pulled him to her.

James' arms came around her, a shield, a security blanket, a promise of safety. He smelled perfectly like him. Skin warm from their dancing, the lingering scent of his cologne, and even with her eyes closed one deep breath told her she was okay. Another reminded her that he would tear down the world to keep her safe, and a third brought the clarity to her mind that he'd just orchestrated the death of the one man who might still want to see her dead.

Or, at the very least, a broken, mindless slave like Anthony had always promised.

"Anthony Williams is dead," she repeated the words against his chest and felt his arms tighten around her.

"Yes, baby. They're both dead." James pressed his lips to her hair, breathing deep before he spoke a little softer, "I had to be sure before I let the security team go."

Leaning back, she pulled out of his firm grip enough to see his eyes again. "You did this because I asked you to stop having the detail follow me everywhere?"

"I've wanted this for a while—"

"We've been offering since you got home," Jake interrupted James, and she peeked over her shoulder at him, finding Jake's expression strained. "We *wanted* to do this, which is why it's our wedding gift to you, Thalia."

"I told you I would pay you," James' voice was tense, but Jake waved him off.

"The guys said no. This was for our favorite badass," Jake's voice softened as his eyes moved back to hers. "Every one of the guys wanted to be here today, to see you whole and happy, but every single one of them insisted on handling this. We didn't get to kill the other asshole, but we got this one, and knowing you're safer because of it makes all of us happier."

Thalia's ribs ached, her lungs tight, and for an instant she could feel the sticky texture of Marcus' blood on her skin, the duct tape on her arm, the chill of that fucking warehouse. Too many memories close to the surface, buzzing like irritating insects, and James relaxed his hold on her as she tensed, but she held onto his shirt a little tighter. Needing the anchor of his presence to pull her back from all of the fucked up images in her head.

"Baby?" James spoke softly, not moving an inch to either pull her closer or lean away from her grip on his clothes.

"I'm glad he's dead." The words left her mouth, and she swallowed past the bitter taste they left. "I don't know what that makes me. Good or bad, brave or weak, but I'm glad he's dead. I hope he suffered."

"We made sure it was abdominal. He suffered." Jake didn't even flinch as he spoke, and she envied the clarity he had, because her mind was still whirling.

Too much chaos.

Too much history.

A wedding and a murder.

All of her light and all of her darkness colliding.

"We don't have to talk anymore about this, I should have waited to tell you. I just —" James stopped talking when she leaned onto her toes to kiss him. For a moment he was stiff, but as she tugged at his shirt, he finally tightened his arms around her again and returned it. She felt herself melt, tasting him, breathing him in, every inch her perfect knight in scuffed armor.

Just imperfect enough to be perfect for her.

"Thank you," she whispered against his mouth as the kiss ended, and she felt the groan in his chest as he hugged her against him.

"I would do anything for you. I love you." James leaned her back from him for a moment, seeking her eyes. "You understand that right? This wasn't some kind of petty vengeance, this was about protecting you and keeping you safe, because I will never let you be at risk." *Again.*

The final word was unspoken, but he might as well have said it. In one of those rare moments in their relationship, she could read him like a book. All of the guilt, the torture he'd put himself through over Marcus written across his face as clear as day. Turning, she saw a similar expression on Jake's face.

Guilt for not stopping him first, guilt for not getting there faster, guilt for not being the one to end his life. Both of them had been tearing themselves apart over a dead man, and so they had turned their minds to the lingering threat and made sure Anthony would never be one again.

If that's not love — raw, powerful, real and dangerous love — what is?

"This was… a lot to take in," she said, and Jake cursed under his breath.

"I knew I should have fucking waited, I'm so sorry, Thalia, I nev—"

"No." Shaking her head, she tried to form the words fast enough to avoid another interruption. "Today was perfect, I just had no idea it was coming and so I had to process, but you have no idea what this means to us, *all* of us."

"I know, I wish I had been able to do this sooner for you and James."

"She's not talking about us, she's talking about the other girls, Jake." The quiet confidence in James' tone made her smile. Not just because he was completely right, but that he'd known it without even needing to verify.

A smile tugged at her lips and she nodded to confirm James' comment. "Anthony is dead, and I'm married to the love of my life. It's going to be the most popular post in the history of the website."

"How many other girls?" Jake asked, and while she and James were smiling now, he still held the slightly haunted look she'd seen in his eyes the first day they'd met.

Without asking, Thalia turned away from James and wrapped her arms around Jake's waist. She felt his body jerk in surprise, his arms up and away from her, but, slowly, they came down to rest around her shoulders, lightly hugging her. "Anthony stopped taking girls long before you found me, Jake. You couldn't have done anything, but today you made a lot of women very happy. I want you to know that this wasn't just for me, and I'd like a copy of the document to post for them so they believe it."

"I can email it to you," he replied, voice slightly dazed, so she hugged him a little harder.

"Thank you. For being there that day, and for being here for me today. And wherever your guys were today, tell them thank you too?" Her voice was slightly muffled against his shirt, but he laughed low.

"Shit, Thalia, you know all you have to do is call."

"If I need someone killed?" she joked.

"Yes," Jake answered. Definitely *not* joking. His arms tensed as he held on a moment longer, and then he let her go, allowing James to pull her back toward him.

"Just promise me no one is at risk for what happened, that no one is going to get in trouble." Thalia meant the words, regardless of the positive outcome she didn't want to see a single one of those men suffering to eliminate one *potential* threat — no matter how dangerous Anthony was.

"It's already cleaned up. Trust me, no one is mourning his loss, badass." Jake looked over her shoulder, lifting his chin. "I think your friends need you, and if you don't mind I need to make some calls." He held out his hand and she placed his phone in it as James tucked her against his side.

"Thank you, Jake." James shook his hand and then their mercenary groomsman grinned at her.

"There's a surprise wedding gift in the lot, no label because we don't do that, but you'll know it's from us when you find it." He chuckled as he glanced down at the phone. "I've got some guys to update on how your big day went."

"They can't possibly care that much!" Thalia laughed, but Jake's raised eyebrows halted it.

"I was told I'd get my ass kicked if I didn't get pictures of you in the dress, and smiling, and eating cake." Jake shrugged. "What can I say? The guys like the strong ones."

"I get that," James said, smiling at her, but she turned back to Jake as he began to walk away.

"Wait, your wedding gift isn't ticking by chance, is it?" The joke seemed to confuse the man for a second, and then he started laughing.

"Cute. I didn't know you were funny." Pointing at her, he walked backward a few steps. "You'll know it, I promise, badass. And you both better keep my number."

"Just in case," James agreed, and Thalia nudged him.

"We'll invite you and the guys for dinner the next time you're in London!" She waved back to him as he walked away, and she turned around to find Kalen and Maggie halfway between the dance floor and them. "Do they know?" she asked.

"Kalen knew what I was planning, and he tells Maggie almost everything, so I'm sure they do. No other reason they'd be waiting." Leaning down he kissed her cheek. "Ready to talk to them?"

"Yeah," she whispered, and he turned to wave at their two closest friends. The people who were more than friends, more of a strange, kinky family that fit their lives perfectly.

"Come on!" James called over to them, settling in one of the chairs at the table, but before she could even think about it he had tugged her onto his lap. "I need to hold you right now, is that okay?"

Relaxing against his chest, feeling the warmth of his body, surrounded in the strength and security of his arms, their wedding bands glinting in the light, Thalia just smiled. "I couldn't imagine a better place to be right now, Master."

"Good, because I don't plan on letting you out of arm's reach for a very long time."

"The honeymoon is two weeks, isn't that long enough?" She laughed as Kalen and Maggie took chairs with them, but James' pinch to her thigh made her yelp.

"I can extend it if I want to, pet. Keep pushing and see how long I keep you in the room and away from the beach and the water—"

"Alright, alright! Yes, Master! I understand, as long as you want. I'm perfectly comfortable anyway." There was no hiding the smile on her face as she settled back against James' chest, focusing on the vibration of his voice instead of the individual words as he recounted the update from Jake. The only time she broke in was to ask for her tablet to update the website, and James agreed to swing by the flat to get it.

Everyone went still, and then burst into laughter.

For once *she* was the one who knew exactly what was going on, while James was left utterly confused. Watching Kalen explain this was going to be entertaining.

Chapter Eleven
THALIA

"Stay here," James commanded before he moved into the hotel room, holding the door wide for the man to push the luggage cart inside.

Thalia leaned against the wall in the hallway as she'd been told, her thighs pressed together in anticipation of what he had planned. He'd whispered *so many* dark promises against her ear on the drive over while plucking pieces of confetti from her hair and dress. Each brush of his fingers had been torture, and she'd pled in a hushed voice for him to touch her, or to let her touch him.

Which, *of course*, had caused him to stop completely. Smiling beside her in the car as he intertwined their fingers, putting a full stop to any plans for fun on the drive over.

Now, the steady beat of her pulse between her legs was growing worse as she thought of his hands on her earlier in the day. Those stinging spanks, the plug, the way he'd moved against her bent over the table, the way he'd teased her on the dance floor.

Dammit.

He had wound her up on purpose, and there was nothing she could do about the wetness soaking into her lace panties in the fucking hallway of this five-star hotel at Heathrow airport.

Thalia was mercifully distracted from her condition as the man wheeled the empty cart out of their room, accepting a tip from James before he moved toward the elevator. Without another word James swept her up into his arms, and she gasped.

"You're such a good girl," he purred as he nuzzled against the side of her head, and she melted as he hugged her tighter to his chest.

"What on earth are you doing?" She laughed, holding onto him as he nudged the door open ahead of them.

"Carrying you over the threshold," James answered, stepping into the room with a wicked grin, but he didn't let her down until he'd carried her through the living room of the suite and into the bedroom. Slowly, he slid her down his front, allowing her heels to meet the floor beside the bed, but his hands stayed firmly planted on her backside. "I want you naked and on this bed in ten minutes. Understand?"

"Yes, Master," Thalia replied, grinning, and then he pinched her ass. Even hotter than the first day she'd met him, the black of the tux made his blond hair stand out, his broad shoulders filling out the jacket in a way that made her mouth water. When he released her, he walked out of the bedroom, closing the door without another word.

Oh my God, it's my wedding night.

The thought hit her hard as she stood in the beautiful bedroom. Even though she was *definitely* not a virgin, the importance of the night still settled over her, a thrill rushing through her veins on the heels of it. Giddy, a whirlwind of butterflies swirled in her stomach as her thoughts spun. *What did he have planned? What had he brought from their playroom at home? Did he plan to make her scream and swoon from pain? Was he going to make her beg to come, torment and tease her until she was breathless? Would he make her come until she was begging him to stop?*

So many completely wonderful scenarios.

Dashing into the bathroom, she barely had a moment to appreciate how nice it was before she'd stripped and started cleaning up. Wiping the shadow of mascara from under her eyes, finger combing her hair to try and look a little more presentable. She was tempted to try and dig her makeup bag out of the luggage, but she was pretty sure James had the bags with him in the living room — and she had no idea how much time had already passed.

Giving up on makeup, she gently pried the tape and gauze away from her hip. The skin around the brand was redder than it had been that morning, sore from the clothes pressed against it, but as she ran her fingertip around the edges of it she loved it even more.

Not a trace of the old tattoo left beneath the solid heart shape, and the J and H just above it were perfect, or at least she hoped they would be when they were done healing. The memory of the series of burns from the thin metal brand had goose bumps rushing over her skin. It had hurt, but James' eyes had never left hers, speaking to her constantly as he'd fulfilled her wish.

To wear his initials instead of Marcus' on their wedding day.

Swallowing, she met her own gaze in the mirror, still surprised he'd chosen her. There were the hazel eyes she'd always found to be too dull and boring, the light brown hair that was never quite blonde enough to be pretty, or dark enough to be rich and shining. Awkwardly pale and lean — Thalia never thought she'd know someone like James. Love and be loved by someone like James.

But he *did* love her.

He had chosen her, come for her, rescued her, taught her what BDSM could really be like when it was done in the right ways, for the right reasons. Given her a side of herself that she had never known she was missing, the same side that Marcus had tried to expose with violence and terror. James had saved her, and he loved her, and now he had married her.

Thumbing the band on her ring finger, she smiled down at it, feeling the flush in her cheeks as the emotion welled up. It was silly how much the brand on her hip and the ring on her finger meant to her because she hadn't had a single doubt about their future in a long time. She had known it would be forever since the day he'd held her on his lap inside the helicopter that took them away from Marcus' warehouse.

If he could love her after that, through all of the nightmares and the painstaking mental healing that took so much longer than the physical, he could love her forever. He *would* love her forever, just as she knew there would never be anyone but James for her.

The ring and the brand hadn't changed any of it, hadn't made any real difference, but they still mattered. A public statement for both sides of their lives that they had chosen each other.

Forever.

And she felt so incredibly lucky.

"Pet?" James' quiet Dom voice made her jump, and her eyes went wide in the mirror as she saw his outline reflected in the room behind her.

Fuck.

Turning, Thalia stepped out of the bathroom, stopping when her feet met the soft carpet, her stomach flip-flopping with anxiety. He stood silently, hands on his hips, naked from the waist up to reveal the firm, lean muscle of his abs, his chest, his arms. The soft black pants hung low enough to reveal the V between his hips, making her mouth water, but the stern expression on his face shut it down — she had fucked up. Already.

Disobeying the first command your Master, and husband, gives you after you get married? Great fucking start, Thalia.

Trying to steady her breathing and slow down her heart rate, she walked toward him and knelt slowly, speaking the only words she could, "I'm sorry, Master."

JAMES

James watched her carefully as she approached, her eyes flickering over him before they dropped to the floor as she moved to kneel at his feet. Graceful, beautiful, and so anxious. No fear though, she was never afraid of him, and he couldn't have stomached it if she were — but she was definitely due a punishment and it made him smile that she knew it. Accepted it. Expected it.

He loved her submission as much as her fire. Loved it all the more *for* her fire.

Thalia was a gift he promised himself he'd never take for granted, even as he turned over the possibilities for what the act of disobedience had earned. "Look at me, pet."

Her gaze lifted to his instantly, and he could read the torment in them, the guilt, and as much as he wanted to smile… he kept his face blank. Calm, controlled, just like his voice.

"What had you so distracted that you ignored my command to be on the bed when I returned?"

She shifted on her knees, sitting back on her heels, eyes drifting away from his for a moment as her hands formed fists, and then she laid them flat on her thighs, that beautiful gaze meeting his once more. "I was thinking about today, and the brand, Master. I didn't keep track of the time, I'm sorry."

Cupping her chin, he angled her head back a little further, devouring the sight of her naked form. Looking over the swell of her breasts, the curve of her waist, he saw the brand at her hip and felt his cock twitch.

Mine.

The inner growl had him tightening his grip on her chin, and her eyes flickered closed for a moment, body leaning toward him, but he raised her back up with a sharp jerk. "Eyes open, pet."

She sighed as her back straightened, knees apart, hands open, eyes on his — hiding nothing from him. Thalia had always been incredibly responsive, meant to be a submissive, but James had no doubt that she'd been a masochist even before she knew what the word meant. Marcus had seen it in her, taken her because of it, and he still hated that it was only because of the bastard's obsession that James had even found her.

But, Marcus was dead, and the brand had obliterated the tattoo he'd placed on her skin.

"Stand up." His voice held more of an edge than he meant it to, and the way her brows pulled together, her bottom lip drawn between her teeth as she rose to her feet… it made him want to comfort her as he dropped his hand to his side.

I'm not angry with you, baby. Just remembering the worst of myself.

"How is it healing?" Attempting to gentle his tone, he brushed his thumb over her hipbone, just outside the redness of the irritated skin.

Three days wasn't long enough, but he could see the rough lines of his initials and the small heart in the dark red of the forming scabs. The fact that she'd asked for it, begged him for it, had shocked him at first. He'd refused when she'd first mentioned it, but while she had responded appropriately… it had clearly upset her. She'd moped for days, and he'd started researching. Calling friends to ask if anyone had experience in it, and he had found a resource much closer to home than he'd expected. Nick and Analiese knew a Dom in Germany who did branding. They had even seen one performed by the man that had resulted in a beautiful brand.

"It's sore, Master, but just fine." Thalia's response was soft, obedient, and he knew she was waiting to know the punishment she had earned for not being on the bed, but she would just have to wait a little longer.

"Have you cleaned it yet?"

"No, Master."

"Then go into the bathroom and wait for me, we'll get it re-dressed before we discuss your disobedience." James turned without another look, walking into the living room to dig out one of the bottles of distilled water, and the little first aid kit he'd put together to tend the mark. As he returned to her, he couldn't help but remember the joy on her face as she'd realized why they were at Sean's club. *SW3* had been the only option for something as important as this, and the only place he trusted to be private and secure in London. The fact that his friend had let him rent the entire club out for a steal, losing a full night of guest fees and irritating several of the members, was just one more reason why he valued the man's friendship so much.

"Master, I—"

"You can apologize after your punishment, pet. Or during it, but not now. This is about your health and making sure we take care of the brand." Offering his hand to her, he lifted her from her kneel on the bathroom tile. Tugging a towel free from the wall, he laid it out beside the sink. "Up on the counter, lay down."

"Yes, Master." With the effortless grace that she never seemed to notice, she hopped up onto the counter and carefully shifted until her hips were positioned over the towel, one foot in the sink, the other dangling off the counter. She stayed propped up on her elbows, eyes roaming over the brand, and he felt his lips twitch into a smile before he got it under control.

"Be still," he commanded, ripping open one of the sterile bandages. As he cracked open the water and started to pour it over the mark, blotting gently, he was overwhelmed by the visual of her stretched out on the table inside *SW3*. Surrounded by their friends, she hadn't even hesitated to strip and submit to him before all of them — not like it had been the first time — but it had meant more with the wedding on the horizon. David, the Dom well-versed in branding, had even spoken about the significance of the branding decision, and Thalia had never even flinched. His brave, beautiful wife. "It looks beautiful, pet."

"Thank you, Master. This… having your initials on me, it just— it means *so much* to me. I wanted it more than I can say."

At her words he stopped trickling the water and leaned down to kiss her, their tongues clashing as he set the bottle aside and held her in place so he could nip her lip. Take her mouth the way he wanted to as her moans vibrated between them. "Baby…" he growled, trying to restrain the urge to fuck her on the bright white tiles of the bathroom.

"Master?" she asked, breathy and practically moaning with need.

He could smell her arousal, knew already that if he were to brush his fingers between her lips that she'd be soaking wet, but he forced himself to step back from her and regain control.

Take care of the brand.

Then the punishment.

Then the scene can start and you can have her.

Chapter Twelve

JAMES

James opened his eyes on her again and wondered if she had any idea just how challenging it was to keep himself in check sometimes. How difficult it was when she was panting, and flushed, and parting her thighs like a bloody invitation.

Swallowing, he moved his eyes back to the brand, trying to avoid looking at the swollen lips between her legs. "I'm very proud of you for taking the mark so well, and I want to make sure we take care of it so it heals well."

"Yes, Master." She stayed still, her belly barely moving with her breath, and he tried to focus on cleaning it the way David had told him. Sterile water, sterile gauze, keep it dry and protected until the scabs were hard, which was just one more reason to keep her in bed and out of the water in Bora Bora during the honeymoon. She could take dips, but then she'd need to rinse it off and enjoy the sunshine, or come back to bed with him.

Definitely not a hardship.

As she lay back on the counter, he had a flash of the way she'd been held down at the club. Each of their friends had been present to witness, to hold her still as David seared the brand into her flesh in a series of strike brands.

Every sizzling press of the brand making her body jerk, but he'd held her face so she kept looking at him, his arm braced between her breasts to hold her chest down. Kalen had held her arms, Maggie, Julie, and the other girls holding her legs. Analiese at her feet to watch, while Nick helped David with the torch to heat the brand evenly.

The sheer trust she had in him, to protect her, to keep her safe, to push her limits, but never too far — Thalia amazed him.

Every single day of their life she made him realize how lucky he was to have her, and as he looked down at the wedding band on his hand he knew that they had a lifetime of days ahead of them.

Patting the area dry, he ensured it was clean before he placed a fresh gauze pad over it and taped it down. Light enough to let the area breathe, but keep it protected, and with the things he wanted to do to her he needed to know it was safe so he could play as hard as he'd planned.

Shaking off the memories of the branding, he brushed his fingers over the tape and then slid them up her side, cupping her breast, tweaking a nipple, before ultimately running them over her neck and into her hair. As soon as he tightened his fist she gasped, lips parting prettily as she arched off the counter.

"Up, pet. Time for your punishment." He tugged her hair as she moved into a sitting position and pushed herself off the soaked towel, a soft moan slipping out as he angled her head and walked her forward with him.

Thalia fell into a stumbling step beside him, her steps quickened, because he wasn't going to measure his steps to hers for a punishment — she needed to keep up.

"Bend," he commanded, pushing her forward until she caught herself on the bedding and bent at the waist, the round curve of her ass presented at the perfect height. "Do you understand why you earned a punishment, pet?"

"Yes, Master. You said to be on the bed in ten minutes, and I wasn't." She was squirming, weight shifting from foot to foot, her thighs slightly spread to reveal the glistening petals of her pussy, and he couldn't help but smile behind her.

My little masochist.

She was waiting for the pain, practically begging for it, but he knew how to make her recognize it as a punishment. Walking over to the chair in the room, he picked up the thick leather strap. It was more powerful than a belt, more unforgiving since the implement didn't give as easily, but *that* wasn't what would make it a punishment for her — it was all about the words. "Was what I asked too difficult, pet?"

"No, Master," she answered softly, and her breath caught as he ran the leather along her spine, her hands fisting in the comforter on the bed.

"So, why did you disobey me?" As he asked the question she answered with a whine, ass lifting as he brushed the strap over her backside and down to her thigh. "Answer me," he demanded, sharp and direct.

"I'm sorry! I didn't watch the time, Master. I got distracted, I didn't mean to, I swear—" The first crack of the strap across her ass made her jolt forward, a gasped cry cutting off her pleading apologies.

James felt his cock harden against his leg, twitching as she mewed while the heat settled, a bright red stripe blooming on her skin. *Gorgeous.* "Did you earn a punishment then, pet?"

Nodding against the bedspread, Thalia drew in a deep breath before she spoke. "Yes, Master. I did, I'm sorry. I didn't want to ruin tonight."

His lips twitched as he adjusted the strap in his hand and delivered another stripe below the first, and then another below that. With each line her body jerked, a gasp and a whimper, white-knuckled grip on the simple bedding beneath her. "You haven't ruined it. What are the rules around a punishment?"

"When it's over, it's over." As soon as she spoke the words, her grip relaxed slightly, her body more pliant, and he chose that moment to deliver another strike at the tender place where her ass met her thighs. She yelped and bucked off the bed, arching prettily for a moment before she fell back into position, forehead pressed to the fabric.

"That's right, pet, but I did ask you to strip and get on the bed within ten minutes, which was *plenty* of time to undress and tend to whatever you needed. Don't you agree?"

"Yes, Master. I know I've earned the punishment." Thalia placed her feet flat to the floor, thighs spread, perfectly presented, and he bit back a groan as he looked over the red stripes. *One more for this.*

"Yes, pet, you did." Pulling his arm back, he landed the last stripe across the middle of her ass, over the already pink and sensitive skin, and she groaned into the bedding, muffling her beautiful cries, but his cock still twitched.

She'd held position for him, accepted it, and now he had to discuss what he'd *originally* planned. Walking back to the chair he dropped the strap and picked up the crop. A sharper, more concise pain, and he rolled it between his fingers as he walked back to her. "Did you earn any other punishments today?"

Thalia's ribs froze mid-breath, and he waited, letting the silence stretch as her fingers dug a little deeper into the comforter.

Ah, guilt… what do you have to confess, pet?

"Master, I, um—" Burying her face in the bedding, she mumbled something and he tapped one of the welts firmly with the crop.

"Speak clearly."

Raising up from the bedding, she spoke to the headboard, "I was late to get ready because I snuck off to use my tablet to check on the website."

Snuck off?

James smiled where she couldn't see him, running the crop from her heel, up her calf, over the backs of her thighs, to the welts he'd already set on her skin.

The way her muscles twitched, body shifting as she fought to be still, turned him on. He couldn't help the erection that now tented the front of his pants, but years of practice allowed him to focus on what needed to be done before he could sate himself. "Explain."

Thalia whined in frustration, groaning as she lifted to her toes and then dropped her heels sharply enough to make her ass bounce. "Master, Ailsa brought me the tablet to check on the website, but it was my choice to go into a different room and check the messages and reply. I lost track of time and was almost late to the wedding — but I *did* make it! And I apologized for making Master Kalen worry!"

James fought the chuckle, able to stay silent behind her only because Kalen had already admitted to snagging the tablet that morning and delivering it to Ailsa so she could bring it to Thalia. Their reasoning was sound, and he'd deal with Kalen overstepping his bounds *after* the honeymoon, but the knowledge that she'd hidden somewhere before the wedding was new.

The fact that Kalen had worried? That was… *interesting*.

"Has Kalen already addressed this, pet?"

"No, Master. He said he'd handle it after we returned from the honeymoon. Everyone was getting me into my dress and trying to do my hair and makeup when he came back." Thalia's muscles jumped, contracting and relaxing as he stood in silence behind her with the crop at his side. Twisting, she glanced back at him, and he schooled his expression into neutrality. "Master?"

"I'll discuss that with Kalen later, but you do remember that I told you to leave the tablet at home? And you understand that even though Ailsa was the one to bring it to you, my decision was still in place?" Before he'd even finished the questions, Thalia had turned back to the bedding, bracing as she nodded over and over.

"Yes, I do, Master. And I'm sorry. I shouldn't have accepted it without asking you."

Tracing the crop over her back, he spoke in a quiet, calm voice. "I wanted you to leave it at home so that you could focus on *you*, on *us*. The girls on there are incredible, and I never refuse you when you ask for a little more time to talk to them when we are at home, but I wanted to give you a day without feeling obligated to them. I'd wanted to give you the freedom to enjoy our wedding, our honeymoon, without the guilt I always see in you after you've spoken with them. I didn't make that decision lightly, pet, and I made it *for you*."

"I'm sorry…" Thalia whined, her voice cracking, and he knew she was bordering tears — which were not the tears he wanted — but at least she understood. And understanding was important before a punishment.

"Good girl." He ran the crop along her ass before he pulled it back. "Then this will help you to remember that when I make a decision, it stands. Regardless of who helps you disobey."

Chapter Thirteen
THALIA

"Yes, Master!" She practically screamed it against the bedding as the crop landed, a sharp and heavy impact that made her knees go weak for a moment. The strap had made every inch of her ass sensitive, and it made the crop that much worse, which was appropriate. She had known the moment Ailsa had offered the tablet that she was defying him, but she'd been so hungry to check in, to verify one last time that the women on the site still supported her, wouldn't hate her for being happy… that she'd ignored his command. Worse, she had run off, hidden so that no one could even stop her from it, and she'd almost fucked up the wedding because of it.

As the pain of the first strike spread, she felt tears at her eyes and knew it had nothing to do with the ache. It was the guilt, but as long as he kept going she'd be okay. This would make it better.

Punishment was absolution of the purest kind.

"I am aware that Kalen and Ailsa worked together to make it *easier* for you to disobey, but this was your choice." James' voice was as sharp as the next line of fire the crop delivered, and she whined loudly into the bed. "You could have sent Ailsa back to ask my permission."

"I KNOW!" She shouted as he delivered another strike, and another, and she tried to accept the pain, to stop fighting it, because she'd more than earned it. James didn't even know the panic the girls had felt, the torture she'd put Kalen through as he worried about her and James, dragging the twins around as he'd searched for her. He didn't even know the awful extent of their friends' fear for her. "I really am sorry, Master. I knew it was wrong, I knew and I did it anyway because I wanted to, and I worried everyone needlessly."

"And *that* is why you're being punished, pet." With wicked precision, James landed a strike on her thighs, and then another just below. Thalia sagged against the bed, knees bent, heels off the floor as the tears made the comforter damp beneath her cheeks.

Two mistakes.

Two acts of disobedience on her wedding day.

The torment inside was worse than the ache of the welts, especially since she could feel the wetness pooling between her thighs. Her body oblivious to the reasoning behind the pain, it simply processed James' presence and the impact of the implements the way it always did — the pain and then pure arousal. Funneling all of the spikes of agony and sharp snaps of heat into a tingling tension that wound tight in her belly, coiling low to make her pussy clench around nothing. Craving him to fill her, to fuck her until she felt forgiven and her brain emptied in bliss.

"Master…" she whimpered, fighting the fuzzy allure of subspace, trying to hold onto the aches she felt, ignoring the dizzying after-effects brought on by the strange chemistry of her brain. The same odd reaction that made everything they were work so perfectly.

But this was a punishment, and punishments meant no escape into pleasure.

Not yet.

She needed his forgiveness first, and she'd take whatever he asked of her to earn it. Straightening her legs, she forced her heels back to the floor, lifting into the appropriate position as she sniffled and tried to halt the tears. "Please forgive me, Master?"

Another strike across her ass, then another a little below, and then he landed the last at the most sensitive point, her sitspot, the place where her ass curved into her thighs. But she locked her knees to stay in position even as she gasped and groaned against the bedding.

His touch made her whole body jump, fingers cool against the heat of her skin as he caressed each welt. The broad stripes of the strap, the narrow lines from the crop, and she could feel the texture of her flesh under his hand. Suddenly, his fingers pulled back and his command snapped out, "Come here, on your knees. Now."

As his touch abandoned her she pushed up, shoving her hair back from her damp cheeks so she could turn to face him. James was stroking his cock through the front of his pants, and she ran her tongue along her lower lip as she slid to her knees and crawled to his feet. "May I?" she asked, trying to fight the trembles in her hands from the adrenaline and the rest of the cocktail of all-natural chemicals their play always brought on.

How anyone found pleasure in vanilla sex… she couldn't figure out.

This was bliss.

Painful perfection.

Absolute heaven as she looked up at James' bottle glass green eyes.

"Go on, pet. You can taste me." Before he'd even finished speaking her fingers were in the waistband of his pants, running along the deep V that she adored, and she paused to run her tongue along one line as she pulled down and let go of the fabric in her hands.

James' sigh from high above made a smile tilt her lips, sliding her fingers along his shaft, stroking the length of him, thumb rolling over the head. The twitch of his muscles had her hungry for more, and she licked at him before sliding him between her lips.

"Yes…" he groaned, and she ran one hand up the back of his thigh to pull him into her throat.

The first thrust was all her, but as he wound his fingers into her hair the second was all James. He thrust deep and held still, her nose pressed to his firm stomach as she swallowed around his cock, and the low moan above her was better than anything else in the world.

"That's it, pet." His hips moved back just enough to let her steal a tiny breath before he thrust again, working back and forth in a rhythm that was all about his pleasure and her service, her submission. As James' fist tightened in her hair, she moaned around him, sucking and tasting as much as he allowed with each pulse of his hips. Her nails pressed into the backs of his thighs, because without that anchor she would have slipped one hand between her thighs, to ease the need that had returned to the surface now that her ass and thighs were stinging with welts.

She wanted to come, but she wanted to taste him more, and so even when he cut off her air again, and again, and again, as he held himself deep, her throat working around him — she stayed still. Obedient, accepting, pleading silently for him to continue. To make her throat ache with the strength of him, so that she'd remember every delicious inch when they moved onto whatever he planned next.

"You are mine," he growled, and she moaned in agreement, working him with her tongue as he fucked her face, his other hand finding purchase in her hair to hold her still. "I don't care how often we go to Purgatory or play with Kalen and Maggie, his decisions do not override mine."

Thalia whined around his cock before he cut off her air once more, unable to apologize again, to beg for forgiveness. *I never meant to do that.* Guilt wracked her, the sting of the welts where her heels dug into her ass a dull comfort. Trying to show him how she felt, she let go of his thighs and folded her wrists behind her back.

I'm yours. Completely.

I'm sorry, I'm sorry, I'm sorry.

The words were nothing more than moans against his flesh, but he growled above her, the green of his eyes almost obliterated by his pupils as she looked up at him from her knees. "My sub," he spoke clearly as he pulled back just enough to thrust deep again. "My good girl."

She wanted to agree, to say yes, but there was no air, no space. Another sharp thrust, and his fists tightened in her hair as he started to move in shallow pulses, staying buried in the tight, squeezing confines of her throat. Her lungs burned, her head swam, as he growled.

"*My wife. Mine.*" James shouted and he came, cock jerking deep as she swallowed everything he offered, desperate for air, nails digging into the arms behind her back.

His taste filled her mouth and when he finally pulled free, she gasped, choked, swallowing again as she bowed forward to draw breath. Trying to shake off the swimming sensation in her head. James' quiet chuckle above her made her smile just before he tugged his pants back into place and crouched in front of her.

"Master," her voice broke on the word, throat sore, but he caught her chin, lifting her eyes to his where his pupils were still so dilated that the thin ring of bottle-glass green around them was barely an accent.

"You are incredible, baby, you know that, right?" Brushing his thumb over her swollen lips, she couldn't respond, drawn toward his inescapable gravity, and then he pulled her in. Wrapping his arms around her before leaning her back for a kiss. James captured her mouth, delving his tongue inside without pause, and as he held her tight against him she felt absolved before he'd even said the words. Absolute bliss as they ended up tangled on the floor, James held mere inches above her with an arm braced beside her shoulder — but she didn't care because he was between her thighs.

Desperate need swelled and she lifted her hips, trying to rub against him, but he stopped her. Pinned her to the floor beneath his weight, taking his time with her mouth. Sometimes decadently slow, teasing brushes of his lips against hers. And then the next moment tongues warring, teeth nipping, and he growled when she bit back a little too sharply, caught up in the moment. Both of them panting, eyes locked on each other as he grinned slowly.

"Do you want to come, pet?" James' voice was playful, sated from his orgasm and the act of punishment, but she was still twisted inside.

"If I'm forgiven, yes, Master, please?" she begged, trying to move beneath him, but he caught her hip to hold her still.

"You took your punishment, so of course you're forgiven, but... I don't know if I'm ready to let you come yet." Lifting himself away from her, James grinned in that charmingly mischievous way, her already soaked pussy growing slick.

"I'm going to die," she groaned dramatically, laid out on the floor in front of him as he stood, but he only laughed.

"Get up, pet. I want to touch you."

With that temptation she almost jumped off the floor, trying not to sound too desperate. "Where would you like me, Master?"

"On the bed like I asked." James smiled, tugging the bedding back to fold it at the bottom, leaving a clean, white expanse.

"Yes, Master." Biting back the grin she crawled onto the bed and knelt, but he only tilted his head, gaze flowing over her curves.

"Lay down for me and spread your legs. Arms up." James had barely finished the command before he turned away, expecting her to obey as he moved to a chair near the curtained windows — and, of course, she did. When he returned he dumped an armful of rope and leather cuffs onto the bedding between her feet. "What did I promise you earlier today, pet?"

As he attached the first cuff around one ankle she tried to sort through the chaos of her mind to remember his words. "You promised to fuck me. Hard."

"Oh, you're right. I did." James grinned as he lifted a piece of rope, tying it off to the cuff before pulling her ankle to the edge of the bed. "After what, though? There was a caveat."

Thalia whined, dropping her head. "You promised to fuck me *after* you made me beg, and scream, and plead. But I *have*, Master!"

He finished tying off one ankle and started on the next with a devious grin on his lips. "Punishments don't count in play, pet. You know that." The sharp jerk of the rope made her groan as she propped herself on her elbows.

"I want you! *Please?*" There was no shame in her desperate tone, even as he made her lay back against the bed again, his strong grip pulling one wrist toward the headboard, wrapping the soft leather cuff tight.

"What happens when you get bossy?" James smirked at her, glancing up occasionally as he crouched to tie the rope to the bed frame.

"You make me wait longer, Master." It took more self-control than she thought she had in the moment, but she managed to avoid rolling her eyes.

"That's right, pet. So, will you be a good girl and be patient for me?" He asked as he walked around the end of the bed, abs shifting with each step, and she pulled her bottom lip between her teeth as he watched her in return. Gaze hungry, an amused expression on his face, but she could tell he was thinking. *Plotting*.

"I promise I'll behave."

Chapter Fourteen
THALIA

The low chuckle as he bound her other wrist to the bed spoke volumes about what he thought of her promise to behave. "Tell me, are you wet?"

"*Yes, Master.*" The exasperation fled her voice as his fingers brushed down her stomach, and when his fingers dipped between her thighs she almost shouted in relief. He traced her pussy, dragging her wetness to her clit to start slow, purposeful circles that were just enough to amplify the tension inside her.

"You *are* wet, pet." Moving his hand lower he gently slid two fingers inside her, stretching her, bucking her hips to seek just a little more friction, but it did nothing. He was torturously gentle, his thumb brushing over her clit, back and forth, teasing passes that had her thighs twitching.

Groaning in frustration she jerked against her wrist cuffs, looking up at him in desperation. When he smiled, she let out a little scream and kicked her heels into the bed. "Master!"

"Oh, pet, no patience at all." James pulled his fingers from her and *tsk*'d. "Is it so terrible to have me enjoy each and every twitch of your body? Every little sound you make when you're so wet and wanting?" Wandering to the chair in the corner, leaving her bereft of his touch, his voice had her squirming on the bed.

Wrists twisting in the cuffs she tried to think clearly through the haze of the arousal, through the dull ache of the welts across her ass. "I just want you. Please?"

"You already had me in your throat, pet. You got to feel me, to taste me…" Returning to her, he sat on the edge of the bed and traced the outside of her leg. "Was that not enough?"

The idea that he might edge her the entire night made her whine low in her chest, gritting her teeth as she fought the pathetic stream of pleas she wanted to utter. Instead, she managed a simple, "Thank you, Master. For letting me taste you."

"Such a good girl." Chuckling, James leaned closer, almost kissing her, and her lips parted in expectation, but he spoke instead. "Will you continue to be a good girl for me?"

"What do you want me to do, Master?" She almost didn't finish the question before he kissed her, his fingers delving between her thighs to roll against her clit, sending her hips into jerking pulses as she sought oblivion. He continued to rub her as he broke the kiss, his breath brushing over her lips.

"I want you to obey me, and *not* come until I give you permission. Understand the rules, pet?" James' pupils had dilated again, that thin ring of dark green beckoning her to the very edge of her sanity as heat coiled tight between her legs.

"Yes, Master. I understand." It felt like damnation to speak the words, but there was no other choice. She'd already disobeyed, *twice*, on today of all days, and this was her chance at redemption. Yes, she was forgiven, but this was about proving to herself that she could obey, that she could show some self-control.

Of course, that idea felt completely ridiculous when he made a low sound in his chest and slid his fingers back inside her. James' lips closed over her nipple and she arched, moaning until he bit down and a brief scream escaped her. "I love the sounds you make."

"Master…" she sighed, trying to focus on the way he stroked at her g-spot, toes curling as he applied a little more pressure and she gasped, just in time for him to bite down once more. A zing of electric tension, fireworks popping in her nerves, making her twitch, jerk against the cuffs without even meaning to move.

Sweet agony.

Pulling his fingers free he leaned up, hovering them before her lips.

"Taste," he commanded, and she opened. The tang of her own juices flooding her tongue, as she sucked his fingers in, running her tongue over his digits, and he growled, pulling them free to take her mouth again.

Demanding, hungry, one knee landing between her spread legs as he leaned over her to control the kiss.

Between her legs she felt something new, small and cool, and then it kicked on and she practically screamed against his lips. "Oh, *fuck!*"

James smiled down at her as the little vibrator kicked to life, her body trying to contort around it, and he looked between them, eyes roving over her curves as she struggled to fight back the fresh sensations.

"Beautiful," he mumbled before his mouth closed over her other nipple, drawing it in, and she tugged against the cuffs, feeling the rope rubbing against the edge of the bed.

Nothing to be done, nothing but accept it, and then his teeth bit down again and it was like electricity rushing through her nerves.

Pain and pleasure intertwining until they were impossible to distinguish in the lust-fueled haze of her brain. The magic he worked as the vibrator buzzed at her core, the tingling rush that followed every nip of his teeth, she was breaking apart — and somehow she knew he was only getting started.

Her whimper only amplified as his teeth lifted and his hands roamed, pinching her other nipple, then sliding down her sides to squeeze at her waist.

"I can't..." she whined, but he just chuckled as he adjusted on the bed to rest between her thighs.

"I know you will, pet. You like obeying me, don't you?"

"Yes, Master, I do, I just—" Her words cut off, stunned by the sensation and the sight of him shifting down the bed until his breath moved over her pussy. *I am so screwed.*

"Do not come or I will leave you soaked and wanting until we land in Bora Bora." James held her gaze for a moment before his head dipped and his tongue made contact, licking in one long, devious swipe through her wetness.

All of tonight, and then twenty-seven hours of flying before they landed on the island.

There was no doubt in her mind she'd lose it if he made her wait, and also no question that'd follow through if she disobeyed.

Again.

But every flick of his tongue had her shivering, the insistent buzz of the little vibrator becoming pure torture as her nails bit into her palms. Then he closed his mouth over her clit and she screamed, choking it off as she pressed her lips together, but it was a sudden and blinding pleasure.

Too much to take, *more* than she could take. She was sure of it as her body torqued, hips twisting and lifting before his strong hands forced her back to the bed, pinning her so that he could continue tasting her.

Ecstasy and torture rolled into one, a fucking doomsday device under his tongue, and she cried out, begging incoherently. "Please, *please*, I — *fuck!* — Master, I can't, I can't, I can't..."

"Do. Not. Come." James lifted just enough to look at her and she whimpered, biting down on her lip before she collapsed against the bed.

The visual of him between her thighs had only made it worse, mouth wet with her, blond hair a seductive mess atop his head. She wished she had her hands free to run them through it, to hold on, to give herself some center, but she was spread wide.

Completely and utterly at his mercy.

The vibrator was incessant, his mouth on her clit a painfully perfect rush that had her pleading to herself to wait. Deep breaths did nothing to abate it, especially not when his thumbs dug into her thighs, holding her still for him.

James knew every inch of her, knew every trick to her body, and it was going to ruin her.

Every cell in her body tensed, concentrating on the tiny bundle of nerves that filled her awareness until there was only the pleasure and the agony of holding it back. Like patching a fractured dam with papier-mâché — there was a limit to what she could take.

"MASTER!" she cried, pleading for permission, and he sat up, pressing something that amped up the vibrations inside her. Tears sprung to her eyes, desperate not to come, not to fail him.

"You will not come until I'm inside you, understand?" James' voice was cool, clear water in the maelstrom inside her head. A spiraling storm that threatened to consume her, panting breaths and buzzing nerves, but he worked the rope and one ankle was free.

"Yes, yes, Master. I'm trying, but—" Her other ankle came free and he grasped her legs behind the knees, bending them up toward her chest, and then out to spread her wide. As she whimpered she saw he was smiling. A wicked, gleaming smile as he looked down at her.

"Listen to me, Thalia. As soon as I'm fucking you, you may come as many times as you can." Taking his time, James slowly eased those soft black pants down his hips. The deep V angling down to his hard cock, and she lifted her hips, wanton and needy, but he had already come and he teased her. "I love the way you look right now, pet."

"*Please*," she begged, but he only chuckled.

"All flushed, your beautiful eyes wide, the way your short breaths make your chest rise and fall…" Leaning forward he braced a hand to the side of her ribs, catching one leg over his shoulder as he brushed his hard cock against her clit in a merciless tease. "The way your body reaches for me, and I know how much you want to come."

"Yes, I do—"

"But you won't until I give you permission." James reached between them, his thumb stroking her clit as his erection pressed into her belly. A scream escaped between her teeth, trying so hard to obey, to be obedient, to *not* come without him inside her.

Just hold on.

The constant hum of the vibrator was going to be the end of her as he leaned down to kiss her, the clash of his tongue to hers a lightning strike, their moans caught in their mouths. Hers desperate and urgent, his satisfied but still hungry. He broke off to growl, "Beg me, pet."

Drawing in a deep breath she whined and then babbled out every useless thought. "Please, *please* fuck me, Master. I need you, I need to feel you inside me. I have to or I'm going to snap. Please, I don't want to disobey you, I don't want to disappoint you, I just need—"

In one single movement he tugged the little vibrator free and he hovered at her entrance, hard cock teasing, stroking, but then he pressed forward just enough for her breath to catch. "I love you," he rumbled, and then he thrust deep. Soaking wet, she provided no resistance as he filled her to the brim, folding her legs even further as he plunged inside.

"*Ah*, Master, *fuck*, I love you too!" Thalia arched off the bed as much as she could, fists tightening on the other side of the cuffs that still kept her arms drawn tight, and then he pulled back and rocked forward and everything blazed into white light. Every muscle tightened, ecstasy thundering through her veins to fill every spare inch of space inside her. The tension amplifying to a crucial point, a dangerous tipping point, before it exploded into a million tiny dots of electric energy, humming through her nerves as the orgasm crashed through her.

So much teasing, so much delicious pain and pleasure, interwoven until it was indiscernible.

Somewhere outside of herself she could hear the moans and sighs and whimpers as she came, but it was all blurry. Hazy as James brushed kisses against her neck, continuing to thrust, fucking her through the first orgasm and straight into the second. Barely able to catch a breath at the surface before she was flooded again. Bliss, pure and wonderful, her soft cries caught against his lips as he captured her mouth, but she didn't care about breathing as her body pulsed with light.

Each sinful thrust was a delicious friction, angled perfectly to send her past the breaking point until she was nothing more than liquid heat as James bit down on her shoulder and came deep. His cock jerking inside her as he found her lips once more, sighing her name against them as they both held still, linked. "You're mine," he whispered.

"Forever," Thalia answered back, her body languid as he slid from her, but he stayed right beside her. Warm and perfect, each brush of his touch over her skin exactly what she needed.

In a few moments he had the rope untied from the cuffs on her wrists and she curled up on the bed. Exhausted, delirious from all of the decadent pleasure and delirious pain, she still fought sleep as she felt James move in close behind her.

He tugged the sheets up and then leaned back to flip off the light beside the bed, even though plenty of light flooded in from the bathroom and living room. "Baby?" he whispered, brushing her hair back from her face as she fought to keep her eyes open.

"Yes, Master?"

A soft chuckle and he brushed her cheek, tilting her chin up to capture her lips in one more, gentle kiss. "You do know you've made me the happiest man alive, right?"

Smiling as she fought sleep, she shrugged a shoulder. "You may be the happiest man, but I'm the lucky one."

"I thought we cleared this up today," James mumbled as he wrapped an arm around her and tweaked a nipple before his arm settled at her waist.

"We did, I announced it first." Yawning, Thalia ended up laughing as he groaned and pulled her closer to his chest.

"You know, I hope that these bungalows Katherine suggested have enough space between them… because I plan on making you scream like that for the next week and a half."

Unable to stifle the laugh, Thalia twisted at the waist to look up at him. "You'll kill me if you torture me like that for a week and a half."

"Oh, pet, don't be dramatic. You'll be just fine." James grinned, mischievous and loving. "Do you really think I'd ever put you at risk?"

"Never," she answered with complete confidence, smiling as she turned back to the pillow. "I love you, James. I never thought I'd get this kind of happily ever after — but then again I never thought I'd meet someone like you."

"If anyone deserves a happily ever after, baby, it's you." Pressing a kiss to the side of her head, James drew up the covers and wrapped her in his warmth. "And we both know I'm the lucky one. Now sleep, because tomorrow we start forever, and that's a very long time."

"Hmm…" She sighed, yawning as her eyes closed. "With you, I don't think forever will be near enough."

"We'll just have to see, won't we?" James kissed her shoulder, and she smiled, letting sleep overtake her. Tomorrow was the long flight to their honeymoon, nine days in paradise, and then they'd come home for forever.

A forever with James.

A forever where they started a family.

A forever filled with every wonderful and kinky thing that made them *them*.

It was the kind of future she had never expected, the kind of future that they had both fought for, loved each other hard enough for, all so that they could live happily ever after.

The End

Bonus Content

✦

Oh, lovelies, can you believe The Thalia Series is over? I can't. It took years to make it a reality, and while James and Thalia's story is complete, there are several fun bonus short stories following this note to keep the fun going a little while longer.

- **The Branding:** Three days before the wedding, James and Thalia had a very special, very private ceremony with their friends from Purgatory. It was not just to erase one of the dark memories of Thalia's past, but also to solidify their relationship in the world of BDSM in a way that so few couples do. After all, these two are one in a million.

- **Christmas at Purgatory:** This is a fun, ménage erotica short story set at Purgatory, the submissive training school run by Kalen and Maggie. I wrote it as a little Christmas present for Thalia's fans back when the story was on Literotica. It would have occurred somewhere in Salvaged by Love, Book 3 of The Thalia Series. I hope you enjoy this naughty little romp!

- **A Kalen and James Flashback:** So many readers have asked for a peek at what Kalen and James were like when they were young and out on the prowl, and so this flashback is from the very first Summer the two men met and wandered through the BDSM clubs of Europe. It's fun, but heartwarming, because we know that both men end up with their happily-ever-afters married to the submissives of their dreams.

- **James at The Auction:** During the Auction scene in Security Binds Her, Book 1 of The Thalia Series, we only see it from Thalia's perspective, but I *have always wanted to share James' POV. As Livia Grant said, this was sitting in my head for over three years, just waiting to be written, and I'm so excited to share it with all of you. It really shows the darkness that existed in him before Thalia entered his life, and I hope you love it as much as I do.*

If you're still hungry for more of this world after you finish these extras, then look for The Beth Series, which follows Beth Doherty who is mentioned several times in The Thalia Series. While the first book 'Breaking Beth' is *very* dark, covering her captivity with Anthony, the rest of the series will focus on her finding her light, just like Thalia did.

Want to find out the dark & twisted truth of what happened to Beth when Anthony had her? Start with Breaking Beth!

Want to skip the pitch black darkness and see what happens when Beth meets Jake and his team? Start with Damaged Doll!

Enjoy these short stories, lovelies. Thalia and James have been a part of my life for longer than I've even had what *anyone* would call an author career, and I love them so hard. I know for a fact I would not be where I am if Thalia and Marcus had not crawled into my head one night and demanded that their story be written. For the record, if someone ever tells you that reading 'naughty' books never gets you anywhere, I'd like to place myself forward as an example.

It's brought me more than I could have ever dreamed.

Thank you for all of your support, lovelies. I know exactly how lucky I am.

Jennifer Bene

THE BRANDING

The Branding
THALIA

Three Days Before the Wedding

"Analiese!" Thalia leaned forward in the limo to get the other woman's attention, almost shouting to be heard over everyone else in the car. "Where's Nick tonight?"

"Meeting us," she answered, a small smile tugging at her lips. "He wouldn't miss this."

"Miss what?"

"Oh, no." James tugged her back against the seat. "Don't try and get Analiese in trouble now, you'll find out what's waiting for you soon."

"Come on!" Looking over at him, Thalia groaned. He had his prince charming smile on, wearing a black on black suit cut perfectly to his frame, but she ignored how sinfully gorgeous he looked and turned toward the sea of knowing smiles on her friends' faces around the limo. "I don't get why it has to be a surprise."

"Because it's more fun that way," he answered, tucking her tight against his side. "Just relax and enjoy yourself, tonight is about you."

"Actually, it's about *both* of ye," Kalen corrected, grinning as he nudged James.

"True." Nuzzling against her neck, just below her ear, James brushed his lips over her skin, trailing his hand up her thigh. "And there are so many things I want to do to you tonight, pet." The low purr of his voice sent a flush of heat to her cheeks, and a flurry of kinky thoughts through her head.

"Like what?" she whispered.

"So impatient." He squeezed her thigh, just firmly enough to ache, and her hips lifted from the bench seat before he pressed her back.

"Master…" A whine tainted her voice as his fingers worked their way under the hem of her dress, a quiet hum of pleasure answering in his chest.

"Tonight is *our* celebration, and I want to taste you. I want to hear you cry out in pain, and gasp in pleasure. I want to hear you beg for release." He nipped her skin, and a shiver rushed through her, pussy clenching in response to all he promised.

"We're not going to dinner, are we?" Thalia asked, breathless, and his soft chuckle was right against the shell of her ear.

"No, pet, we are not."

"One of the clubs?" She whimpered as his fingertips traced her panties, her breath catching in her lungs.

"Such a smart girl."

Licking her lips as her mouth went rapidly dry, Thalia felt her heartrate pick up. "Why are we all in black tie then?"

"Because it's a special occasion, pet. *Very* special." James moved his hand back to her knee, pressing a kiss to her cheek as the limo rolled to a stop. "And we're going to stay right here while they get things ready."

"Right, we should go in, sir." Maggie's cheeks were flushed as Kalen slid his hand from between her legs, catching her mouth with his for another kiss.

"Yes, blessing, yer right." Kalen turned to the rest of the group in the limo and grinned wildly. "Antonio, if ye will get the door?"

"See you in a few." Antonio winked as he stepped out, before helping a smiling Julie onto the sidewalk, and a moment later the limo was empty except for the two of them. The door shut with a loud clap, and Thalia was filled with a tingling, nervous energy.

What do you have planned?

James smiled, turning on the seat to face her as he took her hands in his. "Do you remember when Kalen said I was making one of your wishes come true tonight?"

"Yes, Master."

His eyes were dark, bottle green when he lifted them again. "I've put together something very special to do that, but I want you to know that if I misunderstood, if what I have planned is *not* what you want — I expect you to tell me."

"What… may I know what wish this is?" she asked softly, barely able to hear herself over the pounding beat of her own heart.

"It will be very clear as soon as we go inside, pet. I just wanted a moment to ensure you understood that this is about you and I, about my commitment to protect and care for you as your Dominant." Lifting his hand, he tucked a strand of hair behind her ear before cupping her cheek to keep her eyes on his. "And while your submission has never been a question, I think that this is what you were hoping for when you told me you wanted to be mine."

"Forever," Thalia finished, and the prince charming smile was back, but with a much more wicked gleam.

"Yes, pet, forever." The kiss was warm and soft, a promise, and even as lost as she was trying to think of what he could possibly have planned for tonight, she knew that James meant every word. That he would never put her at risk, never betray the complete trust she had in him.

He was everything she hadn't known she wanted, needed, in her life — and she wanted to be his forever. However that looked tonight, she already planned to say yes.

Another lingering kiss, and then the dull vibration of his phone interrupted them. Pulling it free of his pocket, he let out a slow breath. "Alright, they're ready for us. Remember what I said."

Biting her lip, Thalia nodded, fighting the torrent of butterflies in her stomach. "I'll be fine, Master."

James chuckled, tugging her lip free with his thumb. "I'm sure you would be, pet, but this is still your choice."

Nodding, her nervous energy making her antsy to be stuck in the car, she practically bounced on the seat. "Yes, Master, I understand. Can we please go in now?"

"Of course." The door opened, and it felt like a blur as the limo pulled away behind them and James led her into one of their favorite clubs in the city. Smaller than many, exclusive when it came to the memberships, and absolutely beautiful.

Yet, in all the times they had been there, she had never seen the foyer this empty. The bar was vacant, the door for coat and bag check closed, but the warm, golden light still glowed across the rich carpets. Master Sean, the owner of *SW3*, waited for them wearing a black on black suit, his hands held in front of him.

"Good evening." He inclined his head, smiling. "Are you ready to go inside?"

James reached over and took her hand, squeezing lightly. "I believe we are."

"Wonderful, everything is prepared as requested." Sean led them down the hall beside the stairs, pausing where one of his security personnel guarded the entrance to the club. "If you need anything, you know simply to ask, but otherwise the dungeon is yours for the night."

"Thank you, Sean." James shook the man's hand, and Thalia offered a small wave and a smile, before they started down the well-lit, lushly carpeted stairs.

"Did Master Sean say the dungeon is ours?"

"Yes, pet, it's just us tonight." The answer was soft as they approached the bottom of the steps where the final door stopped them. "You, me, our friends, and one special guest."

"Wow," Thalia whispered, unable to imagine the cost of renting out *SW3* for an entire evening.

Winding his fingers into her hair, James suddenly clenched his fist and bent her head back sending a tingling ache down her spine that made heat flood between her thighs. "Just remember, pet, you are mine regardless of what you choose. Understand?"

"Yes, Master," she breathed.

"Good girl." The softest of kisses brushed her lips before he broke away to open the door, moving her into the room ahead of him with his fist still wrapped in her hair. The lights were dim across most of the dungeon, but a single spotlight flooded a table draped in black cloth. All of her friends stood to the sides, forming a pathway to the table and the serious looking man standing behind it.

Words wouldn't have come even if she'd tried to speak. Her throat was dry, nerves buzzing in anticipation, as James led her toward the table. Everyone that had helped her and James along were there, smiling silently, which was an impressive feat for Chloe and Lauren who stood on either side of Brad near the door. Ethan and Clair stood opposite. Then Nick and Analiese, Julie and Antonio, and finally at the end of the path by the ominous table were Kalen and Maggie. Standing on either side of it like they would be during the wedding. Best Man and Matron of Honor, except tonight it truly felt like they were bringing the magic of Purgatory into *SW3* for the night.

"Strip and kneel, pet." James commanded as he released her hair, but he tugged the zipper of her dress down a few inches before he moved in front of her.

"Yes, Master." The answer was automatic now, her submission wrapping around her like a comforting blanket. This was always when her mind went quiet, when the world melted. When James looked at her like that, when his voice thrummed with power, she was free. No more questions, no more nerves, just a perfect calm.

Her black dress fell in a pool around her ankles, followed by her panties, her bra, and then she stepped out of her heels. Kneeling, she folded them together, and Maggie moved forward to gather the material from her and set it aside.

Forming into a proper kneel, Thalia rested her hands on her thighs and bowed her head, but James wasted no time in lifting her chin so her eyes were on his. Pupils dilated with that thin rim of bottle-green that told her just how aroused he was to see her like this.

This was who they were at their core. Forever.

His lips curved into a quick smile before he released her chin and looked up at the group. "I want to thank you all for coming tonight. As all of you know, our relationship did not begin under the easiest of circumstances."

Heart pounding, Thalia stared up at him, shocked to hear him address aloud what they had only quietly discussed among the trusted few in this room — and not at all with the stern man standing behind the table.

"It was a dark beginning for someone who brought so much light to my life, and even then I do not think she understood just how much I adored her. For a time, Thalia *only* saw herself as my slave, and I cherished that submission." James turned to Kalen and held out his hand, and his friend opened a large black, jewelry case. "In honor of that submission, that gift she gave me, I gave her this collar."

The platinum, braided circlet he lifted made her breath catch. The spotlight glinted across the metal and she knew her eyes were wide looking upon the item she now only wore to clubs like this — but back then, she had worn it everywhere. Had *needed* it everywhere they went, and even then she had barely been able to function.

"Often, relationships like ours culminate in a collaring ceremony, but Thalia and I did things a little differently. Our relationship began with that level of submission." James moved closer, and someone lifted her hair from her neck.

Turning slightly, Thalia saw that it was Julie smiling behind her as James clasped the cool metal around her neck, brushing his knuckles across her chest as he released it. The weight of the collar was a comfort, a sedative against the nerves clanging inside her, and she was silently grateful for it as Julie stepped back. Smiling down at her, James took a deep breath.

"Our challenge was in having Thalia recognize how important she was to me, in believing just how much I wanted her to have a life… to *live* her life with me." His words almost brought tears to her eyes, and as Kalen and Maggie stepped forward to stand beside him, she had to bite her lip to fight the emotion as he said the next part. "And so we went to the only place that I knew could help us… we went to Purgatory."

"When I learned what Thalia had faced, what James had taken her from, I admit I was unsure if I could do what my old friend asked." Kalen's brogue was softer than usual as he stared down at her, eyes warm as he winked. "But I saw the fire inside her, the strength, and I did my part to help her be James' partner as much as she was his submissive."

Maggie cleared her throat, the short, black dress she wore flaring at the hips and barely touching the tops of her thighs. "And every one of ye here helped with that in one way or another. Most of us were there in Thalia's first week at Purgatory. We saw the deep submission, and we also saw her commitment to James." Brushing her hand down James' arm, Maggie smiled. "And we saw James' commitment to Thalia."

Kalen picked up the dialogue with a nod. "That's right, blessing. So, we honored that commitment. We supported them, accepted Thalia into our strange little family, and pledged to be there for each other."

"And we are forever grateful for that," James spoke solemnly, and Kalen rested a hand on his friend's shoulder.

"Before the ceremony tonight, we ask that each of ye express yer commitment to stand by James and Thalia as they continue to grow in their relationship as Master and slave, Dominant and submissive, and *soon* husband and wife." Kalen raised his voice, waving his hand to the small gathering. "If ye do, state it now."

"I do," Julie piped up almost instantly, cheerful, a vibrant smile on her cheeks. Antonio grinned and nodded next to her as he repeated the words.

Analiese and Nick spoke softly at almost the same time, "I do."

"I do!"

"*I* do too!" Lauren and Chloe talked over each other, giggling on either side of Brad as he inclined his head.

"As do I," Brad added.

"I do," Ethan spoke, gripping Clair's hand who had quickly been brought into the fold once he had brought her to a meet-up at Purgatory. So much sweeter and kinder than Marisol had ever even pretended to be.

The girl shrugged, smiling at Thalia as she spoke. "Of course I do."

Kalen and Maggie stepped forward, each of them pressing a kiss to Thalia's cheeks. "We will always be here for ye both," Kalen added, and then they both stepped back into the lines at the sides, and Thalia was flushed, overwhelmed, as she looked up at James.

Her Master, her Dominant, her lover, her future.

"We are so lucky to have all of you in our lives, and we know this, but as Thalia reminded me earlier this evening — there are still things that taint the light that each of you bring to our lives." James held out his hand for her and she took it, her brows pulling together as she stood. "That darkness that brought us together will never truly disappear."

"Master..." she whispered, and he squeezed her hand tight.

"And it should never be forgotten, but I will always do everything I can to ease it. To push it back, to protect you from it." James' free hand slid down her side until his thumb pressed in at a point on the inside of her hip, and Thalia's heart stuttered, skipped a beat, and then picked up harder.

Did he mean...

"Thalia, *pet*, you asked me months ago if I would put a mark on you. One that would erase the Williams Brothers' mark." All the air left the room as his thumb dug in sharper at the point where their insidious tattoo still stood in dark contrast to her pale skin. James had not even needed to glance down to find it, and her head swam at what he was offering. "I told you then that I knew you were mine, that *you* knew you were mine, and it wasn't necessary to erase it... but if you thought I missed the disappointment in your eyes — I did not."

"I —" Thalia tried to speak, but her voice failed her and he squeezed her hand in his a little tighter.

"Tonight, I want to do just that. To erase their mark, to ensure that it cannot taint the memory of our wedding day. I want to mark you as mine, but this is your choice, pet. I promised you on the day I met you that I would never do a thing without your consent, and this is no different."

"What is it, Master?" Thalia asked, her nerves making her tremble even as he lifted his hand from the tattoo on the inside of her hip.

Turning slightly, James reached over the table and the man handed him a long, dark rod, but the end held one of the solutions she'd researched and her breath caught.

"A brand." She answered her own question, running her fingertips over the thin metal that formed a mirror image of James' initials, *J H*, only there was a small, solid heart that was perfectly sized to cover the tattoo Marcus had embedded in her skin.

"We are all here for you, if this is what you choose, baby." James stepped close, releasing her hand to hug her tight against his front. "I know what this means to you," he whispered, "and Nick and Analiese brought David from their club in Germany just for this. He knows how to do it, he's done it for many others... if you want it. *Only* if you want it."

Thalia swallowed, breathing deep against his chest, surrounding herself in him for a moment as she closed her eyes and listened to his heart. The heart of the man who had seen her strength from half a world away, who had saved her, nurtured her, protected her, given her everything in his power to help her build a life after she had lost it all. The same man who had done everything in his power to save her when everything had gone wrong, who had built her back up, fought for her — the man who loved her more than anything. Who wanted both halves of her, submissive and girlfriend, fiancé, wife.

And now he was giving her the freedom to never have to look at their mark on her skin ever again. What else was there to say?

"I want it."

James barely let her finish the sentence before he was kissing her, and it was hard, a possessive kiss that almost bruised her lips as he took her mouth. Tongues clashing, his arms strong around her, the metal of the brand pressed into her back — there was nowhere else she would rather be.

Nothing else that was more perfect than this.

He released her, eyes steady on hers as his brows pulled together. One more mental check in his strange ability to read her like an open book, but whatever he saw must have satisfied him because he nodded and stepped back.

"Up on the table, pet." James helped her climb up, and her friends moved closer.

As soon as she lay down, Kalen caught her wrists and pulled them above her head to press them to the table. "Ye will have to be very still," he answered her unspoken question at being pinned.

Looking down the table she felt Julie press down on one thigh, Analiese and Maggie each taking an ankle. Then Antonio took a place next to David as James handed across the branding iron.

"Thalia?" David spoke for the first time, his voice warmer than she'd expected, with more of a German accent than Analiese carried.

"Yes, sir?"

"I have questions for you. Do you understand the brand is quite permanent? That this is a serious commitment between you and your Master?" David had not moved, his eyes on hers as if he were evaluating her.

"Yes, sir. I understand. I want this." She nodded, and he waited for a moment before he nodded again.

"Then we continue." Turning to Antonio he spoke more quietly. "Shave and disinfect the area."

At the first cold swipe on her hip, Thalia was hit with flashbacks of the yellow toned bedroom from Marcus' house. The desperate look Kaia gave her when

Thomas had prepared to tattoo her. Her first look at the tattoo that would mark her as Marcus' property. His product, *his slave*.

His.

The whimper that slipped out was uncontrollable, but James was right there, hands on either side of her face as he stared down at her. "I'm here, baby. I'm not going anywhere, are you okay?"

Nodding, she fought past the emotional tidal wave cresting inside her. "Yes, Master, please. I want this, please?"

"Antonio just has to get you ready, okay? And then it will be done. Just a few strikes of the brand. Remember?"

"I remember." She swallowed, focusing on all of the research she'd done. Tattoo removal, cover-up tattoos, and branding. All of the ways to erase Marcus' ownership of her, even though she'd never forget what had brought her and James together. Never forget the weeks of hell she had spent with the man.

A brand had been her suggestion, and James had been the one to pull back from the idea… but clearly he had done his research since. Prepared. Planned for this gift so that her wedding day wouldn't be marred by the ink on her hip. The same ink that had earned Kalen's rage, that had made James flinch, more than once, even if he thought she'd never noticed.

Every inch of her was shivering, but she focused on James' eyes. That perfect bottle glass green. The blond tousle of his hair just brushing his brows as he leaned over her, whispering comforting things to her that she couldn't quite process as loud as her heart was pounding. Either way, her mind was too focused on the weight of their friends' hands on her, the fingertips of those not holding her down reaching to brush her skin so she knew they were there.

Surrounded by more love than she had ever thought possible.

The loud click of a blowtorch made her jump, but everyone's hands tightened on her skin, and she pulled her eyes from James' to watch David rotate the brand through the flame. Antonio held it steady, and she watched as the dark tone of the metal slowly began to glow at the edges. "I need you to consent once more, Thalia."

"I consent to receiving James' brand, just please cover the mark." She met the man's eyes as calmly as she could, even though her racing pulse and the tremble of her muscles were things she couldn't fight.

"Thank you," he answered, and then he turned his eyes back to the brand. Watching as it turned a dull red, then he lifted it from the flame and Antonio laid one hand to grasp her thigh. "Hold her still," David demanded.

Everyone tightened their grip, and James forced her eyes back to his, cupping her cheeks. "I love you."

"I love you too," she whispered as she felt the heat of the brand close to her skin, blistering and terrifying. Then there was a moment of sharp, searing pain where her entire body tried to contract, her teeth clenching tight against the urge to shout, but her friends held her tight to the table — and then the pain passed, and a second later David lifted the metal. A dizzying rush followed, making her head swim, the memory of the pain still fresh.

"Don't let go," David commanded, and Thalia tried to remember to breathe as Antonio lifted the flame once more and the man rolled the brand through it.

"You're doing so well, pet. Just hold on." James' weight pressed her into the table, his forearm between her breasts, holding her chest down.

"Thank you," she whispered, clenching her teeth as he lifted the brand away from the fire.

"Hold her tight."

Another hover of the impossible heat, another searing press, another unavoidable contraction of her body as she cried out.

Trying to stifle it, she kept her teeth clenched, and the brand was already lifted before she opened her eyes again.

Fire. Heat the brand. *Press.*

At the third strike she screamed, unable to keep her teeth clamped against the shock of pain. David had pulled the brand away before she'd even finished the whine, tears rolling from the corners of her eyes into her hair. Uncontrollable.

"I want this, Master. I want this." She locked her eyes on James, recognizing that he had been constantly speaking soft words, encouragement, love.

"Almost done, almost. You are so strong, and I love you so much." His eyes flickered to David, and she turned to see him rolling the brand through the fire again. Her limbs jerked before she'd even thought about it, a subconscious effort to avoid the pain even though she wanted the results. Wanted the tattoo obliterated, wanted to wear the mark she'd asked for.

This is James' mark. James' initials. My Master. Mine.

I chose this.

Opening her eyes she saw his, and could see the pain reflected in them. The concern, the worry that this might be too much, and so as the heat grew close to her skin she gasped. "I love you!"

One last sear of her flesh, and she would have torqued off the table without the pressure of her friend's hands holding her in place. And then it was over, the heat fading into an ache at her hip, the lingering scent of the burned skin unpleasant but important.

It was done. Marcus' tattoo burned away. The last physical evidence of his touch erased.

All that was left was the scar on her arm, the pink line that reminded her of her commitment to James. Her attempt to escape, and *that* she had never cared about. That jagged line was all about survival, but the tattoo had been her submission to Marcus. Her obedience.

His property.

His – and she only wanted to belong to James.

The lingering ache on the inside of her hip was a simmering heat, but with her heart racing, and the adrenaline rushing through her she could barely feel it anymore. Most importantly, James was still there, meeting her eyes, concern pulling his brows together.

"I'm okay," she whispered, and he kissed her. Deep, intense submission spiraled through her as she pictured the mark on her hip, her Master's lips pressed against hers.

It was everything she'd wanted.

He pulled back and she watched David smear something across the mark, but before he could drape the dressing across she pulled at Kalen's grip on her wrists. "Wait, I want to see."

"Let her up," David responded and as soon as Kalen released her she propped on her elbows to see the raw, red burn of the brand. The heart had been carefully placed and there was not a hint of ink left from Marcus' tattoo.

Tears welled as she dropped back to the table, pressing the heels of her hands against her eyes to hide them. "Thank you," she whispered, and then she felt him taping the loose gauze in place, accompanied by the gentle rubbing of her friends' touches on her arms and legs.

"Are you happy?" James' voice was tenuous against her ear, and she knew it was his hand on her belly, his thumb rubbing back and forth.

"Yes, I swear. I — I'm just so glad it's gone."

"I am too, baby. I am, too." James pressed a kiss to her cheek, and she moved her arms to wrap around his neck so he would kiss her again, and he did. Warm, gentle, and absolutely perfect.

"You have the directions for care, and as long as you follow them it will heal just fine." David was smiling when James stood up, and the man's eyes stayed on hers. "Thank you for allowing me to be a part of your branding, Thalia."

"Thank you for doing it, sir." She gave a small smile, and he lifted her hand to his lips to press a kiss to her knuckles.

Kalen cheered. "I think it's time to celebrate!"

"Amen!" Maggie repeated, and everyone stepped away from the table except for James.

"You look so beautiful, pet." His hand slid down until he brushed her folds, parting them with a slow swipe. "Do you feel up for more play tonight?"

"Yes, Master," she purred, reveling in the sensation of his deft touch against her clit.

"How much play?" James asked the question, but he thrust two fingers inside her hard and she moaned, arching her hips off the table with only the slightest twinge from the brand.

"Whatever you want, Master. Please?"

Chuckling softly, he slid her wetness over her clit and started to rub her in earnest. "I just want to make you happy."

"You do, you always do." She nodded, fists clenched at her sides as all of the endorphins spiraled, swelling to match the heat in her skin, the heat that pooled around the mark. So much tension, so much pleasure as he plucked her with the practiced ease of a lover who knew his partner inside and out.

Whimpering, she squirmed, and then Kalen caught her wrists once more, hauling them high as he smiled down at her. "Stay still for your Master."

"Knees apart," James added, and Thalia gasped as she spread them, his fingers picking up speed to make her gasp and sigh, barely aware of the eyes on her as her back arched from the table.

"Come for me. You've earned it, pet. I want to hear it."

All of her tension, her anxiety, the bitter memories he'd done so much to erase — all of it blurred and melted resulting in a spiraling heat that focused between her thighs, amplified by the devious way his fingers moved. "Master!" she cried out as it crested, a trembling tidal wave of emotion and lust, and then it broke over her in silken bliss.

Ecstatic and shivering.

Mindlessly happy.

Filled with light and warmth and buzzing joy, she bucked off the table, tugging at Kalen's grip on her wrist. Coming hard against James' fingers just on the heels of the flash of pain from her movements, the lingering ache of the brand. It was exactly what she'd needed, and Thalia found herself laughing quietly as she dropped back to the surface, James' fingers delving deep again.

Soaking wet.

Just one more mark in the ever-growing column of proof in her masochism.

"By God, you are so beautiful." James kissed her again, and she hummed a moan against his lips, their tongues tangling, before Kalen interrupted them with a loud laugh.

"Don't ye think the girl deserves a drink after all that? Let her up, James!"

It was Kalen who grabbed her hand and turned her so she sat up on the table, but she was relieved to see Analiese was already naked, as were Lauren and Chloe. The security personnel that were busy setting up the bar in the corner just made her grin at James. "I can't believe you rented *SW3* for the whole night."

"Where else could we have done this? Our playroom isn't near large enough for everyone." James chuckled as he took her other hand to help her off the table. The two men towered over her, and she just shook her head.

"You two are trouble when you are together."

"Always," Kalen agreed, winking as he held a hand out for Maggie.

"How much trouble do you want to get into tonight, pet?" James asked, leaning down to nip at her neck, kissing his way higher to her ear.

"I have no idea," she answered honestly, and he pulled her back against his chest by her ribs, keeping his arms high.

"Want a little stress relief?" Maggie asked, tucked under Kalen's arm. That red mop of curls matching the heat in her cheeks. "Because watching that branding was incredibly hot, and ye know how much I like to watch."

"Naughty girl," Kalen growled, a hand slipping between Maggie's thighs. The hem of her black dress hitching up as he stroked her — no panties in the way. A whine escaped as Maggie's knees almost buckled, her head leaning back against his shoulder as he held her up with his other arm. "What do ye want, blessing?"

"I want to come, and I want to watch," she pleaded, and he laughed.

"In that order?"

Nodding, Maggie bucked her hips and he lifted her enough to slide his thick fingers deep. Thalia's mouth opened as she watched Kalen stroking, thrusting with his hand buried between Maggie's legs, and she wanted to drop to her knees for a closer look but James held her firm.

"Please?" Thalia asked, and James chuckled. The men made eye contact for a moment, and then James pushed her gently to her knees, directly in front of Maggie.

"Want to taste?" Kalen asked, and Thalia nodded as Maggie begged incoherently. James held her chin gently, tilting it up as Kalen slid his fingers free and moved them between her lips. The tang of Maggie's taste flooded her tongue and Thalia closed her lips around Kalen's fingers, sucking softly as he slid them in and out.

"Sir!" Maggie begged, and Kalen plucked his fingers free before lifting one of Maggie's legs, bracing her against his chest so she was steady.

"I thought you wanted to play with Thalia tonight, blessing?" Kalen purred against her ear as Thalia looked up at them both at almost the exact moment they looked down at her.

"Up to play, pet?" James asked, but Thalia was already leaning forward toward the apex of Maggie's thighs, it was only James' fist in her hair that pulled her back. "Naughty girl, you know you have to ask. Answer me."

"Yes, Master!" There was a little too much snap in her answer, and James wrapped his hand gently around her throat, angling her head back by her hair so she was looking at him.

"Careful. I wouldn't punish you tonight after the brand, but that doesn't mean I won't keep a count of what you're owed. Want to try that tone again?" James was all Dom voice. Cool and calm, with the growl of arousal that had her whimpering in desperation.

"Yes, Master. I want to play. May I *please* taste Maggie?"

"Such a good girl." He smiled at Kalen and then released her throat, nudging her head forward with his other hand. "Go on then, make Maggie happy, pet."

"Yes, Master." Thalia didn't need him to say it twice, she leaned forward and licked slowly through her folds, fighting the smile when Maggie whined and her hips twitched. She tasted even better than the hint she'd gained from Kalen's fingers, and with the next swipe of her tongue she had flashes of Maggie between her thighs the last time they'd played.

Maggie had called it *stress relief* then as well. The two of them tangled in the bed, giggling as they stroked, licked, nipped each other. A rapidly alternating power dynamic that had been exhilarating and fun in a much different way than their Doms were. Kalen and James had been watching from the wall, shoulder to shoulder, so sexy. So hot to be watched as Thalia had drawn cries from Maggie, and they'd raced each other to see who could make the other come first.

The memory made her moan against Maggie, concentrating her efforts on her clit to feel the way Maggie tried to buckle, but Kalen held her aloft. Sweet tang on her tongue, she reached up and slid two fingers deep, curling them to brush her g-spot. "Oh, God!" Maggie cried, and Thalia smiled before she continued.

It had been too long since she'd had the chance to play with them. Wedding planning and the twins and the distance between Purgatory and London made it challenging, but as she flicked her tongue against Maggie's clit she knew they *both* needed this. Her friend had nowhere to move as Thalia teased her, alternating between long sweeps of her tongue and a torturous, teasing focus on her clit, drawing it into her mouth to make her beg. Stroking and thrusting with her fingers as Maggie's pussy clenched her, rippling as she got closer. With the wall of Kalen's muscle at her back, her leg trapped in his strong grip, Maggie couldn't move away — not like she *really* wanted to escape this.

"Please, Thalia!" Maggie whined, and Thalia took pity on her, shifting on her knees so she could stroke in rhythm with her tongue on Maggie's clit. In a moment her friend whimpered and then cursed under her breath as she came. Shivering, shaking, moaning, the tight squeeze as her hips bucked, then Maggie went limp with bliss. Both of them breathing hard, smiling, and when Kalen kissed her Thalia sat back on her heels.

"Thank you, Master," Thalia spoke softly, looking up at James just before she slipped her fingers between her lips, cleaning Maggie's taste from her fingers. His pupils dilated, fist tightening in her hair as he watched her mouth.

"How did I get so lucky to have you, pet?" James pulled her up from the floor, licking his way into her mouth to moan against her lips. Maggie's taste on her tongue, it was sinfully hot, making her squeeze her thighs together, wanting him inside her. Wanting to keep playing. But first she simply submitted to his dominating kiss, taking her mouth by storm as he nipped and brushed his tongue over hers. "*Bloody hell*, I am going to make you come over and over tonight."

Panting, she swallowed and nodded. "I want that."

"Of course you do, pet." He grinned, prince charming and the devil rolled into one, and then he released her to grab her hand, following Kalen who was carrying Maggie toward one of the couches.

Kalen settled her in his lap, and then James pulled Thalia into his. The girls knee to knee, leaning on the chests of the men they loved more than anything. "That was fun," Kalen laughed, his eyes glued to Maggie, who he propped up for a moment to tug her dress over her head.

No bra either.

Maggie had definitely come with a plan, and it made Thalia smile. "Yes, it was, Master Kalen."

"Will I get to watch you, sir?" Maggie's voice was still soft post-orgasm, but the wicked tilt to her lips showed her excitement as she leaned back, completely naked against her husband, her Dom.

"That depends on what James and Thalia are up for." Kalen's eyes met James' over her head, and Thalia looked up to see him smiling. They were plotting in that odd, silent way that the two men had formed over the years. Two Doms making plans about their submissives without even a word spoken.

"Master Kalen, Master James, we brought drinks." Lauren approached, holding a glass of red wine and a glass of whisky.

"Yeah, after *that* show we figured you could use it, because — holy shit — that was hot." Chloe had the same set of drinks in her hands, and then the two girls lowered to their knees gracefully. Lauren in front of Kalen, Chloe in front of James. Their giggles, and devious grins, sort of shattered the sedate submissive looks, but Brad was standing a few feet behind them with a matching grin.

"Your idea?" James asked Brad, and the man shrugged as he tucked his hands into his pockets.

"Joint effort," he answered.

"Thank ye, ladies. Very nicely presented." Kalen smiled as he leaned forward to take his drink, and then they all gathered the glasses from the girls.

"How do you feel, Thalia? That was... amazing to watch." Lauren's eyes were big as saucers as she looked at the square of gauze.

"I feel pretty good right now, actually."

"Hey, uh, sorry to interrupt, but Master David wanted to know if it was okay to bring his submissive downstairs? And I think Master Sean wanted to come say hi as well." Analiese was standing behind the couch, and Thalia laughed.

"Are you asking me?" Sitting up in James' lap she looked at him and he nodded.

"It's your night, pet. Are you okay with them being a part of it?"

"Of course! It's Master Sean's club, and Master David just gave me the brand I've been wanting for months, they should be a part of tonight." Thalia rolled her eyes when Analiese cheered and turned to run for the door to the stairs — completely naked.

Looking around Thalia couldn't believe she had friends like this. So unbelievably open and loving and caring. It was the kind of family you got to choose instead of the one you were born into, and in just a few days she'd be married to James. The thrill that sent through her made her turn and kiss him, and he smiled against her mouth before he took over, pulling her to him so he could kiss her the way he wanted.

After a moment James broke the kiss and looked over at Kalen. "We need to make sure Sean doesn't snag the main platform, because you've already teased Thalia about sharing tonight."

"Tease?" Kalen laughed, loud and boisterous. "I didn't feking tease yer sub, I meant it. My blessing wants to watch."

Squirming on James' lap she felt the heat building between her thighs, and it had nothing to do with the brand. It was imagining them against her again, the feel of them both pushing inside her. Practically delirious with need, Thalia licked her lips and begged, "Please, Master?"

"You want us, pet?" James tilted her head toward his again, lips hovering over hers in a way that made her shiver.

"Yes, *please*..."

"When you beg like that, how could I deny you, pet?" Then he kissed her, his wicked promise scalding her tongue with temptation as she melted against him, moaning into the meeting of their lips. James was perfect for her. Wicked and charming, sexy and sweet, and he loved her.

And soon they'd be married. Bound together, but she felt more free than she ever had.

The End

CHRISTMAS AT PURGATORY

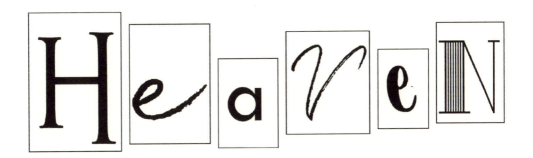

A little reminder from Thalia & James' first visit to Purgatory:

With the full light of the morning flooding in, everything in Kalen and Maggie's house was easier to see. Beautiful carpets, framed photos of trips and smiling faces of friends and family. Above the front door were letters in different shapes and styles that read 'HeaVeN.' Thalia was staring at it when a hand wrapped around her hip and she knew it was James.

"They call their house 'Heaven,' even though the rest of the property is 'Purgatory.'" James spoke quietly in her ear, answering the question she hadn't even asked. She leaned back a little against his chest, soaking in the warm comfort of his body against hers.

"That... makes sense," she murmured.

"I agree." James twisted her by the hips so she could see Maggie and Kalen at the table. He was standing behind her while Maggie bent over the table adjusting the plates.

Kalen pressed himself against her and Maggie let him push her to the table with a grin. He followed forward and kissed across her shoulder blades, mumbling something that made Maggie laugh and lean up suddenly. Kalen laughed too and delivered a sharp swat to her ass before letting her up. Then they kissed, and kissed again, before grabbing seats and looking over at her and James as if nothing sexual had happened at all. Two incredibly happy, loving people.

Thalia wasn't surprised that people who came to Purgatory with tendencies toward dominance or submission looked at Maggie and Kalen and wished for a partner like that. Wished to find a similar balance. It did look like heaven to be that comfortable with someone else, to be accepted completely for who you are; kinks and all.

Acceptance. Isn't that what everyone wants?

Christmas at Purgatory

THALIA

Christmas Day

Eight Months After the Auction

Thalia lifted the large pot off the stove and almost dropped it. It was incredibly heavy, and half full of boiled potatoes that Maggie was going to help her turn into *mashed* potatoes.

"Ye got it, just pour them into that colander!" Maggie turned back to the oven and yanked the door open. "Oh, shite! Hurry up, I need ye to clear some counter space." Thalia nodded and carefully tilted the pot over the colander in the sink. Steam rose up in a cloud, Maggie was cursing to herself about the turkey, and music was blaring from the speakers in the living room. It was chaos, utter chaos, and Thalia loved it. She'd never had big holidays at home, especially not after her mom died and her father spent most holidays awkwardly trying to ask her questions during commercial breaks of whatever was on TV. She had spent most of her Christmases in an undecorated house unless she was able to escape to a friend's. But that was even weirder, because their family just stared at her and felt sorry for her.

This was the Christmas Thalia had always imagined.

Loud, crazy, and full of laughter and people who loved each other. Maggie and Kalen had wound garland up the stairs, around the fireplace, and they had a giant tree lit up with lights. There was a wreath on the door, a pile of presents under the tree, and a mountain of food that Maggie had insisted Thalia help with. She was supposed to be learning how to cook from Maggie, but if she was honest she was really just a glorified assistant.

"Where do you want to put the turkey, Maggie?" Thalia left the potatoes in the colander and set the empty pot in the other half of the sink.

"Over here, cover the carrots and move them somewhere!" Maggie was flushed. The kitchen was really hot, but since it was freezing outside it wasn't too bad. Thalia rushed to move the carrots and Maggie hauled the turkey out of the oven and replaced the space with it. It was golden and smelled amazing. Her stomach rumbled in anticipation.

They were moving around each other with ease in the big kitchen, Maggie was laughing and half telling her to do things, and half doing them for her. If Maggie had let Thalia do everything, dinner would never be ready by the time Kalen got back from his evening visit to the few holiday residents of Purgatory. She and James were personal guests this time so they were staying with them at their home and not in the Dormitory.

"Ladies, it smells amazing in here. Are you sure I can't help?" James leaned in the doorway and Maggie shoo'ed him with her hands.

"If I needed your help James Hawkins, I would ask for it. This is my kitchen, now out. Out!" Maggie was insistent but laughing as she said it, and James lingered long enough to smile at Thalia and shrug before he turned away.

"I think the potatoes are done?" Thalia put down the masher and shook out her arm. Maybe Kalen should incorporate cooking into the sub training because she was pretty sure she had just completed an arm workout. Maggie swept over, tasted them and let out a cheer.

"Yes! Brilliant!" With a heavy breath Maggie turned to survey the kitchen. It was a wreck, it would take hours to clean, but they'd done it. They'd made Christmas dinner, serving dishes and containers were stacked everywhere. A feeling of accomplishment washed over Thalia, she'd never made a dinner like this and the chaos of pots and pans were her trophies." I'm glad you two were able to come, Thalia." Maggie smiled at her as they started separating out the various dishes into two serving sets — one for the Dormitory and one for Kalen and Maggie's table.

"I am too. Honestly, I'm grateful we ended up coming to Purgatory. The original plan was for me to meet James' parents and..." Thalia bit her cheek as she trailed off, focusing on sealing one of the dishes.

"Not ready for that yet?" Maggie asked, looking over her shoulder at her.

"Ladies! I'm not interrupting, I come bearing liquor." James had a glass of whisky for Maggie and a glass of wine for her. A blush rushed up Thalia's cheeks as she hoped he hadn't heard her comment over the Christmas music in the living room. She knew he'd been working while they were cooking, and she could only cross her fingers that he'd been too engrossed in that to listen closely.

"Thank you." Thalia grabbed the wine and leaned up to kiss him. Maggie grabbed the other glass and with his hands free James took the opportunity to wrap his arms around Thalia's waist. She tasted the scotch on his lips, on his tongue, as he intensified the kiss. She moaned into his mouth and then Maggie cleared her throat.

"We're not done yet, James. Can ye keep it in yer trousers for a bit?" Maggie rolled her eyes, shaking her head as she started separating the dishes again.

"Of course, I can. At least until after we eat." He grinned at her before he returned his sea green eyes to Thalia. His hand slid down and he squeezed her ass through the dress. "I love you, baby."

Pure joy. That's what she felt every time he said those words. The stupid smile on her face probably expressed it well enough, but she pressed another kiss to his lips before she responded. "I love you too. Now I really should finish helping Maggie." James nodded, his eyes roaming over her one more time before he backed out with a slightly dramatic sigh and returned to his laptop in the living room.

Maggie lowered her voice, turning to make sure James had left. "So, not ready for the parents yet?"

Thalia shrugged and whispered back, "I don't know, Maggie. I was still trying to figure out if I was ready for that, and then his parents ended up going to Morocco for the holidays and it kind of sorted itself out." She sighed. "At least he *wants* me to meet them? I mean, he wants me to meet everyone. His friends, his co-workers, his sister, his parents."

"That's a good thing, right?" Maggie was leaning back against the counter, all of the serving dishes covered for their dinner. Thalia took a drink of her wine to try and settle her nerves.

"It's a very good thing. I mean, I love it. I love him! I love that he wants me to be a part of his life, that I don't embarrass him, that I'm what he wants, and he's what I want, and we have each other." She bit her lip, stacking the food for the Dormitory together and avoiding eye contact. Somehow Maggie always knew what she was thinking.

"Is there a 'but' in there somewhere?" Maggie prodded.

"But what if his family doesn't approve of me?" Thalia tipped up her wine and finished it, lowering her voice even further. "Family is important. It's *big*, how do I know they'll like me? And what happens if they don't? I don't want to be some issue between them."

"We like you."

"You and Kalen are different, and you know everything, and his family *can't* know everything." Thalia grabbed for her wine glass again, but it was empty. She looked over at Maggie's whisky in confusion. "You haven't touched your drink."

"Oh! Yeah, I'm just hot. Ye can have it, it looks like ye need it." Maggie laughed and handed the glass over and Thalia took a burning sip of it. "I know James' parents, and his sister Katherine. They're nice people, Thalia, I'm sure they will love ye."

"You're right. Of course, you're right. It's stupid. I'm being stupid." Thalia finished the whisky with a cough because she needed to relax. Everything was perfect right now. She was surrounded by a real Christmas, and friends, and the love of her fucking life was sitting in the living room while she was whining about the one day, the *some day*, when she'd have to meet his parents. She was freaking out over a maybe, over a possibility, when what she needed to do was pour herself another glass of wine and continue gossiping with Maggie like they had been most of the day. There had to be more tidbits about Julie's elaborate wedding planning that Maggie hadn't shared.

"MAGGIE!" Kalen's voice boomed from the front door and Maggie's eyes lit up, well, like it was Christmas. Thalia rolled her eyes at herself as Maggie darted out of the kitchen like a sprite and she followed her into the living room laughing. "Ah, blessing, that took me longer than I thought. How's dinner coming along?"

As Thalia walked in the room she saw Maggie wrapped in Kalen's arms, three Doms standing behind him in big coats, and James lounging on the couch with his laptop balanced on his knee. Maggie kissed Kalen fiercely before pulling back with a broad smile. "Dinner is all packed for them to take to the Dormitory. If ye all will come with me?"

"Thanks, Maggie." Two of them spoke at once and she quickly kissed Kalen again before bounding back into the kitchen to boss more people around. Maggie was totally in charge of her house all day, to the point where it was difficult to imagine her as a sub sometimes. If she wasn't married to Kalen, Thalia might even question whether they played, but even when Maggie was in bossy mode, she still reacted to Kalen's Dom voice.

They'd had a lot of giggling discussions about it. When their men got all Dominant, Thalia and Maggie melted. So did Julie and Analiese at that. Really, it was probably a universal sub trait. Instant warm puddle around a confident Dom. Brad was even succeeding at that with Chloe and Lauren.

"Hi, baby." James spoke up, and Thalia looked back at him to find him smiling at her. *Her* confident, smart, sexy, loving, perfect-for-her, Dom. "I've missed you today." James reached out his hand for her and she let him pull her onto his lap. He'd moved the laptop to the table and focused all his attention on her. It made her want to glow.

"I've missed you too. Did you and Kalen have fun earlier?" Thalia squirmed on his lap as his hand slid up her thigh under the edge of the dress. Even though the house was crowded with people he continued, and James pinched her thigh to remind her to be still. She had to bite down on the noise she almost made so she wouldn't attract further attention.

"Yes, shopping in Kalen's playroom is always fun. It's like a live catalogue." James' lips pressed against her shoulder, his teeth grazing her skin as he moved his mouth up her neck. "You will have some late Christmas presents when we get home."

"I already said you don't need to get me anything, you and Kalen and Maggie bought me a yoga studio! That's *more* than enough, for this Christmas and the next ten! AH!" Thalia stifled a moan as James' questing fingers finally found their way to her panties and his deft touch brushed her clit expertly. She wanted to spread her legs, to lift her hips to urge him to continue, but the house was packed and she could clearly hear the Doms stacking food to carry back. Not to mention Kalen had only wandered into his office for a moment.

"Baby..." James' lips were against her ear, his fingers rubbing slow, tantalizing circles over that bundle of nerves. "Don't argue with me on presents. It's Christmas, and I sincerely think you're going to like what Kalen and I have for you later." His nip on her skin accompanied by that dark promise made her moan as she grew wet under his fingers.

"James... what—"

"No. Don't ask. It's not a present if you know what it is." His voice was all clear control and it sent a shiver through her that was not helping the soft waves of pleasure he was creating between her thighs.

"Please?" She lifted her hips, unsure if she was asking to know about the present or asking if he'd push her over the edge.

"James Hawkins!" Maggie was leading the Doms to the door and turned to stare at them, as did everyone else. Thalia pinned her knees together with a fierce blush, trapping James' hand. "What happened to keeping it in yer trousers until after dinner?"

"Mine is still in my trousers, Maggie. And Thalia isn't wearing any." James chuckled and it broke the staring contest. The Doms laughed, glancing at each other as they stepped out into the cold and Maggie just rolled her eyes, shutting the door behind them.

"Quit being a bastard, James, and help me get all this food our girls made onto the table." Kalen was still laughing as he walked back to the kitchen and James moved her off his lap with a quick swat to her ass. She was blushing, and flushed, but she didn't really care. They'd played at enough clubs, been around enough people as they watched or were watched. It didn't matter because with James it all felt easy. Not just easy, it was *fun*.

Dinner was delicious, and they'd have leftovers for days. They opened crackers before they got to the presents. Small, brightly colored tubes that came apart with a loud pop, the smell of powder, a paper crown, and a little toy. Thalia's had a whistle, and it may have been dumb but she wanted to keep it. It was her first cracker, her first British Christmas, and her first decent Christmas since her mom had passed. Maggie was wearing her bright green paper crown and somehow made it look regal. Her mop of curls holding it up like she was meant to wear it.

Presents were opened. So many fun and beautiful things — the best of which, for Thalia, was a mockup of a large ad that would run when her yoga studio finally opened. James refused to tell her how much the ad campaign would cost. Analiese had made the actual advertisement, Julie had helped create the logo, and Maggie had helped Thalia pick the name. *Nirvana*. More than anything Thalia loved it because it was a labor of love, between her and her friends and James. It was all of theirs, even if they kept insisting it was *hers*.

Another glass of wine later and she was nestled next to James on the couch, Maggie was sitting on the floor surrounded by scattered wrapping paper while she leaned against Kalen's leg. He was on the other end of the couch, taste testing a bottle of Scotch that James had given him, and their laughter was winding down from another of Kalen's stories about James. This one had involved a lot of sangria, a trip to Spain, and a session at a club called *Culminante* that had been complicated by the arrival of the sub's boyfriend. It had made James curse when Kalen started to tell it, and it was worth it to listen to the two bicker like the old friends they were over the details of the story.

When they were done laughing James spoke against her ear. "Baby, I've got one more thing for you." He shifted behind her and then there was an envelope in his hand. It was plain, off-white, and had his elegant script across the front. It was addressed to her.

"What is it?" She turned in his arms to find his eyes that deliciously dark green that told her whatever was in the envelope had his thoughts already well into no clothing territory. Thalia felt the blush in her cheeks as she took it from him, turning it over to slide out the note.

> *Thalia,*
>
> *The last time we were here at Purgatory you had a dream, a fantasy, which you shared with me. I promised you that if you made it through the program, I would do my best to make it happen. I would, and always will, do anything for you. Creating an opportunity to play with Maggie and Kalen was easy. If you still want it, all you have to do is tell me.*

Love,

James

Her heart was beating so hard in her chest she could feel it shaking her. Was he serious? Was James serious about this? Her head spun, but heat pulsed between her thighs. She wanted it. How many times had she thought about the dream she'd had? The cropping she'd taken from Kalen? The hungry way Maggie had looked at her after? The things Julie had told her she and Maggie did? Her lips parted as she pulled in a breath and she turned in his arms again.

Not an ounce of jealousy, or concern, or worry on his face. A smile crept over his lips as he trailed a hand up her arm to cup her face. His eyes were still bottle-glass green. She knew he and Kalen had shared for years, that he wouldn't be upset with her for saying yes. They were so much stronger than petty jealousies and insecurities. They were strong enough to recognize the desires in the other person and do everything in their power to make them real. And that's what James was offering her. Tonight.

Officially. Best. Christmas. Ever.

"I want it," Thalia whispered and a low groan rumbled in James' chest as he leaned forward to place a chaste kiss on her lips. His restraint was obvious when he didn't take it further. Then he pulled back and looked past her to Kalen and nodded slightly.

"What's going on? What did you get, Thalia?" Maggie was up on her knees, looking between the three of them with wide blue eyes. Kalen leaned forward, his hand moving into Maggie's wild, red curls. Her entire attitude shifted, her lips parting, a soft murmur slipping from her as he craned her head back. Kalen kissed her neck, but Thalia saw him pulling his own envelope out of his back pocket.

"Hush, blessing. Ye have a present too." He was grinning at her when her eyes widened and she cheered, snagging the envelope from Kalen's fingers as he released her hair. Maggie tore into it with an excited wiggle, and Thalia couldn't imagine what hers said. Was Kalen asking her permission? Had she wanted something else? Her eyes trailed across the paper and then a blush crept up Maggie's cheeks. She glanced at Thalia for a second before looking up at Kalen.

"Sir?" The note was in her lap, her fingers crinkling the edges.

"Up to ye, Maggie." Kalen murmured, his broad shoulders angled forward as he leaned on his knees to be closer to her.

"What does *yours* say, Maggie?" Thalia sat up as Maggie's blue eyes landed back on her. At first Maggie didn't respond, then she moved until she was in front of Thalia, looking up at her from the floor. It was the most submissive she'd ever seen her, and Maggie was *only* looking at her.

"It says that, as long as yer okay with it, I can play with ye. And later, Kalen and James want to play with ye." Maggie bit her lip and it drew Thalia's attention to her mouth. Cupid's bow lips, pale pink, her cheeks speckled with freckles and flushed in her nerves. It reminded her of how Maggie had approached Kalen after the cropping, asking permission to touch her, and he had refused her then. Thalia hadn't been *healed* yet, she hadn't passed Kalen's program. The answer had been no, but now it was yes, and Thalia wanted to know what Maggie's lips tasted like. She wanted to know what Julie had meant about it being *different* than kissing a guy, especially a Dom.

She opened her mouth to speak but changed her mind. Words weren't enough. Thalia reached forward and cupped Maggie's face — and kissed her. Maggie let out a surprised sound, tense for only a moment before she softened against her mouth. Thalia had never been this bold, but she wanted to prove to Maggie, to prove to *everyone* in the room that she was no longer fragile. There was no 'Handle with Care' sign on her forehead anymore. She didn't want any questions on her state of mind, she didn't want any special treatment. Maggie leaned back and Thalia followed her forward off the couch. When she lay down, Thalia leaned over her, her knees landing on either side of Maggie's hips, leaving Thalia straddling her. Maggie's mouth opened to hers and the kiss deepened, a quiet moan slipping from them both as Maggie's hands slid into Thalia's hair. They held each other in the kiss, nipping lips, smiling at each other, before returning to it.

It went on and on, Maggie's hands wandering down her sides to her hips, to her bare thighs. Thalia took the chance to kiss down Maggie's throat and she arched under her. It was different in ways, but the same in others. People were people, and what felt good, felt good. But Maggie was soft in the ways James was hard, her moans were light and sweet. The bite of Maggie's nails against the skin of her thigh as Thalia nipped her collarbone was sharper. Thalia moved her hand to Maggie's breast, duplicating what she knew she liked with herself. Her thumb brushing over the hardening bud of her nipple through the fabric. When she squeezed gently Maggie pulled her mouth back to hers to kiss her again. Their breaths were shorter, excitement making their hearts race, her skin tingling with the anticipation of something new and different. Then Thalia felt a sharp grip in her hair that pulled her firmly up and back from Maggie. She let out a whimper as James tightened his grip slightly.

"Thalia… did I say you could kiss Maggie?" Cold, clear, Dom voice. James was leaned forward so that his mouth was brushing her ear. Heat pooled between her thighs because she knew he wasn't upset with her, this was just about who was in control — and it was most definitely him.

"No, Master," Thalia breathed, looking down at Maggie who was flushed and breathing hard as she watched James tug Thalia up by her hair.

"Correct. On the couch, Thalia." James kept his hand in her hair as she sat back down between him and Kalen.

"Present, Maggie." Kalen's voice was loud even when he wasn't trying, deep and commanding, and Maggie pushed herself up into a kneel, interlacing her fingers behind her head.

"Pet, am I to understand that with your little display you *would* like to play tonight?" James' voice sent a shiver through her. She was a warm puddle, and from the way Maggie's eyes were focused on the floor, her body taut with tension, Maggie was as well.

"Yes, Master, I would like to play tonight." Thalia barely finished speaking before James was kissing her. It was reassurance, and heat, and promise.

"Maggie, what would ye like to do with Thalia?" Kalen's voice boomed behind her and Thalia gasped against James' lips before he pulled her tighter to him.

"May I taste her, sir?" At the request from Maggie, Thalia immediately shivered. She wanted to answer 'yes,' but James' mouth had hers busy and Maggie was asking her Dom.

"Strip first," Kalen commanded, and James nipped Thalia's lip as he pulled back to watch, moving his mouth to her ear with a grin.

"Happy Christmas, baby," he whispered against her ear and she felt the smile on her lips, accompanied by the rapid beat of her heart as she watched Maggie undress. Still beautiful. All soft curves with the swell of her hips, her larger breasts as she took off the pale pink bra. After she slid the matching underwear down she dropped to her knees again, her thighs spread apart, and Thalia found herself staring. James nudged her. "Your turn, pet. Stand and strip."

Thalia nodded and stood from the couch, realizing she was directly in front of Maggie as she pulled the dress over her head. Her bra came off next, and then Maggie's hands were at the edge of her underwear, looking up at her for permission. Thalia dropped the bra to the side and nodded her head a little, and Maggie smiled so big that Thalia couldn't help but giggle. The sharp spank as her ass was revealed made her gasp and she turned to see a grinning James.

"Couldn't resist. Now sit back down, on the edge, Maggie wants her present." James tugged her hand until she sat back down, and then his hand moved to her right thigh, lifting her leg until it draped over his.

"Going to be a good girl, lass? Maggie has been waiting for a long time." Kalen's voice rumbled to her left as he took her other leg and trapped it on the other side of his so she was spread wide in front of Maggie. Thalia could only manage a nod as she leaned back on her arms.

James pinched her thigh and Thalia yelped. "Answer him, Thalia."

She looked at James first, his expression was smooth, unreadable, like he usually was in the middle of a session. It made her heart pound harder. Then she turned to look at Kalen, his tawny eyes sliding down her body before meeting her gaze. He was totally in control too. She licked her lips and made herself speak. "Yes, Master Kalen, I'll be good."

A smile tilted the edge of his mouth before he looked down at Maggie. "Maggie, ye can do what ye like with Thalia, but yer not allowed to touch yerself right now."

"Thank ye, sir." Maggie nodded, her hands releasing from behind her head to slide up the insides of Thalia's thighs. Their eyes met, and Maggie just smiled as she lowered her mouth, her tongue sliding smoothly between Thalia's lips, splitting her pussy with a warm, wet swipe. She ended the first long lick with a brush over her clit. Thalia couldn't close her mouth, panting as Maggie returned to her, tugging Thalia to the very edge of the couch. Kalen and James balanced her, their hands on each of her thighs. A moan rose up out of her as Maggie focused attention on her clit, two fingers sliding easily into her soaked pussy. Soon, Thalia was rocking her hips against Maggie's mouth — she was really, *really* good at this. One advantage to knowing what it felt like, apparently it meant you knew what you were doing.

"Oh God..." Thalia moaned and let her head drop back, her hands clenching in the cushions of the couch. James was watching her as she squirmed, the teasing licks of Maggie's tongue making her whimper and moan in rising pleas.

"Do ye like it, Thalia?" Kalen's voice was close to her ear, his fingers pressing firmly against the soft skin of her thigh. It made her moan louder, biting down on her lip as Maggie grazed her teeth over her clit before sucking it back into her mouth.

"Yes, Master Kalen, yes, very much!" she cried out as Maggie thrust a third finger inside her, her hips rolling, her breath coming faster as that incredible tension built inside her, rushing her toward an orgasm she wasn't sure she was allowed. Maggie seemed to notice and redoubled her efforts, the strong draws against her clit, her fingers curving inside her until Thalia's legs were shivering on the edge. "Please, may I come? Please?" Thalia wasn't sure which Dom she was asking, she just wanted permission.

"Hold it back, we're enjoying the view." James had laughter in his voice, his hand returning to her hair to twist it and keep her from leaning forward.

"It's a very pretty sight. Just wait." Kalen was definitely chuckling under his breath.

They were asking the impossible. Thalia tried to push back from Maggie's mouth, to get a moment of respite from the steady pulse of pleasure as Maggie drew on her clit, her fingers stretching and stroking inside her to build her higher and higher. Kalen and James only tightened their grips on her thighs, keeping her firmly against Maggie's talented tongue.

"I can't! I can't!" Thalia whimpered, her back arching, moans slipping between her lips as her thighs fought to close against their strength. Maggie could have held back, she could have eased up the incredible pressure on her clit or slowed the thrusts of her fingers inside her — but she didn't. An instant later Thalia's body locked up as her orgasm crashed over her, a crippling wave of pleasure making her cry out and strain against the hands holding her in position. Maggie's tongue continued, more gently, coaxing every last ounce of pleasure out of her orgasm, until Thalia was whimpering and shivering.

"Stop, Maggie." Kalen's voice was low and rumbling, and Maggie leaned back. Her lips were swollen and her chin was wet, and she was grinning. She knew exactly what she'd done, and her own harsh breathing and bright flush spoke of how turned on she was, but she kept her hands flat on her thighs.

"I'm sorry, Ma—" Thalia started to apologize but James covered her mouth with his hand, silencing her. He shook his head slowly.

"Tsk, tsk, pet. Now you've earned a punishment." His tone was wicked.

"That she has. Maggie, since ye were so good, would ye like to watch Thalia be punished?" Kalen stood up, reaching for Maggie to help her up from the floor. She nodded and Kalen kissed her hard, Maggie's soft moan buzzing between them. Thalia blushed as she realized Kalen could taste her on Maggie's lips. James stood and scooped Thalia off the couch suddenly, holding her against his chest with a smile. Kalen just leaned down and threw Maggie over his shoulder, which sent her into peals of laughter. His hand landed sharply on her ass. "Quiet, blessing, or I'll gag ye for the rest of it."

"Is that a promise?" Maggie taunted as he started for the stairs. Kalen's laughing sigh spoke volumes of their relationship.

"If ye want to be gagged, keep it up, and I'll also pick exactly what toys ye get to use while yer watching." Kalen's voice was back to deep and commanding, but Maggie's soft moan showed that wasn't exactly a threat.

"You okay?" James whispered against her hair as he followed Kalen up the stairs with her in his arms.

"Do you really have to ask? That was... amazing." Thalia felt a shiver rush through her and James chuckled.

"That was part of Maggie's present, yours is coming up, pet. After Kalen and I punish you for being so *very* disobedient." James' lips were on hers as they stepped into Kalen and Maggie's personal playroom. It was the size of a large bedroom, a king-size bed dominating the middle of it. There were four, thick posts at the corners, and a series of chains hanging above it. Chairs lined the wall in front of the bed, some with restraints. Thalia was blatantly staring around the room as

James let her down from his arms. Kalen flipped Maggie back to her feet in front of one of the chairs.

"Do ye plan on keeping up the attitude, blessing?" Kalen towered over Maggie. His broad shoulders and barrel chest making her look tiny as she stared up at him with a gleam in her eyes. Maggie was *very* feisty, but Kalen loved the challenge. They were happily married after eight years together, and the key to that was never being boring.

"I am yer sub to do with as ye wish, sir." The words were right, but Maggie's cocky little smile was anything *but* submissive.

"Oh... Maggie." Kalen laughed, dropped into one of the chairs without arms and had Maggie across his lap in an instant. His hand came down hard and fast in a series of sharp spanks that had Maggie kicking and moaning and yelping. When he stopped, his hand rubbed over the hot, pink skin and Thalia found herself staring again. James moved behind her, his erection pressing against her back as he slid his fingers between her thighs. She was slippery from the orgasm downstairs, and her legs shook slightly as he moved his touch over her clit.

"Sir! Please?" Maggie cried out over Kalen's lap, and Thalia could see his fingers working between her thighs. But he pulled back, and James did as well, leaving both subs whimpering.

"After all that? Yer lucky I'm still letting ye come while we play with Thalia, blessing." Kalen was smiling as he let Maggie move to her knees on the floor. He stood and his heavy steps went to the cabinet against one wall. Inside were floggers, and crops, and drawers of God-knows-what. Kalen pulled open a few drawers before turning back to Maggie with a grin, his hands full. From where she was standing she could see a dark toned dildo that looked uncomfortably large, and a smaller blue one. Kalen set all of it on one of the chairs, then walked over to a different chair and dragged it until it was centered to face the bed.

"Sir?" Maggie whimpered as Kalen affixed the dildos to the chair that had obviously been designed for it. The larger in front, the smaller a little behind. Then he handed a small bottle of lube to Maggie and crossed his arms.

"Ye can do it, no arguments. If ye want to come, this is how ye will do it." Kalen's voice was firm. Maggie's mouth opened like she might try to argue but then she nodded, applying lubricant to both before she moved onto the seat on her knees. She straddled them controlling her descent while keeping her eyes on Kalen's.

Thalia couldn't breathe as she watched her, and the rhythmic brush of James' fingers over the small of her back was sending chills over her skin. Maggie took the tip of the thick dildo in the front, a soft groan slipping from her. Then she reached back, more lubricant on her fingers as she prepared to take both dildos at once. Her soft whimpers as she eased down, breathing carefully as she stretched over the two invading toys, were incredibly hot to listen to. As she lowered, Maggie brought her legs forward one at a time and held her weight up by the arms of the chair to ease down the rest of the way. Finally, with a low groan, Maggie was seated on the chair. A sheen of sweat covered her, her hips rocking slightly while she panted and whimpered. Kalen knelt in front of her to attach cuffs to her ankles and lock her to the chair. "I'm leaving yer wrists free so ye can touch yerself if ye want to, Maggie. But ye lost the chance to go without the gag. Open."

"But, Sir—" Maggie started, her eyes wide, but Kalen cupped her chin to silence her.

"Open," Kalen commanded and she did. It wasn't a large ball gag, but when it was between her teeth, she wouldn't be able to speak. Kalen strapped it behind her head and then pressed a kiss to her forehead. "Ye are so beautiful, Maggie. I love ye." His words were quiet, and Maggie's murmur back was an obvious return of the affection. Thalia was sure Kalen spoke fluent gagged sub, anyway.

"Just remember, pet, everything that happens tonight, everyone is okay with. If you're not okay, just use your safe word, alright?" James whispered against her hair. He was always trying to watch out for her, to protect her. She could barely focus on him, her body so tense with watching Maggie and Kalen, having him pressed against her back.

"I promise that I'm perfectly fine, Master," Thalia whispered back and his chuckle rumbled against her back.

"Then get your ass on the bed, on your knees in the middle. It's time for your punishment." James stepped back from her, pulling his shirt off in a smooth movement that had her very distracted. The deep V above his jeans made her salivate as he turned and walked to the cabinet so she could watch the muscles of his back move under his skin. She suddenly realized she was ignoring a command before a punishment. Not the smartest move.

Kalen was pulling his shirt off as well though and she couldn't look away, the warmth of the room was comfortable for her since she was naked, but she was glad it meant they needed to lose some clothes. Kalen was heavily muscled, with a thick chest, strong arms, and broad shoulders. Like some ancient warrior. He glanced at her as he walked toward the cabinet again and she instantly climbed onto the bed.

Now was not the time to be slow to respond to commands.

Thalia watched as they talked quietly by the cabinet, both of them removing shoes and socks. Then they laughed. Kalen looked over at Thalia and his voice boomed in the room. "Thalia, present."

She spread her knees wider and interlaced her fingers behind her head. Her pussy was soaked from the orgasm, and from watching Maggie, and from the pending promise of what was coming. She'd already had pleasure, now it was time for the other half of what she craved. And this time it would be Kalen and James, together, deciding how to punish and push her.

"Face the wall, put your back to Maggie so she can watch." James' clear voice had her moving until she was in position. He climbed onto the bed and stood up in front of her, his cock tantalizingly in front of her, just on the other side of the fabric of his pants. As he reached up for the chains, giving them slack to bring them low enough for her arms he grinned down at her. He knew exactly what standing in front of her like this did to her. Her mouth watered.

"Arms up, Thalia," Kalen ordered, and she raised her arms so James could slide the soft lined leather cuffs over her wrists. A few adjustments and the chains were taut enough to keep her arms above her head without making her arms so straight that she lost circulation. When he was satisfied, James lowered himself in front of her, his hands trailing down her arms, over her shoulders, her breasts, her sides, until they stopped at her hips.

"Remind Kalen of your safe word, pet." James leaned his head to the side, kissing over her shoulder, up her neck until his face was hidden in her hair as his lips trailed sucking, biting kisses. He was going to leave marks.

The slap of a crop behind her made her jump. Kalen must have popped it across his hand. That was going to leave marks too. Her body thrummed with the promise of it. "Chair, Master Kalen, it's chair."

"I remember," Kalen rumbled behind her, and Thalia could hear the faint moans and whimpers stifled by Maggie's gag. She must have started moving. "Move her back, James?"

James bit down on her shoulder making her gasp before he kissed the spot and stood again. Thalia looked up to watch James shift the chains connected to her wrists backward on an elaborate set of cables above the bed. As he pushed the chains back, Thalia shuffled back until Kalen put a hand on her back to stop her.

"Good?" James asked, his eyes dark as he looked down at her.

"Yes. Why don't ye go pick something, eh, James? I'll get started." Kalen's voice was deep behind her, and before she could prepare the sharp sting of the crop landed across her ass. She cried out and an echoing muffled cry came from Maggie. Two more followed, hot lines burning into her skin as she bit down on the groans. The next two landed a little harder and Thalia was squirming, tugging against the chains, listening to the rattle of them above her. The sharp stings faded and Kalen spoke again. "First five. Thalia why don't ye tell us why yer being punished?"

"Yes, pet, I want to hear you say it." James was back, standing behind her. The thought of everyone staring at her backside as those five lines appeared on her skin made her shiver.

"I came without permission, Master Kalen." She gasped a breath as she felt the heavy thud of a flogger land against her ribs. Her skin bloomed heat where James had laid the lash. "I'm sorry, Master!" Another thud on the other side, it was heavy and the strike shook her. The next three landed across her back in a pattern she knew was James' hand. Each thud rocked her body, heating her skin and making her nerve endings wake up. She whimpered when he stopped, trying to absorb the sensations, but Kalen didn't give her a moment.

"We're at ten." James said as Kalen brought the crop down a little harder in rapid succession. One, two, three and she was shifting her weight from knee to knee, tears pricking the edges of her eyes as she cried out.

"Please!" She was breathing hard when he paused, the muffled sounds of Maggie moving and straining for her own orgasm were impossible to ignore.

"Who made ye orgasm, Thalia?" Kalen asked, the tip of the crop trailing down her spine. She shuddered as her skin was already sensitive from the flogger.

"Maggie," Thalia mumbled, and Kalen brought the crop down hard across the place where her thighs met her ass. It stung sharply and she let out a short scream, whining as it faded.

"Louder," Kalen ordered.

"MAGGIE!" she shouted and Kalen brought the crop down across her thighs. Thalia yanked on the chains, whimpering as the line of fire settled into her skin. Maggie was moaning steadily behind her, the wet sounds of her movements summoning the image of her form rising and falling in the chair. The dildos moving in and out of her, and Thalia pictured Maggie's hand slipping between her thighs to rub her clit. Her red curls falling forward as she worked toward her pleasure. It had Thalia panting, but the hard thud of the flogger across her shoulders brought her back to reality. It was almost too intense as the second and third landed. The deep, body shaking thuds of the flogger contrasting with the bright, sharp lashes of the crop. Her body was humming, sensation flooding her. The last two had Thalia moaning steadily, leaning forward away from the blows, resting her weight on the chains.

"We're at twenty. Check in, pet." James' voice was lower, arousal evident in his tone. She loved being able to hear that he wanted her, that it was a struggle for him to hold back. A hard grip in her hair lifted her head. She hadn't even realized she'd let her chin fall to her chest as she recovered.

"Thalia, we need ye to check in." Kalen's voice was stern, demanding. It woke her up enough to evaluate herself. The ten lashes from the crop were settling in her skin, warm and a little sore, but fine. Her entire back was tender from the flogger, but she was still more than okay.

"I'm good, Master, I promise." To make her point Thalia made herself kneel straight again, not leaning against the hold of the chains. She heard James' voice speak quietly to Kalen, and a moment later the crop landed on her back. She hissed a whimper through her teeth, clenching her fists on the other side of the cuffs. Then the flogger landed across her ass, heavy and sharpening the sting of the welts Kalen had landed there. Crop, flogger, flogger, crop.

"Breathe, pet," James corrected her and she forced a breath, but it came in on a whimper and out on a series of soft pleas. The flogger wrapped around her hip, then matched on the other side. She was shivering when a hard swat of the crop made her jerk forward, the fiery line refusing to settle into her hot skin. Her backside must have been bright red from shoulder to knees, and she was waiting for the next lash when a muffled cry and a long, low moan came from Maggie. Thalia tried to control her breathing, to slow the tears on her cheeks as she listened to Maggie writhe and whimper in pleasure.

"One more for Thalia, Maggie. Open yer eyes. Watch," Kalen ordered in a low voice, and then another hard crop lash landed where her ass met her thighs. The spot was always sensitive, but now it was brutal and she screamed before the cry settled into whimpers.

"Please, please, please, I'm sorry, Master, Master Kalen, please..." Thalia was babbling, and she jumped when someone's hand ran down her back and over her ass. There was a texture to some of the welts, and she moaned softly as they began to rub her skin.

"That's forty. Think you've earned your present, Thalia?" James was close to her, it was his hand rubbing her skin. She could hear Kalen speaking to Maggie but couldn't understand him through the buzzing in her ears.

"Have I, Master?" Thalia's question was soft, she was bordering on subspace and her voice reflected that dreamlike state she was so close to. James heard it and slid his hand between her thighs, thrusting two fingers sharply inside her, which wasn't difficult as wet as she was. It snapped her head up though and she moaned.

"I think you have." His fingers continued moving inside her, the heel of his hand rubbing against her clit until her hips were rocking in time with his thrusts. She was moaning quietly, biting her lip to fight the urge to beg. Begging now might just make him drag it out, just to hear her beg more. "Kalen, want to let her down?"

"Of course." His voice came from beside her and then he was on the bed in front of her. His tawny brown eyes locked on hers and he tilted her chin up. Then he kissed her. It was a surprise, she hadn't expected it. His beard scraped against her skin and the sensation was different, especially as gentle as he was. Only their lips were touching, his hands back at his sides as he waited for her to kiss him back. When she did her moan buzzed against his lips as James chose that moment to slide his fingers from her and begin circling her clit. Kalen's hands were large and easily wrapped to the back of her head as he held her face so he could kiss her in earnest. His tongue sought hers and she tugged against the cuffs, wanting to touch him back, wanting to touch *someone* as James drove her higher. Each teasing slip of his fingers back inside her was torture, each thrust whether gentle or sharp made her moan against Kalen's mouth. When James noticed she was relaxing into the touch of his fingers, he would draw her wetness back to her clit and renew her whimpers.

"Master Ka— Master, *jesus*, I need—" Thalia couldn't think straight between the two of them, and they were barely teasing her. Her body was electric with tension. Kalen lifted her chin so she had to look at him.

"Say please." He brushed his thumb over her lip and she swallowed.

"Please, Master Kalen?" She would have said anything if it meant they'd stop teasing her, but that seemed to work. Kalen stood up on the bed in front of her and she became very aware of the erection in his pants. When he uncuffed her the rush of blood to her hands made her roll her shoulders. James removed his hand from between her thighs and held his fingers in front of her lips, she opened her mouth to suck them in, cleaning her taste from him as Kalen watched from above her. The moment wasn't lost on her, especially not as Kalen began to unbutton his pants. She moaned against James' fingers as he moved them in and out of her mouth, and Kalen slid his pants down to reveal his erection.

Kalen went commando? Of course he did.

James pulled his fingers from her mouth and massaged her shoulders and her neck for a moment as Kalen tossed his pants off the bed. "Do you want to taste him, pet?" James asked and Thalia nodded as Kalen gripped his cock and stroked it just inches in front of her mouth. She leaned forward to taste and James jerked her back by her shoulders. "Beg him."

Kalen smiled down at her, stroking himself slowly. He was thick, the head of his cock dark and leaking precum that she wanted to catch with her tongue. The words tumbled from her. "Please, Master Kalen, may I taste you? Please? I want to taste you."

Maggie whimpered and moaned behind them.

"Absolutely. Why don't ye put on a show for Maggie?" Kalen stepped to the side, and James twisted Thalia until Maggie could see them both. Kalen's strong hand reached up and grabbed a chain to balance, and then his hand was on Thalia's head, pulling her toward him. She wrapped her hand around the base of his cock and he groaned, opening her mouth to pull him in. His growl was low and loud, and Maggie moaned too. Thalia drew him back, and then in again, a little deeper with each dip of her head.

"Into your throat, pet." James cupped the back of her head, and Kalen tightened his grip in her hair as he pushed deeper. He was thick and she panicked for a second, choking before she made herself swallow. Kalen groaned, easing back and then pushing forward harder. "Good girl," James whispered and his hand moved between her thighs, thrusting two fingers inside her from behind. The hum of her moan made Kalen thrust harder, back deep into her, then he let her breathe before he thrust again.

Thalia rolled her hips, seeking more from James' touch as she tried to keep her focus on Kalen's cock in her mouth. He tasted like hot, male flesh, his precum trailing over her tongue every time he pulled back from her throat.

"Stop." Kalen pulled her back by her hair and she was left panting, whimpering, and moaning as James continued moving his fingers inside her. She was looking up at him, pleading with her eyes because she couldn't form words. He crouched down in front of her, his thumb running across her swollen lips before he grinned. "I'm going to fuck ye, Thalia. Ready for that?"

She nodded quickly, but James took his hand from her and spanked her hard. It stung fiercely atop the welts already there and she whimpered, turning to look at him. His eyes were dark, his expression intense as he tilted his head. "Is that how you respond to a Dom, pet? Answer him properly."

"I'm s—sorry. Yes, Master Kalen, I... I want you to fuck me." She spoke quietly because she was shivering on edge, they'd teased her to the brink, and all she wanted to do was fall over. Kalen smiled and pulled her forward by the back of her neck, his mouth covering hers again in a dominating kiss. When she leaned toward him, he grabbed her and pinned her to the bed. A tremor rolled through her as his knees pushed hers apart. Flashbacks to her dream had her rolling her hips up, but no fantasy could match the heavy weight of him on top of her, the strength in his arms as he pinned her wrists above her head, the way James watched her with a flush in his cheeks as arousal strained his control. James handed Kalen a condom with a grin and he tore the foil with his teeth, but her eyes couldn't leave the dark green of James.' He noticed, and it made his grin turned devious.

"Thalia, do you want both of us?" James asked, leaning closer to her. Kalen held himself above her, his knees widening hers just a little more as she arched her back, nodding furiously. "Say please."

"PLEASE!" she cried out and Kalen thrust inside her hard. He stretched her and it bordered on painful for a moment, then he rocked his hips back on a low moan and thrust forward hard again. He filled her and she closed her eyes as she arched up against him. Maggie cried out against the gag, her rhythmic, low moans signaling she'd found a second orgasm. Thalia wanted hers. She lifted her hips against Kalen's, his thrusts sharpening that edge inside her as her welts rubbed against the sheets. James had moved over to Maggie, pushing her hair back from her face, whispering to her. Thalia knew he was checking on her, but she couldn't focus as Kalen slammed hard inside her again. His mouth trailed down her neck to her shoulder, his beard tickling and scratching across her skin until each shift of his body against hers was like an electric current.

"Do ye want to come, Thalia?" Kalen spoke between thrusts, his voice strained as he held tight to the control he had.

"Yes, please, please, Master Kalen, please let me come," Thalia begged, rolling her hips up to let him thrust deeper.

"Let her come, Kalen." James called over to them and Kalen chuckled above her before he grabbed onto her hip and shifted his thrusts so the next movement was directly on that bundle of nerves inside her.

"Oh God, oh *fuck*, oh God…" Thalia babbled desperately as she tensed, pulling against the hand Kalen was using to pin her wrists above her head. Her body was tightening, painfully holding her over the edge of orgasm, her clit pulsing to the rapid beat of her heart until she could only whimper as she sought the precipice. He backed off, shallow, slow thrusts that held her there, his lips teasing her as he kissed across her collar bone, ducking his head down to capture her nipple and draw it tight into his mouth. Her muscles shook as she waited, breathless, for the orgasm to break over her. Then he bit down on her nipple and thrust hard, and she was tumbling. Crying out with a moan as her mind blanked, suffused with the sparks of pleasure that raced up her spine, the heat that flooded between her thighs as she shook under him. Lost in bliss and breathless pleasure.

"Fuck," Kalen groaned and let go of her wrists, dropping his weight on her hips to still her shifting movements. She was panting when he pressed a kiss to her lips, quieting the little moans that were still slipping from her as the echoes of pleasure slowed. With her mouth against his he rolled so she was on top of him and her body stilled. The shifting of the bed clued her in just before James' hand landed on her back, and lubricant trickled between her ass cheeks. She rocked and Kalen groaned.

"Be still, pet." James pressed a finger against the tight ring of muscles and she gasped against Kalen's lips, and then she bent her head down, pressing her forehead against his chest as James stretched her. Kalen was still buried inside her, making the pressure of James' second finger as he slid it in that much more intense.

"I don't know, I don't know if —" She was babbling against Kalen's hard chest, and James' hand rubbed soothingly over her back, and Kalen cupped the back of her head, his fingers in her hair.

"You'll handle it, baby. Relax." James worked his fingers inside her, stretching her little by little. He wasn't rushing her, and Kalen was barely moving inside her.

Their breaths and her shivers as the sensations increased were the only movements. "Take a deep breath, pet."

She did, and he moved his fingers back. She heard a condom wrapper tear, and then he was pressing against her. Thalia's hands fisted the sheets on either side of Kalen's ribs, but he lifted her face so she looked at him. He looked hungry, his cock buried inside her, but he was holding onto his own control not to move too soon, and he was trying to calm *her* down as he spoke gently. "Breathe."

Her ribs expanded and James pressed inside her, it was a burning ache, an impossible fullness as he eased forward. Thalia whimpered, and Kalen captured her mouth in a kiss, not letting her go until James was in.

"Fuck, fuck, fuck, fuck..." Thalia panted when Kalen released her lips. He moved first, Kalen sliding back and thrusting up inside her. All three of them groaned, and Maggie joined them.

"Language, pet." James bit her shoulder and moved. Her body was shaking already. Too much sensation. Kalen was moving too, his thrusts growing harder and harder. Each lift of his hips pushing her back onto James, and then forward again. James moved more gently, letting her adjust, but soon she could feel the tension in his body against her. He was fighting to control his urge to push her, but she felt fine. Sore already, but fine. The next time he went to thrust, she pushed back hard and he growled, his fingers digging into her hip painfully. His voice was rough. "Is that what you want?"

Kalen thrust upward. "She's not going to break, James. Are ye, Thalia?" His hand was at her neck, pushing her chin up as he squeezed her throat gently. She shook her head. She wasn't fragile.

"God, I love you, Thalia." James' lips were against her back, and then he thrust hard. She winced and cried out, but Kalen was thrusting hard too. They moved inside her, and she was so full, impossibly stretched, the feeling sharp and then they pulled back and her body was shivering, needing more, just a little more. Their groans were increasing, their hearts pounding against her skin, and she couldn't hold on. She was going to break apart.

Her body locked up as she came, tightening down on them both and their groans echoed the cries she made, heat pulsed down her spine, washing over her to leave her gasping and shaking. Fuzzy in her lust as shivering aftershocks rocked her. Kalen thrust deep, growling low, and she felt his cock kick inside her, his hand holding the back of her head to keep her against his chest as James continued to move inside her. His fingers were digging into her hips, and she pressed back against him. Thalia pushed up onto her knees as Kalen slid from her and James had greater control over her movement. A few more hard thrusts and he pulled her sharply back against him. She cried out, whimpering as she felt him come, his cock pulsing.

"Bloody hell..." he cursed, his body tight against her as he leaned over to press a kiss on her back. They were all still for a moment, and then he took a shuddering breath. He kissed down her spine as he slid from her and she realized how shaky she was.

"Holy shit," Thalia breathed and rolled to her side. Kalen leaned over her with a grin, then he pressed a kiss to her lips.

"That was fantastic." His voice was way too loud, but she couldn't help but smile back. He rolled off the bed and went to rescue Maggie who was whimpering and squirming in the chair.

"You are so incredibly hot, baby. Have I told you that lately?" James had taken care of the condom and was pulling her back against him. Every cell of her skin was humming, she was welted and sore and aching, but she laughed.

"You tell me that all the time." She laughed louder when he nuzzled against her neck and bit down playfully.

"I'm sure I don't say it nearly enough." His words filled her with light. He had made her fantasy come true, and not only enjoyed it with her, but seemed as exhilarated as she felt. Under all of the exhaustion anyway.

"I love you, James, and it is ridiculous how hot you are." Thalia grinned and looked over her shoulder at him. His blond hair was a mess, and he arched a brow at her.

"I am *not* ridiculous." He nipped her skin, and she laughed. The pressure of new weight on the bed made Thalia look back to see a very exhausted looking Maggie being laid down by Kalen, who crawled onto the bed behind her. The two pairs faced off in post-orgasmic bliss.

"That was a brilliant Christmas present. I've no idea what ye two will do to top it next year." Maggie smiled before she yawned, cuddling back against Kalen's chest as he wrapped an arm around her. "Oh, and I beat ye, Thalia."

"Huh?" Thalia was smiling, but she was confused as she stared at Maggie.

"I came four times. Ye came three. I win." She grinned and Kalen bellowed a laugh, kissing her neck.

"I love this woman."

"We should all have a drink and then turn in for the night, we've earned some rest." James sat up, his hand running down Thalia's side as she pushed herself up, feeling every aching muscle that would be reminding her of her Christmas present for days.

"Ah, we're good. Think we'll just go to bed." Maggie blushed and sat up with Kalen.

"Oh my God." Thalia stared at Maggie whose eyes widened as she stared at her.

"What?" James was tugging his pants on from the floor, his absolutely clueless face looking between Thalia and Maggie while Kalen's mouth was firmly shut.

"You're fucking pregnant! THAT is why you didn't drink the whisky James brought! And I never saw you take a *sip* during dinner or presents! You. Are. Pregnant." Thalia was shouting, a huge grin on her face as she knelt on the bed, not even remotely caring that she was still naked.

"I don't know what—" Kalen started, but Maggie smacked his arm.

"Oh, hush, Kalen. She knows." Maggie rolled her eyes and grinned. Thalia squealed and tackled Maggie with a hug. Kalen sat up to get out of the way and James walked over to slap him on the back.

"Congratulations, Kalen! You should have told us!"

"Holy shit, how far along are you?! You know Julie is going to demand to throw the baby shower. Do you want a boy or a girl? Oh my God! Can you even have a kid here at Purgatory?!" Thalia was babbling with excitement as she sat up from an equally naked Maggie, who was laughing too hard to answer any questions for a moment.

"We're only eight weeks, and we weren't going to tell anyone until at least twelve. So, no gossiping with the girls. *Especially* Julie! I'll end up with a nursery theme that I had nothing to do with." Maggie blushed bright red, and Kalen pulled his pants on before he stared at her and crossed his arms. She smiled apologetically. "And Kalen was only trying to keep it a secret, like I asked him to."

"Which made hitting me very unnecessary." Kalen was almost pouting, but he was too proud to keep it up. "I'm going to be a dad!" They all cheered, grinning in bliss. Thalia was already picturing a little redhead with Kalen's unique honey-colored eyes. Super cute kid, or kids. Who knew?

"And I think as long as we keep the wee one out of the Dormitory, and the play room, they'll be just fine at Purgatory." Maggie shrugged, pushing her curls back over her ears. "I'm really excited that ye figured it out, I actually wanted to tell ye. But everything says not to, and it was killing me to keep it in all day!"

"Next time just tell me!" Thalia laughed, climbing off the bed to stand by James.

"Well, remember this the next time it takes you six hours to call us with news. Like when ye two decided to actually admit ye loved each other and all that. We were sitting here in suspense most of the day!" Maggie gave her a look that challenged her to argue, but Thalia didn't even bother.

"We're just so happy for you guys." Thalia couldn't stop smiling, and she laughed when Kalen scooped Maggie off the bed, holding her in his arms. He leaned down and kissed her and it was clear they'd be amazing, if not very unique, parents. That kid would never want for love, and it would probably have more adopted aunts and uncles than it could handle.

"We love ye both, and we would have told ye as soon as we hit twelve weeks." Kalen shrugged, looking down at Maggie with a warm grin. "And I'm going to spoil her rotten while she lets me."

Maggie yawned again and Thalia followed suit.

"It's time for bed, we can talk more at breakfast. I'm sure the girls will talk for hours about it tomorrow." James interlaced his fingers with Thalia's, tugging her toward the door.

Kalen nodded, tucking Maggie under his chin as she leaned against him. "Have a good night, we'll see ye both in the morning." James was pulling her through the doorway when Kalen spoke up again, "Hey! One more thing."

"Yeah?" Thalia asked.

"Happy Christmas." He grinned, and they all said it back as they wandered, exhausted, to their rooms. It was a *very* happy, merry, wonderful, brilliant Christmas.

The End

A KALEN AND JAMES FLASHBACK

A Kalen and James Flashback

JAMES

Sixteen Years Ago

"Another round!" Kalen's voice was too loud even for the crowded bar in the club, and the petite bartender cast an annoyed glance toward him. They were in the basement of some abandoned, early twentieth-century warehouse. Neon lights flashing, music booming until there was barely an inch of mental space to think.

Which, for the moment, wasn't such an issue.

Thinking meant remembering that his summer holiday was coming to an end, which meant another year at University, another year of trying to be perfect, and *more* pressure from his father to join his company.

Taking a long swallow of his drink, James glanced over the crowd. A mix of nationalities, a chorus of languages all blurred by the heady pulse of the music. So many beautiful people crammed into this dingy place, all looking for the same thing.

Freedom.

Eastern Europe had so many little holes like this, and he and Kalen had passed through the doors of half of them at least. James was still sipping his beer when his friend planted another full pint on the bar behind him. "Drink!"

Grinning, James caught Kalen's arm halfway to his mouth with the fresh round. "I thought you wanted to find some fun tonight."

"I am finding fun, ye just don't find it the same way I do." Kalen winked and James rolled his eyes and pointed to the pair of dark-haired beauties, both clad in skintight outfits, eyeing the two of them up from across the floor.

"Are you quite sure about that?" James smiled at the taller of the two girls, and she turned to whisper to her friend. The writhing bodies between them did nothing to ease the weight of their interest as their eyes found them once more — and, based on the twitching of his cock, James was definitely interested as well.

"Well, hell, James. Why didn't ye just say so?" A loud laugh preceded the almost painful backslap that landed square between his shoulder blades. Kalen was one sip away from being too drunk to have any fun at all.

"Put the drink down, mate. I think we have other plans." This time, James didn't even need to touch his friend's hand. The other man put the beer down without question, his thick arms crossing over his barrel chest.

"So we do." Kalen raised a hand, bending his fingers in one quick snap, and the girls walked forward like he'd tugged invisible leashes.

Leashes. Hmm, maybe later.

"Are you quite sure your head is ready to play?" James kept his voice low, and Kalen huffed out a breath in response.

"I could drink ye under the table twice over, Brit. Dinnae get in the way of me and *that* bonnie lass." Kalen's accent always grew worse the more he drank, and James watched him as he eyed up the women walking over — although neither of them seemed the least bit nervous about approaching two men who were clearly not here for the dancing.

"Don't frighten them off, all right?" Those were the last words James could get out before the girls were right in front of them, smiling and looking at each other with the knowing looks of long friends. "Hello, ladies."

The taller of the two moved a half-step closer to him, her dark eyes almost at the level of his. "Are you here for the party?" she asked, a thick accent dragging out the vowel sounds as she forced out the English.

At least she could speak it.

"We want the other party." James reached forward to tuck a sleek, dark tendril of her hair behind her ear. It felt like silk against his fingers, her skin still chilled from the night air outside. "We just want company."

"We could be good company." Her friend spoke up, easing closer to Kalen who opened his arms to let her run her palms over his chest. The bastard packed on muscle without any effort while James always stayed lean, and the women gravitated toward his newfound friend on the regular. Kalen's grin showed that he was clearly happy about the contact, and the fact that both girls could communicate.

In Slovakia it had been harder to find English speakers — not like that had stopped them.

"I wanted company too." As if emboldened by her friend, the girl in front of him stepped forward, her pretty lips parting as she took a breath. For a moment, all James could picture was what her mouth would look like when she cried out in pain, and then in pleasure. It was an enticing visual, a temptation, and what had this summer been for except to indulge in temptation and sin?

Dark eyes, gleaming black hair, and James brushed the girl's cheek with his thumb before he slid his fingers into the back of her thick waves and tugged just enough to see her eyes close in pleasure. *Perfect.* "Then maybe you should come with me, beautiful."

"Yes, sir," she purred, and he was undone. His cock was already at half-mast inside his jeans, and the leather sheath she wore as a dress was barely covering enough to be counted as such — but he didn't care. He needed to drown the edges of his world, and behind the curtains at the back of the dance floor was everything he needed to make it happen.

Turning his head, he saw Kalen and the other girl kissing, both of his huge hands engulfing the sides of her head as he held her in place, but the dance floor of this club was *not* where they had planned to spend their evening. "Kalen, are you ready?"

Detaching himself from the girl, he caught her by the back of the neck to hold her still, that dazed look crossing her face that he'd seen on more than a dozen others in the two months he'd known Kalen Reid. "I'm more than ready, James. Are ye?"

Cocky bastard.

"Let's go." Angling his head toward the back of the room, he turned the girl in front of him and swatted her ass to get her moving. The little shiver that ran over her as she started forward made him smile. *Oh yes, this would be a lovely evening.*

The back area of the club was broken away only by a set of thick curtains and a burly guard, and neither did much to quiet the booming music of the DJ on the other side — but here the snap of floggers and whips mixed in with the heady beat. Curled in his lap, Jolana was practically purring. He'd tried to start out slow, but when she'd taken every spank of his hand with barely a wiggle of her hips, James had sought out the collection of toys with an eager eye.

A butter soft deer flogger had barely made her whimper.

A thicker one had only drawn a yelp.

And then he'd slid a bamboo cane from a container, wiped it down, and listened to her scream.

She was beautifully marked, ass and thighs, and when she had begged in broken English for him to fuck her, he couldn't have held back if he'd tried. Condoms were his rule, and he'd convinced Kalen of the same despite his distorted Catholic upbringing, but it paid off in situations like this. In some random city of the Czech Republic he'd fucked Jolana until she'd come twice more, and then he had finally let go.

Unleashed his iron self-control and made her cry out as he'd thrust against her bruised ass and thighs, holding her hips in place as she'd braced against the wall.

It was a bloody miracle they hadn't hit the floor when he'd come buried deep, as the world went white and the pounding rhythm of the music had faded for a moment to leave only his racing pulse. She'd come here for the same thing, not even bothering to share her name until he'd demanded it when he was still holding the first flogger.

That was the magic of these clubs. These temporary oases in a sea of rigidity leftover from Russian oppression. A new wave of youth breaking free of old rules with loud music, and leather, and whips, and BDSM.

Glancing over at Kalen, he couldn't help but respect the guy. He cradled the other dark-haired girl in his lap like something precious, stroking her hair and singing to her softly — yet another thing Kalen outmatched him on. The man could carry a tune like all the Scots, and what did he have to offer?

James looked at the girl in his arms, her head against his shoulder as she recovered under the cover of his button-down, and he knew he couldn't sing to her, couldn't make sweet promises, but he could do the aftercare right. Both he and Kalen had learned the importance of that early in the summer.

Find someone who wants what you want to give, and then give it to them. Watch their reactions, listen, never push it past what they can really handle. Listen for their chosen safe word.

Respect them. Care for them. Hold them when the play is done. Ensure they are okay.

But no matter the gentle side of it, there was no way he could do this back home. No way he could be *this* man in London where his parents were. This was for holiday. This was for men like Kalen without the weight of a family name weighing them down.

It wasn't something that James Thomas Hawkins, son of *the* Henry George Hawkins, could do.

This was a fleeting taste of freedom, and in a week or so it would all be gone, never to be had again. Back to his reality, to his courses and his schoolwork, and his *obligations*.

As if his friend could sense his thoughts, Kalen looked over at him and their eyes met for a moment. The warm smile that had first made him buy the bloke a drink crossed his face, and Kalen shrugged and looked at the two women, wordlessly encouraging him to just enjoy it.

'Stop feking thinking,' the man's voice echoed in his head. How many times had he said that in the last few weeks? Demanding that James stop trying to be so perfect, stop trying to be his father, but it was difficult. It was hard even with a beautiful submissive curled up in his lap, murmuring softly as she shifted and the vicious welts across her ass woke up.

Pulling her closer to his chest, he checked that his shirt was covering her appropriately, likely more than that leather sheath had in the first place, but she was his for the moment, and that meant he was going to protect her. To watch over her — even if it were only for a little longer.

"*Musíme jít domů, Jolana.*" The girl in Kalen's lap spoke, and Jolana lifted her head, twisting to turn and face her friend, exposing herself in the process.

"*Nyní?*" Jolana asked, and James kicked himself for not learning at least a little Czech before they'd stumbled into the Republic. Still, when she leaned up and kissed him gently he returned it, tugging her a little closer so she could understand without the language barrier how much he appreciated her trust. She was the one to cut it off. "We must go to home now."

"Of course. Thank you, Jolana. For tonight." He smiled at her and she kissed him again before slipping off his lap, standing nude in the room without a single flicker of self-doubt. But, why should she? She was gorgeous, all soft feminine curves and round breasts as she looked for her underwear and the dress.

In a matter of moments the two girls were dressed, and he and Kalen were standing. "Can we take ye home?" he asked, but the girls waved the offer away.

"No. This was fun, yes?" Kalen's girl asked, and he grinned and pinched her ass where her welts still ached. The sweet yelp from her lips was clipped short by her laugh.

"Very fun," Kalen answered.

"Are you here next week?" Jolana asked, and James shook his head, already knowing they were heading back toward central Europe the next day.

"My apologies, beautiful, but we have to head home too."

"England?" she asked, a softness in her voice that made something tickle in his chest.

Why did she sound sad?

"I'll be in London, Kalen back in Edinburgh." James shrugged, plastering on the aristocrat smile that had pulled women toward *him* all summer. "But I don't think I'll forget tonight."

Even if I forget your name.

"Well, you are good." Jolana held up his shirt for him, and James took it with a shrug.

"Thank you, but I'm not sure that's the right word for me."

Laughing, Jolana caught her friend's hand and locked eyes with him for a moment. "It is the right word. You are good, I know." Winking at him, she turned and followed as her friend led her out of the back area, through the curtain, and into the storm of noise in the main club space.

Sunrise was a few hours away, and in an hour or so they'd start shutting things down, packing everything away so this club could disappear like it had never been. The dilapidated couches they had lounged on might be left behind, or piled into the backs of trucks, James and Kalen would never know.

And it really didn't matter.

"Drink?" Kalen offered, and James shrugged, knowing he'd pick up the tab either way.

"That sounds like a brilliant idea."

A few minutes later they were back at the bar, except now the dancers were a little less energetic and the music slightly more docile, although the volume was still loud enough to make his bones vibrate. Kalen ordered two scotches, and whatever amber colored liquid they poured was definitively *not* scotch but was a strong enough alcohol to numb the edges of reality now that the submissives were gone. "Yer thinking again," Kalen chastised as he pressed the glass into his hand.

"Term is starting soon, I've got to head back." James took a sip, hissed at the harshness of it, and tried to stare out at the crowd and not the man who had quickly become his friend.

"Right, yer fancy University that makes ye *so happy*." A quiet scoff preceded the other man taking a long drink of the liquid, except Kalen didn't even flinch at the acrid taste.

"I thought you had given up on mocking me."

"Nah, I mostly stayed quiet so ye would keep buying our drinks!" That loud, booming laugh drew eyes toward them, but Kalen didn't care a bit. Then the man settled his gaze on him, his voice turning more serious. "Ye shouldn't try so hard to be someone ye don't want to be, James."

"You don't understand."

"Yer right. I dinnae grow up with money, or all yer aristocratic prestige, but I *do* know when someone is the same and yer just like me, James. If ye can't see that after all this, I dinnae know what ye want me to say." Shrugging, Kalen turned his eyes to the crowd, leaving James to his own thoughts and the bitter alcohol that was supposed to pass for decent scotch in this corner of Eastern Europe.

He'd been raised on nice things, nice liquors, nice manners — none of which fit in with the things he had always known he enjoyed. The look of a woman tied or bound, the sweet sound of a feminine cry when he delivered the pain they craved, their moans of pleasure when he gave exactly what they needed. All of that was what made him happy, but it wasn't reality. It was for back rooms. For underground basement holes like this makeshift club.

It was a new millennium, yes, but the world was ever the same.

The expectations weren't changing.

Especially his.

James took another long drink, the burn barely registering amidst the blur of his thoughts, but he managed to form a few words. "I'll miss you, Kalen. After I go back, I'm going to bloody miss *this*. Every bit of it."

"Oh, yer my brother now, whether ye want it or not. We dinnae share what we have without being brothers, and that means yer with me for life." Kalen lifted his glass into the air like he'd made a proclamation to some waiting audience, and James could do nothing but chuckle and lift his glass as well.

"Cheers to that." He grinned and settled back against the bar. Remembering the times they had shared a submissive, striping her body, pinning her between them, making her come and clench them both. It had been good, the whole bloody summer had been wonderful. "Alright, brother. We still have about a week to make our way back to London. What do you have planned?"

"Planned?" Kalen's booming laughing came again, but it was infectious and the others around them were smiling despite their irritation. "I have nae planned a single step since I left Edinburgh, and I found my way to ye, so I dinnae think I'll plan much at all."

"Well, then what about tomorrow?" It was hopeless to fight the tugging of his lips as he smiled at his friend, the man who had called him *brother*, and who understood him more than any relative by blood ever had.

"Someone spoke of another event in Munich on Wednesday." Kalen lifted his eyebrows, rolling his head until they were looking at each other again.

"Munich is southwest, we need to be headed back toward England."

"Will the world end if yer a few days late, James?" With a grin, Kalen opened the door to temptation like he had so many times before, but it didn't take much to get James to walk through. He'd behaved for so long, been the dutiful son for so long… this holiday had been the first time in his life he'd felt like a real person instead of a puppet. Some Pinocchio with golden strings tugged by his parents, bowing and obeying every whim.

But he was never meant to bow, he knew that now.

In his core, he knew he was meant for more.

He was meant to be a Dominant.

Just like Kalen was.

"We can go to Munich." James nodded, laughing when Kalen let out a cheer and turned to order another round. They'd had their fun with a pair of beautiful submissives, and the hotel room was reserved, waiting for them to stumble back.

This time, Kalen had the good sense to order the local vodka and it tasted much cleaner and made both of them a little less homesick for the good whisky of their countries. Tapping their glasses, Kalen leaned against the bar to take a deep breath. "Ye know, I was sure I was broken when I left Edinburgh. Damned and cursed…" A long beat of silence followed his words, filled by the music still pounding loudly against the earthen walls. "But ye understand, don't ye? This thing we both want. What Elita and Jolana wanted."

"I understand," James agreed, but it was bittersweet. Once he and Kalen had found the right connections, it hadn't been hard to find the next party in the next city. The next submissive, or pair of submissives, or orgy of similarly minded people. It was like an undercurrent in the world, pulsing just under the surface, and one simply needed the right set of words, the right address, the right date and time to tap into it.

Any other day of the week, this place would be a vacant building. Abandoned post-World War II. Some useless factory from the USSR days, coated in snow outside so dense that James still wondered if the girls they'd let leave without an escort had warm enough clothes to protect them. But, they had been given the address, the date and time, the right words to say — and here they were.

Twisted wishes satisfied.

James smiled to himself, staring down into the clear liquid in his glass as he spoke, "I really will miss this when it's over, brother."

"Who says it has to end? Ye can find a girl like that in London, ye just have to look."

Scoffing, James glanced at his friend. "Like you can find a girl in Edinburgh?"

"Scotland is different, and ye know that."

"Say whatever you like, Kalen, we both know that *this* world, that girls like *this*, are few and far between, and we're going to have to give it up eventually." His next drink had a satisfying burn to it, settling into the heat already thrumming in his veins, beckoning him toward the oblivion of getting fully pissed so he could block out his future for a few more days.

"Ye dinnae think ye will marry a girl like this?" Kalen laughed again, but it was lower, more subtle. "Ye would be miserable if ye married someone else."

"Maybe I'll never get married then, it's not like I have to." Shrugging, James upended his glass and turned around, waving at the woman behind the makeshift tables and shelves that served as the bar in this place. She was already pouring when he heard Kalen huff out a breath, turning as well.

"We both know yer parents will want ye to marry."

The narrow, pointed truth of it would have hurt more if he weren't already near drunk. "They have Katherine for that."

"What about the family name?" Kalen asked, and the weight of reality returned despite James' growing inebriation.

"Fuck the family name. No one will want me for me." James snagged the next drink almost before the bartender had let go of it, taking a long draught. All of the painful realities he'd tried so desperately to escape piling one on top of the other in his mind. "They'll either want my family name, or our money." He stole another drink as he stared at the smooth grain of the bar top. "...or they'll want some aristocrat to smile at their dinners, to bring some elegance to their home, and I just *can't*."

"James—"

"You know it's true, Kalen, even if it's not the same as your issues. When I go home, I'm going back to the proverbial silver spoon and all that comes with it." James raised a hand at the room around them. Leather clad, alcohol infused, where the soft cries of submissives from beyond the DJ seemed to blend with the music like they were meant for it. "This world will never pass for acceptable."

"Ye dinnae know that, James."

Lifting his eyes to his friend, he shrugged and tossed back the last of his new drink, welcoming the blur that waited beyond it. "I don't know what woman would be able to handle both halves of me. The aristo and the dominant."

"She's out there, just like there's a woman waiting for a poor Scotsman who is a shitty Catholic." Kalen tipped up his own glass to finish it, and the both of them rested their glasses on the bar top for a refill, which the bartender seemed to sense without any direction.

"You still go to church every Sunday, Kalen. Don't think I haven't noticed."

The other man laughed softly, nodding at the woman behind the bar before he lifted his glass. "Yeh. I've been burning priests' ears from Warsaw, to Rome, to Edinburgh itself. It doesn't make me any less damned, or any more worthy of a good woman." Kalen faced him head on before adding, "But yer different, James. There will be someone for ye, even if I never find a woman for me."

"It seems to me we're both snookered then."

"Ye mean we're royally feked," Kalen summarized as he tilted back his drink.

"Although the Queen might disagree, I'll have to say *yes*." James left it at that, knowing that another drink was coming on the heels of this one, and likely another after that. By dawn they'd be well and truly pissed and asking for directions back to the hotel in broken variations of English and German and Russian.

Because who would ever want all of the strings attached to someone like him? James Thomas Hawkins, hopeless dominant *and* heir to his family's power and control with all the messy society rules and expectations that came with it.

Many would want one, without the trouble of the other, but one thing he'd learned running around Europe with Kalen was that the two halves could not be separated.

He was all or nothing — which meant most likely he'd be all and *alone*. Forever.

The End

JAMES AT THE AUCTION

James at The Auction

JAMES

After almost an hour driving out of the city and deep into the American countryside, James was surrounded by trees and abandoned by his GPS as he drove slowly up the sunlit drive to Marcus Williams' house.

Everything looked so picturesque. So perfect, and yet it was the exact opposite.

This was hell, and he was driving straight into it.

He was a monster for even being in this car, on this drive, in the goddamn country. There was no excuse for coming here. No justification for why he'd opened the website again to look at the cameras — but once he'd seen her sleeping he hadn't been able to look away. Late afternoon, in his office of all places, he had pulled up the feed out of desperation. Too many nights alone, too many unchecked fantasies running through his mind with no outlet, and then… *her*.

She looked so peaceful in sleep, the sheets half across her, revealing her breasts to the cameras along with the sleek curve of her waist just before it dipped under the fabric. His cock had kicked to attention, painfully hard under the desk as his fingers had tightened around the small device. Hating himself, but leaving it open, he'd propped it against a tape dispenser and gone back to work. Trying to pretend he was a good man, trying to convince himself he was innocent, even though a captive girl slept in that prison with its beautiful façade.

The movement when she finally awoke and climbed out of bed caught his eye, and he immediately turned away from his monitor to watch her on his iPad. *Wrong, so wrong.* Every fiber of him, every echo of Kalen's angry rants in his head, told him to turn it off. Condemned him for ever logging back in, but her fear was palpable. A portion of him even enjoyed it, and he hated that part of himself.

Still, he'd watched.

Watched as the camera angle had changed as she checked herself in the bathroom mirror, gloriously naked, but already marred by Marcus' brutish methods. He had almost slammed the iPad face down, but then she'd attacked the door. Screaming, raging, and he had given in to temptation even further. Plugging in his headphones and inching up the volume to listen to her desperate, angry voice.

Bloody perfection.

When Marcus finally opened the door, he'd smiled to watch this woman stand up to him, argue with him — and then she'd slapped him.

His heart had stopped. In awe of her strength, unsure of how long the bastard had even had this girl, but from then on he had been unable to look away. Canceling meetings, claiming a personal emergency to stay at home and watch her. Ruining his sleep schedule, ignoring his friends, his parents, his job, just so he wouldn't miss a moment of her.

Thalia.

She was glorious. Submissive, yet brave. Incredibly responsive, but unbroken. She was not some broken doll of Anthony and Marcus, she was still whole. Real. And in so much danger.

The emails he'd sent to Anthony had been curt but pointed. There was no doubt he still hated the man, *both* of them, but he wanted her out of their hands. He wanted her free before they ruined everything good about her, distorted every natural submissive quality that Marcus had seen in her when he had kidnapped her.

It was more than wrong to watch him hurt her, assault her, force himself on her. It was worse that he was hard as he did, that he found his hand drifting to his incessant cock as she moaned and cried out. To be aroused by the way she begged and pleaded in that soft, desperate voice.

But he had. Over and over.

He'd come more times than he could count in the last week to the sounds of her cries and moans, but Anthony had caved to his requests for an early auction. No doubt in an effort to pry Marcus away from her, for even James could see he was attached to her, but now it was time. He had flown halfway around the world to get her away from him, to buy her from them, and he could only pray that she wasn't as damaged as she'd appeared after Anthony's brutal torture.

As he pulled up to the house, a luxurious home that looked half-log cabin and half-modern construction, he was disappointed by the number of other vehicles already parked outside. Parking, he contemplated grabbing the bag of women's clothes from the backseat, but he knew that would be too presumptuous.

Leaving it behind, he climbed from the large vehicle and locked it with a press of a button. His heart raced at the idea that soon he would be in the same room with her, and the bastards who had ripped her from her life. Violated her and blackmailed him the last time he'd tried to confront them about their brutish, false version of BDSM.

Calling on every skill he had to control his expression and mannerisms, he knocked on the front door. Anthony answered, and although he had the gut instinct to hit the man, he managed a polite smile and a nod. "Anthony, I see you invited others."

"You're not the only one interested in purchasing the slave, Dr. Hawkins." His empty eyes swiveled to the room full of men as he opened the door wide.

"I see," he replied as he stepped inside. Refusing to show how irritated he was that Anthony had clearly baited other avid watchers into coming to this auction. An auction for a real person. Not a willing submissive, but a brutally kidnapped woman forced into slavery.

"Marcus will bring Thalia out soon. Until then please have a drink and enjoy yourself."

"Thank you," James lied, offering a polite nod as he turned away from the monster who had orchestrated this entire empire of nightmares. Violence and rape, that's all they did. The sheen of BDSM across the top of it was a worse lie than anything he may speak aloud in this hell of a house, and it took effort to remind himself why he was here.

Thalia. The girl.

Somewhere amidst the obsessive watching and the guilt-ridden erections, he'd decided he was going to save her. Rescue her. As if he could ever be some fictional version of a white knight after every dollar he'd spent funding their grotesque operation. It didn't even matter if for the last year and a half it had been blackmailed out of him… he'd still paid. He'd still opened it on desperate nights, in weak-willed moments, and even though he'd hated himself for every failure — he had still opened it the day he'd seen Thalia for this first time.

Being in this living room was only further proof of his own evil, but if he could save even one of the women his fortune had allowed to be taken and violated then maybe he could forgive himself.

Even if she never did.

Not bloody likely.

Ignoring the selection of alcohol set out, he meandered around the room, making polite conversation until one particular guest of the Williams brothers remarked on how much he'd like to whip the girl bloody to make her submit. It had taken all of his self-control to step away from the bastard and plant himself in an oversized black armchair. The fact that it was the same one Marcus had spanked Thalia in her first night in the house was not lost on him. He had watched the archived video where she had touched herself on this very carpet, had seen as he attached the handcuffs to the thick metal brackets embedded on the side and spanked her until she'd come despite her fear.

A natural submissive. A natural masochist.

Thalia was special, precious, and she'd spent a week being brutalized by these monsters.

Will you be any different? The question hovered in his mind and he swallowed, wondering if it wouldn't be wise to grab a glass of whisky just to settle his barely contained rage, but then he heard the others around him fall into a brief moment of silence as she entered the room. Crawling on hands and knees, head down like something straight out of his worst fantasies.

He pressed his fingers into the leather arms of the chair as she knelt next to the bastard who had done so many horrible things to her. The multi-colored bruises across her body made his stomach turn. Arms, ribs, hips… so many marks from the asshole who dared to call himself a Dom. A Master.

Kalen would rip the man limb from limb if he had the chance, but it would end badly. All of it. And right now, he needed to focus on the girl — which wasn't a hardship. Every line of her body screamed submission, but he could tell she was looking at him. Her head lifted just enough for him to catch her eyes and he forced himself to stay in the chair and beckon her with his hand.

Thalia instantly looked up at Marcus, silently asking his permission, and he saw the man mouth words as he glared at him. Disgust, rage, all of it was painted across his features, but a moment later the girl was crawling to his feet. The room watched, but he was barely aware of it as the breath caught in his chest and she settled before him.

A wet dream come to life, a slave for the taking, and he wanted her. Wanted to buy her, to place a bid already to get her out of there, but he didn't even know how far gone she was, or if she'd go with him peacefully. Bloody hell, he didn't even know if he could handle this if he left with her, or what he'd do if someone else in this room was actually able to outbid him.

Unlikely, but possible.

Pushing all of his distracting thoughts to the back of his mind, he spoke. "Hello, Thalia. I must say you are even more beautiful in person." It was an understatement, because she was everything he wanted. His cock was twitching, waking up just at the sight of her breasts rising and falling with her silent breaths, and then she spoke.

"Thank you, sir." It was like a jolt of electricity to his nervous system. To have this woman kneeling before him, to be able to reach out and touch her if he dared, but he knew what would happen as soon as Marcus' patience waned.

"He will not let me talk to you long, so I'm going to get right to the point. I've enjoyed watching you on—" He stopped, catching Marcus' gaze above her head. There was nothing but rage in the man's stare, but he wasn't here to engage with him. He was here to take Thalia, and that meant not stepping on the bastard's toes. *Yet.* "Wait, you don't know your Master's name, do you."

She shook her head slightly, fingers digging into the weave of the carpet underneath her bruised knees. "No, sir."

"Interesting," he lied, unable to take his eyes from Marcus as the man fumed, and he smiled because he knew she didn't know the bastard's name and he knew exactly how to build some level of connection with her. Leaning close, he spoke softly. "Well, my name is James. I think you should know my name... but remember not to use it."

"Yes, sir," she whispered, and he wanted nothing more than to scoop her into his lap and promise that the other monsters in the room would never get their hands on her again. That he'd protect her, at least from everyone but himself. Maybe even himself, if he could manage the self-control to let her go. To not touch her, taste her, give her pleasure at his hand and make her cry out like Marcus had.

But had any of her pleasure been real? Had it all been forced? Had she been drugged as well as raped?

Swallowing, he made himself speak so he didn't lose the opportunity. "I've enjoyed watching you on his cameras. I have questions though... has he given you any drugs while you've been here?"

Her head lifted, and the most perfect hazel eyes met his. Wide and innocent, terrified and confused, her intense gaze had him curious and he felt his brow lift just before she dropped her gaze back to the floor. "No, sir, no drugs that I am aware of, and I'm sorry I looked at you, sir." She swallowed, tense and scared at his feet, and he hated it. He wanted her eyes back on his, wanted to see her smile, laugh. He wanted her safe, and right now her muscles were twitching in mindless fear that he was going to hurt her because she'd violated the bastards' rules.

Easing his fingers into her hair, he felt her flinch, but she didn't pull away as he gently pet her, trying to soothe her and reassure her that he would never hurt her. At least, not in any way she didn't *want* be hurt. Finally, her shoulders relaxed a little and he felt his own tension ease. "So, you're trained to keep your eyes down, that's fine. But you don't need to be worried. I obviously surprised you with the question. I'm not upset with you." Continuing to move his fingers back and forth on her scalp, he smiled because she was leaning toward him. Craving the gentle touch, like any abused creature would, but if she were his that would never be a problem. She would receive all the love he had to give — whether it came at the end of his flogger or his tongue.

Still, she was silent, and he lowered his voice to continue explaining. "I only asked the question because you've been incredibly responsive to this lifestyle, Thalia, and I didn't know if that was natural or chemically induced to attract the attention of those at this little party for your debut." Dragging his nails over her scalp he scanned the room of other monsters planning to bid on her, settling his gaze on the bastard who had promised to whip her until she bled. The man's gaze was squarely on her back, where he could see random bruises beneath the waves of her hair. Clenching his jaw, he forced his eyes back to her. "And everyone here is looking at you, Thalia. I think you've made quite the impression." *I know you have.*

"Thank you, sir," she whispered, and he hated the softness in her voice that told him how nervous she was. It was fear. Of him, of Marcus, of Anthony, of all the bastards in the room whom he was pretending to be different from.

He wasn't different, but he had to know the truth. "I understand you didn't plan to end up here, but I need you to be honest with me. Do you enjoy it?"

Silence filled the space between them, even as her hips shifted slightly in a way that made him curious if she were wet or not. Finally, she spoke. "I don't know, sir." More shifting, and then an even more insecure answer. "Maybe, sir?"

Leaning forward, he gently touched under her chin to lift her gaze to his. Multi-colored hazel eyes flicked between his, her paralyzing fear so clear that he could taste it, and he knew he shouldn't like it, but he couldn't help but smile because he could erase that fear. "Your Master has always had a talent for finding women with a natural inclination toward submission. I've never found myself particularly interested in one of his girls until you though."

Not a total lie. He'd watched other women — *victims* — but he had never harassed Anthony to push an auction sooner or flown halfway around the world to buy one. He'd just threatened to expose them and been blackmailed to keep paying.

Although the choice to keep watching was his own.

"May I ask a question, sir?"

"Yes," he answered, grateful for the distraction from his own tormenting thoughts.

"I don't know what to do, I just need to know — can you tell me why you are interested in me, sir?" The way her eyes widened as she finished, the little gasp before she held her breath, it all told him how terrified she was to even ask the question, but he really wasn't sure how to answer.

"Thalia…" He sighed, pulling his touch from her chin to allow her eyes to drop if she wished, although they stayed on him. "You are feisty. After all, I saw the incident with your Master's patio door. And as far as obedience? I would say that you are lacking."

But you are perfect to me.

Those words he could not say. It would cross a line he couldn't uncross, and there was no justification for him to do so. She hadn't said she wanted to be with him, and she had no idea how wealthy he was, or that he'd come here just to get her somewhere safe, or any reason to come with him other than his word. He just wanted her to know that he wanted *her*. Reaching forward he took her chin between his forefinger and thumb, gently tilting her face until she met his eyes. "But I don't like women who are completely broken down. There's no passion left, no spirit, and that's no fun at all."

Tracing his thumb across her bottom lip took too many liberties, pushing the boundaries of what Marcus would even remotely allow. At any moment he might rip her away, might order her back to his side, and he had to make her understand.

Pulling his hand away, he gave her a reassuring smile. "That's why you caught my attention, Thalia, and I have abandoned quite a bit of my work in the last week in order to watch you."

The girl leaned toward him, seeming as eager as he was to feel more of her, but he could only shift in his seat to adjust the erection misshaping his pants. She wore the bastard's cuffs, his collar, and he had already made her scream that she was his over and over. James' rage over that was inescapable, yet he pushed it down like he had his own guilt, and everything else that the Williams brothers had stirred up in him.

Brazenly, he reached forward and stroked the collar around her throat. "If I wanted to touch you, what would you say?" He hoped she understood his implication, but for once she didn't hesitate with her answer.

"It would be up to my Master, sir."

James stifled the urge to laugh, because she knew well enough what Marcus would hurt her for, and fucking around with a random guest without his permission was one of them. "He's trained you well. If he gave permission, would you be okay with it?"

"Ye— yes, sir," she stumbled over her answer and he tried to swallow his own desire.

"That's... very good, Thalia. Look at me," he demanded, and her eyes snapped up instantly. It was a satisfying bit of obedience and he leaned back in the chair so that he didn't cross a line that would have Marcus in a rage.

"Yes, sir?" she murmured, wide-eyed and beautiful as she waited for his next command.

Fuck it. He leaned forward and threaded his fingers into her silken hair again, holding just firmly enough to keep her eyes on his. "I want you to know that your Master and I have had conflicts in the past about how he acquires his girls." Clenching his teeth, he forced himself to leave out just how familiar he was with what Marcus had done to her. "I haven't watched his cameras in a while due to that conflict. But I saw you slap him, and I was impressed by you, as foolish as that move was. After that... let's just say I was hooked."

He grinned, because *that* he couldn't stop no matter how hard he tried, and the way her lips parted, as if she were inviting a kiss made him hungry for her. But all that left her mouth was more subservience. "Yes, sir?"

There was little patience in him on most days, and with Thalia on her knees in front of him he had none. It was time to see if she could be saved. "I know you don't know me, but I'll ask you not to panic. I'm going to speak to your Master."

"Yes, sir," she said shakily and he ran his fingers ran up the back of her neck as he stood. Her skin was so soft, and she was precious.

Priceless.

But he'd have to name a price anyway.

Marcus straightened as James approached, defensive and angry before he'd even opened his mouth, and he seemed surprised when James offered to shake his hand.

"Dr. Hawkins," Marcus growled, feigning civility as he grabbed onto James' hand and jerked once in a tight-gripped shake.

"I'd offer to let you drop the formality, but I don't think either of us want to be that familiar." James looked at Anthony and gave him a slight nod, not even offering to touch the monster who'd done worse things than Marcus ever had — at least on camera.

"You think you can come to my house and talk to me like this?" Marcus fumed, but James simply shrugged a shoulder.

"My interest in coming here has everything to do with Thalia, and nothing to do with you." Turning to Anthony, he continued without pause. "And I want your permission to touch her—"

"You've *been* touching her for the last ten minutes, asshole."

"—to touch her, *and* taste her," James finished, ignoring Marcus' interruption, but the man's rage finally overflowed.

"No! Fuck no, you can't." Marcus raised his voice and took a half step forward, but Anthony's hand came down on his shoulder, gripping just hard enough to control his younger brother.

"Marcus…" There was a warning tone in Anthony's voice. "Dr. Hawkins is a bidder just like anyone else, and therefore we must at least showcase her talents live."

"I told you this was not the time—"

"Excuse us for a moment." Anthony cut off Marcus' next rant and pushed him toward the dining room.

James nodded, but spoke before they could walk away. "If it affects your decision at all, I'm happy to just buy her now, for twice what you made on the last girl, and enjoy her in private at my hotel."

"We will take that under advisement," Anthony replied, forcing Marcus to walk with him toward the kitchen doorway. His own anger was simmering, a boiling sea of disgust and hate as he watched the two men walk away. Being in this house was making his skin crawl. Touching Marcus, speaking to Anthony as if he held any respect for the man made him feel dirty.

Which, he was.

Everything about this situation was cocked up, but he wasn't going to waste a single moment he could have with Thalia. He had to get her on his side, had to make sure she would go with him if he asked. Turning on his heel, he walked quickly back to the chair and reclaimed it, immediately threading his fingers into her hair. She practically purred, and for a second James could see the attraction to pet play, because with Thalia kneeling by his chair like a loyal pet he was rock hard. Yet, he couldn't take his eyes off Marcus and Anthony, reading their body language with ease. Rage and desperation rolled out from Marcus, while Anthony was cold as always, and clearly irritated with babysitting his emotionally unstable brother.

In truth, they were both unstable, just in different ways, and both of them were monsters.

'As are you,' his head reminded him, and he tore his eyes away from the bastards to look down at Thalia. The proof of his monstrosity, the evidence of his dark desires, but she could also be his salvation… if he could save her.

"Thalia, do you know the man who was with your Master?"

"His partner," she answered, pressing her hair into his touch and he took the hint, gripping tighter to make it sting just a little. She squirmed, and his cock kicked against his fly in response to the sheer sexuality of her soft gasp and rolling hips.

He laughed under his breath, because he was just as enthralled by her as Marcus. "You are so responsive, and your Master is revealing too much of himself. Normally that man that was standing next to him is here to help train the girls, but your Master didn't let him touch you." He tugged lightly at her hair until she looked up at him, craving the intense gaze as her breath came in little shallow pants. *Gorgeous.* "Why do you think that is?"

"Master told me this party had to happen, but that he would keep me safe from his partner. He... he said he shouldn't have let his partner hurt me in the chair." Thalia froze, mouth open in shock for a moment until her face collapsed. Those beautiful hazel eyes brimming with tears, she bit down on her bottom lip and he leaned a little closer so that he could block out the wolves circling her. With his free hand he cupped her face and tugged her lip from between her teeth.

I would always keep you safe. If you were mine, no one would ever harm you again.

James pushed the thought away, because she wasn't his yet, but her expression was sweet and desperate for comfort, which he was happy to provide. "Don't worry, pet." He felt his lips twitch up in a smile that he'd used the word aloud. "I won't tell him you told me, and I thank you for your honesty. Would you like to know what I asked for that has him so upset?"

Releasing her chin, he returned to running his fingers through her silken hair, and she whispered a soft, "Yes, sir."

The girl was staring at the floor, the picture of submission and obedience, and he smirked as he leaned close to whisper in her ear. "I told him I wanted to taste you." A sharp intake of breath, another shift of her hips as her hands curled into small fists on her thighs. He chuckled softly, fighting the urge to taste the delicate skin behind her ear. "And your Master didn't want to share you. So, I offered to buy you right then. He and his associate are discussing it."

Thalia turned toward him. Her perfect mouth so close he felt her exhale against his lips as she spoke. "Sir?"

He pulled himself back before he did something foolish, well more foolish than this entire insane trip. The plan was to save her, to get her away from them before they broke her beyond repair. *She's what matters.*

"I know all of this started badly for you, that you were forced into this. I've never been happy about that aspect of their enterprise." Stroking her cheek where he'd seen Marcus strike her more than once, he was haunted by the *other* things the man had done to her. The belt, the orgasms, the way she cried out and begged so sweetly.

Bloody hell.

He shook his head a little, trying to clear it of the vibrant visuals. "I want you to know that with me you could have something consensual, but I will be honest that my appetites are very similar to his. What would change is your right to stop it. You could stop me with a word." *And I would always stop, I would never force you.*

Above her head he saw the brothers approaching the room again, and he wanted to take her away from them right now. Wanted to pull her into his lap and keep her safe, but the rage on Marcus' face promised violence, and he would not make it worse for her. Leaning closer to her, he spoke quickly, "My request has him quite upset, so I need you to be brave, no matter what happens." He glanced up at them, knowing they were going to take her away in just a moment, so he looked into her terrified hazel eyes as guilt clawed him from the inside.

Now or never, James.

"Do you want to stay with him, Thalia? Answer me," he demanded, urging her to speak, and she leaned closer, all her curves answering him, but he needed to hear it. Needed her consent, her permission.

"THALIA! Come here!" Marcus' voice was like a yank on her leash, her body actually jerking as if she felt it, and he took his hands from her to try and stem the virulent anger the man had in his eyes.

Don't you dare hurt her.

Staring across the room, he forced his most neutral, in-control, cold expression and held onto it, because it was taking everything in him not to drag her back to his side where she belonged. The view as she crawled to the bastard was the worst temptation, and he almost stood up when Marcus ripped her upright by her hair. Her sweet cry made his cock twitch, but he wasn't some base animal with no self-control, and he hated Marcus enough to push away the lust he felt for her.

"It seems my newest girl, Thalia, has already attracted an offer my friends. Would any others like to bid?" Marcus' hate wasn't even thinly disguised as he glared across the room at him.

No self-control, Marcus. That has always been your foil.

"What was the offer?" One of the men near a wall asked, and James fought the urge to look at him. If he appeared desperate, it would ruin the negotiation completely.

"The current offer is — substantial. My brother is very interested in accepting it, but as the party has just started we don't want to end the festivities so soon." Those sounded like Anthony's words coming out of Marcus' mouth, but there was no missing the raw edge in his voice.

"We haven't even seen her in action up close, how do we know your little camera feeds have not been edited?" A South African man to the left spoke next, and James pressed his fingers into the arms of the chair so he wouldn't move.

"Excellent point," Marcus growled and shoved her to the floor, forcing Thalia to catch herself on her hands with a gasp. *Bastard.* Unfortunately, James knew she had taken much worse, and as she pushed herself back into a kneel Anthony stepped forward to speak to him.

An intense exchange passed between them, and then Marcus shoved his way past Anthony as he moved toward the kitchen. Thalia's panic was visible from across the room, and his stomach twisted as she shouted, "Master! Please!"

Marcus paused for just a moment before he disappeared through the doorway, and then Anthony had his hands on her. Fisting her hair as he leaned close to whisper something that made her go still with fear.

Thalia replied with a shaky, "Yes, sir," and then Anthony let go of her to clap his hands together, eyes moving around the room.

"Friends, you know that my brother and I provide consistently well-trained submissives. Thalia, as you've observed, is especially responsive." He walked slowly to the center of the room, onto the black carpet where he stopped a mere five feet away from James, and then he snapped his fingers. "Come here, Thalia."

She was crying silently, only a slight hitch in her breath breaking the silence of the room as every man focused on her crawling to Anthony's feet. The sway of her breasts, the way her nose grew pink from the tears — it shouldn't have turned him on, but it did, and James hated himself for it.

"Down," Anthony commanded, and Thalia bent forward to put her forehead against the floor, but she was still sitting on her heels. Sighing, Anthony grabbed her hips and lifted her ass into the air, and the Frenchman behind her took a step to his right to get a better view.

Thalia was terrified, her entire body flinching as the bastard started fingering her in front of everyone, and he didn't even care.

"Gentlemen, she's already wet and we haven't even played with her yet." Anthony's self-satisfied tone made James angry. If Thalia really was wet, *he* had made her that way, not Marcus, not Anthony — *him*.

He should be the one touching her, and he would give her pleasure instead of fear. He'd draw out sweet, soft cries from her, not whimpers and panic. It was clear he wasn't the only one unimpressed by Anthony's skill with her as one of the men huffed and spoke. "The girl is not being very responsive today, is she now?"

"Maybe you scared her too bad. That's been an issue for you before, hasn't it?" The South African on the left was smirking, and James fought the urge to smile at Anthony, but the urge fled when he moved forward and held her against the floor by her neck. No longer even pretending to want to give her pleasure.

"She's given us a little trouble, as you all know, but we have turned her around rather quickly. She just needs a little incentive to behave." His fingers tightened and she yelped, and James was on his feet before he could stop himself.

Keeping his tone calm, he tried his best to look and sound casual as he moved a little closer to her. "If you wouldn't mind, I'd be happy to do the demonstration. It is what I asked your brother for, after all, and I am the high bid." James paused to look around at the other men. "As long as no one else objects, of course?"

"Let the Brit show her off, he got the ball rolling on this party anyway." That comment came from the man who had described how much he wanted to whip her until she bled.

A quiet sob escaped Thalia as Anthony stood upright, tugging the cuffs of his shirt down over his wrists. "Of course, you should have the opportunity."

Walk carefully, James.

"Thank you." He inclined his head to Anthony and moved beside her, tracing a gentle path down her spine to ensure she knew it was him. "Thalia has been quite responsive to her Master, you are right. I think she's just feeling a little shy with everyone here." *And terrified of you bastards.*

Winding his fingers into her hair, he gave a soft tug and commanded, "Up." She obeyed perfectly, and he did what he'd wanted to since the moment she'd looked up into his eyes — he guided her back to the chair and pulled her across his lap. "Spread your knees."

Another command that she followed without question, and it fed the monster inside him to have her under his control. To have her in his arms, pressed against his cock as he tugged her closer. Running his hand over her ass, he loved the way she twisted but he tightened his grip in her hair.

"Stay still, Thalia."

"Yes, sir," she answered quickly, a breathy purr to her voice that told him she'd stopped crying already, that maybe she trusted him enough to believe he'd keep her safe. Maybe.

Please trust me.

It was a silent wish that he wasn't violating her as he slid his hand between her thighs and rested his palm over the heat of her pussy. She'd said he could touch her, that if given permission she would say yes, and he had to believe it. Pressing a little more firmly between her legs, she did exactly what he'd predicted — she wiggled her perfect ass and he lifted his hand and spanked her. Not hard, barely hard enough to leave a blooming pink mark on her pale skin, and he soothed it with slow circles. "Stay still," he admonished, suppressing his smile as she settled again.

Nodding, she spoke softly, "Yes, sir." *So submissive. So perfect. So mine.*

Returning his hand to her pussy, he kept every touch infuriatingly gentle. Distracting her from her fear, from Marcus and Anthony and the men steadily moving closer to watch every small twitch of her body. Listening to every sweet sigh and whine as he teased her. "What do you want, Thalia?"

"More, sir," she breathed, tilting her hips a little, and he immediately spanked her. A little harder this time, but there was no panicked writhing, she wasn't trying to get away. In fact, he could smell her arousal now and it had his cock straining for release.

"Of course, if you stay still." Inching his hand over her ass, he dipped one finger between her folds. That low, quiet moan was torture, but he didn't care. Rewarding her obedience with a brush against her clit.

"Sir?" Thalia was panting, soaking wet, and there was not a single man in the room that did not have his eyes on her.

"Do you like this, Thalia?" he asked, applying just a little more pressure to her clit.

"Yes, sir!" She moaned and a buzz of side conversations picked up, but he wanted her focused on him, on this moment, *his* touch. Changing his tactic, he slid two fingers deep into her slick heat, groaning as he felt her clench around him. Turning his hand, he brushed her clit lightly with his thumb and her hips jolted forward, seeking more, but he denied her. Pulling his hand away to deliver a harder spank.

"Her skin colors beautifully."

"Perfect handprint."

Their commentary was accurate, but he wished this first scene was in private. Just the two of them, so that he could reassure her, and tell her just how beautiful she is, how deserving she is of safety and protection and the right to consent. That urge had him rubbing her clit harder this time, teasing her entrance with his fingers as he held her down over his lap, fist tightening in her hair as her breaths grew shorter.

But then she bucked against his lap, torturing his cock as she disobeyed, and he removed his hand to land another swat to her ass. "I'm sorry, sir," she whined, sounding even more lovely than she ever had on the cameras.

"You are lovely, Thalia." *Understatement.* She was glorious, and he thrust his fingers back inside her, reveling in the moan that escaped the moment he touched her clit again.

"Thank you, sir," she said on another moan, leaning her head forward against his grip on her hair, and he gave the masochist in her what she wanted. A harder pull, a spike of pain to contrast against the pleasure he focused between her thighs. "Sir, may I come? Sir?" Desperate and breathy, begging in all the right ways, and he continued touching her even as she squirmed and panted and moaned.

He would do whatever it took to have her, to keep her. Any amount of money, *anything*.

"Come for me, Thalia," he commanded, and as he found her g-spot with his fingers she came hard. Arching, writhing, moaning and whining, and he kept his eyes glued to her even as the men that were too close for his comfort were groaning along with her. Wolves salivating, but he couldn't deny that he was still craving more of her.

Removing his touch from her slowly, he slid his fingers between his lips and finally tasted her. Closing his eyes to the monsters around him for a moment to just savor the warmth of her body, the sheen of sweat on her skin, and the tang of sweetness coating his tongue.

"Thank you, sir," she said softly, breaking him from his reverie, and he laughed a little as he ran a hand over the pink marks he'd left on her ass, doing his best to ignore the bruises and lingering evidence of Marcus' abuse.

Still, he was in the man's house, and she was technically his property. As wrong as that was.

Summoning a smile, he answered her, "My pleasure. You taste so sweet." Squeezing her ass gently, he did what he knew he had to. "You should kneel again, pet."

That word again. As if she were already his to protect and care for.

"Well, you've seen her perform. Do we have any other bids?" Anthony's voice was still cold, but he didn't even look at the man. He couldn't take his eyes away from Thalia as she got her breathing under control.

"Two-fifty US," the black man with the French accent was quick to answer, but James wasn't concerned.

"That is not enough to surpass the current bid."

"Three-hundred." The American with the penchant for whips was next.

"Just tell us how much the Brit fucking offered," a man from behind the chair growled.

"Four-hundred and twenty thousand US." Anthony glanced at James, and he met the man's eyes. "You did say twice what the last girl sold for, correct?"

"I did." For once, James felt no awkwardness about his family's fortune because it meant it was very unlikely anyone in the room could outbid him. Even if they wanted to empty their bank accounts for her.

"Four-fifty," the American countered and James waited for Anthony to turn to him once more.

"We have a new high bid. Will you counter it?"

"I need an answer to a question I asked her before I bid again." Looking down at her, he softened his voice. "Thalia, do you want to stay with your Master?"

Panic took her. Her shoulders jerked like she was crying, but he couldn't even hear her as she looked around until she found Marcus against the wall. The bastard just stared at her, arms crossed. Intimidating and threatening without a word spoken. After all, she still bore all the marks of his 'training.'

Thalia seized up on the floor beneath him, and he saw the tears falling and knew he was going to lose her if he didn't act.

"Thalia…" Slipping from the chair he crouched in front of her, touching her chin to get her to look at him. To focus on him. "I'm only asking for your honesty. Do you want to come with me?"

Please. The plea was unspoken, but he hoped she could see his sincerity. Could trust that he would keep her safe, would treat her well, would care for her just as he had with her secure over his lap.

Her breath shuddered, and for a moment he was sure she would tell him no, but then tear-filled hazel eyes met his and she nodded slightly. "Yes, sir."

"NO!" Marcus shouted, but James stood fast.

"I'm taking her. I'll outbid anyone, understood?" He met Anthony's gaze first, and then looked around the room. Daring any of the monsters to try and challenge his assets, but they backed down.

"She's not for sale!" Marcus stomped forward, shouting at him from the other side of Thalia.

"She, in fact, is, and I accept the bid," Anthony replied, but Marcus was beyond reason. He grabbed Thalia's arm and tried to yank her to her feet, and without a thought James' hand shot forward and wrapped around Marcus' wrist.

"Don't touch my property, Marcus." There were a few quiet gasps as he used the bastard's name, but it was worth the danger of retaliation just to get her away from him. Gently helping Thalia to her feet, he tucked her behind him, keeping himself between her and the brothers.

"Thalia, please, just stay with me. Things will be different, I promise, just choose to stay," Marcus begged, but Thalia pressed herself closer to him and he knew she would not fall for this façade.

Anthony approached, trying to control the situation, and a moment later Marcus reared back and punched him hard enough to send him to the floor. "Fuck you, Anthony!"

James hid the self-satisfied smile, and took a step back from them, nudging Thalia backward as she clung to the back of his shirt.

It only took a moment for Anthony to be back on his feet, still displaying no emotion as he wiped at the blood on his mouth. "Take Thalia and leave, Dr. Hawkins."

"NO! Thalia, do not leave," Marcus ordered and walked toward them, but Thalia clung tighter to him and Marcus froze. The fact that he was actually surprised by her reaction only proved James right.

"I told you your methods weren't perfect," he growled, enjoying the way he paled as his eyes shifted. Turning around, he ran his hands down Thalia's arms, leaning down to meet her gaze as she drew in panicked gasps. The fear was going to push her into shock if he didn't take action. Rapidly unthreading the cuffs, he abandoned them on the floor and gave her a reassuring smile. "Let's go to the car and talk."

Thalia didn't speak, she barely even nodded, but it was enough. It was consent, and he leaned down to lift her into his arms, heading for the door as the other men stepped aside.

"The auction is over. We look forward to continuing a business relationship with each of you. Drive carefully."

Not bloody likely, James thought as Anthony dismissed the other men. Stepping out into the evening light and the fresh air, he took a deep breath and held her tighter to his chest. "I am sorry that did not go more smoothly. I knew he was attached to you…" He laughed softly against her hair. "I just didn't know how much."

She was dazed, unresponsive, and he was worried she was regretting her decision. The only way to comfort her was to prove it to her, to prove that he wasn't like the other monsters. Yes, he'd watched the feed from the Williams brothers. For years. But he hadn't known it wasn't consensual until a little over a year before.

Still, how could he ever explain to her that he'd known she was being assaulted and still watched. Still flown halfway across the world to buy her like she was chattel.

Tucking her into the passenger seat, he shut the door and moved to the driver's side, watching her carefully for any outward sign of distress, of fear… of him. "Thalia," he tried to get her attention, but she was staring out the window in the other direction.

Sighing, he started the car and turned on the heat to try and make her a little more comfortable, but after another long minute of silence he couldn't handle it.

"Thalia?" he raised his voice and her head snapped to look at him.

"Yes, sir? Um, I mean, Master?" Her voice shook and he reached over to cup her chin, keeping his touch light.

"Calm down, pet. It will take a bit for us to get to know each other, and while I wouldn't call myself gentle…" He moved his hand into her hair, winding his fingers through to tug until he knew she would get that tingling buzz across her scalp. "I am understanding."

Her lips parted, perfectly pink, and he couldn't resist anymore. He pulled her toward him and took her mouth, kissing her with all of the pent-up aggression and lust he'd held back for the sake of the auction. Tightening his grip in her hair, he felt her moan against his mouth. She melted into his touch like she was meant for it, and he knew he could crush her with his attentions if he weren't careful. This would be a delicate dance. Risky and dangerous, but she was worth it.

He just needed her to know that she was more than property to him. She *wasn't* property, even if he had spent half a million US dollars purchasing her.

Bloody hell, this was already so complicated.

"All I ask from you is six months. Give me six months as my submissive and then you can decide if this lifestyle is for you." It was abrupt, likely too forward, but he didn't want to let her go yet. He wanted at least the *chance* to see if this could be something real. The chance to show her what a real Dom was like, what things could be like when done with her consent.

"You? What? I can… what?" Thalia stumbled over her questions, wide-eyed in the passenger seat, and he wanted to kiss her again, but he held back.

"Six months. Commit to me for that long, and then you can choose. Go free, figure out what vanilla life you want to live. I'll even help you rebuild it." *I'd give you whatever you needed to try and fix this.* "Or… you can choose to stay with me. My original offer doesn't change, this *will* be consensual." He brushed his thumb over her lips. "You can always stop me with a word."

"What word?" she asked softly.

"Your choice, pet." He smiled at her, and for a moment he would have sworn he saw lust in her eyes, and she was still so very naked. Taking his hands from her he reached into the backseat for the shopping bag of clothes he'd had the concierge pick up for him.

"Chair," she answered just as he handed the bag to her, and he laughed a little. Slightly confused at the odd choice of safe word.

"Why chair?"

"I'd like to focus on good memories of that word, instead of bad ones."

His stomach dropped as the scene of her in Anthony's torture chamber played in his head. The screams he'd ripped out of her echoed in his ears, and he had to admit he was grateful to Marcus for stopping it when he did. The bastard could have killed her, shattered this beautiful woman. Clearing his throat a little, he leaned across the car, and said the only thing he could think of. "You're very brave, pet."

Then he kissed her, capturing her mouth, but she wasn't passive this time. Her hands pushed into his hair, and she kissed him back with all of the hunger he felt. It was overwhelming, addictive, and he wanted more. Without thinking, he'd reached between her thighs to find her clit, smiling against her mouth as she moaned and arched in the passenger seat. Hips lifting, desperately seeking more, and his cock pulsed, threatening to embarrass him if he didn't stop.

Growling, he pulled back, unable to take his eyes off her breasts as they rose and fell with each pant. The shine on her thighs from his touch, from the orgasm *he* had given her.

Self-control, James, self-control. You have to be patient with her.

"You should put the clothes on so I don't make a poor decision, and then we can leave." Forcing himself to face front, he adjusted his cock in his pants to try and find a comfortable position for the long drive back to the city.

"Yes, Master," she panted and he watched as Marcus walked out onto the front porch.

If there had not been a few other lingering cars in the drive, and his brother inside, James was absolutely sure that Marcus would have killed him to take Thalia back. There was something unsteady in the way he watched her through the windshield. A few minutes later he realized Thalia was still, staring back at the monster who had done so many terrible things to her. "I understand why he's so angry. You're incredible, Thalia." James brushed her cheek as he started the engine, and then backed the SUV away from the house so he could turn down the drive.

Thalia leaned against the door, staring out the window as she spoke quietly. "He told me that too, Master."

The word irked him a little. It was as if she had already put him in the same category as Marcus, but he would ensure she knew he was different. Sighing, he leaned over and gently tucked a strand of hair behind her ear. "He may have said it to you, Thalia, but I plan to show you."

The End

*"There are darknesses in life
and there are lights,
and you are one of the lights,
the light of all lights."*

— Bram Stoker

Acknowledgements

I honestly don't even know how to start these acknowledgements. Seriously, how do I even remotely capture all of the people who helped make The Thalia Series happen? It's going to be hard, but I am going to try anyway, lovelies. If I forget you, just know that every single person who has ever commented, reviewed, or messaged me about Thalia has their fingerprints on this series and me as an author. There's no escaping it, because we are nothing without the people who have shaped us.

Starting out though, I have to go back to my two real-life besties of over twenty years. Blake and Sarah. You guys supported me when I was writing random stories in high school, and you always told me they were amazing — even when they weren't. Both of you are so fucking talented in your own ways, and we are one powerful trio. There's a reason we wear each other's marks on our skin, and it's because we were meant to meet. We're bound for life, chosen family forever, and I will always be grateful that you supported me and my dirty little Thalia chapters when they were in their infancy. Sarah, I thank you for getting just as turned on by it as I did and making the first batch of beautiful Thalia covers with your incredible fucking talent, and Blake for supporting us in our kinks *(even though it talked about gross hetero sex)*. Thank you guys for loving me and always being my safety net. Lobe and Lapollen 4 ever (PS – we need a Mumtaz date, like stat).

Next are all of my Literotica peeps. I'm sure I'm going to miss some, but Tara Crescent is the first of them. She dragged all of us out of the dark and into the bright and scary world of publishing, holding our hands every step of the way, and she will forever be my publishing Yoda, even though our paths in romancelandia have diverged quite spectacularly. To Eris Adderly/Rochelle, MJ/Jim the Brit, Anne

A. Lois, Jenni Tatum, Justine Hollander, Sophie Kisker, Richard North, Catriona Spencer, Esther Calder, Christine Hart, and I know many *many* more… each and every one of you have inspired me, helped me, lifted me up, given me late night dirty thoughts, or just in general been the right people at the right time in my life. The world of Literotica is a dark and dirty corner of the internet, and I feel so damn lucky to have stumbled upon it when I was *way* too young to see it, and to have joined it as a writer later when I was a much more *reasonable* age. I couldn't possibly detail the ways each of you have impacted me as an author, but I know that you have and I am so fucking glad we met.

Livia Grant, you are my Type-A soul sister. My psychotic, overworked, self-destructive twin, and I honestly don't know if I'd be sane without you in my life. I probably would have imploded or given up on writing before now if I didn't have you to siphon off some of my crazy and let me know I'm not alone. I'm sad I never read your amazing writing when we were on Literotica together, but you know how much I love it now (Black Collar Press, ftw!) and I love that we still came up from Lit together. You are always there for me, and I try to always be there for you (even when I fail), but I love you and you're in my family forever now. After all, you've been in bed with me!

Myra Danvers / Waterburn / my lovely chaos demon… even though you are far away in the frigid North, I still love you so hard. From the first day we met when I fangirled so hard over you that I most definitely freaked you out, to the incredible bond we've formed over the interwebs, you have helped me in ways I can't describe. I love you to the dark pit and back.

Addison Cain, my dark and twisted sister. You make me feel normal when we talk about our totally insane story ideas, and I love you so fucking hard. You are such a fierce friend, and I would choose you to go into battle with any day of the week. You're never getting rid of me now, but I think you know that already. I don't know what I'd do without you, and srsly, I'll stalk you if you try to leave me! :D

Niki Roge. I swear, it was an aligning of the cosmos that brought you to the forefront of my life. You are an apocalyptically powerful lady, and I'm not sure how many karma points I cashed in to have you at my back, but I'll happily pay it back over several lifetimes to keep you. There's no doubt that my author career has been bolstered and supported by you, and I will always be grateful to you. Thank you for loving me, even at my worst, and for putting up with ALL of my shit. I know I don't deserve it, and I hope you know how much I love you. Circle of Trust always. <3

Laura Hidalgo… Girl, I don't even know what to say about you. I know that there were some epic strings getting pulled to get us connected when we did (and I owe Marissa Honeycutt big time for the introduction). You are right in the middle of the shit with me, and you are so damn fierce, and strong, and I cannot imagine a better chick to have in my life, and at my back, than you. I hope you know that I will always have your back, and that I love you for more than just your incredible artistic talent with covers, but for who you are as a person. I am damn lucky to know you, and although our friendship is new I can already feel it bone-deep. I love ya, Laura. No doubt about it.

To Alta Hensley, Zoe Blake, and Sue Lyndon who put up with my weirdness, my awkward insanity, and my general dark fucked-upness, while also *always* answering my questions and being constant author friends — just know that I love you. I love you so fucking hard, and I have absorbed you into my inner circle, which means I will always fight at your side and support you. I love you guys so much, probably to an uncomfortable amount for you, but… hey, noncon is how I roll.

Finally, but definitely not the least, to ALL of my amazing reader friends who have taken the time out of their busy lives to contact a random author just to say they liked a book. I don't know if I can put into words what your Facebook comments, tweets, emails, and personal messages have meant to me. There are days when I have felt so fucking low and I go back and re-read them just for a pick-me-up. It may seem small to you guys, or even weird/crazy that I love them so much, but I appreciate the time you take more than I can say. It's like getting a ray of light in the darkness that tells me I'm not stupid for pursuing this dream of writing. Saying 'thank you' to that seems so worthless, but it's all I have, lovelies.

So, thank you. Thank ALL of you for supporting me, whether you knew about this series from the beginning or are just now finding it, just know that I appreciate you and any message you send me.

I love each and every one of you.

Jennifer Bene

About the Author

Jennifer Bene is a *USA Today* bestselling author of dangerously sexy and deviously dark romance. Living in Texas with her daughter and their three dogs, she spends her days avoiding the heat and writing about bad boys and brave girls while drinking wine.

She's known for her intense, dark stories, dangerous villains, dominant heroes, and feisty heroines. Whether she's making you laugh, cry, or sweat through a sizzling scene, Jen always delivers a twisty, spine-tingling journey with the promise of a happily-ever-after… *eventually*.

Don't miss a release! Sign up for the VIP Reader List and get new release alerts and access to free books, bonus scenes, and exclusive giveaways at:

www.jenniferbene.com/newsletter

You can find her online throughout social media with username @jbeneauthor and on her website: www.jenniferbene.com

---

She also writes dark paranormal / fantasy / omegaverse romance under the pen name Cassandra Faye.

www.fayebooks.com

Also by Jennifer Bene

The Thalia Series (Dark Romance)
Security Binds Her *(Thalia Book 1)*
Striking a Balance *(Thalia Book 2)*
Salvaged by Love *(Thalia Book 3)*
Tying the Knot *(Thalia Book 4)*
The Thalia Series: The Complete Collection

The Beth Series (Dark Romance)
Breaking Beth *(Beth Book 1)*
Damaged Doll *(Beth Book 2)*
Scarred Siren *(Beth Book 3)*
Marcus *(A Dark Prequel)*

Fragile Ties Series (Dark Romance)
Destruction *(Fragile Ties Book 1)*
Inheritance *(Fragile Ties Book 2)*
Redemption *(Fragile Ties Book 3)*
The Fragile Ties Series: The Complete Collection

The Wonderland Series (Dark / Taboo Romance)
The Cheshire Cat *(Wonderland Book 1)*
The Forbidden *(Wonderland Book 2)*

Dangerous Games Series (Dark Mafia Romance)
Early Sins *(A Dangerous Games Prequel)*
Lethal Sin *(Dangerous Games Book 1)*

Standalone Dark Romance
Imperfect Monster
Corrupt Desires
Reign of Ruin
Mesmer

Jasmine

Crazy Broken Love

Dark Suspense / Horror

Burned: An Inferno World Novella

Scorched: A New Beginning

Noxious *(Anathema Book 1)*

Mephitic *(Anathema Book 2)*

Viperous *(Anathema Book 3)*

Anathema Codex: The Complete Series

Appearances in the Black Light Series (BDSM Romance)

Black Light: Exposed

Black Light: Valentine Roulette

Black Light: Roulette Redux

Black Light: Celebrity Roulette

Black Light: Charmed

Black Light: Roulette War

Black Light: The Beginning

Black Light: Unbound

Black Light: Roulette Rematch

Black Light: Crossover

Black Light: Roulette Finale

BOOKS RELEASED AS CASSANDRA FAYE

Jennifer Bene also writes dark paranormal/sci-fi romance as Cassandra Faye. You can find her books below and see more about this pen name at: www.fayebooks.com

The Clarity Series
(Dark Omegaverse Reverse Harem Romance)

Alpha's Clarity *(Clarity Series Book 1)*

Alpha's Promise *(Clarity Series Book 2)*

Alpha's Bond *(Clarity Series Book 3)*

Alpha's Trust *(Clarity Series Book 4)*

Alpha's Secret *(Clarity Series Book 5)*

Daughters of Eltera Series (Dark Fantasy Romance)
Fae *(Daughters of Eltera Book 1)*
Tara *(Daughters of Eltera Book 2)*

Standalone Paranormal Romance
Hunted
One Crazy Bite
Dangerous Magic